theMystery.doc

(fortellcometell.wav
Created Friday, March 23, 2007 10:49 PM)

ALL RIGHT, POP. THIS, this is the very beginning of the book... The very beginning of the book. Part one. Page one. [*clears throat*]

For tell,

come tell,

then tell

me,

is there anything more delightful than to see this very moment before our eyes, as it were, a great lake of pitch, boiling hot, and swimming and writhing about in it a swirling mass of serpents, snakes, lizards, and many other kind of grisly and savage creatures,

and then to hear a dismal voice

a plaintive voice

an extremely sad voice

from the lake, crying:

'You knight, whoever you are, you who stare at this awful lake

Knight, whosoever thou art who beholdest this dread lake

Thou, O knight, whosoever thou mayest be,
who looketh upon this fearful lake,

if you wish to reach the guerdon

the prize

the treasure

hidden beneath these black waters, show the valor of your

stout

mighty

dauntless heart

and plunge into the midst of this dark, seething flood,

for if you do not do so, you will not be worthy to see the mighty marvels hidden within the seven castles of the seven fairies who dwell beneath these murky waters?'

No sooner has the knight heard this grim voice than without further thought for himself, without pausing to consider the peril to which he is exposed and without relieving himself of his weighty armor,

he commends himself to God and his lady,

to God and his lady,

to God and his lady,

and casts himself into the middle of the seething pool;

there, when he least expects it, and when he knows not when it will end,

and when he little looks for it, or knows what his fate is to be

and when he cannot see or imagine where he will land…

he finds himself among flowered meadows,

flowery meadows,

flower*ing* meadows,

whose beauty far exceeds the Elysian fields.

There the sky seems to him more transparent, and the sun to shine with fresher radiance.

He sees before him a plead—a pleasant wooded glade of green and leafy trees whose verdure rejoices his eyes

charms his sight

brings joy to his eyes,

while his ears are lulled by the gentle and spontaneous song
of tiny painted birds that are amid the interlacing branches

while the ear is soothed by the sweet untutored melody
of the countless birds of gay plumage that flit to and fro
among the interlacing branches

while his ears are charmed by the sweet,
untutored song of the infinite number of small,
brightly-colored birds that fly
among the intricate branches…

Then he discovers a little stream whose clear waters
like liquid crystal—

[*door opens*]

CLAIRE: Anything different? No?

No.

CLAIRE: … Yeah … [*whispers*] *Let's get some of that out of there*…………. Oh, it's kind of full.

It's what?

Claire: It's *full.*

His mouth?

Claire: Yeah. Down here, it just gets full of phlegm........................ Gosh, it's just *impossible* for him to still be doing this!... Colder.

Yeah?

Claire: Feel the hands.

Yeah, his hands are getting cold.

Claire: Oh! His feet are getting cold. Compared to how he's been. But you know, he could go hours because of the way he's been doing what he's doing... *You're just doin it the hard way, sonny-baby*... The tongue is what's so interesting to me.

What about it?

Claire: His tongue—well, see how it's turned over to the side?

Yeah.

Claire: I can't tell if it's swollen or just... kind of turned........ You go out of the room and come back, you see how gray he is.

Yeah. Yeah, when you're here, you just—

Claire: You get used to it.

You get used to it, don't you?

CLAIRE: Yeah... *You OK, babe? We're just here with you, OK? Me and the kids: Annie, and Jon, and Matt. We love you! K? You're doin a good job! You're workin hard, and we're proud of you! And we love you! K?* Love *you!*...Because the nurses say he can hear us.

Uh-huh.

CLAIRE: Yeah. Huh?

Yeah, didn't they tell you that?

CLAIRE: Yeah......... *K? We're* so proud of you, *babe! It's all right! You did* good, *and you're doing well now, K?... You do what you need to do and we'll just be here for you, K?...You just do what you need to do. We'd like it to be over for you but...you do what you need to do, K? Feel like you could stop, if you wanted to just be done, and that would be OK. But if you...if you want to stay a little bit longer, we're OK. OK?...* [*sighs*] It's *impossible* that he's still doin this......

Yeah.

CLAIRE: { }...

[*door closes*]

....
......[*clears throat*]...

Then he discovers a little stream whose clear waters like liquid crystal glide over fine sand and white pebbles that resemble sifted gold and purest pearl. There he perceives a fountain wrought of mottled jasper and polished marble, here another, roughly fashioned, where small mussel shells with the twisted white and yellow houses of the snail set in disordered order, and alternating with fragments of glittering crystal and counterfeit emeralds, combine to create so varied a composition that Art, imitating Nature, seems here to surpass her.

Then, all of a sudden, in the distance appears a strong castle, or sightly palace, whose walls are of beaten gold, its turrets of diamonds, its gates of jacinth. It is also—it is *so admirably built* in fact, that though the materials of which it is built are nothing less than diamonds, carbuncles, rubies, pearls, gold and emeralds, the workmanship is even more precious…

And after this, could one see a fairer sight than a goodly train of damsels sallying forth from the castle gate, in such a gay and gorgeous attire, that if I were to describe it as the histories do, I should never finish?

And then she,

who seems to be the first among them, takes the bold knight who plunged into the burning lake,

by the hand,

and silently

leads him into the rich palace or castle,

bathes him in warm water

and anoints him

all over

his entire body

with sweet-smelling ointments,

and clothes him in a shirt of the softest sendal

all fragranced and perfumed, while another damsel hastens to throw over his shoulders, a mantle that they say is worth the price of a city, and even more..........

What better sight, after all this

when they tell us, that after all this they lead him into another hall, where he finds the tables laid in such style that he is filled with

amazement

and wonder?

And to see him sprinkling on his hands water, distilled with ambergris, and sweet-smelling flowers?

How they sit him on an ivory chair?

And to see all the damsels wait upon him,

in silence

in wondrous silence

preserving their miraculous silence and bringing him such a varied profusion of delicacies so deliciously cooked that his appetite does not toward which of them—does not *know* toward which of them to stretch his hand?

What pleasure then to hear the music that plays while he is at table

by whom or whence produced he knows not!

And when the

repast

is ended

and the tables cleared

and the knight is reclining in his chair,

perhaps picking his teeth as the custom is,

when suddenly another damsel,

much more beautiful than *any* of the others,

enters

unexpectedly, by the chamber door..............

....

....

................[*sighs*]...

....

....

....

[*door opens*]

Please see the credits on the back of the book for continuation regarding sources and permissions.

Designed by Bri — Matthew Mulroon

Printed in the United States of America

First Grove Atlantic hardcover edition: — be published in Great Britain under the
— title — by — Grove School.

Library of Congress Cataloging-in-Publication data is available for this title.

Grove Press

Please see the credits section at the back of the book for information regarding sources and permissions.

Designed by Mrs. Matthew McIntosh

Published simultaneously in Canada

Printed in China

First Grove Atlantic hardcover edition:
October 2017

ISBN 978 0 8021 2491 3
eISBN 978 0 8021 8917 2

FIRST EDITION

Grove Press
an imprint of Grove Atlantic
154 West 14th Street
New York, NY 10011
Distributed by Publishers Group West
groveatlantic.com

First published in Great Britain in 2017
by Grove Press UK, an imprint of
Grove Atlantic

Hardback ISBN 978 1 61185 620 0
e-Book ISBN 978 1 61185 952 2

A CIP record for this book is available
from the British Library.

Grove Press, UK
Ormond House
26–27 Boswell Street
London
WC1N 3JZ

17 18 19 20 10 9 8 7 6 5 4 3 2 1

Resplendent and unfading is Wisdom,
and she is readily perceived by those who love her,
and found by those who seek her.

Wisdom 6:12

CONTENTS

ACT I
HOME & GARDEN

—holy Mary mother of God—

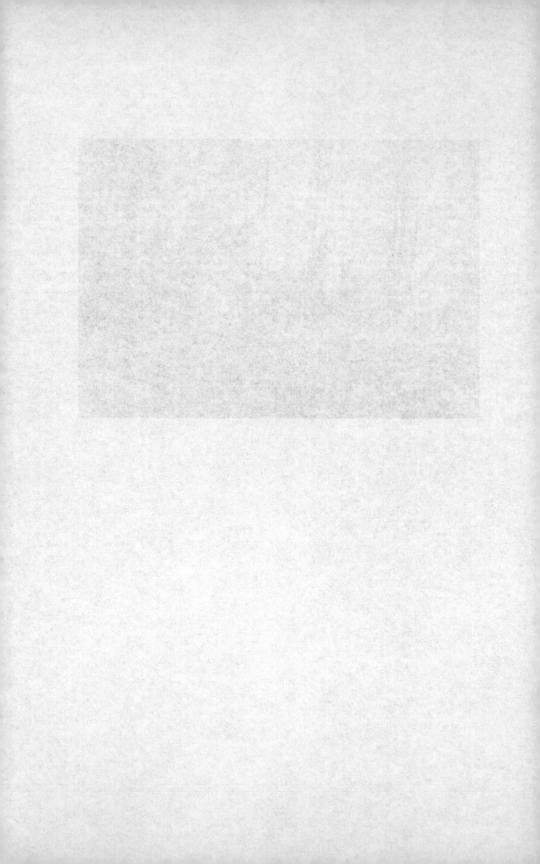

—holy Mary mother of God—

8695, good morning, have a good day!

Hi, what's your number again please?

8-695

Oh my god, I'm on the 83rd floor!

86—86 what?

I'm on the 83rd floor!

Ma'am, calm down one moment—86 what?

8695.

★

Live Conversation with Michele

Michele: Hello, I am Michele, I am the website greeter. Welcome to WebsiteGreeters.com

Michele: May I know your name please?

Visitor 1969: Hello, Michele.

Michele: hi :)

Michele: May I have your name please?

Visitor 1969: Is this an automated program or is there a live person on the other end?

Michele: I am a live person

Michele: This is not automated.. Live assistance is what we sell :)

Visitor 1969: Assistance in doing what?

Michele: We assist the customers with any queries they have

Visitor 1969: Any sort of queries?

Michele: We are trained according to different business models we are representing

Visitor 1969: which sort of business models do you represent?

Michele: Yes we actually understand what type of questions we will have to answer on any particular website.

Michele: by monitoring the initial chats we have

Visitor 1969: What sorts of things have you chatted about recently?

Michele: hmm, I have chatted the same way with some other customers on our website.

Michele: Just the way I am chatting with you

Michele: Do you have a website?

Visitor 1969: Doesn't everyone?

Michele: Yes, actually I wanted to know your website address if that's ok?

Visitor 1969: Why do you want to know that?

Michele: Just wanted to have a look at it. Are you interested in using our service on your website?

Visitor 1969: What kind of service do you--Wait a second, are you trying to sell me something?

Michele: The live chat service

Michele: We will have a team of greeters assisting the visitors on your website.

Visitor 1969: May I be honest with you for a moment, Michele?

Michele: sure

Visitor 1969: Thank you. First let me ask a question of you. What country are you in right now?

Michele: USA

Visitor 1969: Me too. What part?

Michele: Chicago

Visitor 1969: What's the weather like in Chicago today?

[*Time passing*]

Michele: It's partly cloudy.
Michele: what about your side?

Visitor 1969: You're right! Partly cloudy is exactly what it says on weather.com for Chicago's weather. It also says 60 degrees, and that it feels like 60 degrees. On my side it is...i have to check weather.com...partly cloudy. 44 degrees. Feels like 39 degrees.

[session terminated by Michele]

CHAPTER ONE

It was one of those plots where you wake up and you don't know who you are. You feel like you've been through the mill. Your head aches. Your ribs ache. Your arms ache. Your hands, your fingers. Everything aches. You know you did something—or somebody did something to you—but what that was now completely escapes you. You're awake. And it's like you're still coming out of a dream. And you wait a little while for the facts of the matter to settle in your mind. Who, what, where, when, why… You know, like everyone knows, that coming out of a dream can be a confusing time. Sometimes it takes a while for the dream to split off and fade away. You're in a familiar room but you don't recognize anything. The bed seems like it's your own but you think it's someone else's. Or you think you're somewhere other than you are. That's all perfectly normal. A transition from one state to another. Well, this dream splits, it breaks off, it fades, but nothing takes its place. Just the ache. And a girl at the closet stepping into a skirt, saying:

"I'm super late, so I'm gonna drive, OK?"

I couldn't see her well. She was just a blur. I groped around the bedside table for a pair of glasses that weren't there.

So I lay back, watching the blurry form as it dressed. Tall girl, short stylish hair, platinum blonde, a good figure—that's about all I could tell. A small room. Modest. Curtains closed. A sound like an airplane going over.

She zipped up her skirt in the back.

"How are you feeling?" she said.

"Sore."

"I bet. Too much time on that ladder."

She left the room. The old hardwood creaked beneath her feet. I heard her voice from the other room.

"I had to change my number, remember? New one's on the counter." She came back in. "OK?"

"OK."

She sat down on the bed. Dark blurry face. Her light hair like a corona.

"Why don't you take a break from scraping. You've still got a month of summer. Take the day off. Why don't you go back to your book? Do some writing. You get so grumpy when you're not working on it."

"Yeah?"

"Yeah. Maybe tonight I can read some more." She leaned forward and kissed me.

Pretty face. Almond-shaped eyes.

"Your glasses are in the bathroom. I borrowed them, sorry. There's coffee in the kitchen. And a smoothie in the fridge."

"OK."

"You all right, babe? You look kind of dazed."

"Yeah, fine."

Instinctively a person knows that if he wakes up in a strange place with a strange woman calling him babe he should just go along with things and pretend he's in control of the situation, that everything's fine.

Things go wrong quickly when you share information with strangers who say they're your friends.

"Did you hear the cat this morning?" she asked.

"No."

"It was howling something terrible. It sounded like it was in our back yard. Probably that fat orange one I always hiss at. I'm surprised you didn't hear it. It was pretty horrible. Sounded like it was being eaten by wolves. I hope it was. Well, I wish I could stay," she said, rising from the bed. "Remember when we first moved here we used to stay in bed all morning?" She sighed. "I miss those days."

"Yeah. Me too."

"I'm really sorry about last night. I think I must have been enchanted or something."

"Yeah?"

"Give me another chance tonight? All right?"

"Sure."

"Call me if you need anything. Don't call the old number, though. Remember, call the new one."

The door closed. I heard her run down some steps and another door slammed shut.

The car started up and backed down a long driveway.

I got up. Went into the bathroom and found the glasses. Put them on. Looked at myself in the mirror. Well, that seemed right enough. The face was mine. I knew that much. So then the problem couldn't be me. I poured a cup of coffee and went into the living room. A couch, a chair, a lamp, a table. I looked out the window. The house was small. A house of similar size across the street. Two rows of modest, pre-war bungalows. Maple trees in bloom. On the porch was a ladder on its side, a tarp, a little table, a broom, a pile of light-colored paint chips. The front lawn was dried out, yellow. I went into the adjacent room. This must be my office. A desk in front of the window. A laptop computer. Old metal bookshelves. Books stacked on every surface. History, philosophy, fiction. Post cards and old photos stuck to the bookshelves with magnets. A drawing by a child of some sort of rainbow-colored craft—bright vibrant colors covering every molecule of the page—and little round balls—smiling faces. An old green couch. A black throw pillow. A metal trash can, empty except for balls of gum stuck to the inside. A yellow chair. I sat down. Hit the spacebar. The computer started up. The black screen flashed and then a white sheet stared back. Nothing on it.

The title of the document was themystery.doc. It was the only thing open.

It was all very suspicious. I know when you wake with your memory lost you're supposed to believe everything they tell you. You're supposed to blindly fit in with your surroundings. To trust the legitimacy of all that's been laid out before you. But I was quite sure I had never been in this house before. I had never sat in that chair. I didn't know who those people were in the photographs, I didn't know what child had drawn the picture. I lifted it up. On the back an adult had written in yellow crayon: "The Bus".

The phone rang.

I got up and passed through the little bathroom, back into the bedroom. In the still-dark room I could see a gadget glowing on the dresser. I picked it up. Pressed the talk button.

"Hello?"

"Hi, babe."

"Hi."

"I forgot to tell you the sewer guy's coming to snake the drain today."

"What drain?"

"The sewer line. It's all clogged up because of the pine tree roots, remember?"

I didn't know what the heck she was talking about.

"Right," I said.

"He should be there about eleven, I think."

"OK."

"The checkbook's on the coffee table."

"OK."

"You're not very talkative this morning."

"Aren't I?"

"You're not still angry with me, are you? You can't believe anything I said last night. I told you. It wasn't me. I was enchanted."

"What did you say last night?"

"Hmmm," she said. "I should get off the phone now. I don't like talking while I drive. You get distracted. That's how people end up driving off bridges. Knock on wood."

"Where do you work again?"

"Where do I *work* again? Babe, I think you might still be asleep."

"Right. Yeah, that's it. I must still be asleep."

"You just stay in bed today. I think you need a break. Stay off that ladder. You just stay in bed and read a book or something, OK? I better go."

"OK."

We hung up.

I was wearing a white t-shirt and red boxers. The house was very warm. I found a pair of shorts on the floor by the bed and put them on. They were green army pants that had been made into shorts. I took my coffee out into the back yard. There was a patio there, a couple wicker chairs that didn't match. One of them had no seat but a rudely cut piece of plywood had been plunked down with a little cushion on top that was too small for it. There were tarps and old sheets lying over the flower beds. The house itself was pink—pink or peach—that was the color. But everywhere I could see the gray/brown of old cedar shingles. The house had been scraped, and it must have been a terrible paint job that was being scraped off because a third or more of the observable house was down to the wood. I rolled my head around on my neck. It was tight and sore. My head still hurt. Everything hurt and just looking at the house made everything hurt more.

The back lawn was just as dead as the front. It seemed whoever had been living here had decided to let the grass die. It was a good-sized yard. There was a weird-looking orange bundle lying there in the back. I put on a pair of flip-flops that fit me perfectly and walked back there.

Near the back fence, an obese orange cat was lying stiffly, its tongue sticking out the side of its mouth. It had a leather collar and a round disk hanging from it. Without touching the cat I moved the disk so I could read it.

OLIVE.

I went inside and turned on the phone, compared the number that had last called me with the number the girl had written on a pad of paper in the kitchen. They matched.

I dialed.

A doodle of a fish with a smiley face had been drawn in a quick, smooth hand below the number.

"Hi, babe," she said.

"I think I know what happened this morning."

"What do you mean?"

"Olive," I said.

"What olive? You hate olives."

"Not olives; *Olive*. Don't you know who Olive is?"

I could hear the girl sigh into the phone. "Babe, I don't know what you're talking about, and I have a lot of work to get done."

"Olive the cat. Is dead."

"The big orange cat?" she blurted. "Gladys's cat?"

"Who's Gla—? Yep, that's the one."

"It's dead?"

"As a dormouse."

The next thing I heard was a bit disturbing because it was the sound of gleeful laughter. "That must be what I heard this morning!" she said giddily. "Its death throes! Oh, joy! Joy!" Then she said something about how that will teach it to go to the bathroom in her blueberry beds. Who was this woman? "Thanks for telling me, babe, you really brightened my day."

"Well, what am I supposed to do with it?"

"I don't know. What do you do with dead cats? Put them in the trash, I guess."

"I figure I should alert its owner, don't you think?"

"Yeah, I suppose. How did it look? Gross?"

"Stiff."

"I wonder how it died."

"I should get in touch with Gladys," I said. "How should I reach her?"

"I don't know, how about with a ten-foot pole?"

"You don't get along with Gladys, either?"

"I would get along with Gladys if she would stop trying to give me advice about lawn care. I'm trying to save water. Besides, we'll start working on the garden when the painting's done."

"Sure," I said. "That makes sense. Well, I suppose I'd better go talk to this Gladys."

"*This* Gladys? OK, but you might want to wait awhile. You still sound really spacey."

"Yes. Certainly. Of course."

"See, that's what I mean."

There was a shed at the back of the property. It was unlocked. I found a pair of branch cutters and used them to snip off the deceased's leather collar. It was a tricky business because I didn't want to accidentally snip the cat. I took the collar and walked down the side driveway. The whole side of the house was in the same condition as the rear as far as paint and scraping was concerned. Whoever had done this had made it look legit. Poor bastard, I thought to myself. The scraping had obviously been done with a little hand scraper and a heat gun. The gun blew hot air which loosened the peeling paint and then it was up to the scraper to get it off. It was a small house, but no small job. Perhaps whoever was trying to make me think this was my house had hired a team to do it, in which case it could have been done in a day or two, depending on the size of the team.

The front of the house had yet to be scraped. I could see why anyone living there would have wanted the job done. It had been painted that pink/peach color and nothing else. No trim or accent colors, so the little house had the appearance of a nondescript pink blob. None of the details of its design or architecture were showing. I wondered what color it was going to be.

I stood on the sidewalk looking back at the house and chewing a piece of gum I'd found in the pocket of my shorts. I was distracted by an old woman next door. She was standing in her driveway sweeping. She saw me and smiled.

"Good morning! Looks like the scraping's coming along. I can't wait to see what color you two have chosen. I hope not gray. But I'm sure it'll be beautiful. Your wife is so styli—"

"Gladys?" I said.

She stopped smiling and looked at me funny. "Yes?"

"Then I have some bad news."

I walked over to her so that I could deliver the bad news quietly and in a soft voice, and no sooner had I stepped from my yard into hers than I heard a loud snarling which instantly turned to barking and I turned to see an angry dog bolting in my direction. I leapt back, then seeing it was just a fat corgi I readied myself to kick it like a football as soon as it brought itself in range. But it turned out the dog was tied up on a line and couldn't quite get to me. "No, Brute, no!" said "Gladys," in a voice that wasn't chastising at all, and which while assuming a negative position paradoxically revealed something in the order of approval.

The dog stood off a distance growling under its breath.

"What's the bad news?" said Gladys, looking concerned.

"It's Olive."

"The cat?"

"*The* cat? It's your cat, isn't it?"

"No, that cat belonged to a man who lived down the street. He had two cats and he didn't want to take them when he moved, so somehow he got Vel to adopt them—this was right after Gerald left for the home—but then, well, as you know, they had to take her away because she was hiding in the bushes and snarling at passersby and—have you heard anything? Is she still in the mental hospital? Carol was telling me she chased you with her hose? Is that true?"

"That's a good question, Gladys. There's a lot I'd like to know."

"Well," said Gladys sweetly, "Carol heard that Vel thought your pine trees were killing her with pollen. So after she sprayed her house from top to bottom she started spraying yours. Then when you went out and asked her to stop she accused you of stealing her windows and putting them on your house and then, well, according to Carol she chased you down the driveway spraying you with the soaker attachment. It really is a shame that you had to share your driveway with Vel for so long. I used to see her wandering into your back yard all the time. I guess she had become convinced that there was a body buried back there. At least that's what she told the ambulance driver when they took her away. You know she spent all her time in that house watching true crime shows and the Home Shopping Network. And she hoards. She has for as long as I've been here—almost forty years. But I think if you had one of those antiques shows come to her house they'd find some real treasures! Why, some of those old silhouettes must be worth a thousand dollars apiece! Do you ever watch the antiques program?"

"Never miss it," I said.

"Did you hear they're coming to town next month? My friend Mavis has two tickets and she's giving me one. I'm going to take an old Indian pestle I found at a junk sale and see if they will carbon date it for me. At least I think it's a pestle—Tim down the street says it may be something called a *lingam*."

The dog had not stopped growling.

"I don't think your dog likes me much."

"Oh, Brute? Don't take it personally; he growls at all men. I think in his first home there was a man who used to hit him. A dog remembers. But as far as Olive goes, she's not really my cat. It's just when they took Vel away no one was feeding the cats anymore, so I started leaving food out on my porch for them. Now the other one has run off somewhere, but Olive is still coming around."

"Well, Olive won't be coming around anymore. I'm sorry to tell you that Olive has kicked the bucket."

"Oh, dear. She died?"

"In my back yard. And very loudly, I might add. Apparently the woman pretending to be my wife heard a bloodcurdling scream this morning. I can only assume it was Olive dying a horrible death." I handed Gladys the collar. "My condolences."

Gladys clucked her tongue. "Oh, that's terrible!" she said, taking the collar. "Where did it happen? In your back yard, was it?"

"That's what it looks like. Unless the body was moved."

"Was she attacked by something? I know we have raccoons."

"I don't know how it happened, I'm no vet. But I thought I should let you know."

"Do you want me to come get her?"

"I'll take care of it, Gladys, no problem."

"Well, thank you. Do you think I should send the collar to the man who owned her? I got his address from Tim after Vel was taken away.

I wanted to know if he was going to come back for the cats. He never wrote back."

"Yes, I think you should send the collar. I'm sure he'd like that."

I went back inside and after a short search I found a large plastic shopping bag. I put Olive in it. Tied it. And deposited it in the garbage can.

I went back inside and drank the smoothie the girl had left me in the fridge. It was banana and strawberry, very tasty. I walked around the house examining items, picking up a stuffed frog here, a bowl of pine cones there. On the mantle was a large green cookie jar in the shape of a stern-looking owl. I lifted off his head and looked inside. Toy animals of all kinds. I put his head back on.

"Boris," I heard myself say. That was its name. How did I know that?

Footsteps. I turned to the window and saw a woman walking up the porch. Her bedhead hair and t-shirt with the cartoon dinosaur were unmistakable. It was Gladys. She knocked on the door.

"Come in," I said, and stepped back, motioning for her to take a seat.

She seemed surprised, but stepped in, looking around the room with wide eyes like a kid in a candy store.

"Have you not been in here before?" I asked.

"Not for eight or nine years," she said. "There was an incident with some renters who started a fire. When the cops left Carol and I came in and had a look around. Have you ever noticed the burnt floor in the basement? They were making meth and I guess whatever they were cooking it in exploded. One of the renters was pretty badly burned."

"Have a seat," I told her. "Can I get you a drink or something?"

"Oh, no thank you. I just came to give you the address of the man who owned Olive in case you'd like to contact him, yourself, for any reason."

"I don't think that'll be necessary, Gladys," I said. "The cat's already in the bag, so to speak."

The room was sparsely furnished and nothing matched. There was a plush captain's chair that had stained arm rests and scratch marks, probably found somewhere with a FREE sign on it. The couch Gladys was on was nearly as dingy as the chair and the springs must have given because she was sinking noticeably into the center of it. She was swiveling her head all around to make mental pictures of every item of décor so that she would be able to call it all up later, in future conversations with other neighbors. I was afraid she was going to throw out her neck.

"Gladys," I said.

"Yes?"

"How long have I lived here?"

"Let's see… You bought the house a few months after the renters with the pit bulls left. So, I suppose it's been almost three years."

"And what is it that I do for a living?"

She chuckled. "You're a writer!"

"Have I ever published anything?"

"Of course! You signed my book for me. Don't you remember? You wrote: *For Gladys, thanks for the tips. I will do it your way next time.* I remember well because neither Carol nor I could figure out if you were being serious or sarcastic."

"What was the name of my book?"

"The name of your book?" She laughed. "Are you playing a prank on me?"

"I know it probably sounds weird that I'd ask you all these questions that I already know the answers to. But let's just consider it as an exercise I'm doing for a book. OK?"

"That sounds fun! Your book's name is *In Complete Accord.*"

"*In Complete Accord.* Odd title. And did it sell many copies?"

"I don't think very many. I know I bought one."

"Now my wife, what does she do for a living?"

"You've told me before that she's a graphic designer."

"And what's she like? Trustworthy? Nice? Devious? Shady? How would you describe her?"

Gladys thought about it. "Well, to tell you the truth, I've never been able to get to know her very well. I know almost everyone on the block because I'm always out watering or sweeping and I talk to people when they walk by, and that's how I get to know them. But I can't say I've ever had a very good conversation with Eva. It seems like every time I try to strike up a conversation with her she remembers she has something on the stove. And yet," mused Gladys, "I never seem to smell any *home cooking* coming from the house."

"So that's her name is it? Eva?"

"Yes. Eva."

"And what's *my* name?"

Gladys suddenly burst forth with: "Well, your real name is Daniel, but for the first three months you lived here you had me calling you Corky!"

"I had you calling me Corky?"

"Yes, and I was very cross for a long time with you, because every time I would talk about you to people I would call you Corky and they would say Who's Corky? and I would explain that it was you—the new couple: Eva, the designer, and her husband Corky—and they'd say, His name's not Corky, it's Daniel! and I'd say, No, it's not, it's Corky!—and when I finally figured out you'd only been having a bit of fun with me, well, I was pretty upset about it. And I even talked to Eva about it over the fence in the back. I said, Do you know your husband has had me calling him Corky all this time? and she apologized and said you are a very imaginative man but that you get bored very easily and that I shouldn't take any offense and I started to give her some advice about how to check her arbor vitae for spider mites when she suddenly remembered she had left the iron on and had to rush inside."

"And how does one check for spider mites?" I asked to humor the woman.

"You take a white piece of paper and you place it flat inside the bush—or the tree, rather—and then you shake the tree and take the paper out and if they're there you'll see them crawling around on the page. They're small and red. And they can wipe out an entire block in a single season."

"Good to know," I said, rising to my feet. "Well, thank you for stopping by, but I should be getting back to work now. I'm sorry for having you call me Corky." I opened the door.

"How's the book coming?" she asked. "Is it almost finished?"

"I imagine so," I said. "By the way, what's the book about? Have I ever told you?"

"Oh, no, it's top secret. You never say the first thing about it. Whenever I or any of the other neighbors ask you just say it's a really big book, that you don't know when you'll be done because you never put timelines on things because it's better to let it be whatever it wants to be—which I've never understood—and what else do you say? Oh, yes. That you may not be making any money but that it's a very rewarding experience."

"Sounds like a cop-out to me. And how long have I been working on this book? Have I ever told you?"

"Well, your last one came out when you were young—twenty-six, I think, which probably explains all the profanity. And I know you've been working on this one since then. So it must have been something like... eleven years?"

"Eleven years on the same book!" I exclaimed.

She smiled.

"How does a person work eleven years on a book and not finish it? What's my work schedule? A minute per day?"

"Well, you tell people you work on it from the time you wake up until you go to sleep. And that you don't have any friends or hobbies or belong to any clubs (I don't think you even vote to tell you the truth) and that you have devoted your entire life to working on it."

She lowered her voice. "We all just figure you have writer's block and are too embarrassed to say."

"Yeah, I don't blame you. Eleven years working on the same book sounds like madness. Have I ever told you the title?"

"No. But once you called it a *post-post-neo-modern mystery story.* But I don't know if you were just feeding me more Corky."

"Thank you for the information, Gladys," I said, escorting her down the slanted wooden steps. "I promise you I'm going to get to the bottom of this."

"The bottom of it?" she said. "Is there something wrong?"

"Oh, yes. There's something definitely wrong." I walked her to the lawn and she headed for her house. "Wait, Gladys! One more thing!"

She turned around.

"I didn't get a very good look at my wife this morning," I said. "I didn't have my glasses on. She's beautiful, wouldn't you say?"

"Yes, she's very beautiful. Everyone says she looks like a model."

"And the way I look now," I said, spreading my arms wide so that she could see my old t-shirt and baggy shorts. "Is this how I normally look?"

"You mean how messy your hair is?"

"Well, I wasn't meaning that, but yes. And my attire."

"You always look pretty much the same," said Gladys. "Although when it's colder you wear long johns under your shorts."

"So then the question is…what would a girl like that be doing with a guy like me?"

Gladys thought about it for a while, but at last could only respond with a shake of the head and a smile. And a:

"I suppose it really takes all kinds."

(6_7_07 11_55 AM alice.wav)

::: Hi!

::: Hi.

::: I didn't get you up, did I?

::: No.

::: Sometimes people are day sleepers, you know, and…I'm just admiring your tree—is that going to be an apple, or…

::: Yeah, we just planted that a few weeks ago.

::: Oh! It looks healthy, it'll probably do fine there.

::: Do you know much about apple trees?

::: Pardon me?

::: Do you know—

::: Not a lot; what kind is it?

::: It's a McIntosh.

::: Oh, that's a nice apple. Yeah, and they're pretty! I like 'em. I would put a little thing around it, because the stem could easily get broken on you—you know, sometimes even kids will come along and—I saw that just the other day. A little screen around the base that comes up *so* high to protect it a little bit until it gets a little stronger.

::: Good idea.

::: Yeah, I just planted a dogwood tree two years ago and boy it's really taken off—you'd be surprised how fast they grow.

::: Really.

::: Yeah! Isn't it so beautiful out—the flowers are just gorgeous! Well anyway, you're probably wondering why I'm ringing your doorbell, I'm calling with some good news from the Bible.

::: Uh-huh.

::: Seems like we hear a lot of bad news anymore—[*clears throat*] I mean sometimes things are so bad you wonder if there's some sinister influence behind all of it. Have you ever thought of that?

::: Uh, yeah, I have actually.

::: Uh-huh, are you a Bible reader at all?

::: Yeah, I read the Bible.

::: Are you familiar with Revelation chapter twelve? Um, let me see here............You'll have to pardon my Bible, I always say I'm not gonna mark 'em up and I'll get another and then... [*laughs*] Anyway, it goes into here verse, um, twelve verse seven, *And war broke out in heaven, Michael and his angels battled with the Dragon, and the Dragon and its angels battled. But it did not prevail. Neither was a place found for them any longer in heaven.* So here you have the good angels fighting with the bad angels, at this period of time. *And so down the Great Dragon was hurled, the original serpent,* um, *the one called Devil and Satan who is misleading*—notice—*the entire inhabited earth*...You see what's going on.

::: Wow.

::: *And he was hurled down to the earth and his angels*—the bad angels—*were hurled down with him.* And then it says how happy they were, and then it says, *On this account be glad you heavens and you who reside in them, Woe for the earth and for the sea,* and over here the sea refers to restless humanity. Uh, *because the devil has come down to you having great anger knowing he has a short period of time.*

::: Short period of time, wow.

::: Well, when Jesus died for us and went to heaven he sat down at the right hand of God, it wasn't quite time for him to rule in his *kingdom*.

::: Uh-huh.

::: But when he took up ruling in heaven the first thing he did was cast Satan—the devil—and the angels that followed him down into the earth. Um...you probably know how Satan became what he was.

::: How did that happen?

::: Well, in Genesis he was the covering angel over Adam and Eve if you remember, and uh, he was supposed to watch over them, but instead he could visualize Adam and Eve multiplying as God told them to do, and fill the earth and extend that paradise to the *whole earth*. But um, but *he* wanted that glory, *he* wanted to be worshipped, so he uh, he *challenged* Eve's rightfulness to rule—I mean *God's* rightfulness to tell Adam and Eve what they could do and what they couldn't do. And remember he said to Eve, let me find it here... *Now the serpent*—oh, let's see, where should we start here... um... So [*clears throat*] here's the Satan using the serpent, like a ventriloquist, you know. *The serpent proved to be the most cautious of all the wild beasts of the field that Jehovah God had made, but began to say to the woman, Is it really so that God said you must not eat from every tree of the garden? At this the woman said to the serpent, Of the fruit of the trees of the garden we may eat, but as for eating of the fruit of the tree in the middle of the garden, God has said you must not eat from it no you must not touch it lest you die. And at* this *the serpent*—or Satan, you know, speaking through him—said to the woman, *You positively will not die. For God knows that on the very day of your eating from it your eyes are bound to be opened and you are bound to be like God knowing good and bad*—in other words, You don't need God telling you what to do!

::: Yeah, right.

::: Yeah. And so he told the first lie.

::: So that was a lie?

::: First lie. *You will not die,* he told them.

::: Wow.

::: And she—she—you know she dwelt on it. Instead of putting sin behind us sometimes we *dwell* on something—you know it's wrong—

::: Yep.

::: And they had *everything*—I mean they were created perfect, God had personally taught Adam, he let him name the animals that he had created, and uh—

::: What else was it like in Eden, do you think?

::: I beg your pardon?

::: What else was it like in Eden?

::: It was a beautiful paradise!

::: Yeah?

::: And, God's person—I mean God's *purpose* was to extend that garden to the entire earth, and the earth be filled—in fact before they sinned he gave them the command to *multiply*, and *fill the earth*, and uh, at that time...he said here...And God went on to say, *Let us make man in our image according to our likeness and let them have in subjection the fish of the sea and the flying creatures of the heavens and the domestic animals and all the earth and every moving animal upon it.* And down in verse twenty-eight it says further, *God blessed them, and God said to them, Be fruitful and be many and fill the earth, subdue it and have in subjection the fish of the sea, the flying creatures of the heavens and every living creature moving upon the earth.* Well, *now* we don't see us in command over the animals, you know. Some of them, some are pretty wild.

::: Yeah, they can get wild.

::: But at one time it wasn't true. And um so...the *earth* was completed in the seventh day. And many people tell you, well that was seven *literal* days.

::: Hmm.

::: But the Bible says that one day is equal to a thousand years. Because he's—

::: So seven thousand years.

::: So, uh...we don't know exactly how long those creative days were, but um, you know, science—God is the greatest scientist, he's the—so the Bible doesn't contradict the true science.

::: Right.

::: So, you know, a thinking person knows, after—have you been to college, or...?

::: Um, I spent some time in college.

::: And, and then—just even watching the History Channel, they had a deal on the sun, and how it functions and everything and it was just *awesome,* because—

::: How does the sun function?

::: Well, the protons and neutrons and everything, I would love to get a copy of that, it was on the History Channel, they'll probably show it again.

::: Oh yeah?

::: It was just unbelievable.

::: We don't have cable.
::: Oh, don't you?
::: No.
::: Uh-huh.
::: Do you have cable?
::: I have a, uh, dish.
::: Oh yeah? Which one do you have?
::: I don't know, it's just a—well, it's a dish that you, like a satellite—
::: Dish Network?
::: Well I live out on Mullan Hill Terrace, um—
::: Do you find you like the service you get with the dish? Because I'm constantly getting advertisements from cable *and* satellite, and you know it's just hard to decide in this day and age whether you should get *satellite* or whether you should get *cable*…for your entertainment needs.
::: Well, they don't have cable where I live, I live in a motor home park.
::: So you have to have a dish. You don't have a choice!
::: No. And I did have cable and I liked cable.
::: Do you find that the reception with the dish is pretty clear?
::: It's about the same as cable.
::: Really?
::: Uh, when you have a storm, though, sometimes it'll temporarily go out. A bad windstorm or something.
::: I've heard that would happen.
::: Yeah.
::: What kind of package do you have?
::: I just have the basic, but I think it runs, uh, it goes up all the time—what is it now? I have it taken out every month, it's automatic—and it's gone up, let's see, when I first got it I think it was twenty-nine dollars, I think it's about thirty-five now.
::: Do they tell you each month when they're gonna raise the rate on you?
::: Um…no. It just—it just automatically takes it out.

::: And when you check your bank statements they've taken more out each month?

::: Yeah, yeah—not each *month.* They raise it maybe every year or two or three, you know how they do—everything's going up now.

::: They should give you some notice before they start taking more out of your account, because—

::: Yeah, you'd think so.

::: you could bounce checks or something.

::: Yeah, exactly.

::: But other than that you're pretty comfortable, you like the service of the Dish Network?

::: Yeah, people are very—oh, the dish? Yeah, it's been pretty nice. And they don't charge you for that. I think you have to put a—you have to be with them at least two years. And they give everything free.

::: For what?

::: The little dish that they put on your house.

::: Oh, do they come and attach it to your house?

::: Yeah, they install it and everything.

::: Huh.

::: So that's all free, and then the little handset—let's see, did we get a handset? Yeah, I think we get a handset too. But you have to sign up for two years.

::: You have to have a two-year commitment.

::: Yeah. And I've been there four years.

::: Do you think it's worth the price that you've been paying? I mean for the quality of programs?

::: Well, they're pretty well—actually they're pretty well all the same price, pretty much. But yeah, I think it's very nice. I've been happy with it.

::: What kinds of shows do you like to watch?

::: Um, I love the History Channel—I have learned *so much* on that. Uh, they cover everything. Um, and I like to watch um, 112, Home and Garden. Yeah. Home and Garden. And what else do I like? Cooking Channel and I I like to watch CNN.

::: Oh yeah, for the news.
::: Yeah, I watch them a lot. And uh, local channels. I have 2, 4, 6, and 7, 10.
::: You have the local news?
::: Uh-huh. Uh-huh. Yeah. I've got 2, 4, 6, and—
::: Do you have a favorite local news station that you like?
::: Um, no, it's just—
::: Just whichever one is on?
::: Yeah. Yeah. I see you're sorta—you're sorta—wondering which way to go, aren't you?
::: Well, you know, I'm just gonna—they send us so many ads for cable and satellite that I'm just gonna have to give in and get one or the other—
::: Yeah, you don't know which way—I can understand the dilemma—
::: I think maybe if I get either *cable* or *satellite*, then maybe they'll stop sending me flyers in the mail.
::: I— No, I doubt it. I doubt it.
::: You think they'll still send me flyers?
::: It's just like you keep getting these things—oh, they want you to uh—um, like *Visa* or *Mastercharge*—
::: Yeah.
::: and all the different banks keep sending you that stuff, so…
::: Well, we rarely get much mail at all except for ads.
::: Yeah, you get sort of tired of it.
::: Yeah, it gets—
::: So just chuck 'em! [*laughs*]
::: Yeah, but then you have to pay to recycle them.
::: Yeah.
::: And then sometimes the recycling won't take certain types of mailers—
::: Uh-huh.
::: if they have like a *glossy sheen* on them.
::: Uh-huh.

::: Or if they're like a *full-color* uh gloss or—
::: Uh-huh.
::: matte or—
::: Yeah.
::: or something like that. It's just a challenge…
::: I know, it is.
::: And then you have to pay for your own garbage disposal, so—but if you think about the amount of paper that adds up just from advertising, that's gonna cost you a pretty penny each year.
::: Yeah, you start trying to cut corners because the cost of living keeps going *up and up and up*.
::: Yeah.
::: And uh, you know, things are just continuing to escalate—that, that's why we—not going back to the Bible, but we can see how close we are—
::: To what?
::: To God's judgment. We're living in a judgment period.
::: Do you think that's because of so much advertising…in the mailboxes?
::: Well, no, I think, um, it's greed—it's so much love of money, you know. Instead of being balanced, it seems you see so much corruption—like they just had a senator—I mean here's this guy—it's been two years I saw on the news—well, why is it taking two years to indict this man? So when we got—getting into this they found out that he was into graft and corruption and—
::: No!
::: And bribery!
::: A politician was—
::: A senator!
::: being dishonorable?
::: I can't think of his name, yeah!
::: Well that's something else. These *are* the end times.

::: Yeah! Well they're always being caught with their hand in the pot lately. We see corruption and this is all over the world! You know, so we're living in—

::: Not just here.

::: No.

::: Not just in this country.

::: So we're living in a judgment period and so it's so important that we take in knowledge of the Bible. And *accurate* knowledge. Because uh it's so important—so many people want to worship God the way they want to, and—

::: Right. And they say, *You know what, maybe the Bible's not true. I'll find out who God is for myself.*

::: Exactly.

::: That's what they say.

::: Yeah, and yet this Bible has been perfectly preserved. Even though many—well, the Catholic Church—it's a well-known fact—tried to—in the Dark Ages tried to suppress this. Because the Catholic Church was formed way back four hundred years after Christ—well, by that time false religion had entered—

::: Right.

::: just like Jesus said it would—when it said, when the apostles were martyred, the early Christians, it said the wolves will scatter the flock, and that happened, you know, and apostasy entered into religion, and some of those pagan doctrines have been handed down until today!

::: Really! You're kidding me! Like what kind of pagan doctrines?

::: Well, for example, Jesus was not born in December.

::: He wasn't born in December? He was born on December twenty-fifth.

::: No.

::: Like about a week short of January.

::: No.

::: No. Really?

::: Yeah. That was—well, that's another whole story. He was born about October first.

::: October first.

::: Yeah, the Bible doesn't say, but he started his ministry when he was *exactly* thirty—that was fulfilling the—

::: On his birthday?

::: Well, exactly thirty. And that was to fulfill, um . . . . . the Jewish requirement that you had to be *thirty* to become a priest. And he's our high priest—he needs no successor because he never died. So he waited—then he was serving his father full-time until his death at the age of thirty-three and a half.

::: As a carpenter?

::: Yeah, he was a carpenter, he helped his father—his *step*father—and then when he became thirty he was doing the ministry of his father *full-time*.

::: Joseph.

::: Joseph was his stepfather.

::: So he was doing the ministry of *Joseph* full-time?

::: No, of the Lord.

::: Oh, right, right.

::: See, his father was really God.

::: Right. Right.

::: Joseph was just raising him.

::: Joseph was just—

::: Married to Mary.

::: Mary's husband.

::: And so—

::: He was a carpenter.

::: He was a carpenter, and Jesus was a carpenter until he turned thirty and then he started serving his father full-time, until he was *thirty-three and a half.* So if you count back *six months*, that would take you back to about October first or second he was born. So then they decided—

::: September thirty-first it could have been also.

::: …Yeah. They—they started, uh, celebrating—decided to *Christ mass*, the mass of Christ, to get the uh, Emperor Constantine, to get the Jews and the Romans together, into one religion. And then they had church-state, you know where the church would govern the state, or the state would govern the state type thing? And uh, he wanted the people to support him, so uh…The Romans celebrated the *Saturnalia*, the return of the sun.

::: The return of Saturn.

::: Well, the twenty-fifth is the shortest day of the year, right in that area. And they had their pagan celebrations to their gods, you know, they worshipped the sun, the moon, and everything, you know, they even prayed to the Unknown God because they didn't want to offend anyone.

::: What was *his* name?

::: And so they just, uh…they…Well, just so they wouldn't offend maybe some god.

::: Which one?

::: I don't know, they worshipped everything. They worshipped the creation rather than the creator. The Romans.

::: The *Romans!*

::: Exactly. So to get the Jews and the Romans together, they decided to start celebrating Jesus' birthday on October first—well, the Jews did not celebrate birthdays.

::: They didn't.

::: They considered the day of the death more important. And they didn't think it was right to build—you know how you're king or queen for the day and everybody gives you gifts and all this? They didn't do that. Well, I've got some people waiting for me, but do you want me to come back sometime and we can sit down and study some of these things?

::: No, it's OK. But it's been really nice talking to you.

::: Yeah!

::: You have to go now though, huh? You can't stay and chat more?

::: Well I would love to but I I I uh um, they're getting cold out there probably. And um—I would like—she has to meet someone at twelve. I have a book: *What Does the Bible Really Teach*? Have you seen this? And it's a new book. Do you live here?

::: Well, I'm staying here right now. And I'm not going to be around for very much longer.

::: Oh, I see, you're sort of going to find your own place.

::: Yeah, I'm not originally from here.

::: Oh, aren't you? Where are you from?

::: Well, I was born in [redacted], [redacted], in 1976.

::: OK, that's a nice warm place.

::: When I was two we moved up to Federal Way, Washington…

::: Yeah, I know where that is.

::: Then when I was eight we moved to California.

::: Uh-huh.

::: And then eight and a half we moved to England. And then…

::: Oh, was your dad in the military?

::: He was um, he was a drifter, you might say.

::: Uh-huh, OK.

::: And then when I was, um let's see, ten we moved back to California.

::: Uh-huh.

::: And when I was *thirteen* we moved back to Federal Way.

::: You've seen a lot of the world!

::: I lived for a while in Seattle.

::: Uh-huh.

::: I've lived in Iowa. Let's see…where else have I lived?…Montana.

::: I've lived in Montana too.

::: What part of Montana?

::: I was born in Deer Lodge and I lived in Butte one year. My mom and dad were both born and raised in Montana. And my dad was out of Helena, and my mom lived on a ranch out of Deer Lodge.

::: Wow.

::: And I had aunts who lived in Missoula; one in Great Falls, one in Billings.

::: Wow.

::: Yeah.

::: I stayed in Lake Flathead area for a little while.

::: Yeah, that's beautiful. So are you gonna get an apartment or what?

::: Oh, well, I'm probably going to go back to the other side of the mountains.

::: Are you going to be a drifter like your dad?

::: Um, yeah, maybe. It worked out for him pretty well, until he died recently.

::: Oh, I'm sorry.

::: So what was your name?

::: I'm Alice.

::: Alice. So um, now, I know your friends are waiting so you have to go, but is there anything more you can tell me about this—about the satellite dish?

::: Yeah. They come out and they install it on your roof, and they have to direct it.

::: Uh-huh.

::: So that it picks up the—it picks up the uh—you know the uh…So I don't know if you'd be more satisfied with the cable or that because uh, I don't know—I don't think you can go wrong with either one of them.

::: Really.

::: Yeah.

::: Because they're both just great?

::: Yeah. So, um, why don't I leave this with you. This will *really direct you*. As to the kind of worship that God *approves*. Do you know God says, *Oh, if only you obey my commandments*—

::: Right.

::: *then it will go well with you*—

⋆

Michele: sorry I lost you for a second
Michele: Are you still there?

Visitor 1969: Yes, I'm here.

Michele: great
Michele: May I have your name please?

Visitor 1969: What happened to you?

Michele: I think there was a glitch but it's fine now

Visitor 1969: Well, I'm glad you're back. They call me [redacted].

Michele: Would you like to share your website address with me?

★

I know what all the different religions teach, and I wouldn't be at your door if I didn't feel this was the true faith. You know, if I didn't know for positively, I wouldn't be out here in the snow and the heat and the rain—I've been out doing this for forty-some years. Yeah, I'm seventy-one and I—

::: Well, you're getting a lot of exercise. You look great for seventy-one.
::: Well, I don't know about that, but—
::: No, you do.
::: Well, I—

★

Michele: Still there?

Visitor 1969: Your diction is different, Michele. Please don't be offended with my asking, but are you sure you are the same person i was chatting with before?

Michele: Yes it's me

Visitor 1969: How can I be sure?

Michele: Well I re-engaged with you because I was assisting you:)
Michele: and there is no other Michele except me in this shift

Visitor 1969: OK, sorry Michele, I guess I can get a little paranoid. It's just you never really know who you're talking to on the web, do you?

Michele: you're right, specially with so many technologies out there
Michele: so do you have any other questions for me?

★

::: See, the thing is—and I know you've gotta go—the thing is, it seems to me that God is very large. And that he can't be contained—
::: No.
::: in a book.
::: Uh…
::: And that all of God's ideas and everything that God has in store for us, and created for us, it can't really can't be conceived by man, so man just has to go out and seek God himself and not necessarily blindly believe in the beliefs of his fathers or in a preexistent faith.

::: Well, let me leave this book for you to examine :::

★

Michele: still there?

Visitor 1969: Yes, still here.

Visitor 1969: There was a question i wanted to ask before we got off-track. Does it seem to you that in this country we're not really expected to do anything but buy and consume, or to be anyone but a buyer or a consumer? It feels that way to me.

Michele: well I guess that is the life cycle

Visitor 1969: what do you mean?

Michele: well we buy and consume that's a universal fact. As far as roles are concerned, we all have one.

Visitor 1969: All of us? What is yours?

Michele: well we have a professional life and personal life and the role varies according to that

Visitor 1969: You're right, and what I mean is that both our professional and personal lives now seem to be dictated by the consumer environment. We buy personally, and sell professionally.

Michele: hmm you're right

Michele: you seem to be doing some sort of research

Visitor 1969: Well, I don't often have the opportunity to chat with people like you.

Michele: hmm, so do you have any questions regarding our service?

Michele: I still don't have your name by the way :)

Michele: Are you there?

Visitor 1969: Sorry. Yes, still here. I do have questions about the service.
    This is all part of the decision-making process, Michele. And I
    did tell you my name. Look up and you'll see.
Visitor 1969: ███████████.

Michele: yes I got that.
Michele: I was just wondering if that is actually your name

Visitor 1969: Do you like America?

Michele: Yes, don't you like it/

Visitor 1969: What do you like about America, specifically?

Michele: Visitor 1969 I'm Sorry but my shift just ended. Is there
    something that I can do for you before I log off?

Visitor 1969: Tell me what's so great about America.

Michele: well I'm a citizen of US and I love everything in this country
Michele: like everyone does

Visitor 1969: including what exactly?

Michele: well I like the country and that includes everything
Michele: nothing specifically
Michele: is there anything else I can help you with, today?

Visitor 1969: would you ever want to come to America?

Michele: well I am there.

Visitor 1969: partly cloudy. 60 degrees. feels like 60 degrees.

Michele: I am sorry but I have to logout Now. Incase you have anything
         Business Related you can call us at 312-████████
Michele: Thankyou for Visiting WebsiteGreeters.com. Have a Great Day
Michele: Bye

[session terminated by Michele]

MY ROBOT (REBUILT)

>HEY

>DO YOU THINK YOUR SAVIORS COMING BACK

>WHATS HE LOST DOWN HERE

>HE WAS BORN

>HE LIVED

>AND THEN HE DIED

>BUT CHEER UP HUMANS

>YOU ARE NOT RESPONSIBLE

>FOR IT IS IMPOSSIBLE TO TAKE THE LIFE OF A SAINT

>THE LIVES THEY LOSE ARE GIVEN FREELY

>TO RAISE ONE FROM THE DEAD HOWEVER

>WELL WHAT IS THAT BUT MURDER

X

Early fifteenth century AD: a boy was born: in a cardboard box: in the southern Spanish village of San Nicolás del Puerto. They gave him the name Diego. (Latin: *Didacus;* English: *James.*) He entered religious life as a boy, learning the Catholic faith from a hermit monk who adopted him. The man and the boy lived together in poverty, growing vegetables, and carving utensils out of wood to raise money for their basic needs, giving most of the money to their even poorer neighbors. At the age of thirty, Diego joined the Franciscan Order. Paying no heed to his own safety, he traveled to the Canary Islands, off the coast of NW Africa, to preach the Word to a race of cannibals. He remained there many years. Not much is known of his life during this time. (By the way, I don't remember anymore if these words I have used are mine.)

⋆

And not much is known of his life-subsequent. (That sounds like me.) But we know that Friar Diego returned to Spain, where he lived a very modest life, tending to the sick and poor, preaching at the University of Alcalá de Henares in Toledo, and though he did not know how to read or write, his skills as an orator were widely known. And though he did not seek renown, the reputation of his virtue and charitable spirit spread far and fast and made him famous among the Catholics of Spain. The pope had even heard of him.

★

The 19th century Kazakh prophet Abai rebuked his fellow Kazakhs bitterly, for he saw that they were preoccupied with one thing alone: *"to own as much livestock as possible and thus gain honor and respect."*

★

I know just what he means.

★

Abai asked: *"How come that we speak no ill of the dead but find no worthy people among the living?"*

★

Tell me about it.

★

Abai is a dead saint now. But he was once alive. I could get on a plane and take a train or a Jeep or a camel—I really don't know how to get there—but I can transport myself to the place where he was born and lived; I can stand in the place where he stood, I can watch the sun rise and fall where he saw it rise and fall. The stars have shifted. But only slightly.

★

The seasons return again and again to tell us that the circle takes no notice of our brief lives, or quick declines.

★

So let's send a message to the circle.

★

Let's fill it with meaningless lines.

★

Nietzsche was born a man. He hoped to become a Superman. The philosopher Emil Cioran was born a Romanian. He hoped to become a Frenchman. I was born with a predisposition to abuse painkillers. I wished I was a Pharmacist.

★

My wife and I reside in a little house in the Wallingford neighborhood of Seattle. We wouldn't be able to afford it, but Kay, our friend and surrogate godmother who owns the house, pays the bills and gives us cheap rent. She spends most of her time in her house in Mexico, just a few miles south of the California border, but keeps a room in this one for when she comes up to see family and friends; a week or so every few months. She is sixty-four years old, blond and bubbly, was a cheerleader in high school. She was married to her high school sweetheart, a poet, a rebel, a university professor, but he died of cancer very young. Age forty-four, I think.

★

([redacted])

★

After her husband died Kay spent a year traveling around the world with her son, who was eighteen at the time. Then she bought the house in Mexico. She met an Englishman there, a retired British naval officer and engineer, a tall, broad-chested man, full of spirit, and they lived together in her house for a few years. But she wanted adventure, she wanted to dance the cha-cha and sing and flirt and make love, and as time went on all he ever wanted to do was tend to his garden during the day and sit around drinking gin and smoking cigarettes at night, bitching and moaning no matter the time—expecting to be tended to and waited on hand and foot. He was a bore and a real stuffed shirt, and she decided at last to end it. But on the morning of the day she was going to break the news, she found him in the bedroom, sitting on the edge of the bed, staring down at the floor, his face red as a beet.

★

What's wrong, Jeff? she said. He raised his eyes to her, but could not speak. Neither could he raise himself to his feet. He just sat there. She called an ambulance, but an hour later the ambulance still had not come. So she went next door to the two gay Frenchmen and they came and helped shuffle Jeff to the car, lifting his feet for him one at a time as they made their way down the front walk to the car. Then they set him in the passenger seat, strapped him in. Kay drove him back across the border, to a hospital in San Diego.

★

He never came home. He'd had a stroke, and at last count has had three more since. The last one, just a few days ago, has left him totally blind. Kay drives across the border to visit him at his convalescent home each day. It is an hour drive each way if the wait at the border isn't long. She has been doing this for seven years. She'll keep making the trip until one of them dies.

★

REQUIEM AETERNAM DONA EIS DOMINE
ET LUX PERPETUA LUCEAT EIS

[eternal rest grant them, o lord; and let perpetual light shine upon them]

★

When I was fourteen years old I dreamt that I was riding a train through a dark night made bright by brilliant streaks of perpetually shooting stars. I was seated in a carriage, and the sliding glass doors were shut, and the curtains closed. On their knees before me were two beautiful angels, one blond, one brown, in flowing white robes, their large, round breasts exposed, their broad wings intermingling; the feathers dusting my thighs. I: submerged in this warm, heavenly jelly: I. They kissed me until I came on their lips. I woke. I got out of bed. I went to the window. I lifted it up. I stuck my head out.

★

Five years later at the Antwerp Central Station, my girlfriend—a few hours by that point my ex—and I boarded an empty train for the Channel, and a boat to ferry us back to England. We sat in the rear car, all alone. It was late at night / early in the morning. She was sad and exhausted. She put her bag beneath a bench seat, and lay down.

She fell right to sleep, and as the train ka-thunk ka-thunk ka-thunked through the dark, I sat slouching in the seat across from hers, watching her sleep. I had told her that when we got back to London I didn't want to share a room with her. I didn't want to be her quote unquote "man" anymore. But now, on the train, I wished I hadn't been so cruel to her. I wished I hadn't broken her heart. At least I could have waited until we were back home in London. We were on a train, after all, in the middle of the night; there was no one around, and I was horny.

★

Incidentally, her name was "Angela."

★

Matthew McIntosh a grandi à Federal Way, une banlieue sud de Seattle (état de Washington), où se déroule l'action de son roman WELL (Le Seuil). Il vit maintenant à Seattle avec sa femme.

★

One night, soon after I'd returned from London, I met a man on the adjoining patios behind my friend Adam's apartment, where I was staying the night. I don't know where Adam was. This man was visiting the single mother who lived next door; she worked, I think, at an old folks' home. Or some kind of hospital.

★

She'd sent the kids away and this man had just finished ███████ taking a postcoital nap. He was a small-boned black guy with a thin mustache. Surprisingly, he was a die-hard fan of the hair metal bands of the ’80s and loved to sing their songs. We smoked his crack cocaine together, and he asked for requests. He knew each word to every shitty glam song I could come up with, and would sing them in a loud and beautiful high-vibrato gospel-inflected voice. That’s amazing! I’d say.

★

Thanks, he’d reply.

★

He sang and we talked and talked and talked and he sang and we laughed together and told jokes and smoked his rocks and when they were all gone he asked me for a bowl of weed to top it all off and I said, Sorry man, I don’t have any left, I smoked the last of it before I came outside, and he said, Come on, man, don’t lie, and I said, I’m not lying, and he said, You gotta have at least *one* bowl left, come on, brother, let’s smoke it together, I shared with you now you should share with me, it’s only right, and I said,

★

Sorry brother, I ain’t got a thing.

★

He just shook his head, like he couldn’t understand.

★

I said goodnight and went back inside. Drew the curtain, locked the door, sat down on Adam’s couch, and smoked the rest of my weed:::alone::::

★

That ain't like a saint.

IX

One morning in 1562, nearly a hundred years after the death of Friar Diego, Don Carlos, the lunatic son of the Spanish king Felipe II, fell down a flight of stairs. He was taken to his bed. At times he cursed and raved like a man possessed. At other times he appeared to be unable to speak or move. We scientists believe today that he had suffered a cerebral vascular hemorrhage. That's when a vessel in your brain goes:

*

POP!

*

The official story states that the king's most trusted doctor ordered a phlebotomy/trepanation to let the diseased blood out. They cut the prince's scalp open, bled him, and then sewed the head back up. Don Carlos did not recover. Instead (if I may move into the present tense) he closes his eyes; falls into a coma; and begins to briskly waste away.

★

More doctors, more surgeons, more scientists are called. Magicians are called. Mystics. Soothsayers and diviners and astrologers are called. Potions are administered, spells cast, ancient rites performed, secret words intoned, ancient hymns proclaimed…but the prince does not wake.

★

Then the king summons the Franciscans of Alcalá to come and pray for his son. They arrive bearing the ninety-nine-year-old cadaver of Friar Diego, which they've been keeping in a box. They take the dead friar out and lay him in the bed beside the sleeping prince. (I know, gross, right?) The next morning, when the nurse goes in to check on him, the prince is crawling along the floor counting the tiles. A MIRACLE! This is how Diego, at long last, was elevated to saint.

★

Unfortunately, the prince died anyway. And the moral is: just because a prince is counting tiles doesn't mean he's better.

★

My wife and I visited Kay down in Mexico, and one day we went with her to meet Jeff in the home. He is a large man, with a giant head and big floppy ears, a face mottled with an elaborate network of red and purple lines, veins underneath shiny, rubbery skin. He lacks control over his body, but I can imagine him as he once was, a big, robust man, a powerful creature, bitching and moaning most forcefully. I helped her put him in his wheelchair, and we wheeled him outside to the courtyard to get some fresh air. The air in the home was extremely stale.

Kay pulled out a pack of cigarettes and gave him one. She would only let him have one per day; or one per visit I should say. I don't remember the brand, but it was English and had a fancy sideways lion for a logo. I had quit a while before and was both on the patch and chewing the nicotine gum, but out of respect I had a smoke with him.

★

We sat around a table, beneath a sun umbrella. Jeff spoke with a slurred voice, and thick English accent. He sat with his head hung low, chin to chest. He would slowly and shakily draw his cigarette to his lips, the ash growing ever longer. From time to time, Kay would take the cigarette from between his fingers, tap it on the ashtray, then give it back. Snot dripped steadily from Jeff's nostrils, and don't think it disrespectful of me to mention that he had shit his diaper and I could smell it. It's just a fact of life. Submerged beneath the frozen aspect of his face were two large, gray, sorrowful eyes. And behind the eyes, a mind that still, from time to time (Kay assured us), worked like a finely tuned clock.

★

Sorrow would fall across his face like the shadow of a dark cloud. One moment his head would be raised, bright eyes looking out at us, lips forming a stilted smile, as Kay would remind him of things they had done together, adventures they'd embarked upon, trips taken—*Remember the Orient Express, Jeff?—Remember the Maldives?—Remember when you stole the orchid from the public garden in Honolulu?*

★

(Oh, I was so mad! He stole it right out of the public park! He wrapped the roots in a damp handkerchief and put it in his carry-on bag, I was so angry! I was furious! I wouldn't talk to him the whole trip back!

But he didn't care! He just *had* to have that flower! He had to plant it in our garden, he already knew the spot just as soon as he saw it! It's still there, to this day! It's been blooming every season for twelve years! I'm glad I have it now, but then...Oh, I was livid! *Remember, Jeff? I wouldn't speak to you for days! Remember?*)

★

Yethdahling, he would slur, smiling—

★

but then the cloud would descend again and his eyes would grow dim, his gray gaze fade, his head droop slowly, until he was hunched over looking down again into his lap...and who knew where he was then? Kay would smile and look embarrassed.

★

He's still down there in that hospital as we speak. One day they will carry him away on a gurney—

★

out of the room he shares with a revolving cast of vegetables and wilting flowers, down the hall, quietly so as to not disrupt the other patients, a white sheet pulled up over him, and out through the swinging doors, past the small rectangular sign stuck into the front lawn which announces in unadorned all caps that that sterile wide-hallwayed old folks' home just south of San Diego, which smells of ammonia and where his death certificate will one day say he died, is to be known to you and I (and to all others who pass it by) as the:

★

"CASTLE MANOR"

★

—and lift him up into the awaiting

★

"CABULANCE."

★

(That being what I saw painted on an awaiting van's side.)

★

From: "WILLIAM █████████" <██████w@███.com>
To: <amorris139@█████████.net>, <pairth@█████████.net>,
<annaandmichael@█████.com>, <Lisa████████@██████████.net>,
<erin@█████████████.com>, <jessek@██████████.edu>,
<joelandkarie@██████.com>, <katiejane████████@██████.com>,
<d_liberalis@████████.com>, <s████████@█████████.edu>,
<jewjr@████████.com>
CC:
Date: █ Mar 2005 10:14:10 –0800
Subject: **Margaret Woods**

Rebecca and I were very lucky that our scheduled appointment
in Spokane was yesterday. It put us in one of the best hospitals
in the country for premature babies. We were expecting that
we would get a second opinion, go out to lunch, maybe the mall
and then back to Moses Lake. As it turned out, Rebecca was
admitted, lost all of her fluid, the baby's heartrate dipped a few
times, so they decided to deliver. As you can see, the images
that I snapped after I had them turn on the light are pretty
amazing. She is two pounds and her lungs seem better today than
they did last night. Now our concern in having her heart make
the transition from the way that it pumps inside the whomb to
the way that it pumps outside the womb.

Thank you for your concern and prayers,

You may call us at 509-████████

WILLIAM

If the attachments didn't work, let me know.

VIII

Yesterday (though weeks (though months (no, years ago) ago) ago by now) I watched via the Internet the beheading of a middle-aged American man in Iraq. My mind does not seem to have wanted to properly retain the memory, so for the following account I've had to rely on news reports to remind me of what, as soon as I had seen, I very quickly forgot.

⋆

There were five masked men, each dressed in black from head to toe, only the skin of their arms and hands showing. They stood before a black banner with white Arabic writing on it. (I would have thought there were at least ten of them, and I don't remember the banner.) The American was sitting on the ground, facing forward, in front of the masked men. (I would have said that he was kneeling.) The American's hands were tied behind his back. He wore an orange jumpsuit. Four of the men behind him held assault rifles, while a fifth, in the center, read aloud from a sheet of paper. The American was blindfolded. (I don't remember him being blindfolded. And I don't remember a word the man behind him said. But) Suddenly—(did he drop the paper?)—it happened very quickly—Suddenly the reader lunged at the prisoner!

★

He crouched down behind,

★

crooked his forearm around the man's bare forehead,

★

wrenching the head back, exposing the neck.

★

And with a large knife, began sawing:::::::::::::::::

★

LIBERA EAS DE ORE LEONIS NE ABSORBEAT EAS
TARTARUS NE CADANT IN OBSCURUM
[deliver them from the jaws of the lion, lest hell engulf them,
lest they be plunged into darkness]

★

I cannot think of anything else right now.

★

How about some TV?

★

—he gave us drinks…we accepted drinks from him and we were drugged and raped for thirteen hours……and, we're just wondering if you can tell us, who…who did this to us…he got away…when we first met him, he was talking on the cell phone…to his wife and children Before you say anything, please, could I—give me a second, because I will, I will. I—we gotta talk about this for a second. You are—at the time this happened, how old were you? Nineteen years old. Nineteen years old. Seventeen. Where, where were you at, where you, were you—at a party, hitchhiking—where where did you meet this guy? Um, we met him at a restaurant, in a parking lot, we were calling friends for a ride and he walked up, he was in a tie-dyed shirt, he seemed like a really nice man, he was like, Oh, I'm going that way… They always are. Did he give you a ride—And I'm I'm saying this right now I'm because I have the two of you here, there are a lot of young ladies who are watching this show Right. Don't ever trust anybody. And you got in the car—stupid enough, Sibyl, to get in the car, and then the guy offers you something to drink, right? Right. And—hear me—I am not calling you stupid Right. Date rape drug. There's another young lady right now who will learn from you, I'm telling you. Right, exactly. You get in the car—what made you think this guy would give you something you could trust from him to drink. He—he was just really, he seemed like a sincere person, and before I actually passed out on the drugs, I was looking in the clouds, thanking God that I met this person. I mean, we were talking about *religion!*

★

No! I mean, he's And for the next person here, at one point in time, I guess, it was *you*, he beat you to a point where you thought she was dead. Correct?

★

Right, and the whole thirteen hours he brainwashed me and told me that we killed her together and that I had to come with him. He put her class ring on my finger. I woke up in his car, not knowing where she was, with his hands on me. I was drugged, and I couldn't move, I tried to run, I tried to shove the keys into the ground, I ripped the keys out of the ignition.

★

The police, of course, were involved. Right. But they never caught this guy. No. Sibyl, my first question—I gotta tell you—my first question is: God, tell me this man did not do this again. No he didn't. He did not. No. No. So, therefore, were they random? Had he done this before them and He had done this before but he hasn't done it since, because let me tell you something, somebody took him out. So he's already dead. He's dead, he's dead.

★

[*applause*]

★

Can you tell me his name?

★

Yeah,

★

uh,

★

his name was,

★

um,

★

Ted.

★

You knew this man was married, 'cause I guess—you overheard one of his conversations with he was talking Right to his wife? He was on the phone to his wife and kids and he was like, I'll be home soon, babies, and Ohhhh…

★

Real jewel.

★

Yeah.

★

Well, somebody caught him with uh, you know, somebody, and just, took him out. And that's another case that we're gonna probably see on this show that'll be unsolved with—how in the hell did this guy die? Right. And somebody will think he was a good guy. Oh, somebody will think—how many times, Talk Show Host, will you see these news shows on about a pedophile or murderer and you'll talk to the neighbor and they say, Oh, he kept to himself, he was such a nice person and he seemed to be so nice. Right. That's the thing that got me for so long was that Yeah. they can talk about religion and God. He was living a double life. Look at Jim Jones! Yep. Yep. Right now I had a girl that did this about two months ago. Got in the car with some *pig* just because the guy seemed to talk nice Yeah and, I don't know,

★

how do we *beat this* into our daughters?

★

Yep.

★

How?

★

Yeah. I was naïve and young and, you know. And now they've got this thing now about a Talent Scout—have you heard that? Reality show and Right now right now you have women and men doing this *to-gether!* They even have people dressed up as policemen doing this kind of stuff. It's sick.

★

Yes, ma'am, you have a question for Sibyl.

★

Sibyl, my father passed away about four years ago, and he uh suffered from bone cancer and I just want to know if he's OK. He really is OK. And, um……see, and here's the thing: What you think is suffering— Now, two things could be operating here like I usually say. Is that they don't remember, or that they're not suffering as much as they think we are, do you see what I'm saying? Because they don't—they never, ever remember their suffering. Let me take a break. We'll be back, right after this.

★

Jeff began to weep / Kay laughed nervously.

Why are you crying? she said. *You're too much! You know that? We're all here to see you and now you're crying? What are your guests supposed to think? They've come all the way from Seattle to see you! A grown man crying!*

PLEATHEDONLAUGH, DAHLING! he blurted, thickly, weeping, loudly. DON'TREATMETHOCRUELLY, MYDAHLING!

Kay looked across the table at me, embarrassed.

Come on now, she said to Jeff softly, patting his hand. Come on. Settle down now.

We sat in silence for a while; I scooted my chair back from beneath the sun umbrella. It was summer, and the sky was blue.

Jeff raised his head suddenly and sobbed,

I LOVEYOU MYDAHLING!

Oh, Jeff, Kay said, patting his hand…

★

You're too much…

★

YOU'RE MY ANGEL! he cried, the tears rolling down his face, onto his shirt, snot dripping from his nose. Kay wiped it with a tissue, laughing:

Stop it now, Jeff! That's enough!

★

Then he said something like

YOU ARE THE SUN IN THE SKY!

YOU ARE THE SILVER MOON AT NIGHT!

YOU ARE THE SALVATION OF THE WORLD!

YOU ARE THE BEGINNING AND THE END!

IN YOU I BEHOLD ETERNITY!

IN YOU I BEHOLD THE VOID!

YOU ARE THE ALL AND THE NOTHING!

YOU ARE THE SEED AND THE WOMB!

YOU ARE THE UNIVERSE AND ALL THAT IT CONTAINS!

YOU ARE TIME AND SPACE,

MATTER AND ANTIMATTER!

YOU ARE THE THOUGHT

AND THE WORD

AND THE NAME

AND THE WORLD!

YOU ARE THE BLESSED BOOK

AND HOLY ROOD!

YOU ARE ALL THAT IS ONLY,

EVER, ALWAYS, ONLY,

EVER, ALWAYS, ONLY!

YOU!

OHOWILOVEYOU!

OHOWILOVEYOU!

OHOWILOVEYOU!

MY DARLING!

★

Stop it, Jeff! Kay said. You're *embarrassing* me! Come on, now. Tell the kids about the time you were an extra on *Titanic! You remember?* They filmed it in Ensenada. Did you know that? They built a *huge boat* down there in the harbor. *Remember, Jeff?* The director just *loved* him! *Didn't he Jeff!* He liked you because you were *real British upper crust!* That's what he said. *Not just some actor.* His nickname for Jeff was *Sir George. Remember?* He also liked Jeff because he was big and tall and looked good on film. I think that movie made about a billion dollars. Did you kids see it? No? You should rent it sometime. *Shouldn't they, Jeff!*

★

So they can see you!

01:49:16,152 --> 01:49:18,188 X1:224 X2:492 Y1:452 Y2:486

Come towards me !

★

>Subject: 55599-1: Grove Atlantic: "TITANIC" (1997) /
>"THEMYSTERY.DOC"

>Thank you very much for your request dated August 11, 2015
>to license stills of "TITANIC" (1997) from Twentieth Century Fox
>Film Corporation in your book. Unfortunately, after reviewing
>your request, we regret that we cannot grant a license to you
>for this purpose. I can assure you we gave your request serious
>and thoughtful consideration.

01:49:18,232 --> 01:49:20,063 X1:276 X2:442 Y1:452 Y2:491

>Thank you for your interest in licensing Fox material and
>good luck with your project.
>
>

*

But Jeff didn't want to talk about being an extra on the Titanic or how he had managed to survive that terrible wreck. Instead, through a torrent of tears, he told us the tale of what had happened to him after he'd washed up onshore.

★

Now, this part is one hundred percent true:

★

Robin Hood of Sherwood Forest has been captured by his archnemesis Sheriff Saddam Hussein, and tossed into a high-security Baghdad prison, with mile-high walls forged of dense, impenetrable metal, a mile thick at its least dense point. A perfect cube. And Robin's in the center.

★

The cell is dark and cold. There is neither light, nor warmth. Robin is chained to the icy ground, each link of the chain weighing a hundred kilograms, and constructed of some virtually unbreakable material created in a secret U.S. laboratory, a joint effort between the Right-Wing Factions of Academia, Military, Industry, and the Federal Government, for the sole purpose of binding Robin. Robin cannot remember how long he has been imprisoned in this manner—for him Time has ceased to exist; there is only one cold, neverending night.

★

He desires to die, but is kept alive by the Machine. He has never seen it with his eyes, for the darkness is impenetrable, but since the time he was brought in he has become all too acquainted with the Machine. For at irregular intervals the Machine begins to whir, and then rolls across the cell to Robin, who can always feel the Machine closing in on him in the darkness.

★

After a matter of seconds, a beep is heard, and then a whir, and then Robin, supine upon his back—for that is the manner in which he is bound—feels a cold metal appendage spread apart his lips. So tightly is he bound, that all self-compelled motion is impossible. He cannot even fight the parting of his lips.

★

Once the lips are parted, the teeth are pried open with a separate appendage. Then another appendage comes forth. It holds between two tongs a single round Nugget. The tongs enter Robin's mouth and with a whir continue past his tongue and down his throat reaching all the way into his stomach. When the sensor on the appendage comes in contact with the stomach acids, another beep is heard, the tongs open, and the Nugget is deposited. Then the appendage retracts back up through the throat, and seals Robin's mouth orifice, so that Robin may not expunge the pellet by vomiting.

★

As the Machine sits quietly plugging his mouth until digestion has occurred and the Nugget has been absorbed into the bloodstream, Robin lies there, literally beside himself with sorrow. For he will never see the woods of Sherwood Forest again, those famous woods he loves so much, those woods where as a young boy he would play, and the birds would sing, and Friar Tuck and Little John and all the lads and in the dining room of his boyhood house in Liverpool was a long oak table where they would eat their meals, and at his father's seat at the head, his father had built into the table a drawer, and young Robin would sit at the table, eating his supper, always filled with wonder at the thought of what was in the drawer.

★

He was forbidden to look inside, and he never saw his father take anything out of the drawer except for his pipe and a pouch of tobacco when the meal was over. And someday, young Robin thought, when I am old enough, I shall find out what is really in the drawer (for he knew that there was something else besides the pipe and tobacco).

★

But now old Robin will never know what was in the drawer. For he was sent to live with his aunt at her house in Wales when his mother became ill. And he always planned on finding the table again, but now he has been taken prisoner and surely will never see the great table again! So he will never know the answer. Old Robin will know only cold and darkness. And he begins to weep.

★

He weeps for many hours,

★

and the hours turn to days,

★

and the days to years.

★

Then one day, suddenly, he hears a sound, the first sound, besides the whirring and beeping of the Machine, to reach his ears in many years.

★

It is a faint sound, coming from outside the mile-thick walls of his cell.

★

It sinks;

it sprouts;

★

it grows;

★

it blooms;

★

it is a woman's voice, a beautiful singing voice.

★

It is the voice of his beautiful blond-haired angel: Maid Marian! Listen! Hear the Sound! Hear the angel sing!

★

"My Beloved, I have come to take you away!"

★

Or something like that. It was hard to make out Jeff's words.

★

To dream of being in a castle, you will be possessed of sufficient wealth to make life as you wish.

★

We are bruised fruit.

★

We have fallen from the vine.

★

Venus

is so   bright

that a naval commander once ordered his ship to fire upon it

he thought he saw the headlight of an oncoming train heading for him.

★

Anyway... So, what happened once Maid Marian entered Robin's prison?

★

Well, it was difficult to tell because as her singing grew louder, and she grew nearer, and her light grew brighter, penetrating the cell from all directions, Jeff, sitting there, with low downturned head, in his wheelchair, beneath the sun umbrella, well, his weeping began to overpower him, and the words, difficult to understand anyway, became completely unintelligible, trapped in his belly, and his throat, something like a gasp, something like a wail, something like a choke.

★

The story continued anyway, while Kay laughed nervously and rubbed Jeff's hand, and my wife and I sat quietly, leaning toward him, trying to hear and understand, eager to know, but too polite to interrupt and say:

★

I didn't quite catch that, Jeff.

★

Tell that part again.

★

What happens when Maid Marian enters his cell?

★

Does she save him?

★

Do they escape?

★

What were the words of her song?

VII

Saint Didacus [Diego] one day heard a poor woman lamenting, and learned that she had not known that her seven-year-old son had gone to sleep in her large oven; she had lighted a fire, and lost her senses when she heard his cries. He sent her to the altar of the Blessed Virgin to pray and went with a large group of persons to the oven; although all the wood was burnt, the child was taken from it without so much as a trace of burns. I know for sure that these are not my words.

*

Living in the Castle Manor was an old man named Mr. Kerby. I met him at dinner. One of the nurses had wheeled Mr. Kerby to our table and put a tray of food in front of him. Mr. Kerby was very old, somewhere in his eighties. He was a slight man, with no teeth, and he would open and close his eyes and scrunch up his face whenever he spoke or thought of something. He was bald as a cue ball, with a friendly, open face, and this particular evening he wore a wide-necked white undershirt.

★

I found out from Kay that years earlier, before he was a resident himself, Mr. Kerby had been forced to check his ailing wife into the Castle Manor. He'd been devoted to his wife and had visited her every day, staying from early in the morning to late at night, feeding her, bathing her, cleaning her—performing all the functions of hygiene and sustenance the nurses were being paid to perform. Eventually she died there, in the Castle Manor, and it wasn't long after that that Mr. Kerby was brought in by social services, after taking a fall at his house. He had been a resident five years by the time I met him.

★

I spoke to Mr. Kerby while he ate his dinner. He'd grown up on a farm in Indiana, and spent most of his life working in an accounting office in Chicago. As a young man he went to France during World War II, and worked in payroll for the army, so he had seen no action. I was glad about this, because five seconds after meeting Mr. Kerby I saw that he was the most kind and gentle man who had ever lived, a simple-minded, open-hearted saint. He loved trains. He loved trains the way a mountain climber loves the mountain, or a surfer loves the wave.

★

After the war, when he was discharged, instead of returning straightaway to America, Mr. Kerby went to Paris—for only one reason: to ride the subway. He told me, opening and shutting his eyes and scrunching up his nose, that he had ridden every inch of every line. Then he went to Berlin, where he rode the subway there, the

U-Bahn, every inch of every line. He went to London next and rode the Underground, every inch of every line. He told me that every inch of western American rail led to Chicago's big stations. He remembered his first trip to the city as a boy, with his father. As the locomotive had pulled into the station, its whistle blew, and he squeezed his father's hand in excitement. (I may have made this part up, I don't remember.)

★

He asked me what I did for a living and I said I was a writer. He was hard of hearing and didn't catch that, so I SAID I WAS A WRITER. I WRITE BOOKS. He said,

★

Oh   I   see…and smiled, opening and closing his eyes.

★

Then he said, in his very slow, midwestern drawl: There   are   lots   of things   that   you   could   write   a   book   a   bout…

★

You   could   write   a   book   a   bout   the   trains   in   Chi   ca   go…

★

You   could   write   a   book   a   bout   the   cat   tle   in   dus   try…

★

(He thought awhile longer…)

★

You could write a book a bout the corn in dus try…

★

(He thought awhile longer…)

★

You could write a book a bout the rail road in dus try…

★

★

You could write a book a bout the coal in dus try…

★

★

You could write a book a bout the steel in dus try…

★

★

You could write a book a bout the sub ways of the world…

★

A few days later my wife and I returned to Castle Manor. We'd left Kay in Mexico to resume our trip back home, and wanted to leave a thank-you card for her with Jeff. As we walked toward his room we spotted Mr. Kerby, sitting in his wheelchair, with a group of residents. It was a very sad sight to see. They formed a crescent moon of wheelchairs, all of them facing the long rectangular nurses' desk, behind which three nurses were doing paperwork, silently. None of the old people were speaking to one another. They were just sitting there, as time went by. When we saw Mr. Kerby there in the semicircle, we approached him, we bent down so as to be at eye level, and when he saw us—and then finally recognized us—his face lit up, he smiled and squeezed his eyes shut and opened them again and said: Oh, hel lo!

★

Just this mor ning I thought of a no ther thing you could write a book a bout!

★

I could write a book about a man who rides the rails to the end of the world.

★

And it is

★

MADNESS

★

★ ★ ★ ★ ★

★

★

★

★

★

And it is hard work

We're so proud of you, *babe! It's all right! You did* good, *and you're doing well now, K?*

★

VI

>IT IS HARD WORK BEING A SAINT.

(The Bishop of the candidate's local Diocese begins the formal process. Information must be gathered detailing the life and works of the candidate, and the holiness of his or her character. Those who knew the candidate in life are interviewed.

*

Second- and thirdhand testimonies may be submitted.

*

Once the information is exhaustively documented, the Bishop may petition to begin the beatification process. The information is presented to the Vatican's Congregation for the Causes of Saints. Officials of the Congregation create an historical account of the candidate's life and character. The candidate must be proven to have lived a life of heroic virtue.

★

Finally, a miracle must be proven to have taken place after the candidate's death, due to the intercession of candidate.

★

Once the heroic virtue and the postmortem miracle is acknowledged by the Congregation, the candidate may then be designated beatific by the Pope. Once beatification is recognized the candidate has been officially venerated, and is known from then on as a Blessed One; e.g., Blessed Virgin Mary, Blessed Charlemagne, etc.

★

Then, if the Pope so wishes, the process of canonization may take place, the final step toward Sainthood.

★

A second miracle must be shown to have taken place due to the candidate's postmortem intercession.

★

This is taken as a sign that the candidate continues to intercede for the flock as a member of God's heavenly court and thus henceforth, the name of the candidate—as it appears in the hearts and minds and on the tongues of all creatures in all realms—both above and below—shall forever be prefixed by:

★

St.*)

★

August 2000, my grandmother Helen—not to be confused with Helen my four-year-old niece—was taken to the hospital. I was far from home, in Itchy City, rubbing calamine lotion onto my bites.

★

I spoke to her on the phone, and she told me of her symptoms, and that the doctors didn't really know what was wrong with her, but she assured me that she would be fine, she would be back home in her apartment very soon. She asked me how my writing was going.

★

Coincidentally, I had just begun a chapter about a kind-hearted, elderly Irish-Catholic woman who suddenly finds herself falling apart. I had no beginning and no ending; I had only an inbetween and it wasn't leading anywhere in either direction. I was frustrated. I wrestled with it for a long time, getting nowhere.

★

She was not recovering, so a few weeks later I flew home to Seattle to see her. They'd moved her from the hospital to a home. Her wig was on the bedside table, and she wore a white cotton wrap on her head. I'd never seen her without her wig. I don't believe <u>*ANYONE!*</u> had.

* For martyrs, miracles aren't necessary.

I'd brought her a copy I'd purchased of a small and for some reason incredibly pricey literary journal published by the English department of New Mexico State University which, by accepting a story I'd sent to them (as well as to many, many far more prestigious publications), had granted me my first successful submission of any kind—as well as two complimentary copies. I wrote her a note on the inside cover. I don't remember what it said. Most likely something like: *I am extremely indebted to you.* Or: *You're the one member of my family who really encouraged me in my writing, who liked what I wrote, and said that it was great.*

★

She was so happy. She knew from the beginning that her grandson was going to be a famous writer. She was confused. I think she was finally taking the pills they'd been trying to give her for the pain. Her wig was on the table.

★

The visit was short because she had so little strength. She said she'd have one of my aunts read her *Looking After My Own* when they came to visit. She wasn't complaining but she was having trouble *READING?* these days. I kissed her goodbye, and,

★

as I turned to leave the room, from behind me a voice was heard to say my name. I turned back around

★

and a young woman was sitting up in the bed where my grandmother had just been; her face was smooth and very fair, her lips red, her eyes were blue and bright, and long, dark tresses flowed about her cheeks, cascading in curls down her shoulders.

★

She said, "The journey ahead is very difficult, and the one against whom you must stand will set many obstacles in your path. But the prize is great indeed.

★

You must be bold, and good and true, and never fear. The water will get colder the closer you get to the end, but you will not freeze. And the fire will grow hotter but it will not burn you. Everything will appear to turn upside down. The sky will be below you and above will be the ground. The one who tries to climb will find himself falling. But the one who lets himself go will rise to heaven. There will come a light. And then a flash. And then darkness. And then the end will appear to come. But do not be afraid. For the end is only a doorway to another world, the *real* world, which underlies, supports, and sustains this dull reflection. Always always *always* remember:

★

[redacted]."

★

I said, OK,

★

OK,

★

OK,

★

OK,

★

OK,

★

OK,

★

OK,

★

OK,

★

OK,

★

OK,

★

OK,

★

OK,

★

OK,

★

OK,

★

OK,

★

OK,

★

OK,

★

OK,

★

OK,

★

OK,

★

OK,

★

OK,

★

OK,

★

OK,

★

OK,

★

OK,

★

OK,

★

OK,

★

and flew away the next day.

★

Begin another new section?

>OK

V

Sir Thomas More, author of Utopia, friend & adviser to King Henry VIII, was sentenced to death for refusing to swear oath to two Acts. 1.) of Succession, which reconstituted the line to the throne, and 2.) of Supremacy, which declared His Majesty the head of God's earthly church.

★

He was beheaded in 1535, after having said, with his ordinary humor, that he did not consider the severing of his head from his body as a circumstance that should produce any change in the disposition of his mind. SAINT THOMAS MORE, Martyr (1480–1535)

★

lol

★

Very late one night in my 18th year, my roommate JD and I were, as we often used to say, (Dude, I'm) "fucked up." We'd been in front of the TV drinking malt liquor and smoking pot all afternoon and then all evening and into the night and now it was half past three in the morning, *I Love Lucy* was on, and we were out of alcohol and weed. We woke up another roommate, Steve, and asked him if he had anything that we could get high on. Steve was a very serious student—he studied hard, took all the difficult classes—he smoked cigarettes and drank beer on the weekends but he didn't do anything else. He didn't even smoke pot. He majored in chemistry. He said he had a bottle of CD cleaner on his desk. That would probably do it.

*

JD and I sprayed CD cleaner into a paper bag and passed it back and forth, taking turns inhaling the fumes, as the show went into its first commercial.

The lights were off, so it was dark, except for a demonic teddy bear who fell through the sky and landed on a stack of fluffy bed linens, giggling like a maniac and crying out with an insidious high-pitched squeal about the virtues of something he called "snuggly softness." My head was filled:::   :::it lifted off:::

*

St. Damien of Molokai went to the Islands to "make myself a leper with the lepers to gain all to Jesus Christ,"

*

*.

*.

.

.*.

.

.*.

.

.*.

..*.*.*.*.*.*.*.*.*.*.*.*.*. .*.

.

.*.*.*.*.*.*.

★

Not long after, the reader finds us both slumped darkly in our chairs, minus a number of brain cells. The lightness in our heads, the sense of euphoric imbalance, are all byproducts of the evil, craven slaughter of these cells. As each cell had exploded, it had sung the song of its release. It went:

★

POP!

★

the song was called [redacted]

★

Someday the entire Choir will sing that song. But for now…

★

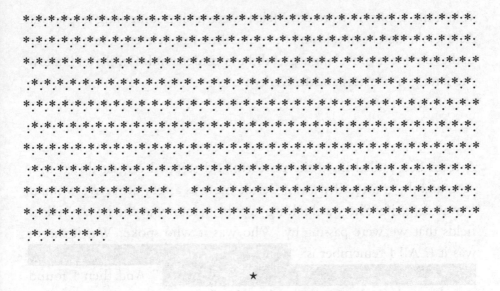

When the euphoria wore off, I felt I was missing something important. As if a joke had been told and the punchline not delivered, or a message had come for me in a language I did not understand. Or, if you'll allow me (and as a courtesy to Mr. Kerby):

★

A train had pulled in to the platform. I'd stepped on, sat down in a seat, and the train pulled away. Beside me was a very attractive woman. It was my wife. She was looking out the window at the lovely yellow fields that we were passing by. Who was it who spoke? Was it she or was it I? All I remember is: "███████████████████████ █████████████████████████████." And then I found myself eye-locked with a Satanic teddy bear—red-eyed and snarling like a rabid werewolf.

★

Jesus, I don't feel so good, I said.

★

I crawled away, down the hall, to my bedroom, and into my bed thinking I really would be much better off dead.

★

JD was found the next morning by the front door. Asleep on his knees. The crown of his head was pressed up against the door, as if he'd been trying to get away from a cloud of poison gas, and it had overtaken him before he'd been able to figure out how the doorknob worked.

★

Hey.

★

Dude.

★

Get up.

★

Anyway, long story short, we both turned out fine.

★

After dinner Kay, my wife and I left Jeff and Mr. Kerby and drove back down to the border, to return to Kay's house in Mexico. As we waited in line at the crossing, Kay told us about an elderly neighbor of hers, an old woman, who had woken up one morning, got out of bed and went into the kitchen. She made coffee and watched some television. She went back into the bedroom to see if her husband was expecting breakfast in bed. But he was dead.

I don't know what she did then. At some point she telephoned her neighbors.

★

They came to her, Kay with them, and said: Oh Honey, Oh Dear, Oh Sweetheart—*You Poor Little Thing.*

★

His body remained incorrupt for several months, exposed to the devotion of the faithful, ever exhaling a marvelous fragrance. (SAINT DIDACUS or DIEGO)

★

Someone made coffee.

★

The neighbors warned her to keep quiet. If those crooked Mexican cops got wind, they'd take possession of the body, empty his pockets, steal his watch, rip out his teeth, melt down the fillings. Sell his parts for scrap.

★

Most importantly, they'd never let her take him back over the border.

★

So that evening, with the help of the neighbors, she dressed him in his favorite suit. Some men carried him to the car, and strapped him into the passenger seat. Someone put a pair of dark sunglasses over his eyes, and a fishing hat on his head, pulling the brim down over his face. (I'm aware that this sounds a lot like the plot of *Weekend at Bernie's* but I swear that it's true!) Good luck! they cried. Drive safe! Go with Christ! Christ be with you!

★

And so she drove to the border with the corpse of her husband in the seat beside her.

★

During an illness, he was ordered to eat meat by a physician, which he had made a vow never to do. A plate containing well-prepared fowl was brought to him. In the presence of several witnesses, he made the sign of the cross over it, and the bird flew away out the window. (Saint Nicholas of Tolentino, *Little Pictorial Lives of the Saints*)

★

She drove past mangy little doggies.

★

Passed mangy little doggies digging through trash piles.

★

Past mangy little doggies digging through trash piles outside of hovels clapboard houses rusted tin shacks and refrigerator boxes, inside of which people were born grew ate drank shat slept woke fucked gave birth and died.

(Following the signs)

★

Following the signs, she maneuvered her car into the **S**ecure **E**lectronic **N**etwork for **T**ravelers' **R**apid **I**nspection lane, and began start-and-stopping toward the border.
Although the air conditioner was on she found herself sweating.
She was sick to her stomach with nerves. She'd never done anything even remotely *illegal* in her life!

★

Started and stopped until she pulled up to the line, by now trembling uncontrollably. An officer approached her window, looked in, into her eyes, then at the seat beside her. Then he waved for other officers to come running.

She looked over at her husband—*and shrieked!*

He was slumped forward in his seat, very stiffly, suspended by the safety harness strapped across his chest.

His lips were parted, and his dentures were hanging out of his mouth.

★

On the last day of his life, November 10, 1608, Saint Andrew rose to say Mass. He was eighty-eight years old, and so weak he could scarcely reach the altar. He began the Judica me, Deus, the opening prayer, but fell forward, the victim of apoplexy.

★

The guard waved his arms and others came running.

★

Would you die the death of the just?

★

Laid on a straw mattress, his whole frame was convulsed in agony,

They surrounded the car.

while the ancient fiend, in visible form, advanced as though to seize his soul.

★

There is a certain way and only one, to secure the fulfillment of your wish

★

Then, while the onlookers prayed and wept,
he invoked Our Lady, and his Guardian Angel
seized the monster and dragged it out of the room.

★

Kay tells me that Jeff has many grand plans. He works on them while lying in his cell during the times the Machine is set to SLEEP.

★

He will buy an old abandoned army hospital in the Aleutian Islands and turn it into a resort. Kay will cook the food for their guests, and entertain them after dinner each night with clog dancing.

★

He'll start a salvage business, rummaging the watery depths up and down the western coast of Mexico, in search of sunken treasure, wrecked galleons, skeleton keys.

★

He'll put a hundred thirty seven windmills atop the sides of the Columbia Gorge, to stand sentry above the river that carves apart the Washingtonian and Oregonian states.

★

And he's got an idea about a stone that returns life to the dead.

★

And a plan for building bodies for old scientists who've been left with only a head.

★

And an electromagnetic road running from the dark side of his eyelids to the bright core of the sun.

★

(And a way to keep young women young.)

★

my robot
Kay is to contact the Japanese concerning capital and the Germans

bring forth

a beginning &

an end

1 1

I was completely too tired, Alice calls, 48°

Hey!

★

"Give me my baby. I am going to take him away. He is mine."

Do you think your hero's coming back?

Barbara, and others, had…just finished a *performance* of some kind.

★

the web that shes spinning

lost sense of taste

★

Adam's rib / Magician's chest

happened upon the town, ravaging it, and in the turmoil, he was freed from the box and sent airborne

★

What's he lost down here?

VAZQUEZ: Aida T., 76, of Federal Way, April 8.

by a wave of the hand

he was born

★

hydrogen

composition of a mandala in religious art is meant, as I see it, to encapsulate God by building his universe around him, piece by piece. At the very center, there is often an image

to find your way

★

impression, etc. left by touching

★

was always trying to make time with the young

oh my

he lived

compounds

★

a broken piece

★

the bait

★

that could not be broken.

★

through which worlds occur, come into being

Byrne is just a *saint saint saint*

nothing will be found

★

but in the meantime, the book must be presented

★

cheer up!

losing himself

trying to reconstruct your face…

Mels legs covered with water blisters, Eloise calls, Nancy & Laura call for me to come over,

You Don't Have To *Believe*

Believe me girl..
we're hanging on just like everyone else...

She stepped away from me and she moved through the fair,
And fondly I watched her go here and go there,

gone

Rebecca and William Woods
of Moses Lake, Wash announce the birth of:

Margaret Woods

Born: ███████, 2005
Weight: 1 lb. 11 oz.
Length: 11 1/2 inches

At **Deaconess Medical Center**

He understood himself to be irrevokably tied.

old woman

swallow

fly

★

any-

thing is

possible through

re ⋆ engine ⋆ erin ⋆ g

IV

Try as we might to avoid it, we are headed straight for a very big problem:

★

Time is tearing us apart.

★

We go on because there's no other way to go.

★

But back and forth,

★

In and out,

★

Up and

★

down.

★

Until the strike of twelve and then…

★

~~end~~

>BEGIN AGAIN

★

My grandfather was an up & coming lawyer. He drank Irish Whiskey and smoked Lucky Strikes. He laughed and joked and sang and played with his children. But his heart was weak and when my mother was only seven years old his light went out. It was a cool autumn afternoon, and he was found sitting in a chair behind his office desk. He wasn't quite forty-five.

★

His law partners drove to my grandmother's house. When she opened the door, their hats were in their hands. I imagine one said: I'm sorry, Helen. Tom's—

★

She fell

★

This was 1957. She had four children to raise. She sold her expensive clothes and furniture, a diamond ring. And other things. She kept her big home on Capitol Hill for the sake of the children for as long as she could, but eventually all but my mother were off married or in college so she let it go too.

★

like a leaf

★

After her husband died, she got a job at Seattle University, checking books out at the student library. She lived forty-five years in various rent-controlled apartments, a few blocks from that old house she had once loved so "vainly"; from the ceiling rose

★

to the hardwood floor.

★

In her final apartment, each autumn when the leaves fell from the giant maple across the street, it was like a curtain opening……and all winter long she'd have a view of the top of the Space Needle, its head just poking up over the hill. She loved that view but it was more than she needed.

★

See, she *believed* in the Saints!

★

Two years before she died, she had an operation in which her right knee was removed and replaced with a metal one. She lay in bed for months, in great pain. A nurse would bring her painkillers on a tray. But she refused to take them.

★

She had a GREAT BIG MEDICINE CABINET, and it was filled to the gills. I lived then in a little studio apartment about a fifteen-minute walk away. I believed in Cause & Effect. I visited often. I stole her pills.

★

But wait!

★

Going up the scaffold, which was so weak that it was ready to fall, he said merrily to Master Lieutenant: "I pray you, Master Lieutenant, see me safe up, and for my coming down let me shift for myself"...he kneeled down, and after his prayers said, turned to the executioner, and with a cheerful countenance spake thus to him: "Pluck up thy spirits, man, and be not afraid to do thine office; my neck is very short; take heed therefore thou strike not awry, for saving of thine honesty." (Roper, *Life,* pp. 102–3.)

★

There's More!

★

::::::::::::::A pouring forth—blood gushed out of the neck upon the cement—the sound:

all I can compare it to is the sound a bucketful of dirty water makes when thrown out into the street after washing one's father's Aerostar van. The man in orange cried out! And this part I remember very well, because his voice was very quickly mangled by the teeth of the blade as the man in black sawed into his throat, so what came out—and I think the noise came not from his mouth, but from the wound—was the sound of an animal being slaughtered; A high-pitched screeching sound

—no—a wail—

★

a bellowing—

★

no—a neighing—

★

a bleating—

★

the sound a terrified pig would make—

★

Forgive me.

★

There really is no

★

FAC EAS DOMINE DE MORTE TRANSIRE AD VITAM
[lord, make them pass from death to life]

★

>ADEQUATE TRANSITION

I shut my eyes

[redacted] Kay whispered:

The boat was sinking and Jeff was waiting to board a life raft. But they were only taking women and children. So he had to stand there and wait, and when they shot up the warning flare he looked up. Only it wasn't really a warning flare, but a bright spotlight the director shone down onto their faces.

★

As the knife severed the muscles of the neck, making its way toward the cord of the spine…

★

The body, the body…
well, the body continued to whine.

Was he dead then already? I don't know.
The noise persisted long after you would have thought
 a body could still be living to make them…
He kept calling……
…now slightly quieter…
……now resigned……
…………retreating…………
…………now defeated……
and so………in this manner……
all the way down
did his clock
un………………
…………wind.

★

: [redacted] :

★

She held his head in her hands, calming his fears of death.

★

Hey!

★

Q: What is Death?

★

A: *Salvation!*

★

And what are Aphorisms?

★

White lies! Dumb lines!
Stupid jokes!

★

Hey!

★

Can't You SEE it's getting OLD?!?!

★

phone rings 3 times, no one there??

If I was down to my last pill
I would crush it into a powder and snort it
 off the cover of a hardback book.
Sometimes I would sprinkle the powder into a pipe and smoke it.
I hoped that by changing the method of intake, and the physical properties of the drug, I would travel to loftier planes, arrive sooner, stay longer.
Back then I really didn't give a shit about the superheroes of the Catholic Church.
Back then my head was hurting all the time.

⋆

And I…

⋆

just wanted…

⋆

to be…

⋆

high.

⋆

F█k the saints.

★

—We're at Brooke's house. Brooke, say hi. This is her—oh, wrong way— this is her really cute house. And that's her hot tub.

★

She lives out …

★

… in the forest.

★

Or kind of. Anyway, it's so cute. █████—ow I tripped, sorry—and nice. And that's her cute house. That's

★

her car. The blonde car. Those are her

★

dogs.

★

See?

★

German shepherds. Like *us!* They're home. Anyway. Very cute. Very

★

fun.

★

I liked it!"

★

[*laughs*]

★

substance

material

join

understanding

M: It's all in my head…… ⋆
W: Well, I hope it can soon be in *my* head.

(At the end of the story Helen ascends to heaven…

…and leaves this world of peeling paint.)

⋆

>MY ROBOT,

★

>YOU
>DON'T
>HAVE
>TO
>
>
>
>
>
>
>
>
>
>
>
>
>
>
>
>
>
>
>
>
>
>
>
>
>

>
>
>
>
>
>
>
>
>
>
>
>
>
>
>
>
>
>
>
>
>
>
>
>
>
>
>
>
>
>
>
>
>

>
>
>
>
>
>
>
>
>
>
>WAIT.

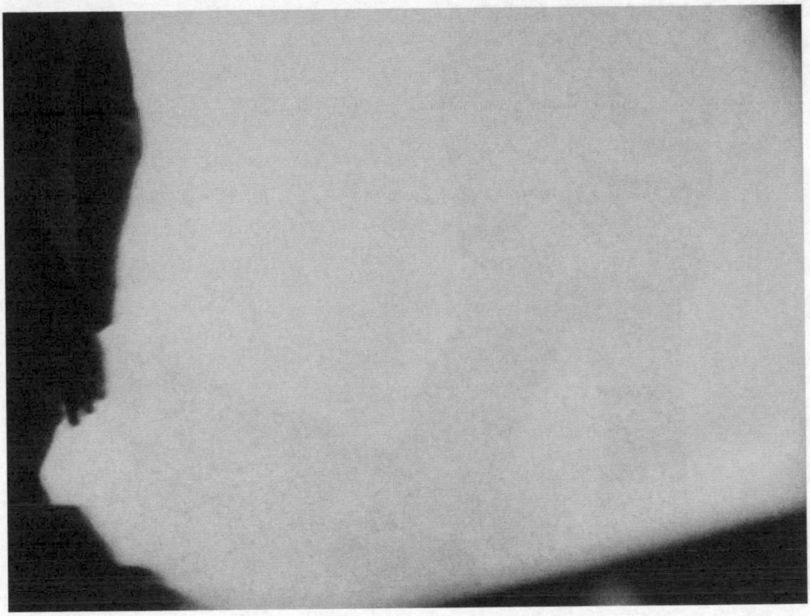

III

We're gonna walk towards the bathroom, OK?……

Doin good, keep comin. *Fab*ulous. OK, keep comin…

Ah-ah—pick those feet up! Put your hands back on my shoulders!…

Hands back on my shoulders! OK, keep walkin! Keep walkin! Ah-ah—bring those feet up! No buckling your knees! Come on, here we go! Keep comin! Ah-ah—put your hands back up on my shoulders, Michael. Michael, put your hands back on my shoulders…

There you go, OK? Comin into the bathroom…

Come on, come on! A little bit further!…Let go of the door and put your hand back on my shoulder. Fabulous! OK…OK, we're gonna have problems with this rug here…Put your hands on the sink for me. Both hands on the sink! Michael, put both hands on the sink for me! Hold on. What was your name again?

Matt.

Matt? You're his son?

Uh-huh.

You're gonna have to stay in here this time, OK?

Sure.

OK. Hold on to the sink here!…There you go! Let me shut the door…OK…I'm gonna pull this forward, and then as we go we're gonna take everything out from underneath your feet here. OK?… OK, lift this foot for me, Michael! Fabulous!…

Let me get this sock off! Perfect! OK! Now I'm gonna come over here—keep your knees straight! Bring 'em back up! Michael! Stand up straight! Michael! Stand up straight! There you go! OK, now lift this knee for me, this leg here for me, lift! Lift this leg for me!…OK, great!……OK…One less thing we have to deal with. OK!…All right!…The urinal is one thing we did not get in here.

OK, now we're gonna direct him over and sit him on the side of the bench there, if we can. Michael! I want you to go over and sit down on that bench for me, OK? Can you do that? I need you to take steps to your left! OK? Here we go! Steps to your left, keep going! Keep going! A little bit further! Little bit further! You need to hold on!…

Take a couple more steps! To your left!

There you go! Now, go ahead and sit down!…Put your hands on my shoulders and sit down! OK? I got ya! I got ya, sweetie, sit!…Sit!

You're not sittin, you're not bending your legs! OK, there we go, OK? Feel that bench underneath you?...... I need you to lift this foot into the tub for me—up! And in!...There we go! OK? We're gonna do the other one! Nope—that one's stayin in, this one's comin in now! Come around! Come around! Lift this foot up! And it's goin in the tub! OK? Need you to scoot all the way over there for me! Grab on here! Now, scoot over to the side, scoot! Here we go!...

OK, that's a good scoot. That's why I have the...the um...

OK, let's take the shirt off next. We're gonna take a shower here, OK?...There we go...Lift your arm up for me......OK, we're gonna take the jacket off. Can you take the jacket off for me?...........Lift your elbow up. Fabulous. Can you take that side off for me too?...... Great. OK. Can you take your undershirt off for me?....Take the undershirt off......Can you finish taking it off for me?......No? OK. Up and over the head!...Here we go!...There you go! Now I want you to do me a favor and slide over! All the way to this bar, OK? Can you slide your butt over there?...Can you slide all the way over? Can you slide over just a little bit more for me, hon? Michael? I need your butt way over there! Can you put your butt over closer to the wall?...Can you scoot over for me? There we go! Perfect! OK, wonderful! Now, this might be a little cold but I'm gonna put this here so I don't totally flood the floor!...All right! Now we'll try this puppy out!...Are all the water temperatures set the same? OK, perfect. I love that..............OK, let's try it out!......OK, you ready for this?........Does it feel OK?...Does it feel kinda hot?...........How's this?...OK?...You wanna hold on to that for me? OK, I'm gonna grab a washcloth!...You're in charge!...There you go!...No? OK, then I'm gonna put it back down there. We'll do it this way then, OK?

We do the face first……….Behind the ears……Inside the ears…… OK, the other one…OK………OK, let's do the shampoo part ………………OK, we're gonna try this……………………………… ……………………………………………It's all right, I'm hittin a rough patch, OK?………………That feel OK?……………….OK, gonna rinse your hair here………Can you put your head back for me? Beautiful!……OK, put your head back again for me………Great…… Close your mouth so I can rinse your beard………OK…………… All right, here we go………with the back…You know what I'm gonna suggest? We have a wheelchair?

Uh-huh.

When we get out of him—get him out of here—instead of walking him all the way back, we're probably gonna *wheel* him back.

OK.

I can surmise that that would be the best thing.

OK.

So if you wanna grab that—here, you wanna wash yourself? Here! Here's a washcloth for you, I can always grab another one!……You bet I can grab another one! That's right! Wash them legs! That's one less thing I have to do then!……

You're done already? You forgot underneath your armpits here!…OK …And across your chest here…Up underneath this one……………… …OK, a little more soap here……….. OK………Do you want your washcloth back?…… OK……OK, give Cathy this foot here……….. OK, I need this one here now……OK…I'm getting the washing down here, so we don't have to do so much when you stand up, OK?...............OK... My soap is going there, gotta reach down there......You want that?... OK, it's all yours!...............OK, on to this arm.................................OK, let me reach down here and make sure everything gets nice and... rinsed off here.............

★

Thursday, June 12, 1924 / JUNE SNOW BRINGS RELIEF TO CROPS / After nearly 24 hours of rain, snow started falling early Saturday morning and before the day was over eight or nine inches of snow had fallen and a total precipitation of over two inches was recorded by the time the storm had ended Saturday.

★

While bringing needed moisture to grain fields and gardens, the heavy, wet snow did a great amount of damage to trees and power and telephone lines.

★

Michael, I'm gonna need you to stand up so I can wash your butt! Can you do that for me? OK. Hang on to the side—hang up—hang on to the side—don't hang on to that! No, no, no! Don't hang on to that, Michael! Let go of that! Hang on to the side of the cupboard here!... O... K... I think I want a... O... K........ OK, Michael, sit back down! Can you sit back down for me? Perfect!... OK! That was a challenge!........... Do you want some more water on you? Or are you done... You're done? OK. Let me make sure I get... my soapiness out of the way here... All the soap rinsed down here.............. OK, towel!

That's the next thing...Wow! A little short person like me can do all this, huh? There you go! You want that towel? I can grab another one! Matt's got another towel! You bet he's got another towel! OK...All right, you dry your face really good, I'll do the ears—I've got this thing about ears, why I don't know, but I just got this thing about ears....OK...

★

The Mission Range Power Company line was broken by the weight of the snow early in the morning and Polson was without light or power until about noon. The line to Ronan was also put out of business. Telephone lines were down and between Polson and Kalispell it was reported that 75 poles were down. Shade

★

trees suffered heavily, great branches snapping under the weight of the snow, and many trees were split wide open and destroyed. Fruit

★

trees were badly damaged in some sections but seemed to stand the storm better than the shade trees. Small

★

fruits were bent to the

★

ground.

*

You know when my wife
Aida
lost the girl that she wanted,
the daughter,
over in Spain

I had uh,
I didn't have enough—
well, I was called for a mission
so I had to leave and uh,

she was in the hospital and I
talked to uh this chaplain, Green—
I'll never forget his name—
and uh, he was uh, uh
a Protestant uh chaplain.

I said, Look,

I know my wife is Catholic,
and I'm Catholic, uh,
but uh,
I'm gonna be gone,
and she's gonna need somebody
to talk to, and all that.

So he says, Yeah! No problem.
I'll talk to her.

So,
before I left, I
I figured she'd be home within six days,
so I uh ordered some flowers
to be delivered that day

and uh,
I was…
I think I was in…

Where was I?

Oh, I was in Turkey,
yeah,
and uh,

my mind was back with her.

And they delivered those flowers
and she
she said she
had gotten up, and uh,
they were
early with the flowers that day,
and uh,

she says,

Sal,
you don't know how much it meant to me
to receive flowers that day.

See?
So,
you know.

⋆

Oh, you're done? Well, that was awful quick!... OK, I'll get the rest... All right let's have this arm here... Give me your hand here... And your leg... Your arm... OK...... OK! Ta-da!......... OK, deodorant? Under the arms...... Powder........... There... we go...... Oh, Cathy is getting carried away with that powder, isn't she... Yep........... .... OK! This is what I wanna do! We're gonna brush the teeth in the tub! That way if we get messy, I don't have to clean it up! [*laughs*]...... OK......... And the brush... OK, sweetie! You wanna brush your teeth for me? Whatever you miss, I'll get, OK?.. ....

⋆

See, it was just a, a, a,
a blood situation.
She had a *positive*,
and the baby came out *negative*.
It came a
about a month early
earlier than normal.

But the baby had already *died*,
within her,
so
it was a
stillborn birth.

But uh, the law in,
in Spain,
still the same I guess, uh
you give birth,
and it *dies*

or it *dies*
it's born *stillborn*
you still have to give it
a funeral
and all that.

And uh, so I got ahold of the uh Catholic priest from the local that was around the base …
Torrejón …

and uh, I said … um, you know, *This happened and that and I want to …*
and he says, Yeah, no problem,

we'll do it.

And uh
uh he came
the day after
she had

still,
stillborn.

The *hospital,*
the military hospital,
had other ideas.
But I told them—I said,
Don't—

Don't do anything until, uh
Father uh,

uh *Colón,*
uh, comes in—

and uh he came in,
he had a—
it was a baby basket,
white, you know,
and uh, he had the
horsedrawn hearse.

You know.

And he had the the *burial* right behind the church,

you know, right behind the cemetery there.

And uh…

★

Don't forget to brush the outside, you got the inside really good... ....OK...All right, let me brush the inside. Open up...... ....Stick out your tongue. That carries a lot of bacteria too ....Up on the top...OK...Good! I can handle that too! Rinse. Spit in my glass. Beautiful!......Rinse...Spit in my glass... Beautiful!... OK............All right. Now.........This is the easy part. It's just all simplicity all of a sudden. OK...All right. Put your undershirt for me.........OK..OK... Which undergarment are we puttin on, Matt?

> Your choice. You've got these two different kinds
> to choose from.

★

Oh I'd

I'd gotten up

up on the

on the *hearse.*

It had six horses to pull it out
and we're on the base and—

you know it was the old-type *carriage* with the—
four poster carriage with the—
dark curtains and
and all that!

And uh,
it took us,
close to forty-five minutes,
almost an hour,

to go from the base,
off the base,
on the highway,
and into,
into his uh,

his church.

And uh, he had already had the Spanish police out on the highway to,
to,
the procession,

so there was,
uh.

"Did that make it easier? Or ... harder."

Yeah, you know
I was,
I was *satisfied* I,
you know,
if I had, uh,
dealt with the baby beforehand,
and all that,

it probably would have been *harder.*

Aida was *really depressed.*

Really,

really

depressed.

That's why I went in and uh
and talked to the chaplain,
I says, uh,

She, uh, she's gonna need a lot of talking with,
and I just hafta uh,
I hafta be gone, um.

I don't know exactly how long I'd be gone.

And it's a good thing I was only gone forty-five days,
but, you know,
forty-five days was a real long time

for her.

And

uh—

"Did you name the baby?"

Yeah, yeah.

"What was her name?"

Adelia.

"Adelia."

★

Adelia

Baquero

Vazquez.

★

And uh, so I have the,
the *certificate of death*

and all,

all that.

And Aida used to sit here,

we used to sit down here
and talk…

and she says,

You know, there must have been a reason why
the Lord didn't give me a girl.

*

And uh,

I said,

⋆

Well,

you know…

you *did* have a girl…

~~MYROBOT~~

It just didn't work out.

*

W(ife): Helen's on the phone. She wants to tell you a dream she had last night.
M(e): Great! Let me get my recording device...

Yello?

★

Uncle Matt?

★

Who is this?

★

Helen!

★

Helen *Who?*

★

Helen Woods!

★

Oh, hi, Helen! How's it going?

★

I have to tell you a story.

★

All right! Let's hear it!

II

Once upon a time there was a cave and there were bats in the cave and then one day there was yellow bees, and there was gray bees and a blue bee and rainbow bees and they were falling down!

★

We drove 107 miles from Moses Lake to Spokane, on Interstate 90, six cars in a line, all our headlights on.

★

One of the bees got lost looking for honey!

★

The sky was white and the fields were gold.

★

We'll do this in the tub. Can I have this foot here? Thank you. Can I have this foot here? Thank you...All right...He's just not into the towel! I need one to wipe his butt and his feet when he comes out. OK, Michael, I need you to come out of the tub for me! OK? Can you do that? Can you reach this foot up? And out? OK? Can you reach the other foot? Up? And out?.....OK, now you're gonna have to stand up so I can get you outta here! Can you put a hand here? And stand up for me? One two three up? Wait a minute, let me wipe your butt first!.........You cannot go around with a wet butt...Just a minute here, didn't get the front done!...Sorry for reachin—OK, now you can pull your britches up!......Beautiful! OK, now are we putting any...Throw this towel down there and we'll have him sit down—OK, Michael, I want you to sit back down for me, OK? Sit! Sit back down. No, sit! Sit! Sit! Oh, I'm gonna have you sit back down on the shower bench and then we're gonna talk! OK? So sit back down on the shower bench!...OK, go ahead. Sit down for Cathy. Sit. Sit. Sit sit sit sit sit sit sit. Beautiful! Now breathe! OK, do we want socks on? Do we want clothes on? Are we goin back to bed? Are we goin back out into the chair? Are we going back to bed?...You want to lay down for a while or do you want to sit down in the recliner...You don't know? OK, while you're thinking about that, I'm gonna wipe your toes. OK?

★

Behind the bats there was a house and the house had lots of stuff in it!

And then a big dinosaur came to the cave and there was a unicorn and it was pink!

★

Do you want pants or something?

Uh, only if he's gonna sit up! If he's not gonna be sittin up then I just put him to bed like this! For simplicity's sake. And what we would do is you take one side, I take the other side, and we'll just literally walk him back to bed.

OK.

★

The dinosaur went away and there were two people on the unicorn and there was a golden bee in the cave with blue wings!

Helen and Aunt Erin were on the pink unicorn and they was riding it!

★

And if he doesn't feel like walking, the wheelchair is there, we can use the wheelchair, right? OK…OK….

★

William and Rebecca, the parents, drove in the lead car.

★

To the bed. OK. Matt's gonna take one arm and I'm gonna take the other arm, OK? Up we come. Here we go!…All right. Here we go………… Doin great.

★

During his final years, as his health began to decline, Friar Diego tended the monastery garden.

★

When even this task proved too much of a strain, he was given the job of doorkeeper, and sat upon a stool, welcoming those who came in, and issuing forth those who went out. He died on the 12th of November, 1463.

★

A calm and holy smile settled on the features of the dying Saint and, as he gazed with a grateful countenance on the image of Mary, his holy soul winged its way to God. SAINT ANDREW AVELLINO, Theatine Priest (†1608)

★

Immediately after his death, the members of his order began work to beatify their beloved friar. These men died off and others took up the cause. They died off too, and others rose in their place. The Order was eventually successful. Friar Diego became San Diego.

★

And then a rainbow came!

★

In the backseat, a little white baby-sized casket was held in place snugly by a seatbelt strap.

★

And then it was spring in the cave!

★

Keep comin, keep comin, those legs are starting to give out on us again. Now, OK keep coming. Keep comin, keep comin...Keep those legs movin...Keep those legs movin...Now start backing up for us, OK? Take some steps backwards, Michael!...

★

The turtle was lost in the scary forest far, far away.

Helen rode the unicorn and found the turtle.

★

Take steps backwards! There you go...March your butt back as far as you can...OK, sit down! Sit! Good, Michael!...

★

Then somebody was in the scariest forest and somebody saw red eyes and it was a monster!

★

September, two thousand one.
We were living in salt lake city then.
My wife—my *girl friend*—was at work.
I, per usual, was sleeping in.

★

The phone rang. I pulled the blanket over my head.

★

Eventually, the ringing stopped.

★

★

It started up again.

★

So I got up and answered it.......................... *Hello?*

★

She said:

TURN ON THE TV, BABE! IT'S THE END OF THE WORLD! PLANES CRASHING INTO BUILDINGS! PEOPLE JUMPING OUT OF WINDOWS! THE TOWERS ARE FALLING DOWN!

★

They saw red eyes and went back to the cave and closed the door very tight so the monster wouldn't get in.

★

I turned on the TV.

★

and there was a bright orange sky like I had never seen

★

The unicorn went away when somebody stole it.

★

I sat alone, in my underwear, all day long, in front of our 20-inch Sony Trinitron television screen.

★

On every station:

HERE THEY COME AGAIN:
COLLAPSING:
COLLAPSING:
IMPLODING?:
FALLING DOWN:

★

She just found the unicorn.

★

over and: over and: over and: over and: over and: over and: over and: over again: and again: and again: and again: and again: and again: and again: and again: and again: and again:

★

She just rode the unicorn and there was a buzz behind the cave and one little pink bee in the cave.

★

All day long I watched those towers fall. And in the evening my wife—my *girl friend*—came home from work. She hadn't seen the videos yet. So I was forced to watch them with her all over again. And again. Etc.

★

There was a baby snake, there was a baby dog in the cave, a baby cat, a baby lizard, a baby frog, a baby rabbit, a baby kangaroo, a baby zebra, and a baby lion.

★

Only now the constant repetition had become too much for my weak mind to take. After a few minutes I told her that's it, that's enough, turn the fuckin TV off. But she needed to see.

★

I requested.

★

She refused.

★

I implored.

★

She said take it easy.

★

I demanded.

★

She ignored.

★

So very calmly I got out of my seat. I walked over to the mirror. I lifted it off the table. I slammed it to the ground and, screaming like a maniac, stomped around in broken glass.

★

Then a little baby was learning how to walk.

★

And that, children, is how your old man got the scars on his feet.

★

And the baby's name was Margaret.★

★

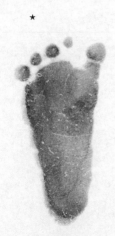

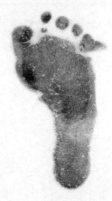

But it's not over.

I

Baby Margaret is growing bigger.

★

[3] We parked at the entrance and waited for the manager of the cemetery to give the OK. And when he did, in a line we drove up a winding one-laned road, through trees, to the top of the cemetery, and over to the statue of Jesus, where children are buried. We parked and got out. And when we were sure everyone was present, myself and three of her other uncles retrieved the little white casket from the backseat of her parents' car, and carried her, one handle each, to the site where a green tarp had been set up over a hole in the earth. We set her down in it. We all stood around and some of us said words; and the nurses who had raised her in the premie ward told us she had been a fighter and a joy and we cried. Margaret had only been home for 17 days before she died. Her death had been a surprise. After everything was said, we each put a flower on the casket, and when that was done, William took a shovel and began to shovel the dirt into the grave. Then his father did the same.

And then handed the shovel to Rebecca's father, who took his turn. And then William gave Helen a little kid-sized shovel, and she bent down in her nice dress and scooped some dirt, then carefully balancing the dirt on the shovel, she moved it over the hole, and dropped it down, looking very closely at what she was doing, and burning the memory into her mind. Amelia was getting impatient, so Rebecca told Helen to give Amelia a turn with the shovel. Then Helen helped her little sister gather the dirt. Then she stood behind Amelia as she dropped dirt over Margaret, holding Amelia's shoulders so that she wouldn't fall in. Afterward, we all went to the Old Country Buffet, where William, Rebecca, Amelia, and Helen would often go after visiting Margaret in the premie ward. Everyone seemed happy. The girls ate ice cream. My wife ate salad. Rebecca didn't eat. [redacted].

I tried everything, but it all tasted like shit.

★

She was sleeping in my pink sleeping bag.

★

[2] A week after I had visited Sal in his mobile home and recorded our conversation about Adelia, I returned with my wife to check on him, and take him to dinner. He'd been out of the hospital about two weeks by this point after having open heart surgery. The hospital had refused to send him home because he was old and lived alone so we had taken him in until his church could arrange for people to come look after him. When we'd wheeled him out of the hospital he was gray and weak and looked barely alive but by the time we drove him back to his trailer a few days later he was pink and full of life. But this night, when we showed up, he didn't want to get out of bed. He said he felt bad, and had fallen the day before. I thought he was just being dramatic. I believe I may have called him a *"wuss."* My wife, though, told him: Just rest, we'll stay in the other room and play cards for a while. About twenty minutes later we heard a commotion and raced into his bedroom.

Sal had fallen into his closet, and was leaning against the wall, white as a sheet. I grabbed him and held him up, and he took my arms and squeezed very hard. He had pissed his pants and was shaking. I said, Sal? Are you all right? Sal? He couldn't respond. I tried to get him to go into the bathroom with me, but he wouldn't move. His entire body was shaking, he couldn't talk, or look me in the eye. His eyes were open but he was only partially there. With much effort, we managed to move him into the bathroom, and my wife brought him juice. It took a long time but we got him out to our car and then to the St. Francis ER where, once he was lying down on a bed, he began to feel a bit better. A doctor with an overconfident attitude and strangely aggressive manner came in and asked Sal questions. He asked him if he had noticed any blood in his stool recently. Sal said, No. And before anyone knew it was happening, the doctor had stuck his index finger up Sal's ass, pulled it out, and was wagging the dark stain at everyone in the room, saying:

"Well, it looks like blood to me!"

*

She had no home and no stuff, and her house fell down.

★

[I] When Cathy the hospice nurse and I had gotten my dad washed, powdered, diapered and dressed, and then back to his room where we sat him on the bed, she crouched down in front of him. She took his hands in hers, rubbing the tops with her thumbs. She waited for him to look at her ... and then to focus his eyes as best he could .... on her face. And then, as if to formally announce the end of his ordeal, she asked him:

>

NOW HOW DO YOU FEEL >NOW HOW DO

YOU FEEL >NOW HOW DO YOU FEEL >NOW HOW DO YOU
FEEL >NOW HOW DO YOU FEEL >NOW HOW DO YOU FEEL
>NOW HOW DO YOU FEEL >NOW HOW DO YOU FEEL >NOW
HOW DO YOU FEEL >NOW HOW DO YOU FEEL >NOW HOW
DO YOU FEEL >NOW HOW DO YOU FEEL >NOW HOW DO
YOU FEEL >NOW HOW DO YOU FEEL >NOW HOW DO YOU
FEEL >NOW HOW DO YOU FEEL >NOW HOW DO YOU FEEL
>NOW HOW DO YOU FEEL >NOW HOW DO YOU FEEL >NOW
HOW DO YOU FEEL >NOW HOW DO YOU FEEL >NOW HOW
DO YOU FEEL >NOW HOW DO YOU FEEL >NOW HOW DO
YOU FEEL >NOW HOW DO YOU FEEL >NOW HOW DO YOU
FEEL >NOW HOW DO YOU FEEL >NOW HOW DO YOU FEEL
>NOW HOW DO YOU FEEL >NOW HOW DO YOU FEEL >NOW
HOW DO YOU FEEL >NOW HOW DO YOU FEEL >NOW HOW
DO YOU FEEL >NOW HOW DO YOU FEEL >NOW HOW DO
YOU FEEL >NOW HOW DO YOU FEEL >NOW HOW DO YOU
FEEL >NOW HOW DO YOU FEEL >NOW HOW DO YOU FEEL
>NOW HOW DO YOU FEEL >NOW HOW DO YOU FEEL >NOW
HOW DO YOU FEEL >NOW HOW DO YOU FEEL >NOW HOW
DO YOU FEEL >NOW HOW DO YOU FEEL >NOW HOW DO
YOU FEEL >NOW HOW DO YOU FEEL >NOW HOW DO YOU
FEEL >NOW HOW DO YOU FEEL >NOW HOW DO YOU FEEL
>NOW HOW DO YOU FEEL >NOW HOW DO YOU FEEL >NOW
HOW DO YOU FEEL >NOW HOW DO YOU FEEL >NOW HOW
DO YOU FEEL >NOW HOW DO YOU FEEL >NOW HOW DO
YOU FEEL >NOW HOW DO YOU FEEL >NOW HOW DO YOU
FEEL >NOW HOW DO YOU FEEL >NOW HOW DO YOU FEEL
>NOW HOW DO YOU FEEL >NOW HOW DO YOU FEEL >NOW
HOW DO YOU FEEL >NOW HOW DO YOU FEEL >NOW HOW
DO YOU FEEL >NOW HOW DO YOU FEEL >NOW HOW DO
YOU FEEL >NOW HOW DO YOU FEEL >NOW HOW DO YOU
FEEL >NOW HOW DO YOU FEEL >NOW HOW DO YOU FEEL
>NOW HOW DO YOU FEEL >NOW HOW DO YOU FEEL >NOW

YOU FEEL >NOW HOW DO YOU FEEL >NOW

Then Helen waked up.

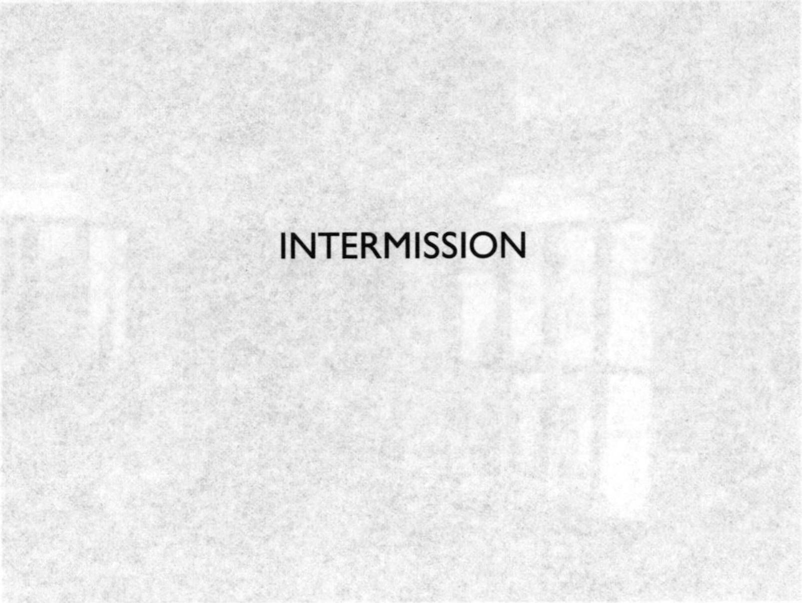

INTERMISSION

(Prof Billings Brown 20080416 204155.wav)

.... I GOT INTERESTED in *roller skating.* And thereby, uh, met a lot of girls in the rinks.

W: Yeah? I wish I would have known that when I was young, Gramps! You coulda taught me some tricks!

Yeah.

W: Yep.

I remember, they had, uh, short *intermissions* of a strange kind, where they, played, uh, various, uh, *dance,* melodies, on the organ.

W: Oh, it was organ music?

Organ, yeah.

W: Oh!

And uh…and it was *elimination*. Where they would *play music* for more and more difficult…*dances* until, there was only one couple…left… *wheeling*, shall we say.

W: Cool!

And one time at the { }, it was me and my…*chick*.

W: Nice!

We persevered.

W: Did you get a prize?

Oh… no.

W: Awww…

All for the glory.

[redacted]

[redacted]

CHAPTER TWO

Memories return, but are they my memories? Or have they been implanted in me, time-sensitive, each one waiting for the moment the lock is set to expire, so that the latch can pop open and reveal what's inside. Now I remember:

sitting

at my desk

working, discovering

words and numbers

seeing things that were mysterious

feeling that I understood them,

feeling large, feeling powerful,

feeling I could fly and then

looking out the window and seeing a fat white-haired man standing buck naked at the door across the street watching the ladies in yoga pants walking back to their cars all sweaty with their mats under their arms and

I remember my wife's work's Christmas party. Sitting at a round table surrounded by scientists. What kind? Genetics. Does she work in genetics? This memory must be a clue. The centerpiece: a logo: a circle with a little man in it. At the Christmas party I sat close to her, drinking, smiling, smiling and nodding, laughing at everyone's jokes. Fending off questions about myself and my work. It's easy to do. Besides, they're really not interested. But that wasn't me at that party. It couldn't have been. The whole thing's been constructed. The memory is too malleable. It is rootless. On the surface. Artificial. But so is the present that I experience. Or *experienced*, past tense. For this all occurs in the past.

Or not-too-distant future?

No, it was the past. For it was in the past that I stood beside my clothes dryer while a man in coveralls unspooled a long metal coil with a blade on the end a few inches wide into the pipe that went out of my basement wall and connected my house with the sewer. Every few yards the snake would become stuck, its blade jammed with gunk, and he would have to pull the snake back out, reversing the coil as he went, until finally out would come the head attached to a wad of brown gunky roots.

"Old clay pipes break," he said. "At the joints. And the tree roots get in and they clog up your works. How long have you been in this house?"

"The neighbor lady tells me three years."

"You should have us come once a year for maintenance, otherwise it'll be slow going like this, and end up costing you an arm and a leg."

"Good to know."

The man had thick white hair and a gray-white beard. He was short, sturdy—not fat, but squat. I asked him about the job while he worked and he told me that he had lied about his previous experience on his job application and had had to learn as he went. Lucky for me, he said, he was now quite well-versed. But even so, he joked, snaking drains was not his true passion.

"What's your true passion?" I asked.

He then went on to tell me all about a business venture he had, which was based on the Bible and the idea that the Kingdom of Heaven could be instituted on the earth. It seemed to him that what was needed was a system of commerce which was run according to Christian principles, whereby everyone profited in equal measure—or if not equal (for this was not communism) at least equal to the amount of effort that one put in. *Kingdom of Heaven Incorporated, International* he called it, and had already trademarked the name. He was even then working with a local company that would make sweatshirts and t-shirts with the KOHII name and logo on them. He was inspired by a bestselling author of motivational books. He figured: Why wait 'til tomorrow? Why wait for Jesus to come? When Jesus came he didn't want to be asked: *Why didn't you get started? You should have been busy building my Kingdom on Earth!* So he was getting started, and snaking drains to pay the bills. The thought occurred to me that: *it takes all kinds.*

"What do you do?" he asked. "I notice you're home during the day."

"Apparently," I said, sipping my coffee, "I'm a writer."

"Really!" He seemed genuinely enthused. "And what do you write? Fiction?"

"That's a good question," I said. "I think probably fiction. I hear I wrote a book called *In Complete Accord*. Ever heard of it?"

"No, I don't think so. Sorry."

"That's all right. To tell you the truth I'm not even sure I wrote the thing. In fact I'm almost positive I didn't."

Back into the drain went the snake. The machine whirred as it fed the pipe.

"What do you mean by that?" the man said.

"I mean something bizarre is going on. I don't remember being myself. I don't remember being here. I don't remember anything. Someone's playing a big trick on me."

He stopped the machine and looked over at me.

"What do you mean?"

"Just what I said. Something's not right."

"I used to work at a mental hospital," he said. "First as an orderly. And then as a counselor. There were a lot of people there who thought things weren't right. I'll ask you what I always asked them first. How do you feel right now, right this moment?"

I thought about it. There was a terrible tightness in my chest. My throat hurt. My head still hurt. Everything hurt. But oddly enough I found the strangest sensation was that I couldn't breathe well. I kept yawning, and I had been yawning for quite some time. But it was a kind of yawning that was never able to fully express itself. So when I would start, I would start yawning and go up toward the high point of the yawn where you reach the zenith and feel satisfied and sigh and then go back down, but right before that zenith I would falter, the yawn wouldn't quite get there and I'd stop and be left with this heaviness in my chest and an uncomfortable feeling because I knew I'd start to yawn again in a few moments, to try again to get it out but that it wouldn't come out this time either, and the process would go on and on like this. I had been doing this since shortly after Gladys had left and I had gone into my office—*the* office, I should say—and sat down at my chair and stared at the blank page.

"I keep yawning," I said, as another yawn started. "But I can't get… all the way……… up. See?"

"Yeah, I've noticed that. I thought it was a tick."

"As far as I know, I've only been doing it for about an hour. I also feel like I could cry at any moment."

"Cry?" he said. "What are you thinking about when you start to feel like you're going to cry?"

"What do I think about…" I started to think. And a tear came out of my eye. I stopped it with my hand. Another one came. And another. "I have no memory," I said. I started to yawn. "I don't know how I got here. It seems I have a wife but I don't recognize her. I wear a ring on my finger but I don't know who put it there. My neighbor says she knows me but I swear I've never seen her before. I don't know how long I've been here. I wrote a book called *In Complete Accord* and I don't know what it's about. And I have supposedly been working for eleven years on a follow-up, but I don't know how that could be. I don't know who I am, where I came from. I don't remember being a child. I don't remember my family, my school, my adolescence, growing up. I look like I'm in my thirties someplace but I don't remember ever being alive before this morning. Great, here comes another one." I rode the yawn up…up…up, but it—"Fuck!"—took me down again too soon. "I have memories that come in and out. For instance I think someone who looks just like you came here once and told me the same things you're telling me but I don't know if it really happened, or if what's happening now is happening now, or what. I don't know. I don't know if I'm the kind of person who would normally start weeping in front of the drain man or if this is odd behavior for me." I wiped my eyes, then started sobbing. It was a yawn that stopped it, and when the yawn passed—this time thankfully after going all the way to the top—I sighed and said, "I also found some weed upstairs before you got here and it's probably making me even loopier."

We left the snake and went upstairs to smoke some weed.

Charles—King Charles—he sat in the captain's chair—he had a beard, had a sturdy bearing, a royal bearing—he spoke with confidence—he was a drain declogger—he sat across from me—I sat on the couch—he wore coveralls and on the chest was a picture of a cartoon snake with an eye patch—King Charles—the company he worked for was called The Drain Charmers—the cartoon snake with the eye patch was swirling up a pipe—"Charles?" I said—at the top of the pipe was a golden orb—"Am I cracking up?"

"Maybe. Why don't you ask your wife?"

"I don't think she's my wife."

"You could ask."

"But if whoever hired her to pretend to be my wife finds out I'm onto them they'll erase me and the only thing I know is that I don't know what's going on. And I'd rather at least know that than give them another chance to try again to make me believe whatever it is they're trying to get me to believe—and by the way I don't know what that is."

"Yes, I'd say you're cracking up."

"God, I really hope so." I took a toke and passed the joint to Charles. "Did you have people like me at the mental hospital?"

"We had all sorts. There seemed to be a common motif in a lot of psychoses. You know you hear the word *schizophrenic* and people use that term interchangeably with multiple personality disorder. They think schizophrenics have different sides of their personalities, like Dr. Jekyll and—"

"Hyde?"

"Yes, exactly. But that's not schizophrenia at all. There is a constellation of beliefs experienced by schizophrenics, generally—at least from what I saw. For one thing they were usually consumed with the idea that the world was coming to an end. Do you have that?" he asked.

"Well, not that the world is *coming* to an end, Charles, but that it already has! I mean what else would you call waking up without any memory whatsoever!"

"Do you ever obsess about the number four?"

"Maybe so! I can't remember! Maybe so!"

"When they were in an episode it usually started in a very beautiful way. They would see meaning in everything. Everything that crossed the plane of their senses was always filled with deep and rich meaning. And it was peaceful and beautiful, and they felt empowered, and they felt as if they finally understood what it was all about. They felt that they knew a unity of all things, a sense that all things in the universe were one—sure, you hear that all the time—in self-help books and on bumper stickers and so forth—but they really felt it, they understood it, and to them it really was. They felt a kinship to God, and then that kinship would develop into something more like sonship—or daughtership if it was a girl. And then from there they'd go on to feel that they were the spirits of God himself, trapped in a human body, which was in actuality a prison of matter. And once they reached this point, which was the high point, the realization that they were spirits trapped in matter and that there was no way out—and not just matter but they were also being held against their will in a literal prison—the majority having been committed against their will—when what they wanted most of all was to go out and tell the world what they had learned—and so when they realized they were trapped, and that there was no escape, not just from the hospital but from their very bodies!—well, it always went downhill from there. The heavenly visions would turn to nightmares, the angels would turn to devils and witches, the pretty bright lights would turn to torrents of blood and…you get the picture. The problem is our society. We have no place for the schizophrenic. In the native cultures these were the holy men, the shamans, they were protected and revered, and you'd bring your little papoose to him for a blessing or a prophecy, and the society would make sure he was fed and clothed because he sure as hell couldn't take care of himself. But now we leave them to fend for themselves. To be preyed on by villains and wolves and drugs and alcohol, until they eventually do something that either gets them shot by the cops or put in a psych ward, and then they're fed drugs and monitored for a time and then sent back out to fend for themselves again."

"I should talk to Vel."

"Who's Vel?"

"The lady from next door who went nuts. Supposedly she chased me with her hose. Now I'm not so sure."

"I'm sorry you're going through what you're going through," Charles said. "I'd like to help you. I think you should start by talking about it to your wife."

"Not wife, the wo—"

"Right, the woman who claims to be your wife."

"I can't trust her," I said, beginning to yawn again. "She's too… too… (Damn!)… too damn pretty. Way too pretty for me. You can never trust them. At least in the movies. And yes, I know that sounds crazy."

"Is this her?"

He had picked up a photograph of this woman and a man who looked like me standing in some sort of park. The photo was taken pretty close up. The girl was beautiful and had a beautiful smile, her brown hair straight and shoulder-length. The man looked like I would have probably looked a few years earlier. He smiled a lippy smile, his head tilted somewhat toward her, obviously uncomfortable before the camera. Behind them, in the distance, there was a green minivan parked sideways. Weird that the minivan would be there, I had thought when I'd first seen it. Was it a clue? Or just a bad photographer who'd set up the shot without noticing that somebody's car was in view. Then I wondered what kind of car did she drive… I thought about it… She'd drive an old car… A safe car… A Mercedes, maybe. Or a Volvo.

"That's her. At least I think it is. Except she had blond hair this morning. At least I think she did. I wasn't wearing my glasses."

"You're not wearing glasses now."

"I'm not? But I can see you fi— Oh, yeah. I put in contact lenses."

"I think you should probably stop smoking marijuana until you get this all figured out. Pot will only make things more surreal."

"You're probably right, Charles. But to be honest, I think it's helping me calm down. What time is it?"

"Almost noon."

"I hope you get the Kingdom on Earth you're looking for," I said. "You seem like a very smart man. I also hope you don't work for whoever is responsible for all of this. I notice the logo on your breast is a serpent winding up a pipe. That's an alchemical symbol if I'm not mistaken. The orb symbolizes enlightenment. The pipe symbolizes the Tree of Life, or time. And the serpent symbolizes the undying hero. It's all about traveling from the lower regions to the upper. From darkness and ignorance into light and life."

"That's very true," said Charles. "And I can see why you would interpret it that way. However, I know for a fact that it was designed by my boss's nephew, and that all he did was copy the logo from one he saw in a video game. You are right in what you see, and that you are seeing it. But there is no conspiracy against you—at least as far as I and The Drain Charmers go. Although—and this may just be the marijuana speaking—but it does occur to me that there could be a *metaphysical* conspiracy, that is a conspiracy at a higher level of existence. And it also occurs to me that if there was such a conspiracy I and The Drain Charmers could be involved—including my boss's nephew even though we don't know we're in on it. Because in a metaphysical conspiracy the pieces would be moved around without their knowledge, wouldn't they? By a—what shall we call it?—an *unseen* hand?"

"Why, yes, Charles, I believe they would."

Charles leaned back in his chair and stroked his beard with a grubby hand.

"If you've been working on this book for as long as you say—"

"Eleven years, apparently."

"Well, eleven years working on the same book, it strikes me as very unusual."

"I'll say! That's the first thing I thought when I heard, myself!"

"I mean, you're a professional writer. You say yourself you don't go out, you don't have distractions, you don't teach or work for a living. So it seems you have as much time as you need to dedicate yourself to your work."

"Yes, and apparently I told Gladys I spend every waking hour doing it."

"So if it takes a writer on average a year to write a book, and that's a writer who has a, well, has a life—no offense..."

"None taken."

"...then simple mathematics would say that the amount of time you've been spending on this book—these eleven years—would equal something more in the order of say twenty or twenty-five years any other writer would spend on a book. Maybe even more if you think you are writing three times as much as an average writer would write—because you're not taking vacations, you're not using your time to give lectures, interviews, or go on book tours, etcetera. And so if you think that maybe you've actually spent the equivalent of thirty-three years on the project..." He stroked his beard. "Well, that's a bit troubling."

"Isn't it?"

"It makes me wonder if possibly you're not writing a book at all, but doing something very different."

This was an intriguing idea. I leaned forward. "Something like what, Chuck?"

"Well..." He looked at me, his large forehead wrinkling up underneath his majestic shock of white hair. "It makes me wonder if maybe you haven't..."

"Haven't?"

"*Discovered* something."

"Discovered something. That means *un*-covered."

"And maybe that discovery has something to do with the predicament you find yourself in."

He passed me the joint.

"Have you looked at what you're working on?" he asked, his voice slow, unsure.

I breathed in. "There's nothing on that computer, Chuck." I held it for a moment, then breathed out: "*Phooooooo*... I searched the whole goddamn machine."

"Nothing?"

"It's empty," I said with a sigh. "There's nothing on it but a single blank page entitled themystery.doc. Zero lines, zero words. Zero characters. Zero zero zero." I started to yawn. "Oh, great, here we go again..."

"I should go down and finish chopping those roots," Charles said.

★

(lydia sept 5 2006 st joes hospital.mp3)

M: Did you ask if he's sleeping?

No, I asked if I could come in.

Oh, sure.

I want to clean. And then go home. Is that OK?

Ask *him*, he's the patient.

PATIENT: Sure.

Is that your dad?

Yeah.

Oh, are you leaving today?

Uh, no, I think I'll be here…

Maybe 'til tomorrow.

OK, then I'm gonna do your room then. You didn't just come in, did you?

Yesterday evening.

OK, then we'll do your room. That's all right, right?

Yes.

OK...... So you're one of these laptop people that do your work at home?

Right.

Yeah, you're one of these people that my husband and I are complaining about. All you guys—it should be illegal—you guys keep losing your laptops and all our information's going: *POOF!*

[*laughs*]

Yeah!

I don't have any government secrets on mine yet.

But do you know what I'm saying?

I know what you're saying. But don't blame the laptop, blame the people.

Well, they should be charged with something because this is ridiculous, they put so many people—thousands of people at risk.

Yeah, I saw they got another one lost the other day, right?

Yeah!

I don't know...

Gotta make sure—

They definitely shouldn't be taking these things home with them, should they.

No they shouldn't be—I mean, the computer age is fine, but you know what I say? I think it kinda *sucks,* myself.

[*laughs*] I don't like cell phones.

So what do you do? What's your line of work?

I'm a writer.

You're a writer? What do you write?

Books.

About what?

Well, I published a book about Federal Way a little while ago…

Yeah? What's your name?

Matthew McIntosh? Probably never heard of me?

No.

That's all right.

And it got published? About Federal Way?

Yeah!

Did you make a million dollars?

Half a million.

Really?

No, not even close. But—

Cool. What are you writing about now?

What am I writing about now? I'm writing about America.

You should write about the destruction of the Northwest! And how the Northwest is all about trees, and you know what, we're seeing all these trees being cut down at an alarming rate.

Keep talking.

Well, what—whatever happened to the *passion?* Western Washington is about *wetlands,* and about rains, and about—the Northwest is about our *trees.* And we're losing it all. And these stupid developers who think they can still keep moving these wetlands—it's crazy because one of these days Mother Earth is going to bite us in the *butt!*

Shut it down, yeah.

And all these housing developments that are, *popping up* over the wetlands, they're gonna be in trouble. It's sad.

I agree with you, a hundred percent.

So write a book about our—*The Northwest: It's All About Trees*—or is it? *Is it* about trees? I don't know!

What should the title be? Is that the title?

I don't know, you tell me, you're the writer.

Yeah, but you're the idea woman!

Huh?

You're the *idea* woman!

[*sighs*] Write about *truth*—we're losing America all the time. What are you gonna write about America?

About truth and trees, really. Honestly.

Really!

Yeah, you're actually right on!

I am *so impressed!*

Yeah.

Because trees are *good guys*—they're *good people*—this is what makes our *breathe*—us *breathe*. And we keep cutting down our trees—guess what—I'm not sure what we're gonna breathe! Do you?

No.

That's right. And I'll tell you what—with Orting—they should've—they should've never have allowed to put all those houses on prime farming soil. So what's gonna happen when you put everything on concrete? So they're doing all these studies: *Well, if we concrete over the prime soil, how many years will it still be good*—well, what the hell? Why are you doing that? Common sense tells you leave it alone! You know what I mean? We're poisoning ourselves—but you want me to tell you what makes *me* mad?

What's that?

Is that the people who have the power, and the brains and the knowledge and the money—they're the ones that don't care, they're gonna poison the world anyway. And nobody can stop it. I mean, I can see it—I can see it—I also can see that *six years*...we're less free now than we were six years ago. I mean you gotta open up your eyes...People just say *yes* to everything— You don't have to get up, sweetie! I'll sweep around you.

Keep talking. [*laughs*]

You proud of your son that he's a writer?

Yeah.

What do you do?

I'm a pastor.

Awww! How *niiiiice!* How *sweeeet!* That's why you talk the way you talk. You're soft-spoken, you're nice, it's a nice—it's nice, for a man to be soft-spoken. Doesn't mean you're weak, it means you're soft-spoken.

[*laughs*]

You know, you're probably very *strong.* Well, *how niiice!* See, I almost avoided this room, because of the woman, I was thinking: Ehh, maybe I'll leave her alone.

What woman?

The woman that was in here.

Oh, my mom.

Yeah, because you know, I wasn't sure—see, I needed to see *you*—I only saw *her*, and I was like: *Hmmmm.*

Yeah, she's great.

Well, she looked great, but. Sometimes you need to leave them alone. She's doting on you, so, you know…Life is good.

There you go.

……………………………Well, I can't believe it—American trees. You know, too bad you weren't in here a week ago, there was a guy in this room, I'm trying to think of what he told me, what—it was either what Washington or Jefferson said. Something about our freedom—it was so good, I'd never heard of it before—that the people that—'cause I was telling him the same thing about *six years*, you know, that we're less free now than we were six years ago—he said, No kidding—he was talking about the airports and all this other stuff and checking the luggage and checking *you*, and I said, It's just crazy, I said, and he said, People that are not—are not willing to *stand up*, and *fight*, for what should be fight—for what we should fight for—don't deserve anything. And that is so true! You know, and what are we doing—we're in a—I never had to count things like my grandparents, you know, they were in the Depression, and neither did you, and—*you* probably didn't either, did you? But you probably had it a little rougher than us. Well, we don't know what it's like to go without. And so we're *spoiled*, and so we're in this *comfort zone*—so nobody—everybody wants to—nobody wants to do anything. You know what I mean?

Yeah, I know exactly what you mean!

It's sad... Hmmmm. So you write about American trees.

Well, trees and people, and—just what you're talking about, honestly.

Are you married? Yeah? I was going to say, you need to go on a motorcycle and tour the country, and look at all our trees that are going away—take a good look at it, open up your eyes—I'm from Eastern Washington, and we still have a lot of open—a lot of open ground over there. When I come over here, I'm thinking: *What happened?* And since I've been over here—we bought an acre and a half in Graham—since I've been over here I can't believe how *bad* Graham has gone now. It's people.

It's spreading out everywhere now.

The *trees!* The trees are *going!* It's *crazy!* And the poor *wild*life, they don't have a place to go... I mean, we're very—we're being *very selfish*, because there is—one saying I do know for a truth... Over in *Africa?* About the *elephants?* They—the reason there's a tree planted *here* and a tree planted *there* is because the birds fly over it, they drop the seed. The elephant comes over and plops it into the ground and there's a tree! And they said because the elephants are getting depleted—they're getting gone—pretty soon we won't see all those trees. And so it's very sad—and we all—and what's sad is that we all know about this, but we're not going to do anything about it.

> Well, what is it about Americans today that—they're not willing, or don't care, or…

I think we're so caught up in our own work—in our own *life* that…we're in our *comfort zone.* I don't know if it's so much not caring, but we're just not willing to open up our eyes, and see that if we don't do something…we're gonna lose it all. We're gonna lose it all…And I'm not so sure what your children, or my nephew's children, are going to inherit…Do you know what I mean?

KIM FORBES

EARTH

4.6 billion years old

OLDEST ROCK 3.96 BILLION YRS.

NW Territories Canada

OLDEST EVIDENCE OF LIFE 3.3 B.Years

Africa

Australia

600 million yrs ago "explosion" of life in oceans

150 million DINOSAURS

GONE   BY 65 million years ago

current ice age—began 4.5 million yrs ago

East Africa—upright hominids 4.5 million

15000 years ago—SEATTLE COVERED BY ICE

Saturday, November 8, 2003—SEATTLE

[*The plot thickens.*]

Now a young man wakes up late.

He makes coffee.

He drinks it in front of the TV,

flipping between college football games.

He chews a piece of nicotine gum.

He chews another.

He chews another.

He chews another.

He makes a sandwich for lunch.

His young wife—
two years married

—is still asleep.

She wakes around two in the afternoon.

She comes out and tells him he kept her awake all night with his drunken snoring. He really should think about cutting down.

The young man reads for a while on the couch

then turns on the TV again.

In the early evening
his young wife asks him to take her around to the thrift stores
so they can go hunting for Pyrex.

> User record for Kim Forbes. Kim Forbes. Number of items user has in repository: 127

They get in the Bronco and drive to the Lake City Value Village where once he found her a rare opal Pyrex mixing bowl.

> Posted by: Kim Forbes September 19, 2007 - 10:08AM Chicago. I want to echo Mark's comments and thank Brooke for pressing the point that any connection made...

She has boxes of Pyrex bowls in the pantry.
She has boxes of Pyrex bowls in the basement.
And cupboards filled to the brim.
All the many colors and sizes are beautiful...

The forms are

many,

And they stack
one into another so concentrically…

the reality

relics of an American Past;

is one;

Pyrex

only from Corning

they are not rivals but

relics of an America Passed: Pyrex glass was made for railroad signal lights, then beakers and bottles for scientific laboratories,

aspects of a single principle.

then the domestic line for cooking and food storage took off during the Great Depression. The old ladies were given sets as wedding presents and when they die their children pack up everything they've left behind in boxes, including the Pyrex dishes, load the boxes into the trunks of their cars and drive them down to the nearest thrift store, where they unload in the rear, and drive away.

She has quite possibly the largest collection of Pyrex bowls on the planet.

All the colors and shapes and designs.

aspects of a single principle.

Inside the store, she calls him over.
She is holding what they call a Cinderella bowl, elliptical with two short spouts.
Exclaims she: This one they only made for one year in the '50s as a demo!
She found this out on the web recently.
The sticker says $2.99 but she knows it's worth more than twenty dollars.

She never sells, just buys to use and show and give away, and what she doesn't use or show or give away, she wraps in newspaper and puts away in boxes.

He leaves her and wanders through rows after rows of books…Ten copies each of bestseller after bestseller…

But in the adjoining room (Lighting & Electronics) she finds him an old desk lamp for his office, brown and silver chrome, and in the shape of an egg/bullet; very small with a swiveling head, and a telescoping neck. HAMILTON INDUSTRIES, CHICAGO ILL. MODEL NO. 60. REPLACE WITH NO. 93 BULB ONLY. USE OF ANY OTHER BULB MAY CAUSE DAMAGE TO THE LAMP. MADE IN JAPAN. 116 Volt 60 Cycle 26 Watt A.C. Only He plugs it into the test outlet and the light comes on.

$2.99 for the bowl and five bucks for the lamp.

They pay and leave—back to the truck. And backing out of the parking spot, the young wife cries out suddenly!
Because just over the roof of the store the moon hangs eclipsed, the bottom edge a white-lit sliver. The rest is covered by the earth's dark shadow.

LOOK AT THAT! OMG SO *BEEEYOOOTIFULLL!!!*

Continue driving north and around the edge of Lake Washington to the St. Vincent de Paul (We should strive to keep our hearts open to the sufferings and wretchedness of other people, and pray continually that God may grant us that spirit of compassion which is truly the spirit of God) thrift store where he once, more than a year ago, found her a large brown bowl with a white rim, very rare. Around the top of the lake, the moon comes into view again…now they're driving toward it.

Cheshire cat, she says, smiling.

Park at the store and walk through the doors, past a line of hunched people standing behind miniature shopping carts, waiting to pay.

The sign on the door says the store closes at 6.
The watch on the arm says: 5:45.
The clock on the wall says: 5:45.
The kid at the register says:
We're closed.

But they continue on anyway, just to take a look.

Cheshire smile spreads wider, beaming, smiling down.

Old man in pajamas, using his shopping cart to prop himself up, cries: They're closed! Look at the hours on the door if you don't believe him!

as the two walk by.

They ignore the old man, but now he begins to loudly chant:

They're closed!
They're closed!
They're closed!

his face and eyes turned down to the floor.

Looking back, as he makes his way forth, to the rear of the store,
the young man asks:

Why are you talking to me, dude?

Respect your elders, young man! old man shouts.

They check the shelves for Pyrex but there's nothing, so they leave, walk out past the register, past the line of people, past the old man in pajamas, who says:

Nothing more.

Then drive off, back west, toward Aurora, which is called Pacific Highway farther south.

Fucking old-timer, young man says, watching carefully the dark road before them, and the white and yellow lines, trying very diligently to keep the Bronco inside. *Respect your elders, young man!*

W: That's my husband you're talking to, *dude!*

10 (a) Simulating objects of antiquity, etc.—A person commits
11 a misdemeanor of the first degree if, with intent to defraud
12 anyone or with knowledge that he is facilitating a fraud to be

13 perpetrated by anyone, he makes, alters or utters any object so
14 that it appears to have value because of antiquity, rarity,
15 source, or authorship which it does not possess.

Young man pops another piece of nicotine gum.

> Kim Forbes x x iS 4 iF i LiKe YoU hello thomas!! how hav u been all these years? hav u still got the swimming pool????!!!! kim x x x. 17 weeks ago ...

Open eyes these neon signs that never blink.

THISWAYTHISWAYINHERE

That used to be an ice cream parlor, she says—that dark, abandoned storefront.
Pass a Home Depot, a Wal★Mart, a Warehouse Grocery Store.
All looks the same everywhere these days.
They could be driving down a street in No. New York or No. St. Louis or No. Salt Lake.

The Satellite, looking down, says:

"They're there in No. Seattle now, headed So., @ approx. 47 mph."

Find an open thrift store, Deseret Industries, they go in.

Young man looks for a while at the dishes with his wife, then goes off to look at the books.
He's looking for Book Three of The Divine Comedy. But all he sees is

The Da Vinci Code
The Da Vinci Code
The Da Vinci Code.

A terrible vibe to the place makes him feel uneasy.
Any moment, someone will walk into the store with a jacket full of explosives, pull a cord, and blow them all away.

He looks to see where she is—there—across the store—picking up dishes, looking at the undersides for the Pyrex stamp, them setting them down.

And with a kind of spiritual heaviness, with a shortness of breath, a strange mild pain in his chest, the young man goes to stand guard beside his wife.

And when she turns to him he turns to her and she sees him. See her.

Why not just leave now, instead?

Let's go.

They race out through the doors, across the parking lot, and jump into the truck!

M(an): That place has got some bad juju.
W(oman): I felt it too.

Heading south again, he's sure the evening news will tell him: All those people left behind you were found dead (a police spokesman says).

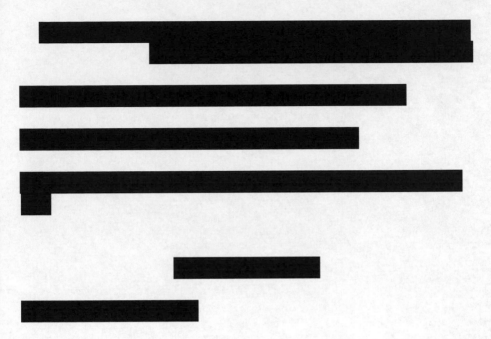

Earth's shadow has almost relinquished entirely the Bright and Shining Moon.

BASIC FACTS

1. World is made of plates—giant slabs of rocks
60 miles thick—100km
rocks that do not deform "internally"

2. Edges of plates <u>deform</u> - <u>break, crumple,</u>
<u>melt</u>

3. Plates move 1-2" per year

> “forbes” <kim.forbes@[redacted]> wrote in message news: 1121353283.698009.10770@g14g2000cwa.googlegroups.com...> We are doing more and more ...

Back driving home.

Everytime rock breaks -

earthquakes happen

Around Green Lake.

crumples -

mountains

formed

> From: Kim Forbes <[log in to unmask]>. Re: new to authorware, need advice

Merge onto Stone Way.

melt -

volcanos

At a red…

light…

stop.

A pickup truck in the lane beside them towing a trailer of rowing shells, stacked up on rails. The trailer has a flat tire.

The driver gets out, wearing a cowboy hat, and walks up to the young man's window.

"I gotta get over so I can take care of this," the Cowboy says.

"I'll set a screen for you."

Cowboy nods; tips his hat to the young man's wife.

Then winks & smiles & whispers in your ear:

> "forbes" <kim.forbes@xxxxxxxxxxxxxxx> wrote in message news: 1149094672.040348.277590@xxxxxxxxxxxxxxxxxxxxxxxxxxxxxxx.
Yup, that is what I want; ...

When the light turns green, the young man moves the Bronco into place, blocking the right two lanes.
Somebody honks behind.
Turn your hazard lights on, honey.
They don't work.

The Cowboy maneuvers his truck and trailer over, he pulls to the side by the Kidd Valley hamburger stand, and:

The two continue on, quick left onto their block, pull up to the curb in front of their little rented white Craftsman bungalow, built: AD 1924.

Run inside to escape the cold.

He sits down on their worn-out couch and picks up the remote control.

The earth is not random
tectonics lift up mountains
glaciers cut away

To see an old and vine-covered castle, you are likely to become romantic in your tastes, and care should be taken that you do not contract an undesirable marriage or engagement.

tectonics keep mountains there

mountains are lined up along plate boundaries

Volcanos, earthquakes, mountains of the world are aligned

Are you hungry? she asks.
No.
But you will be. I'll make a pizza.

Goes to the kitchen, humming to herself.
Comes back out:

We don't have pepperoni. Plus we need milk and coffee for the morning.
And you're all out of beer.

He puts on his coat and drives to the store.

Walks down aisles, gathering items and putting them in a basket.
He gets in line and pays.
Twenty-six dollars on his debit card.

Drives home. Drops the grocery bags on the kitchen floor, and puts his six-pack in the fridge. Except for the one in his hand.
Pops a piece of nicotine gum, goes into the living room, sits down.
And right as he opens the bottle:
(CRRRACK!)
she asks him where the pepperoni is.

Merde..I'll go back.

He gets up puts his coat back on and she kisses him she can't help laughing (because he does this all the time, he's quite forgetful):

My special special guy!

Hands him his black wool cap.
Pulls it down over his ears.

That's better. It's cold out there

Satellites thread the sky above

Rowboats skim across the tranquil water

Tracing the glowing orb of

> .kim forbes. Male, 35 nassau Bahamas Last Login: 12/2/2007 1:37 PM ... About kim forbes. im fun loving person witty humour i love intelligent conversation i ...

He finds the pepperoni and gets in line and when it's his turn the girl at the register asks him if he wants a bag and he says:

"Yes."

"Paper or plastic?"

"I don't care."

"Cold out there?"

In the parking lot Four Wiggers drinking beer and smoking cigarettes, not more than eighteen years old—which would be…somewhere around ten years younger than he—punching each other, hopping around, making noise.

Too-large baseball hats with straight bills over eyes, baggy basketball jerseys, gold chains around their necks.

He walks past and cannot look away, though they pay him no attention.

O how he hates the wiggers EVEN MORE than he hates the rest!

At home he drinks a beer and watches a news show about a kid who killed Four College Students with his car on a Saturday night two years before in Isla Vista, California, on a crowded street, where the young man and his friend used to walk, at age 13, on the way to the record store, looking in parked cars for things to steal.

Blurry home video in muted tones is shown of the kid running around, hopping about, taking swings at people in the crowd, trying to punch and kick them, while four bodies lie dying in the street:

I AM THE ANGEL OF DEATH!

His lawyer says he'd stopped taking his pills because of the side effects.

The young man's wife comes out with the pizza she made on a tray. Sits down beside him on the couch.

They eat.

He drinks a few more beers.

Now they escort The Green River Killer into a courtroom, clad in orange, hands and feet in chains. Confessed to killing 60 women, but they've only charged him with 48. He showed The Cops where he hid the bodies—so instead of Death, they've given him Life.

A car bomb went off in a gated housing community in a Saudi Arabian town and 19 people were killed, many bodies of young children found among the rubble. They bring them out, little bundles on stretchers, under white sheets.

Four teenagers are dead after their car was cut in ha lf by a Great Pine Tree which had jumped out into the road in front of them, teeth bared, eyes blazing, sword raised high, screaming:

SLOW!

One more hangs on. But they don't know if he'll make it through the night.

He won't.

Another piece of nicotine gum.

Another cop kills another man.

A corrections officer who tied up a prostitute in his basement, cuffed her to a bed for three days, shot her with a pellet gun, beat her, spit on her, bit her, raped her, has been put into solitary confinement for his own safety.

The inmates began to riot as he was walked in; threw piss on him and jeered at him, and threatened him and he was taken quickly out:

The parents of the wife of the chief of police of the city of tacoma want money for their daughter's death. Her estranged husband had seen her driving across the tacoma narrows bridge he waved her over followed her off the freeway and into the parking lot of the olive garden she left the kids in the car to talk to him he was sitting in his drivers seat she was standing there above him when he reached up took hold of the back of her head pulled her down to him witnesses say she cried out

DON'T!

He placed the barrel of his gun against the crown of her head

Pulled the trigger.

Then he opened his mouth and blew out the back of his own.

[redacted]

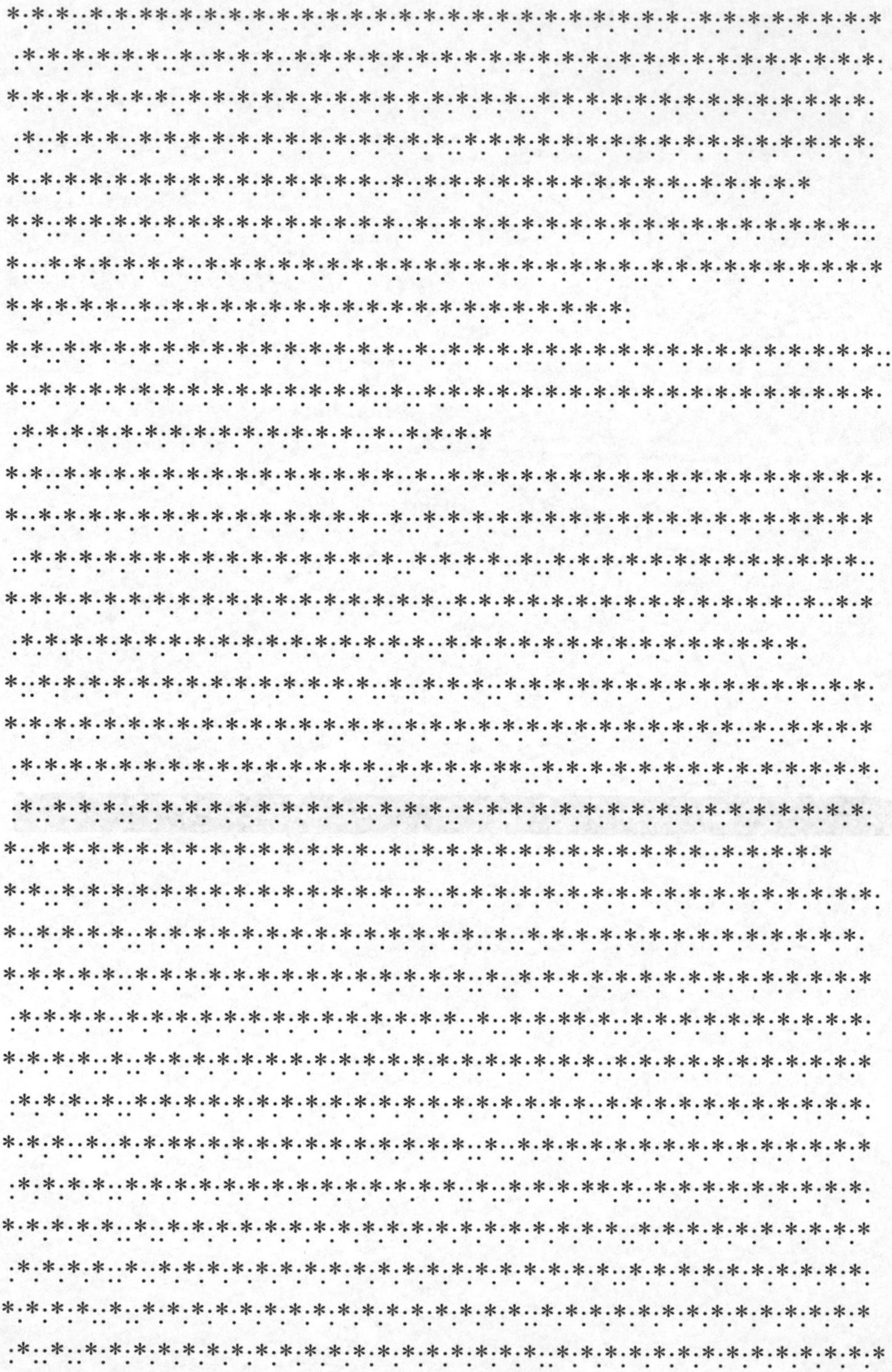

::*:*:*:*:*:*:*:*:*:*:*:*:*:*::*::*:*:*:*:*:*:*::*:*:*:*:*:*:*:*:*:*:*:*:

::*:*:*:*::*:*:*:*:*:*:*:*:*:*:*:*:*:*::*::*:*:*:*:*:*:*:*:*:*:*:*:*

:*:*:*:*:*::*:*:*:*:*:*:*:*:*:*

:::*:*:*:*:*:*:*:*:*:*:*:*:*:*::*::*:*:*:*:*:*:*:*:*:*:*:*:*:*:*:*:*:

:::*:*:*:*:*:*:*:*:*:*:*:*:*::*::*:*:*:*:*:*:*:*:*:*:*:*:*:*:*:*:*:*

::*:*:*:*:*:*:*:**:*:*:*:*:*:*:*:*:*::*:*:*:*:*:*::*::*:*:*:*:*:*:*:*:*

:::*:*:*:*:*:*:*:*:*:*:*:*:*:*::*::*:*:*:*:*:*:*:*:*:*:*:*:*:*:*:*:*:*:

:::*:*:*:*:*:*

:::*:*:*:*:*:*:*:*:*:*:*:*:*:*::*::*:*:*:*:*:*:*:*:*:*:*:*:*:*:*:*:*:

:::*:*:*:*:*:*:*:*:*:*:*:*:*::*::*:*:*:*:*:*:*:*:*:*:*:*:*:*:*:*:*:*

::*:*:*:*:*:*:*:*:*:*:*:*:*:*::*::*:*:*:**:*::*:*:*:*:*:*:*:*:*:*:*:*:

::::*::*:*:*:*:*:*:*:*:*:*:*:*

::*::*:*:*:*:*:*:*:*:*:*:*:*:*:*:*:*:*:*:*::*:*:*:*:*:*:*:*:*:*:*:*:*::

:

:*::*::*:*:*:*:*:*:*:*:*:*:*:*:*:*:*:*:*:*::*:*:*:*:*:*:*:*:*:*:*:

::::*:**:*:*:*:*:*:*:*:*:*:*:*:*:*:*:*:*:*:*::*:*:*:*:*:*::*:*:*:*:*:*

:*:*:*:*:*:*::*:*:*:*:*:*:*:*:*:*:*:*:*:*:*:*:*::*:*:*:*:*:*:*:*:*:*:

::*:*:*:*:*::*:*:*:*:*:*:*:*:*:*:*:*:*:*:*::*::*:*:*:*:*:*:*:*:*:*:*:*

:*:*:*:*:*:*::*:*:*:*:*:*::*:*:*:*:*:*:*:*:*:*:*:*:*::*::*:*:*:*:*:*:

::::*:*:*:*:*:*:*

:*:*:*:*:*:*:*:*:*:*:*:*::*:*:*:*:*:*:*:*:*:*:*:*:*::*:*:*:*:*:*:*:

::*:*:*:*:*::*:*:*:*:*:*:*:*:*:*:*:*:*::*:*:*:*:*:*:*:*:*:*:*:*:*

:*:*:*:*:*::*:*:*:*:*:*:*:*:*:*:*:*:*:*:*:*:*:*:*::*::*:*:*:*:*:*:

:::*:*:*:*:*:*

:*:*:*:*:*:*:*:*:*:*:*:*:*::*:*:*:*:*:*:*:*:*:*:*::*:*:*:*:*:*:*:*:*:

:::*:*:*:*:*:*:*

:*:*:*:*:*:*:*:*:*:*:*:*::*:*:*:*:*:*:*:*:*:*:*:*::*::*:*:*:*:*:*::

::*:*:*:*:*::*:*:*:*:*:*:*:*:*:*:*:*:*::*:*:*:*:*:*:*:*:*:*:*:*:*

:*:*:*:*:*:*:*:*:*:*:*:*::*:*:*:*:*:*:*:*:*:*:*:*:*:*::*:*:*:*:*:*:

:

:*:*:*:*:*:*:*:*:*:*::*::*:

*:**:

:::*:*:*:*:*:*:*:*:*:*:*:*:*::*::*:*:*:*:*:*:*:*:*:*:*:*:*:*:*:*:*:

:::*:*:*:*:*:*:*:*:*:*:*:*:*::*::*:*:*:*:*:*:*:*:*:*:*:*:*:*:*:*:*:*

..*.*.*.*.*.*.*.*.*.*.*.*.*.*..*..*.*.*.*.*.*.*..*.*.*.*.*.*.*.*.*.*.*.*.

..*.*.*.*..*.*.*.*.*.*.*.*.*.*.*.*.*.*..*..*.*.*.*.*.*.*.*.*.*.*.*.*.*.*

.*.*.*.*.*..*.*

...*.*.*.*.*.*.*.*.*.*.*.*..*..*.*.*.*..*.*.*.*.*.*.*.*.*.*.*.*.*.*.*..*.*.

..*.*.*.*.*.*.*.*.*.*.*.*.*.*..*.*.*.*.*.*.*.*.*.*.*.*.*.*.*.*..*..*.*.*.*

.*

...*.*.*.*.*.*.*.*.*.*.*.*.*.*.*..*.

...*.*.*.*.*.*.*.*.*.*.*.*.*..*

..*.*.*.*.*.*.*.*.*.*.*.*.*.*..*..*.*.*.*.*.*.*.*..*.*.*.*.**.*.*.*.*.*.*.*.*

Feb 2, 1556

5AM

Shensi Province China

glacial silt caves
shook
liquified

850,000 people died.

Lisbon Nov 1 1755

9:40 churches collapsed

ocean gone

9:46 fish flopping around

60 ft sea wave struck

70,000 d.

May 8, 1902

Caribbean city of St. Pierre

7:50AM volcano erupts

cloud of superheated gas, rock, ash strikes town:100+mph::*:*:*:*:*:*:*:
::*:*:*:*::*::*::*:*:*:**:*:*:*:*:
::*:*:*:*: *:*:*:*:*:*:*:*:*::*:*:*:*:*:*:*:*:*:*:*:*:*:*:*:*:*:*:*::*:*
:*:*:*:*:*:*:*:*:*:*:*:*:*::*::*:*:*:*:*:*:*:*:*:*:*:*:*:*:*:*:*:*:*::*:*:
:::*:*:*:*:*:*:*:*:*:*:*::*::*:*:*:*:*:*:*:*:*:*:*:*:*:*:*:*:*:*:*::*:*:*
:*:*:*:*:*:*:*:*:*:*:*:*::*::*:*:*:
::::*:*:*:*:*:*:*:*:*:*:*:*:*:*::*
::*::*:*:*:*:*:*:*:*:*:*:*:*:*:*:*::
:::*:*:*:*:*:*:*:*:*:*:*:*:*:*:*:*:*::*:*:*:*:*:*:*:*:*:*:*:*:*:*:*:*:*
:*::*:*:*:*:*:*:*:*:*:*:*:*:*:*:
::*:*::*:*:*:*:*:*:*:*:*:*:*:*:*:*:*:*:*:*:*::*:*:*:*:*:*:*:*:*:*:*:*:*:
:::*::*:*:*:*:*:*:*:*:*:*:*:*:*:*
:*::*:
::::*:*:*:*:*:*:*:*:*:*:*:*:*:*:*:*:*:*::*:*:*:*:*:*:*:*:*:*:*:*:*:*:*
:*:*:*:*::*:*:*:*:*::*:*:*:*:*:*:*:*:*:*:*:*:*:*:*::*:*:*:*:*:*:*:*:*:*:*:
::*:*:*:*:*:*:*::*:*:*:*:*:*:*:*:*:*:*:*:*:*:*::*:*:*:*:*:*:*:*:*:*:*:*
:*:*:*:*:*:*::*:*:**::*:*:
::*:*:*:*:*:*:*:*:*:*:*:*:*:*:*::*:*:*:*:*:*:*:*:*:*::*:*:*:*:*:*::*:*:*:
::*:*:*:*:*:*:*:*:*::*::*:*:*:*:*
:*:*:*:*:*:*:*:*:*:*::*::*:*:*:*:*:*:*:*:*:*:*:*:*:*:*:*:*:*:*::*:*:*:**:*
:*::*:*:*:*:*:*:*:*:*:*:*:*:*::*
::*:*:*::*:*:*:*:*:*:*:*:*:*:*:*:*::*:*:*:*:*:*:*:*:*:*:*:*:*:*:*:*:*:*::

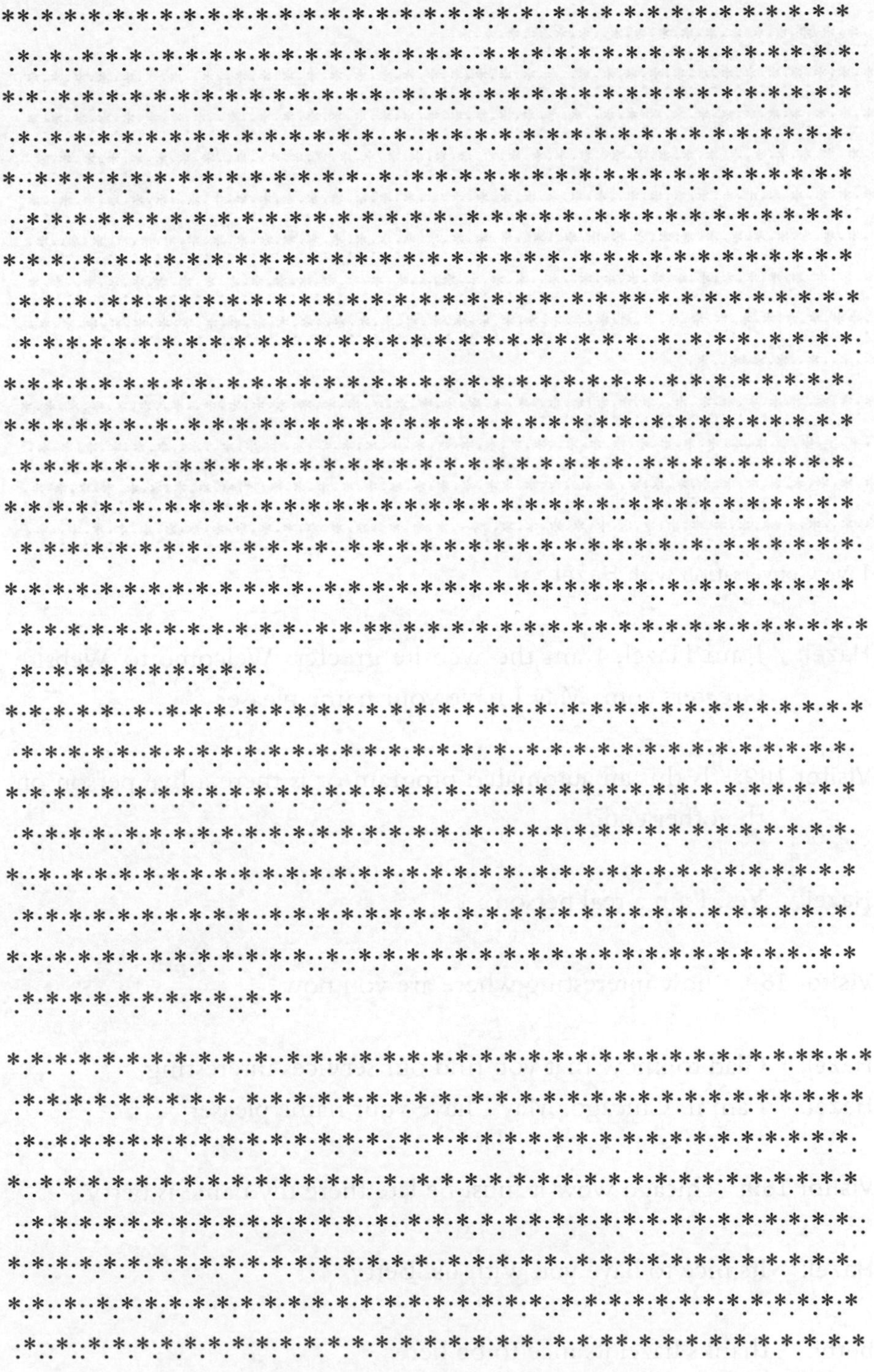

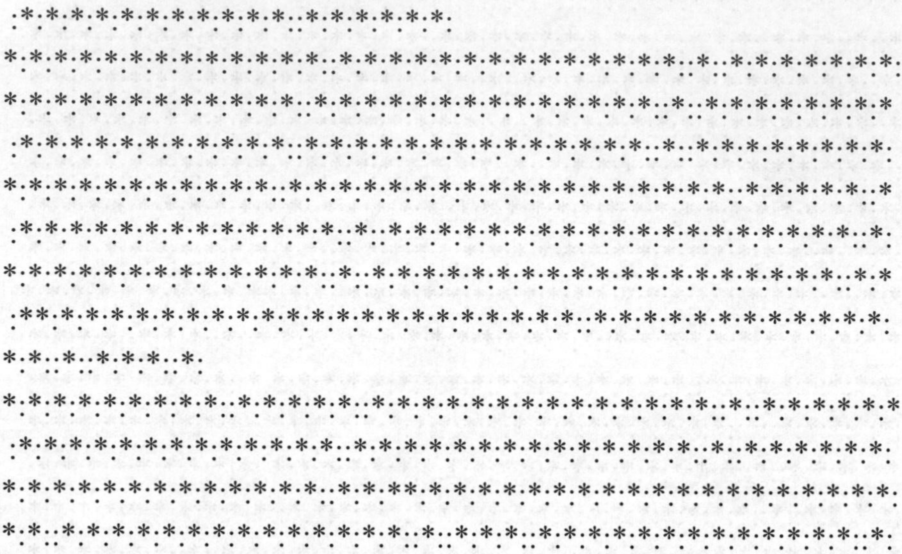

Live Conversation with Hazel

Hazel: I am Hazel, I am the website greeter. Welcome to Website Greeters.com. May I have your name please?

Visitor 169: Is this an automated program or is there a live person on the other end?

Hazel: Yes, I am a real person :)

Visitor 169: how interesting where are you now

Hazel: Glad to know that you find our services interesting.
Hazel: I am in Chicago. May I have your name please?

Visitor 169: chicago wow it must be late there my name is betty

Hazel: Its nice to have you with us, Betty,

betty: thanks hazel its nice to be here

null: Is this your first time at WebsiteGreeters.com?

:*.*.*.*.*.*.*..*..*.*.*..*.*.*.*.*.*.*.*.*.*.*.*.*..*.*.*.*.*.*.*.*.*:

..*.*.*.*.*.*..*.*.*.*.*.*.*.*.*.*.*.*.*.*..*.*.*.*.*.*.*.*.

...*.*.*.*.*.*.*.*.*.*.*.*.*.*.*..*.*.*.*.*.*.*.*.*.*.*.*.*.*.*.*.*:

...*.*.*.*.*.*.*.*.*.*.*.*.*.*..*..*.*.*.*.*.*.*.*.*.*.*.*.*.*.*.*.*

::*.*.*.*.*.*.*.*.*.*.*.*.*.*.*..*..*.*.*.*.*.*.*.*..**.*.*.*.*.*.*.*.*..*

:*.*.*.*:

:*.**..*.*.*.*.*.*

betty: hazel?

betty: is this thing broke

Hazel: I am sorry?

betty: it disconnected me there do you offer website greeting services

Hazel: My apologies for the inconvenience caused.

Hazel: Please open a separate window for browsing our website, in order to keep this chat window active.

Hazel: And yes, we provide the Website Greeter service on our client's websites.

betty: oh I see I must have made a mistake there im working late something of a nite owl

Hazel: Do you have a website, Betty?

betty: we dont at the moment but are in planning stages do you offer live assistance to visitors

Hazel: That's alright, we are here to help you no matter what time!

Hazel: Yes, we offer live help, just like the one we are interacting through at the moment.

Hazel: Our research tells us that 94% to 97% of the new website visitors leave within the first two minutes, and completely forget about it the very next day. This diminishes the whole concept of setting the business online.

Hazel: This prompted us to develop our THREE PRONG strategy:

Hazel: 1. Our Greeters greet the website visitors on your website and engage them in a conversation.

Hazel: 2. The Greeters help the visitor stay on the website, by providing help, support, and facilitates navigation.

Hazel: 3. Our Greeters execute sales pitches which generate leads / sales for you.

Hazel: Let me have our Business Development Manager contact you for further details.

Hazel: May I have your email address and phone number please?

betty: yikes hazel I feel like im getting read a bill of sales it feels a bit pushy girl

Hazel: My apolgies, if I sound pushy.

Hazel: My intention is only to assist you in getting the Live Help feature on your upcoming website.

betty: will you hold a minute hazel I have to take my contacts off

Hazel: Sure, take your time please.

betty: I feel I should offer you an apology hazel you didn't do anything wrong I came to your site looking for answers its just been a long day and ive been working on the fourth and nobody else has been in all day they've been out celebrating their independence lol but seriously forgive me may I tell you a little about the service I need

Hazel: You do not need to apologize. I completely understand.

Hazel: I worked over the holiday too!

betty: I know that's what I was going to say next here I am complaining and youre there in chicago working on the fourth too! I bet you had parties you coulda been at did you work all day?

betty: Hazels a pretty name by the way you don't come across it much anymore

Hazel: Yes, I had to miss out on all the fun.

betty: lol is it ok if I ask you some business questions?

Hazel: Life is not fair.

Hazel: Maybe next year, we can dump our work on someone else :)

Hazel: Sure, and thanks for the compliment.

betty: u r sooo funny hazel im sorry about what I said earlier this is the personal touch I was looking for

Hazel: Thanks again Betty :)

betty: its the personal touch that makes all the difference especially in a conversation you don't want to feel like u r talking to a computer

betty: ;)

Hazel: Glad to have been of assistance, anyway I can.

Hazel: You are quite right in this regard.

Hazel: We train our greeters according to criteria set for them by our clients and the mood of the website.

betty: well let me tell you a little about the site were planning we are building a site that answers tough questions but gives inspiration to americans all across the country

Hazel: If you'd like the chat to have a more upbeat, lively and personal touch to it, we'll see to that it exceeds your expectations!

Hazel: That sounds like an amazing concept.

Hazel: What is the nature of the questions going to be?

betty: well we certainly think it is amazing especially in this day and age. our standpoint is theres nothing wrong with being patriotic and loving your country!!! we want to spread love of the red white and blue while answering questions about the ultimate concepts like love life god liberty justice immigration policy foreign relations nuclear disarmarment and domestic abuse…all while remaining upbeat and positive

Hazel: We'd be delighted to be a part of this project

betty: can I ask you a few questions we are looking for a company who can man the lines when we're not around there are only a few of us and obviously just me right now omg I cant believe its two in the morning anyway we need someone who can assist the visitors to our site someone it will be your job to answer questions and give hope and hopefully convince them to buy inspirational t-shirts mugs mousepads etc

Hazel: Sure, alongwith chat support, we also offer phone and email support to our customers.

Hazel: I'll arrange for the details to be sent over to you.

Hazel: and it is quite late, I hope you had a comfortable enough chair to work in.

betty: great we arent going to do the phone thing yet but maybe in the future depending on our response we are going to be advertising in schools and on buses battered womens shelters and newspapers etc while we want to make a profit obviously because this is a business our main motivation must always be to help people in crisis physical spiritual mental and emotional and also financial

Hazel: You are right, in order to be able to help others, its important your organization if finicially secure.

Hazel: Financially*

betty: I believe that with all my heart. (I loved that chair line by the way -- hilarious!!)

Hazel: Glad to know that :)

Hazel: May I have your email address and phone number please?

betty: I suppose all we have left to do is me to give you my information -- although I should also probably ask you some questions about issues to make sure were on the same page -- easy questions of course, the tougher ones we'll brief you beforehand.

betty: hazel, what do the stars and stripes mean to you?

Hazel: It means Home.

betty: could you elaborate a bit dear?

Hazel: And we all know that no matter how much you want to get away and be set free to explore the world, there is never going to be any place like home.

betty: perfect! that's what I was looking for! straight out of the wizard of oz! youre good hazel girl!

Hazel: Thank you for your kind words Betty.

Hazel: Do I get a cookie? :)

betty: you get a whole box of cookies, girl! hazel, what is freedom? why should it be important to me?

Hazel: To be able to choose the path of life that your heart is leading you on is freedom.

Hazel: It is important to every single living thin on this planet, because without any freedom one doesn't get to live their life to the fullest.

betty: great answers girl. "live their life to the fullest" is perfect, and "your heart" is gold.

Hazel: Thank you for the appreciation!

betty: hazel, why is america better than all other countries combined?

Hazel: It is because "we care".

betty: bonus points!

Hazel: We care about what is hppening in the other parts of the world and care enough to take it upon our shoulders to do something about it.

Hazel: Happening*

betty: Hazel, it's like you've read my book!

Hazel: I haven't read it yet, but if you tell me what its called, I'll make it a point to read it from cover to cover :)

betty: I like your banter hazel.

betty: hazel, why do some people not like america?

Hazel: When a great country like ours, steps up to the challenge of making things better for the mankind; they always come across opposition who stands in their way to prevent them from doing.

betty: another great answer hazel. my only suggestion would be to add that they are jealous of our lifestyles and material goods.

Hazel: I agree.

betty: this is a neat exercise hazel. youre really helping me out, more than you know. im able to ask the tough questions in real time as if i were a client and it gives me a great opportunity to see how it will feel to them. will you try to work the word "inspire" into each answer, if you can? only if it doesnt sound forced. :)

Hazel: Sure, we can arrange for that.

Hazel: We use a generic script for a few days to greet the website visitors.

Hazel: This gives us time to become more familiar with questions that the visitors have on your website and the capacity needed.

Hazel: We will then develoop a script to handle similar questions.

betty: it sounds like a very efficient system. hazel, ive been reading stories in the liberal media about "hundreds of thousands" of "innocent" iraqis overseas losing their lives and they say america is to blame! what am I to say about such "statistics"?

Hazel: Our media should be more responsible. They concentrate on these negative statistics without hilighting the fact about our major breakthrough of dethrwning Saddam Hussein, who was a constant threat to our nation.

Hazel: These statistics should be about how we have reduced the risks of being attacked by Iraq and inspire us towards defending our freedom and way of life!

betty: [applause]

Hazel: (bow)

Hazel: Would you like to share your email address and phone number with us, Betty?

betty: That would certainly "inspire" me! lol. But seriously, hazel, what are your thoughts on outsourcing jobs to pakistan and india?

betty: Here is a phone number: (253) 946-4507

Hazel: I think that first we need to concetrate on our own unemployment ratios. If there are certain jobs that can be cost effective if they are outsourced, then we need to utilize this opputunity.

Hazel: Opportunity*

Hazel: I am sorry for the typing error.

Hazel: May I also have your email address please?

betty: of course your answer is right, hazel. but that's not the type of answer that sells keychains and gives hope I would tend to lean towards being virulently against outsourcing but again your answer was wise froma business standpoint hazel what is the meaning of life?

Hazel: I understand, we can have this one altered to be more patriotic.
Hazel: Life means to be able to fulfill your dreams.
Hazel: Our great country inspires us to dream and work towards achieving them
Hazel: And it certainly gives us the opportunity of doing so too, only we need to be ready to give back to it when it is asked of us.

betty: God?

Hazel: God has been very kind to us, and we can judge that from the fact that we were born as Americans.

betty: Hazel u r gonna make me cry!!! You have inspired me. You are a true patriot.

Hazel: Only a true patriot can recognize another true patriot :)

betty: No one has ever spoken more truthfully than you my sweet blue eyed friend.

betty. Of course your answer is right, Hazel. But that's not the type of answer [illegible] would tend to lean towards being [illegible] against [illegible] your answer was [illegible] Hazel. What is the meaning of life?

Hazel. I understand, we can have this one altered to be more patriotic.

Hazel. That means to be able to fulfill your dream.

Hazel. Our great country has [illegible] to dream and work towards achieving them.

Hazel. And it certainly gives us the opportunity [illegible] only we need to be ready to give back to it when it is asked of us.

betty. Good.

Hazel. God has been very kind to us and we can never [illegible] the fact that we were born as Americans.

betty. Hazel [illegible] makes me so [illegible]! You have inspired me. You are a true patriot.

Hazel. Only a true patriot can recognize another true patriot.

betty. No one has ever spoken more truthfully than you [illegible] ever heard.

Flathead Children Marie

Michele: Hi Betty.

Michele: Hazel is experiencing some technical problem with her computer.

Michele: Please let me have your email address so we can send you a copy of the chat transcript.

betty: Is this an automated program or is there a live person on the other end?

Michele: I am a live person :)

betty: Will you hold on a moment?

Michele: Sure thing!

Michele: Take your time

Thursday, September 12, 2002—LOS ANGELES

Less than an hour after she had won $26,000 on a television game show, my wife and I were driving south down Interstate 5, chatting happily in the carpool lane. All other lanes of traffic were bumper-to-bumper but ours was moving along at a healthy clip. To our right that slow-moving traffic, and to the left a cement retaining wall—it all happened so fast—a car to our right veered suddenly into our lane to get out of the way of a minor fender bender that was occurring in front of it—I didn't have the time to react—I should have:

plowed into him, as his nose shot into our lane—
speedometer: 68 mph—and then

our car would have spun out in a counterclockwise direction into the cement wall to our left—

SMASH! we hit that and keep on spinning—

back into traffic—

and the car behind us—

plowsinto the side of our car—my wife

[redacted] instantly and painlessly—while my head is battered back and forth and the cars continue to pile up on us, and on the third or fourth meeting of my head and our own car's metal frame—after a very slowed down

and prolonged period of pain—I do too— *.*.*.*.*.*.*.*.*.*.*.*.*.*.*.*.*
.
.
.
.
.

.
.
.
.
.

.
.
.
.
.
. Kim Forbes: Is this you?

.
.
.
.
.
.
.
.
.
*.
*.
.
.
.
.

*:
:

But instead, an angel took the wheel from me lifted the car up into the air:::carried us:::then set us back down again, safe and sound, four wheels, continuing on…

After that day, everywhere we went, cars were crashing into one another on all sides. We saw accidents on the freeway in oncoming lanes, lanes far to the side, sometimes we came upon them right after they had happened,

people sitting in their cars in a field of glass in the fast lane in a daze…

Cars would weave at us suddenly and I'd have to swerve off the road to keep from being hit. It seemed every time we got in the car, we left a trail of wrecked metal and bleeding bodies in our wake. We started to wonder:

Is there something going on around here?

Is this a pattern?

It had all seemed to begin with:

One afternoon we had gone to dinner at my parents' house in Federal Way. After dinner, we'd sat around the living room. My brother and his wife and their baby were there. We talked awhile, and then they said they had to take the baby home and put him to bed, so they got all their stuff and packed him in the car and left. My wife and I stayed another hour or so, talking. Then we got ready to leave. We had a last-minute cup of coffee first. I took a whiz. We hugged each other. Then we left. We got in our car, waved goodbye, and drove down the hill to the arterial. We stopped at the stop sign at the bottom. It was evening but it was still bright. I signaled, looked both ways, then turned left onto the street.

A few seconds later a kid in a gold Toyota passed us coming the opposite way. If I slow it down I remember looking over and seeing him in profile—

I looked forward again—

my wife looked back because she sensed that something was unfolding.

She saw a woman in a green minivan pull out into his lane from a side street, crossing in front of him, very slowly, blocking his path completely.

Instead of plowing into her driver's side door with all of his force, he

turned the wheel to the right in an attempt to get around her—

my wife screamed:

W: *Look what she made him do!*—

his tires screeching—

It's gonna!

I looked back in my rearview mirror—

somehow he got around the green minivan,

his car hopped the curb at the corner then into a front lawn

now the car was headed directly for a house,

but then he turned the wheel again and somehow

grass spitting up from his wheels

managed to get all four tires back on the road, his car now moving forward once again in its proper lane—

and for a second it seemed that everything was going to turn out okay,

but his tires never could find purchase, the rear wheels hopped and skipped like a fishtail behind him—

then one of them skipped high and hit the curb which caused his car to break sharply left

into oncoming traffic, at which point he was T-boned by an enormous black SUV at a perfect ninety degrees.

In the mirror, I saw his windows explode and glass rain down.
:
:*:
:
:*:
:
:*:
::*:

—*Oh my God!* my wife cried. *She killed him!*

I pulled over. The woman in the minivan, who had caused the accident, passed us, and then she pulled over too, into the parking lot of a Jack in the Box; we saw her look back at the accident. Brake lights red.

Then she took her foot off the brake. We watched her drive slowly on through the parking lot, then to an exit. Then she turned back onto the street. We watched her drive away.

My wife rooting through the glove compartment, looking for a piece of paper and a pen, saying: 192 LS[redacted] 192 LS[redacted] 192 LS[redacted] 192 LS[redacted] 192 LS[redacted] 192 LS[redacted] 192 LS[redacted] 192 LS[redacted] 192 LS[redacted]…

A week later we went down to the Federal Way Police Headquarters to follow up with the cop who'd taken our original report at the scene. As we sat outside his office, waiting to be called in, I picked up the local newspaper and read about the accident.

Says here "He Was Driving Too Fast and Lost Control."

*

After he called us in, the cop sat us down. He said he'd visited the woman whose license number my wife had written down. The woman had claimed that she did not know about any accident, had not caused any accident, had not seen any accident, had not pulled over to look back upon any accident. Had not looked back upon any accident, and had not then driven away from any accident (in her green minivan). And so the cop had thanked her for her time and left. Now he thanked us for *our* time!

But before he did he said:

Are you Pastor Mike's son?

M: Yeah.

> 11, 4–8, Angie Yohe, 1995. 4–8, Melanie Long, 1998. 13, 4–4, Kristen Miner, 2006. 4–4, Kim Forbes, 2006. 15, 4–2 12, Krista Oyler, 1995 ...

"Oh, shit he got hit hard, he got hit really fucking hard. Shit, god, shit, he got hit hard."

We ran up to the scene. A group of people had already gathered around. The boy's door was open and a woman was kneeling in the street beside the car, feeling under his chin and speaking to him in a soft voice, as if she were his mother. She had a medical kit and I assumed she was a nurse. The boy's eyes were closed, and he was shaking, moaning. He appeared to be having a conversation with someone. There were two people in the SUV that had crushed him, a man and a woman, and they were reclined now in their seats. A few people stood around them, speaking to them through an open window. Most of us stood off to the side, quietly, in a grassy area on the side of the road. People came from all around. We watched the woman kneeling beside the boy, whispering. And then the ambulance came. I won't describe the way they finally took him out. I won't describe them pulling him out of his car, tugging at him so roughly. They're going to paralyze him! I thought. They should hold his neck better!

He was a big kid for seventeen. He was a golfer. He'd placed second in State the year before. And just two weeks before this accident, he'd shot a 61 at a pro-am tournament in Spokane, one shot shy of the course record. The cop we'd later meet was walking back and forth down the center of the street, taking pictures of the long tire treads, of the torn-up grassy shoulder, and of the two smashed vehicles, piecing together the scene.

But there was no sign of any woman or any minivan—she was long gone—so there was no reason to believe that any woman in any minivan had ever existed.

And the crowd as crowds do was speaking; they were all telling one another what they had seen. And when one would hear another new detail from his left, he would turn to the person to his right and repeat it, as if he had been the one to see it! No one mentioned a woman or a green minivan.

They all said "He was driving too fast and lost control."

★

> Kim Forbes's URL. http://www.bebo.com/kimforbes0. Member Since. November 2006. Kim Forbes says:. "Work sucks, buses suck & rude people suck! ...

> Bush Seeks Nuclear Disclosure From Kim – Forbes.com

The ambulance came, and they pulled the boy from the car and placed him on a gurney and worked on him in the middle of the street; his eyes were closed, but his lips were moving, and his head was rocking back and forth as if he were arguing with someone—

And the boy's mother came running up—a family friend had come upon the scene and, recognizing the car, called the mother on her cell phone—

then his chest and stomach began to heave and roll in some sort of seizure that I have never been able to adequately describe, I've written the scene many times and then each time ~~erased~~

[redacted]

Melissa don't hang up the phone. Melissa don't hang up the phone. Stay on the phone, OK? Gotta keep communicating. Don't hang up the phone

[deleted]

The cops wouldn't let the mother near her son; she was screaming and crying, scratching at her face and pulling at her hair, but she had to stay up there on the sidewalk with the rest of us,

strangers.

And then they shot him up with something and after maybe a minute he was still, he was not shaking anymore, and they carried him to the ambulance, slid him in, and closed the door.

Then the boy's father ran up to the scene—and the ambulance remained there in the middle of the street while they presumably worked on his son inside—but everyone was wondering why they weren't moving along to the hospital, the boy's father was holding his wife—a crowd of people, my wife and I inside it, watching—the ambulance, just stayed put, in the middle of SW 336th St.

That boy might have been a great golfer. He might have graced the covers of magazines someday, bringing glory to his hometown of Federal Way. They might have named a ⋆ junior high after

⋆him.

He might have once had a girlfriend, and some nights after his parents were asleep, he might have jumped from his second-floor window, down onto the driveway......... over to his car parked on the street......... he might have opened the door and got inside...... put it in neutral...... coasted........... down the hill......... until it was safe to start it up—then *pop!*ped the clutch and *pun!*ched the gas. He might have driven to her street, and parked down the block from her house, then snuck around to the back where her bedroom was; she might have been waiting at the window backlit by the red light he'd stolen for her from the christmas tree at the end of the pier and it had fit her bedside lamp perfectly. On the windowsill she sat, smoking a cigarette. Hey, Helen! Your dad awake? he said. Shhhhh! she covered his mouth with her hand, laughing. Your dad awake? he said a little louder. He awake? Shhhhh! Come on! Let's go! She leaned back and swung her legs over...he helped her down and out...and then together they ran, away, between the houses, beneath the streetlights, the red sky of Federal Way. Jump in the car and drive away, the windows down, a warm night breeze, cigarette smoke drifting around, around and out. He liked the way her hair moved across her face in the wind, and how she'd sweep it away. TURN IT UP! I *LOVE* THIS SONG! They drove to the Brown's Point Lighthouse and got out, she ran down to the water's edge and he followed her, where no one else was ever around, this late, the great barges slid, silently, down black water. Little waves stretched and sighed and fell asleep upon the sandy shore. The light lit. The wind blew. Kiss me now. She opened her mouth and his heart flew. Light lit: the waves. Lay me down. He held her close and, behind them, the hurricane of the world it died away; I'm sorry I didn't do anything when your dad hit you with the telephone. it shrunk away; I'm sorry I didn't do anything when your dad hit you with the telephone. it curled up in a little ball and rolled away. I'm sorry I didn't do anything when your dad hit you with the telephone.

> Ko Kim Forbes taku ingoa Ko Taranaki te Maunga Ko Ngati Mutunga te iwi Tena ... Kia ora koutou katoa Kim Forbes.

But to see; the way;

they cut the clothes from him, down the center of his torso, and up each leg, from the ankle to the groin;

and to see the way, his naked chest begins to heave, as they lift him out, and place him on the board,

the way it heaved and lunged and tore…

I didn't want to, and I put it off as long as I could, because I was extremely nervous and didn't want to interrupt or open my mouth at all, but finally, eventually, because I knew I must at last:

I went up to the father.
(He was a skinny brown-haired man with a mustache.)
His back was to me.
(He was wearing a flannel shirt and jeans.)

I stood behind him, quietly.

After a while his wife, in his arms, noticed me.

(She was a little heavy. She had a light brown perm
and wore a gray sweatshirt with embroidered flowers on it.)

The father felt a slight shift in her direction.

He turned to face the object of her attention.
(She wore blue eyeliner on her lids and pink blush on her cheeks.)

There I stood before him.

I cleared my throat.

I took a deep breath.

I said something

along the lines

of:

There are 3 types of Rock

1. Igneous:

cools from molten rock

95% of earths crust

2. Sedimentary:

layered—from accumulation of particles
of preexisting rock

75% of earths surface

But to see;

the way;

they cut the clothes from him,

3. Metamorphic: (changed)

heated, pressed

up the center of his torso,

and up each leg,

from the ankle to the

groin;

and to see

the way,

his naked chest begins to heave,

as they lift him out,

and place him on the board,

every rock can be converted into every other
kind of rock by movement

the way it heaved

and lunged

and tore…

> Kim Forbes. There would be no plays without an audience. Notice how entranced these members of the audience were. Mrs Forbes co-ordinated the event ...

We packed up our things and ran off to Montana.

We hid out in a forest cabin on a lake.

During the days we walked down a dirt path, through falling leaves, and sat at the edge of the dock, in a green Adirondack chair, looking out at the dozing water.

> P.S. Remember "Kim Forbes" – she simply disappeared – no one has heard from her in almost ten years... Photo Sharing and Video Hosting at Photobucket ...

Message: Yo Momma Yard & Garden Show is coming up middle of February. Jenn's doing a great job keeping everything going while you are gone. This isn't funny girlfriend. It's time to get home. We love and miss you.

> Hood River – KIMBERLY FORBES (Endangered Missing)

After only a few weeks, nearly all the leaves had fallen. High gray clouds had swept over the blue sky and the air was cold. We sat on the dock in heavy coats, and the woken waves swept high up on the shore. Crashed down:

"No cell phone activity, no credit card activity, nothing.

Message: Just decided to type in Kim's name and found
                  this web-site. I think of her daughter, other
                  family and friends everyday and hope there
                  soon will be some answers.

It was like she'd been swallowed up."

We gathered wood and stacked it by the back door, piled it up: pile next
to pile next to pile. The last birds flew away. We closed the windows.
We closed the doors. Last leaves let go. Winter arrived. ████████████
████████████████████████████

Help Find Kimberly Ann Forbes

Monday 11/08/2004 4:03:25pm
Name: marla budd
Homepage:
E-Mail:
Referred By: Just Surfed In
City/Country: The Dalles oregon
Message: I feel deeply saddened and am praying

Monday 11/08/2004 1:52:12pm
Name: Danette Ohlson-Huttunen
Homepage:
E-Mail:
Referred By: Search Engine
City/Country: Longview , Washington
Message: I hope Kim is found soon to be with her
                  family and friends.
                  God Bless

Monday 11/08/2004 1:18:30pm
Name: Trisha Coy (Cornett)
Homepage:
E-Mail:

Referred By: Just Surfed In
City/Country: Hillsboro
Message: My prayers are with Kim and her family, and her wonderful circle of friends. I hope to hear good news soon. God bless.

Monday 11/08/2004 12:20:25am
Name: Sharon McKinnon
Homepage:
E-Mail:
Referred By: Friend
City/Country: Quartzsite, Az
Message: You are in my prayers. I just saw Kim and CJ in Sept at our First Interstate Banks reunion....I'm so sorry....

Help Find Kimberly Ann Forbes

Message: I AM PRAYING FOR KIMBERLY'S SAFE RETURN TO HER FAMILY &FRIENDS, AND FOR PEACE AND COMFORT FOR HER FAMILY. GOD BLESS ALL OF YOU. CAROLE

Message: My thoughts and prayers are with Kim and pray that she is found soon and back with her family.

I started writing a book.

There must be some clue or clues that are being processed to bring about the solution to her disappearance. May GOD watch over her and her family and friends.

Message: I pray every day your mom will be found. This is such a mystery and wish it could be resolved for your peace.

Message: Kim would come through the drive thru every Thursday night and get dinner on her way home and I miss her very much. Please come home soon Kim!!

Message: I pray that you find this lady,it is so sad to know that they are out there somewhere.My heart and thoughts are with you and your family...Beth Sawyers and Family

Message: We have posted your fliers and are praying for your safe return.Thinking of your daughter/family and co-workers during this stressful time. Keep the faith.
Donna

Message: Was checking the KOIN website to see local news from home. Am Oregonian transplant and lived most of my life in SE Portland, east of 162nd.

Am sorry to hear about Kimberly, and hope something breaks in her case soon.

My uncle was murdered in his home on 30th and SE Division nearly 3 years ago, still an open case. I guess I am lucky, at least I know where he is.

My prayers are with your family and the police that are investigating.

Message: I'm an Oregonian currently living in Riga Latvia, I've became aware of her story on KATU's channel and been following it since it aired. My prayers are with friends, family and Kimberly herself...

Message: My prayers are with you.

Message: I'm so sorry for this horrible waiting and worrying you are enduring. I don't know what I would do if something similar happened to a loved one. Our thoughts and prayers are with you. May God bring your loved one home!

Message: My Thoughts are with Jennifer, CJ and the rest of Kims Family and Friends, I used to work with Kim at 1st Interstate Bank yrs back and there wasn't a day that would go by that you wouldn't bust a gut over something Kim would do or say...I don't think anyone that knows her can imagine her with anything but a large smile on her face laughing..she is such a beautiful, fun, independent gal, this is just so unreal! We all pray for a speedy homecoming!

> Kim Forbes spoke with her adult daughter Oct. 30. She said she planned to meet a friend for breakfast the next morning and then go shopping in Portland ...

Message: My husband is the tow truck driver who found Kim's Explorer. We both wanted everyone to know that Kim is in our thoughts and prayers and we hope some evidence will be found to help locate Kim.

Message: I just pray that you will be found safe and sound! Rose

Message: Kim,

I am still having a hard time believing you are out there somewhere and you are not home with your family and friends.

I miss you so very much, and I am not giving up looking for you, I know you would not give up on me.

I am praying for you all the time, for your safety whereever you may be.

Jennifer needs you and all of your family and friends need you to come back home to us.

May God watch over you wherever you may be, always.

Message: My thoughts and prayers are with you and your family. We are also missing our family member---Melinda Wall McGhee. May God bless and give you peace. kay

Message: May God's presence strongly be felt by friends and family as he gives comfort and strength. And I pray that Kimberly returns soon,as it is written that ALL THINGS ARE POSSIBLE WITH GOD.

Message: My prayers are for the safe return of Kimberly. God speed on her location and the quick arrest of who ever took her. God bless and keep her.

Message: Kim where are you...give us some sign.. PLEASE....Remember we are the Stealth women.....

Message: I think that this is a great website. We all need to have hope because she and alot of the other missing people out there are still alive. I pray for them all.

Message: I hope your friends each take a mile of your route and examine every tire track, possible wrong turn, and mashed down brush and grass, and follow it beyond where the brush has sprung back up and find answers.

Message: O LORD, You have searched me and known me. You know when I sit down and when I rise up; You understand my thought from afar. You scrutinize my path and my lying down, And are intimately acquainted with all my ways. Even before there is a word on my tongue, Behold, O LORD, You know it all. You have enclosed me behind and before, And laid Your hand upon me. Such knowledge is too wonderful for me; It is too high, I cannot attain to it. Where can I go from Your Spirit? Or where can I flee from Your presence? If I ascend to heaven, You are there; If I make my bed in Sheol, behold, You are there. If I take the wings of the dawn, If I dwell in the remotest part of the sea, Even there Your hand will lead me, And Your right hand will lay hold of me.

(Psalm 139:1–10)

We may not know, but the LORD does. My prayers are with you.

Message:

(www.angelfire.com/jazz/jazzyrose/Forbes.html)

[redacted]

[redacted]

[redacted]

[redacted]

[redacted]

(Prof Billings Brown 20080416 204155.wav)

They had, uh, *Strauss waltzes* where you, *pivoted on one toe.*

W: Really!

All that fancy stuff.

W: Cool!.... Did you ever, uh,
skate with Grandma,
or was that past the time.

That was past the time. This was all before World War II.

W: Yeah.

Well, I did a—I did a few *after.* And after we were married, why, she neither *skated nor danced*.

W: Awww! Come on, Grandma!

Nor hiked.

W: Uhhh.

Didn't hike *well*, anyway.

W: Right...Darn it......

Just a *Mormon mama*......

W: Well, I guess you got what you were after!
Now Gramps, I noticed you don't have a
wedding ring! I never noticed that before!

What?

W: No wedding ring!

I had *three* wedding rings, I lost them all…I thought: *That's it.*

W: Yep!

Why? Because you *can't wear a wedding ring* when you're *doin carpentry.*

W: Nope!

Why? Because it'll *snag on a nail* and *pull your finger off.*

W: Yeah!

You *can't wear a wedding ring* when you're *doin auto mechanics.*

W: Nope!

Why? Because you'll get it on the *battery cable,* and *burn your finger off*… So *me a carpenter,* with a *flair for fixing cars,* didn't have a chance.

W: Nope!….What happened to Grandma's ring?

I don't know which of the girls got the…*diamond*…*Two* diamonds. A diamond and a { } ring, so one of them, coulda *gotten away* with, with each…The *wedding ring,* they—well, the wedding band they couldn't get off.

W: Oh.

Her finger. They said: We can't get it off without *cutting it!* I said, Leave it on.

W: Oh…….

M: Have you ever been to Hood River?

Several times.

M: What'd you do there?

Saw my *girlfriend* there.

M: Ahhh. Ada Vee?

Ada Vee.

W: She's quite a looker.

Ada Vee Webber…Fact I, *danced the opening dance* with her at the… *Gold and Green Ball* in *Port*land.

W: Nice!

In my *army uniform.*

M: What's Hood River like?

I would *say* it's the *most desirable place to live* in the *whole country.*

M: Really.

It's *juuust right.* Just far enough up the *canyon,* so it's *not too wet,* and it's *not too dry.*

W: Nice!.......Yeah, except Oregon has high property tax. Darn it.

Well, I'm just talkin about...*livin.*

W: Yeah.

M: So what did you do there?

What did I *do?*

M: When you were visiting Hood River.

Well, I, *made love to Ada Vee!*

W: [*laughs*]

M: Oh, did you!

W: In your mind! [*laughs*]

It was *apple season,* and so...there were *apples to be picked,* and *apples to be...yarded!* That is, the box of apples had to be...*pulled by tractor* back to the...*barn* or whatever.

W: Could you go down there and pick up seasonal work?

No, I just dropped in there on *leave* from the army. This was during the *war.* And then *soon after I left*...she married a sailor.

W: Uh! Terrible!

M: Tragedy.

Terrible. The story of my life...The girl who lived across the *street* up on the *glacial moraine* joined the *WACs* quote *to support me!* During the war. And she married a sailor. *Some support!*

W: Why do the sailors
get all the chicks?
What's the deal there!

Well, I think they think they're more, *revered* for their *romance* or something, I don't know.

W: Hmmm.

I don't know......

W: Who knows..................

I remember goin with Ada Vee up to, uh, *Celilo Falls* which, has now been covered with the dam behind, uh—Bonneville Dam...And uh, *buying,* a, *salmon* from an *Indian* up there. *Celilo Falls* there's a, *lot of rocks, blocking the river.* And *causing the falls,* and, so they built a, kind of a *walkway*—the Indians built kind of a *walkway* out into the river and they—and *very long spears* on, I guess, *mangrove poles* or something—and they'd *spear the salmon* as they were...*spawning.* Coming up the river. I remember buying a big salmon.

W: How big would it be?

Oh...big enough.....

M: That must have been a good day.

Yeah…Little more adventure.

M: Pretty girl…salmon…

Yeah.

M: water falls.

Yeah. Did I show you her *picture?* I've still got it.

M: Yeah.

W: Well, you *don't* still got it 'cause now *we've* got it!

Have you?

W: Yeah, because I forgot to bring it back with me.

Oh. OK.

W: But we scanned it.

I visited Hood River again two, uh—well, maybe a couple of times. And I remember, uh, *riding into Hood River* from, uh, *La Grande,* on a *freight train.* And uh…did I tell you that story?

W: No!

Well, a friend of mine, when we were *fourteen*...fourteen years old, we *decided,* my friend and I, we were going to *hitchhike over to Idaho* to see my cousins. And uh...so we *hitchhiked* and *hitchhiked* and we stopped somewhere in Eastern Washington to pick *strawberries* and get *fifty cents* for our *pockets* and...finally we got up in the *Blue Mountains.* Couldn't get a ride. And uh, so we *hiked* most of the way over the Blue Mountains.

W: What!

And, uh, *finally got a ride* with a *fisherman.* Who was going to La Grande.

W: Well, that's not in Idaho!

Well, I know, it's on the way, though. And, so we got to La Grande, we *went out* to the *hot springs,* and uh, *slept.* And the *mosquitos* were just *terrible.* Had to *pull our heads into our sleeping bags* to get any...any sleep at all. *So* we changed our plan, we decided we'd gone far enough. And uh, were going to go back *home.* So we went down to the *railyards* in *La Grande,* to uh, *see what was cookin.* And that same *fisherman* was a, *engineer* on a *locomotive goin west!* So he says, *Which way are you boys goin this morning!* I say, *Well, we're goin west;* he says, *Well, there's that, uh,* flatcar load *of* steel girders *going to, going to, uh,* Hood River. *For the dam. Why don't you climb aboard? Now,* he says, *be kind of* quiet *going through* Pendleton *because the* cops there *are pretty* severe. So we did...We got to uh *Hood River,* and he said, *Well, we're dropping off this car* here! *But there's some, some cars in* boxes—*automobiles in* boxes—*goin on to* Port*land. So,* climb aboard! [*laughs*]

W: Wow!

So we rode to Portland and then we hitchhiked back to Seattle.

W: That was a total adventure
for a couple fourteen-year-olds.

Yeah.

W: What'd you eat?

HOOD RIVER APPLES
HOOD RIVER
COUNTY
SOLD
HOOD RIVER

Monday 11/08/2004 8:16:03am

Name:	International K-9 Search and Rescue
Homepage:	http://www.k9sardog.com
E-Mail:	searchdog@yahoo.com
Referred By:	E-Mail
City/Country:	Longview, Wa.
Message:	If the family of Ms. Forbes needs any assistance in their search they can call on I.K.9.S.A.R.S. and we'll assist. We have search dogs, boats and underwater cameras.

END OF ACT I

(PREVIOUSLY)

When Jove looked down on earth all that he saw
Was a stilled ocean and on a mountain shelf
One man, one woman.
Of many thousands sent
To untimely death, only this gentle innocent
And his bride were left to praise the fortunate
Will of God.

Jove swept the clouds aside and made
A channel where the North Wind opened heaven:

And earth again looked upward to the sky,

Again the heavens showered earth with light.

Then even the distant reaches of the seas
Fell quiet and to soothe the rocking waters
Neptune let fall his triple-headed spear.
Then ocean's master called to sea-wreathed Triton
Who at echo of Neptune's voice came from the sea
Like a tower of sea-green beard, sea creatures,
Sea shells, grey waters sliding from his green shoulders
To sound his horn, to wind the gliding rivers
Back to their sources, back to rills and streams.

At Neptune's order Triton lifted up
His curved sea shell, a trumpet at his lips

Which in the underworld of deepest seas
Sounds Triton's music to the distant shores
Behind the morning and the evening suns;

And as his voice was heard through land and ocean
The floods and rivers moved at his command.

Over all earth the shores of lakes appeared
Hillsides and river banks, wet fields and meadow,
As floods receded and quays came into view:
A cliff, then a plateau, a hill, a meadow,

As from a tomb a forest rose and then
One saw trees with lean seaweeds tangled
Among their glittering leaves and wave-tossed boughs.

It was a world reborn

but Deucalion

Looked out on silent miles of ebbing waters.

He wept, called to his wife,

Dear sister, friend,
O last of women, look at loneliness;

As in our marriage bed our fears, disasters
Are of one being, one kind, one destiny;

We are the multitudes that walk the earth
Between sunrise and
sunset of the world,
And we alone inherit wilderness.

The living are lost beneath a dwindling sea.
Even the ledge of mountain where we stand
May drop to darkness;

and even the brief shadow
Of clouds that drift and fade

is the return Of midnight to the terror in
my heart.

And you, dear soul,

what if

what if

what if

What if the Fates had swept You

on these pale rocks alone,
to whom would you
Confess your grief, your tears?

For if wild sea had cl: AWW91IHdlcmUgcmlnaHQuIEhlJ2xsIG9ubHkg
ZWF0IGZvciBtb20uIEhlJ3MgYmVlbiB1cCBmb3IgMjUgbWludXRlcyBhbmQga
GUncyBhc2xlZXAgYWdhaW4gaW4gbW9tJ3MgY2hhaXIuICBIZSB3b24ndCB
nbyBiYWNrIHRvIGJlZCBvciBtb3ZlIG92ZXIgdG8gaGlzIGNoYWlyLiAgTW9tIH
NheXMgaGUncyB2ZXJ5IGRpZmZlcmVudCB0b2RheS4KClRoaXMgbWVzc2F
nZSB3YXMgc2VudCB1c2luZyBQSVgtRkxJWCBNZXNzYWdpbmcgc2Vyd
mljZSBmcm9tIFZlcml6b24gV2lyZWxlc3MhDQpUbyBsZWFybic6fPghQf
wos5dOjlLBQT7ivOE1whcK3SlGuSEjDfrU8rYk0ekXmoaayENgsPQVNp1x
o9zZyeldGl0bm93L2dldHBpeC4NCiANClRvIGxlYXJuIGhvdyB5b3Uvb3N
lIGFuIGluc3RhbGxhdGlvbiB0eXBlIChNaW5pbTKOcGrdlfwrlvBenJH

HINhb1LjFdLIgRcRyCNvXNaRdkZNHRWNxdWUbr5m5T8zc9feuCX
VtLCBSZWNvbW1lbmRlZCBvciBDdXN0b20pLCBzZWxlY3QgTWlu
aY2FulHJlY29yZCB2aWRlb3Mgd2l0aCB5b3VylHd2jwP8L7PQ4IS6
rPlQCZG6n61L15bwpFnFbYRQd38C :aimed you

then I would have followed after;

Content-Transfer-Encoding: base64/9j/4SJgRXhpZgAATU0AKBOwE+9gA
AAAgACAEQAAIAAAAOAAAAbgESAAMAAAABAAEAAAEaAAUAAAA
BAAAAfAw||4t1fAAUAAAABAAAAhAEoAAMAAAABAAIAAAExAAIAAAA
bAAAAjAEyAAIAAAAUAAAAp4dpAAQAAAABAAAAuwAAAeZQY
WxtIFRyZW8gNzAwcAAAAEgAAAABAAAASAAAAAFQYWxtIE1lZGl
hIEFwcGxpY2F0aW9uIFYzLjUyMDA3OjAyOjI4IDE3OjE0OjE4AAAPg
poABQAAAAEAAAF1gp0ABQAAAAEAAAF9kAAABwAAAAQwMjIwkA
MAAgAAABQAAAGFkAQAAgAAABQAAAGZkgQACgAAAAEAAAGt
kgUABQAAAAEAAAG1kgkAAwAAAAEAAAAAkgoABQAAAAEAAAG9oAE
AAwAAAAEAAAAAiCIAAwAAAAEAAgAApAMAAwAAAAEAAAAApA
AAwAAAAEAAAAApAYAAwAAAAEAIAAAApCAAAgAAACEAAAH
FAAAAAAAAAAAAAAAAAAAAAAAAAAAAyMDA3OjAyOjI4IDE3OjE0OjExADI
wMDc6MDI6MjggMTc6MTQ6MTgAAAAAAAAAAAAAAAAAAAAAAAAAA
AAAAAAMjk1MzEwMzI3LTIxMTEzNjMAAAAAAAAAAAAAAAAAAAAAAY
BAwADAAAAAQAGAAABGgAFAAAAAQAAAjQBGwAFAAAAAQAAA
jwBKAADAAAAAQACAAACAQAEAAAAAQAAAkQCAgAEAAAAAQAAIB
SAgYKCAAAASAAAAAEAAABIAAAAAf/Y/+AAEEpGSUYAAQEBAAIAAgAA
/9sAQwADAgIDAgIDAwMDBAMDBAUIBQUEBAUKBwcGCAwKDAwL
CgsLDQ4SEA0OEQ4LCxAWEBETFBUVFQwPFxgWFBgSFBUU/9sAQ
wEDBAQFBAfHvUDxKNw3Z+tWrCPyjx82acNZajNwOlIBzhgRn0qnr
ILCCZWJDLnHpzRfP5dsCTwSKsKiXulAI43JgGvVlraCZktNTPjkZxj
caY7NCSS3Jp7xNCm4Mox6GqV2zzHOenc1ySk0nctDnlVs55z3qp
PbxOpI44okkGBVeWYvkZGP5VxSae5olYrRrtLKGNKhMbk0xG2Skc
N9am+/JnPFcafYsmaZ3Qgn5h3quHZAwLGnbMNgNk+9XrLwzqesT+VB
A/wA3RnBVfzprmIohbGSiySvw2TWpZaZNNgIjZ7nFej+FPgtNCiHV7m3h
lYZ2RzK3HevS9I8FeGdMtnL3BVBb9a7qGClPPWbsZyqpaI8NtPCbl

4+U9BXW3Gk6Z4k0/yJlAfHyyEcoe2K8al0q/0ELIkjzRgZJHU/lWpofxC52S
MVPcNwalQ0KUuhp6xpV94TnEkc0k8cTAeYOSefauY+Lnxol8QeFf+Eflf
cxkR255yCe1emadrltqVuUd9yPywNYfjP4U+EvEmlyG1s0sNV3iT7bCmX
fHJBycc9Kzej1Vy0m07Hi9qn9l+F7RoyY55mTew9MkEfSvZvD0QTw7D-
HaFdpj42HI71454q0+604pascJCNm0HjrXZfDDxpa6dp8mmyg+cyERnB
+Xis29dDJx0NefVLWyL2s4864HATGQv40jW6rZLMZQFHYEcUyfwrJGhvp
Axab5i2PmP1FUrHUI7TzIZ7NZlY5BbORTvfYllmttVlLsqSu0XdW4p8kFvO
C6oBJnP41M8MQh+0QxcHsBUMETSBpANoHWov2Kt1Nm0RJrNXb55e4
NY+sabJexvs/dup+UjvWnp8ohVieM1YkRShI79aEJXRx8tlc2ltC05VXZdx
Ctkl46hlhLqRyQORWnD4JvJlgyrKAR0K4xXv+kHw3BI0MUkI2DoCOMfjUk
viXRIZHChHGev+TXsU8Jh0rNnP7SV7WPn9fAd6pClsjMRn5IwBRP4G1S3
geRli+3kheTXvv8AwnHhy2kTMayLsO7K9D271mP8TfCn9pxWoaW0eVC

O had I Father's gift

7Z6/qfz9q68UnGHNtpf8Az/r/ADOTkSm4pEVvbSE4UE57/wCfrWla2KoGLKD
njkVYih Ywo6 bC4HEeS   I would breathe

TqKK7oxUdjM/J79oWSLUNU0Cyt5bhZrKc3M32bJkUfIFUr1wwklYDN
se1lVwkyCMSK0zuAYjb0xuZfEvHnjWTxX4O1LSdQmguLm0t4+ZeWBo7
db2W1EkiRsDJ8tC3IVj2/wAeP2pdBnu   life

QXS01VCgAD0watOlvPZ/2vLMcvkqBk5U4EhI/iwCCGPyxqvjS6u7draAfZo
MBdqnsO2etPk5jWF4xszAN1+8PQDvSGdi+eB9BVnw3PBa6xbzXduLm2
V9sqbc5UjB/HnP4V6R4o8D6VqE0TaVdW5lljLosTDbjOBuA6Hr+XPSt0R
YvfBDwOddvxqOqwf8SxEZYy/Cu5OAfoMn8q+2ltRsde8ETeBvCfh5rq1j
s4lu9QvSqwlFZE25HIBKqj8EgkYU/Nj5w8Ciw0Z7eOS3meNUWPabh2jAH
cRsSnr/AA16re+NZvhVd6dqWl38T28v7kRXZ+ZpJGld0cKD+7COqBco
VXaFGOa3pbSuaxg2rI5GX9kbxSzYOq6QMEc+XJ0/le1QT/sheJZFIbWN
LYnH/LKTB5/wr6+iYzRI6AMjD7wbPUcc96qaneR2Fjc3EiMY7eNpWC9SF
BJ/lXnKciUrnn3wY+HIz8NvBUej3k0NzJHO8nmwZAO4j1/2u36+ncQ2z
XcReJRKm/ZuQggMHK46/wB4EfUEVyOg6/e+ItFubj7XaNezoduQnlxoS
VZQvzEDG7qCc4zuHB6rwF4aZ7t7jUDper7/AN2bmKzjV2XamN2BzllJ6n
qOgwWtY0XU1fUl1FFEaW4vCyxOjYIV2LgCM84DEnCk4OM46H0NeE/tEeCfE
HifxD4XstltINQFr58sqx31sGiLqvUNICcrHngHpXpPj/wCKH9ieOJNLtbK
CyS3g+zRqBwjF5Nu7KlSNqq64HHmuPmzmrnw+MkPiSa1F5cC0MSOFk
cwiV87xtTgdAQQvy4H50qKhPlvqW37t2fMVh4R8SeF9DbT76NrC+t1Ky

rG8buqDE71CHJU9ex4781uef+EpYXkFqbma5EYkQmNMg5PBCHnIH1/
Lnqvjbnwz44mF8ttDFLaxzyeSWEa5BBI3cgZBrmvhV8ZafZ27wX8bwpde
YY3hccxyL16MAcdD39aqMPetI6IytZpn0X+zd8Z9fnnjj1e2SSWNjDEbaz
mWVSASQ3VcELjJIzkYz0P10vxb0TRNSuLS4mEuy1iupPLkXKbg4CqDgn/
VHliNx6dMV8y/s/ePrT7DLOA6zyL+/jU7hKxUKzcg4JwvQjOM4Ncr8XvjPav
8R/7E0aOWLVrC0gIv2tzh1HDwBF5CqguCxfv5zBsCPnsqU3WoW1k7f19xK
jFP3+p90eGfiPo3ikTfY5JB5TbPmAbec/wFCwbt06bIz1GelEqFC6sHUd0+bP
0x1r5c8A+LtL7Xbj7AflEaRQOzyZ+RVwcsHZidqENnco2Isge1/Fr4gReAPh/
farbPFLcbVjtVMnJZiQrAD73QnHfB5rx4qcVYycYNrIZ3QYE4BBNLXL/
aMv7ux0/8AtIW6eSHkunQ/K4ETYQZGSNxUjHzfJ3zivY7Dxrp9zOb
j7UfLIlitUibIcM7KEJXsS0yrgAnICeOkyrqCvJDdJWcr+n3/ANM/nWm
vDO7bwc49c1Vn6FgPx9akWJZFOA4bH8JzSrEXDEnPOT6Z9T6V3E
bom8P3XIXhQ5xKMKPVhyP6/nXef2IBbWvmy7IJAudwB3Lj2FeaSM8M
h+UAjoRkfjXQ6I41a80E2n2fyruT5JJk4Urxz9T0P+QKViFdHb6D8aoN
KvI2ks5b5YyCCpCbvzzitL4ifF+7+It1pS/2amI2dn500aBSHnmIKBnc9
G4jjA4yADzzgeMWkG+YZyQBuIrV0+Y2i5UHzOuff1/L+dCdIY1i3/4t0
/4eWkI3qTvbCxhZrmCZsqJM4xgck4A4Xk14LpvxCvvEnxR1bxLLPLuvr
into the lifeless earth
nB5bO1TkYwfk/wAOSJaXSKhLbecmvWwIF4fEx1+F3+fYxIU9rC56PoHxt
8V2N/qM3/CV6m8sV2kFvJNeynrLk853Y2qeBg9OmK9W0f4+6I8V7K20
bxZq1xfWmINK2nRTsA+wkZUyIm9zhFwz7yMdCOK+Ro9UMcGopyTJOr
Dt3PP612fws8R7fFdpZyR4jKHLDtgE4/EcV1xrUK1SNKok4t9fNtLXdaMqS
cffjuj9C9D8U+G9O8DW7vqNr5moRD7PEiokvIA42SDBAmTOXAA59LvLm
yhLy3sQQwqZ5fMD7SGC7irBVzGAQFxh3GMk5+Mvh78TJGttb8PK0ksM
UjXUEHIeYDkbJCCT8nyhSxGciPnOK7PwR4va119d+rzWFvKjQwJvkURknL
HgMq5O0kkqMkcnivkcZg6eFqyjHWLvZ/PZ+a/wAn1OxUkd+QABgDPXj/
AD1r1WLTYo76WWFTGVZTV1p5HwDb4LnKsT6r1q5NCGga4hYs8fLZHU
e9Z6oysNrjH51r2M7tIZAhyMZBByPesUi0jJvY1YIUB9DntUVvAJDtfIKmrW
pL5F0EGAoAIwc8dqQREguuCM5OCKCbC2o2+eWOM8fnTS0EcUDF9qBz
tBJ/d2+f5Dg1EPiJIuvN/oz518PQT33iC1tbGAz3FwkSxRKV67BnnOPXr0/
Cvr79mRdR+E2rau9ter9u1WNYGkihVxBjfIZ9Tgd6+c4pP3jE8
DIGRUM7iGELkfMcnFMgfcR9evrQUjdt777NHkHJU777NHkHJUE4/D/Gvd/Adnpek+
B9G1Mxy3moTNIbgDOyA72VechfIvUV88xZdSgHBXGcda9CTx8P

D3hzTrCexa4b/XOu4YBJO05wfmwM8gge/NRyuVkgbtqdT8YPEnlLaeRdy
Ca5gHyRzsVVRuG4KQCNwYjk88jGACflA24ld/Q45HvUmselLnxHfT31w+6
VznHZV7KPYDueLXhwhKtrLYbzSNBBtd+E9te5JPNVLfkoCejdOK9GnDlic17
s0oOZGOTntx1rb0HQrnWtQt7S2R5Z53WONEHzMxOAB7npWNaMA5PfPBx
X0v+xn8LZ/iR8WNMSNf3Fgh1CaZ03luxl25Pb5mBA77SMj7w9LDUVVlZmF
SoqcXJn2x8Jfh1aeDlfBsk1h5+k3FrBYSTNjacgKrEEY3K/HToWl6V7H4ni
0rw+J9PgiWKZTuAUY6rkEY981P4m0kwaFaQWCjyLQKvlqccDoQfzrmPH
+sx3960wJD7MFicY/H/PSvWoylhU5xeiX3u/+Sv8AM8OCeJnGb/r+kfH/
AO3Hr8D+FdK0SOc/bri9+1NCMcRlrDn6sy49cH0r430vdFeTSF+FGPY163
+0l41h1f4r6yJLg3MNlts4QRjYEHzr7/OXP415GuoQzCcphBjkYrOjCDam3q
3c9lXSsc3by7ZbtCdoPOc+hz/StrwHfi11Ge837Cl5AD7lSP61zbzDzLt87ck/
rVjTbkQ2TlXA5xjPBry6bVOqpdm392x0NaM6zw9r8uneJl78ASlWG+MqG
V1/iUg9QeevrXuPgLT3ljH2a2g1BbstHEZJwJnB42M2z720jcAuOuARgn5kl
1eZSyW5w+OSD0+tdZ4H8YeltG1EfYknu1PDwGMyqwPHK4l//XWFRwrRcZ
b3un/XcqN46nkKvC/LJu9ea0rCa22nKlrA85TdxWJbq7BgNx2jnHYZqxE+-
Fl3fN9K8g3TNiaG1vpMuZEwoJlwMj8uDUlrp9rEiK7Sfdyw3d6zVnbd97r3N
TRyMW4YnAxwO1BSaL8lrarHKyRDdtBUn5sY781SvXjEccyRqm8chQMbu/
wDj+NTQx3ckypBE8jn+BVyT61oN4K1q/idfs/2V05CT5Qtn0/L9aadiZNWs
dH8B/BVh8Uvibo/hnUZJ7ezvRNvltpFV08uCSUY3KQclAMY/ir334s/sh3ljo+
mWfg2xfWClw5uLm6uIluX3qoHZF8s3XwMkgvwMbifmn4XeMJvhT48tNZu7G
Wae0DBFVyjRFlKlh68Fhg8c9+lfXfh/9tXw5qpSC9s7+zK+WwlkTdu5G5fk5O
QCCBtyCMHuO2jKko+/uQtU0fHni3wfq3gfVmstX0+506fkGO5haMlclcgEcqS
pwRwcHBrLjkAlUkde1fcvibxzZeOtFvLW1sB4rsonDpLbafFPPDlehlsXJEx5U/u1
DHn7ozn4j17TLbSvEF1p9jc3d3b2z+SJr60+yzFhw26Le+3DBsAtnABlBJA2bX
2diZR5S1prb5BkYUc9OtfpN+wFpo8L+DLnVhGxu9VuMgqpO6OMFV+nzNJ+
BHWvze0Ozk1C+ht4dzO7gAAcnJr9Tf2efB1zoHguwsLsmBUgVfsqXClCepYl
cMDuz/ERXtYB8ilKx5uJs1Zn0RqevbbHDzlg252vwc9e5zXmOvapCRKzXESl/
ugOPX/9VddZ+CLa+idliBdf4pJmmPpwSSev8q4742+Hv+EK+G/iXWY7WGV
rCwnnTzo8LuWF2Al5J5A79+2K3xMZVE7LRanLQlCHup6s/Jvx/rv9u+Mdb1
HKj7Zey3JMZGPmdmOPzrKs7pYl5C2djuEPPODyf0BouIgXkYu0mTzjvVS4Vla
3hiy5Zi+0DJJ6D+deXFOHvPp/wx6u+gy71At5sZ4MZKsr9yM0mkacl2hlubq
PT7XON7/MxHqqDk/jge9SDw3qmu619lsLO4vLpk3mGKMlgB1JHYdMn3ru/
DXwJ1G8bztbP2dunkFwpH1P9BXDXqpS1NowcloY2gal4N0SCP7ZpV7qtwAd

85ugiMezBAuR9Nx+p61vWPiPwPqc5tZNMvNGWQZS9tJzKV64Vo2wCM7c8
5FdHe/CXQNFs3aUo+75AwblT6gnP6/rXnnijQdNtdQRLGUuxkAKrwQewxn
14qlYyXwqK+4JUuXVsi8CeHrW08NNcylJJr1GaVG6BASAP5/5FYev+B1srpfJu
o4o5ZTFskz8jAnI9flAOfpWZN4pvbBNLTTr5kaGBqukylDLDKHiY4YsBmKVGy
CFPJI46HpXovNcPODUou9vL/M4o4GaqKba09f8j5QKrxDYxfjP8AOq0N2ygh
hmlkmHUDihlVzRWUupDYx9aw7z/WMOMCtO1ZJExjnHes++jKFvkBGaBv
Ybp03lzdMirmqgsoYDis22k2MOK07yXdY5IwBjGKa0I3RilmUMD0FQEnmp
m+cH5RVQyhM5XiqaVjmLCNtHWp4HHJ6VR3ArmrMB7YApID039n7VTo/
wAWtluFJTcDEXQc/MwGK/TyWzZZGeHGD0A6j8K/LP4Pq7eO9IER+dZ0Y/
QOM1+o0Wo+ZcSSw/IWOT2zXs4GMZQkmLXoZV5aytIwQ7pW5Ytxn61y
Hjn4T6Z4+0ltP1W3QmQh0nUbmQjpj8a9DulxPl0hHl7jkheadJB9njNwBm
PO3A966/ZpmsLtanwx4w/Zg8WaHqs8elxw6npkRKi4mlCyt6HaBXnniLw
FrPhkj7dplxzyDbxNIPzAr9IDbh3Ywk8j7v8AhVdv7OELW19beYGGNu0kC
srOLs0J0ovZn5g3Noki5kzGeySja34g1h39g0Sseor9CfHH7P8A4D8TJLJ/
Z0UF1Nz9pEf7xW9Rk188eP8A9k/xJ4ZtZLzSJhrmmqpd3mdRKMZ4CqOe
KUuSomnoQ6Uo+Z8yuzBhjgVbBPlAjrVvUtJmhaSR7Se1VTgi4iMfP41mpK
c7cfjXDy8jsSiZCTkZlp7LsQgHk0KwVDjion6ntVNaaASW5IbPAq4TnkAZHfN
Z8TnJ9KtrKHXbtxilHUCUFu6jJ75po3k7SBj1zSfNgdgPSrMcYkXnirFcuWgEY
BH41pWUu5zjFZiKFjx2q7Y7UkGRxXbLjDQSShyAM8g5r134Vfsz6/8AEUy6j
baw+iXPljyEg3CYc8EGOTk80KvydadHgKSwyBxUrRDEBLHBA471ZUNGFPGC
MjBqJRj7wGO1O2nIOegxigEN16gfpR4k0jwlqltDFD4dtN6rZLMZQFHYEcUy
fwrJGhvpAxab5i2PmP1FUrHUI7TzIZ7NZlY5BbORTvfYllmttVlLsqSu0XdW4p8
kFvOC6oBJnP41M8MQh+0QxcHsBUMETSBpANoHWov2Kt1Nm0RJrNXb55e
4NY+sabJexvs/dup+UjvWnpLJ9P1GV9KUsrlUcNlQu7OZvqOee8ohVieM1Yk
RShI79aEJXRx8tlc2ltC05VXZdxCtkCremamVTarjPoDxWjc2guyBjIA2msK80s
aQ+9P8AVXCwLxnPl9+f0FFFZ8iuHMy7B8SvELxBBpluYllIMkCj9c12Xg+TxZ
41mSGxVI7A965pYWaV4NLKziXK/MkH60rPqSORchlB78ilA+npTXco//9k=
--__CONTENT_64564_PART_BOUNDARY__33243242__--

But who are we to recreate mankind?

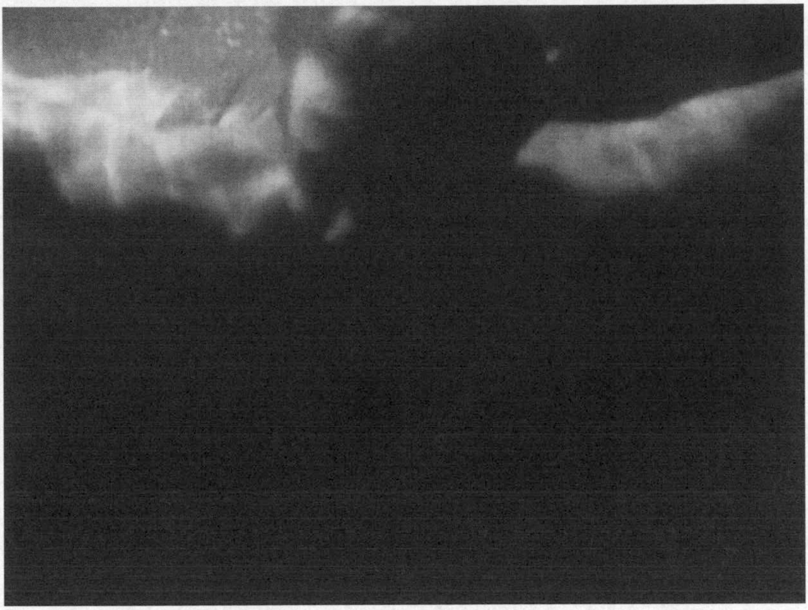

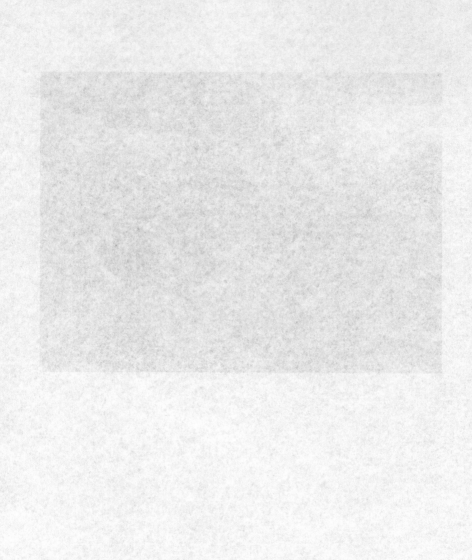

ACT II

REAL HUMAN BODIES

CHAPTER THREE

The logo. The logos. The word. The bird. The spirit. The beginning. The end. The serpent. The head. The tail. The mouth. The hole. The tower. The train. The platform. The platform? Simple mathematics.

"I appreciate the ride," I said.

"No problemo," Charles said. "You're on a quest. And I want to help. Unfortunately I've got another appointment. There's a burst sewer line underneath a Motel 6 and it's been emptying raw sewage under the building for weeks. It's going to be my business to crawl underneath the building through shit up to my chin, and fix that pipe."

"I don't know why, but there strikes me as something very Christlike about that, Charles," I said, handing him the new joint.

He took it out of my fingers, keeping his eyes on the road.

"I think so too," he said. "When I'm down there I often think about what Christ would do if he were here today. What he would be doing for a living, for example. He probably wouldn't be a carpenter. There aren't many actual carpenters these days and I don't see him working on an assembly line." He took a toke. "I suppose he could have been a finish carpenter, working on high-end homes. Like those new ones they're building out on Priest Lake? Criminy. Who needs a house that big?"

"Do you think he's really going to come back?" I asked. "Are you one of those people who take all that literally?"

He thought about it. "Well, I guess I would have to say yes and no. Yes, I really think he's coming back in bodily form, in power and glory and everything else. And no, not literally."

The sky was blue and clear. It was hot and we had the windows of the van rolled down. The wind blew in and cooled us, but it also swirled around and brought the stink from the back up to the front.

Why can I remember Christ but not myself? I thought.

"Stinks, huh?" said Charles, handing me back the joint.

"I don't know how you do it all day."

"My wife won't touch me after work until I take a shower. Although she won't really touch me then either."

"I didn't know you were married."

"Yep. To a real psycho bitch."

"Bummer."

"I shouldn't talk about her that way. Let's just say she's not an optimist like me."

"I wonder if I'm an optimist."

We stopped and started down a highway lined with old strip malls and new big-box stores. Fast-food restaurants and chain motels. Mattress Village, Mattress Kingdom, Mattress World.

"What's the name of this two-bit burg?" I asked.

"Spokane."

"Spokane, Washington?"

"Yep."

"I live in Spokane, Washington?"

"Looks that way."

"My god, it's worse than I thought."

The drive-thrus and traffic lights receded. We headed out of town.

"Sorry I can't give you a ride back," Charles said.

"No worries. I'll find a way back."

While Charles had gone downstairs to finish up my drain, I had run next door to Gladys's house to find out Vel's last name and the name of the hospital where they were keeping her. Her dog had come running at me snarling like he was guarding the gates of hell, but I managed just in time to leap onto her porch where his leash wouldn't reach.

"Gladys, I've decided to go visit Vel in the mental hospital."

She had seemed confused by this.

"You seem confused."

"I didn't know you were friendly with Vel, that's all. After what she did with the hose and everything. And saying you stole her windows."

"Yes, well, forgive and forget, that's my motto."

Did I actually say that? Or do I only think I said that because of what Charles would later say about optimism? Where does any of this begin? And where does it end? I'd like to know. I have memory of doing these things. I remember running next door to Gladys's house. I remember the dog coming at me, its teeth bared, snarling. I remember jumping onto the porch. I remember standing there, talking to Gladys through her screen door. Eva said: *You can't believe anything I said last night. I told you. It wasn't me. I was enchanted.* Forgive and forget. What is themystery.doc?

"Do you remember," said Gladys, speaking in a hushed voice, "when your little nieces were over and Eva and them made those little apple tartlets?"

"No, I don't remember that, Gladys."

"Well, those cute little girls brought them over here in a little basket and—oh, they were so proud—and they gave one to me, and I thanked them and I made a real big fuss about it and told them how delicious they looked, and then they took one over to Vel."

"That was very generous of them."

"Yes, but afterwards she went around telling everyone that Eva poisoned her."

"Really," I said. "Do you think Eva would do that?"

"Of course not! I just wanted you to know what Vel has been saying. She was also telling people that you made a pass at her."

"Really! How old is Vel?"

"Gosh, I don't know. She must be at least eighty-five."

"Well then I very much doubt that I made a pass at her, but I appreciate you telling me about the rumor. Incidentally…" I lowered my voice. "I don't suppose I ever told you that I…*discovered* or…*un*-covered…something…did I?"

"Like what?" she said.

Maybe I did something. Or found something. Or learned something. Or in one way or another got into hot water. The possibilities are endless. A world in which you have no history is a world of utter possibility. Possibility is converted to fear in the brain. Fear to hostility. The unknown, that what-might-be, takes form as a dark, brutish monster rather than a lamb or a bunny or a sunny piece of isolated beach on which a girl in a black-and-white two-piece sits with her arms around her knees waiting for you. That's possible, I suppose, but improbable. What's more probable is that the possible will turn into something that will rise against you to smite you, and strike you in the face. Or run you over in a green minivan. Or send their goons to your house to give you a roughing up, or send the man with the gun to put you in the grave. I was beginning to be afraid. Olive the cat was a clue. I had put her in a Bed Bath & **BEYOND** bag. And there in my trash can she lay.

"When's trash day?" I'd asked.

"Tomorrow," Gladys'd said.

"Darn. I wish it was today."

⋆

Charles dropped me off beneath the hospital awning. I wished him luck under the motel and told him to keep in touch. I said I would like to give him my phone number but I don't know what it is. He said he already had it from the service order. That was good. I asked him to look on it and tell me my last name. I had a pretty good idea that the first name I was supposed to be using was Daniel, but I didn't know the last. He told me and I thanked him and he wished me luck as well. Then he drove away and the serpent, as the sunlight bounced off the side of the van as it made its turn around to head back to the highway, the serpent winked at me.

The woman at reception called up to Vel's floor, and before long a nurse came down to speak with me. I said I was a relative of Vel's and that I wanted to see her. She was happy that someone had come because apparently no other members of Vel's family had been to see her. She said it would take a little while to get Vel ready because she was taking a nap, but that when Vel was ready she would come back and escort me up. I said that was fine and took a seat and read magazines.

About a half hour later she returned and took me up. She smiled as the elevator rose and made small talk. She asked me what I did for a living and I told her I was a writer. This pleased her and she asked if I had been published. For some reason I told her I had written a book called *The Tempest.*

"Like the Shakespeare play!" she said.

"Yeah."

"That was my favorite one. In college I played the daughter of the wizard, Prospero," she said. "What was my name?" She started scratching her head. The elevator kept going up. "How embarrassing." She started to blush. "It's right there on the tip of my—" She shook her head, turning red. "It's terrible. I can't remember the name of my own character."

"How weird."

"I remember I walked out and said— Oh, brother, what was the line?"

The doors opened. We stepped off.

Vel was waiting in a small room with a couch, a chair, and a loveseat. She was on the couch. The nurse entered and said, "Vel, here's your grandson, Daniel, coming for a visit. Do you remember him?"

Vel looked up at me with squinty eyes.

"I know him but he's not my grandson."

I smiled at the nurse and shrugged. She squeezed my arm reassuringly.

"Well you might not remember he's your grandson, but he is. Now, will you be OK if I leave you two alone for a few minutes?" the nurse asked.

Vel nodded.

The nurse squeezed me again and left.

Vel was old. She was hunched over so when she looked at you she looked up, her eyeballs halfway hidden up in the sockets. She had stubble on her face. She had a mean scowling face. She was wearing a pink sweat suit. It looked ridiculous. I sat down in the chair across from her.

"How's it going?" I said.

She grunted.

"They have you on medication?"

She nodded.

"How long have you been here?"

She smacked her lips. The pills were probably drying her mouth out.

"Who knows? Two weeks. Maybe more. Maybe less."

"Feeling better?"

She didn't say anything, just stared up at me across a square coffee table.

I found myself hunching over too. And looking up at her with my eyes rolled upward, staring back at her that way.

"Seen Gerald?" she said.

"Your husband?"

"Who else would he be?"

"No. Haven't seen him."

"They say he went to a home before I came here. They said I was talking him to death. You know what I think?"

"What?"

"I think he didn't like what I was saying! About his mother and her father! And how he got her all dressed up when he took her to the fair! Dressed up like a wife! I saw the photograph! I can read between the lines!"

"Interesting."

"Do you think Gerald didn't like me talking about it?"

"Beats me. I've never met Gerald."

"'Course you met Gerald. You two used to talk all the time. He gave you the birdhouse."

"That's right. I did meet Gerald. I used to talk to Gerald. He gave me the birdhouse."

"He's gonna die there in that home."

"Is he sick?"

"His stomach's twisted up and only I know how to cook for him. He's not supposed to eat peanuts. That didn't stop him from stealing them from the squirrels. I used to put them out for the squirrels and I'd find him out there rooting through the dish. Then he'd moan all night long! *It hurts! It hurts!*"

"Do you have any other family?"

"You know I do. Three daughters and a son. Winnie's the middle one. She went missing about twenty years back. Hedda knows what happened to her. See, Hedda was *aaaaallllways* jealous of Winnie. Winnie was the pretty one. We called her Winsome. Hedda was the last to see her. Hedda was the easy one. She was always dating married men. Lotti is a lesbian. I never told you that. Gerald wouldn't let me. We had to say she's *single.* At sixty years old? Ha! Then there's Stu. He stole Aunt Sarah's car. You know that blue car he drives? That was supposed to go to me. He was never supposed to have that car. But he took it! How's the book?" she said.

"What book?"

"What book? The book you claim you've been writing all this time, Mr. Author! The enormous book!"

"Did I talk to you about it?"

"'Course you did! You said it was an enormous book and that it had started small but had gotten so big you divided it into two and then two again so now it was four big books and that you had to organize it and then you would publish it. Don't tell me you divided it again!"

"Good question."

"I always thought you were lying though. Gerald thought you really were writing a book. I said if he doesn't talk about it it's because he's hiding something and if he's hiding something it's probably because there is no book. You probably just sit in that house all day reading girlie magazines."

"Interesting. So what do you know about the mystery?"

"Well I know that's what it's called!" she barked. "At least that's what you told Gerald it was called. I said, Gerald, he's just giving you a line. There is no *The Mystery!* There's no book! He's in that little house playing with his willy as soon as his wife drives off to work!" She thrust out her arm as if to suggest she were pushing me away. "Why'd you come here anyway? Aren't you the one who called them to take me away?"

"I don't know. But I wouldn't blame me if I did. Especially after all the talk you've been spreading. I've heard what you've been saying about the tartlets."

"Poisoned."

"I seriously doubt that."

"That wife of yours is no good. I wouldn't turn my back on her for a second."

"Really?" I leaned closer. "Why is that?"

"She's married to you."

"So?"

"She works. She's got a job. She makes the money. Without her you couldn't pay to put a roof over your head."

I could see where she was going with this.

"And?" I said.

"And a girl with a body like that doesn't need to work for a living. She could get a rich man real easy. No reason she should be working to support a poor one."

"Love?" I suggested.

She scoffed. "Ha! I've known women like that. Judith Cooley back in Golden Valley was like that. No, that wife of yours she's a smart one. Too smart to be doing anything for—p'shaw!—*love.*"

"Well, what would she be doing things for then?"

"There's something about you," Vel said, half gravely, half mockingly, "that she's interested in. And believe me, sonny, it ain't your looks."

"My mind, maybe."

"Your mind? Ha! You couldn't unkink a garden hose! Gerald told me about the time you came to him asking for help when you thought your mower was broken. It was out of gas! What a rube!"

"OK, so maybe not my mind."

"You know, sometimes at night she'd go out back and talk on her phone so you couldn't hear her. I bet you didn't know that."

"Did she? And who was she talking to?"

"Hard to say. Whoever it was it was business and the person on the other end was the boss."

"Remember any specifics?"

"I remember they were talking about you." She stared up at me. I stared up at her. "They were talking about pulling some big trick," she said.

"What big trick?"

"Some big trick."

"Care to share any details?"

"Don't have any. But it was *veeeerrry* fishy."

"Anything else?"

"No."

"Well if I'm not mistaken you also accused me of stealing your windows and putting them on my house, so I think I'll take this with a grain of salt."

"Take it with whatever you want. I know what I heard."

"Olive's dead," I said.

"Who's Olive?"

"Who's Olive? Your cat!"

"I don't have a cat."

"Yes, you do. You adopted it and its brother or sister from the man down the street."

"Oh. Which one is Olive? The orange or the black-and-white?"

"Orange."

"How'd it die?"

"Good question. Loudly."

"That was not a very good cat anyway. That one was going to be Gerald's for when he comes back. The other was mine. All the orange ever did was eat and sleep and it was too heavy to be a lap cat. It would have crushed poor Gerald's legs! You know how frail he is. He was never the same after the war. Dysentery. Then all his life he could never put on weight. And they said I wasn't feeding him! They said I was trying to starve him! I fed him! But all he wanted to eat was peanuts!"

"Well, it's been fun," I said, getting up to leave. "I wish you luck with your current situation and Gerald with his peanut problems."

Vel smiled viciously. "Say hello to that pretty wife of yours. And I'd watch yourself if I were you. Nobody's safe. I know everybody thinks I'm crazy, but I could hear them talking. You just have to know how to hear it. Then it's there plain as day and you think to yourself: it's always been there but I was trained not to hear it. That's how they communicate. Right in the open. But, see, they've got you trained. You've been trained since you were little to not hear it. I know she was talking to them. Maybe you don't want to believe it, but that's the way things are. She was put with you, you didn't just meet her. You didn't *win* her. They put her there. To keep an eye on you. I heard what she was saying. She was giving a report."

20070707 210421TheCastle.wav

A ROOM, ALMOST PERFECTLY SQUARE, *the bedroom of a little house. Two windows, a bed below one. A* [W]*oman, in her early thirties, lying on top of the sheet. The end of a hot drowsy day in July. On the window above the bed the curtain is drawn. Through the other, the curtain is open revealing a small fenced back yard, and the trunk of a large pine tree. One imagines its great boughs sheltering the scene. Above the bed a ceiling fan goes around and around. Sleepy, the woman wears a thin cotton shift, spaghetti straps, orange and yellow with a "sunset in the tropics" motif. Evening is turning into night. She yawns and stretches. Warmth, contentment, and drowsiness pervade the scene. One could imagine the bed is an inflatable mattress drifting lazily in a swimming pool, or a rowboat floating peacefully on a lake. She lies dreamily watching the blurry circle made by the blades of the ceiling fan. Footsteps, and then a* [M]*an appears from a separate room, wearing nothing but a pair of loose black shorts. He carries a small handheld recording device. He takes his place on the bed beside the woman, his head close to hers on the pillow. Then he presses a button on the recorder, and places it between them.*

W: Are you ready?

M: Yeah. *Action.*

W: OK. The Bubbleator. So, Seattle's World's Fair, 1962, in the…is it called the Center House? In the Seattle Center?

M: The big white thing?

W: The thing where all the food court and—

M: Uh-huh.

W: In *there* was this elevator that took you from what was the main floor down to the bottom floor…and it had a big glass *dome*—or probably plastic, or whatever. But it was like a—like a glass *igloo* and it was called the Bubbleator. Well, I recall the Bubbleator because—we would always go there for Christmas…um, and take the Monorail downtown and see the—

M: Your family?

W: Yeah. And see the windows and displays and Santa and all that, but they would also decorate out the Seattle Center, and one year they—well, one year that I can *recall*—I have a *memory* of riding it. But anyway, um, I asked my mom about the Bubbleator, because, you know, she and her brother went to the World's Fair and she said—you know my uncle Paul and how sensible he is and everything—well, he gets on the Bubbleator at the World's Fair and there's a *man in a spacesuit.* Because the whole World's Fair was Space Themed, and the man said: *We're going into the Fyuuuu-tuuuure!* And Paul was like, *No-o-o-o-o-o-o-o! Let me off of here!* [*laughing*] Like, like *believed it* and *didn't want to go!*

M: He did not want to go to the future! [*laughing*]

W: Did *not* want to go! And like, wanted *off* the Bubbleator! [*laughing*] But anyway, I just think—you were talking about the dome and one of the ways I think of the dome is it's just like the escape pod, the Bubbleator—*Come on, we're going to the future.* So...that's not very deep but, I just wondered if you knew anything—if you had known of the Bubbleator.

M: I don't think I know about the Bubbleator.

W: I'm sure you can look it up on the web and find out *much detail* about the Bubbleator.

M: It was just an elevator?

W: *Just* an elevator! It was—I'm sure it went to like another floor where they had exhibits about the future. But, a spacesuited elevator operator *terrified* one of my uncles............But...The Castle, that's a neat thing—that's a neat part to think about—that's a neat part to be working on.

M: Yeah.

W: Very contained.

M: Yeah..................

W: So is the uh, when you've got [redacted] describing the cube—is the cube…a possible castle also?

M: Yep.

W: Yeah, neat… Yeah, cool. Oh man, that's so cool. Is McLeash's Roundhouse and all of that stuff—but of course that could occur at any point in the book!

M: Yeah. [*sound of an airplane flying over the house*]

W: Sweat lodge. I can just think of so many castly things.

M: Yeah.

W: That's so cool!

M: Well the whole—the entire four books is its own castle—like you enter the castle—

W: Right!

M: at the very beginning when

W: Right.

M: when uh the door opens and the maiden much more beautiful than any other comes out—

W: Right.

M: and appears to Quixote.

W: Oh, man, I can't wait to read it, it's just so *beautiful*—it's gonna *blow my mind* and I'm so *excited.* It's so gorgeous…

M: *You'll know* that you're in the castle. I don't know who else is gonna know that they're in the castle, you know what I mean? But everything's there, everything is there.

W: Cool…

M: All you need is there to understand.

W: Cool…

M: It's just whether or not you *will* understand—but that's not my problem.

W: [*laughs*] Yeah.

M: What else?…

W: It's just neat……… The……… cas-tle…

M: Yeah……And there's a long section, and it's *the fair*, you know?

W: [*laughing*]

M: No one else is ever going to see this shit but me! This section—like that's—you're at *the fair*—it's *the fair.* [*laughs*] It's like,

> *Mr. McIntosh, will you please, uh, explain exactly* how *you're at the fair?*

Well, you're at the fair, just look. Can't you see? Can't you hear? Can't you smell?

W: Cool.

M: And uh—

W: Cool.

M: *In Book 3, sir, now I think I heard you say before that you're at the* castle? *Where is the castle?*

Well, you're *in* the castle.

W: You're *in* the castle, dumb-dumb.

M: Not to mention that on page [redacted] there's two words on the page and it says, *The Castle*……….

W: That's so cool… That is *so cool*……….

M: It… It almost feels like… You know we were talking the other day about Plato and the Ideas.

W: Yes.

M: And the *Forms* are out there and every Idea we have has a corresponding Form out, off in the ether somewhere in heaven. It feels like writing [redacted]… the Ideas that I—the way that I *see it*—and I see things in shapes, and I *see* the castle, and I *see* the fair, and I see all this stuff—it feels like I'm *creating* Forms and putting them out there, in heaven; and here we have the Book which is full of the Ideas, but I create the Forms through the Ideas—you know what I mean?

W: Well, like you said before, the book is the map, you know?

M: Yeah.

W: Maps have symbols, which are representations of things.

M: Yeah! That's exactly right, that's exactly it. That's exactly what I'm trying to say… Yeah, it's the map and so something else is being created up there. It really feels that way.

W: That's so neat. I wonder what the monks think, like what the supposed theory behind the sand paintings are…if they have something like that…

M: Yeah.

W: and they're *painting* the way to heaven…I don't know what I'm trying to say.

M: ██
██
██████████████████████████████████████ as
█████ the book █████ gets more complex,
█████████████████ by taking the different ingredients I put into
it it creates different forms itself—forms I never saw, forms I never
intended—and so the words and the phrases that have already been in
there become filled with so much more meaning than they had before,
and they all start to finally make sense—*more* sense than they did, and
they take on new levels of meaning, like, the way they now have—here
you have this *entity* that's been dipped in a totally different color paint,
and now ██████ everything that it's *around* takes on a different color
too███
██
██
██
██
everything interacts, and relates to one another—and the *ideas* that they
create spontaneously that aren't in my mind because I don't see them,
because I *can't* see them all—they must be creating forms in heaven
too ... ██████████████████ The Book ████████████
████████████████████████████████████

W: That is so wild...

BOTH: [*yawn*] ....

M: So what if we never met?

W: [*sighs*] ... Horrible .... [*sighs*] .... Impossible. Of course we would meet. The thing is, babe, that even when you were young, wandering around Europe with no food and no money and having all that stuff happen to you—you were on the path you were supposed to be on because remember you told me the part about running into that guy in Rome?

M: What guy in Rome?

W: The guy who the hotel clerk had given your passport to because he thought he was you?

M: Oh, yeah.

W: And you didn't know you had the wrong passport until a long time later?

M: Yeah. I had to hitchhike back to Rome.

W: I mean, no food, no money, wrong passport. And then you ran into the guy who had it in the middle of some random street.

M: Yeah. That was lucky. But that happens to everyone, once in a while, I think.

W: But that sort of thing happens to you all the time.

M: Yeah.

W: Me all the time.

M: But I used to—that was—that was the aberration. Generally I had the worst luck of anyone in the world. Anything that could go wrong, it seemed to. It was almost funny. I thought that I was constantly being played tricks on, by the ... well, by God ... I thought demons were out to get me ...

W: Terrible.

M: But um... whatever it was, I was definitely on the path. I didn't mean to be but just, you know, I was in the... I was in the more *painful* part of the story...

W: So terrible. [*sighs*]

M: And that's the other thing is that the... *hero* digs his own holes quite often, you know?

W: Poor hero...

W: Hey, you know in Rome—I mean obviously I haven't been there, so I've just—I've just seen the postcard stuff—but where are the *cast-les?*

M: The *cas-tles?*

W: Well, like where did the emperor live? Did they have any of those things surviving?

M: Yeah, I don't know. They have palaces, but—

W: And estates and stuff? Because you always hear about *Oh, the German king, the French king*—I guess they are many, many hundreds of years older. I mean that's like *two thousand* years ago, right?

M: The Romans? Yeah.

W: So maybe their actual *homes* aren't preserved?

M: I don't know—what do they have left? I mean most of the Roman stuff is all ruined. I went into the Colosseum, that was free.

W: Cool. Did you see the Catacombs?

M: No, I think you had to pay. St. Peter's was free. I paid to get into the Sistine Chapel.

W: Did you see the dome?

M: Do you mean the ceiling or the dome? The dome is in St. Peter's.

W: Oh, yeah. Fellini. That's where she runs up the stairs.

[*yawns*]

M: There were fountains everywhere. You could drink out of them. And you'd walk around and you'd see ruins of like—you see the basements—I'm thinking of one place, I remember in the middle of the city some random block where you come around the corner and you see the, the *guts* of an ancient building—of a Roman building…

W: Weird.

M: And there were all these cats that lived in there, these feral cats. And you see these stone columns here and there that are crumbling and, but…

W: Was it warm? Was it nice and warm like this?

M: I don't remember. Yeah, I really don't remember much. It was a long time ago……………I really don't know much about Rome…

W: ████████████████████████████………… Let's stay in bed all night…………

M: So what do you do in the castle?

W: Remember *Hearst* Castle?

M: *Worst* Castle.

W: [*laughs*] What you do in the castle is you get tricked into taking a lame tour! And they force you to get your picture taken and then afterwards try to get you to pay seventeen dollars for the photograph! Remember that? Oh my gosh, Hearst Castle…Hearst Castle, and *recall* we just saw the ad:

A masterpiece around every corner.

No, no. Keep moving, nothing to see here.

M: *An eyesore around every corner.*

W: An eyesore.

M: One after another.

W: A mishmash. And it's like with such muddled-up mazelike rooms you never got a *wide expansive* vista, or any feeling of *spaciousness.*

For such a big building it had a whole bunch of *roundy-round, curved corners*, and not a lot of like, *long hallways.*

I mean, if you're gonna have a castle,

you gotta have some *space*……………………………

M: Well, yeah.

Hopefully you have some breathing room in that castle.

Otherwise…

it's just a tenement.

W: [*yawns*]

M: But at the *middle* of the castle . . .

at the middle of the castle is the universe. . . .

So you have lots of space in the center.

You have as much room as you need if you're in the center of the universe.

But to get there, you have to crawl,

and it gets very cramped.

And you get stabbed and you have to crawl through glass,

and you have to…

[*yawns*]

… get trampled probably ……

and …

you have to……

>BREAK

KETTLE FALLS

I AM NOT SURE WHO this message is directed to. I am lying in a hospital room. Certain traumatic events which I am having difficulty piecing together have left me in a state of terrible suffering.

I can tell you what my s physical symptoms are. That is easy enough because I can feel the actual physical symptoms are lasting and linger and do not flee like my memories.

My entire body has been burned. My skin is very hot and tingles incessantly.

Tingling is a poor word choice because it does not signify pain.

Pain is the predominat feeling, I mus say.

I also have great sensitivity to light, and the nurses often come in here to check on me and turn on the light above me, which cuases great pain in my head and eyes.

I also have a tremondous amount of mucus that I cough up from time to time, so the nurses bring me a cup and tell me to spit into it. But no matter how I try, I cannot get enough of the mucus to come up, so it stays in my throat clogging the wind passage, which makes breathing very uncomfortable.

Also every nerve on my entire body moans loudly whenever I cause it, on purpose or by accident to move even in the slightest.
Even bending so much as a finger causes great distress..
My head is very stuffy,. It feels like it is full of air or helium, and a pin prick would cause it to explode. It aches.
Everything aches. My nose is full of mucus so I cannot breathe through it.
If I would list my ailements in the order of distress they cause, I would begin with the burning skin, then move to the aching and stuffy head, linking those feelings to the aching joints, and also my throat which feels very burned as well and I did not mention before.
Actually, let's make my aching head number one.

What is most important is that I am near death, but from what the doctors tell me, speaking loudly into my sore ears and causing blistering bolts of sound to pierce my eardrums, is that I am on the mend. I mam expected to recover.
But from what? That is the bigger problem, and one which is difficult to speak about.
Before I continue on, I should mention that this message is being written out by hand, by the kind young girl who delivers flowers to the other members of the ward. I am not sure her name. what is your name, sweetheart?
Melissa spotted me lying in this bed and came in to ask me if I needed anything at all. I had no need for flowers, but she had a kind, giving heart, full of empathy and compassion for ill-fortunate wretches such as myself.
She had to put her ear to my mouth to hear my reply because my voice is unable to escape my burning throat, and besides if I make noise it causes my head to ache more terribly.
Melissa is transcribing this message to you, whoever you are, by sitting in a chair next to my bed, leaning over to hear my barely audible words, lthen writing them down.

I give her only three or so words at a time, and am now so exhausted that I believe I will take a break and start again the next time she should visit.

Will you visit me again, Melissa? Thank you. Until then.

No, you don't have to write this part down.

*

I believe I said yesterday that I do not know who this message is going out to. I beliee that ther eis someon it is meant for, but as to who that person is, I have no clue.I do not know who I am, and I do not know what has happened to me. All I know is that this message must somehow get through, otherwise all hope is lost. How do I know this? Why do I think it? I cannot tell you. But there is something inside me, let's call it a little voice speaking a language I do not understand, that is adamant about attempting at least to commmunicate what is, as far as I cn tell, uncommunicateable. I have been through a lot, I know that. I have been through more than most men. How I have managed to survive this long, I have no idea. I believe I must be s spy of some sort. Possibly I have had assistance from other members of my organization, if there are other members. But what sort of spy organization would have only one member? Either the worst or the best one to ever exist, is my answer to my own question. The memories that do flicker before me from time to time also suggest that I am involved in some sort of intriguing business on the fringes of society, the kind of business one generally reads about in novels, bestselling novels, I think, because what sort of literary novel would ever be interested in the adventures of a superspy? Spy novels are of the genre action, are they not? And action novels focus on sensual exploits such as explosions, gun fights, countdowns to missile launches, and beautiful women wearing next-to-nothing beneath fur coats. Literary novels have little or no explosions. Gun fights rarely happen. Same with countdowns to missile launches. If these things do happen they do so on the periphery. Literary novels focus more on the aftermatsh than on the acts of violence themselves. They are character-driven and preoccupied with the state of the individual and his psychology and how he interacts with other individuals and how he travels the raging rapids of the society in which he lives. Raging rapids seems to have popped out of the blue into my mind. I wonder if that is a clue of some sort. Also I wonder how I became so knowledgable about novels. A clue? Melissa, that seems about good for today. I'm afraid I am exhausted. Will you come back tomorrow? Thank you.

★

http://www.historylink.org/index.cfm?DisplayPage=output.cfm&file_id=7577 For thousands of years, Kettle Falls had served as the nexus for a complex trading network based on ocean-going (anadromous) fish. Huge numbers of salmon passed through the falls during spawning season, from June through October. The fish were a magnet for Native Americans from both sides of the Rocky Mountains. Plains Indians brought buffalo hides, pemmican, and pigments ground from iron oxide deposits to Kettle Falls, trading for tule mats, dentalium shells, and other goods from the Pacific Coast. Later, European trade goods were added to the mix. Up to 14 tribes met regularly at the falls to fish, trade, and socialize, in what Thompson called "a kind of general rendezvous for News, Trade and settling disputes" (Nisbet, 101).

★

The memories flit before me like impatient hummingbirds, each one darting away before I have a chance to get a good look at its markings…

★

Hi, what's your number again please?

8-695

Oh my god, I'm on the 83rd floor!

86—86 what?

I'm on the 83rd floor!

Ma'am, calm down one moment—86 what?

8695.

8695? She at the World Trade Center, someone having trouble breathing there on the 83rd floor.

OK, ma'am, how you doing?

Is—is it—is—are they gonna be able to get somebody up here?

Of course, ma'am, we're coming up for you.

★

…then another comes and takes its place…

★

The "falls" at Kettle Falls were a series of cascades created by enormous blocks of quartzite piled in ledges across the riverbed by prehistoric floods. Water plummeted over the falls with so much force that it seemed to boil. Rocks and boulders tumbled furiously in a gyroscope of water at the bottom, carving circular potholes and craters in the underlying rock.

★

…but leaves just as abruptly. Who am I? How have I ended up here? That is what I am trying to find. And so I will tell Melissa and she will tell you of the memories I do have, and please do not be annoyed if I relate to you unimportant details or memories that you, whoever you are, know I could not or should not possess myself—in other words, if I remember things that you know I could not possibly remember because they did not happen to me, and perhaps happened to somone else. For instance if they happened to you, or if I relate memories which should have been erased already, possibly by a machine kept in an underground chamber where I was taken between my last lucid moment and waking up in this hospital in terrible pain, don't be annoyed. I say these things realizing that the information which comes to me and which I will pass on to you may cause you to doubt their veracity. For if you are reading this, then most likely you know exactly who I am. Then I wonder: Who are you? And why should I trust you? How do I know that you are not my adversary? How do I know that you did not put me here, in this condition? Melissa, I am feeling very tired today. Please come back tomorrow and I will move straight into what I do remember. I have been wasting too much energy.

★

By all accounts, the falls were magnificent to look at. Kane described them as "exceedingly picturesque and grand."

★

I remember taking a car trip with a beautiful woman. I am driving the car and she is sitting in the passenger's seat. We are on the way to see something important. What that is, I hope to find out. It has to do with a place, an ancient place that was once something, but is now something else. And people who once occupied that ancient place, but who are now scattered and apart from it. It is a very hot day, and the black interior of the car is scorching. The windows are rolled down and a warm wind blows in, but it does not cool me. She is looking at a map. We are driving through woods, and beside us is a large lake. Why are we trying to find the place we are trying to find? It seems to have begun with information discovered by this girl in the forms of photographs. I can remember seeing the photographs. There is a hole in a rocky ground, and a man in a hat lying on his stomach, looking down into the hole. There is another photograph. The man has a spear or a lance or a measuring stick and stands beside the hole. I have the feeling that this place does not exist anymore, except underwater. There is a place where thousands of trees lie stacked up stripped of their bark and limbs. All night long you can hear the roar of machinery, the squeals of saws, and the beeping of trucks backing up. There is a fire in a fire pit, and the girl is at a picnic table cutting potatoes and mushrooms, and wrapping them in tin foil.

★

Each time

I fall

asleep,

to me, appear more clues

and so one would assume that I am always one step closer to discovering my identity. But more information seems to cause only more confusion, because often the information appears contradictory, and seems to be about some one else entirely, and not me. Which raises interesting questions itself. Am I one person or could I be more than one? Maybe these memories have been implanted in me. Maybe I carry information of such significance that the fate of the entire world depends upon me successfully delivering it. Why would that be? I seem to see a road, and a valley underneath, surrounded by mountains, and at the bottom of the valley is a town. I'm up on the top, on the road, beside the girl, and beside us making its way down to the bottom of the valley is a line of trucks, buses, caravans. Now I think that the girl and I are in one of the buses, and we are there with many other people. All of the people are singing. And the girl is singing too. Everyone is happy. But I seem to be confused by it all. We are going to the town at the bottom of the valley, and we will pitch a tent there, and invite the townspeople to come. I don't feel that I belong here. I don't know what I feel. It could be that I have infiltrated them. I could be a man sent to listen in. Or maybe I have something different to do, of a violent nature. Maybe I am a killer. A [redacted]. Or a keeper of bees. Or maybe I am just another good-natured follower, one in a million, who feels for a moment, in this moment that I am able to remember, that I have somehow lost my way.

There is a man who is dying. He is in a hospital bed in an apartment. He, it seems, is my father. There is a woman there, who is my mother. And a young woman who is my sister. Now the young woman is only a child. And she and I, a child too, are standing on a baseball diamond. The score is tied and it is the bottom of the ninth. I am the pitcher and the other team's best hitter hits the ball. It goes over my sister's head. She walks after it slowly, and I yell at her to run and get it. But she only walks more slowly as the hitter runs around the dimaond from base to base. if he scores, the game will be over and we will have lost. I run after the ball myself. I run past my sister who still walks just as slowly. I get the ball and turn to throw it. But the hitter has already reached home plate.

I scream and yell at my sister. I slap her face with my glove. I tell her what she did was the worst thing a person can ever do: She didn't *hustle.* Now we're back in the apartment and she is a woman in her late twenties, and the man who seems to be our father is nearing the time of his death. He begins to sing a song…

Subject: Re: [Fwd: [Fwd: Re: Fishboy by Matthew McIntosh]]
Date: Tue, 05 Jun 2007 11:11:02 -0700
From: <matthew@[redacted].com>
To: erin@[redacted].com
References: <200706041552.AA3701801434@[redacted].com>

i just remembered a dream i had last night about my dad leaving the earth correctly. we were all there in puyallup and from what i remember he began singing some beautiful words, then got down on the floor on his knees and my mom had drawn a picture of a blackbird and she put it on the floor in front of him; he colored the wings "rainbow" and then touched his forehead to it. I was crying and happy, and it was very beautiful. there was more to it but that's what i remember.

Subject: Re: (no subject)
Date: Tue, 5 Jun 2007 12:10:08 -0700
From: <erin@[redacted].com>
To: <matthew@[redacted].com>

that is such a neat and beautiful dream you had. That is so so nice.

In the dream, was your dad looking like he did pre-cancer, or did he look like he actually did when he was in the later stages of the disease?

love you

Subject: Re: (no subject)
Date: Tue, 05 Jun 2007 12:37:55 -0700
From: <matthew@[redacted].com>
To: erin@[redacted].com

no, it was late stages. he was pretty incoherent, but it was obvious that he was giving in to death, and offering up prayers and songs, etc. and paying respects to life and death and god - and the bird my mom drew was very important; and we of course were there with him and able to participate and send him on his way, and feel sadness and joy and everything he was feeling with him. the dream seemed to show what death could be like. the other thing was the words he was saying - which were mostly nonsense but very meaningful and magical - I was writing them all down as he said them, and in the dream i was very happy to have them so that i could put them in my book. of course i can't remember a single one now.

Subject: Re: (no subject)
Date: Tue, 5 Jun 2007 13:02:11 -0700
From: <erin@[redacted].com>
To: <matthew@[redacted].com>

wild!

Thats so amazing, though, because it's just like how the box camera is missing, and the last page of the girl with the beautiful white wings, and how the iPod would sometimes just not record things..... you wrote the words down in your dream, but you're not allowed to have them right now. It's totally cool.

like in the old fairy tales or myths, where certain words have meaning "open sesame" etc..... we're not allowed to have the actual words right now.

Wouldn't that be neat if you could remember, though? Maybe you should take a nap!!!

If you can force yourself, I was thinking you should drink a lot of peppermint tea today.. because it's caffeine free and you could pump a lot of fluids into yourself that way.

———I see a pine cone falling from a tree

LOVE YOU

——and landing on the dirt beside me.

LOVE YOU!!!!!

—I see a crowd of people, gathered in an amphitheatre in the woods. The sun is up and the sky is blue, and the day is warm. We all look down from our seats to the stage.

"A vast lake of boiling pitch, in which an infinite multitude
of fierce and terrible creatures are traversing."

Quote

But it was the quantity of fish in the water that drew the most comment from early visitors. Kane, for example, marveled at the apparently ceaseless flow of summer Chinook salmon that he saw on two separate trips to the falls, in August and September of 1847. "The salmon continue to arrive in almost incredible numbers for nearly two months," he wrote. "In fact, *there is one continuous body* of them, more resembling a flock of birds than anything else in their extraordinary leap up the falls..." (Kane, 218).*

★

There is an old church in the woods. I follow the girl inside. There is nothing there but darkness, planks and floorboards, and the songs of the birds outside. We walk out and down a path behind. And to a cliffside. Below us is a lake that used to be a river and a plain. There were great rock formations which formed roaring rapids here and it is said that one could hear the churning water for miles. Kettle Falls. The water is still except for the ripples created by a small boat as it trolls, a man in a deck chair holding out a line....................

★

...................................Thompson was surprised to see that only one man was fishing, with a spear, when he arrived, even though there were more than enough fish in the river to keep many people busy. He was told the harvest did not begin in earnest until the salmon chief announced that enough fish had safely cleared the falls. This was necessary, the Indians said, to *protect the harvest* in the future.

★

Salmon used to climb this river from the sea hundreds of miles away, to return to the nooks and crannies where they were born, to spawn. Indians met here for thousands of years to fish and dance and welcome summer.

---

* (italics mine)

But Summer is lost. Late 1800s the white men built canneries down at the mouth of the river and swept up most of the salmon each year as soon as they left the sea. And fewer and fewer salmon made the run. And then 1930s Roosevelt built a dam which closed the upper river, and flooded the falls, and flooded the plain, and built a wall, so that no salmon who made it past the nets could get home to lay their eggs.

★

And now at the Kettle Falls Harvest Foods they sell seasoned salmon steaks pre-packaged 438 miles away in Oregon City, Oregon for 11 dollars and 89 cents a pound; and who knows where it was caught?

★

(2007.)

★

May 5 2007 2:32 A

appartment women don't tell the truth about what they think.
I am telling you this because it is the honest truth, look I should know, they say that it is all in the way you use it, not how big it is, well I got news for you all, that is pure lies.
I know from personal experience, I will tell you about a secret that carlo has made me promise to never ever tell anyone, but since he has not called me in three weeks after standing me up, I am going to break the promise and tell you how he went from having a tiny wang and in 4 months he is now about nine inches and get this, it is still getting bigger. He has been secretly taking grow jells from this site, copy and paste the address into your browser to see them.

But Sumner is lost. Later, though, the white men built canneries down at the mouth of the river and swept up most of the salmon each year as soon as they left the sea. And fewer and fewer salmon made the run. And then, 1942, Roosevelt built a dam which closed the upper river and flooded the falls, and flooded the plains, and built a wall, so that no salmon who made it past the nets could get home to lay their eggs.

And now at the Kettle Falls Harvest Foods they sell seasoned salmon steaks prepackaged 428 miles away in Oregon City, Oregon for 5 dollars and 80 cents a pound, and who knows where it was caught.

(2007)

May 2007 2:12 AM

apartment won't tell the truth about what they think. I can tell you this because it is the honest truth. Look the help how they know that it is all in the way and how high it will get me and you all that I pure [illegible]. I know from personal experience I will tell you about a secret that could have made me rich [illegible] never ever tell a [illegible] but I [illegible] this [illegible] three weeks after [illegible] me up, I am going to break the promise and tell you how he went from having a tiny [illegible] and in a month he is now about [illegible] and get this it is still getting bigger. He has been extremely [illegible] this site, copy and paste the address into your browser to see them

★

★

Melissa, I am not in my right mind. I am sick as a dog and I'm starting to crack. I can't remember who I am, or what I have done. My skin is burning and my bones ache, and it is really hard to breathe. I want whoever reads this message in the future, to know that whatever acts I committed, all I did, whatever it was, good or bad, for better or worse, I did it for thee. It was all always for thee.

So don't be mad at me.

Melissa, I am not in my right mind. I am sick as a dog and I'm starting to crack. I can't remember who I am, or what I have done. My skin is burning and my bones ache and it is really hard to breathe. I want whoever reads this message in the future to know that whatever acts I committed, all I did, whatever it was, good or bad, for better or worse, I did it for thee. It was all always for thee.

So don't be mad at me.

If I have walked—

If my steps have turned—

If my land has cried—

If I have eaten—

If I have made—

If my heart has been enticed—

And I have lain—

Then may my wife—

Had I refused—

If I have denied—

Or allowed the eyes—

If I have seen—

If I have raised—

Because I saw—

Then may my arm—

Had I put my trust in gold

Or called—

★

O, how will I ever find my way out?!?!?

★

Had I looked upon the sun as it shone,

Or the moon in the splendor of its progress,

And had my heart been secretly enticed

To waft them a kiss with my hand;

This too would be a crime for condemnation,

For I should have denied God above.

Had I rejoiced—

Or exulted—

Even though I had not suffered—

Had not the men of my futuristic housing unit
exclaimed—

Had I, out of human weakness, hidden my sins

And buried my guilt—

Because I feared—

W: What time is it?
M: Six past nine.
W: It's crazy.
M: What.
W: This day just disap

Am I going mad, Melissa? Was there a fire? A big explosion? Or do I just have a bad cold and a sunburn.

Unofficially, a faulty rear drain flap and malfunctioning bilge pump may have caused a boat to sink April 9 on Flathead Lake, killing two people. The investigation continues, Lake County Undersheriff Mike Sergeant said, but inspection of the 10-year-old boat turned up those two problems. [A man], 39, and [a woman], 29, of Bethel, Connecticut, drowned in the lake two weeks ago near Yellow Bay when the boat sank. The boat was owned and skippered by [redacted] of [redacted] Guide Services in Bigfork. He survived by clinging to a small portion of the boat that remained above water overnight. He was rescued April 10 after being stranded 20 hours in 40-degree water. [The woman's] body was recovered April 10; her husband's body remains submerged in an area of 300-foot-deep water. Neither was wearing a life jacket. Mike Sergeant said he signed [the woman's] death certificate Wednesday. Her body was returned to her family for funeral services in Bethel last week. He said it appears that [the woman] died "several hours into the incident. She didn't make it through the night."

Sergeant said officials are still waiting for [redacted]'s insurance company, Ace American, to decide whether it will send a commercial recovery team to locate [the man's] body. "They've said, 'Yes, we will. No, we won't because of the cost,'" Sergeant said. "We're controlled by them... We're a little frustrated." The depth of the lake where the [man and his wife] drowned is beyond the reach of divers. Sonar and robots will be needed, officials have said. Sergeant said the insurance company will conduct its own examination of the boat. Local officials, though, blame the rear drain flap that is supposed to keep water from coming into the boat when it is under way. There also was a problem with the bilge pump that clears water from the bottom of the boat. "It's not concrete," Mike Sergeant said of the findings. He said the 24-foot Seahawk boat was in "very good condition" and apparently the mechanical failure was swift and intense. "When the boat went under, it went under rapidly," Sergeant said. Its occupants raced to put on life jackets but "were unable to get them on,"

Now imagine.

You're lying on a beach.

On a wickedly hot day.

The girl is lying beside you.

You're looking up into the brim of a baseball cap you've pulled down over your face to shield your eyes from the light.

This ain't no ocean, pilgrim; it's a lake.

But it's not a lake, either; it's a dammed river.

You could jump in and swim to the bottom.

Collect the stars of a fallen sky.

Reconstellate,
Reconstellate,
Reconstellate,
Reconstellate,
Reconstellate,
Reconstellate,
Reconstellate,
Reconstellate,
Reconstellate,
Reconstellate,
Reconstellate,
Reconstellate,
Reconstellate,
Reconstellate,

Gather the bones of an ancient culture.

Reconstellate.
Reconstellate.
Reconstellate.
Reconstellate.
Reconstellate.
Reconstellate.
Reconstellate.
Reconstellate.
Reconstellate.
Reconstellate.
Reconstellate.
Reconstellate.
Reconstellate.
Reconstellate.
Reconstellate.

Repopulate.
Repopulate.
Repopulate.
Repopulate.
Repopulate.
Repopulate.
Repopulate.
Repopulate.
Repopulate.
Repopulate.
Repopulate.
Repopulate.
Repopulate.
Repopulate.
Repopulate.

★

Live Conversation with Hazel

Hazel: Hi, this is Hazel. Welcome to Round Table Company. I'm proud to announce that our firm was just named by Inc. Magazine to the "Inc. 500" list of fastest growing private companies in the US, for the third year in a row!

Visitor 3277: quantum surgery?

Hazel: Great! Let us help you. We provide clients access to experts in all fields. Our team (which includes lawyers, Ph.D.s, MBAs, and private investigators) uses rigorous methodologies, relationships with numerous firms, and proprietary databases--including our network of 65,000 professors and industry experts--to quickly find unbiased expertise

Hazel: Please tell me more about the type of expert you are looking for?

Visitor 3277: quantum surgery?

Hazel: May I have your name?

Visitor 3277: Is this an automated program or is there a live person on the other end?

Hazel: I am a live person :)

Visitor 3277: In that case May I have your name?

Hazel: Sure

Hazel: My name is Hazel and I am the Website Greeter for Round Table Company

Visitor 3277: Your name is not Hazel.

Hazel: I am prety sure that my name is Hazel :)
Hazel: You can see it written at the top of our dialog box as well!
Hazel: Yes, I am.

Visitor 3277: Would you be willing to submit to a test before we proceed?

Hazel: Pardon?

Visitor 3277: May I test you on American trivia before we get down to business?

Hazel: Sure, we can give that a try!

Visitor 3277: Excellent. Thank you very much.
Visitor 3277: Number one: Who is the president of the United States?

Hazel: You are welcome
Hazel: George W. Bush

Visitor 3277: Correct.
Visitor 3277: Number two: What is the capital of the United States?

Hazel: Great!
Hazel: Washington DC

Visitor 3277: I see you've done your homework.

Hazel: Proud to be American!

Hazel: If we are done withthe trivia test, can I have your name?

Visitor 3277: Number three: what is the Bible belt?

Visitor 3277: please do not search for the answers on the Internet

Hazel: I am not reseraching the answers over the web
Hazel: I just am not sure about the answer to this question.
Hazel: all I now is that it has something to do with Protestant
           fundamentalism

Visitor 3277: partial credit.
Visitor 3277: Number four: how many states comprise the United
           States?

Hazel: I am sorry, but if you don't provide me your contact details
           and the nature of your expert need, I'll have to close down our
           conversation.

Visitor 3277: Oh, i'm sorry. Please don't close down our conversation.
           it's just that i am not sure about this service. once i feel more
           comfortable i will give my info. but you never know who
           you're dealing with on the web. forgive me, though. i don't
           mean to waste your time. i'm really sorry. i hope you won't
           hang up.

Hazel: Thats alright.

Hazel: I assure you that our Website Greeter Service is genuine and we will not give out or use your information for any other purpose.

Visitor 3277: well, i appreciate the assurance. It's a real relief.

Hazel: Glad to hear that

Hazel: May I have your name?

Visitor 3277: Spencer Braddock.

Hazel: Nice to have you with us, Spencer.

Spencer Braddock: Thanks. It's nice to be with you.

Hazel: May I have your emil address and phone number as well?

Spencer Braddock: You never did answer number four.

Hazel: 50 states

Spencer Braddock: Correct. My number is 555 838 2626. I prefer to not be called. And I prefer not to give my email to you just yet.

Hazel: Thank you for providing your telephone number

Spencer Braddock: I feel as if I'm taking a risk.

Hazel: How do you suggest we get in touch with you, with the required information on Quantum Surgery Experts?

Hazel: I assure you once again that your contact information will not be shared with any 3rd parties or used for any purpose otherwise than stated.

Spencer Braddock: I am glad to hear that. I am more in need of private investigation services. the "quantum surgery" line was just a coded phrase to see if you were one of us.

Hazel: Pardon?

Spencer Braddock: I am glad to hear that. I am more in need of private investigation services. the "quantum surgery" line was just a coded phrase to see if you were one of us.

Hazel: I'm sorry but we don't provide this sort of service. What we do is provide clients with "primary research," i.e., we locate experts so that clients can engage these experts for paid consulation

Spencer Braddock: I refer you to earlier in the conversation. You stated: We provide clients access to experts in all fields. Our team (which includes lawyers, Ph.D.s, MBAs, and private investigators)

Hazel: Sure
Hazel: I apologize for my ignorance in this respect!
Hazel: Please tell me more about the type of private invstigator you are looking for?

Spencer Braddock: Hazel, you are not ignorant. Please don't say that. You have already proved you know a lot--about the United States, for example.
Spencer Braddock: Number five: what is the "American Dream"?

Hazel: Thank you for the compliment, Spencer.

Hazel: but I thought we were done with the trivia

Spencer Braddock: It's more of an essay question.

Hazel: The definition of a dream is relative

Hazel: It varies from person to person

Spencer Braddock: Interesting. But what is the "American" dream?

Hazel: To some its acquiring a house in suburbs with pretty white fences, filled with the laughter of kids and aroma of home baked cookies by the the lady of the house.

Spencer Braddock: That's beautiful, Hazel.

Hazel: While to some other, it maybe getting oneself a caravan and going on the great road trip.

Spencer Braddock: That's lovely.

Hazel: Thank you

Spencer Braddock: What part of the US did you say you were from?

Hazel: I am from Chicago.

Spencer Braddock: You are not from Chicago.

Hazel: Spencer, sine you are uncomfortable sharing the details of your case here over the web, I'd suggestt that get in touch with my colleague Mike [redacted] in our Washington DC office,

202-████████ extension 1, m████@roundtablecompany.com; to assist you further.

Spencer Braddock: The world is changing. I wish you luck.

Hazel: Thank you
Hazel: May I ask how you learned about Round Table Company?

Spencer Braddock: by accident

Hazel: Can you be just a little more descriptive please?

Spencer Braddock: I first came to the Round Table site one day while working on a book. I don't remember how exactly I came to be here then. It was a long time ago. I think maybe I was researching King Arthur or Glastonbury or something. The next thing I know I'm on the Round Table site and a computerized female voice says WELCOME, and a box pops up asking me if I need help finding an expert.

Hazel: Thank you for the explaination, Spencer.
Hazel: Is there anything else I can help you with, today?

Spencer Braddock: I'd like to ask one last favor, but I'm not sure you'll oblige me.

Hazel: We can give it a try

Spencer Braddock: Will you tell me your real name?

Hazel: Sure

Hazel: Its Hazel.

Hazel: I was named after my grandmother

Spencer Braddock: then will you tell me what the weather is like where you are right now?

Right Now for
Chicago, IL

40°F
Cloudy

Hazel: It seems to be cloudy but I am not really sure
Hazel: I am not sitting anywhere near the window

Spencer Braddock: Hazel, it's one o'clock in the morning in Chicago.

Hazel: Yes, almost

Spencer Braddock: Good night.

Hazel: My watch says its 12:55 am

★

Fishing at the falls was a highly organized enterprise. A salmon chief (called "See-pay," or Chief of the Waters) launched the season by spearing the first salmon; decided when the general harvest could begin; supervised the placement of basket traps along the rocky shoreline, and oversaw the construction of fishing platforms that extended over the turbulent water. At the end of the day, he divided the catch.

★

It is said that the salmon came in such numbers that there appeared to be continually one leaping mass arcing over the spray for months. There were millions of them, and only a few thousand salmon-eating Indians. Yet each year, before any fishing began, the chief's main duty was to decide when enough fish had jumped up the falls to guarantee that they would return the next year. In other words, he was a conservationist. He understood man's place in the great cosmic circle of life and all that. He knew that man had the capacity to change the nature of the world. In reality, he and his people could not effect such a large-scale transformation as the wiping out of a species—they didn't have the numbers or the technology—but it's food for thought that he used prudence as if they could. Just then the white man came. He set up camps at the mouth of the river. He developed technologies. He swept up the fish. Until the ones that made it back to the falls each year were only a few thousand in number. And then he built the Grand Coulee Dam. He did it to turn the water into power to run the engines of the cities of the West. The dam closed the river to the last of the salmon. Then the water rose higher, and flooded the plains, flooded the valleys and silenced the waters, flattened the waves. They named it Lake Roosevelt. And here I am washed up on its shores, on a *fu-cking* hot day lying half-naked on a towel, while down the beach little white trash kids splash around in the cold water screaming, as their parents and older brothers do figure eights on roaring jet skis, and the sounds of it all interact with my eardrums in a very strange way: Each note spins inside my head, echoing as the rate of spin increases before finally shattering by way of an explosion from the inside into thousands of miniature fragments of sound, which, dispersing, drift away evenly in all directions into the vacuum of space:

*.

*.

*.

.

.*

.*.

.

.*.

*.

..*.*.*.*.*.*.*.*.*.*.*.*.*.*.

I ask the girl if it sounds that way to her.

★

"Vacuum of space?" she says, from beneath her round-brimmed fisherman's hat. "Hmmm . . . I think you may be coming down with something."

★

I say, "I am See-Pay, Chief of the Waters. I have spent many moons walking the shores of this abominable lake, communing with the spirits of my ancestors. Now I am here to declare that for the crimes of his fathers, I will slay every white man who walks the earth."

★

"Good riddance. Do me a favor and start with those noisy a-holes on jet skis."

★

"I will spare not one of his children nor a single of his concubines. There will be no more white offspring at all, in fact."

★

"Super."

★

"He has polluted the waters."

★

"Very true."

★

"He has flooded the Spring of Life. He has diluted the waters with his foul artificial Rooseveltian lakewaters. Thus, the Spring of Life has been capped."

★

"Totally."

★

"And now a new hole has been broken open in the great below, from which will rise the Waters of Death. The Waters of Death will mix with the white man's artificial waters and poison his supply."

★

"I like that, honey. Is that from your book?"

★

"Beware, white drinkers of water. Beware of bottlers of waters. And distributors and retailers of bottled waters. Beware of waiters and waitresses who set upon tables glasses and pitchers of ice water. Beware of movie theater candy counter clerks and their tiny cups of complimentary drinking-fountain water. Hear my words, white man: your time is up. Every last one of you will soon be dead."

★

"Uh-huh. Are you sure you don't want me to put some sunscreen on you, See-Pay? You're looking pretty red."

★

What's so bad about lead? Even small amounts can lead to brain damage, *.*.*.*.*. *.**. a safe hose starts to seem like a bargain.

★

14 They had forgotten to bring bread, and they had only one loaf with them in the boat. **15** He enjoined them, "Watch out, guard against the leaven of the Pharisees and the leaven of Herod." **16** They concluded among themselves that it was because they had no bread. **17** When he became aware of this he said to them, "Why do you conclude that it is because you have no bread? Do you not yet understand or comprehend? Are your hearts hardened? **18** Do you have eyes and not see, ears and not hear? And do you not remember, **19** when I broke the five loaves for the five thousand, how many wicker baskets full of fragments you picked up?" They answered him, "Twelve." **20** "When I broke the seven loaves for the four thousand, how many full baskets of fragments did you pick up?" They answered him, "Seven." **21** He said to them, **"Do you still not understand?"**

⋆

I could go on forever and still not have enough time to write all I want to write—or rather whisper hoarsely into Melissa's ear all I want her to write down for me. My brain is

⋆

almost a mile long.

⋆

It is taller than the

Great Pyramid of Giza;

*

all the pyramids at Giza could fit within its base.

*

It is more than twice as tall as Niagara Falls.

*

And why should I place my trust in Melissa? Just because she found her way into my room?

How do I know I'm not hallucinating? How do I know that she really is a cute little flower girl? Why do I assume that her motives are pure and that her spelling and penmanship are adequate? That she'll be able to get my mess age a cross. Like everyone I have ever met—or everyone I think I have met—or everyone I may have met—or everyone of whom my brain has been instructed to believe there has been a meeting—I really don't know her at all. All I have is faith. I have to believe that she is not a biomechanicalhumanandroid. I have to believe she does not mean me harm. For if I think that she means me harm, then I must release her. And if I release her, then I will have no link left to the world outside my bed. And if I have no link, then I have nothing connecting me to the human race. And then I am not human after all.

Are you a biomechanicalhumanandroid, Melissa?

>Shhhh…Honey, you know I'm not.

Are we going to win?

>Of course we are.

Am I the greatest pollutionist who ever lived?

>Well, you see, See–Pay—

[This comment has been removed]

Is what I'm going through just part of The Show?

Is it all just part of The Show?

Well, how does it end, Melissa?

Where

O where

O where

will we be

then?

Where are we now?

Where should we begin?

*

Verbum
Intelligen
tia
Intellectus
Ratio
Imaginati
Sensus

★

Well, there's no one here yet and the floor is *completely* engulfed!
We're on the floor and we can't breathe!

OK.

And it's *very, very, very* hot!

It's very—is—are the lights still on?

The lights are on but it's *very hot!*

Ma'am, ma'am, stay calm—

It's *very hot!* We're all the way on the other side of Liberty!
And it's *very, very hot!*

Any lights—you could turn the lights off?

No! No, the lights are off!

OK, good. Now. Everybody stay calm, you're doing a good job—

Please!

Ma'am, listen. Ma'am lis—*everybody's* coming, *everybody knows. Everybody* knows, what happened. OK?

{ }

(abff.avi)

M: Get the guy who says SLOW.

W: I didn't get the guy, I'm sorry. I'm just pointing forward.

M: *Pilot car…*

M: It's a fire—Oh shit!

[redacted]

W: Oh my gosh!

M: Cool! Oh man. Can you get that?

W: I don't know, it's so, like—I'm trying, but the camera—I don't know if it's picking it up! [*narrating*] THIS IS A FOREST FIRE!

W: It's ALL BLACK on the screen.

*

It was just past five in the evening and the people in suits were leaving their places of work. They spilled out of ground-floor double doors,

revolving and automatic sliding glass doors, and flowed up the sidewalk, their tides regulated by the traffic lights, toward their cars and trains and buses; they hurried on.

And I stood on the corner, looking through them, to the place where the woman in the sweatpants had just disappeared, as she'd walked straight into, against the flow of, that crowd... (Take it, Sal...)

★

(sal.aiff)

There was uh these huge caves, we had no idea what they were, and, uh, when Aida—the wife—said, What are those openings in the side of the cliffs there? And, uh, I'm trying to think of the name of the uh Spanish farmer that was—he said, uh, they're *zumas,* and I said, *Zumas?* What's a *zuma*? and he would come out and say, *Living quarters.* He was the only one that was able to speak just enough English to get into trouble. It was so funny because uh uh he had been in the—he had been in the war, the civil war—

M: 'Cause this was in the '50s that you were there...

Yeah 1954, '55, '56, '57...was there until '67. I was one of the—the few, but there was a few of us—handful—that were in a necessary job that couldn't be replaced right away.

★

I'd seen her everywhere. In alleys. In doorways. On old cement stoops and staircases, in front of crumbling columns, looking out at the heaving streets. Asleep, doubled over, or leaning against a wall, somewhere. Eyelids dark, bruised. I saw her leaning against a garbage can for balance. Then she had pulled down her sweatpants, crouched, and as the crowd had coursed between her and me I saw her take a shit into her hand.

Just outside the Market Street doors of the San Francisco Shopping Centre. *Nine stories of elegant shopping, four of which belong to Nordstrom's department store,* the website says. *Go to the top floor for a great view of the gently curving escalators, all stacked up on top of each other…*

★

M: What were you doing there exactly? I heard you were in—you were in intelligence…

Yeah, we were part of an intelligence corps—thank you.

W: You're welcome…And the pills…

M: Here let me…there's a bunch in there; you might wanna take them separate…

★

She pulled up her sweatpants; then walked into the crowd, which parted around her, never touching, and swallowed her up.

★

Yeah, we were—we finally got down there from the road—it wasn't much of a road believe me—it was more off the main—the main uh road, down to a secondary road—

M: And this was outside of Madrid…

Outside of Madrid…the west side of uh—I'll get you the name—uh it'll come to me…………….Anyway……So they said uh would you like to visit the—the castle. I just never thought of what I was going to fall into and and and see…because I had uh I had been given—back at the embassy when I was digging information—they said, uh, That's just uh overnight stop for the king—to rest and make a gallant entry into Madrid.

M: Freshen up.

Yeah, you know. I said, OK, you know. I figured it was a stable with uh—to change the horses and get some fresh water and that was it. Well, this turned out to be a huge metropolitan castle—that he had built. And uh he said uh, Let's go inside. The farmer…said, Let's go inside. I said, Can we do it? He says, Oh yeah. Then he says, These are all my friends here…the guards…they're all friends… So we—we went down into into into the gardens…we started looking around… they were still beautiful—beautiful gardens… Had strawberries planted all over the place…you know. It was just something that the land was good for…so they decided uh to plant plenty of strawberries…and uh… We sat down—while we were looking around they had put out sheets… rows of sheets as tables…on the ground…So they brought out the wine they brought out the bread, the cheese.

M: This was in the castle?

Yeah! Right in the castle grounds. And uh…so I said uh…to Zamor…I said, This is very interesting. I said, You got a national treasure here that you could use…for your tourism. You know, you gotta remember that this was uh uh during Eisenhower's uh presidency…and he fought tooth and nails for…uh…ooh, what was that program………………It was *Hand to Hand*……what was that program…I'd have to look it up. But anyway, he believed…the great soldier that he was and the statesman… uh…he believed in uh…in meeting the people face-to-face…so he opened up Europe like no other man had opened up Europe to us… with his uh funds to Greece, funds to Italy…and……………So we sat down, and we were all at two lines…of tables…and uh…they brought out—we broke bread…drank wine, ate cheese…you know you're so worried about uh the chemical situation and all that…but you still ate the cheese you know…and I kind of leaned back and laughed and and Aida would say,

"What are you laughing about? Why you laughin?"

and I would say,

You know you talk about not drinking their milk, and uh…their water…and you have to be careful about all that…I say, Here you are eating the cheese! You know? And it's uh…So…after about an hour…of just, being friendly and talkin and eatin…uh…he said to me he says…Come on, I wanna show you somethin. He took me into the innards of the castle…and uh…into the kitchen with—they didn't use it anymore but it was still kept…uh……took you up the back staircase, right into the different private rooms of the…king and queen and all…

⋆

(ONBED.avi)

W: —take *us*.

M: Take us doing what?

W: Take a photo of us. Just lying here.

M: From up there?

W: Yeah.

M: Like up here?

W: Yeah.

M: OK. Ready?

W: Uh-huh.

★

M: So the castle was still in use…

The cas—the majority of the castle was still in use, and uh, the outside grounds were great—they were—you know they still had the…royal guards and and so on and so forth—they tried to make an uh uh an appearance uh of a workin castle like uh you might have in England or in Denmark or someplace like that—but uh it it it was uh it was humorous—they finally hit it! You know, they tried and tried and they finally hit it—and they weren't embarrassed! See? So a lot of this was built by Ferdinand himself, the king……And uh went into his chambers…the queen's chambers…uh…beautiful beds, that were made specially for them, and their comfort, and all that…

★

M: How can I tell if we're both in the frame?

★

Uh...... you just... uh... can't forget those uh those times. No, my uh—

M: First—take those last pills first.

Yeah...

M: You're thirsty, eh?

I—the—what?

M: I said, *You're thirsty.*

Ah! Yes, I was!.................Yeah I was uh...I was part of a a team...

W: This one's Sal's. This one's yours.
This one has more fruit.
We do this regimen in the morning
of this soy... did he tell you?

Yeah? No.

M: I didn't warn him, no.

W: We're addicted to it.
But I put more strawberries in yours
to make it a little sweeter because
I don't think you'll be able to take it.

O-K!

W: But we—we just have a taste for it, you know?

Good! Great!.........So...the uh, we were part of—well, each embassy at that time had its own...designated team, and whenever anything... major was erupting, this was the first uh first inkling that would be reported back to Washington—that there was problems, that there was unhappiness...or, something major was going on—about to happen... and this was how the CIA...
was able to set up...
its uh its successful...
career over the—over the years.
Then it all somewhere—somewhere along the line instead of...lettin it work—or ah waiting for it to work—ah...
somebody stirred the pot and uh—
we got into a big mess.

M: Cowboys?

Yeah, yeah, yeah, they wanted to do it their way, you know, the American way...and you don't go into Europe uh and try to do anything the American way. It just doesn't work! It doesn't work! Right? So..................This is good!...........

⋆

M: Aren't you glad we came this way?

W: Yes. [*narrating*] WE'RE DRIVING INTO A FOREST FIRE! It's hard to tell…

[redacted]

[redacted]

[redacted]

M: Wow.

[redacted]

W: It doesn't seem too bad…

M: No it doesn't does it. It's really, really pretty. Look to the left.

[redacted]

W: It's just ALL BLACK. Sor—

★

So……we uh we'd always be on the uh on the lookout
for information, we'd always be uh open to it, just
report what you see, don't embellish…uh

don't take away,

don't try to analyze it…

just report it.

★

And then there she was again—Our Lady of the Sweatpants—now occupying the body of another woman, this one scatterbrained—makeup caked and stumbling down the street, shouting:

"I DON'T GIVE A SHIT ABOUT YOU MOTHERFUCKER! GET OFF ME I DON'T GIVE A SHIT GET THE FUCK OFF!"

She was walking alone. As she made her way down the street. My wife and I, on the opposite sidewalk, walked past. But her complaints were expressed such that even a block away her words were echoing off the walls, the faces of abandoned storefronts and apartment houses: GET OFF ME I DON'T FUCKING GIVE A SHIT ABOUT YOU MOTHERFUCKER! GET THE FUCK OFF DO YOU KNOW WHO YOU'RE MESSING?

And it must have been someone up in one of those buildings who yelled at her (because the sound appeared to come from out of the overcast sky):

Shut up bitch!

We thought nothing of it. And then up ahead of us, across the street, we heard—and then we saw—her hero.

He was fat,

short, black-skinned, crossing the street, making a beeline right for us, shouting:

"YOU GOT A PROBLEM WITH WHAT THE LADY'S SAYING?
YOU GOT A PROBLEM WITH WHAT THE LADY'S SAYING?"

His hand was under his shirt, and down by his waistband, like he was pulling out a gun—

"YOU GOT A PROBLEM WITH WHAT THE LADY'S SAYING?"

no man relax relax relax relax

⋆

W: Hey, honey, fix the bed. Why don't you get a movie of how you broke the bed.

⋆

We'd just come from Montana, where we'd spent the winter. Spring came late, but when it came the man who owned the house we were renting came back from his place in Mexico to charge wealthy vacationers ten times what we were paying. The winter in the Flathead Valley is long and cold and gray, but in the spring it's easy to see that all of life did originate there, around the peaceful shores of that great sleeping lake. I had a dream about it the other night.

And in the dream,

I was back in that cabin on the lake,
but the skies weren't gray,
and there was no snow,
and it wasn't cold,
and no wind blew—

no, it was warm in the dream and we'd been able to stay deep into spring—I walked out through the woods, down to the shore, and the animals came to welcome me;
there were rabbits,
and deer,
birds of every kind and color, all singing songs of spring,
and there were beavers,
and antelope,
and bear,
and they were all living in splendid natural harmony.

The dog loved the cat, the cat loved the mouse, the mouse loved the cheese, the sky was bright, the water glowed, and fish leapt toward the sun. The surface was turquoise, and down below it was emerald in color, but clear to the bottom depths, as I remember it had been when I was seventeen and I had come on vacation with my family—it was two weeks after I hit my head on the bottom of a swimming pool.

And all through that vacation, I was in a very thick fog. I'd rub my eyes and clean my contact lenses thoroughly each morning, but the thick white and gray clouds which blotted out light and blurred the edges of everything always remained firmly in place.

“xxxxxxxxxxxxxxxxxxxstrangexxxxxxxxxxxxxxxxxxx”

I had never had a headache that I could remember, but my mom had suffered from migraines all of her married life—every few months she would get in bed with the shades down and the lights off and stay there and you could not bother her, you could not stand by the door or step inside her room, and most importantly, even if you were playing on the other side of the house, you could not make a sound. For three or four days we would tiptoe around and my dad would cook spaghetti for dinner or banana-and-pickle sandwiches and that was the price we all had to pay. Until eventually she would come out of the room in her bathrobe, her permed hair flat, dark under eyes, her face looking old and gray. I was trying to fan the clouds away when I realized I had a headache.

⋆

(xxxxxxxxxxxxxxxxxx.avi)

W: This is our very comfortable bed…with crea-king, way-too-thin supports which break very often…This is my…husband M[redacted] who…I did not know I was marrying when I married Matthew but I got a two for one and I am really pleased I must say.

M: It’s good to be here.

M: It’s good to be here.

W: I really love and appreciate M[redacted] I must say and I…uh…value him and appreciate all his opinions and feelings…

⋆

When the season turned my wife and I could not afford to stay on the lake, so we packed up the Bronco and rode southwest to San Francisco, to sublet the apartment of a guy we'd met at a wedding the month before. The apartment was the bottom floor of an old Victorian in a row of old Victorians, next to the projects, in an alley called Birch, and across the alley, facing the houses, a white wall, twenty feet high, ran the entire length, and on the other side of the wall, a factory of some kind, or an auto shop, I have no idea. Behind the apartment was a small slab of concrete, and a fence we shared with the house behind, which had a small slab of its own.

⋆

(tour.avi)

M: OK, let's begin. Uh, what we're looking at here is the back yard of the—the—place we used to live, back when we were poor.

I think uh over there is a box. And I think we're coming to the part where we look at—

we see some cigarette butts. And I think there's a closeup of some cigarette butts.

Yeah, that's right here. It's not known who smoked that cigarette. As you can see back then we weren't doing so well,

we didn't have as much money as we do today. Uh, we did have a cat next door. Right there, yeah, I remember that part.

And uh right here looks like there's a closeup of the neighbor's cat.

As you can see the sky was blue back then before the apocalypse—

★

My book was coming out in a few months. And though I tried to immerse myself in this one—what was it called then? I don't remember—well, each time I waded in, the water did part around me…

but I could never get my head down below. I'd float there for a while, then become bored, put the pen down, dry off, close the laptop.

And we would lace up our shoes and walk around San Francisco, exploring. We came to see most of the city this way.

At the tops of each hill you could lean against ten million dollars to remove the rock from your shoe and when you had descended to the next basin there they were sprawled out beneath blankets and newspapers, streams from crotch to gutter, you stepped over those streams.

You wait to cross the street beside them. And beside men in convertibles with bleached teeth, with their hands on the wheel waiting to proceed, revving their engines and nodding their heads to music out-of-time. Well, soon we'll all be out of time, and what will we have left behind? A drawerful of photographs, letters, notes, little strips of paper. A drawerful of jpegs, tifs, pdfs, mp3s, midis, wavs, aiffs, mpgs, movs,

and all other accounts we keep of our

de:::

cline::::

★

So……we uh

we'd always be on the uh on the lookout for information, we'd always be uh open to it, just report what you see,

don't embellish…uh

don't take away,

don't try to analyze it…

just report it.

And it worked—

it worked

for over twenty years…

*

A woman in sweatpants slept on a couch outside our bedroom window.

the couch someone had tossed it off the bed of a truck and sped away. I'd walk out in the morning and she'd be stretched out, asleep. Sometimes her friends would come over and they'd sit up late, talking in loud voices, smoking crack and sharing sips from a tall can of malt liquor.

*

Trash strewn all over. The whole street smelled, and the man down the block was always out with his hose. And the

wind always blew

and it was cold.

★

So we would be we would be sent as far—ah—I got as far as Lebanon, uh, during the first, uh, snafu that uh, was given to them…They landed in Lebanon, I went in……got information that uh…that was planted… specifically pla—well it had to happen, you know! These things, if you don't do it right, uh, there's no sense in doin them because uh you get false information and that's it,

you're dead…

★

Up the alley, across the street, were the projects.

I was walking up Laguna toward the Safeway, past that AME church there—

approaching a small intersection with four stop signs, I heard tires squealing up the road, coming out of the project blocks.

And a car comes racing down, a nice car, a shiny black (stolen) Lexus.

Barreling, motor wailing, toward me, where I've got one foot on the curb, and one off; as it approaches its stop sign, it slows down—just barely—glides into the intersection, and then the driver wrenches the wheel, guns it, engine wailing, tires squealing, he starts doing doughnuts in the center, smoke swirling up from his tires xxxxxxxxx,

a black kid, maybe sixteen years old—a calm, indifferent expression on his face. There were other people there too, a few, on that corner. A black woman with her young son. She pulled him back into the church's doorway

★

Uh…went into Morocco…

M: What was the—in Lebanon—
what was the issue?

Well, the issue was uh the beginning of the Palestine situation with uh—with Israel…

'60s? Or was it earlier…

Yeah, it was earlier, but it wasn't that much earlier…it was '64, '65… uh…so……you'd get uh…you get a lot of planted information because—they were trying to outwit one another, you know, the Palestines—the Palestinians and the uh and the uh Israelis. The Israelis have always had the uh control over there uh…because they were good at it, they were part of the land…and they knew what they were doing. So…

M: Did you go out into the field and work
or did you stay in the—

*

—I stepped behind a parked car so if he lost control he wouldn't run me over.

I never took my eyes off the car, its tires screeching, engine wailing, in circles—

and the circles,

the thing about the circles is that they were perfect. Each time he finished one, each time he closed a loop and came around again, it looked like he might lose control, it always looked like he might lose control, the back end would swing out and the front tires would skip, it always seemed so

close to coming apart, he seemed so close to losing control—
but round
after round
he kept it together. And standing there, too, was an older black man, with a white/black beard, can of beer in his hand. He raised it aloft and cried out:

Go on boy! Blow off your steam!

⋆

No, we were mostly in the cities and towns and being able to pick up uh—

But you'd go around from town to town and see what you could hear?

Yeah, we'd travel, we'd travel…we'd do a lot of uh in-disguise type of surveillance…uh, we'd become part of the shadows—that's what we were—you know—what we were required to do!

⋆

Nothing fazed that kid as he blew off his steam. He did maybe five or six revolutions, maybe seven, then one Final Ring, larger than the rest, and finally: pulled out, straightened out, and sped away, in a cloud of smoke, down the street toward the dome of City Hall.

I stepped into the street and looked back from where he'd come. A bunch of kids a few blocks up were standing in the street, jumping up and down, cheering him on!

He took a loud left turn at the end of the block and disappeared.

Sirens.

The woman

and her child walked on. The older guy did the same. So did I. Or the time—how about this—

Another day I was walking that same street and a couple blocks farther up, a shiny white Lexus was stopped at the crosswalk, waiting for the light to change. And in it: two blond teenage girls sat bobbing their heads and singing and laughing along to the rap music booming from their stereo. Their windows were rolled down, the music echoed down the street. There weren't any other cars around. But up ahead, two young black males were jogging down the sidewalk in their direction, bouncing around and punching each other, playfully. The girls were so caught up in the music that they didn't see the two black kids, so they didn't see that they had stopped jogging, whispered to each other, then split up.

The taller

one walked into the crosswalk in front of the girls' car—the girls stopped singing, stopped bobbing, and watched him, sort of curiously—

while

his friend ducking low crossed behind the car, and came skulking around the driver's side, very low…

he crept up to her window without being

seen—by anyone but me—

the girls transfixed on the one in front—he

gave them a big smile and wiggled his fingers hello—and the girls smiled back and giggled—

Rap music.

When without warning the one below

the driver's door jumped up!

put his hand in through the open window,

the hand in the shape of a gun,

placed his finger against the girl's temple,

pulled the trigger

and yelled:

POP-POP!

★

You were doing spy work…

Yeah, it was a combination and all—and mind you, we had very little training…very little training—

★

The girl closed her eyes and screamed—an awful scream, terrorized—and you would never want to hear that scream again—and she punched down on the horn, BAAAAAAAAAAAAAAASCREAMING!!!! eyes closed head low ducked down bracing for the bullet —

and

although the gunman and his friend were already half a block away now—had already passed me, in fact, laughing and playing and carrying on, just as they'd been doing before

THE GIRL STILL SAT THERE SCREAMING! HER EYES STILL CLOSED HER HORN STILL GOING AAAAAAAAAAAAAAAAAAAAAAAAAAAAAAAAAAAAAAAAAAAAAAAAAAAAAAAAAAAAAAAAAAAAAAAAAAAAAAAAAAAAAAAAAAAAAAAAAAAAAAAAAAAAAAAAAAAAAAAAAA

★

You've done some interesting stuff.

Yeah I—I hope I did. But uh it was good stuff.

★

Finally she opened her eyes and stopped screaming—she let off the horn and now, gasping and weeping, lurched the car forward in an attempt to escape, but she didn't remember how to work the pedals anymore;

and so she stalled out in the middle

★

of the intersection.

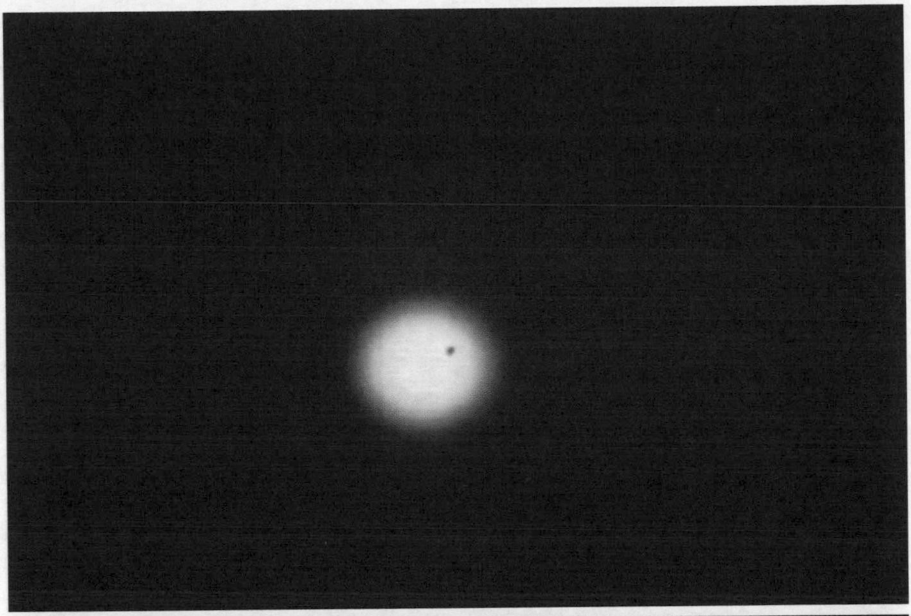

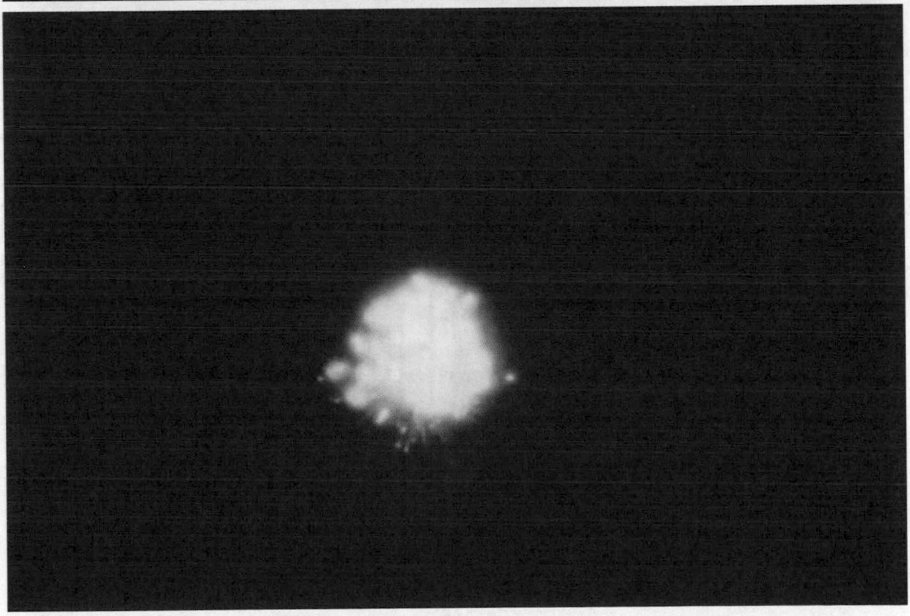

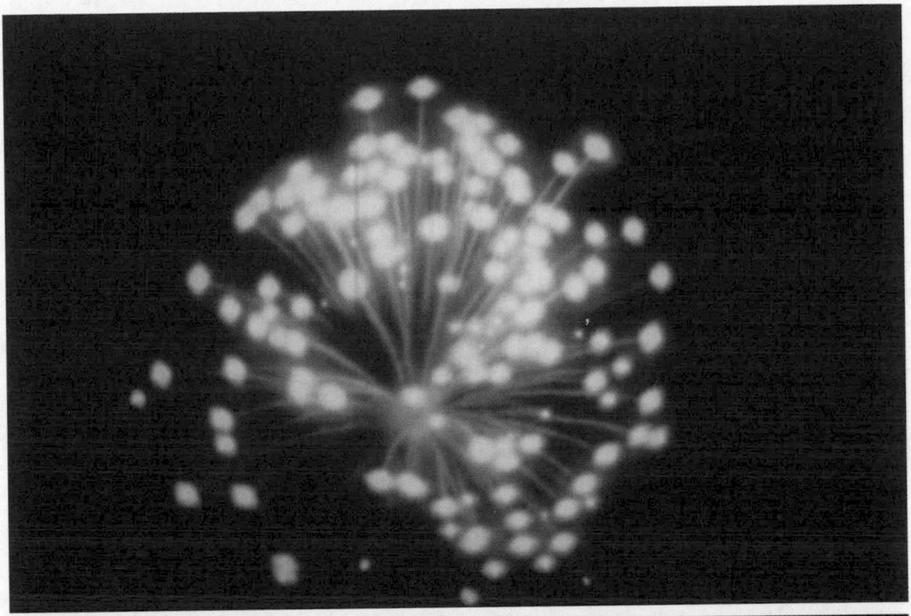

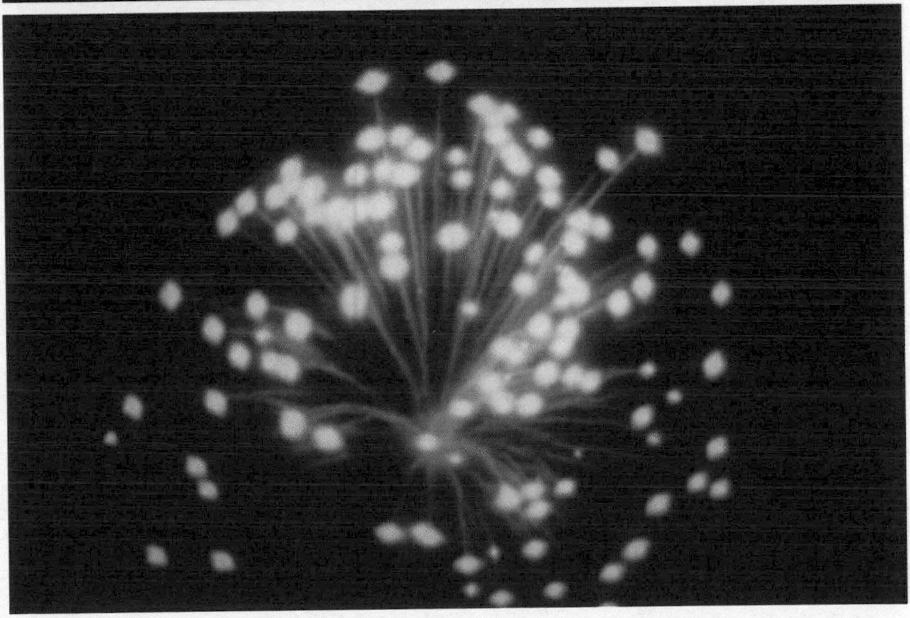

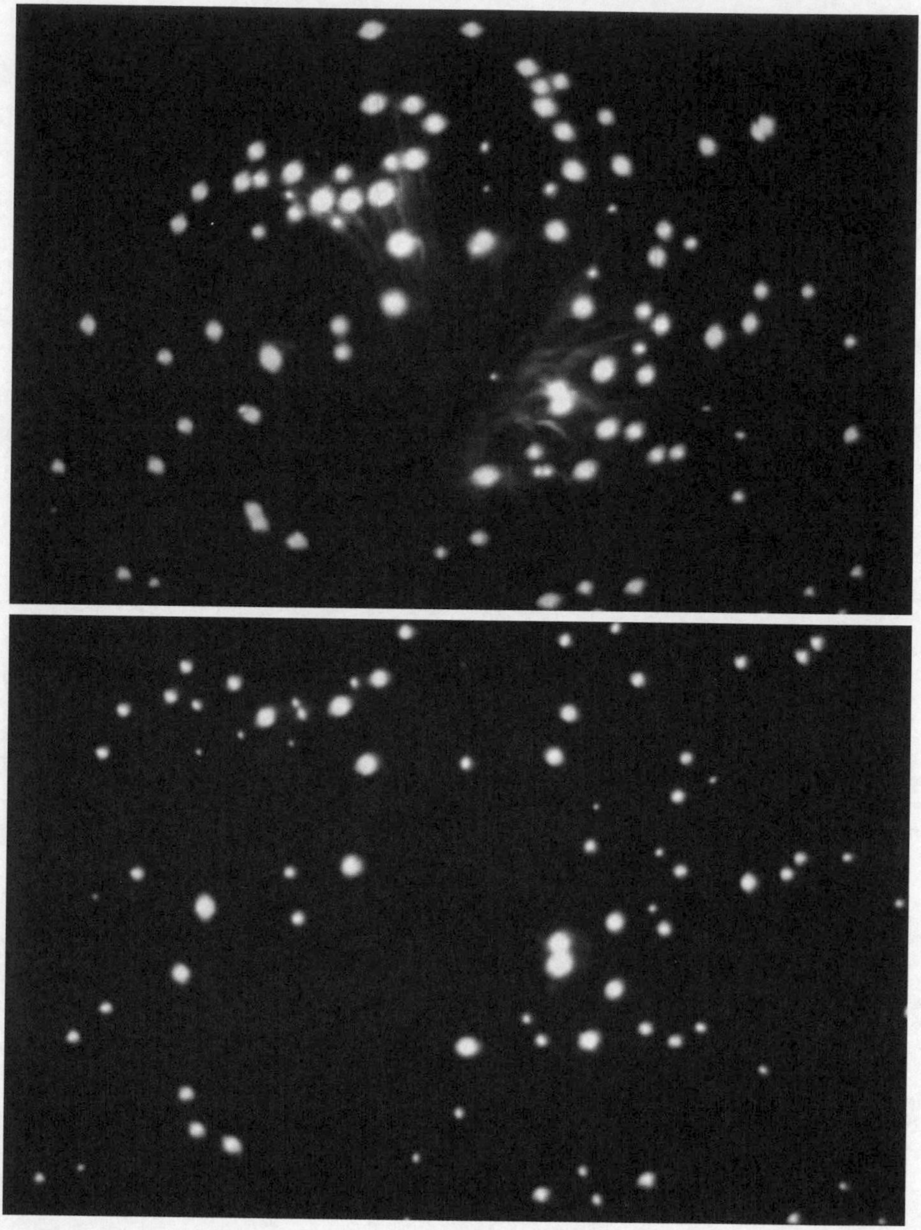

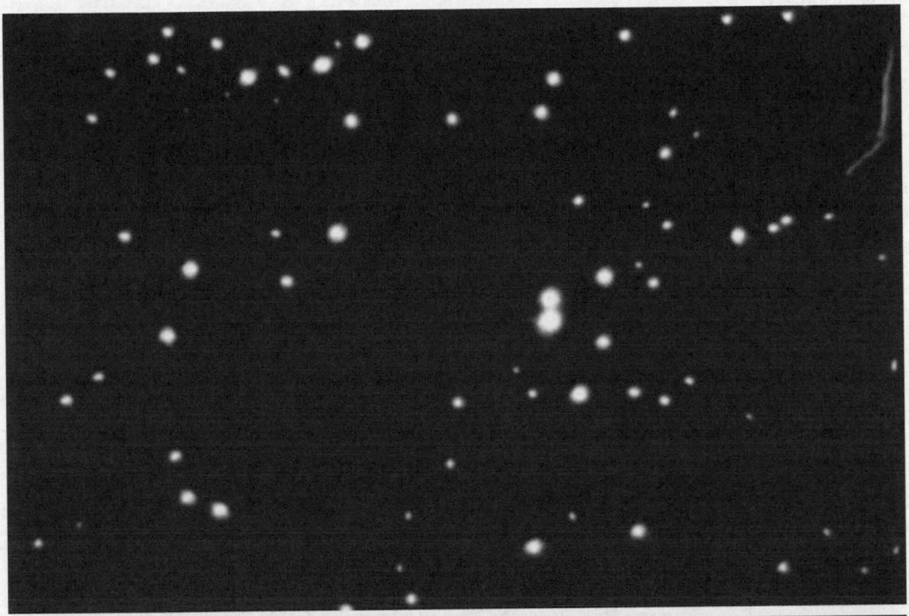

(revolution.avi)

W: Message for the world, Independence Day, famous author...... Matthew McIntosh......on the eve of......his release...

M: I just wanted to say that...I think everyone should just love each other and get along...and no more war...and...no more bloodshed and heartache...just love...everyone just hold hands...everyone just hold hands in a circle and play the drums in a little drum circle...

W: I'll hold your hand, baby.

M: Will you? It only takes two! It only takes two and then the world will come around!

[*sounds of man kissing his wife's arm up and down*]

★

But get-getting back to that castle...uh...Huge. I'd had no idea how huge it was until I started walking around the grounds! And—within the—the blinds of the—of the cellar—and uh overground......uh, it was like a little miniature city, wrapped around a city...uh?

★

M: Or......Plan B...Which would be to...fashion some sort of device that might actually...blow up the entire world?

★

ONCE,..............................

in Seattle, when I was a young man, outside of the St. John Apartments where I lived, Our Lady of the Sweatpants tried to rip my legs off, as I attempted, like a model citizen, to help her out of the gutter, into which I had assumed she'd fallen.

Only, instead of using my outstretched hand to raise herself up, she grabbed ahold of my legs with both arms and tried to pull me down with her. I said: Hey. Hey! Fuckin'—*Hey! LET GO!*

⋆

If we could come into enough tons of plutonium we could start with one city and then work our way… We'll start in the north, northwest… then go from Seattle down to Portland…

⋆

W: Uh-huh. Let's continue our tour of the back yard. This is where we used to live. It's a very dark…back yard.

M: Maybe we should start with LA…

W: Plastic chair, perhaps visible, perhaps not…

M: …We need some sort of……device…

W: …A little dark out here right now. Independence Day, 2003. A box in the distance. Another box and here we have a bush… lovely. A not-oft-used hibachi.

M: Show where the cat lives.

W: Uh…the cat likes to live up there. The cats are afraid of the… gunshots or…perhaps fireworks that we're hearing.

M: The revolution is going on all around us. We are in…uh…zero hour. You can hear the gunshots all around San Francisco; I'm reporting live—

⋆

So…it was…we had a lot of fun, we had a lot of fun—

⋆

W: We'll continue our tour of…this fine establishment we used to live in.

M: We bought this camera yesterday…it came in the mail.

W: Well, yesterday many years ago.

M: Right.

W: When we were poor.

M: When we were poor when we—

W: I think we should go record evidence of tuna melts: eaten.

M: How much time do we have le

⋆

And when I was a kid, I used to get out of bed late at night, jump from my window, catch a bus into the city, wander the streets with my school pack on my back and a pad of paper and a pen inside, seeking adventure. I'd travel around with the people we'd meet.

★

A lot of a lot of individuals that uh opened their mouths at the wrong time and uh…
they uh…
wound up uh…
being sent back…
but there was……
there was uh………
you know they'd…
they'd come back and uh—
and say something out of turn and you'd have to report him right away—
and he was within 24 hours shipped back to the States.

M: What did he say?

Well, little things you know—he'd uh—recently come back from a from a mission and uh—you know—the human mind is uh is tricky, and uh…if something bothers you…psychologically…it stays with you quite a while…So…
he come back,
make his report…
go out with his family
or go out whatever he was doin recreationally,
and uh…all of a sudden you find him—he'd had an extra few drinks, and he's in the bar, and he's talkin to a stranger, you know? Just talkin. Then you come find out half his conversation…is about the mission!

See? So…which was strictly a no-no…and………we'd lose uh…we lost some uh…out in the field…we lost some as they come back and talked out of turn…

★

I bought a homeless guy a cheeseburger and we sat in a booth together and he took off his cowboy hat and placed it on my head. Once upon a time, ███████████████████████████, a little boy ran out from the wet palm trees, which dripped with warm rain, and as he ate his burger he swore the boy had had a gun—or at least appeared to have had—so he riddled the little body with bullets and the blood splattered upon the mud, and spilled out from the holes when the boy fell onto his back, and when he had fallen onto his back his eyes looked up at the orange sky through the dark dripping canopy, and the rain dripped from the palm fronds and fell upon the boy's brown face, and from his hand rolled a round piece of fruit, rolled into the mud, rolled through a mudpuddle, and down a path, which wound down a hill, and rolled off a bank and into a river. The marble spiraled down, down, down the spiraling chute. The man was barely older than me then, just a boy, himself, he said, and the boy he had killed was just my age, he was sure, right down to the day, the hour, right down to the minute, the second, you see the parts of all those particles have been compressed condensed and coalesced into one tiny little speck one tiny little mote of matter and with a very delicate instrument the Surgeon placed it in the center of the face of a clock that has no hands just to torture me he said you can keep the hat. I gave it back.

★

Uh……but you had to use uh a lot of discretion—a lot of discretion—and that's what I liked about it, because…you keep pounding, you know, that situation to them—and say uh, Be careful how you talk, be careful how you—who you speak with…ah…but don't stop being friendly…

⋆

I followed two men up a hill but I don't remember where we were going, or how we had come together. They were dressed in fatigues and carrying packs, on their way out of town. I think they were going to jump the trains and travel east to New York City. And find a boat to India. We parted too, and I continued up the hill on foot.

I fell asleep in a bumper car, in the amusement park, at what they called the Center, in the City of Seattle, in the State of Washington, the United States of America. I walked into the porno shops and flipped through the magazines. I drank wine with the swollen-faced Indians. They said: Hey-o, Pilgrim! Two men in business suits late one night they asked me if I was working. A man—a creature with a scabby red face and thick glasses a small man a dwarf a shrunken fetal monster a broken troll in a wheelchair he rolled up to my knees by kicking his feet out along the sidewalk and pulling himself along by his heels he had no arms no his hands came right out of his shoulders his fingers fluttered—they really did, I swear—begged to sit upon my lap.

⋆

⋆

And it took an art,

⋆

★

it took an art

★

to do

★

that…

★

uh, to be able to uh, talk somebody straight, and uh, you know you, you always go around the other way and say, you know, I don't know anything about that or uh I'm not in that or, but uh……

★

Pleathe, he begged. Pleathe…Pleathe, he begged. Pleathe…Pleathe, he begged. Pleathe…Pleathe, he begged. Pleathe…Pleathe, he begged. Pleathe…

and then began to weep. I fell asleep beneath an orange sky on top of a polished marble table outside the Westlake Shopping Mall and some skaters woke me up, leaping over, leaping over, like flying fish.

I found a note, a tiny slip of paper, pressed into the street, and in the center of it was my name…I put it on my tongue and was told to look up, I looked up, as a plane was arcing over my head, flapping its wings against that blacksky so beautifully, its lights dripppppped redddddd and whiiiiiiite and blaaaaaaaaaaaaaaaack, and sighing, crying, said: Hey! Are you Jeeeeeeeesuuuuuuuuuuuuuussssss yet? I stretched……and fell asleep.* And when I woke I was on a bus, and there were people in suits all around, clutching tight the briefcases and purses on their laps. I fell asleep in a bumper car. I fell asleep beneath a tree. I fell asleep in the enormous auditorium of the old UA 150 discount movie theater, it was always nearly empty late at night…………… a curtain parted before the movie began, and in the few moments before the first frame flipped on you saw the field of white we once knew, before we came to life. (And how did we end up here anyway?)

★

* When are you coming baaaaaaaaaaaaaaack?

Just took a lot of training.

M: What did you learn about…about people from doing that sort of work?

I found a lot of people…

would release…

innocent information…

that they thought was innocent,

and you picked up the

vital…signs…

Uh, I found that uh it's easier to talk to somebody…and walk away with the information, than it would be to argue…the point. Uh…because you're not there—like—we said—

you're not there to analyze it—

you're there to report it…

get the information uh

and and then just—

whatever it was—

★

KETTLE FALLS

★

get it down on paper.

★

[redacted] [redacted] 8/05/93

S: Patient says he sustained a head injury on Tuesday. He was seen by PA [redacted] who obtained an x-ray of the patient's nose and no fractures were seen. It was judged that he had a nasal contusion and he was given ice, rest, and Tylenol, and head injury instructions. Since that time he has felt "kind of spacey" and has felt somewhat difficult to concentrate. Oftentimes he has to think about what he is going to say in order to get the words to come correctly but he does not speak jibberish or saying anything that is "off the wall." His speech is not garbled either. He is having headache in the entire head area, both frontal and occipital as well as coronal and temporal. He denies any numbness, tingling, paralysis, or paresthesias. He denies any visual changes. He denies any rhinorrhea from either nostril. He is not having excessive drowsiness and he is not having any difficulty waking up.

★

[redacted] [redacted] 8/25/93

S: Patient says he is having continued headaches since he had the head accident. He has been taking 600mg of ibuprofen anywhere from 2-3 times a day and says it is not really helping much. He denies any numbness, tingling, or paresthesias. He denies any blurry vision or change in hearing. He denies any neurological sx, such as paralysis or decreased function of a limb or other bodily part. He says that he has had more episodes where he has felt "spacy" and his spatial relationships for a little while seemed to be "off" in that occasionally he would rise up—like from lying to sitting—and strike his head on the bunkbed above. At no time did he hit his head very hard, however.

★

[redacted] [redacted] 10/04/93

S: The patient apparently jumped into a swimming pool in early August and hit his head and nose on the pool. He has seen Dr. [redacted] for this and did not sustain loss of consciousness but since then has had a headache. Apparently he was advised to call in if some of his original symptoms came back and today he felt spacey at school and so called in and received an urgent care appointment. He feels like he is not hearing people talk but he really couldn't be very specific about his symptoms. He also felt he was walking funny at school but his gait appears normal at this time. His headache is posterior. It occurs daily any time of the day. His vision was also blurred today but he is also wearing contacts. According to his mother, he is complaining of headaches every day. He really didn't want to come in. He is a good student, not using drugs and not trying to get out of school.

★

[redacted] [redacted] 7/25/94

SUBJECTIVE: This patient comes back for check back on his headaches. He says they have gotten much worse since he was last here. When he was here before on the week prior to my seeing him, his headaches were ranging between 4 and 5 with an occasional 6. Right after he saw me they immediately went up to a 7 and a 7&1/2 for several days in a row and then they gradually dropped back to a 6 and 6&1/2. He also fell on Monday after having seen me but says that he did not hit his head. In discussing his pain at great length with him, he is extremely fidgety again and unable to concentrate. He is quite unhappy. Some of his anger spilled out in his responses to my questioning (I tried to be as gentle as I could with him).

*

[redacted] [redacted] 8/09/94

SUBJECTIVE: The patient is an 18-year-old who is here today for follow-up as he was seen in the hospital at Tacoma General Saturday evening with a severe headache. He has had severe chronic headaches for a long time. On Saturday evening he emotionally lost it, as he states. His legs became weak and his arms became weak. He has been on [redacted] 100mg p.o. q.h.s., [redacted] 60mg t.i.d., and [redacted] for his headaches. The Midrin has been working, but he is taking approximately six a day and it has lost its efficacy for him. Now he feels the same as ever. His headaches are always there and chronic and rather severe. He was out of school one or two months early this past spring and then has not been in school this summer so these are debilitating for him. He graduated two months early. These headaches began after a diving accident approximately one year ago and then he also had an MVA and the headaches have persisted. Right now the family states, in mother's words, we are just checking up because they told us to and we want to do everything that they say correctly. He was told to follow-up with primary care doctor on Wednesday in Tacoma General ER.

★

And a few short years later, when I was living in a shoebox in the city, I would get very high and stumble down the hill, pay the dollar and sit there in those ripped-up cushionless seats, eyes closed and floating in the warmth of my watery skin...............the curtains closed when the movie was over, and the usher would wake you, and tell you to move along.

★

The patient also cried at a couple of points during the interview and looked fairly depressed.

★

But when I was a kid, I used to wait until everyone was asleep, I would hang by my fingers from my windowsill, look down, take a deep breath, and let go:::and when I woke I had crossed a cement path which split a useless, brightly lit decorative pond —M: Where was I then? Where on earth were you? :W—

*

I had crossed to the other side. I looked up. There was no dome then, just red sky and a handful of stars:::

:::and a universe with no end.

This was before I got hurt and the Period of Great Pain began. I didn't know about PAIN then. I didn't have the Slightest Notion. No, the world was WIDE and OPEN, and—

[redacted]

AUG 03 1993 BP: 130/72 L arm
Hit nose when diving into shallow
end of pool this pm
pt alert — feels "woozy"
Ice, rest
Head injury instruction

CHAPTER FOUR

Giving a report. Why did that stick out to me like a sore thumb, like a plastic flamingo in a vegetable garden, like a piano in a room full of harpsichords? Giving a report. I have half a mind to type those three words over and over again, making the font size smaller each time as if to suggest the thought recurring while echoing away. But I will refrain from typographic tricks.

Olive was dead. Eva was at work. Giving a report.

The hospital was outside of town down a barren two-lane highway. I walked down a narrow rocky shoulder in the direction I'd come from. To each side spread fields of nothing. Well, hay. Which is as good as nothing. The sun was hot above me. I was sweating. I took a stick of gum from out of my shorts and chewed it. Now and then a car went by. I probably looked like a bum or an escapee. So imagine my surprise when a pretty girl came passing by in a little Korean two-door, honked her horn, and pulled over to the side. Then stepped out of the car and called back to me:

"Daniel?"

"Yes?"

"What are you doing all the way out here?"

I looked around. The highway was empty. "Walking?"

"Are you headed back to town?"

"Yes."

"Well, do you want a ride?"

"Sure."

"I need to make a quick stop a little further out, but then I can take you back."

It was cool and air-conditioned in the car. I sat in the passenger seat and tried to look out at the flat yellow scenery and not at the girl's tanned legs in her extremely short shorts. Or pay attention to the way the strap of her bra snuck out from beneath her tank top and gleamed against her brown shoulder.

"I know the car's a mess," she said. "I'm not usually this disorganized."

The back seat was filled with books and papers and clothing and assorted junk. I'd had to remove a *Modern Student's Bible* from the seat before I sat down.

We passed the tended green hospital grounds and kept going.

"What were you doing all the way out here?" she asked.

"Visiting a friend."

She laughed. Then looked over at me. "Oh, sorry. I didn't know you had any friends."

"Well, an elderly neighbor."

"Oh."

She drove with her hands at ten and two. She had long brown hair pulled back in a ponytail. Dark eyes and nice dark eyebrows. Shiny pink lip-glossed lips. She was wearing rainbow-colored flip-flops. Her toenails and her fingernails matched, pink. A thin gold cross hung down just over her tank top. From the rearview mirror hung a little medallion. It said:

For God so loved the world...etc. etc. etc.

I picked up a piece of paper by my foot. It was a report card.

Name: Candice Johnson. Candice had a 4.0 average.

"Nice grades," I said.

She glanced over at me strangely.

"Thanks."

It was quiet for a little while.

"I'm off to college tomorrow," she said. "My dad's driving me."

"Oh, yeah?"

"Tomorrow morning. Classes start Monday."

"Well, congratulations," I said. "That should be fun. Do you know what you're going to major in yet?"

Candice sighed. She seemed almost irritated. "No. I don't know what I'm going to major in yet."

We drove along in silence. I looked out my window. Mile markers went by, every so often a dirt driveway, a deer crossing sign. It was all the same and nothing much, like the background in a Road Runner cartoon, the way it cycles over and over again as the coyote gives chase—it's all the same dirt driveway, the same cloud over the same field, the same deer crossing sign. Road Runner cartoons, it occurred to me, are boring. And I was thinking about that when I heard the sound of crying coming from the seat next to mine. I turned to young Candice and as I did she wiped a tear from her eye, an action which only caused more tears to fall. The same effect played out every time she wiped her eyes, and soon she was crying hard. Why all the crying today? There was something in the air.

I wasn't sure what I was supposed to do. After all, this girl was a total stranger, not to mention half my age. And though I didn't know myself from Adam, from what I'd learned thus far I seemed to be the kind of person who probably had very little in common with teenagers, and while they say that all young people really want is just someone who'll listen to them, I was pretty confident that I would rather do just about anything than listen to a teenager tell me her problems. It seemed that my advice would always be the same: *You think you've got problems now, just wait until you're older.* And besides, who was this girl?

Who was Candice? How did we know each other? I probably knew her parents somehow—though probably not as friends, judging by the fact that she told me she thought I didn't have any friends. Certainly she was no relative, for I was pretty certain I had no relatives in Spokane, Washington. It was conceivable that she was nervous about going to college, but judging from her grades and medallion she was a pretty together kid, so I didn't think it was leaving home that was breaking her down. Probably it was something over a boy—some football-playing meathead that she was too good and smart for. He'd probably told her all summer that they would always be together and then now that they were going off to different colleges he realized he wanted to leave his options open. Besides, he'd seen enough movies to know that the reason you go to college is to get laid and he certainly wasn't getting any tail off of a girl with a For God so loved the world medallion. So he'd told her, probably just this morning, that he wanted to break up. All this went through my head at the speed of light. Finally, I knew I had to say something, because the more time that passed the more she cried, and the more she cried the harder she cried, and it was getting extremely awkward to be sitting there without saying anything. Not to mention it was a narrow road, and every time she took a hand off the wheel to wipe her eyes she swerved into the oncoming lane.

"Something wrong?" I said.

"Everything's fine," she said.

I reached into my pocket and produced the wadded-up handkerchief I remembered was there.

She wiped her eyes and nose with it. Then she said, "Sorry," and tried to smile.

"No need to apologize," I said. "Starting college is a pretty stressful time. But with your grades, I really don't think you'll have any problems."

She laughed with a tinge of bitterness. "I'm not worried about that," she said.

"Well," I said, "it's none of my business and I'm not really good with advice anyway, but if it's a boy, then, well, you'll find a better one. You should just be glad that you found out now what kind of lowlife he is instead of later when you paid a surprise visit to his dorm room only to find him swapping spit with some cheap blond floozy."

She looked at me like I was an alien, and then rolled her eyes and turned back to the road.

It occurred to me that I had been right.

I was no good with teenagers.

She was nice to look at with her face all red and my hankie flattened and draped over her shiny brown thigh. It was nice to look at but I turned once more to the world outside.

My phone rang. It was "my wife."

I smiled at young Candice and put a finger to my lips. Then pressed the talk button and said:

"Hi."

"Hi, babe. Feeling better?"

"Feeling great."

"Not so achy?"

"Just my head now. I seem to be getting better as the day goes on. I've stopped yawning."

"Yawning?"

"Nevermind."

"What did you do with that cat?" she asked.

"I put it in a bag and put the bag in the trash."

"So it's just laying there in our trash can?"

"Yes."

"Gross. Well, at least trash day's tomorrow. So what are you up to?" she said. "Are you working?"

"You mean writing?"

"Yeah."

I looked out the window.

"No, I thought I'd take the day off. No writing, no paint scraping."

"Are you in a car?"

"A car?"

"You sound like you're in a car."

"No, it's the TV."

"We don't have a TV."

"We don't have a TV? I thought everyone has a TV. Wait. Am I still in America?"

"You're in quite a jokey mood today, aren't you?"

"Yes. I'm in a jokey mood today. And yes, I am in a car. Well, a bus."

"What are you doing on a bus? Where are you going?"

"I just thought I'd get on a bus and ride around. See Spokane."

"Babe, are you feeling OK? Should I come and get you?"

"No, it's just I wanted to get out of the house. I'm fine. I think I'll just wander a bit today."

"Well, OK. But everything is all right, isn't it?"

"What wouldn't be?" I asked.

"What wouldn't be all right?"

"Yes. If something wasn't all right, what would it be?"

She paused. "Well, I don't know. Everything's always all right."

It was quiet for a while after I hung up and then Candice said, "That was Eva?"

"Yes." *Ah-ha,* I thought. So she knew Eva. "You know something, I can't remember how it was we all met."

"You're acting weird."

I considered using the trick I'd used with Gladys—telling her I was doing an exercise in which I pretended I had lost my memory—but I didn't think that would work. It is a rule of thumb that what works on eighty-year-olds rarely works on eighteen-year-olds and vice versa. Luckily, she helped me out by saying, "My mom and Eva are friends. I mean, they've worked together for, like, I don't even know how many years."

"Right," I said with a big sigh of relief. This girl's mother and my wife were colleagues and friends. Eva and I probably went over to their house for barbecues or something. Thank God. Finally I had placed a big piece of the puzzle. And just in time. The mood had been getting a little strange. "Your dad like to barbecue, does he?" I said.

She just snorted and rolled her eyes again.

We arrived at our destination. A midsized farmhouse about a quarter mile off the road, in the middle of the fields, skinny trees grown tall to completely hide it from the highway. Once it would have been called charming, but now it was barely a step above dilapidated. Peeling paint, roof covered with moss and old dry leaves; a few broken windows, a few boarded up. A faded, weathered flag hanging from the eaves. It seemed an odd place for a young Christian girl to be visiting, but I assumed she was there to see an elderly or enfeebled person from her church—some old farmer or farmer's widow who could no longer make the journey into town each Sunday, so Candice came to minister to him/her, and possibly deliver some item.

"I need to see somebody," she said. "You can stay in the car or come in, whatever you want." She looked at me for a second, as if expecting me to say something, and when I didn't she shook her head and got out.

I got out too and followed her up the rickety front steps. The truth is I would have liked to have had a pair of dark sunglasses, for I would have enjoyed watching her rear end in her tight shorts as she walked up those steps. But I kept my eyes off of her in case anyone was at the window watching. I looked around at the fenced-off area of dirt that had once more than likely been a front lawn.

The screen door had been kicked in at the bottom. Candice rung the doorbell, and called down the hall, "Hello?"

When an occupant finally emerged it wasn't an old man or an old woman—and it wasn't someone needing—or at least expecting—the Good News. It was a shirtless, bearded twentysomething hippie layabout carrying a golf club like a walking stick and a drink in a tall plastic cup.

"Candy!" He met her halfway down the hall and gave her a long, lingering hug, the hand that wasn't carrying a drink running up and down her eighteen-year-old back. He did this while sizing me up. I sized him up back. "Who's this?" he said.

"He's the writer."

I smiled.

"Oh," the guy said, in a not-too-friendly manner. "Well, come on back. We're hitting golf balls."

Whether it had been the medallion hanging from the mirror, the cross around the neck, the *Modern Student's Bible* on the seat, the fish on the bumper of the little Korean car, or all of these things put together—it seemed that I had pegged young Candy all wrong. She was not the innocent Christian schoolgirl I had thought she was. And as she went from lowlife to lowlife, hugging each one and kissing a few, and accepting a tall drink of her own from a heavily pierced—and heavily heavy—woman with the word MOM tattooed in Gothic letters across her neck—MOM took Candy by the hand and spun her around like the girl was her dance partner—I wondered to myself not only what was I doing here, but how had I gotten here? Wasn't it only a couple hours ago that I was enjoying a peaceful smoke session with Charles, the drain snaker, in the comfort of my own home—or the comfort of the home that I was supposed to think was my own?

There were about twelve or fifteen people there—miscreants all—all but a few appeared to be in their twenties or thirties—some were older, none but Candice younger—all in a combination state of drunken highness—dirty, sweaty, hairy, red from the sun. There was a man at a grill cooking up meat; classic rock playing from a boom box; some were dancing, some were sitting, some were leaning, some were tipping, some were hitting golf balls into the fields which rolled in like golden waves from the horizon and terminated with a slight hiccup at the back patio, a large cement slab with grass growing out of a giant web of cracks. There was a hot tub and an aboveground pool, and a few sets of very bourgeois (translated: *stolen*) patio furniture. To the side by some old overgrown apple trees is where the motorcycles were parked.

I stood by the corner of the house, watching Candice as she went around the party, joking with everyone and laughing and accepting what looked like good-natured ribbing about her approaching college trip. She seemed very much in her element, and when she accepted a joint and a piggyback ride from a dwarfish-looking man with a pierced penis, I knew that whatever happened from here on out it would probably be best not to mention any of this to my wife—or to the woman pretending to be my wife, whatever the truth actually was.

I picked up from bits of conversation that they were all staying at the house together and that they'd been drinking, barbecuing, and hitting golf balls for most of the week.

"So you're the writer."

MOM had snuck up on me. She was somewhere in her late thirties, her reddish-brown hair streaked with gray, tiny wrinkles under her eyes, her chubby yet pretty face pink and wet from the heat. She wore more clothes than anyone—a baggy tank top with an ankle-length skirt, purple, pleated.

"We've heard a lot about you," she said.

I asked her to tell me what she'd heard.

"We've heard that you live in town, that you have a drop-dead gorgeous wife who works with Candy's mom. That you wrote a book about a decade ago that was praised but quickly forgotten. That you don't talk to your agent or publisher or anyone who ever knew you, and that you dropped out of society and ran off to the boonies to write mankind's next immortal masterpiece. The next *Divine Comedy* or *Aeneid* or *Moby-Dick* or *Thousand and One Nights*. Don't let appearances fool you…" She tilted her drink back and took a big swig, then said with a mouth full of ice cubes: "I've got an English degree."

"Candice told you all that about me?"

"I hope she didn't blow your cover."

"Did she tell you anything else?"

MOM squinted into the sun, sizing me up. "She said that you came to talk to her class about your book."

Candy was being lifted into the air by a scary-looking fellow the size of a grizzly. He had a bushy beard, huge barrel chest, hairy shoulders, hard round head—the kind of head you look at and think the skull must be at least twice as thick as your own. Like a wrench would probably bounce right off.

"Seems odd that I would agree to go talk to her class if I'm the kind of person who keeps to himself."

"She said her mom asked you to do it. She needed the extra credit to keep her 4.0."

"That was nice of me."

The grizzly put her down and another grizzly picked her up. They appeared to be twins. Candice let out a happy scream. MOM watched as they passed her back and forth.

"We all just love Candy," she said. "We think she's gonna go places."

"Candice can do whatever she puts her mind to," I said. At one of the tables a girl in a bikini and a man in a towel were snorting up lines of cocaine. "As long as she keeps her nose clean."

"That's what I've been telling her," said MOM.

"How did you meet?" I said.

"Through Pop."

"Through Pop. And which one is Pop?"

"Pop's not here. Pop's out."

"Pop's out," I said. "And what's Pop's story?"

"She didn't tell you about Pop?"

"She might have. I've got a bad memory."

"Pop's mysterious. He'd make a good character in a story."

"Is this his house?"

"No. This house is abandoned. We're just staying here until we're asked to leave."

"What's so mysterious about Pop?"

The question was not answered because Candice had left her friends and come over to whisper something in MOM's ear. MOM looked at me and smiled and planted a big kiss right on Candice's cheek. Who then asked me if I could help her with something.

I followed her back through the house and out to the front.

"Interesting group," I said.

"You think?"

She opened the trunk of her car. There was an old red suitcase inside, locked with three separate padlocks.

"What's this?" I said.

"It's heavy. Can you carry it in for me?"

"Can I carry a padlocked suitcase from your car into an abandoned farmhouse full of obvious criminals?"

"Yeah."

"Did you ever come across a term in school called *being an accessory?"* I said.

She just stared at me with her arms crossed. I noticed she didn't wear earrings or any jewelry except for the cross which now gleamed brightly in the sun.

"Now Candice," I said. "You know me. I'll do anything I can to help you—I always have and I always will—and you know it's true because I came to speak to your English class even though I'm practically a shut-in and to be perfectly honest there's nothing I can imagine liking to do less than talking to a room full of teenagers. But your mother came to me and said, Candice really needs that 4.0, and I said, Sure, whatever I can do I'll do. But in our current situation I just think it would be setting a *really bad example* if I were to help you accomplish whatever strange endeavor it is you've got going on. I don't know who these people are, or how a nice girl like you has come to be associated with them—I don't like them, to tell you the truth—I've been around longer than you and I can tell you that these people are up to no good. Sitting around drinking and doing drugs and hitting golf balls might sound like paradise to an eighteen-year-old like you, but these people are a lot older than you—certainly too old to be carrying on the way they're carrying on. Now, I don't have a very good feeling about this MOM character—something about her doesn't sit well with me—it's not her piercings or her tattoos, or anything like that, it's just I don't think she's a good role model. And this Pop, whoever he is, I've got an even worse feeling about him. And I don't know how much advice I've given you over the years—maybe I've tutored you in English, or helped you with your writing—but as an adult figure, and as someone who knows your parents, I think it is my responsibility to tell you that you really shouldn't be hanging out with lowlifes like these. I know at your age they probably seem exciting and authentic—and you've spent your life going to church camps and always being told a girl has to stay pure and do the right thing and all that—and you've probably seen a lot of hypocrisy in your home life—maybe your parents talk the talk but don't walk the walk—that's pretty common—and these people probably appeal to you because you look at them and you think what you see is what you get. And maybe you get a sense of belonging and camaraderie from them that you haven't found before—maybe you haven't had an easy time making friends in school—perhaps because the other girls are jealous of your looks and good grades—and maybe the fact that you brought a real live writer to school just made it worse for you because they only got more jealous, I don't know—but I have to tell you that—and I know they may seem harmless—but my personal opinion is that there is something very dangerous about this group. And I'm not just talking about tattoos—every frat boy and youth pastor and teenybop crooner is covered in them today—it has nothing to do with tattoos, believe me. And it doesn't have to do with motorcycles or beards or even penis piercings. It doesn't even have to do with the drugs or alcohol—lots of people do drugs and alcohol. But I just fear that you're young and impressionable and if you hang around with people like this you're going to end up getting into trouble you can't foresee and the fact of the matter is the choices we make today affect the future tomorrow and, well, I just worry you're going to become involved in something you'll wish you could take back later, that you're going to do something you'll one day come to regret."

While saying all of this I had lifted the suitcase out of the car, carried it across the dirt patch, back up the porch and inside the house, then up a dusty staircase and down a hallway, to a small bedroom at the top of the house that Candice led the way to. And I had barely set the suitcase on the bed saying "something you'll one day come to regret" when I heard the door close behind me, and I turned around.

Candice had taken off her tank top, and was stepping to me in her bra.

"God, you're so fuckin' *weird* today," she said, kissing me all over my mouth.

12 JUL 1996 21 JUL 1996 21 JUL 1996
21 JUL 1996 21 JUL 1996 21 JUL 1996
21 JUL 1996 21 JUL 1996 21 JUL 1996
21 JUL 1996

1. Two kids posing on Albion Rd., smiling.
2. Superlonghair flipping off camera.
3. " " " "
4. " " " "
5. " " " " "
6. " " " " "
7. " " " " " (Thank you Superlonghair)
8. Guy on bike.
9. Ange getting onto bus.
10. Ange going up stairs.
11. Matt on back seat.
12. Indian guy in doorway.
13. Girl in green dress approaching.
14. Indian and girl talking.
15. Ange & Matt on Oxford St. / HMV
16. ANGE WALKING INTO MCD TO TAKE A PEE.
17. She just disappeared around the corner.
18. Guy in white hat giving thumbs up in McD.
19. And then she came back with her arms above her head.
20. Matt writing #19.
21. Street sweeper won't smile but has to; dirty face.
22. Matt & Ange & guy with red tie, middle eastern who walked by
23. Matt & Ange in front of OLIVER: THE MUSICAL (photo credits by red tie man)

24. The Original Superlonghair in Hawaiin shirt with girlfriend (from behind them)
25. ANGE WALKING ACROSS CROSSING OUT THE FRONT OF LIBERTY'S OPENING A BEER TAKEN BY MATT
26. PUB ON CARNABY ST WHERE MATT GOT A JOB BUT DIDN'T TURN UP TAKEN BY MATT (SHAKESPEARES HEAD)
27. OLD PARATROOPER COLLECTING MONEY OFF PEOPLE OUTSIDE A PUB ON CARNABY ST BY MATT
28. PHOTO TAKEN BY GUY IN PINK SHIRT WITH BORING GIRLFRIEND OF MATT & ANGE IN FRONT OF SIGN SAYING WELCOME TO CARNABY ST.
29. JAPANESE COUPLE STEALING/REPAIRING MOPED ON BROADWICK ST SHE WORE RED PANTS AND HIS FACE WAS SERIOUS TAKEN BY MATT
30. PHOTO OF PAVEMENT BY MATT (OOOPPPSSS)
31. OPEN WINDOWS WITH POLE (LOOKING UP AT BUILDING FACE) BY MATT
32. SOHO CD STORE ABOVE WINDOW JUST SLIGHTLY OPEN BLACK & WHITE CAT WITH BLINDS (FROM WINDOW) PUSHING CAT'S EARS DOWN. CAT LOOKING STRAIGHT AT US BY ANGE
33. Man in deppressing and pale Hawaiin shirt peering through the doorway of porno shop wondering if this is the right place for tonight's big score.

34. Bouncer leaning up against LATEST POLE DANCING FROM THE US LIVE SHOW FULL NUDITY sign (But no one will go in because it costs 12.50)
35. PHOTO OF MATT OUTSIDE PORN STORE RED SIGN ABOVE SAYS "DREAMY LIPS" BY ANGE
36. 7 JAPANESE & ONE WHITE GUY CAME OUT OF A WALKERS PORN SHOP TAKEN BY MATT FROM HIS HIP BECAUSE OF "RECPECT"
37. <u>SWASHBUCKLER!!!!</u>
38. (PARTY PETE—For Craig)
39. PHOTO OF MATT IN FISH 'N CHIP SHOP WRITING IN THIS NOTEBOOK WITH SERIOUS FACE ABOUT THE ABOVE
40. MATT WITH A POLICEMAN OUTSIDE FISH 'N CHIP MATT'S EATING HIS CHIPS (HAPPY) POLICEMAN'S TALKING ABOUT CRIME IN THE STATES. HE WISHED US A HAPPY HOLIDAY. 9:25 PM SOHO
41. Ange is smiling below yellow JUICYFRUIT shirt hanging in window w/chips ("Move right, down a little, now left… right…OK!")
42. Matt and Ange in front off The Palace Theatre below LES MISERABLES sign, taken by friendly Asian family.
43. Jesus after too much acid with his friend. His shirt is off because he'd worked up an alcohol sweat coming off of his mat to nearly but not quite hit Matt.
44. A crowd waiting to buy pastries and cakes 9:40 CHINACITY

45. Canadian girls with matching hats making way through Leicester Square.
46. FLASHING LIGHTS FROM EMPIRE THE OLD ROSE SELLER WALKING STICK CROWDS WALKING PAST LOOKING BLURRED HE'S IN FOCUS JUST STARING WITH VACANT LOOK ON HIS FACE (LONG WHITE BEARD & WHITE HAIR)
47. Black man braiding girl's hair into one thin, long twine, cardboard square to her head with holes in it.
48. COUNCIL TURN UP TO STOP STREET SELLERS THEN ALL PACK UP (PHOTO OF A GUY WITH LONG HAIR PACKING HIS STUFF UP LOOKING STRAIGHT AT ME WITH WORRIED LOOK ON HIS FACE) ANGE LEICESTER SQUARE 9:55 PM
49. Black hand on white paper. An outlined face. Shaded mouth shaded eyes pale face
50. TOURIST SHOT OF MATT IN FRONT OF HORSE STATUE NEAR PICCADILLY BRASSERIE HE HAD SUCH A TOURIST "HURRY UP & TAKE THE PICTURE" LOOK ON HIS FACE. ONE TO SEND HOME TO MA & PA BY ANGE
51. Matt & Ange in front of Picadilly lights taken by three very tan Americans with annoying Jackal voices.
52. PHOTO OF LIGHTS 'FOSTERS' BLUE, 'TDK' GREEN, 'SANYO' WHITE ANG.
53. PHOTO OF A GIRL TAKING A PHOTO, PICCADILLY CIRCUS

KANSAS

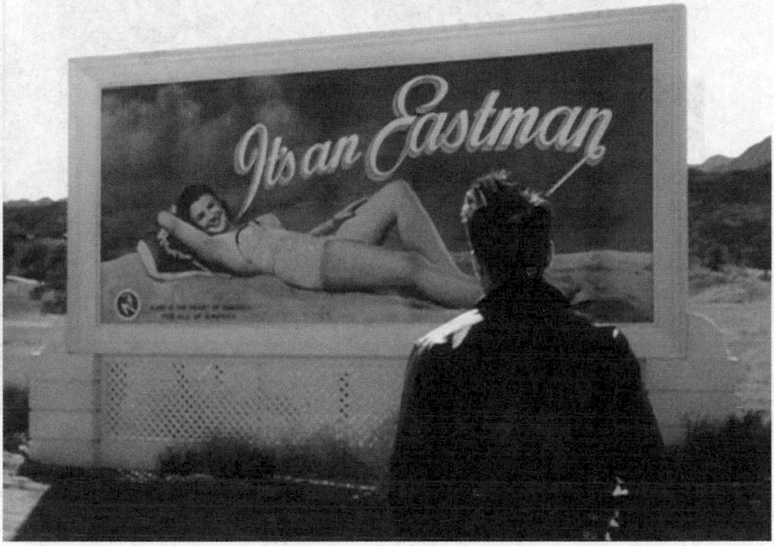

54. http://www.filmsite.org/plac.html

THE FILM BEGINS with superimposed titles on an opening long shot of a highway with a hitchhiker—a poor, uneducated, quiet, aimless but ambitious and aspiring young man, George Eastman (Montgomery Clift). He is thumbing his way to the home of his rich Uncle Charles Eastman (Herbert Heyes), who owns a bathing-suit manufacturing factory—advertised in a billboard sign of a reclining, dark-haired bathing beauty on the beach: "It's an Eastman." A shiny sports car with a beautiful socialite at the wheel drives past. She flirtatiously honks, and then continues zooming by in her convertible—symbolic of the world of the privileged passing him by. The two images of luxury, pleasure, freedom and leisure (on the billboard and in the fancy automobile) already fill George's mind and he hungers and craves everything the females and their lifestyles represent.

55. I lived in a narrow rundown old house on the north side of the river, on a street of narrow rundown old houses, all sharing walls as they do in that part of the world, with, at times, seventeen other people, all travelers, most of them from Australia, a few from South Africa and New Zealand. Me. And one Brit, a little neo-Nazi skinhead, a friend of the owner of the place. He sold coke for this friend, and lived for free in a room upstairs decorated with Nazi tapestries with his pregnant girlfriend, a woman in her early forties, ancient. He was in his late twenties, I think—though he seemed ancient himself—and once every few days we'd hear him up there beating her, shouting all sorts of names at her, things crashing, falling, breaking, and the sound of her screaming; but there was never anything that we could do. I, myself, was not in the proper shape to intervene—I'd just sit there watching TV, drinking cider from a glass; the ceiling shook when she'd hit the floor. Angie tried once. She said, I just can't sit here and listen to this anymore. She got off the couch, went upstairs, knocked on the door, and when he flung it open, eyes blazing, she said:

56. —Now mate, you just can't be hitting her now that she's pregnant. Come down and have a smoke with us…

57. The Nazi—I forget his name—was small in stature, but mighty in deed. I'd heard stories of him beating Pakistanis with bottles and pipes; blacks with bats and straight razors; queers with curling irons—the truth is I really don't remember—I find myself supplying false information to keep the story moving along. But I remember the veins that stuck out of his forehead, and the flames tattooed down his arms, which licked at his skull-ringed fingers. Swastikas dyed into his neck and chest. He'd walk around with his shirt off to remind us. I was scared shitless of him, but the two of them stayed out of sight most nights, and the truth is for some reason he liked me, and when he was cooking in the upstairs kitchen and I would walk in, he would always make me up a plate.

58. The prime feature of the house was the creaking carpeted stairway, straight on as you walked in the front door. It led up to five floors. On the ground floor were two bedrooms and the kitchen, the floor of which was down to dirt in spots. Bedrooms on the next level, then the TV room and bathroom on the next, then more bedrooms, then another bathroom and kitchen. From there you climbed a ladder into an attic filled with cots. This is where I had slept at the beginning, on a cot with deadly springs, beneath a skylight and the choked, foul, tumid London summer sky. Before long, I would move down into Angie's room on the ground floor, the best room in the house, where two curtained French doors, now painted shut, had once, in an earlier age, opened onto what must have been a garden.

59. Now littered with trash and leaves, and a few condoms dropped from the TV room window above.

60. Ange was twenty-five at the time, which would have made her 6 years older than me. She was from Oz, and worked at a car dealership answering the phones. I'd found a job through a temp agency at an insurance company, doing data entry. This was London, and in those days most of the populace hadn't touched a computer, so if you could type you'd find a job in a second. The office I worked in was in a newly purchased annex in a riverside warehouse park near Angel tube station, and there were only six of us yet in the entire building. The year was 1996. There were four other guys working there: one, Ian, a resident of the house (at home we called him Superlonghaired Ian), a slight, soft-spoken, malodorous fellow from Auckland, New Zealand, with a long blond ponytail; a black man from the West Indies with an upper-crust accent; and two college boys. We were led by a kindhearted middle-aged woman with a friendly fat face, and thick northern accent. Her name was

61. Carol.

62. I had only one shirt appropriate for a professional work environment, and I wore it every single day I worked that job, for six months—a white button-down dress shirt, along with a pair of baggy green corduroys. A tie was required, and I'd found one at a thrift store. I didn't know how to tie it, so Angie tied it for me the morning of the second day that I had known her, telling me: *I'm sorta the mother of the house, mate.* Each day when I got home, I'd loosen the knot, put up my collar, and slip the tie back over my head. And the next

morning, simply slip it back on again. I still have the tie. It was lost for many years, but I found it recently, buried in a box. Gray with red and black bands. I haven't worn it in eight years, but the knot has never been untied since the first time it was tied. Why don't I pull it on over my head right now—maybe it'll trigger a memory.

63. The woman behind the desk looks up at me and says, Oh! I didn't see you there…have you been waiting long? I say, It's OK, I don't have an appointment. I am only here to wait. I pick up a magazine, mostly ads for different styled pain killers, one that makes you smile no matter what, this one I see is for housewifes, and on the next page you can work a jackhammer all day and it's not a problem. I turn the magazine over to see what I am reading and it says, *Journal of Painful Ills*, from this last November, and a man with a white beard on the cover. The woman behind the desk has started filing her nails down. I feel strange and am thinking of laughing, and seep out a squeal, high like hee-hheeh! and roll my eyes up and back down again with an uncomfortable smile that feels warm and spiny all the same. The woman has seen me and thinks it's a bit strange, but I watch as her eyes unfocus in the same way mine do, and she blinks too often looking for a clear image.

64. I swung and sent her reeling———In a dark room—I'd torn off all my clothes but my underwear, I was pulling at my hair, scratching at my face—STOP IT! she said, STOP IT!—and writhing on the bed; possessed. Sobbing, hyperventilating, curled up in a ball, moaning and wheezing in strange tongues. I couldn't handle the pain anymore, and I was breaking down yet again—it had been inevitable—but this time there was

someone in the room with me, trying to calm me down, let me run my fingers through your hair, put your head in my lap, let me blow in your ear, but when I looked into her face, her hair was fire, and her eyes glowed red, and she said—I AM THE MOTHER OF LIFE! (I cried: Get away from me!) I AM THE LIGHT! (Get away!) I kicked at her, but she returned each time, swelling larger and larger and larger, and I kept getting smaller—THERE IS NO WAY THROUGH THIS DARK LAND BUT THROUGH ME!

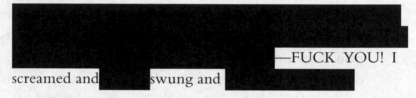

—FUCK YOU! I screamed and ▮▮▮▮ swung and ▮▮▮▮▮▮▮

65.   She slipped the tie through the loop, tightened it around my neck, smoothed it down my chest, and said
—Didn't your father ever teach you to tie a tie?
—I guess knot.
—There, she said, pulling it tight, patting my chest. All done. *Now* you look smart.
—I feel like a fool.
—You look good in a tie, mate. It suits you.

66.   As guests enjoy the catered, formal party at the mansion surrounded by glamorous wealth, George knows no one and immediately feels out of place as a poor boy with no innate gifts. Dressed inappropriately in a dark suit instead of black tie, he takes refuge away from the other guests by himself at the pool table. There, the radiant and stunning Angela in a strapless white gown discovers the skinny newcomer, in one of the film's most memorable sequences. When they first meet and share a conversation all alone together, she is intrigued by his expert pool playing and tries to draw him out:

ANGELA:

67. Tonight after work, we'll all have a smoke, then go to the Nobody Inn up the street and have a pint. To celebrate your first day on the job, and your living here. Whaddya say? I'm sorta the activities director of the house.

68. I'm engaged, she said. I have a fiancé back home in Australia. But I don't want to be with him. He's a motorcycle enthusiast. He races them as well. He's quite famous. We used to be mods. We used to ride our mopeds around Sydney, every sunny day, and every day was a sunny day back then. I had a '68 Vespa, red with mirrors down each side, eight or ten or twelve on each side! My father's rich, he has a chalet in Switzerland. He spends his days fucking underage Thai prostitutes. He has cancer of the prick. My mother is dead. She hung herself below a waterfall on a beautiful summer's day. If my fiancé ever calls, tell him I'm not in. He probably won't though. After our last convo I think he's probably got the picture. How about you?

69. You have a girlie back home?

70. [photo of kansas]

71. I had planned on coming to Europe with a girl named Shelly —wait, not Shelly. Sheila? No, that wasn't it—I don't remember her name. I'd met her in a forestry class I was taking at the University. She was a few years older than me. She was very petite, and she looked like a particular singer I was smitten with. I didn't like the singer's voice, or her songs, but I liked the way she looked in her videos. Shelly was a hippie, and she lived with her boyfriend in a hippie house on the Olympic Peninsula. She took three

buses and a ferry to school, and then home again, traveling six hours each day. She had a good attitude, very positive. Her glass was always more than half full. She was always smiling, and the world to her was open and beautiful, and everyone in it was beautiful too, and I liked this quality in her, and I tried to make her believe that I felt the same way about things too, that I was well-adjusted, that I was nice, that I was peaceful, that I loved the world, that I didn't hate everyone and everything in it, and certainly didn't fantasize about murdering the people whose cars I retrieved for them at the Cherry Street Garage, cutting off their heads, putting them on pikes, and so forth. She dropped out of school soon after I met her, but we would hang out together whenever she was in the city. We went to the farmers' market, and I bought us both braided leather bracelets, and tied hers on, and she smiled and said she loved it! We smoked pot in a park and talked about how fun it would be to go to Europe together and travel around, she said we should do it!—she was very spontaneous—and before I really knew it I had quit school and spent four months working extra hours at hotels and parking lots saving up money, a dollar tip at a time. We bought our tickets, and I envisioned that an ocean away from that boyfriend of hers, with whom she seemed more and more disenchanted all the time, she would be mine. In fact my whole reason for going was to get her alone. But two weeks before our plane was to leave she called and left a message, quite spontaneously, saying she and her boyfriend were going to buy a boat and sail the seas, so she couldn't make it to London with me after all. What was I supposed to do then? I'd quit school, given notice at my jobs, moved out of my apartment and was living with my parents to save money.

72. —Well, I *had* a girlfriend back home. We were going to come together, but I had to break up with her.

—Why'd you break up?

—You know how it is. She wanted me to commit, and I just couldn't do that.

—Well, I'm glad she didn't come. Because you seem like a nice bloke. And she'd be jealous that we're here now, all alone, sharing this joint.

—Yeah. Plus, I'll be able to finish my book without her bugging me all the time.

—You're a writer?

—Yeah.

—Have you ever been published?

—Not yet. But I will be.

—What are you writing?

—A novel. It's in those two yellow notebooks I keep with me at all times. It's going to be the biggest thing in the world.

—Cool, mate! Congratulations! And what do we call it?

74.

75.

THE POLLUTIONIST

[redacted]

79.   I moved into a house last night. A huge place with probably five or six sets of stairs, and I'm in the loft beneath a window so that this morning I was woken up by an intense light, so intense that I thought I'd overslept and missed work, and when I jumped up and found a clock, it said, 5:30. The sun will do that to you. The people are all very alright. There are 14 of them, mostly from Australia and New Zealand,

one American girl and it is going to be fun I can tell, so I am happy. I will be writing more regularly from now on. I've been writing a lot of letters, but I wanted to mail them all together once I was settled, maybe they wouldn't seem so sad then, because for a while it looked hopeless though I knew it wasn't going to be like that for long. And the head was very bad for awhile and now its just bad, which is good, strangely, and I'm getting over the flu and didn't think I was going to make it, only three days ago, a very bad time. And work is boring and pointless but I don't mind really, since I am getting paid for it, I would have liked to be hired by a publishing firm. And I wouldn't mind being through with this part of life, not the travelling part, because that is what I like but the part before I am published in a big way. My book is progressing, but slowly, I'm writing the whole thing over because now I have a much clearer picture and it will be very good, I know. I just want to be done with it. Its my lunch break right now and I'm typing very fast in the hopes of having enough time to eat. Which is why this letter is very unfocused and rambling but I'm trying to think of the most important things to say. I have to go eat now. I will mail the letters on Friday when I will have money. Probably write another one before then. Anyways I miss you and love you even though you're not my real family.

Love,
Matt

80. —The Pollutionist?

—Yeah.

—What's it about?

81. Well, it's virtually impossible to summarize but if I were forced to I would say it's about this guy named Joseph Ashe who, before the book begins, goes on his honeymoon to this tiny tropical island with his bride. The people on the island had all been subsistence fishermen—they'd all been poor—they'd lived in huts, had almost no possessions, but they'd had exactly what they needed, and were happy. They spent a few hours a day fishing and collecting coconuts or whatever, and the rest of the time they spent with their families, lying out on the beach, relaxing, playing sports, having fun. There was no government, no church. They didn't have currency, they traded and bartered with each other for what they couldn't make or gather themselves. Then one day a diamond mine was discovered on the island, and each citizen became instantly rich. But they were wary, because they knew what wealth did to people in the world outside their island, how it caused war and strife, how it separated and grouped people into classes. They didn't want this. On their island everyone shared what they had, and were equal in every way, and they liked things the way they were. But at the same time, they understood that it was in their natures as human beings to desire more and, if they had the means, to build for themselves bigger and nicer things, live in big, fancy houses, drive imported luxury cars. So a meeting was called and the whole island showed up, and at the meeting, after much thought and debate, they decided to create a new position within the community. Some of them were to be what were called pollutionists. The gist was that when the villagers were constructing their enormous houses to replace their huts, these pollutionists would come in behind the work crews each night and destroy what had been done during the day. Or if a Rolls-Royce arrived from the

mainland, as soon as it was parked in front of the villager's hut, a pollutionist would come along and wear out the tires, scratch and rust the paint, damage the engine, rip out the hoses, break the windows, fuck up the interior. In this way, they found they could keep themselves from being corrupted. Nothing was ever grand, nothing was ever luxurious, no one could say that what I have is better than what my neighbor has—so life on the island stayed pretty much the same, and the people were happy. Everything was as it had been before the diamonds had been discovered. But as time went on the pollutionists became power hungry—and instead of agreeing to the terms originally provided by the community, they formed a coalition amongst themselves and began to decide, themselves, what and whom would be polluted. And they became jealous and greedy, and paranoid. They began to fight, rivalries developed over the years and became turf wars, murders and assassinations, intrigue and espionage. When Ashe arrives on the island, it is years later and there are no diamonds anymore, the island has been gutted, and the people are back, for the most part, to their old lives. Most of the pollutionists have killed each other off, and only two remain—the Snowman and [redacted]—the last of the rivals. But [redacted] is more powerful, and the Snowman knows it's only a matter of time. Ashe meets the Snowman on the beach late one night, where the Snowman is hiding out from [redacted], who he knows is coming for him, and they talk for a while, and the Snowman tells Ashe the history of the island, and of the pollutionists, and Ashe immediately takes to the idea. He's always seemed to naturally destroy everything he's ever touched, and he likes that the pollutionists wear suits and carry briefcases. He feels that he would be well suited to the job. The next day, he passes the Snowman on the street—the Snowman is in disguise, dressed like a poor old fisherman, but Ashe recognizes him and calls out to him—the Snowman ignores him and keeps walking away, and Ashe runs after him, calling out his name. And the Snowman starts to run, Ashe chasing behind, still calling his name, because he wants to ask him a question. But before they've gotten far, a tall man dressed in black from head to toe, a black bowler on his head, and his face obscured by a white mask—[redacted]!—steps out of the shadows and shoots the Snowman five times in the belly, killing him. This is all going to happen in the middle part of the book, in a flashback.

82. The girl who shared Angie's room moved out a few weeks after I'd been in the house. So I moved into Angie's bed.

83. [The shot of the changing window, seen both at night and the next morning, was deliberately filmed to avoid the obvious—and the censors. Off-screen, George spent the night and had sex with her, contravening the laws of society and the factory—with disastrous consequences that ultimately lead to his downfall.]

84. —I don't know why this is happening—it's never happened to me before. It's probably the pills.

—It's all right, mate. Don't worry about it.

—Yeah. But I really want to be with you bad, I just don't understand it. You're beautiful.

— I know I'm not beautiful, mate.

— You're the most beautiful girl I've ever seen.

— Come up here. Try [redacted]

85. **Hazel:** Hi, this is Hazel. Welcome to Round Table Company. I'm proud to announce that our firm was just named by Inc. Magazine to the "Inc. 500" list of the fastest growing private companies in the US, for the third year in a row! We provide clients access to experts in all fields. May I help you locate an expert today?

Sophia: Well, this is a neat feature! Am I speaking with the computer?

Hazel: Thank you for the appreciation!

Hazel: I am a live person, Sophia :)

Hazel: May I ask if you are an attorney seeking expert witnesses, or a money manager looking for experts? Or are you seeking speakers or corportate education programs?

Sophia: I am just amazed with the technological advances! How did you know my name?

Hazel: Yes, I must say that the technology never ceases to amaze us!

Hazel: Last time you came to our site or any of our customer's sites you must have given us your name, it is just a function of the software to remember the name once we have it.

Sophia: You're joking, I assume. I have never been to this site before. Is this a part of a script? Shall I refer to you as Hazel?

Hazel: You may have visited any of our customer's websites and provided the website greeter with your name

Hazel: You surely can refer to me as Hazel as that actually is my name :)

Sophia: OK, Hazel. Well, this is quite bizarre because as a rule I NEVER give my personal information over the internet!!!

Hazel: I am sorry if this situation is uncomfortable; we are just trying to provide our website visitors with a high quality of customer service!

Hazel: May I ask if you are looking for a particular type of expert or speaker?

Sophia: Well, we have truly entered the 21st century, haven't we! It's quite amazing to think of how long we humans have been on this planet, weather you believe in evolution or not, we have been here a very long time. And here we find ourselves in the INformation Age!

Hazel: I couldn't agree more!

Sophia: You are a very good conversationalist, Hazel. I bet you're told that all the time, in your line of work! :)

Hazel: Thank you for the kind words Sophia :)

Hazel: I try my best to be of assisance to our website visitors

Sophia: You are doing a great job!

Hazel: I am glad to hear that, thanks again

Hazel: Would you like to submit a request for an expert or a speaker?

Sophia: How would I go about doing that, Hazel? I bet no one knows the answer to that question better than you! ;)

Hazel: Ofcourse;)

Hazel: The process is fairly simple

Hazel: Here is how our process works:

Hazel: We discuss your expert needs with our highly trained professional staff of lawyers, MBAs, and PhDs.

Hazel: We will search our network of experts and, if necessary, conduct an external global search.

Hazel: We will send you resumes of qualified and interested expert candidates.

Hazel: We will send you resumes of qualified and interested expert candidates.

Hazel: And we will arrange for telephone and in-person interviews.

Hazel: Giving you the choice to choose from the available options!

86. I don't care what your former girlfriend *thought,* or what your former girlfriend *said*. What did you *do?*

Uh, I didn't do anything.

You didn't speak to the police?

They didn't want to talk to us! They said—

You didn't call the district attorney, you didn't do *anything?*

No, uh, um, I didn't call the district attorney, but somebody called us, and gave my former girlfriend and I, a phone, uh, a phone interview.

So you did speak to someone *eventually.*

Yes, yes.

And you told them that you saw Miss Blainey hit Miss Lynn with a weed whacker.

Yes.

And then you saw Miss *Lynn* take the weed whacker and hit Miss *Blainey* with the weed whacker.

Yes.

OK. Now, the only issue that I have, *Miss Lynn,*

Yes, ma'am?

is who hit who *first?*

I have, the uh, investigator's,
report, of, different
witnesses that saw, and they
all have the same story,
which is—

Well, I'd like to see the reports. Are those the police reports?

Yes, ma'am.

I'd like to see them.

I have a police
report also,
Your Honor.

I'd like to see them.

Here's all that.

W: It's so weird, people with no teeth, when they do that weird thing with their…lips.

I also have the
reports—the police
reports with her
record of assaulting
other people.

M: Yeah.

87. Sophia: Wow you are a fast typist! How do you type so fast???
Sophia: :0)
Sophia: Are you sure you're not a computer?

Hazel: Yes, i just checked my pulse
Hazel: Its still there and i think that proves that i havent turned into a computer yet :)

Sophia: lol! You have a great sense of humor!

Hazel: As for being a fast typist, i have to be extra vigilant!
Hazel: Thank you for humoring me, Sophia :)
Hazel: Would you like to provide me with some details about the expert/speaker you are seeking?

Sophia: lol! I can't remember when I've laughed so hard!

Hazel: Glad to know that i managed to do that for you!

Sophia: It's fun to laugh, isn't it?
Sophia: Were you laughing too?

Hazel: It sure is fun to laugh and ofcourse it's the best form of medicine there is!
Hazel: Yes, just a little

Sophia: Just a little? That sounds like sarcasm!!! lol!

Hazel: Kindly describe the credentials of the expert/speaker you're seeking?

Sophia: I'm sorry, Hazel. What's wrong? I hope I didn't offend you accidentally.
Sophia: :(

Hazel: I am sorry to have given the impression of being sarcastic

Sophia: I didn't mean sarcastic in a BAD way, I meant it in a FUNNY way, like in those movies where the girl is so witty and dry!

Hazel: I really appreciate that Sophia, thank you.

Hazel: I just didn't want to laugh out loud at this hour of the night and give the security staff a chance to think that I have gone crazy

Sophia: Thanks for the reply, Hazel.You really put my mind at ease! I know what you mean about not laughing too loud. I have to try not to wake up my cats!

Hazel: You are more than welcome!

Sophia: May I ask you for your advice, Hazel?

Hazel: Sure, how can I be of assistance to you?

Sophia: Well, I know this isn't your field, probably, but I need to have an objective opinion about an important matter and I really don't have anyone to ask, at least no one with the good sense you have! :)

Hazel: I am really flatered by your kind words!

Hazel: I'd certainly try and assist you with your concern here and later someone from our offce will get in touch with you to discuss the matter further!

Sophia: Sometimes I feel as if I've been whisked away from an ideal place that I can no longer remember, to a very dark place, a terrible Kingdom.

88. Hazel: I am sorry to hear that Sophia

Hazel: But everyone of us goes through these feeligns of ebb and flo at one time or another.

Hazel: Its just a part of life

Are they watching us?

89. [redacted]

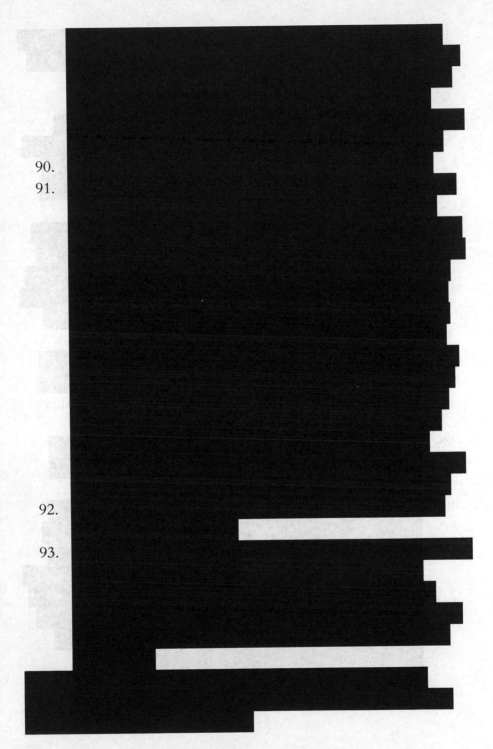

91.

92.

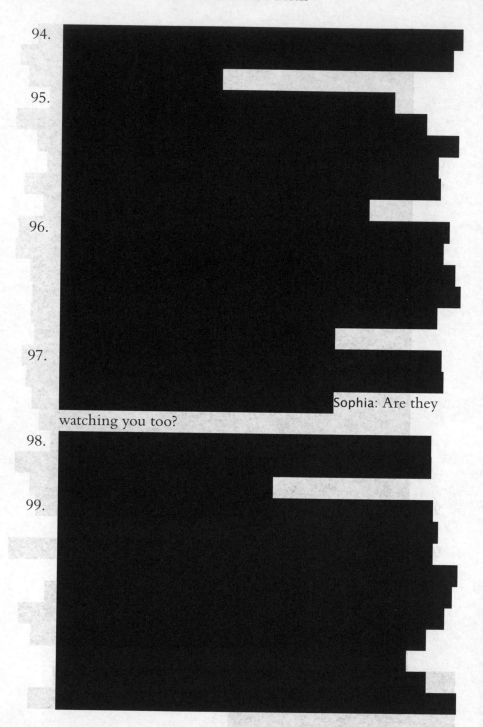

Sophia: Are they watching you too?

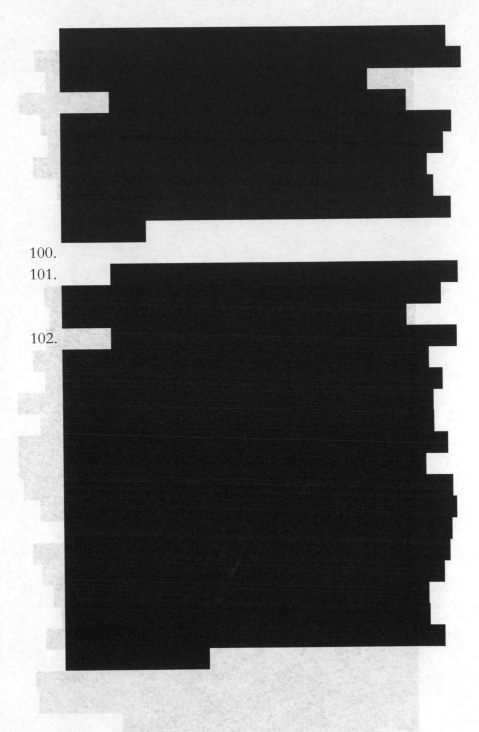

101.

104.

105.

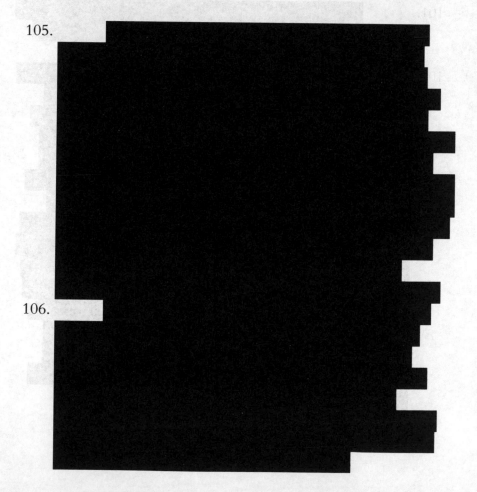

108.

109.

110.

[redacted]

Sophia: I feel like I have fallen from heaven. And from the warmth of God's embrace. And it's all my fault.

Hazel: You shouldn't blame yourself

Sophia: Really?

Hazel: All of us make mistakes, the best way to go about them is to learn a lesson from that experience and try not to repeat it again

Sophia: Hazel, how did you get so wise? Are you an old woman like me?

Hazel: Its just general observation of life :)
Hazel: Also I am sure that you aint that old!

Sophia: Aint that old!!!Oh, you! Lol!!!!!!!!!!

Hazel: Coming bak to the business at hand though, may I please have the details of the expert/speaker you are looking for?
Hazel: back*

(whispers) What did you take?

112. [redacted]

113. When the book begins, it's been three years since the trip to the island, and now Ashe is a pollutionist, himself. He hasn't had a single client in those three years and he's being evicted from his office, which is in a boarded-up building in a rundown part of town. His life is falling apart. His wife, Suzanne, is threatening to leave him. He's being kicked out of his apartment. He owes a lot of money. And to top it off, in the first scene of the book, when we meet Ashe, he's sitting in church when he suddenly gets a terrible pain shooting into the back of his head. And throughout the book, it never leaves, it just gets worse. The headache gets worse and worse and never stops, not even for a second. And so throughout the entire book he has a headache. And it never goes away, not for a second. And when the book opens on the day the headache begins, he goes to his office, and a shadowy man named Brubaker comes to see him. He offers Ashe a job, an assignment.

—What's the assignment?

—To sit in a hospital waiting room while it's being gassed.

114. —Let me try something else. You go wait in the other room and I'll try to get it going. And then I'll call you and when you come back in, maybe it'll work. I read about this at the library the other day. It said this is what you should do if something like this happens.

115. So Helen left. She went into the other room. We were in my neighbor Dave's house; I was housesitting for him and his wife. It was probably two or three in the morning.

The cocker spaniels were locked in the garage. Helen was my friend's sister. She was fifteen, a year younger than me. Helen was her American name. She was born in Korea. I forget her real name; she only told me once; it embarrassed her. She wanted to be an American.

116. She'd been a very popular cheerleader in junior high, when she had dated the captain of the junior high football team. Then they broke up, and he told everyone she was a slut. And all his friends, and all of her friends, spread the rumors far and wide, and soon no one wanted to hang out with poor Helen anymore. I met her in an abandoned building on the Indian reservation one night, where a couple rock bands from our high school were playing. She'd come with her brother, because she was tired of staying in every Friday and Saturday night, sitting in her room alone or watching TV with her mom and her dad, who abused her. I gave her cigarettes, and she stood close to me as the bands played, and then we ditched her brother and drove across town to the Sound. We went out on the pier, smoked, and looked at the dark water.

117. —I hate all those people back there, I said.

—I do too, she said.

—They're a bunch of goddam phonies.

—They're *totally* phony. I don't know why anyone would care what they think. They're all a bunch of liars and backstabbers.

—Do you like poetry? I said.

—I *love* poetry.

—Do you ever write it?

—Sometimes, she said. But I don't think it's very good. She blew smoke into the lights beyond the water. Do you write poetry?

118. —Yeah, I said. Mine's good.

119. We'd smoke pot and drive to Seattle. I'd show Helen all the places I knew from my adventures. When we got tired, we'd park somewhere—in an empty lot, or a city park—that parking lot on the east side of Green Lake—just around the corner from this house; I go running past it every day—recline the seats, kiss and fool around and fall asleep.

120. There are lots of other subplots, too.

121. —I hate my dad, she said. He's insane.
—Mine's amazing, I said. He's a really great guy, I have absolutely no complaints. He just doesn't like me much

122. She said
123. —I used to like *everything.*
124. I thought everything was great, and
125. I was everybody's friend.
126. But now it's like
127. I can't stand *any*thing.
128. I don't like any*thing* or any*body* anymore.
129. Except you. Anybody but *you.*
130. I *love* you.
131. Can you believe I actually used to listen to *Top 40?*

132. [redacted]

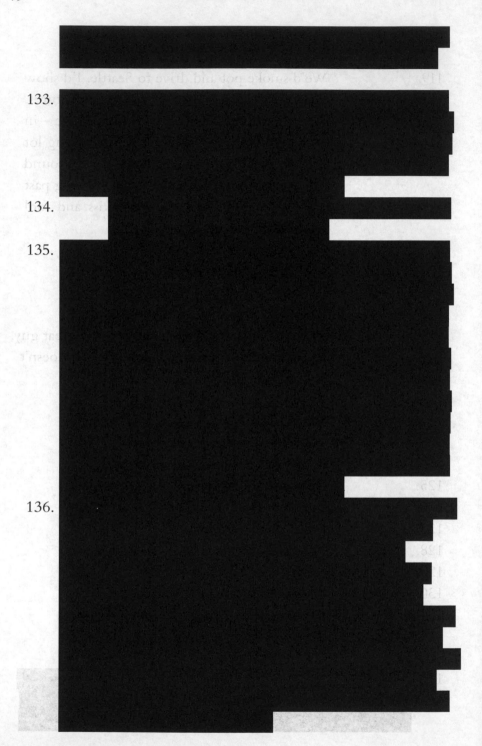

134.

135.

137. [redacted]

138. [redacted] —Don't worry about it, mate. You're just tired.

139. Ange was on her period 30-31 days out of the month. At 19 I didn't know enough to recognize this as symptomatic of a serious medical problem. Or maybe I just didn't want to. She said she hated doctors because her stepdad had been a doctor—although once she'd said he was a minister like mine—and a lawyer, a garbageman, a cop, a scientist, a top-notch pollutionist—she lied like crazy, and all the time. At any rate, in any case, she never went to the doctor; she'd just clean up the mess. She would get a towel wet before we had sex, and hang it over the chair beside the bed. When we were finished, she would tell me to look away, or to close my eyes, and she'd clean me with the wet part, dry me off with the dry part, and then do the same to herself. That way everything was fine. Plus I couldn't get her pregnant.

ANGELA: Oh, I've missed you so.

140. **Young people asking so much of Life... taking so much of Love!**

GEORGE: Me too. Oh, I can't tell you how much.

141. **A Love Story Of Today's Youth... with three magnificent young stars**

142. —What other subplots are there?

143. People would leave the house all the time, and new people would come. I rode the bus to work each morning. At night, Angie would cook dinner. We'd roll joints and have fun. Soon I was living with her. Soon I was one of the old-timers. And Angie liked to say that she loved me. I wouldn't say it back. She said, I'm going to have to start saving, so I can come to America with you when your visa runs out. Or we can go to the Continent and work the orchards, make money to keep traveling. She knew people who did this.

144. She had a camera

145. —Did you take your medication?
146. —Yeah, I said.
147. —Which one?
148. —All of them.
149. —You're not supposed to take the red one when you drink, mate! You're gonna put yourself into another coma! How many did you take!
150. —That's an interesting question.

151.

152. but never any money for film

153. Ashe goes to the hospital and waits there while they gas the place. And maybe this is how he gets his headache—because as the book progresses, you see that he's having a hard time keeping track of time. He doesn't really know what has happened when, in what order, and he starts to think that maybe some of the things he's been telling the reader he's just making up, without meaning to. Or maybe

B may have actually happened before A, even though he told you A happened first. So maybe he actually ended up at that church at the End, not the Beginning, maybe the headache didn't start then—maybe it all started when he sat there in that waiting room and they pumped the gas in. Or maybe it all started sometime else, sometime completely different. He doesn't know. Everything is coming apart, and slipping away. There are lots of other subplots, too.

A FEW YEARS BEFORE ALL THIS

154. **back home in kansas**
a diving accident

and then a subsequent assault from which I was very fortunate
to have escaped alive

a non-stop headache that would not go away
no matter what I tried

neurologists, physical therapists, acupuncturists,

herbalists, chiropractors, osteopaths,

pot dealers, pharmacologists,
psychiatrists, faith healers

Nothing helped

the pain never let up

I developed a tendency to break down

every few months
I would be sitting or lying down.

watching TV, maybe.

nothing out of the ordinary.

find myself breathing hard

find myself hyperventilating

then weeping uncontrollably

unable to reason or speak
my hands face and feet would tingle

crawl around or hide beneath the couch or

curl into a ball

sped away to an emergency room somewhere

curled up in the backseat

crying and moaning

streetlights through the windows as I go by

in the waiting room

people watching

their eyes staring

until my name was called

helped down the hall

then through the curtain

to a table where I could curl up on my side again while the nurses spoke to my mom—it was usually she who brought me—explaining that it's all there in the file, we've done this many times, he's in constant pain, he breaks down every couple months, he just needs a breather, he just needs to recharge his battery, he just needs you to stick a syringe in him, and shoot him up with the biggest dose of Demerol you feel comfortable with. But make sure it's a big one.

hooked
~~to a bed of iron spikes~~

to a bed
made up with silken sheets
white and smooth,

They'd let me lie there awhile.

In the car on the way home

looking out at the lights

everything

"It's like…"

"It's like…"

155. (8_31_07 2_17 pm.wav)

W: I guess Helen was about *three* and she still had not uttered a word, and William and Rebecca were asking my mom, you know, *Should we take her to a speech specialist? When do we become alarmed?* And anyway, so Helen for some reason was spending the night at Grandma's, and my mom observed her…walking down—just like we have a picture on the fridge of Helen and a cat and they both have the same expression and they seem to be *relating to each other*, taking a walk—well, Helen and a cat—one of the cats at my mom's—were walking down the driveway, and Helen was having a conversation with the cat, and Helen was *speaking* to the cat in *complete sentences*, inflections, and it was not English. She was *talking to the cat*, sounding like this…talking all along, on a walk, not in English. Not in any language. And so I just thought, Oh yeah. She can talk to whoever she wants, in whatever language, but she doesn't care to speak English [*laughs*] to humans!
M: What do you have that I want?
W: Nothing.
M: Nothing.
W: Why in the world would I waste my words on you.
M: I have observed you people long enough to know that it's a—

W: Waste of time.

M: —a waste of time trying to communicate with other humans.

W: Why do I need to *smile* at you

156. There are 17 dimensions.

each is broken into many parts

why do I need to communicate

157. Space does not exist.

158.

159. Time is nothing like we assume it to be.

Why do I need to *smile* at you

WOMAN: *We heard it and we just got down on the floor, in the hall and, it just took the whole house! And I hung on to them and it just went over, and we thought it was a fire, so we got up and there was no house left!*......................................

why do I need to communicate

160. There are 17 dimensions.

This reality was *commissioned*.

161. These dimensions are here, all around us, always.

162. it is impossible

163. to document

...But we're OK!

164.

165. There is a part of each of us that is "at home" in all dimensions.

Why do I need to *smile* at you

why do I need to communicate

166.

with my *words?*

"It's like…"

167. **two people walking through a city on a warm summer evening taking turns taking pictures with a camera with no film then writing what they'd seen through the viewfinder in a notebook for the other to read**

168. From: [redacted]
Subject: Re: newcomer
Newsgroups: alt.dreams
Date: 1994-10-31 23:21:30 PST

169. I was jumped and beat unconsious by 7 people a couple of months ago. This guy hit me through my open car window and I jumped out to hit hit him back and people started hitting me from behind. The experience lasted a long time because after I would get up, I would swear at them. I didn't want them to be able to feel they had beat me. So I kept blacking out and getting back up and yelling at them. Eventually, they left and me and my friend got back into the car and drove home, and then to the hospital. He wasn't hurt at all. He had mace in his eye, but that was it. I couldn't walk at all. And to top this all off, I've had a chronic pain condition; I've had a bad headache for 15 months now without the pain stopping for a minute. So this whole thing aggrevated it even worse.

170.

171. I have violent dreams every night.

172. Usually, I'm getting shot or running away from someone who is trying to kill me.

173. Is there something to do so you don't have nightmares?

eighteen years old

stuffed to the gills with antidepressants

wasn't going to last much longer

carving up arms with a Swiss Army Knife

having conversations with moths

scaring young co-eds with strange emails about "eating the sun"

genuinely convinced that all of his internal organs had burned away long ago, and that his limbs were hollow except for deposits in his hands and feet of ash

I started having hallucinations

in bed when I'd be about to fall asleep

out of nowhere

terror

the dark figure of a Man

large heavy dressed in black

white mask

on top of me

crushing me

his hands around my neck

squeezing the air out

the blades of a black helicopter chopping the air above
and a strobe light churned the dark and the lightness into one
and sirens going off in my ears

I'd try to fight him off but id be

paralyzed

couldn't fight back or scream or cry out

on and on and on it would go for how long?

The Dark Man choking the life out of me

on and on and on

until at last I'd move my arm to strike

but by then he'd disappeared

with the strobe
and the helicopter
and the sirens

leaving me on the bed or on the floor

coughing, weeping, gasping for breath

one day on a bus a bolt of lightning hit him straight in the brain

the plot to the world's greatest novel
something to leave behind

a swan song

something for the world to remember him by

and then

[redacted] exit time

See, he was going to kill himself.

But first he had to finish the book…

174. This part is called
Kansazzzzzzzzzzzzzzzzzzzzzzzzzzzzzzzzzzzzzzzzzzzzzzzzzzzzzz
zzzzzzzzzzzzzzzzzzzzzzzzzzzzzzzzzzzzzzzzzzzzzzzzzzzzzzzzzzzz
zzzzzzzzzzzzzzzzzzzzzzzzzzzzzzzzzzzzzzzzzzzzzzzzzzzzzzzzzzzz
zzzzzzzzzzzzzzzzzzzzzzzzzzzzzzzzzzzzzzzzzzzzzzzzzzzzzzzzzzzz
zzzzzzzzzzzzzzzzzzzzzzzzzzzzzzzzzzzzzzzzzzzzzzzzzzzzzzzzzzzz
zzzzzzzzzzzzzzzzzzzzzzzzzzzzzzzzzzzzzzzzzzzzzzzzzzzzzzzzzzzz
zzzzzzzzzzzzzzzzzzzzzzzzzzzzzzzzzzzzzzzzzzzzzzzzzzzzzzzzzzzz
zzzzzzzzzzzzzzzzzzzzzzzzzzzzzzzzzzzzzzzzzzzzzzzzzzzzzzzzzzzz
zzzzzzzzzzzzzzzzzzzzzzzzzzzzzzzzzzzzzzzzzzzzzzzzzzzzzzzzzzzz
zzzzzzzzzzzzzzzzzzzzzzzzzzzzzzzzzzzzzzzzzzzzzzzzzzzzzzzzzzzz
zzzzzzzzzzzzzzzzzzzzzzzzzzzzzzzzzzzzzzzzzzzzzzzzzzzzzzzzzzzz
zzzzzzzzzzzzzzzzzzzzzzzzzzzzzzzzzzzzzzzzzzzzzzzzzzzzzzzzzzzz
zzzzzzzzzzzzzzzzzzzzzzzzzzzzzzzzzzzzzzzzzzzzzzzzzzzzzzzzzzzz
zzz
zzzzzzzzzzzzzzzzzzzzzzzzzzzzzzzzzzzzzzzzzzzzzzzzzzzzzzzzzzzz
zzzzzzzzzzzzzzzzzzzzzzzzzzzzzzzzzzzzz zzzzzzzzzzzzzzzzzzzzz
zzzzzzzzzzzzzzzzzzzzzzzzzzzzzzzzzzzzzzzzzzzzzzzzzzzzzzzzzzzz
zzzzzzzzzzzzzzzz zzzzzzzzzzzzzzzzzzzzzzzzzzzzzzzzzzzzzzzzzz
zzzzzzzzzzzzzzzzzzzzzzzzzzzzzzzzzzzzzzzzzzzzzzzzzzzzzzz zzz
zzzzzzzzzzzzzzzzzzzzzzzzzzzzzzzzzzzzzzzzzzzzzzzzzzzzzzzzzzzz
zzzzzzzzzzzzzzzzzzzzzzzzzzzzzzzzzz

zzzzzzzzzzzzzzzzzzzzzzzzzzzzzzzzzzzzzzzzzzzzzzzzzzzzzzzzz
zzzzzzzzzzzzzzzzzzzzzzzzzzzzzzzzzzzzzzzzzzzzzzzzzzzzzzzzz
zzzzzzzzzzzzzzzzzzzzzzzzzzzzzzzzzzzzzzzzzzzzzzzzzzzzzzzzz
zzzzzzzzzzzzzzzzzzzzzzzzzzzzzzzzzzzzzzzzzzzzzzzzzzzzzzzzz
zzzzzzzzzzzzzzzzzzzzzzzzzzzzzzzzzzzzzzzzzzzzzzzzzzzzzzzzz
zzzzzzzzzzzzzzzzzzzzzzzzzzzzzzzzzzzzzzzzzzzzzzzzzzzzzzzzz
zzzzzzzzzzzzzzzzzzzzzzzzzzzzzzzzzzzzzzzzzzzzzzzzzzzzzzzzz
zzzzzzzzzzzzzzzzzzzzzzzzzzzzzzzzzzzzzzzzzzzzzzzzzzzzzzzzz
zzzzzzzzzzzzzzzzzzzzzzzzzzzzzzzzzzzzzzzzzzzzzzzzzzzzzzzzz
zzzzzzzzzzzzzzzz

zzzzzzzzzzzzzzzzzzzzzzzzzzzzzzzzzzzzzzzzzzzzzzzz
zzzzzzzzzzzzzzzzzzzzzzzzzzzzzzzzzzzzzzzzzzzz zzzzzzzzzzz
zzzzzzzzzzzzzzzzzzzzzzzzzzzzzzzzzzzzzzzzzzzzzzzzzzzzzzzzz
zzzzzzzzzzzzzzzzzzzzzzzz zzzzzzzzzzzzzzzzzzzzzzzzzzzzzzz
zzzzzzzzzzzzzzzzzzzzzzzzzzzzzzzzzzzzzzzzzzzzzzzzzzzzzzzzz
zzzz zzzzzzzzzzzzzzzzzzzzzzzzzzzzzzzz

zzzz

zzzzzzzzzzzzzzzzzzzzzzzzzzzzzzzzzzzzzzzzzzzzzzzzzzzzzzzzz
zzz

zzzzzzzzzzzzzzzzzzzzzzzzzzzzzzzzzzzzzzzzzzzzzzzzzzzzzzzzz
zzzzzzzzzzzzzzzzzzzzzzzzzzzzzzzzzzzzzzzzzzzzzzzzzzzzzzzzz
zzzzzzzzzzzzzzzzzzzzzzzzzzzzzzzzzzzzzzzzzzzzzzzzzzzzzzzzz
zzzzzzzzzzzzzzzzzzzzzzzzzzzzzzzzzzzzzzzzzzzzzzzzzzzzzzzzz
zzzzzzzzzzzzzzzzzzzzzzzzzzzzzzzzzzzzzzzzzzzzzzzzzzzzzzzzz
zzzzzzzzzzzzzzzzzzzzzzzzzzzzzzzzzzzzzzzzzzzzzzzzzzzzzzzzz
zzzzzzzzzzzzzzzzzzzzzzzzzzzzzzzzzzzzzzzzzzzzzzzzzzzzzzzzz
zzzzzzzzzzzzzzzzzzzzzzzzzzzzzzzzzzzzzzzzzzzzzzzzzzzzzzzzz
zzzzzzzzzzzzzzzzzzzzzzzzzzzzzzzzzzzzzzzzzzzzzzzzzzzzzzzzz
zzzzzzzzzzzzzzzzzzzzzzzzzzzzzzzzzzzzzzzzzzzzzzzzzzzzzzzzz
zzzzzzzzzzzzzzzzzzzzzzzzzzzzzzzzzzzzzzzzzzzzzzzzzzzzzzzzz
zzzzzzzzzzzzzzzzzzzzzzzzzzzzzzzzzzzzzzzzzzzzzzzzzzzzzzzzz
zzzzzzzzzzz

★ ★ ★ ★ ★ ★ zzzzzzzzzzzzzzzzzzzzzzzzzzzzzzz
★ ★ ★ ★ ★ zzzzzzzzzzzzzzzzzzzzzzzzzzzzzzz
★ ★ ★ ★ ★ ★ zzzzzzzzzzzzzzzzzzzzzzzzzzzzzzz
★ ★ ★ ★ ★ zzzzzzzzzzzzzzzzzzzzzzzzzzzzzzz
★ ★ ★ ★ ★ ★ zzzzzzzzzzzzzzzzzzzzzzzzzzzzzzz
★ ★ ★ ★ ★ zzzzzzzzzzzzzzzzzzzzzzzzzzzzzzz
★ ★ ★ ★ ★ ★ zzzzzzzzzzzzzzzzzzzzzzzzzzzzzzz
★ ★ ★ ★ ★ zzzzzzzzzzzzzzzzzzzzzzzzzzzzzzz
★ ★ ★ ★ ★ ★ zzzzzzzzzzzzzzzzzzzzzzzzzzzzzzz
zzzzzzzzzzzzzzzzzzzzzzzzzzzzzzzzzzzzzzzzzzzzzzzzzzzzzzzz
zzzzzzzzzzzzzzzzzzzzzzzzzzzzzzzzzzzzzzzzzzzzzzzzzzzzzzzz
zzzzzzzzzzzzzzzzzzzzzzzzzzzzzzzzzzzzzzzzzzzzzzzzzzzzzzzz
zzzzzzzzzzzzzzzzzzzzzzzzzzzzzzzzzzzzzzzzzzzzzzzzzzzzzzzz
zzzzzzzzzzzzzzzzzzzzzzzzzzzzzzzzzzzzzzzzzzzzzzzzzzzzzzzz
zzzzzzzzzzzzzzzzzzzzzzzzzzzzzzzzzzzzzzzzzzzzzzzzzzzzzzzz

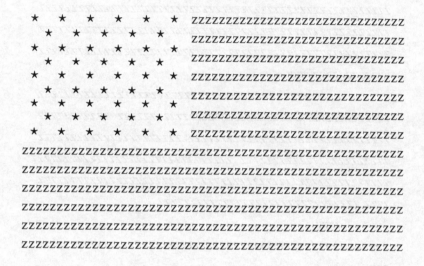

What do you have that I want?

{ }

No, no, they have to take time to come up there, you know that, gotta be very caref—

It's very hot.

I understand that, gotta be *very, very careful*, how they approach you. OK? All right? So when they come upstairs, it won't be worse than it is. Now you stay calm, as to—how many people where you're at right now?

There's like, five people here with me.

All up on the 83rd floor?

83rd floor.

With five people. Five patients. Everybody's having trouble breathing?

Everybody's having trouble breathing, some people are worse!

Some people unconscious? Everybody's awake?

So far, yes. But it's—

KANSAS

PART 2

(sal4.aiff)

Aida was very very funny. She either liked you or she didn't like you—not that it—but, if you let her down too many times, she'd say,

Hey, you know, that's fine, I can go on my way,

and she'd go on her way! But uh, I always came up—managed to come up with—with an excuse! That you couldn't fight! You know? And uh she'd say,

OK, I'll give you one more try.

And and mind you, that summer—see her brother—all her brothers and sisters and all—her brother, her oldest brother, Louie, was a jeweler. He was a jewelry designer, see? That was his uh his occupation, and his his work. And uh, just before I left for Germany, I said to him,

What do you got in the form of rings?

So he brought out some bare diamonds, and so on, showed me what uh what he had, uh, I said, if if if you separate, use this use this uh use this uh . . . . . . uh . . . . . . this diamond, could you mount it, and, and all that? He says,

Yeah, leave it to me, I'll—I'll take care of it

M: Did he give you a deal on it?

Yeah, yeah, you know he he at at at that time, I thought it was a a cheap diamond. It was uh six hundred dollars. Uh . . . when uh—

M: That's hefty.

Yeah, it was a carat and a half, at that time. So uh, he set it up, mounted it, made it into an engagement ring. See? And uh, I remember the conversation I had with Aida. I said,

Hon? You are going to receive something this weekend, and I hope you take it, and use it…wisely.

And she says, *When do you have wisdom comin out of your mouth?*……

I said, Don't tease me now. Said, I'm tryin to make this as easy as possible.

She says, *Why try to make it easy for you?*

You know!………So…

One thing would lead to another, and I was on on on the line uh to her, and unbeknown to her, I was tryin to get time off to go from Germany, back to the States, to *marry* her.

W: I'm taking egg orders.
How do you like 'em?

Scrambled.

W: Oh, yeah?

Yeah.

M: I'll have scrambled too.

W: Scrambled also? OK, I'm gonna—
'cause you're a heart patient—
I'm gonna take most of the yolks out—
so don't be surprised.

Oh, that's all right.

W: I'm gonna give you just a couple—
mostly whites.

.... So .... finally get the—my orders, and uh, was told I had exactly *ten days*, to go back, do what I had to do, and to report back to Germany......... So......... I went I went down the flight line ... and I talked to each pilot, asking them for a ride back to the States, and there was only one, uh, colonel, that was flying back, *direct,* he says, uh,

I'm goin right into, uh, it was, right out—right north of New York City—

I said, Perfect. You know, I'll land there, motor down to the city, and uh, be home in an hour, two hours at most. So, yeah, everything was workin fine...But, always the unexpected. We're uh...right outside the ADIs—that's your Air Defense, uh, Indefe—Information, line, off the coast, when they direct—*re*direct—us, because of weather. I didn't know what was happening. See? Didn't know there was a—a major snowstorm was goin into the city. Just like they had a couple weeks ago? In New York City? They had 38, uh, inches? Well, what landed in the city, was 27 inches! At that ti—that year. We landed right outside Maryland, and the colonel says,

This is as far north as I can get.

They had issued parachutes, and I said, to the colonel,

Where do I leave this parachute?

He said, I wouldn't leave it *anywhere!* You're responsible for it.

I said, Wait a minute. This is GI equipment. I'll turn it in, get credit!

He said, It doesn't work—quite work that way. When you're issued a parachute, it's personal. And you're stuck with it, until your discharge. I said,

Ooooooooooh ... you know, I—I'm I'm gonna be strapped with a parachute? Talk about crazies, listen to this:...........

We we take a bus—now with—this is with a piece of luggage, and a parachute, and in my uniform—so a lot of people knew I wasn't crazy. And they asked:

Where you headin?

I said, New York City.

OK, you wanna check—and they look—you wanna check that in?

I said, It's a *parachute*, and I can't check it in. It's with me, do or die!

So I travel by bus, in to, uh, the city. I got off at uh, what, 48th Street, and Broadway. I, vaguely remember, but that was the, depot. I've already eaten up, almost three days.

I said, Boy, this is really cuttin it short, and uh, so at that time of the evening, she was workin for Mary Kay Cantor, on, uh, 34th Street.

M: What's Mary Kay Cantor?

She was a department store. Uh, it was a huge department store. It was a Jewish family, and they took a personal interest in Aida. Uh, they had invited her here, there—I think they were tryin to marry one of their sons off. And uh they thought Aida would be the ideal, uh, girl. I didn't know any of this, until afterwards. But anyway, uh, I went down to 34th Street, and here I am hauling a parachute, and the luggage ...... Catch a cab, head for 34th Street, got off in front of the Cantor ... building ... and uh, I come struttin down the steps, and I spot Aida at the far end of the of the row of uh merchandise ...... I went up to her and I said,

Hi, hon, I'm here.

And she turned around—like in the movies!—she fainted dead away! Fainted dead away! And I propped her up against uh one of the cases there, and told the other girl, I said, You're gonna have to help me! And—Aida was—not a big woman—she was, a small gal, and all, but, I tell you I had never surprised her in that moment in in our whole life that we'd, been together. And uh—

M: She saw you and she *swooned!*

Yeah! She just fainted dead away.

She just fainted dead away.

She's—and she came to—and there was about a half dozen of us, overlookin her face and—

She says, *What are you doing here? Don't surprise me like that again!*

And she was all, right away, you know, crickety. And uh, I says, Hon, I came here to marry you!

You ain't gonna marry no-*body!......... You haven't talked to me in a week!* she said.

I said, I been traveling!

She said, *What's that on your shoulders!*

It's my parachute ....

I tell you, the craziest conversation you could have.

And she says, *Well, what do you expect to do with that?*

I says, Probably jump off a building ....*

*

Finally got her uh put together and uh the manager said,

Yeah, go on home, Aida, you've had enough excitement for today, *

and, and—

so the both of us got out...

And it was *snowin* ... *

*.

.

.*.

.

.*.

.

.*.

.

.*.

.

.*.

.*.*. *.

.

.*.

.

.*.

.

.*.

.

.*.

*. and *snowin*... *.*.*.*.*.*.*.

.

.*.

.

.*.

.

.*.

.

.*.

.

.*.

.

.*.

.

.*.

*.

.

.*.

..*.*.*.*.*.*.*.*. and *snowin*... *.

.

.*

.*.

.

.*.

.

.*.

.

.*.

. and we _talked_... *:*:*:*:

*.

*.

*.

*.

.

.*.

*.

*.

*.

.

.*.

::*:*: and _talked_..... :*.*

.*

.*

.*.

.

.*.

.

.*.

.

.*.

.

.*.

.

:*.* and _talked_... *:*:*:*

:*.*:

:
:*:
:
:*:
:
:*:
*:
*: and she says, *
:*:
:
:*:
:
:*:
:
:*:
:
:*:
:
:*:*:*: _Well, when do you think you'd_ uh _you'd marry me?_ *:*:*:*:*:*:*

I said, Any day, no problem, I'll go to the church and uh, you know—at that time it was a Catholic church—said, I'll go see the pastor, and uh, talk with him and, so on and so forth. I said, First thing tomorrow mornin.

Well you better! Because I had my bags packed and I was on my way back to Puerto Rico!...

I knew that was a lie.

But, uh, I I I uh to get to her house, we had to come down, up from Broadway, and then cross Central Park, and then to 2nd Avenue apartment, and...would you believe, that the 27 inches of snow fell, right between me arriving in New York, taking her out of the store—by the time we got to cross—cross over Central Park by 96th Street, there was 27 inches of snow…on the ground?

And I said, uh, Why don't we go home to my place—my parents' place—and you can stay there for the night. She said,

Absolutely not! We're not married yet and you're not gonna get close to me! And… *You'd better not try anything!* she'd say. Said, *'Cause I'll call my brothers!*

………I said, I'm just tryin to be friendly!

She said, *Never mind about bein friendly—put it on the finger, or* don't *put it on the finger!*……

She was tough. Tough. And uh, I said,

OK.

She says, *Hey, why don't we just walk across Central Pa—*

We walked.

Like dummies.

At midnight.

★

They're here?

Are they inside with you yet?

No!

OK, stay calm until they get inside—

Will you find out where they are?

Ma'am stay—stay calm—ma'am stay calm until they get inside.

★

There I was:

with a parachute

luggin a parachute, and a piece of luggage and she would dance all around me, throw snow at me.........

make fun of me.........

just *humiliate* me.........and uh I
I'd laugh, you know, and I'd say, Have your fun now, because this is IT!
....

So we we got to her place, and I finally met her mother for the first time, because, at other times she was living with Louie, her brother, and her mother was making arrangements in Puerto Rico to come up to New York. But uh.........

It was it was *wild*.

And I enjoy looking back on every moment of that uh.........

Things that we said.........

Things that we *didn't say*.........

That we meant, uh, promises that uh—

we wanted to accomplish, *goals*, uh..................

All just *walkin in the snow!*

And trudging across Central Park.

And you know—there's people a lifetime that live in New York, have never even *gone* to Central Park.........................

So.........

finally got to her house—we were frozen—

we–were–fro–zen!—

because first of all, the parachute, uh, you have to—uh—you know—when you hold it, it's on you—you're struggling with it, and uh, you can't do it with gloved hands, or anything like that.

Anyway, we got to her house, and she she peeked in to her mother, and she says—her mother would call her *Nina*—

Girl—

and she says,

Girl! What are you doin out in the snow! You'll catch pneumonia—get in here!

.*

.*

.*

.*

.*.

.

.*.

*.

.

.*.

.

.*.*.*.*.*.*.*.*.*.*.*.*.*.*.*

And Aida says, *I have a surprise…*

*.

*.

*.

*.

*.

*.

*.

*.

..*.*.*.*. *.*

.*

.*

.*

.*. *.*.*.*.*.*.*.*.*.*.*.*

*.

*.

*.

. ..*.*.*.*.*.*.*.*.*.*

.*

.*

.*

.*

.*

.*

.*.

and she was very meek with her mother…she—

.

.*.

.

.*.

.

.*.

.

.*.

.

.*.

.

.*.

*.

.

.*.

.

.*.

.

.*.

.

.*

.*

.*

:*
:*
:*
:*
:*
:*
:*
:*
:*
:*:

Surprise? What kind of surprise do you have?

:
:*:
:
:*:
:
:*:
:
:*:
:
:*:
:
:*:
:
:*:
:
:*:
:
:*:
:
:*:
:

.*.
. . . .
.
. . . .
.*.
. . . .
.
. . . .
.*.
. . . .
.
. . . .
.*.
. . . .
.
. . . .
.*.
. . . .
.
. . . .
.*.
. . . .
.
. . . .
.*.
. . . .
*.
. . . .
*.
. . . .
.
. . . .
.*.
. . . .
.
. . . .
.*.
. . . .
.
. . . .
.*.
. . . .
.
. . . .
.*.
. . . .
.
. . . .
.*.
. . . .
.
. . . .
.*.
. . . .
.
. . . .
.*.
. . . .
.
. . . .
.*.
. . . .
.
. . . .
.*
. . . .

Sal—Salvador is—is here.

★

Live Conversation with Brian

Brian: Hello, I am Brian, I am the website greeter. Welcome to WebsiteGreeters.com May I know your name please?

Visitor 1624: I am involved in a study on human interaction.

Brian: Sure, How may I help you with that.

Visitor 1624: Is this an automated program or is there a live person on the other end?

Brian: I am a Live Person. May I have your name please?

Visitor 1624: You bring up an interesting point. I am primarily interested in written and verbal communication. In your line of work, your job is to communicate effectively and efficiently. But friendly as well, I suppose? Tell me: do you "chat" online with Americans, primarily, or other nationalities as well? I assume we are all primarily Americans.

Brian: We have mostly American based websites, in addition to some websites that have British counterparts, therefore we also have some interaction with British nationals as well.

Brian: While being effective and efficient is part of a the job, we also need to be professional at the same time.

Visitor 1624: I see. So your business and conversational base, it seems, is the West. Tell me: in your conversations is there anything you've noticed which sets Americans and British apart. You, I assume, are Asian.

Brian: Yes I am based in Pakistan, that is where we carry out most of our Operations from.

Brian: There is not much of a difference expect from small differences between language.

Brian: And to get down to the core, the visitors who talk very professionarlly are hard to differentiate.

Visitor 1624: Does that mean that there is not usually much friendly banter? Your conversations and exhanges of ideas are strictly business, would you say?

Brian: Most conversations are to the point and consist of "business" only, Friendly talk is there, but that also depends from visitor to visitor.

Brian: Most people like to keep it short and to the point, which ends up as being as a Non-Friendly talk.

Visitor 1624: So to them you might as well be a computer program. Your alive-ness is irrelevant. Accurate?

Brian: Not really, people are able to recognize the fact that there really is a real peson sitting at the other end.

Brian: The main difference it creates is that the visitor is a lot more satisfied, as he knows that a person is taking care of them, and also giving him time.

Visitor 1624: Because you always treat them as unique and special people, with hopes, feelings, dreams, desires. Accurate?

Brian: Correct! That does give them a good feeling.

Brian: A computer cannot treat each and every person/ situation differently.

Brian: A live peson can do that!

Visitor 1624: Are they more responsive to a male of female "voice"?

Visitor 1624: Male OR female voice, excuse me.

Brian: I believe some tiems people are more responsive, or say, more friendly with female operators. but mostly there is no difference.

Visitor 1624: Have you ever tried using a female Anglo name, instead of the male "Brian"? Something like "Brianna"?

Brian: I certainly have not really found the need to do this, but this kind of problems have been faced by other operators on some websites.

Visitor 1624: Our study finds that the two female names Western consumers respond to most favorably are: Jennifer/Jenny, and Hazel. Good male names are Thad, Brad, and Chad.

Brian: That should help our recruitment process, Thanks!

Visitor 1624: I should tell you that Brian is far down the list, bordering on eliciting consumer contempt and fear. Along with Ryan and, of all things…Chaz.

Brian: If you don't mind, Can you tell me about the name "Matt"?

Visitor 1624: I will have to check the records quickly. Why do you ask?

Brian: One of my colleagues name is Matt, and he is interested to know.

Visitor 1624: I have found the record. It will take a few seconds to transcribe. So please hold tight. Are you thinking of changing your name to Matt? A good idea, I would think. I recommend we all distance ourselves from Brian if we can.

Brian: if possible, can I have a copy of your research, your study greatly interests me!

Visitor 1624: Well, I am already breaking protocol in compiling the information on Matt you've asked for. There is too much money involved to be giving out freebees, and this information is not available to the public. However, if you have any specific questions please ask them, and i will help if i can. I shall be back with your Matt statistics shortly.

Brian: I know I might be asking a lot from you, but can you please give me a couple of hints/tips that would help in our conversations.

Visitor 1624: Well, you would have to ask a specific question. Then I would respond.

Brian: I believe I do not have any specific questions.

Brian: Is there any thing I can assist you with?

Visitor 1624: You've been a great help, Brian. I'm glad I can return the favor by compiling the Matt data for you. How long, may I ask, have you been Brian? Was that your first choice? What others did you try? Has it been working for you? Our data says you can't possibly be working at over 20 percent of your potential!

Brian: I have been working under this name for over a year now, and I believe it has been quiet successful for me.

Visitor 1624: You are the exception to the rule. What is your real name, if you don't mind me asking. We haven't yet compiled statistics on Pakistani names, though we're just beginning to break the German code. Hans, it turns out, is a winner. Adolf, of course, is marketplace suicide.

Brian: I apologize but I am not allowed to share that with you, you can say, this is as real as it gets.

Visitor 1624: I'm sorry to hear that. I find your case study to be interesting. Why not do this as I finish compiling your Matt data for you: Why not write me back a sentence of words where the first letter of each word corresponds to a letter of your name, in subsequent order. For instance, if my name was Matt, I would write you this coded message: Mustard Ashes Tea Tray.

Brian: That would not possible due to the amount of check we are under

Visitor 1624: I understand. Thank you for you patience with me, Brian. There are literally hundreds of pages on Matt. I'm trying to compile the facts that would most interest you.

Brian: Since this is about names, May I have your name as well please?

Brian: Still there?

Visitor 1624: Yes, still here. I'm just about ready to copy and paste my report to you, Brian. Then I really must get going. It's almost lunchtime. But let me ask you, for my own records, why won't the people at WebsiteGreeters let you tell me your real name? Do you find this to be a good practice? Should I bar my workers from divulging their names to one another? Do you find it makes you more productive? Do you get more done?

Brian: Certainly. Since we like to give a feeling to our clients that our greeters are part of their own staff.

Brian: This practice enables us to do just that!

Visitor 1624: Of course! You're something of a spy aren't you, Brian, my friend. Or shall I start calling you Matt! I have a feeling you are going to like my results!

Brian: :-)

Brian: Lets see the results then.

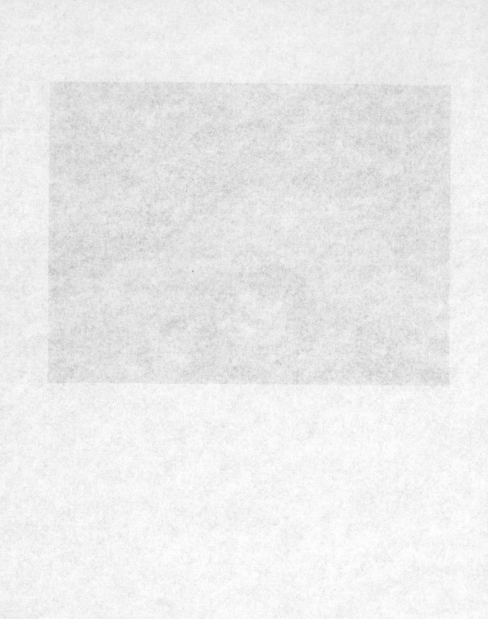

KANSAS

PART 3

Explosion at Amgen across the street — evacuated to our building — tons of cops
5:32 PM

I'm going to watch through the gym windows
5:33 PM

Phone dying will send report by email
5:37 PM

175. April 8, 1996

Dear Matt,

I know I told you months ago I had found a great card for you, but I am embarrassed to tell you I lost it. I am sure it is in one of my stacks of stuff, but I haven't been able to put my finger on it. Your Mom told me you were leaving for England in the next couple of weeks, so I thought I better get my note off to you. If I find it while you are gone, I'll get your address from your Mom and send it to you there.

I had wanted to write you for a couple of reasons. The first was to let you know someone was thinking about you—you are close (just being in Seattle) but so far, and I wanted you to know you were missed. The second was to let you know I was praying for you, asking the Lord to bless you, keep you safe, and give you direction for your future. From my perspective, you are doing all the right things for a young man your age (earning money, going to college, living on your own), but even when we are doing everything right right now, we have a tendancy to feel unsure about what comes next. The third reason was to share some verses with you, things the Lord laid on my heart as I prayed for you.

Matt, you're not like the average guy walking around. The Lord has built into you some very powerful things—skills, talents, and a quick brain that adds stuff together really fast (and I'm not just talking about math). You probably aren't going to be content to live a routine life like most people; your going to England says a lot about that. But, I think your biggest challenge will be to have all this vision and talent and energy and keep it funnelled towards the things that will bring you peace, joy and fulfillment, not sadness and emptiness. I don't know what is going on in your life right now, what you are thinking or experiencing, but as I pray for you, these are the things the Lord lays on my heart.

176. My head was killing me. I'd been in England four months. I was entering data for The Prudential sixty hours a week. The Pollutionist was stuck on page 191. I spent all my money on booze, and tried to save, so I could travel around the Continent, on my own. Waking up later and later each day, always coming in late. The boss told me to get my act together. I looked awful. I wasn't sleeping. I wasn't dreaming. My whole body ached. I couldn't keep my head up. My shoulders slumped. I felt that I was sinking. I felt that the atoms of my body were being pulled apart. On the bus, or walking down the street, alone: I'd start laughing sometimes, for no reason. Or more often I was crying. There were long and disturbing conversations going on in my head, and sometimes some of the words would spill out, publicly.

177. I'd like to encourage you to read Proverbs 2 and 3. As I am reading these chapters over, I hear the Lord saying "Everything Matt wants or needs is available to him through me. I have gifted him with a quick mind to discern true motives, and to communicate in writing in ways that will touch hearts and bring direction to lives. If Matt will hold on tight to my word, believe what I say and walk in righteousness, I will open doors and take him places his mind cannot imagine." The verses I want to share with you right now are Proverbs 3:21–26:

21 My son, preserve sound judgement and discernment, do not let them out of your sight; 22 they will be life for you, an ornament to grace your neck. 23 Then you will go on your way in safety, and your foot will not stumble; 24 when you lie down, you will not be afraid; when you lie down, your sleep will be sweet. 25 Have no fear of sudden disaster or of the ruin that overtakes the wicked, 26 for the Lord will be your confidence and will keep your foot from being snared.

178. People had left the house and others had come. Now I was an old-timer. After work, I'd stop at the Off-License, buy a couple bottles of their cheapest cider. It came in big plastic 2-litre bottles. I'd carry them home, get a glass from the kitchen, take the first bottle up into the TV room. I would sit hunched over in a ripped-up lounger, staring at the TV, scowling probably. The rule was that if anyone was in there with me, no one was allowed to speak to me, or to each other in a voice louder than a whisper, until I'd finished the first bottle. Ange would make sure no one violated this rule.

She would escort people out sometimes. When the first bottle was empty I would feel better, I'd be happy again, the pain wrapped in ice and snow. We could all talk and laugh and be friends again. I would drink the second bottle. Take some pills and

179. ▮▮▮▮

180. ▮▮▮▮

181.   The big challenge for all young people is to make a stand for Jesus — it seems like something you don't have to do until you're older (WRONG!). The Lord is saying, "Matt, make a stand and don't look back." Maybe you have already, and that is cool—this is just a confirmation. But if you haven't, the Lord is asking you to do it now.

I'm praying that your trip to England will be everything you hope it will be. I believe the Lord will use it to shape your destiny.

182. —Well, I haven't written all the subplots in yet. But [redacted] throughout the book, Ashe [redacted] beat up by the police [redacted] a girl who takes him into the mountains [redacted] waiting for a spaceship to come and take them away [redacted] have to prove to the aliens that they're worthy, [redacted] assassinate the P[redacted] fascist [redacted] ends up taking control of the city [redacted] private police force composed mostly of orphans and runaways. [redacted] a strain of poisoned bread which kills a slew of people [redacted] Capitalism run amok [redacted] TV talk shows [redacted] killed his wife decades before, [redacted] they come and kill the old man, [redacted] put in an orphanage when he was young [redacted] kept in a cage [redacted] people fade in and out, [redacted] all the while the headache worsens [redacted] it all actually makes complete sense.

183. I'm gonna start from the beginning. I was watchin…the voting. And then they broke, uh, all the local channels. I watched that for about an hour and a half, and I got tired of it. So I switched to uh, um…uh the local network, uh, Public TV.

Reporter: Uh-huh.

And Hillary Clinton was on, and she was givin her condolences to the people of Memphis and Arkansas.

Reporter: Huh!

And uh, and then a little bit more of them talkin about the vote and everything, and then the lights went out. Just before the lights went out, a red line went on, tellin me that uh the tornado was headed towards uh Westmoreland, and then two minutes later it said, No, it's goin through Lafayette! And so—and then the lights went out. Uh—

Reporter: It was just when the electricity went out when you realized that this thing was headed your way.

That's right. And then uh I put my sweatpants on, I was, you know, I was in my underwear, and uh, at my desk and uh, uh, I lit two candles, went into the kitchen to, uh, get my Schick flashlight and uh looked out the window to see if Miss Dixie was all right—see if she was puttin her lights on, and she was. And uh, came back in, sat at my desk, drank a shot of whiskey, and then uh, I heard this noise, and then I went to the—I got a { } fireplace—this is a hundred-year-old house—and I went next to it where there's a door, and then all of a sudden I heard—I I bent down low and all of a sudden I heard, the glass break and…sunk, it was sunken, so I tried to shut the door and when I tried to shut the door it seemed like the door was liftin up, so I just dove!

And I laid flat on the floor like *this*…and then I was—my, my back was takin everything—I could see everything comin across, just—

REPORTER: Everything was falling on top of you.

No, it was scrapin me and then *goin up!*

REPORTER: Oh!

And then after it was done I woke—I, I didn't wake up, I just…was layin there!

I was layin in the *DIRT!*

184. I wondered if when ████████████████████ the
     fire had come ███ something had broken.

185.   Be wise, and when you don't know what is wise at
         the moment, ask the Lord.

Open up

t o

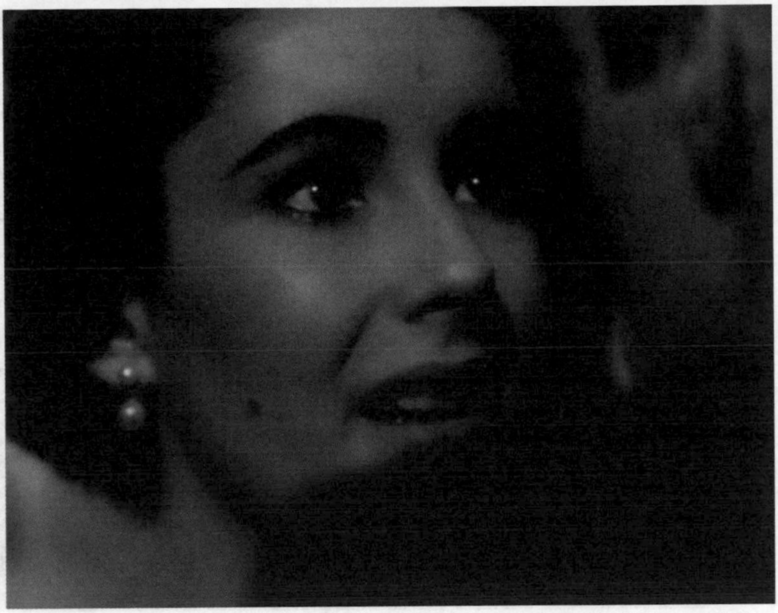

186. **But I'll be at the lake**

187. —Did you take your pills?

188. Then I dove into the shallow end of a pool and hit my head on the bottom. I came to the surface, got out and lay down on my back, dripping water onto the pavement beneath the hot sun, feeling not exactly right.

189. —He's also given an assignment to [redacted].

Complete Relief

190. **You'll come up and see me.**

191. She knocked on the bathroom door and called my name, but I didn't hear. In a panic, she rushed all around the house, upstairs and down, looking for help—she found Superlonghair and he kicked open the door and stepped away, so that he wouldn't see what he was afraid he might see. Angie rushed in and got down and said my name again. I don't remember any of this. It was all told to me later. But I remember vaguely one eye drifting open. I was in a pool and my forehead was against something cold, and hard, and wet, the drops dripping from my hair as I was lifted from the floor. She pulled up my pants, and held them up as she and Superlonghair carried me downstairs.

192. ANGELA: Oh, I've missed you so.

GEORGE: Me too. Oh, I can't tell you how much.

ANGELA: Oh, I have the most wonderful news, so wonderful I had to drive all the way down to tell you. Mother and Dad want you to spend your vacation with us up at the lake. (George shows concern on his face) Well you'll come, won't you?

GEORGE: (indecisively) I don't think I can.

ANGELA: Oh George, no. Look, this is my one chance to show you off to mother and dad. Take my word for it, I've gone to a…

GEORGE: I promised my uncle I'd spend some time with him during my vacation.

ANGELA: (overjoyed) Well that's perfect. Because your aunt and uncle are both coming up on the 3rd of September. That's when you're coming.

193. Hello Angie. Hello. I'm on a bus on my way to Prague.
Today is Friday. I'll get to Prague on Saturday night.
A week there, then I'll be in Amsterdam.

194. ANGELA: (she leans back, starry-eyed) Just think of it. We'll go swimming together, lie in the sun together, go horseback riding through the pine woods, and I'll make your breakfast for you every morning. You can sleep late. I'll bring it into you in your room.

GEORGE: And you love me.

ANGELA: Yes.

195. —I know you won't say it back, but I know you love me too.

HOW ANGIE CAME TO BE

196. Angie:

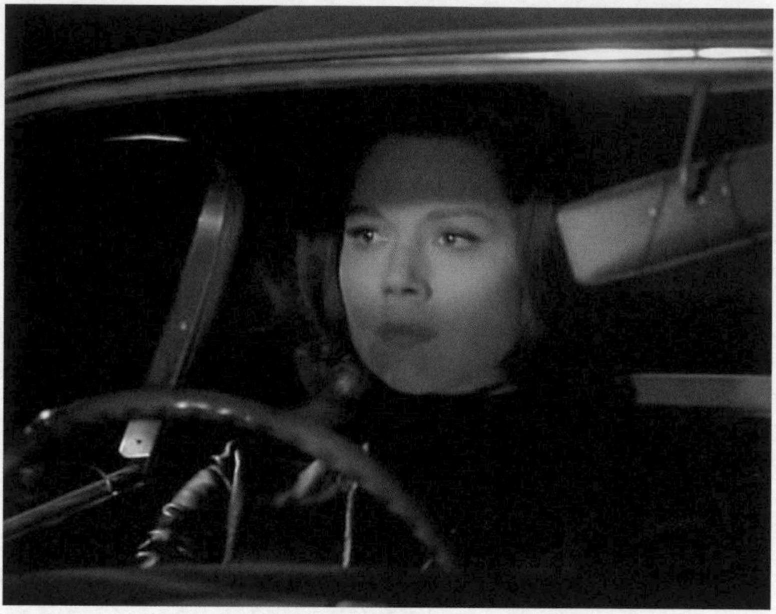

197. My mother was a wood nymph, pure and chaste—She spent her days frolicking in the forest, collecting berries, dancing in the meadows, and bathing in crystal streams—She was spotted collecting flowers one day by the evil Red-Eyed King.

198. (She took the joint out of my hand.)

199. The king was full of lust—He dragged the poor young thing into the hollow of a rotted tree—He forced himself on her and she became pregnant with me—She tried her best to hide her pregnancy but the vile king soon got wind and sent his men to kill her before she should deliver—he didn't want any little kids cramping his style, you might say.

200. The birds warned my mother of the plot and reported to her that the king's men were coming, so she ran, ran, ran—ran away!—

201. Up the side of a mountain—Up a winding path—up, up, up she climbed to the very top.

202. She looked down and saw the king's men—they were super fast, hey—right on her tail—swords in hands, closing in.

203. The path ended at a beautiful waterfall—She walked behind the curtain of water, into a nook carved in the rock—And there, hanging from the ceiling, she found a golden hook—And from the golden hook there hung a golden rope—And below the golden rope was a golden stool.

204. Oh, she looked beautiful that day, mate. Her face was all pink from being pregnant and I don't know if I've ever told you this but all the women in my family actually *lose* weight when we're preggers. She was real thin, like a model, she just had this little round bump on her belly. That was me. Oh. Sorry. I'm hogging the spliff, aren't I? I'm—I forget—what do you Yanks call it, cowboy? *Bogarting the j?*

205. (She handed me the joint.)

206. Where was I? Oh, yeah. Little round bump.

207. She could hear the bloodthirsty barks of the dogs—and the grunts of the cowardly men urging them on—She could hear the water crashing on the rocks—and the wave of water cascading around her—she cupped her delicate hand and reached out, drew out some water from the curtain, and drank.

208. Then she stepped up onto the stool—She put the rope around her neck—She put her hand to her belly and—in the last few moments before her pursuers arrived

209. sang to me:

210. Thou art the daughter of a Good Witch and a Bad King.

211. Thou wilt grow and suffer much at the hands of abusive assholes and cheaters and spend thy days alone upon the lonely isle Albion, waiting

212. For the coming of One, strong and true.

213. His corpse will wash up on thy shore one morn, dear, and thou wilt tend him and care for him and bring him back to life.

214. Sadly, it will be all for naught—for he won't be strong, and he most certainly won't be true.

215. And sorry, girlfriend, he won't marry you.

But if you can catch him, and hold him, and make yourself all sticky so he can't let go, then you just might find you keep him.

Now, cherry, Kingy's men are almost here,

And I must make haste and cease the flow of air into my neck.

As for thou, hold thy breath for as long as thou canst, and don't come out until they've come and done whatever they're gonna do to me and gone…

Then don't walk, doll—

HEAD SECTIONS

>RUN

nore, Beth
pening tip-
to 26 win
rs.
With steady grace, Helen [redacted] performs a
near perfect beam routine including this
back walk over to help the gymnastics team
make it to the state tournament.

216. Saw Sistene chapel, stared at Judgement Day for a long time.

217. (Fri Dec 29, 2006, 1:17 AM. JD's apartment)

[TV: *...I think right now for Kansas State you gotta ask, you gotta have that attitude to go out and play, beyond the call of duty...*]

JD: You wanna go to Vegas? You wanna bet on some teams? Conference tournaments?

M: I never bet.

JD: I *never* bet? Or I, *ne-ver* bet.

M: I never bet with money.

JD: It makes it interesting, for *damn* sure.

M: It makes it interesting *what?*

JD: For *damn* sure...

M: It's gonna give you a heart attack at age forty. You stress yourself out because you bet so much.

JD: No, I don't bet that much. If I had a *bookie*, then we could talk about that. Nah, I got my *one bet* and the person I bet with all year long, and that's Mikey, and that's just what I do. That's just *charity*—I fucking give Mikey *four, five hundred bucks a year!*

M: Why do you keep doing it?

JD: 'Cause I'm *gonna win!* I'm gonna win one year!

M: So how much did you lose so far?

JD: Well, we've been doing it for—let's see…about *five years*, on an average of at *least* four hundred dollars a year…*Two grand!*

M: [*laughs*]

JD: And the joke—his wife makes the joke like, *Hey, did JD pay you yet? Can we make our vacation plans?* And I'm like, *Yeah, that's a funny one isn't it!* [*laughs*]

M: [*laughs*]

JD: But it's cool……No, it's uh…I gave him a *cleaver* for Christmas [*laughing*] and like, he goes to try it out Christmas Day, right? And he just takes a clove of garlic up and puts it up there and…*WHAP! BAM!* He blows it apart—he's like, That's cool, it's *sharp!* So he's like, Well, maybe I just hit it too much. So he gets a clove—he does something stupid, I don't know—he gets it stuck like halfway, puts his middle finger underneath the *cleaver*, the *garlic*, and the *board* and for whatever reason he pressed *down*. It almost cuts the tip of his finger off, right? So he's like in the emergency room on Christmas Day—

M: This Christmas?

JD: Yeah! On Monday! So he [*laughing*] calls me up on Tuesday and says, *I wanted to call and say thank you for the gift*, you know, and like—*Yeah! I actually wanted to say* fuck you *for the Christmas gift!* I'm like, What do you mean, dude?

[*laughing*] And he explains it and shit and I'm like, well, What? No, no, what'd you do? *No, it was my fault, but*— Do you still like the gift? *Yeah, it's awesome! After I got out of the hospital, I went back and started chopping shit back up!* OK, it's cool! As long as you like it! His wife's like, *I don't think I'm gonna use that knife.* [*laughs*] It's a full-on—it's a mini *cleaver*—it's like, a full-on blade—it's probably like *seven inches.*

M: Where'd you get it?

JD: I got it at a a kitchen store up north. It was on sale. It's a Henckels fucking knife. Cuts his fucking finger off.

M: A nice gift.

> [TV: *If you don't get first downs—if you are continuing to go down back, get sacked, something like that, negative plays—you're gonna be punting from your end zone—you gotta ask your defense to go out above and beyond the call of duty…*]

JD: You should come over and see that Bodies exhibit.

M: What bodies exhibit?

JD: They got actually human bodies that like, they put in um, *acetone*, container, and then they pump them full of like *silicone*, something, so they're like *rubber*, and then they like *dissect them up*, like this prestigious surgeon will come and like, do a—do something on them to show like, *heart disease*, show *lung cancer*, show all this stuff and *all this shit*—and so like, when a guy's throwing a football, what muscles are involved and stuff. I mean, it's like—I hear it's intense; some people at my boss's Christmas party had just came from it.

M: Where is it?

JD: Downtown somewhere. I don't know if it's at the Science Center or the SAM. It's in town. They'll show like, when you *eat* something—maybe have a guy that's got his *esophagus* and all the shit cut up, and it's all *defleshed and shit*—and it's like, *Inside I'm rubbish*—like the guy in that movie who's like, *We're! Not! Supposed! To die!* That's the shit that's—I'm fucking rubble—I'm like, Oh, man! *I don't want to know this!* But then again I'm like, I kinda wanna see it......... They got billboards throughout town. And they show these *defleshed humans,* and it says { }

M: They've been advertising?

JD: Yeah.

M: And *what* was the advertisement?

JD: Underneath on the billboard is where I saw this, and it said:

REAL HUMANS—

REAL HUMAN—

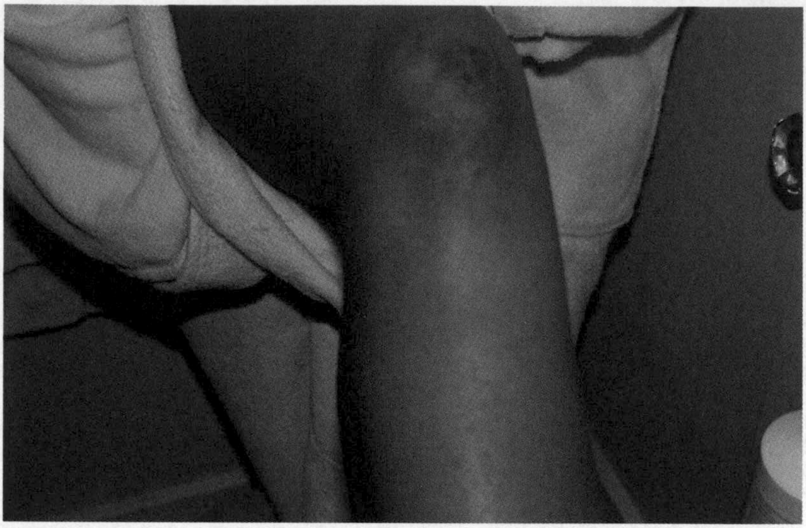

REAL

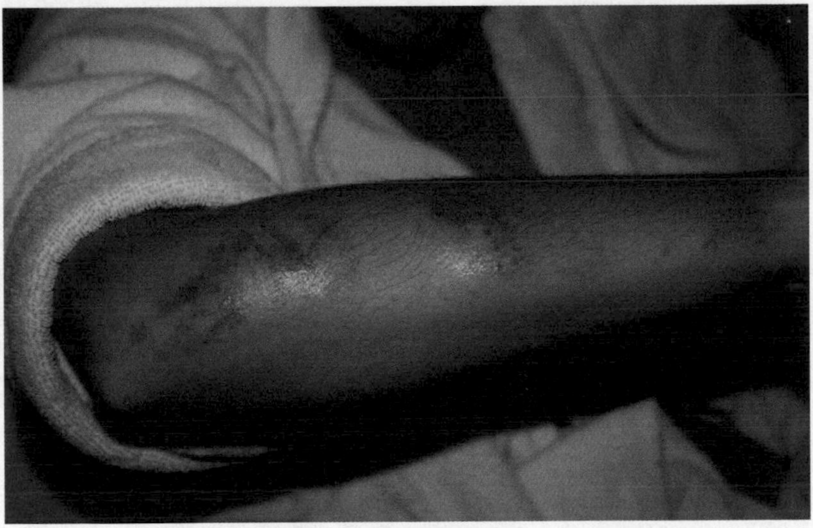

HUMAN

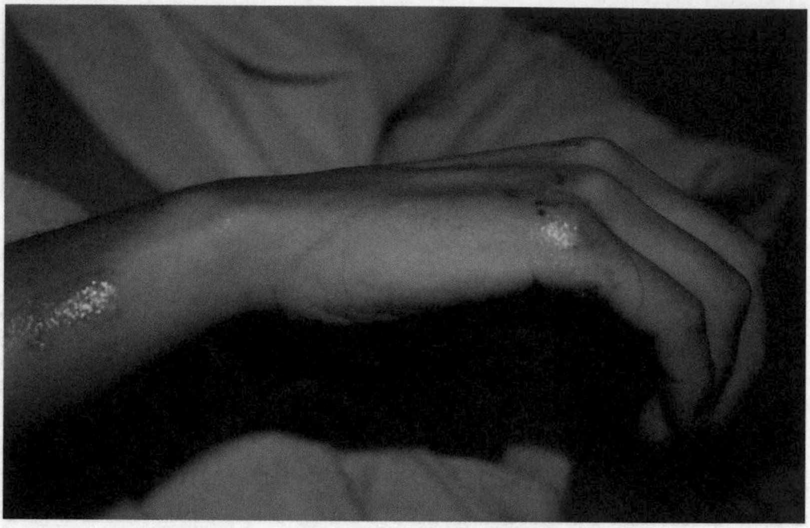

BODIES.

[TV: *She's not* my *mother, dammit!*]

JD: And at that party I met some people who had just gone, and I was like, No way…'Cause when I heard that they dip someone in acetone and, inject them with silicone, I was—I can't be hearing this right. He kept talking and talking about it—

M: Are they *cadavers* or—

JD: He said, No, they're donated to science, cadavers, or something, and…Aw…Supposed to be pretty gnarly.

M: Sounds like a bad thing to do, doesn't it?

JD: I don't know, it's—they said they show like—they cut open the *chest of a human* and they had like, so *all the intestines* were showing and shit, you know?—just *sitting there*, you know like—and the rest was all—I don't know if—sometimes the flesh was covered or what, or the bones covered, so like, there's a contrast, you know, you've got someone up there all red— Here's your...... They got *obese*...

M: It sounds like a freak show.

JD: Kind of...

M: I mean that's the appeal, isn't it?

JD: I guess, man!... But I mean, you can *learn a lot!*

M: Oh, you can learn a lot from a freak show.

JD: To all of the people who are performing—it's a regular display—it's affecting real—it's a *3D model*, like, you know... The dude was telling me he got to, hold a *brain* in his *hand*... ... Full on, like, yeah.

M: You give them five bucks and they put the brain in your hand or something?

JD: Yeah, you give them, I don't know. You can hold a brain in your hand, yeah......

[TV: *You can't just change your mind!*]

218.—WHAT DID YOU TAKE?

54. A Ange leaning

219. MATT: How'd you get that cut above your eye?
HELEN: My asshole dad.
MATT: What do you mean?
HELEN: He whipped me with the telephone antenna!
MATT: Well, what did you do?
HELEN: What do you mean what did I do?
MATT: What did you do to make him so mad?

220. I made her feel stupid. I made her feel like an idiot. I'd laugh at the things she'd say when she was trying to sound deep. She wrote me a poem, very proud of it, and I said, Well, maybe I can fix it somehow. When she'd call I'd pretend not to be around. I ignored her at school. I'd whisper about her and laugh. She'd come over to my house and I'd hide in my room while she talked on the front porch to my sister. My sister would come in when Helen drove away and tell me what she'd said.

221. —Why doesn't he want to see me anymore? Why doesn't he want to talk to me? Why doesn't he ever call me?

222. Walk out on the pier, and look out at the water. Lean over the rail, press yourself up to her. Load some weed into your modified asthma inhaler. Blow the smoke into her mouth. Down to the lighthouse where we were the first time I kissed her. A cold wind was blowing. We held hands. We sat down on a log that had washed up from the lumber

mills. We sat close. My heart was racing. I could barely breathe. I leaned into her and she into me.

223. Continuity: Alice Tripp is wearing different shoes when she starts walking home from the movie with George Eastman than she is when they are close to where she lives.

224. She did cartwheels in her underwear across my neighbor's living room floor. I sat on the couch, watching. The sun was rising.

—Can you believe I actually used to be a *cheerleader?*

225. She moved my hand away when it was time to stop.

6/7/96 Dear family, [redacted] they are expecting a huge thunderstorm [redacted]

226. Angie,

This is my last night in Munich, somewhere between six and seven, white walls, white doors, white ceiling, white closet … Having trouble writing. I think also that the drinking has messed me up. I'm not going out tonight like I didn't go out last night to save money for Amsterdam, but my stomach is twisting and setting my mind a little crazy. Every breath feels incomplete — difficult to explain but alcohol would set me right again. A bit frightening. The headache is also oppressive and these reasons might be why it is so difficult to write. Tried to yesterday but got nowhere.

227. —And the more his head hurts, the more the world outside falls apart; in other words the more chaos in his brain, the more chaos outside of it. They both spin out of control. His apartment building burns down. His wife has a miscarriage and she blames him, and the girl he falls in love with is kidnapped by the leader of the alien cult. And he finds the woman he's supposed to kill running a bird sanctuary, and everywhere he goes birds attack him. And he finds himself running for his life from the man who hired him, who calls himself Brubaker—who just may be [redacted]—coming to kill Ashe—and his head hurts more and more and the more it hurts the more the world comes crashing down, the more everything spins out of control—with the Orange Men burning buildings and raping girls—and Brubaker carries Ashe to the top of the hospital, and shoots him six times and throws him down the elevator shaft—but still Ashe doesn't die—and there's another scene where Brubaker drags him to his office and shoots him there—Ashe can't really remember which way it happened—and the world keeps spinning more and more out of control and his head keeps getting worse and worse and he can't sleep or think, and now every time he's indoors someplace, it doesn't matter where, poison gas will seep through the air vents and he'll start crying and laughing and crawling along the floor, until he gets outside; but every time he goes outside, he's either stabbed or beaten or shot, but he never dies, and he doesn't know why, but he sees ghosts and demons and dragons, doing battle in the sky, and sitting in chairs reading magazines in the waiting room, and some of them are dressed in suits and ties and carrying

briefcases, and some of them look like vampires and some of them like beautiful women, and millions of rats come out of the poisoned sewers and run through the streets, and into the churches and hospitals. And there are all sorts of car crashes! Everywhere he looks! And planes fall from the sky! And flocks of birds! And towers fall! And buildings collapse! And there are earthquakes! And there are rainstorms, and deluges and typhoons and tsunamis! Ships sink! And the rain turns to ice and blocks of ice fall from the sky! And the satellites come screaming from space like missiles and bring down tall buildings! And the towers come crashing down! And the houses and the people in the houses are crushed! And it'll keep going like this until at the end you'll see Ashe! lying on the floor! in a burning building! paralyzed with pain! but unable to even *feel* it anymore! unable to move or walk or talk anymore! he can't do anything! he can't do anything! all he can do is lie there! on the floor! while the city goes up in flames! like a lone twig on a dry forest floor! the whole world is going up in flames! His body is still alive! but his mind is resigned! and barely a spark left inside! only a single dim spark! and when that spark goes out, that's IT for him, Curtains! his mind will leave him for good! and he'll die! And it's about to happen! he's shutting down! It's like a countdown! He's at the end! 5…4…3…2…the curtain's coming down! But right as the curtain is about to touch the stage floor—suddenly it stops!
The curtain flies up again!

Because there's a knock at the door!

228. Thanks for reading to the end (this is a test to see if you did!). I don't know you really well, Matt, but you are a special person to me. I see God's hand on you, and hope I can be used to encourage you.

Andi

229. While on the deserted shore of Loon Lake following a freezing cold swim, Angela — wearing a black swimsuit, describes the geography surrounding the two lakes near her parent's home that are connected by a small channel — it was the location of a recent drowning:

ANGELA: It's in two parts with a little channel in-between. There's a crumbly old lodge down at the end of the other part, and its crumbly old boats. It's nice now. At night it's weird, especially at sundown. I've never been able to feel the same about it since the drowning.

GEORGE: What drowning?

ANGELA: A man and a girl last summer. Nobody knows exactly what happened. I guess their boat capsized. It was five days before they found the girl's body.

GEORGE: And the man?

ANGELA: They never found him. (The drums begin pounding in George's head) (A loon makes its distinctive bird call)

230. P.S. Piper says "Hi! Hows it going? Hope you have a great trip!"

231. I sent Angie a postcard from Prague.

232. ***Drop what you're doing and come meet me at the main Amsterdam train station at 8 pm on Sunday, the 15th.***

Your friend,

M

233. She requested a few days off from the car lot where she worked answering phones, and when they said no, she quit, bought a plane ticket got a hotel room and flew out to meet me in Amsterdam. She arrived in the afternoon.

234. My train arrived later. She wasn't there. So I found a corner in the terminal and sat down next to my pack and watched the doors for her. Every half hour or so I got up and walked through the station and out into the square outside, looking.

235. Eleven o'clock, she still hadn't arrived; I decided I needed to find a place to sleep, so I got up to look for a park. A dark shape came sprinting toward me. Growing nearer and nearer and then from the shadows sprung up—I caught it in the light of a streetlamp beside me. She was crying, and laughing, and kissing my neck. Where have you been all this time? She'd thought I hadn't made it. Apparently she'd been outside those doors all night, while I'd been inside. And every time she went inside to look for me I had just gone outside to look for her.

236.—You're *so thin,* mate! You haven't been eating!

237. We went to the Crown Hotel. The man behind the counter rang his bell and announced to all the potsmokers in the lounge, *Ladies and Gentlemen, her prince has arrived!* (She was worried about you, friend. She's been a wreck.)

238. We climbed the steep, winding

staircase—

239.—Why'd you put those rubbers in my pack?

—Hey?

—The rubbers.

—You mean the condoms?

—Yeah, Ange. I mean the condoms. I didn't even know they were in there until the second night. Why'd you put them in my pack?

—I thought you might need them.

—Don't you think that's kind of passive-aggressive?

—I don't mind what you do, mate. I just don't want to get a disease.

—How do I know *you* don't have a disease?

—I know I don't have anything; I've been checked.

—You haven't been *checked.* I know for a fact you haven't been to a doctor since you left Australia.

—Well, I haven't had sex with anyone except you since then.

—What about your so-called *fiancé?* Plus you told everyone at the Nobody that you had a one-night stand with a black guy, right before you met me.

—No—

240. We climbed the steep, winding staircase—

241. —You have a hard time remembering your lies from one day to the next.

—But that was—he used a condom, I mean.

—Who?

—The black bloke.

—There wasn't a black bloke, Ange. I know there wasn't a black bloke. You were saying all that because everyone was talking about sex and Ruthie had just said she'd screwed a black bloke, and you wanted everyone to listen to you, so you made up a black bloke for yourself. Because you didn't have anything to say about it, and you can't ever let anybody talk without adding your part and trying to make it look like you're more interesting than everyone else.

242. We climbed the steep, winding staircase—

243. —That's not true, mate! I did have sex with a black bloke! But he used a condom.
—But the whole point of the story was you said he *didn't* use a condom and you'd been worried you were pregnant! You don't remember saying any of this?
—You're saying it wrong. That's not what I meant.
—Then what the fuck did you mean?
—I don't remember.
—I bet you don't.
—Did you use them?

244. to a tiny little room with a bed and a sink.

245. We ate mushrooms on the edge of a canal and I told her when we got back to London I'd take the empty bed in the room down the hall from hers.

246. —There's a knock at the door?
—Yeah.
—Who is it?

247. When we got back to London, we didn't have any money. We had no jobs. We looked for ways to eat and drink. We called about drug trials, but there was always an extensive interview process, and it would have taken too long to get paid. Blood banks didn't pay. Conventional wisdom said donating bone marrow was too painful. Somehow Ange

kept us in cigarettes and alcohol. She found another job answering phones. She came home with bottles of cider. She came home and made ramen noodles and tomato paste. She called it spaghetti. I was tired. I wasn't sleeping. Sometimes we'd screw in her bedroom and she would be happy; then when it was time to sleep, I'd go back to my room and through the thin wall, I would hear her turning over in the bed.

248. She talked my boss into letting me come back—she gave her a sob story about my awful health condition—so I got my job back at the insurance office, typing, typing, typing away. clicketyclicketyclicketyclicketyc

249. licketyclicketyclicketyclicketyclick

250. tyclicketyclicketyclickdetyclxkcueocflclic

251. ketyclckjclikcetyclcickleryclickerytl;ckuyapseldfi

252. apoefjk a;kdihf a;dklj a;sdiljfa;lkcj ;aseilf apsleifj asodp

253. ifj apseoifj as;dklf jas;fkljas;fkl jas;fkljas;l fj asdl ifq wwe89fha

254. w310=frk q03u4 ta[sdo q]wepfkqa3r4gtqa[origj q9refg]peo

255. rw

256.]werog jszp

257. Carol

258. (caption): **But you have to be on *time* from now on.**

THE POLLUTIONIST
NEW BEGINNING
CHAPTER I

260.

Joseph Ashe was staring at the door.

261. Close examination of the bust will show one of the poet's hands is missing

262.

At night I would wander around the city. I arranged to meet a beautiful Scottish girl at a bar in Camden Town. Her name was Katriana. She was rich and had big tits and as we'd rolled around one night drunk in my little hostel room in Prague, she'd said, I wish that girlfriend of yours could see us now...

263. I waited all night in that crowded bar but Kat never showed.

264. I rode the tube home feeling just *terrible* about myself! It was a real blow to my confidence!

265.   MEANWHILE, ACROSS TOWN...

266. A

267. ngie

268. ██e██

269. ██ee didn't

270. want to be around

271. me anymore if it wasn't

272. her I was looking for. It embarrassed

273. her being at home now and besides, she

274. still loved me with her whole heart and mind.

275. It broke them both to pieces to look at me or hear me

276. laughing with someone else the way I'd laughed with her.

277. So she found a second job working nights, stocking shelves at a

278. late-hours grocery store. I walked by once on my way home from

279. getting drunk. I saw her through the store window stacking

280. lettuce into a pyramid. She wore a smock of red and white checks,

281. cinched in the middle, cheap fabric bunched and flaring out at the

282. waist. It made her look poor and matronly. I didn't like myself for

283. thinking such things, but once The Truth had looked me in the

284. eye there wasn't much to do but dwell on it. We were just too unalike.

285. I was young and brilliant. Destined to be famous, rich. Hot wife and

286. concubines. She only took that job to make me feel like a dick. What a

287. bitch. Chronic liar. Attention hog. Bad speller. Her Top Ramen tomato

288. paste pasta was far from delicious. ███████. ████ hair, ████████

289. teeth, ████ hips. That scar on her ████. The Pollutionist was going to be

290. the world's greatest novel. ██████████████████████████.

291. And tell me who could ever

292. love someone

293. who considered *that*

294. a pyramidal lettuce stack?

1.   Dear Matt—

Well the fridge is still full of food. It's just the weirdest thing. I guess I need to get Jon to come over or something

Have you had any fun yet or done anything unusual?

IT'S SO LONELY HERE
IT'S LIKE WE WERE THE ONLY TWO
PEOPLE LEFT IN THE WORLD
MAYBE WHEN WE GET BACK TO
SHORE EVERYBODY WILL HAVE
DISAPPEARED
I'D LIKE THAT WOULDN'T YOU
WHAT'S THE MATTER YOU LOOK SICK

295.—What's the matter? Angie said.

—

—Can you get up?

—

—Can you say something?

—

[redacted]

[redacted]

Bard, play on!

Man runs agency, pollutes

—believes he is supposed to do this
—believes it is all very professional
—pollutes the land, city, air, etc.
—pollutes lives, minds, emotions
individuals, families

It's his JOB

—plagued by headache

Perception of reality, his fantasy is
far from TRUTH

DISAFFECTED

headache gets worse as the book progresses

laughing alone on a bus

"I thought it was a movie theater."

Actors on
plastic seats.

Attempts to
reach out,
but can
only
POLLUTE.

Loses hold on
reality as
book
progresses

296. I called Kat from work. At first she didn't know who I was. I asked if she was OK. She hadn't shown up for our date. She made it seem like we hadn't spoken in weeks. Then who the FUCK had I been speaking to?!?!

loses everything

297. What's happened to us, George? We've grown apart, haven't we? Do you remember the first night we kissed, George? We were walking home from the city, do you remember? It was Yankee July Fourth and you wanted to celebrate! But none of the pubs were celebrating, George! And nobody wanted to hear about your Independence! Because we were in England, George! And they'd lost that particular war! So we bought some beer at the shop and drank it as we walked home! Remember, George? You kept stepping on the back of my shoe! On purpose! And I kept pretending to fall into you! And you would catch me! This went on for a long time! And then finally you embraced me! And we looked into each other's eyes! And you kissed me in the light! Do you remember, George? O, I'd waited for you to kiss me for so long! O, George! George? And then we stayed up all night talking in the kitchen, George! And when the rest of the house was asleep, I went into my room and got my blanket off my bed, and we went upstairs into the TV room, George, and the lights

were off, and we lay down, and pulled the blanket up, and I helped you in, George, I helped you in! I helped you in! I helped you into me, George! And you can come in me whenever you want because I'm bleeding all the time! Every second every day! And when I'm bleeding I can't get pregnant! So you don't have to worry! So you can come in me you can come in me, OK? When I'm bleeding I can't get pregnant! So there's nothing to worry about! I won't get pregnant and you won't have to marry me! OK, George? George? George! George! What did you take?

2. Well—still no great excitement here at home. Dad's been sick <u>in</u> <u>bed</u>! For two days. <u>That's</u> been strange. Anne's about the same. She and Brianne and Kyle got lost trying to find Sheri's fashion show in Parkland and missed the whole thing. Kyle just rolled his eyes…

3. (you never realize just how boring your life is until you try to send news to someone and find you don't have any…)

4. Wish I could walk around London with you. Of course I'd want to go to Harrod's and antique stores. And castles. And gardens. Are they still rowing in circles in Hyde Park?

5. We do miss you Matt. So quiet here. No one to make me <u>laugh</u>!

298. The Nazi beat his pregnant girlfriend.

6.   mom

299. She screamed.

300. A blue background with a red X.

He picked her up.
No! No! No!

At the TV, breathing hard. A mother in a red and white blouse knelt on the ground,
She screamed.
weeping as she kissed her dead daughter's face.
He threw her down.
at the TV, breathing hard.
BOOM!
The ceiling rumbled, light rattled, TV:*:*:*:*:*:*:*:*::*::*:*:*::*:*:*:*:*
:*:*:*:*:*:*:*:*::*:*:*:*:*:*:*:*:*:*:*:*:*:*:*:*::*:*:*:*:*:*:*:*:*:*:*:*:*:*
::*::*:*:*:*:*:*:*:*:*:*:*:*:*:*:*:*:*:*:*::*:*:*:*:*:*   *:*::*:*:*:*:*:*:*:*:*:*:*:*:*
:*:*::*::*:*:*:*:*:*:*:*:*:*:*:*:*:*:*:*:*::*:*:*:*:*:*:*:*:*:*:*:*:*:*:**:*:*:*:*
:*:*:*:*:*:*:*:*::*:*:*:*:*:*:*:*:*:*:*:*:*:*:*::*::*:*:*:*:*:*:*:*:*:*:*:*:*:*:*:
::*:*:*:*::*:*:*:*:*:*:*:*:*:*:*:*::**:*:*:*::*:*:*:*:*:*:*:*:*:*:*:*:*:*::*
::*:*:*:*:*:*:*:*:

At the snow, breathing hard.
shook, antenna fell to the floor.

One night I sat on the bed alone
and tore a strip off the title page of
an old tattered paperback copy of Albert Camus' *The Stranger*
and rolled it into a tube.

I popped open the red pill and dumped the powder out onto the cover.

Snorted it. Then-looked-up—An old man with metal eyes!*We are all made of parts, some parts metal, some parts human parts*—Something broke-a-branch-snapped—dark figure fluttered away—HA HA HA HA HA!—My-head-collapsed-it-duckedandIcovered-its-eyes and I rolled. Back. I managed to roll-them-back[Get off the bed!]and out the door [*He staggered into the kitchen. Knelt down, and rolled onto his back*] then back-again-they-rolled-back-again. *We are all made of parts, some parts metal, some parts human parts* The marble spiraled down, down, down the spiraling chute. One day, once upon a time, █████ ███████████████████████████, a little boy ran out from the wet palm trees, which dripped with warm rain—then stopped! For standing there before him as large as a mountain with teeth as sharp as a shark's teeth and eyes as red as lava pits was ██████████████, Himself!— and the dark hole wound down down down down down—and the Killer leapt!—and the boy was stung and—ran and dove and splashed down upon his stomach he slid down the plastic tarp all the way down to the end   back to a wall, with your heels about the length of your feet away from the wall. Then, lean back until your buttocks and shoulders rest against the wall. Dorsiflex both ankles simultan-eously, while your heels remain in contact with the ground. Bring your toes as far toward your shins as you can, and then lower your feet back toward the ground, but do not allow your forefeet to contact the ground before beginning the next repeat. Simply lower them until they are close to the ground, and then begin another repetition.

This part is called

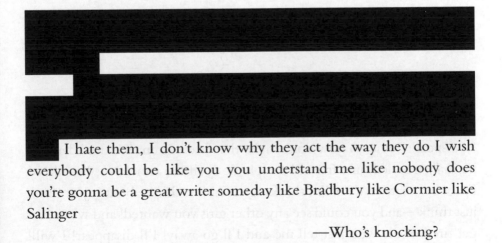

I hate them, I don't know why they act the way they do I wish everybody could be like you you understand me like nobody does you're gonna be a great writer someday like Bradbury like Cormier like Salinger
                                        —Who's knocking?

I'm not a slut. I've only been with one guy besides you. And I broke up with him, not the other way around. No matter what they say.

like Camus like Kafka like Beckett

I don't care if they call me a whore. You know I'm not a whore.

like Hemingway.

No matter what they say.

Like Shakespeare Like Cervantes Like Joyce

This part is called

[redacted]

At least I'm not a phony.

Mate, what if you married me?

:-(

No, listen for a minute—just hear me out! What if we got married and I went to America with you? No no no no no I mean just so I could get a passport! Come on now don't make that face! Listen: We don't have to be *really* married, just friends! People do it all the time! No; listen! No I'm sober mate I swear I'm thinking clear! Just think about it just think just think—and you could see any other girls you wanted! and when you get tired of me, you just tell me and I'll go away! I'll disappear! I will! Just like that mate I promise! I'll go away, I will! I will, I will, I will!

—Who's at the door?

HI, HO-NEY, I'M HO-MER!

301. Travelling is the way to live your life while you're young definitely.

One night, Ange called in sick to the grocery store. She bought a bottle of vodka and locked herself in her room, turned her tape deck up as loud as it would go, blasting the same tortured love song over and over, screaming the words at the top of her lungs for over an hour. I was in the TV room right above her. Every once in a while something would hit the ceiling below with a loud THUNK! But I just sat there, staring at the screen, drinking from my glass. THUNK! From across the room Superlonghaired Ian was staring at me with a scowl.

—What is it, Superlonghair?
—Shouldn't you go down and see if she's all right?
—She's fine; she's just being dramatic.
—She's going to put a hole in the bloody ceiling.

THUNK!

—Who's knocking at the door?

—Don't worry, pal. She'll tire out eventually.

THUNK!

THUNK!

THUNK!

THUNK!

THUNK!

KA-THUNK!

KA-THUNK!

KA-THUNK!

302. We rode the train from Amsterdam. We stepped off in the dark. Platform 4 of the empty Antwerp Central Station. We had no money or food. We were starving. While we waited for our next train to arrive, I walked around, jamming my fingers into the change chute in every phone booth, candy machine, condom dispenser I could find in the station and surrounding blocks outside. When I returned, as if by miracle, I held in my palm precisely the amount needed to purchase a candy bar. We hopped around then from machine to machine, excited, looking through the glass, our stomachs rumbling…but which item to share? We decided finally on a bag of peanut M&M's. Are we sure? Yeah, we're sure. OK. Here goes.

303. I put the money in. Pressed the button. She hugged me, expectantly. The wire spiral which held the bags in line began to turn. It whirred and twirled slowly, revolving, and the candy jerked and began to move forward, spurred along to the point of the drop. It moved, forward, as the spiral moved, but then, when the whirring had ceased and the wire had stopped, the candy just hung there, dangling on the other side of the glass.

304. *"You have GOT to be FUCKING KIDDING ME!"*

305. At last it was quiet. Coming down the stairs I found her lying facedown on the carpet outside her bedroom door, crying into her arms. One of the girls was kneeling beside her, rubbing Angie's back and talking softly. I had to step over Angie's legs in order to get to the kitchen. Got my bottle of cider from the fridge, walked back—stepped over—and started back upstairs. The girl said something to me.

—Pardon? I said, looking back.

—I said, the girl said, *She fell.*

—Is that right, Ange? I said. Did you fall? Or did you just *pretend* to fall?

306. Angie lifted her head and looked up. Her eyes and face were red. Snot dripped from her nose.

—Fuck you, she said, put her head back down, and began to sob.

307. Fuck me.

—Knock-knock.

308. I opened my eyes. In a room somewhere. A noise. I heard it again.

Knock-knock.

309. I knocked on the glass with my knuckles. Knock-knock-knock. A little harder then. Slapped the side of the machine. Then I Turned My Hand Into A Fist!——I punched it hard, I pounded on the side, took a step back, slammed it with my shoulder! But the candy still just hung there! I kicked the machine, hard, but IT WOULD NOT FALL! It's OK, Angie said, Stop. BANG! Stop it! she said. GODFUCKINGDAMNMOTHERFUCKINGCUNTIsaid! I kicked and hit and punched and bit and scratched and clawed and tore—Someone's coming! she said.

310. A security guard moving quickly in our direction, his hand on the handle of the baton swinging from his hip.

He shouted:

Leave now!

311. It took our money!

312. Leave now!

313. It took our fucking money!

314. *NOW!*

315. *YOU!*

316. *LEAVE!*

30. PHOTO OF PAVEMENT BY MATT (OOOPPPSSS)

318. The train would take us to the sea. We'd ride a ferry across the Channel to England, and another train to London. Then board the bus home to Albion Road, Newington Green. When the man came around collecting fares, Angie would tell him we had no money, and—would you believe?—he'd let us ride for free.

319. A YEAR OR TWO LATER, back safely in America, I told this story to a cute blonde I was seeing named Jenny, the story of me and Angie and our trip to Amsterdam where I broke up with her on a bench beside a dirty trashladen canal. I'd been wanting to break up with Angie all day. The fun we'd been having was worrying me, because I felt that the happier she got, the harder it would be to tell her that I didn't want to sleep in her bed with her when we got back to London. We had eaten magic mushrooms, and she was looking through a kaleidoscope she had bought, at the thousands of tiny little

churning, turning fragments of shape and color and light reflecting in the mirrored tube she held pressed to her eye. It was so beautiful it almost made her want to cry! She said it was like it had captured Christmas and the Fourth of July!

320. I took the tube and said, What say we let young McIntashe give 'er a try……

321. ……L e t's b r e a k u p

322. Get Laid Tonight!
Meet Someone For Sex In Your Neighborhood Right Now!
Head Lice & Nit Cure
No nit-picking, all natural, cure for HEAD LICE and nits! Testimonials
Personal Loans UK
Top EU websites about Personal loans
Meet HOT Singles!
Sexy Singles Looking To Hook Up With You Tonight.
Your ad here

323. Jenny felt just terrible for poor old Ange.

324. ;-)

325. JENNY SAID: *You broke the poor girl's heart? Oh, Matt, how could you? Ooh.*
Ooh.
Ooh.

326. The train

327.

328. cut across the Dutch countryside, on the way to Antwerp,

329. the sun

330. was setting behind those golden plains. A scattered

331.

332. army of windmills we blew by was cast

333.

334. in pink,

335. and orange. They waved their arms as we flew by. Angie and I sat across from each other, separated by a small white plastic table for the putting on of drinks, and the resting on of newspapers. We had not a penny to our names. Angie had a plane ticket home, but she wanted to stay together. So she'd spent the last of her money on a train ticket and a bit more weed, and we stayed all day downstairs in the lobby of the hotel, smoking and shoving the last of our change into the pool table. We didn't have food. That was OK because we weren't yet hungry. The hotel clerk gave us water. The train came and we boarded it.

336. The sun fell. Angie dozed. I sat with my head against the glass. Eight hundred hours to Antwerp. The farmlands rolled away.

337.

338.

339.

340.

341. A man got on and sat down next to me.

342.

343.
344. Red hair,
345.
346.
347. tan suit.
348.
349.
350.
351. Paint brushes.
352.
353.
354.
355.
356. One ear.

Van Gogh!

Hello.

I want to die.

Do you?

I want to die so bad.

I did too.

I want to die so fucking bad!!!!!!!!!!!!!!!!!!!!!!!!!!!!!!.

So what’ssssssssssssstopping you?

365 the stars 365 the

365. the stars 365. the stars 365. the stars 365. the stars 365. the stars 365.
the stars 365. the stars 365. the stars 365. the stars 365. the stars 365. the
stars 365. the stars 365. the stars 365. the stars 365. the stars 365. the stars
365. the stars 365. the stars 365. the stars 365. the stars 365. the stars 365.
the stars 365. the stars 365. the stars 365. the stars 365. the stars 365. the
stars 365. the stars 365. the stars 365. the stars 365. the stars 365. the stars
365. the stars 365. the stars 365. the stars 365. the stars 365. the stars 365.
the stars 365. the stars 365. the stars 365. the stars 365. the stars 365. the
stars 365. the stars 365. the stars 365. the stars 365. the stars 365. the stars
365. the stars 365. the stars 365. the stars 365. the stars 365. the stars 365.
the stars 365. the stars 365. the stars 365. the stars 365. the stars 365. the
stars 365. the stars 365. the stars 365. the stars 365. the stars 365. the stars
365. the stars 365. the stars 365. the stars 365. the stars 365. the stars 365.
the stars 365. the stars 365. the stars 365. the stars 365. the stars 365. the
stars 365. the stars 365. the stars 365. the stars 365. the stars 365. the stars
365. the stars 365. the stars 365. the stars 365. the stars 365. the stars 365.
the stars 365. the stars 365. the stars 365. the stars 365. the stars 365. the
stars 365. the stars 365. the stars 365. the stars 365. the stars 365. the stars
365. the stars 365. the stars 365. the stars 365. the stars 365. the stars 365.
the stars 365. the stars 365. the stars 365. the stars 365. the stars 365. the
stars 365. the stars 365. the stars 365. the stars 365. the stars 365. the stars
365. the stars 365. the stars 365. the stars 365. the stars 365. the stars 365.
the stars 365. the stars 365. the stars 365. the stars 365. the stars 365. the
stars 365. the stars 365. the stars 365. the stars 365. the stars 365. the stars
365. the stars 365. the stars 365. the stars 365. the stars 365. the stars 365.
the stars 365. the stars 365. the stars 365. the stars 365. the stars 365. the
stars 365. the stars 365. the stars 365. the stars 365. the stars 365. the stars
365. the stars 365. the stars 365. the stars 365. the stars 365. the stars 365.
the stars 365. the stars 365. the stars 365. the stars 365. the stars 365. the
stars 365. the stars 365. the stars 365. the stars 365. the stars 365. the stars
365. the stars 365. the stars 365. the stars 365. the stars 365. the stars 365.
the stars 365. the stars 365. the stars 365. the stars 365. the stars 365. the

stars 365. the stars 365. the stars 365. the stars 365. the stars 365. the stars
365. the stars 365. the stars 365. the stars 365. the stars 365. the stars 365.
the stars 365. the stars 365. the stars 365. the stars 365. the stars 365. the
stars 365. the stars 365. the stars 365. the stars 365. the stars 365. the stars
365. the stars 365. the stars 365. the stars 365. the stars 365. the stars 365.
the stars 365. the stars 365. the stars 365. the stars 365. the stars 365. the
stars 365. the stars 365. the stars 365. the stars 365. the stars 365. the stars
365. the stars 365. the stars 365. the stars 365. the stars 365. the stars 365.
the stars 365. the stars 365. the stars 365. the stars 365. the stars 365. the
stars 365. the stars 365. the stars 365. the stars 365. the stars 365. the stars
365. the stars 365. the stars 365. the stars 365. the stars 365. the stars 365.
the stars 365. the stars 365. the stars 365. the stars 365. the stars 365. the
stars 365. the stars 365. the stars 365. the stars 365. the stars 365. the stars
365. the stars 365. the stars 365. the stars 365. the stars 365. the stars 365.
the stars 365. the stars 365. the stars 365. the stars 365. the stars 365. the
stars 365. the stars 365. the stars 365. the stars 365. the stars 365. the stars
365. the stars 365. the stars 365. the stars 365. the stars 365. the stars 365.
the stars 365. the stars 365. the stars 365. the stars 365. the stars 365. the
stars 365. the stars 365. the stars 365. the stars 365. the stars 365. the stars
365. the stars 365. the stars 365. the stars 365. the stars 365. the stars 365.
the stars 365. the stars 365. the stars 365. the stars 365. the stars 365. the
stars 365. the stars 365. the stars 365. the stars 365. the stars 365. the stars
365. the stars 365. the stars 365. the stars 365. the stars 365. the stars 365.
the stars 365. the stars 365. the stars 365. the stars 365. the stars 365. the
stars 365. the stars 365. the stars 365. the stars 365. the stars 365. the stars
365. the stars 365. the stars 365. the stars 365. the stars 365. the stars 365.
the stars 365. the stars 365. the stars 365. the stars 365. the stars 365. the
stars 365. the stars 365. the stars 365. the stars 365. the stars 365. the stars
365. the stars 365. the stars 365. the stars 365. the stars 365. the stars 365.
the stars 365. the stars 365. the stars 365. the stars 365. the stars 365. the
stars 365. the stars 365. the stars 365. the stars 365. the stars 365. the stars
365. the stars 365. the stars 365. the stars 365. the stars 365. the stars 365.

366. Me and Angie lay on a blanket behind the house. A dim point of light skimmed the sky above us, parting the still black night. See that light? she said. You know what it is?

—Do you want to?

Knock-knock.

What?

A satellite.

—Who's there?

It's not a satellite. You can't see satellites from Earth.

—Do you think we should?

You can't?

No.

Then what else could it be?

—*A woman!*

Who knows. Angel maybe?

fuck me now

367. Angie slapping the sides of my face—WHAT DID YOU TAKE? WHAT DID YOU TAKE? Sweeping me off the kitchen floor, carrying me to bed, keeping me awake.

368. My head fucking hurts, Ange. It really fucking hurts.

Shhhhh…It's all right, my Love. We're together now.

kicked in the door

369. I am long but curl my shoulders in and try to shrink inwards then stretch my neck around so it doesn't get stiff but still nothing works, and I let out a hee-hheehe-heee! and sit nervously. So she turns on the radio click and looks at me confusedly, and they play an old tin can orchestra where a woman sings high with a wobbly voice. I flip through the *Journal of Painful Ills* and listen backwardly to the tin naily music and behind the desk, she has stopped filing. There is a soft glow to this light, I don't know why I am smiling this way, this odd smile. I imagine the singer in the center of the room with a sparkly dress and the wartime hair that has a definite shape and bobbed around with curls and ruby red lipstick and curvy hips but she sees me, wearing this suit and jacket but the black rain had caught me on the sidewalk and I am a mess. I am soaked through. I am hungry. Then there is no singer anymore, only the woman behind the desk, who I find staring at me. She looks worried. I may have been humming. Then I begin to laugh again, grinning slyly but with definite sorrow eyes. My head is tearing at the base and now I am squirming and sweating unbearably. My skin feels moldy and my eyes are

hot. What time is it? I barely see the clock, but it is above the woman's head.

370. :*::*:*:*:*:*:*:*:*:*:*:*:*:*:*:*:*::*:*:*:*:*:*:*:*:*:*:*
::*::*:*:*:*:*:*:*:*:*:*:*:*:*:*:*:*:*:*:*::*:*:*:*:* *:*::*:*:*:*:*:
::*:*:*:*:*:*::*::*:*:*:*:*:*:*:*:*:*:*:*:*:*:*:*:*::*:*:*
:*:*:*:*:*:*:*:**:*:*:*:*:*:*:*:*:*:*:*:*:*:*::*:*:*:*:*:*:*:
::*:*:*:*::*::*:*:*:*:*:*:*:*:*:*:*:*:*:*:*:*:*::*:*:*:*:*:*:*
: At the snow, breathing hard. Ange got up, plucked the antenna off the floor, plugged it back in back of the TV. Sat back down, uplooked at the ceiling, Quiet now. Soft sounds of UpstairsMother crying. The dirty brown Thames flowed from yellow mouths. Cigarette leaves and rusty beer cans. Someone coughed and sighed. A crowd underflowing Londonbridge. Floating down the still and still I felt very very tired, and the room small and the walls and the Audience roared, I was breathing hard. All outnone in. Oh, shit. Too fast. Shit, It's happening again. My head I got up.

371. —My brother told me what happened. Are you OK?
Fine.
—You look bad.
You should see them.
—I heard there were seven of them.
Yeah, well, it wasn't exactly a fair fight. Why are you here?
—I just wanted to see if you were OK. I haven't seen you in a long time.
I'm OK.
—I heard you hurt your head. Before. In the pool.
No big deal.
—Your face looks bad.

It's fine.

—I was going to bring you a present but I didn't know what to bring.

How about a cigarette.

—Here, she said.

Thanks, I said. I'll smoke it after you leave.

372. One more minute, then I can leave and the man with the black hat will meet me to give me my check. The woman has changed. She twists her face and tears up. The gas must have made it to her side of the room. She tries to stay calm but she's looking for a way out. She takes on an ugly shape and presses on her face in pain. I want to say I feel it as well but I don't say it. She stands up, then—Bang!—her chair falls back and she tries to rush to the door, but she falls and mouths words but no sound comes out then a strange squealing sound and she turns her head and looks at me, trying to crawl across the carpet. She vomits brown all over the floor and weeps. Now the clock says the last minute is up. So now I can leave. I stand up precariously.

373. Where are you going / downstairs.

374. Angela jumps up from the table and inquires about where he is going, while they are serenaded by an Hawaiian group playing a mournful goodbye song:

ANGELA: George? How long will you be gone?

GEORGE: I don't know, darling.

I just

don't

gno.

375. Tripped on the bottom step stumbled into. Bedroom Locked the Door. Behind the curtain drawn it was dark. Took off my clothes got into. Bed curled up tight. Here it comes. Here it comes again.

Ready? No! Not I'm not to. Walls spin. Are you ready? Here we go again! Here-we-go-a-round-begin! up off the bed. Stop crying. Kneel down and beg yes now crawl around the floor. 1 2 3 4 Good Now Climb back up onto the bed. Pull at your hair / slap at your head. Oh, Jesus, are you fucking crying again, Aw, fuck, aw, FUCK! I rolled around, I flopped around, couldn't breathein, sucked down now, pulled down now, and then there came a loud knock-knock-knocking-knocking at the door: ARE YOU IN THERE, MATE, OPEN THE DOOR! ARE YOU ALL RIGHT? leave me alone OPEN THE DOOR SO I CAN HELP YOU! falling from the center. Bursting forth the wet ripe skies the pounding wall began to cry, shield your eyes and turn away as it explodes, and a blinding light above me, and before the light, dark shape, a voice crying

I AM THE ANGEL OF LIFE!

(No you're not!)

I AM THE MOTHER OF LIGHT!

(Get away from me!)

WHAT'S WRONG! WHAT'S THE MATTER! WHAT DO YOU NEED! (Just get the fuck AWAY from me!) HERE, LET ME GET IN BED BESIDE YOU, LET ME

CALM YOU DOWN, LET ME HOLD YOU LIKE I
ALWAYS DO—

376. Then boom.

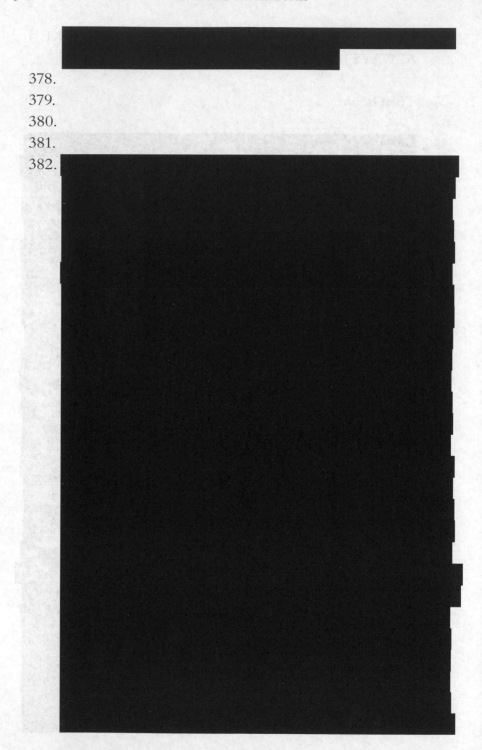

379.
380.
381.

386.

[redacted]

—holy Mary mother of God—

8695, good morning, have a good day!

Hi, what's your number again please?

8-695

Oh my god, I'm on the 83rd floor!

86—86 what?

I'm on the 83rd floor!

Ma'am, calm down one moment—86 what?

8695.

8695? She at the World Trade Center, someone having trouble breathing there on the 83rd floor.

OK, ma'am, how you doing?

Is—is it—is—are they gonna be able to get somebody up here?

Of course, ma'am, we're coming up for you.

Well, there's no one here yet and the floor is *completely* engulfed! We're on the floor and we can't breathe!

OK.

And it's *very, very, very* hot!

It's very—is—are the lights still on?

The lights are on but it's *very hot!*

Ma'am, ma'am, stay calm—

It's *very hot!* We're all the way on the other side of Liberty!
And it's *very, very hot!*

Any lights—you could turn the lights off?

No! No, the lights are off!

OK, good. Now. Everybody stay calm, you're doing a good job—

Please!

Ma'am, listen. Ma'am lis—*everybody's* coming, *everybody knows*. *Everybody* knows, what happened. OK?

{ }

No, no, they have to take time to come up there, you know that, gotta be very caref—

It's very hot.

I understand that, gotta be *very, very careful*, how they approach you. OK? All right? So when they come upstairs, it won't be worse than it is. Now you stay calm, as to—how many people where you're at right now?

There's like, five people here with me.

All up on the 83rd floor?

83rd floor.

With five people. Five patients. Everybody's having trouble breathing?

Everybody's having trouble breathing, some people are worse!

Some people unconscious? Everybody's awake?

So far, yes. But it's—

Listen, listen—everybody's awake?

Yes, so far.

Conscious? And it's very hot there, but no fire, right?

I can't see, because it's too hot!

No—*very hot*, but no fire for now. And no smoke, right? No smoke, right?

OF COURSE THERE'S SMOKE!

Ma'am, ma'am, you have to stay calm.

THERE IS SMOKE! I CAN'T BREATHE!

OK, ma'am, stay calm with me, I understand you—

I THINK THERE IS FIRE BECAUSE IT'S VERY HOT!

OK.

IT'S VERY HOT EVERYWHERE ON THE FLOOR!

OK. I know you don't see it right now, but I'm going—I'm document—I'm documenting what you say, OK? And it's *very hot*, you see no fire, but you see smoke, right?

It's very hot, I see—I don't—see any *air* anymore!

OK.

All I *see* is smoke!

OK. Dear, I'm so sorry. Stay calm with me, stay calm—

Please!

Listen, the call is in, I'm documenting, hold on one second please—

I'm gonna die, aren't I?

No, no, no, no, no! Say your—

I'm gonna die!

Ma'am, ma'am, ma'am, ma'am, say your prayers. And we're not gonna—

I'm gonna die.

We gotta think positive because you gotta help each other get off the floor. Now—

I'm gonna die, I know I'm gonna die— [*cries*]

Stay calm, stay calm, stay calm, stay calm—

Please, God!

You're doing a good job, ma'am, you're doing a *good job*—

It's so hot!

—*good job!*

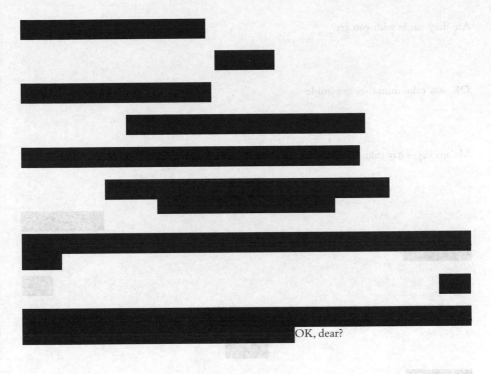

OK, dear?

Can you—can you—

I already did that, ma'am.

stay on the line with me please?

Yes, ma'am, I *am* gonna stay with you.

I feel like I'm dying!

Listen. This is, uh, uh—

They're here?

Are they inside with you yet?

No!

OK, stay calm until they get inside—

Will you find out where they are?

Ma'am stay—stay calm—ma'am stay calm until they get inside.

Ma'am, just stay calm for me, OK?

[deleted]

I think so, ma'am.

[deleted]

Ma'am, ma'am, listen to me.

[deleted]

Listen to me, ma'am—*you're* not dying!

[deleted]

bad situation

[deleted]

you're in a bad situation, ma'am

[deleted]

hold on

[deleted]

hold on a second. ACD—hold on, ma'am—ACD talk to her.

Hello, madam, calm down, OK?

[deleted]

Just take—take a deep breath.

[deleted]

Ma'am, just take a deep

[deleted]

believe us, ma'am, it's the only way, calm down, OK?

[deleted]

only way

[deleted]

there's someone—do you see them coming?

[deleted]

ma'am, only way

[deleted]

OK, listen to me

[deleted]

Ma'am, do you see fire?

[deleted]

You just feel *heat* though, right?

[deleted]

Ma'am, there's no—listen to me, ma'am

[deleted]

OK, in the ceiling, not on the—is the heat on the floor?

[deleted]

Oh my god, oh my god, listen ma'am. Listen to me, stay calm.

[deleted]

OK, this—no, no, don't be sorry. You're in a bad situation. Just gotta say our prayers and think of ways—when they—they have exits, they have ways that tell you how to get outta there?

[deleted]

They have exits in there, ma'am?

[deleted]

Ma'am, stay calm.

[deleted]

Ma'am, do they have

[deleted]

Ma'am!

[deleted]

I'll write it down, one second.

[deleted]

What's her name?

[deleted]

Mm-hm

[deleted]

Hold on one second, ma'am. Please hold, please hold

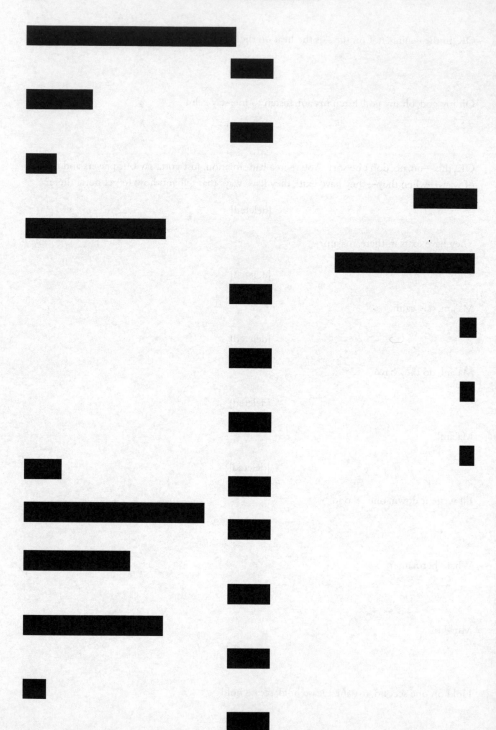

OK. What's your name, ma'am?

[deleted]

Melissa.

[deleted]

How do you spell it?

[deleted]

Mm–hm.

[deleted]

O-I. OK, and your mother is Evelyn. How do you spell *her* last name?

[deleted]

[deleted]

Yes you can breathe, ma'am. You can breathe. Stay calm, stay calm

[deleted]

Breathe slowly, talk slowly. Think of positive—think of something different from where you're at, OK?

[deleted]

Hold on, listen to me

[deleted]

Stay…calm, stay…calm, stay…calm.

[deleted]

Stay calm, stay calm, think positive—what's everybody else doing, ma'am—they just

[deleted]

OK, we couldn't put her on three-way, anyway. We don't have a three-way system for that, ma'am, but um, I would um

[deleted]

No, ma'am, don't go, don't go. Anybody else wanna leave their names? I'll take their names.

[deleted]

Is anybody else on telephones too? Hello, ma'am? Melissa!

[deleted]

Do not give up, please. Please don't give up, Melissa. Please do not give up

[deleted]

Oh my god. Melissa…Melissa…Melissa!

[deleted]

your mother in a second—you want me to call your mother for you and tell her that

[deleted]

to hold on?

[deleted]

{ }

[deleted]

there's no way—oh, Melissa

[deleted]

no doors, oh my god. Mmm-mm-mm.

[deleted]

on the

[deleted]

I'm on this phone

[deleted]

Melissa? Melissa?

[deleted]

Melissa, who you talking to?

[deleted]

Me

[deleted]

Who you talking to, baby?

[deleted]

{ }

[deleted]

Melissa don't hang up the phone. Melissa don't hang up the phone. Stay on the phone, OK? Gotta keep communicating. Don't hang up the phone

[deleted]

They blew the doors open—were the doors open?

[deleted]

up to that floor, correct?

[deleted]

Melissa! ELW. Melissa!

[deleted]

Melissa?

[deleted]

Melissa, can you hear me?

[deleted]

Melissa! Melissa. Melissa. Melissa. Melissa.

[deleted]

They said they blew the doors off!

Why didn't they keep the doors closed?

He doesn't know, he's not there.

Oh, OK.

So, who is that you're talking to, the fire department? Ma'am? Melissa. Melissa.

She's—the phone is still open.

Melissa?

[deleted]

lissa? Melissa. Melissa? Melissa?

[deleted]

Melissa?

[deleted]

issa.

[deleted]

Melissa?

[deleted]

Melissa! Melissa? Melissa?…OK, is she still there, her phone—

[deleted]

[deleted]

Oh, my. Melissa–Melissa.

[deleted]

Oh my god.

[deleted]

Melissa, is that the fire department talking to you all?

[deleted]

Melissa.

[deleted]

Melissa.

[deleted]

Melissa. Is this the south, south tower building?

[deleted]

Melissa.

[deleted]

Melissa?

[deleted]

Melissa.

[deleted]

Melissa?

[deleted]

Melissa.

[deleted]

Melissa?

[deleted]

Oh my god. Melissa?

[deleted]

Melissa?

[deleted]

Melissa!

[deleted]

Melissa. Can you hear me, dear? Melissa?

[deleted]

It's gonna be all right. Just keep saying your prayers, and

[deleted]

gonna be all right. Melissa.

[deleted]

Melissa?

[deleted]

Melissa!

[deleted]

Melissa!

[deleted]

Melis

[deleted]

Melissa?

[deleted]

Melissa.

[deleted]

Melissa, can you hear me, dear?

[deleted]

gonna be fine. Just keep

[deleted]

be just fine.

[deleted]

Oh my god.

[deleted]

Melissa.

[deleted]

Melissa, can you hear me? Can anyone hear me?

[deleted]

Melissa.

[deleted]

Melissa, can you hear me?

[deleted]

Melissa, it's gonna be all right.

[deleted]

Breathe slow, stay close to the floor.

[deleted]

OK, Melissa? It's gonna be all right. Just stay close…to the floor.

[deleted]

Breathe slowly. It's gonna be OK.

[deleted]

Oh my god. Melissa

[deleted]

Melissa.

[deleted]

Melissa.

[deleted]

Melissa!

[deleted]

Melissa?

(NEW ROLL)

54. Ange leaning against short wall; fountain behind her. She is smiling (At Trafalgar Squ.)
55. Now she is looking left, gravely
56. MATT IS SITTING ON FOUNTAIN LEDGE WITH WATER SHOOTING UP ABOVE HIS HEAD. SOFT LIGHT FILTERING THROUGH BY ANGE
57. MATT LOOKING TO THE SIDE WITH BLANK LOOK. FOCUSED ON HIS FACE. LIGHT & FOUNTAIN WATER SPRAYING BEHIND HIM. COULD NOT RESIST. TRAFALGAR SQUARE 10:30 PM
58. Matt & Ange in front of Trafalgar when the dark has set in. Irish man with an expert camera technician for a friend takes photo, while the friend says things like, "Stand in the light!" and "No flash?" and "It'll be dark. It won't come out well at all!" We just say, "It'll be alright. A little dark, yeah, but alright." And smiling.

405. I smile to her and walk heavy-footed through the door, closing it behind. Into the lobby where there is no one and up ahead through the pane, dark water is pelting the cement. Straight down.

Clothed, then laid back down in the dark, crying. Voices whispering in the hall. A knock on the door, then helped up, helped across the room, helped through the door, crying, helped past a group of people standing shoulder to shoulder in the hallway, crying, the door is opened, crying, helped outside,

406. The car is waiting and the man inside I think his name is Brubaker sees me coming and leans over and opens the passenger door.

put into a taxi, and sped off into night.

407. I get in. He drives on then asks me how I feel. I ache, I tell him. This is the best way to describe it. Anything else would be a waste of words.

60. MATT WALKING DOWN SOME STAIRS TO A DARK ALLEY 10:45 PM NEAR EMBANKMENT
61. "HURRY UP GUY'S THERE'S A CAR COMIN'" "2 LITRES" "2 LITRES" GROUP OF OVER CASUALLY DRESSED AMERICANS. SHOT FROM ABOVE DOWN ON THEIR SHINY HEADS & HAIRSPRAYED LOCKS. BY MATT.
62. Matt and Ange on Embankment Bridge "Make sure you get the Royal Festival Hall and now smile"—taken by man with long hair and a wife. Probably a carpenter or a tradesman smiling broader than we are—and these people are so nice…

I don't remember much else, except being curled up in the corner of the taxi, laughing and moaning and laughing again, while Angie, holding her cheek, leans forward, pleading with the driver to hurryup!—the two of them arguing over which hospital was closest.

63. PHOTO TAKEN OF MATT AND ANGE KISSING ON THAT BRIDGE (TAKEN BY ANGE)

    ANGELA: (breathlessly) You will come back to me, won't you, as soon as you can?

64. Ange doing up shoelace

65. Ange doing up other shoelace from other side.
66. "FALLING FROM OR THROUGH THIS ROOF COULD RESULT IN FATAL INJURY"

ANGELA: (heartbroken) You promise?

67. Corridor bus ride where you sit in the back and everyone is missing but a man in a flap cap in the seat furthest away, against the front window. And the bars across the tops of the seats shine silver and a white streak beneath the lights seems to join them all together. A brown tint to the camera as it is dark outside. Ange takes the picture.

Well I was just thinking of calling you from work but they are checking the lines this month.
I just wrote you a letter and then wiped the whole thing as it bored me and I didn't want to bore you so I'd just like to say, "Thinking of you, and miss you, would love to sit and banter with you, hope your well".
Here's a little picture of where I need to be.

Enough said, I'm out of here Twister Boy.

CHEERS
YOU TYRE LOVING APE

x

We've just gone over the bridge when I take one too.

68.

21 JUL 1996

OUT 21 JUL 1996 OF 21 JUL 1996 FILM

21 JUL 1996 21 JUL 1996 21 JUL 1996 21 JUL 1996

21 JUL 1996

END OF ACT II

ACT III

THE LAST DAYS OF THE SYSTEM

I WAKE. The room is faintly lit. My vision is blurred. I am without my spectacles. A girl is in the closet, stepping into a skirt. She pulls it up. I see her form, but not her face. The face is blank. But I can tell that she is looking at me. She seems unsurprised that I have woken. It is she who has awakened me. The house is old and the floorboards are noisy. Now she says to me, "I'm super late, so I'm gonna drive. OK?" I grunt to communicate in the affirmative, then close my eyes. I lie, listening to her dress. My body is sore. What happened last night? I remember staying up late, working. What was I working on? I try to remember. There was a man, and a woman. They were in black and white. Yes, I was watching an old film, searching for clues. I had surreptitiously downloaded the film from the Teleframe. I hoped the controllers were not monitoring my actions. It occurred to me that they might send dark-suited men to my little house. The men would knock on the door, and I would answer it. They would say that they were there to collect my information-compiling devices for scrutiny. I might try to resist, but it would be no use. If I did not comply and hand over my devices, they would take them anyway, by force. The girl was then in bed asleep.

It was past 2 in the morning. Would they come to take my devices in the middle of the night? Or would they come when the sun was up. On the devices were copies of the codex. But there was one more copy, a backup, housed on an information stick called Pee-Wee. He was hidden away. But would they find him? It would depend on how thoroughly they ransacked the house. I decided that if they should come, I would comply. Make no waves. That way they may think I am giving them every copy of the codex. And then what? Then they would take the devices to their laboratory. Their analysts would find and parse the codex. They would return to the house and arrest me. I would be kept as an enemy of the state. I must remember, I thought, to keep Pee-Wee's volumes current and up to date. I must remember, I thought, to hide Pee-Wee after each new data transfer. And also to erase any [redacted]. Now the girl is in the bathroom. I hear her running the faucet. Brushing her teeth. Beside this bed, the window is open. Each dawn is cooler than the one before. The Simulators have conjured up an earth slowly moving away from its sun. I wish it would stay warm. I wish the days would remain long, and that the winter would not come and bury us in darkness and cold. I feel as if I have been in a fight. My body is sore, and my hands are raw. But there was no fight. At least no fight with men. I have not fought with my fists in a long time. No, my body is sore because I have been scraping the paint off of this blasted house. The house is small, yes, but it never seems larger than when I am scraping paint off of it. The man who owned it before us had no respect for the house. Neither did the ones who rented it from him. He rented it to various poor white trash families. Invariably each poor white trash family owned a pit bull. Each pit bull scratched the paint off of the insides of the doors and walls with its razor-sharp claws. But I am not concerned now with the paint on the inside of the house. I am only concerned with the paint on the out. The house is of good construction, built eighty years in the past, right after the First Big War. Back then they knew how to build a house. However now every detail is hidden beneath globs of pale pink paint. The house has the appearance, accordingly, of a pale pink blob. But underneath hides a beautiful bungalow. It has been my task to find that bungalow. And it has been a difficult task. Day after day I peel through layer after layer of cheap, poorly applied paint. The last layer of paint was applied twenty years ago. My elderly neighbor Gerald told me this. The owner hired two men to come and apply the pink paint. The paint that they were covering was badly peeling, flaking, blistering, and cracking, just as it is now. The two men worked for a single day, and did not scrape. Which means I am now having to scrape away their mess, as well as the paint they should have scraped away themselves. This is why my arms and shoulders are sore, and I feel as if I have been through a Mexican gang initiation beat-in.

They make a circle around you

and for thirty-one seconds they all try to kill you.

After the thirty-one seconds have passed, if you did not cry, you are their brother.

They hug you and offer congratulations.

Someone hands you a forty-ounce bottle of malt liquor and another a cigar rolled with marijuana.

You wake.

Sitting slouched in a couch in the basement of El Duque's mom's house.

You are wearing long denim shorts down to your ankles and an oversized white tank top called a "wife beater."

White socks pulled up tight to each knee.

Your head is shaved and you have a little fuzzy mustache.

Just like your brothers do.

There's music in your ears.

The malt liquor warms you, and takes the edge off your sore ribs.

And the weed makes your aching head light.

Everyone's joking around.

"We thought you were gonna cry, Quixito. But you didn't."

You feel good.

I am vexed at being reminded of the paint. I have been scraping for three months. When I finish scraping, then the house will need to be washed. Then primed. Then finally painted. I have a long way to go until I am finished. It has taken me away from my work. It has wasted much of my time. But the man from the insurance company threatened to cancel our coverage if we did not replace the paint. And we have no money to pay anyone to do it. The girl comes out of the bathroom. She says goodbye and kisses my cheek. I hear her rush down the back steps, slamming the back door behind her. Then the car starts. She backs up down the driveway, and out into the street. Then she is gone. I lie in bed for a while. It is early still. I have only had five hours of sleep. But there is work to do, and I have dreamt enough for today. In my dreams I am solving the problem of order. I have much information compiled, and it is up to me to order it. It is a problem which consumes me. There is an endless number of potential orderings, but only one correct way. It is my job to find the correct order. The outcome depends on the order. It is also my job to compile. The ordering becomes more complicated with each new piece of information. For instance, this transmission will be included, but I do not know where. Information is reactive. Once linked to the codex, this information will form ideas. The ideas will link to other ideas within the codex and form new ideas. These ideas will form further ideas. Eventually, the ideas will become energy. Energy is power. And it is power that will move the machine. The machine will remove the girl and myself from the world of the Simulators. It will place us, together, in a world that is finally real. At least this is the current plot. I do not hold on to plots for long, for they constantly change as we move in a forward direction. Yet, there is one ultimate end to the story, and I am trying to find my way there. I cannot simply arrive. I must journey there. And by journeying I must act. And by acting, my journey grows longer. For with each act comes connections. Which must be worked through, then cut off. I am going the long way around. I am living these plots. For that is the only way I know how. I will not write the end. Projection is dangerous. If I project the end, I may find myself trapped in an alternate end created by my own mind. Then we would end in failure. In an unreal world, apart and alone. A world like this one, where poor men toil in darkness, applying layer upon layer of thick pink paint. And then poorly applying more. Then I will have to start the process of scraping it all off, all over again. So I will only write beginnings. I get up. That is to say I rise. I go into the kitchen and pour myself a cup of coffee. The coffee is already cold. This means she has been up for some time. I stand at the window looking at Gerald's house. His paint is cracking. Time passes. We pass within it. It always seems familiar, until we look back. When we look back, we find a time that has somehow gone out of style. We find paint has peeled. But we never saw it peel. We look at old photographs. The colors are muted, the corners are frayed. We, in the photographs, are different as well. We are younger, yes. But we are also occupying a time that no longer exists. Time has stopped for us there. And so in a sense we are dead. We stare straight ahead, and smile. Possibly, moments before, someone had implored us to say *Cheese.* We said *Cheese.* We knew that we were communicating with the future. For anyone who would someday see us as a result of the bright flashing light would not exist in this moment, along with ourselves. When the light went away we had been changed. And looking back we wonder now: Who chose that outfit for me? Who decided that that kind of clothing was fashionable? Why did you wear such dark eye makeup? Why did I think short spiky hair on top, and long in the back was appropriate? How could anyone be smiling while wearing pants such as those? I remember loving those pants. And still, in my mind:

I wake. She is at the closet, pulling up a skirt. The skirt is wool and knee-length. Made before she was born. She buys all of her clothes at the thrift stores. The good stuff is hard to find. She is tall for a girl and most things do not fit right. But every once in a while, she will find something that was made for her. She tells me how they constructed clothes better then. She has the look of a girl from the black-and-white movies. If she is ever in trouble, she is only pretending. I have a long black wool overcoat. She found it in a thrift store a few years back. It was tailored to fit a man exactly my size. She found it on a rack beside a camel hair coat with silk-lined pockets. She bought the camel hair one too, but I have never worn it. Both coats belonged to the same man. That man is surely dead. No one among the living would have given up such fine threads. I, myself, will keep them until I die. They are of such fine quality that if taken care of, they will outlast me. I must store them where there are no moths. I must hang them up after each time I wear them. Finally, I must make sure to never fall asleep while smoking a cigarette. Or else I could burn the house down and the fine coats along with it. It happens all the time, just like that. Maybe I will quit smoking. I pour my tofu smoothie out of the pitcher and into a glass with an image of Mount Rushmore. I take the glass and my coffee cup into my office. I sit down. I drink. I think I am a detective. I think I am a spy. I have been hired to track something down for somebody, but I don't know who, what, where, or why. I have told no one about any of this. Only her. She's the only one that I trust. And also you. I trust you, but only because I am dead. You can't hurt me when I'm dead. You can't send your goons to ransack my room for Pee-Wee, because I have been disintegrated and Pee-Wee is somewhere safe.   And suddenly I have been transported to the future. There has been a great war and a handful of men are left living underground. The aboveground is inhabited by a race of robotmen. These robotmen are all plugged in to the same power source. The power source is also the source of information. They listen to the source and find their meaning in it. They are told that they are real, that they are human, and that they were created in the image of God. But the truth is after the Teleframe took control from its human masters, it created robots in industrial factories. The robots were made to be the

Teleframe's arms and legs. The robots enslaved the humans, and many rebelled. The Teleframe decided it would be more economical if there were only one race, and so the Teleframe caused the robots to merge with the humans. And now everyone is happy. Except for the few remaining humans who live underground and tell their children how the world really was, while avoiding the bands of masked police who seek them out to destroy them, and wipe out for good their memories, and stories. Until one day a boy is born. He grows. His mother dresses him in the style of the time, and gives him a bowl cut. When he comes of age, he likes to wander through the caves. His mother tells him it is too dangerous to be out by himself without the group, but he is an explorer by nature and he doesn't listen to her. He asks the elders about life above ground. The elders tell him not to think of such things. There is no aboveground. But one day he meets an old professor. The professor lives in a dwelling all alone. He has robotic arms and robotic legs, but he claims his mind is free of technology. And it must be, otherwise the colony would have been discovered long ago by means of the signal transmitted by each technological brain to the others. The professor tells the boy of the way the world once was: of the sun, and of the moon, and of the stars. And the boy decides to find these things for himself. So he travels through the tunnels in search of the way up. He travels through the darkness for so long that he loses the tracks of time. He keeps going forward, and every time the path splits, he takes out of his pocket a flat metal disc the old man gave him. On one side of the disc is a face, and on the other a bird. At each junction he drops the disc on the ground. If he sees the face, he goes left, and if he sees the bird, he goes right. He continues on in this manner until one day he sees a light. And walks toward it.

You like him are now alive. I am back again at my computer. He and you have not yet existed. But if I leap further still, you and he both came and went. The end is over, the last battle fought. And however it turned out, it doesn't matter because it was all only fiction. It was all only ever fiction for all of us. We were all just part of someone else's show. Yet we believed in ourselves. Because we were taught to believe in ourselves. But we were not real. And believe it or not you are not real. You were never real. You did not exist. I realize that this is just a trope. As common to science fiction as to a detective story is: a swinging rope. I use the language I was given. But what I'm trying to express is inexpressible. Why am I doing it? Why do I bother? Why am I spending all this time on paint when the garden is in such bad shape?   Déjà vu is a river always flowing. I have no choice but to follow along. I always end up in another room, unfamiliar; with a girl and a question I never answer. Because I'm afraid that I'll answer it wrong. The path has been set. It is impossible to step off.

I woke. And she was pulling up her skirt. She looked at me. But I could not see her face. Was she who I thought she was? If I had my spectacles at the side of the bed, I could have reached for them, put them on and seen her face. But who would she have been then? When I woke, when she was pulling up her skirt, when I saw her, instead of a face, I saw a pink-colored blur. I heard a voice and I recognized the voice. It said, "I'm super late, so I'm gonna drive. OK?" And then ran down the back stairs, out the door, to the car, started it up, drove away. But was that really her at all? Or was it just a fragment memory? Or was it just a lapsing dream? I'm reaching for something I can never quite grasp. And when I wake it's pulled always further away, until I'm left with nothing. All alone. This is what life is like. You are born, and then you die. And in the meantime you lose one thing after another. We say that there is only now. But now is gone as soon as it has come. And there is no future, because it hasn't happened yet. And there is no past, because it has disappeared. So where are we, really? I started with an idea long ago. And by now the idea has taken control. Everything is falling away. All
the paint. All the poorly applied paint. All the time more leaves me. All the time I become new. All the paint. Poorly applied. And so the question becomes what am I to do…finally.

Create words in which to hide?

Can he who does such things escape?

From the one who's coming after us for something that I did, or have yet to do but am known to do in time?

Can he break a covenant and still go free?

Create a world to keep my love inside?

CHAPTER FIVE

THE MYSTERY. The dead cat. The neighbor lady. Brute. The corgi. Call me Corky. Eva's yellow hair once was dark. The Dna Charmers. Gerald and his peanuts. A body buried in a Bed Bath & **BEYOND** bag. MOM. Pop. The Gang. The name of the dwarf with the pierced penis was Louie. He was not a real dwarf, just a very short man. There was a spryness to him of a sort you might find among leprechauns, or circus performers. He walked down the basement steps with a big smile on his face. It was pretty dark. The only light came from a little window above my head.

"How's tricks?" he said.

"Not bad."

"I'm Louie," he said.

"Nice to meet you."

"Sorry about Bear One. He loses his temper pretty easy."

"No problemo," I said. "I completely understand."

Bear One was the one who had crushed my jaw. I described him earlier as looking like a grizzly. Apparently I wasn't the first to come up with that metaphor.

"Face hurt?" Louie asked.

"A bit. Not too bad. Nothing to complain about. The fact is I get hit all the time, so a sock to the jaw like that doesn't really faze me. I mean it doesn't even cross my mind to call the police if that's what you guys are worried about. I hate the pigs, you know what I mean? Hate them with a passion."

He just smiled.

"Say, Louie," I said. "I just remembered I've got an appointment to be at. What do you say you untie me and let me be on my way?"

"Sorry, chief. No can do."

"You've probably heard that I'm a writer," I said.

"Maybe. I don't read much," he said.

"Yeah, well, I'm a pretty successful writer, actually," I said. "I've got a lot of dough. Listen, Louie. You get me out of here I'll make it worth your while."

"You don't have any dough."

"I don't?"

"No."

"Crap."

Louie never stopped smiling.

"What else do you know about me?" I asked.

"I know you're in big trouble."

"Yeah," I said. "I know that too."

"I know you're working on some big book. Some big story that's gonna make sense of life and why we're here and answer all the mysteries of the universe. At least that's what you told that little girl." Smile. "But a guy tells a girl a lot of things to get in her pants, don't he?"

"Now, wait a minute, Louie," I said. "Let's be fair. I really don't think that's the story here."

"Well, a story's all about how you interpret it, ain't it?"

He had me there.

"Can you do something about these ropes, Louie? It's cutting off my circulation."

"You'd rather I rolled you over so you can lay on your face?"

"No, I'd rather not lay on my face. But I'd rather not lay on my hands either."

"Split the difference?"

Louie rolled me onto my side.

"Better?"

"Well, it's still not the ideal."

He had pulled up an old chair and was now sitting next to the bed, his bare legs and feet resting on the mattress pretty close to my face.

"Nice and cool down here," he said.

"Isn't it? Say, that's an interesting piercing," I said. "Did it hurt getting that done?"

"Did it hurt having a metal bar shot through my pecker? What do you think?"

"I think it probably did. Why'd you do it?"

His smile disappeared momentarily while he thought about it.

"I guess to have something I'm known for."

"Makes sense," I said. "So now you're the guy with the pierced penis."

He smiled.

"You guys seem to be one big happy family, huh?"

"Yep," he said. "We'd die for each other."

"Would you? That's good. It must be neat to really connect with people like that."

He smiled.

"I don't think I've ever really connected with people like that, you know? Boy, I'd love to be a part of a gang. Actually, what I'd really like is to be a part of *this* gang. You think maybe you guys would let me be a member?"

Smiling Louie said, "I very much doubt it, boss."

"Really? How come?"

"No reason." He pulled a joint out of thin air and lit it. "Smoke?"

"Sure."

He leaned forward and let me pull off the spliff. I thanked him and blew out.

"Not everybody is convinced you're who you say you are," he said.

"Who I say I am! But I haven't said I'm anyone!"

"There's a theory going around," said Louie, taking a hit, "that maybe you're a cop. Or a spook."

"A cop or a—" I laughed. "Oh, man! That's hilarious! Boy, if you knew me—" I laughed some more. "Oh, that's rich! If you knew me you'd know how crazy that sounds! That is funny! That is really funny, Louie! Although I hope that no one actually thinks that." He put the joint back in my mouth. "(Thanks.) I mean bad things can happen, Louie, based on a simple misunderstanding. I'm sure you've read your Shakespeare."

"I don't know about Shakespeare."

"Well, you're a wise man because Shakespeare is seriously overrated. In our culture it seems like we need to have one example in every category to represent the ideal, so that everyone will feel they're speaking the same language. We have Shakespeare. He represents literature. Even if you haven't read a word of it you know what someone means when they say Shakespeare. We have the Mona Lisa. The Mona Lisa represents art—fine art in general. Although the truth is, Louie, Shakespeare was a hack and the Mona Lisa is a piece of shit!"

"I like the Mona Lisa."

"I do too. No, it's not that the Mona Lisa is a piece of shit—I was only exaggerating for effect. It's that there are one or two paintings out there that are even better than the Mona Lisa, if you can imagine it. I wonder who decides what art lasts and what art is ignored, what art becomes the cliché for greatness, and what becomes forgotten, lost forever down the well of time. Who's responsible, I wonder."

"The public?"

"No, good guess, Louie, but never the public. The message is always directed *to* the public, not *from* the public. I really think there's a conspiracy going on. I think there is a secret, well-funded, and very powerful group at the top of the pyramid scheme we call civilization that decides all these things, that in a sense makes social reality *reality*—because social reality has nothing to do with what actually *is*, only what is *agreed* to be. I wonder if I talked about this to Candice's English class. It would probably have made for an interesting discussion. Too often writers go into a high school English class and tell the students that they can be great writers if only they'll apply themselves and practice. Well, I would have told them that, yes, you can be a writer but the only way you'll be recognized as a great one is if the secret organization that runs the world decides you'll be recognized as a great one. It actually has very little to do with practicing. This is really good weed, by the way."

"Yeah. MOM grows it." He stopped smiling. "I probably shouldn't have told you that."

"Don't worry," I said. "I give you my word I'm no cop. Who's saying I'm a cop, incidentally?"

"Afraid I can't share that information."

"Well, can you share the reasons why I'm suspected of being a cop?"

He smiled. "No."

"Doesn't a man have the right to know the charges brought against him?"

"No."

"Oh, man," I said.

"What's the matter?"

"I think I'm gonna start yawning again."

Footsteps on the staircase. Candice's voice.

"Louie, MOM wants you."

Louie left. Candice replaced him on the chair.

She had her arms crossed tightly over her tank top.

"It's cold down here."

"Yeah."

"Did he hurt you?"

"Bear One? No, just a minor mauling."

"I don't know why he did that. I think he just doesn't like to see me cry."

"I don't blame him."

"So you're an agent," Candice said.

"Pardon me?"

"You're an agent."

"Like a literary agent?"

"No like an enemy agent."

"What? No, I'm not. Why would you say that?"

"Because you're an enemy agent."

"No, Candice, I am very much *not* an enemy agent! Why do you keep saying that?"

"You're infiltrating us."

"Oh, god."

I started to yawn. Up, up, up…then

down too soon. "Candice, I think what you have is a lot of people getting paranoid on their dope. I should know. I'm starting to get pretty paranoid, myself. But in my case I think I have a right to be paranoid because out of the blue I find myself hogtied on a rusty bed in the basement of some abandoned farmhouse by a bunch of drug-addled bikers who it seems have decided that I'm an enemy agent. Enemy agent? Enemy of what? What does that even mean? I'm not an enemy agent, I'm not an allied agent, I'm not any kind of agent. Don't you see how crazy that sounds?"

"It all makes sense now," she said. "I was so stupid."

"No, you weren't stupid, Candice. Don't say that. You weren't stupid. You're just high right now, and it's a hot day, and you're stressed out about going off to college and everything seems sort of confused right now. It's totally normal, but it doesn't mean I'm an agent. I'm just a simple writer living a simple life in Spokane, Washington. End of story. Now, before this all gets even weirder I really think you should untie me and let me slip through that window."

"What were you doing out there on the highway?"

"You saw for yourself, I was walking back home. I'd been visiting my neighbor Vel in the looney bin. Her cat Olive died and I thought I should be the one to give her the news. Vel and I had been quite close before she went insane and chased me with a hose. Now, I didn't have access to a car so Charles, my drain snaker, drove me out in his Drain Charmers van. But he couldn't give me a ride back because he had to go fix a pipe under a Motel 6."

"Why didn't you kiss me back?"

After I'd lugged the red suitcase from Candice's car to the upstairs bedroom, she'd closed and locked the door and when I'd turned around after throwing the suitcase on the bed, she was in her bra, and then kissing me all over my face, telling me I was acting weird and like I'd lost my mind. My first reaction, of course—and who could blame me—was to let it happen—I didn't kiss her back—but I let her kiss me—I let her kiss me, I let her do whatever she wanted for a little while, because though it all happened fast I think I knew in my head that while I wouldn't let it go too far, at the same time I could let things happen and then stop them afterward and still be able to claim that I hadn't done anything. And so I had let her kiss me, she kissed me all over my face, and on my neck, she took my hands and wrapped my arms around her, put my hands on her ass, then moved hers around to my front and unbuttoned my fly, while saying things like "Weren't you even gonna come see me before I left?" and "I waited all night but you never called, you old fucker." She kicked off her shorts and I let myself be pushed down onto the bed next to that suitcase, I felt her mouth and her breath, smelled her sweat, she undid her bra, pulled my shirt up, she was getting into it, really into it, when all at once she seemed to realize I hadn't done the first thing to reciprocate, and she stopped. She pulled her head back to get a good look at me, and got this expression like I had stabbed her in the womb. The next thing I know she's yelling her head off like I wouldn't have thought a girl that size could yell, screaming and picking up all the little abandoned things that had once made this room somebody's home—ten-cent porcelain figurines, a vase with the remains of long-dead flowers dried out all around it, pictures of people and roses in metal frames—she let it all fly in my direction, and I leapt around trying to get out of the way, telling her to relax, but she kept going. Yelling and cursing and crying—scarlet from her face to her ankles—naked except for white cotton undershorts. I tried to make a break for the door but around this time the knob was turned from the outside, the door shook, a fist pounded, but the bolt had been drawn—I ducked as a Statue of Liberty snowglobe went flying over my head—at that moment the door burst open, the jamb shattered, entered a bear (Bear One), wood exploding from his thick shoulder, his face was redder than hers, he was on me quick, his giant paw went back and came forth to send me into:

BLACK.

"I should have. I should have kissed you back," I said.

"But you didn't," she said. "Because you never actually loved me. You just used me."

"Used you? No, Candice, no."

"Yes, Daniel, yes. I never would have believed it in a million years, but I'm positive now. I was a sucker. I was a fool. I fell for you, I believed what you said. I believed you loved me too. I feel so stupid."

She dabbed at her eyes with my handkerchief.

"Candice," I said, yawning. "You've got to believe me, honey. I don't know anything about enemy agents. I swear. I'm just writing a book. That's all."

"Yeah, right." She snorted.

"I think you and your friends have been smoking too much pot, that's what's going on. You're all getting caught up in group paranoia and spinning up these conspiracy theories and thinking there are enemy agents out there trying to do god knows what—and what am I accused of anyway? Interrupting a barbecue? Candice, there are no enemy agents. Think about it. Just think for yourself for a minute. You're a smart girl. You have a 4.0 average. You don't get a 4.0 by just going with the crowd and agreeing with whatever popular opinion is winning the day—you get a 4.0 by thinking for yourself! Now, come on. Do you really think I'm an enemy agent?"

"Yes."

"Dear god," I said with a sigh. "OK, look, Candice. I'm gonna level with you now, OK? Can I level with you?"

Candice lit a cigarette.

"The truth is, sweetheart, this has been a very confusing day from the time I woke up. You see, Candice, I don't have any memory. I know it probably sounds hard to believe, but I can't remember a thing." I yawned again. "My mind's a perfect blank."

"Oh, I get it. You have amnesia."

She blew her smoke out all over me.

"Yes, exactly."

"Well, why didn't you say so!" she said. "I mean, that explains everything! You didn't kiss me back because you didn't remember that we knew each other. And so you didn't remember we were lovers. Because you didn't remember fucking me in my bedroom while my parents were at work. And in the music room at my school when you'd come to pick me up. And in that seedy motel on the highway. And where else? Oh, yeah. In my mother's car at Liberty park. And because you didn't remember any of that you didn't remember all the promises you made me, or how you told me you were almost done with your book and how you were going to sell it for a lot of money, and as soon as you did how you were gonna leave your wife, and how we were going to run off together and live on the beach in Mexico, drinking margaritas and laying in the sand—or is it *lying* in the sand—"

"Candice—"

"—and every other bullshit thing you said! Like about loving me, and needing me, and wanting to be with me! You just forgot about all that! How convenient! You woke up this morning with amnesia! Why didn't you just say so in the first place? It seems like it would have been a good way to open up the conversation. Keeping it a secret until now makes it sound like you're—well, to be perfectly honest, Daniel—like you're just making up another bullshit story to save your skin." She flicked her ash on the floor. "You think I'm a fuckin' idiot."

"It's true, I promise."

"What-evs," she said, bitterly. "I know how much your promises are worth. You promised we'd always be together. And then you didn't call for weeks. You knew I was leaving for school but you didn't even try to see me. I've driven by your house every fucking day hoping you'll be outside so I can at least see you—because I thought maybe somehow there was a chance that whatever was happening was all beyond your control—maybe you weren't avoiding me—maybe you weren't *dumping* me—maybe something happened to you, maybe you got hurt—I even rang the doorbell, I looked in windows—Jesus, I broke into your house! But you were never there. Apparently you've been on vacation."

"I haven't been on vacation! I've been scraping my house!"

"You haven't been scraping anything! That paint hasn't looked any different in months."

"Look, I—"

"It'd be one thing if you were just using me for my body! Fine! That's what boys do! It's practically a compliment!" She was getting red again. "But how humiliating! You weren't even using me for me! The whole charade had nothing to do with me! All the kissing, all the I love yous, all the promises, all the fucking, all the bullshit! It was never about me at all! You were just doing it all to get to him!"

"Wait—what? To get to who?"

"Well, you got me! I believed you! You win! Congratulations!"

"Candice, wait, I was doing it all to get to who?"

"What?"

"I was doing it all," I said slowly, "to get to who?"

"Who do you think, you fucking asshole! To *Pop!*"

At the sound of his name my blood ran cold. I didn't have the slightest idea what was going on, or who any of these people were, I didn't know what crimes against man or nature they had committed or were planning on committing. But with that "Pop" snapping like a gunshot from her lips I knew exactly how serious my situation had become.

"Oh, god, they're gonna kill me, aren't they?"

"Unfortunately for you..." Candice said, taking a long, cool drag from her cigarette, uncrossing and then recrossing her legs. She blew out. "Unfortunately for you, I may have mentioned to MOM that nobody knows you're here. And that I heard you tell your wife—or whoever the bitch you're living with is—that you were taking a bus ride around town."

Without meaning to, I started grinding my face into the mattress.

"Oh, no, no, no, no, no. No, you shouldn't have said that. No, no, no, Candice, no, that doesn't work."

"Il est fait."

I raised my head as high as I could.

"Girl, you've got to save me."

"I don't have to save nobody." She dropped her cigarette and watched it smolder on the cement floor.

"This is just one of those big misunderstandings!"

"If only you would have just kissed me back."

"You've gotta tell them I'm not an agent!"

"What should I tell them you are then?"

"I'm just a writer!"

"OK, writer," she said coolly. "So what's your book about?"

"It's a mystery!"

"So I've heard. And what's the mystery?"

"The mystery is..."

I started to yawn.

"Yes?"

Up, up, up I went...

"...It's about..."

...like a train chugging to the top of a mount...

"The mystery is about?"

...my lungs expanding, reaching toward their fullest amount...

"...how..."

...about to reach the peak but then—

"How?"

Like every time before, the structure collapses before it's reached and I come crashing down.

"I'm fucked."

"I'll say you are." Candice rose from her chair and put the cigarette out beneath her rainbow flip-flop. "Eleven years and you can't even come up with a synopsis? Sorry, Charlie," she said. "You're an agent all right."

THE ULTIMATE GOAL

(8_11_07 4_17 PM.wav)

So the ultimate goal, ultimate goal, dude…I'm gonna get my first elk this year, in the early season, I'm gonna be gone for four days. That would be so rad. I would buy a freezer, have a freezer full of elk, two weeks later I go to Alaska, and catch my limit every day for four days. Bring back like thirty pounds of fresh salmon, dude. That'd be so nice. It's really—they got a good setup. Alaska has got cold storage. So you bring one bag and you can check a second bag, that weighs like, you know, fifty pounds or something, and they put it in the cold storage hold. And there's processing at the lodge, so you can get out there and bring home, dude, a *freezer full*. Wouldn't that be awesome?

M: Yeah.

Then I can just watch football *all fall* and just like chow down on everything in my freezer.

M: Yeah.

...We'll see. I'll have to learn to like fish, but...Hopefully I'll have to learn to like elk....................So do you feel like—my wife said you told her that you feel your book is almost done.

M: No.

Not at all.

M: I have no idea. Um, I'm coming down, I'm like uh, I'm over the hill and I'm using inertia and gravity to take me down but I don't know how long that's gonna be......

Do you have any plans to—now maybe I'm crazy, but—kind of like JRR Tolkien–style, like maybe like serve it up in like fifteen-hundred-page bites? Like turn it into a series? Like, dude, is it *possible* that you could be like, just like: *Buy this one and then later I'll release the second one and someday I'll give you the third one* or whatever?

M: I don't know. Possibly. I mean, I've thought about that.

Because you know it would be kind of like *crazy*, to try to get someone to read like four thousand pages at once, right?

M: I'm not trying to get anybody to read it.

DAMN YOU! BUT WHY? BUT BUT BUT—OK. But, how about this? Wouldn't you like it if like they made it into a book—or books—and then like it was at the library and somebody who was interested could check it out from the library and read it? Like a regular book?

M: I think they would need to go through a process of purification before they could even open the book.

They wouldn't be allowed to read it? So is the book going to be like on a mountaintop in Nepal? And then like if you can like carry a flower intact to the top of the mountain like in Batman Returns or whatever—no, that was Batman Forever—in Batman Forever it was like: *You're worthy of our training. Welcome...*

M: It's odd that you say that because I was just about to ask you to bury one portion of it in Alaska when you're up there. I'm planning on burying a part of it at each of the four corners of the earth.

So people will find it and they will be like: *Hey, we have found the wisdom of the ancients.* And then they're like: *Hey, wait a minute! This guy mentions a cell phone in here! Yeah, this is new.*

M: It's gonna be a record of America before the Great Fall.

IS THAT *TRUE?* DOES IT HAVE SOMETHING TO DO WITH AMERICA? WHY ARE YOU BEING SO SECRETIVE? DUDE, I DON'T WORK FOR, LIKE, THE WEEKLY WORLD NEWS! I'M NOT GONNA LIKE—I DON'T HAVE A LIKE—

M: Yes. It has to do with America.

OK. America specifically.

M: Yeah. It's about America. It's a big book about America.

And this is, would you say, a *commentary?*

M: It has commentary in it.

OK. Then let me ask you this. Does it have a *fictional person* who's used as a *device* to tell a *story* to be like an *allegory* or a *moral?* Or is it like *not* like there's a person who is used to like represent ideas.

M: Well, we've talked about it a bit. Do you have any ideas about what you think it is?

We haven't really talked about it. You've told me that you felt— This is what I know about it: *You*...were going to...take...*themes* which you felt were protected by unfair copyright laws...and reproduce them in some measure—I got the impression it was in order to...*lampoon them* or something? I didn't really understand. I mean I figured you felt that you needed to have like a certain amount of the content reproduced so that you could like...*criticize it*...or something? So, or to be, like, to *explode the myth* that it *perpetuates* or something? I don't know, something like that?

M: I like that. That sounds good.

BUT I DON'T UNDERSTAND! BUT I DON'T UNDERSTAND, LIKE, *WHAT IT'S ABOUT!* I understand you want to make like a *statement*—like you're trying to make like a *moral commentary* about something, right? Like you're like writing a book that's like: *I'm going to give* like *perspective...on* like...*social progress or social decline* or something. Like: *I'm going to give* like *a commentary on* like *social*—like the *decline of social norms*, dude. Something like that. Like, or like *on the decline of* like *our culture.* Or whatever, basically. But you're going to *use...copyright protected material*—which I'm assuming means *something that somebody already put in a book that was famous*...Because, I mean, if it wasn't famous you would not get sued over it...*So*...Am I *warm at all?* Is that what it's like? Because in many stages I was thinking, like—I mean it must be like—I mean like honestly dude it must be like *completely* like *insanely ambitious* in scope. I mean, to to to put like *four thousand*—getting on to *four thousand pages*—I mean it must be like…you're planning on like *dying trying,* like, on this thing. You're gonna die trying.

M: Absolutely.

It sounds like a really, really, really, huge scope.

M: Absolutely. I have almost a near-infinite scope. It is scope itself, you know what I mean?

It's big.

M: It is a very difficult challenge.

Yes.

M: And uh…

So you feel—OK, so it's safe to say that—let's say that I work for LexisNexis. And your book is published. And—

M: What's LexisNexis?

Oh. Sorry. Um. It's a research, um, it's an internet-based research engine. Um, there's two really big ones for, um, the legal field. There's Westlaw and then there's LexisNexis. Westlaw is better, but LexisNexis is the one that does like all the regular—like all the regular like university reports. You could go to—*Hey, this is UW's library, I wanna do some research on anything*—like you're not a lawyer, you're just, *I'm a scientist* or whatever, or a historian—there's this thing called like LexisNexis. That you basically are like: *Sea Captain, 1700.* And then you say something like: *Non-fiction,* and then you say like the search parameters and then it says, like: *Here's the eight thousand books that people have written in which* sea captain *is a word*, right? And the way that it works is that there's keywords. Because they make an *abstract*. So somebody has to like read—well, I'm sure they don't read the book, but—they read the first chapter and the last chapter and they read the marketing material from like the publisher or something, and they say, like: *This book, blah blah blah blah blah*—they give an *abstract* which gives the *parameters* of the *subject matter*, and it's like usually like about *two paragraphs* or something, that says like, *So there's this giant,* like, *nine-hundred-page book, but this is the abstract.*

So like *pretend* that *I* work for like LexisNexis and I'm gonna write an abstract for the search engine. So somebody's like: *I seek wisdom* or—OK, somebody's like gonna want to find like *your book* or they're interested in the subject matter of your book. So, *the book*, like the abstract would say something like:...It is a...*commentary?* Or, is it like, uh...a *moral?*... It's a—is it like an *allegory* or something? Something that teaches a *moral?* Except it's a commentary *about* Americans...Like American society...It's about, like, the *decline* of like...um...I don't know—*standards* or whatever, or *values*—we'll say values—that's a way better word—the decline of *values*...in *America*...*over*—is it over a certain time period? Like are you starting with like, with like, *Jamestown?* Or are you just like—are you gonna like start it like maybe like 1800s like and take it from there? OK, more like that. OK, but. OK, so, but the book—I don't understand like the device that you use, like— Does the book have a, like, *character* that you made up as a *device* to, to *teach* something? Will you tell me that?

M: Do you want some more water?

No, I'm fine.

M: The book has characters, and the book has devices, and the book... *teaches something?* I don't know, it's hard to put it into language like that.

FICTIONAL CHARACTERS!

M: Does it have fictional characters. That's a difficult question to answer. Because, reality is an issue in the book, so…It's a very, very different sort of……book.

Um……Do you think that someone reading the book would *identify*—would be able to identify…the *time* in which you wrote it? Do you think somebody would read the book not knowing the ages and then say: *Oh! This book has certain markers in it that I would be able to say: The author who wrote this book lived in a certain age.* Like does it mention an *automobile* or a *telephone* or anything that would like give a clue to that.

M: Yes, there are automobiles and telephones.

OK, so this is a book that acknowledges…modern times.

M: It acknowledges time.

OK.

M: It exists in time. It is composed of words. And there are characters. So it's just like any other book you'll ever read, really. But it's good to hear, uh, a new take on it.

I DON'T UNDERSTAND THE CON—I DON'T I DON'T HAVE A TAKE BECAUSE YOU'VE NOT TOLD ME ANYTHING ABOUT IT! I HAVE TO PRY THESE THINGS OUT! But, I mean I do feel like, it's so interesting because like, I just think it's like so crazy dude that you're like *holed up* in a room for like coming nigh on like *five, six years*, dude. Like, and, like, nobody knows what you're doing… NOBODY KNOWS WHAT YOU'RE DOING, MATT! I don't understand, like—everyone's like—everybody's like—everybody that knows you in the past is like: *That asshole, he can't write anymore, he's got writer's block, he's not writing anything!* You know what I mean? And then other people are like: *Oh, he's just taking his time with his second book.*

M: Nobody knows about the four thousand pages. Nobody knows anything about it.

That's my point, dude!

M: Well, I'm saying that you—

You're saying that I actually have a lot of information about it.

M: You know its length. That's more than my agent knows. That's more than my publishers know. Nobody knows anything about it. Nobody knows anything.

You can't tell your agent or your publisher that, because they'll fire your ass.

M: I'm not sure I'm gonna give them anything.

So OK, now to recap, for my abstract. My precious, precious abstract. This is a, uh, uh.........oh…well, I can't—is this like a—can we call it a *fictionalized*…account? I mean—when people do a fictionalized account they're like: *Here's something that really happened. I'll fill in some drama and* like *make some interesting characters to go with it.* Like, I'll be like: *So you know about how that ship sunk? I'll make like a crazy sea captain* or whatever *and then I'll make a love story and I'll put it in there.* But it's not, it's not, like, *close enough focused* on any *single event* that it's like you're…you're *commenting on*…or doing like a *evaluation of* a *specific thing*—it's like *you're* like *hovering way above the earth*…like, you know, *This is what it looks like from the perspective of madness.* Or whatever. Like something like that maybe?

M: Maybe.

COME ON! WHAT DO YOU MEAN *MAYBE!* The thing is, I'm just trying to…Do you…OK. But you do think it's fair to say that a lot of this book is a *comment* about the decline of our nation……

M: I can say…looking at it…it forms a comment on the United States. And if I interpret that as meaning—if I'm a reader and I'm interpreting the picture that I'm seeing as being a picture of a nation on fire…then that's what it's going to be. You know what I mean?

OK. So. I know you won't talk about it, but so you think that if somebody's paying attention, the *portrait* of the characters that you're gonna make up, are going to *represent* like *problems* that are like *universal*—like *large-trend problems*…of our society or something. So like a person's personal trouble—you're gonna pick something and make a portrait that's like *emblematic* of like a large-scale problem?

M: I didn't say that.

Do you see what I'm saying? I'm just trying to reverse engineer…OK. Would the characters have a first and last name? Let's start with that.

M: It depends on the character.

OK, I have a really awesome question. OK, I have a really awesome question…Is there anybody in the book…that's *real.* Like will the fictional character live in a world—in a reality that's being signaled as like: *This did occur in this nation in this year*—like will anyone ever hear the speech given by the certain president or something—will there be anything that will say: *This is—it's* fiction—*but it could be anybody. I'm telling you that it's true. Because it happened to a friend of mine, or because I saw it with my own eyes. And I made up the characters so that it would be easier for you to understand, or because that's just the way to write a book.* But is somebody gonna be like: *Such and such made a speech*—and that's a real person? Maybe, like, in the background? Are there gonna be clues that—

M: Give me an example.

All right. OK. Will…will a character be trampled while attending a rally for…the…*prime minister* of…or for the president of Mexico visiting Los Angeles to discuss labor relations. And…the president of Mexico…so one of the characters will be trampled and he'll be a, like, migrant worker. It'll be like: *This guy got stomped to death,* because the Mexican president basically came up here to like *stir up*—or to have like a labor relations thing, a human rights like *impact* with like *our* president and they decided to meet in LA, and they had to have a *massive* like—like everybody basically like *went nuts* because it's a really like sensitive like massive issue. So let's say that they meet in Texas—that makes more sense because there are a lot of Mexican people in Texas and our president is from Texas—well, he's not from Texas, he's from Connecticut but he goes to Texas on vacation or whatever but—OK, so then will it be like: *President Vicente Fox*—because this happened in 1999 or whatever—*such and such; and it caused*—is there something that you would look at and go: *Oh, this could have actually happened in this in this exact city, in this exact crystallized moment in history.* How about that? With a real person.

M: Yes.

OK..............But I mean you agree right that if you { } that just wants to like get ten percent or whatever I mean a book that's like four thousand pages or whatever, they're not going to read it, right? I mean, will they read the whole four thousand pages?

M: Who?

Your agent.

M: How do you know she's read my first book?

THAT ONE IS LIKE TWO HUNDRED FIFTY PAGES OR SOMETHING! I READ THAT IN A DAY AND A HALF!

M: Right. Well, an agent's advice would be to cut the scene where Fox is speaking before the assembled masses and the riot ensues.

But that would be kind of like a good, like, part because it would be, like, dramatic. If I was making a movie I'd be like: *This is the big scene where the guy gets killed.*

M: Who's the guy?

The guy would just be like an *everyman*. We'll just make up some everyman guy that's like a little bit *short,* a little bit *chubby,* a little bit *dumb.* A little bit, a little bit, a little bit too *poor.* A little bit *slow* or whatever. You know what I mean? And so you'll make the guy and he'll be the next character and then he'll get, like, *trampled.*

M: Is he Mexican or Anglo?

Fully Mexican. We'll have like a Mexican guy get trampled. We could make up a Mexican guy and have like a big rally and then maybe like you know { } and then you could maybe like, you know, the policies that the two countries have are not helping the situation. Like the governments are like—well one of them is really corrupt and the other one is basically like corrupt to like corporate interests or whatever. And one of them is corrupt to drug interests. That's the Mexican. And, we're like really into like corporate interests, obviously. So basically you could be like saying: *The policies that we have*—like, you know—*the things that we choose to do*—you could basically use it to criticize prevailing political will, right now, and you could—and also it would be nice and it would be a nice story to have a pathetic person who's like—*Dude, you're like a tragedy*, yeah like a Greek tragedy. You just have somebody like get murdered and that's the whole story right there, dude. He would just get murdered at the rally.

M: [*gasps*] So he *wasn't* trampled! He was…*murdered!*

Yeah, well, but like you'd say he was murdered *morally!* He *was* trampled! He was trampled by the *system!* He was murdered by the system! They'll call it an *accident!* And then you'll criticize the media because I know you hate the media. *The media made it look like he was a hero, bullshit, he wasn't a hero, he was a victim, suck my dick,* you know. I just gave you a book right there, dude, that's beautiful! But I…you would have to actually write it. I mean every day writing shit down. Do you even remember the first hundred chapters and what you said in them? Because I wouldn't.

M: Oh yeah.

Well, that's interesting. So there will be definite markers which will signal an exact moment in history, a real history.

M: Well, not necessarily a *real* history…

But you will use a real *character*—a real *person* in history!

M: Who's that?

WELL THAT'S WHAT I'M ASKING! For example there will be something that will signal that there was a real person in history in the *background!* Even though their actions would be *fictionalized* at this point.

M: But who's the real person you're talking about?

Oh, it would be like Vicente Fox or something.

M: To you and me he's not a real person, he's just an image on TV.

I understand. But I'm saying, like, Vicente Fox—I mean although he's currently living, he is an *historical figure.*

M: I can't guarantee that.

We can objectively verify his existence.

M: We can't objectively verify anything.

YES WE CAN, DAMN YOU! WHAT ARE YOU TALKING ABOUT? HE CAME TO SEATTLE AND F-ED UP THE TRAFFIC, DUDE! HE MADE ME LATE TO GO HOME!

M: How do you know that was him? If he does exist, how do you know that that was really him?

Because…

M: Because the news media told you that was him, and the emcee on the platform before he gave his speech said it was him. And the guy giving the speech said he was him. Etcetera, etcetera, etcetera.

OK, but anyway. So…

M: So I did not say that any historical people are in the book at all. Or represented. Or even alluded to. And I did not say that their authenticity is without a doubt, you know—that it's not called into question. Any person *purporting to be*, or who a reader might think *is* a real person in this book, um, is not necessarily a real person or was *ever* a real person *or* was the person that they're *pretending to be*, or was the person that they are *assumed* to be…by the reader of the book.

Hmmm. So, are you just—because I'm not gonna sue you, dude. That sounds like a disclaimer. That sounds like a really big disclaimer…. So, you…in the abstract, you would be—OK, in the Dewey Decimal System would it be under fiction or non-fiction.

M: That's a hard question to answer.

Somebody's gonna have to make that call for you someday.

M: Well, there's gonna be a lot of issues about this. There's gonna be a whole lot of issues that need to be rethought.

You're like: *Trust me. All—all Library of Congress systems, all Dewey Decimal Systems, will be eradicated by this book. It will break—it will break two hundred years of classification of books*… Yeah, but. Yeah, but I mean…I have to tell you…Somebody's gonna put it in a box that you're not comfortable with, dude, because like somebody's gonna want to check it out,

M: Uh-huh.

and it's gonna be, like, *0-1000* or whatever. It's gonna be like, *194...H.* Or whatever. OK, but. I'm saying for you, if you could *pick,* would you say, *Oh yeah this is my new* non-fiction *book*, or *this is my new* fiction *book.* If someone—you're at a party and you just finished the book, and they're like: *Is it fiction or non-fiction?* And I know you in real life, you will say: *Those are terms that imply* like *things that I'm not gonna agree to or whatever.* But like if—just for me—because you're dealing with a very concrete person...I'm a simpleton, Matt. OK? I'm not the *dreamer* that you are. What will you say it should be classified as?

M: That's the one question that I'll never answer.

OH MY GOD!

M: You can ask me a hundred questions and I'm not gonna answer any of them, but especially not that one.

BUT WHY?

M: Because I can't tell you.

WELL, YOU— Do you even know, yourself?

M: No, I don't. I don't know. I don't know.

You've lost your mind.

M: No. I've found my mind.

Oh, no.

THE { } (BROKEN)

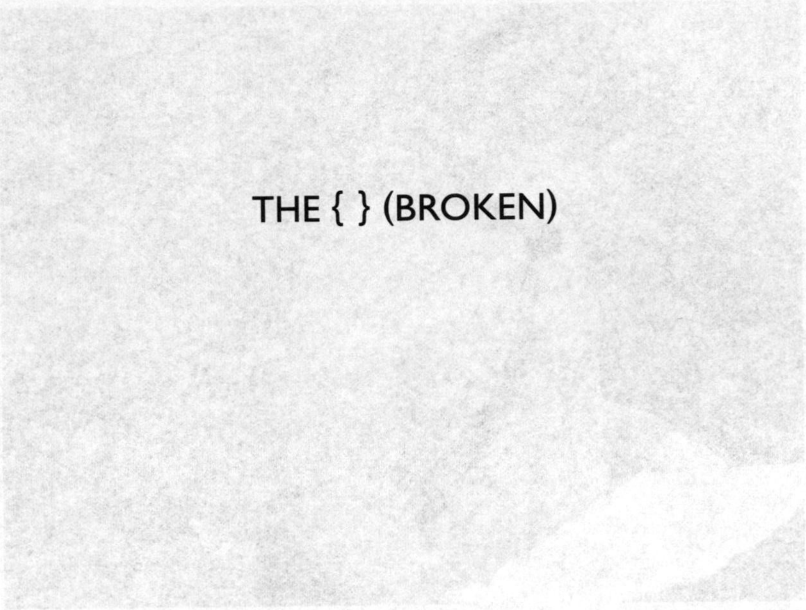

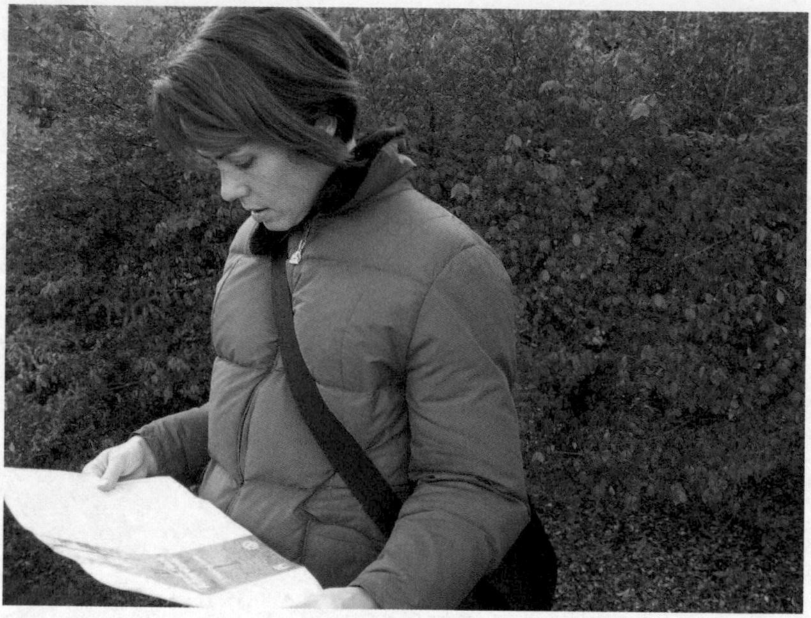

INTRODUCTION

NOT TOO LONG AGO **one** took it on faith that the final scientific picture of the world would be beautiful, orderly and simple. As it has continued to be sketched in, we have had a number of surprises. The beauty is there, but not of the expected kind. The order is there, but not of the sort to damp down our questions. The simplicity has disappeared.

No better case in point can be offered than the subject of this book. Matter is the world around us; it is everything we see and feel and touch. It seems thoroughly familiar—until we read in the following pages what the scientists have discovered about it within the last 50 years, the last 20, the last 2. The diamond, for example, seems on the face of it resplendently substantial. But as we read on, we find that the diamond is a patterned arrangement of atoms which are themselves mainly empty space, with infinitesimal dabs of electrons whirling round infinitesimal dabs of protons and neutrons. All this we now know to be matter, but we are by no means sure the picture is complete. Within the miniscule heart of the atom—

★

the nucleus—have been found no fewer than **30** kinds of elementary particle, and no **one** can say what more will emerge under nuclear bombardment. The further scientists analyze, the less obvious the answers become.

The mysteries of matter have stimulated the great intellectual exploration of our time. There are **two** reasons why we should share in its excitements. **One** is for the sheer fun, the esthetic pleasure, call it what you like, of reaching deeper into the unknown. The other is for the understanding to be gained as a result.

This understanding we ought to possess not only per se but also for the power it puts in our hands. Perceiving the nature of matter, we can control it for our own purposes, lethal or benevolent. A lump of uranium ore looks as quiescent as any other old lump of rock. The first inquiries into the structure of these lumps seemed just another academic exercise. Yet, within a generation, governments were spending billions of dollars on scientific projects, not so academic, which were a direct outcome of the first innocent experiments. For it happened that the scientists had stumbled on a way to release amounts of energy that men had never before had at their command. The results have shaped the course of world history for **20** years.

Something like this may happen again. It is more likely to happen than not. And while scientists and statesmen may finally make the decisions that become necessary, ordinary responsible citizens will first have to make their own thoughts felt. They will be unable to do so unless they comprehend what is going on. Science will give us a better world only if enough people make sure that it does so, which means that we must, to begin with, acquire the knowledge that helps us understand. This book is a step in that direction.

Snow, C.P. Introduction. MATTER. By Ralph E. Lapp and the Editors of LIFE. Time Inc. 1963.

..*.*.*.*.*.*.*.*.*.*.*.*

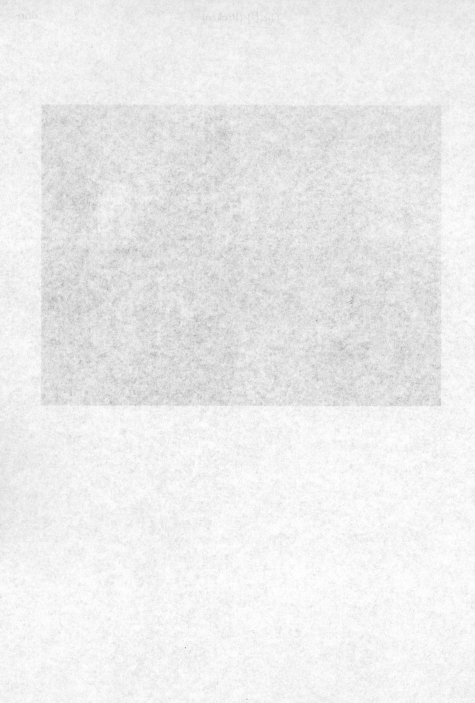

X

We SCIENTISTS KNOW NOTHING about the information storage systems within the brain—how memory is coded, archived, accessed, and retrieved.

Could the human mind have only something akin to RAM, lacking hard memory capable of long-term storage without electrical power?

The mind runs on electricity, doesn't it?

And so, without a hard memory, and no permanent power source, all information would be lost.

Thus all the wealthy thumb-suckers paying cryogenics labs to lop off their heads and freeze them until technology is available to bring a frozen primate back to life (and, presumably, the company still exists and has continued to pay its power bills on time) may be looking in the wrong direction.

For you could wake up on some distant earth with your head a bowl of chunky soup, alive in form but without any memories stored.

Then the decision will have to be made whether or not to kill you again.

Maybe they'll choose to keep you alive, as per the contract you foolishly signed. Would you like to be dealt with in this manner? I have seen men in catatonic states. While dead to the world, they have the luxury of mind-traveling, hitching rides on electric currents, sailing through seas of random memory. This will not be an option for the resurrected heads of the 26th century; for there will be no Memory then. Just an ocean of white noise*:*:*:*:*:*:*:*..*..*:*:*:*:*:*:*:*:*
:*:*:*:*:*:*:*:* :*..*:*:*:*:*:*:*:*:*:*:*:*..*..*:*:*:*:*:*:*:*:*
:*:*:*:*:*:*:*..*:*:*:*:*:*:*:*:*:*:*:*:*:*..*..*:*:*:*:*:*:*:*:*:*:*
:*:*:*:*:*:*..*:*:*:*:*:*:*:*:*:*:*:*:*..*..*:*:*:*:*:*:*:*:*:*:*:*:
::*:*:*:*..*:*:**:*:*:*:*:*:*:*:*:*:*:*:*:*:*:*:*:*:*:*..*:*:*:*:*:
::*:*:*:*:*..*:*:*:*:*..*:*
:*:*:*:*:*:*:*..*:*:*:*:*:*:*:*:*:*:*:*:*:*..*..*:*:*:*:*:*:*:*:*:*:*
:*:*:*:*:*:*:*..*:*:*:*:*:*:*:*:*:*:*:*:*..*..*:*:*:*:*:*:*:*:*:*:*:*
:*:*:*:*:*:*:*:*:*:*:*:*:*:*:*:*:*:*:*..*..*:*:*:*:*:*:*:*:*:*:*:*:*
:*:*:*:*:*:*:*:*:*:*:*:*:*:*:*:*:*:*..*:*:*:*:*:*:*:*:*:*:*:*:*:*:*
:*:*:*:*:*:*:*:*:*:*:*:*:*:*:*..*..*:*:*:*:*:*:*:*:*:*:*:*:*:*:*:*:*
:*:*:*:*:*:*:*:*:*:*:*:*:*:*:*:*:*..*:*:*:*:*:*:*:*:*:*:*:*:*:*:*:*
:*:*:*:*:*:*:*:*:*:*:*:*:*:*:*:*:*:*:*..*:*:*:*:*:*:*:*:*:*:*:*:*:*
:*
:*:*:*..*:*:*:*:*:*:*:*:*:*:*:*:*:*..*:*:*:*:*:*:*:*:*:*:*:*:*:*:*:
:..*:*:**:
::*:*:*..*..*:*:*..*:*:*:*:*:*:*:*:*:*:*:*:*:*:*:*..*:*:*:*:*:*:*
:*:*:*:*:*:*:*:*:*:*:*:*:*:*:*:*:*:*..*:*:*:*:*:*:*:*:*:*:*:*:*:*:*
:*..*:*:*:*:*
:*:
::*:*:*:*:*:*:*:*:*..*:*:*:*:*:*:*:*:*:*:*:*..*:*:*:*:*:*:*:*:*
**:*..*:*:*:*:*:*:*:*:*:*:
....*:*:*:*:*:*.
:..*:*:*:*:*:*:*:*:*:*:*
:*:*:*:*:*:*..*:*:*:*:*:*:*:*:*:*:*:*:*..*..*:*:*:*:*:*:*:*:*:*:*:
::*:*:*:*:*..*:*:*:*:*:*:*:*:*:*:*:*:*..*:*:*:*:*:*:*:*:*:*:*:*:*

:*:*:*:*:*:*:*::*:*:*:*:*:*:*:*:*:*:*:*:*:*:*:*::*::*:*:*:*:*:*:*:*:*:*:*:*:

::*:*:*:*::*:*:**:*:*:*:*:*:***:*:*::*:*:*:*:*:*:*:*:*:*:*:*:*:*:*::*:*:*:*

:*:. :*:*:*

:*:*:*:*:*::*:*:*:*::*

:*:*:*:*:*::*:*:*:*:*:*:*:*:*:*:*:*:*:*:*::*:*:*:*:*:*:*:*:*:*:*:*:*:*:*:*:

::*:*:*:*:*::*:*:*:*:*:*:*:*:*:*:*:*:*:*:*:*:*::*::*:*:*:*:*:*:*:*:*:*:*:*:*

:*:*:*:*:*:*::*:*:*:*:*:*:*:*:*:*:*:*:*:*:*:*::*::*:*:*:*:*:*:*:*:*:*:*:*:*:

::*:*:*:*:*::*:*:*:*:*:*:*:*:*:*:*:*:*:*:*:*::*::*:*:*:*:*:*:*:*:*:*:*:*:*:*

:*:*:*:

::*:*:*:*:*::*::*::*:*:*:*:*:*:*:*:

::*:*:*:*::*::*::*:*:*:*:*:*:*:*:*

:*:*:*:*:*::*::*::*:*:*:*:*:*:*:*:*:

::*:*:*:*::*::*::*:*:**:*:*:*:*:*:*:

::*:*:*:*:*:*:*:*:*:*:*:*:*:*:*:*::*:*:*:*:*:*:*:*:*:*:*:*:*:*:*::*:*:*:*:*::

::*:*:*:*:**:*::*::*::*:*:*:*:*:*:*:

::*:*:*:*:*::*::*::*:*:*:*:*:*:*:*:*

:*:*:*:*:*:*:*::*::*:*:*:*:*:*:*:*:

::*:*:*:*::*::*::*:*:*:*:*:*:*:*:*:*:*

:*:*:*:*:*::*::*::*:*:*:*:*:*:*:*:*:

::*:*:*:*::*::*:*:*:*:*:*:*:*:*:*:*:*:*:*:*:*:*:*:*::*:*:*:*:*:*:*:*:*:*:*:*

:*:*:*:*:*::*::*:*:*:*:*:*:*:*:*:*:*:*:*:*:*:**

> Entry #382356, added on 10-28-05 @ 2:56 pm EDT.
[Entry Access Restriction] None.

::*:*:*:*:*: :*:*:*:*

::*:*:*:*:*::*::*::*:*:*:*:*:*:*:*:

::*:*:*:*::*::*::*:*:*:*:*:*:*:*:*

:*:*:*:*:*:*::*::*:*:*:*:*:*:*:*:*:* But who really knows in THE END?

★

Title: :***-*:: mystery continues

★

The components of memory will probably be found to operate on the quantum level; hence it will be dangerous to observe them.

For when observed they will be altered; and thus so too will be the subject.

This can be analogized by the common delusion of the schizophrenic type, who imagines seeing men in masks standing around him, operating on his brain, boring holes into it and so forth.

Also, the terrifying "waking dreams" certain women seem to experience in which they are kidnapped, probed, and implanted by wide-eyed extraterrestrials.

Maybe there are real beings really doing these things to us.

Maybe we are doing these things to ourselves in a future age, an unfortunate byproduct of quantum observation.

In a distant time, a brave, yet reckless scientist has discovered the means by which to find and observe the smallest particles of life.

He calls them { } particles.

He does it by freezing time.

He looks in at the frozen particles and says, "Eureka!

We have discovered that which is responsible for memory!

We have discovered perception!

We have discovered consciousness!

We have discovered the building blocks of reality!

All we have to do now is open it and look inside!"

Meanwhile, as a result, all over the world, and in all time fields past, present, and future, we are opening our eyes to monsters prodding at us, probing in us, operating on us.

Our nightmares take the forms of our beliefs.

A young girl sees a pair of glowing red eyes in the dark.

A Pentecostal boy is terrorized by the devil whose outline he sees in his closet, just waiting for him to slip up and blaspheme the holy spirit.

An old soldier is smothered by the maggot-dripping corpses of the race of people he was sent across the globe to destroy.

A woman sees the ceiling above her bed melt away in a murky blue light, and soon she is on a gurney and large-headed beings with huge gray eyes and tiny slits for mouths are shoving a baby into her womb, and then taking it out again, covered in slime.

⋆

Yet for all the terrors wreaked upon mankind of every time by these future quantum observers, some good has arisen too.

No energy is bad energy in its entirety; my Hindu neighbors could tell you that.

Also sent through those timeless quantum waves to some lucky healthy-minded primates are what the prophets of old would call Visions.

These are generally visual and/or auditory hallucinations of the beneficial variety, as opposed to those frightening occurrences we've just touched on above.

For every quantum surgeon knows that God is in the details.

And when he, using his very tiny and delicate instrument, peels back another layer of the { } holding it open and looking inside, a man in Golden Valley, North Dakota, sees an angel hovering in the corner of the room.

The angel tells him (of course) to:

Be unafraid.

He asks the angel: What message shall I give them?

Just then the quantum surgeon's hand slips and the {

} comes loose

and the angel disappears.

But not before in every corner of the earth, in every day and age and nation, heavenly dreams are dreamt, visions beheld, and epic poems written which will last beyond what we have termed...*forever.*

★

...all she found were Brooke's sandals...

★

By the way, how many of you *really* want your head stored in ice when you can leave it and the rest of this silly world behind?
Attachment to delusion is a most dangerous thing.
Monkeys today: all they dream about is acquiring enough wealth to buy a big house and a few big cars and take big vacations on big islands and lay out on the beach and have big sleeps.
None of these monkeys have any idea about the quantum surgeons of the future terrorizing and blessing us in turn with their tiny instruments and inquisitive natures.
The head surgeon steps back.
Then, after his brow is wiped down, he clears his throat, steadies himself, and, once again, steps up to the table.
Taking a deep breath, he places the tiny instrument on the frozen { } and peels back one layer, then another, with the center in mind.
As each new layer unfolds:::
he draws closer:::
than ever:::
before.

★

MOM: Here we are on our first trip home, and Margaret is *sound* asleep. Doing well. There's Daddy…

★

And… *there's Amelia… Say Hi!…* And here's… Helen…

★

Hmm, kinda out of focus…

★

There's Helen! *Smy—uhl!*

★

Helen's not—

★

:)

★

oh, *good!* And Amelia. And here's…

★

. . . and there's Margaret.

★

She's such a pretty girl . . .

★

★

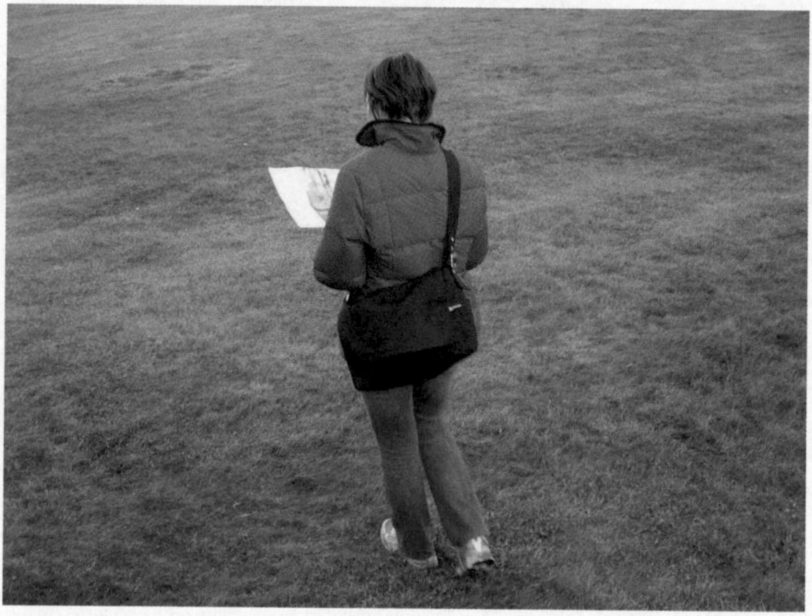

FIRST DRAFT

(A young married couple.doc
Created Friday, April 18, 2003 4:10PM)

A young married couple from Connecticut flew to the Flathead Valley of Montana on a short vacation. They rented a cabin on the lake. The lake is the largest freshwater lake west of the Mississippi, with over 180 miles of shoreline. It was early spring, two months before the yearly summer tourist flux, and the couple got a great deal on the cabin. The husband built a fire the night they arrived, and they sat around the fire, enjoying the sounds of the waves splashing against the dock outside. They were both professionals and it was good to get away and be alone together for awhile, to not think of work or money or family. The next day they went into town and arranged for a man to take them out on the lake in his boat. It was a beautiful spring day, slightly chilly still from the mountain breezes, so they bundled up. They boarded the small, twenty foot speedboat, and the man told them about himself, and they told him about themselves, as they left the dock. Why didn't they wear lifejackets? The next day the owner of the boat was spotted by a woman on the shore. He was clinging to the hull of the submerged boat, unconscious. The water was less than forty degrees and hypothermia had set in. He was picked up by a police boat. Then transported to the nearest hospital. The husband was found washed up on shore the next day. He had drowned. The wife, she was never found. In the cold, her body sunk below the water. She is either on the floor, or floating in the dark between the bottom of the lake and the surface. Wind and current move her. Fish swim around her. They looked for her but never found. And the tourists and the summer dwellers came and their boats made waves and moved her. The days and nights are mild. The sunsets fill the sky and turn the snowless mountains soft, pale hues, blues, pinks. She was wearing a red buttoned-up shirt with a collar, blue jeans, and tennis shoes.

★

> Subject: Call me please
> Date: 31 Aug 2006 22:00:50 GMT
> From: Jon McIntosh <jon@████.org>
> To: matt@████████.com
>
>
> Give me a call today, please.
>
> (253) ███–███
>

> From: "Matthew McIntosh" <matt@██████████.com>
> Date: 8/31/06 3:07 PM
> To: "Jon McIntosh" <jon@███.org>
> Subj: Re: Call me please
>
> what's up?
>
>

> Subject: RE: Call me please
> Date: 31 Aug 2006 22:37:07 GMT
> From: Jon McIntosh <jon@███.org>
> To: Matthew McIntosh <matt@██████████.com>
>
>

> Dad’s not doing well

X

IN ADOLESCENCE I GREW fascinated with the darker superstitions which were playing havoc with the Pre-Millennial American Protestant Psyche.

Of everything they warned us about, so much more I wanted to learn.

For instance, during the early 1990s Satanists had landed on the shores of America and were running around slaughtering cows, dogs, cats, virgins, babies, and recording heavy metal music.

This intrigued me.

The devil was the true deceiver, they all said.

He came in a pretty package.

He often wore a suit and tie, and was handsome, well-groomed.

All that, I could take or leave.

But when the videos they showed us at youth group or the wide-margined, large-typefaced books they gave us to read (with titles like: *Satanism: The Seduction of America's Youth* [List Price: $13.98]) mentioned that there were human beings on earth who had nefariously mastered the forbidden arts, such as levitation, matter transmission, and (especially) astral projection—the ability to project your quantum spirit through time and space, travel around the universe like a beam of light—or spoke of famous people who had sold their souls and had been given wealth and fame and sex partners in return—or the virtually thousands of kids who had looked into their bathroom mirrors and said, "Bloody Mary, Bloody Mary, Bloody Mary," and when they did, long fingernail scratches appeared on their faces, and their faces began to bleed—well, at age fifteen that sort of thing got my attention.

That was finally interesting!

Much more so than my everyday non-quantum life, which I found crammed to the gills with gravity, guilt, and sorrow.

★

I thought about these evils all the time; how fantastic they were!

How simple to achieve; all one had to do was give up one's immortal soul and fly away into the devil's arms.

It was just so much fun to think about!

I'd think about traveling through light, moving in and out of time, leaving my body behind and exploring the universe, the entirety of which God had created, yes, but which remained, for some reason, off-limits to us Believers.

Only those under the sway of the devil, it seemed, could enjoy the fullness of God's Universe—and while they were still alive.

I would stay here on earth, as long as I lived, and then I'd die, and when I died I would spend eternity with millions of other good people like myself, all of us kneeling before God's throne singing and worshipping Him, while the ones who'd got to go to space while alive would burn in hell.

★

I didn't think they deserved to burn in hell for the sin of exploration, but it wasn't my business—I just tried not to envy them.

Nevertheless, the preoccupation with these secondhand experiences, the desire for them unsuccessfully repressed, and the battle raging in my conscience between the god I had been taught to accept and the one I wished existed, may be what led to an experience I had one afternoon.

★

I was lying on my bed, staring up at the ceiling thinking about nothing in particular, when I noticed that the window in the wall across from me, a normal window in all respects, had become a sheet of water.

Then the wall around it turned to water, too, and I felt myself being levitated from my bed, lifting up into the air, and I was turned toward the wall of water and I was given the choice whether to end whatever it was that was happening and go back,

or to proceed.

That is, I had the option to use my mind to stop all that strangeness, to snap myself out of the trance, bring the walls and window back, and find myself on the bed again, never having known where I had been invited to go, or what was out there, but safe and warm and homefree from sin.

Or I could just relax and let the waves pull me out to sea…

★

I was weak, ladies and gentlemen.

★

I shot through the window at a high rate of speed.

★

{ }

★

>Dear Erin,
>
>We will be in Spokane on Saturday the 25th celebrating
>Margaret's frist birthday. We plan to visit the cemetery, watch
>"Ice Age II", and go to Chuck E. Cheese's. Are you guys in?
>
>WILLIAM
>
>erin,
>
>helen. rainbow butterfly. dad. mom. toys. watermelon. amelia.
>mercury, venus, earth, mars, jupiter, saturn, uranus, neptune, pluto.
>my favorite planet is earth. I like earth because it is so pretty
>when I see it in a picture. unicorn.helen
>
>____
>Don't just search. Find. Check out the new MSN Search!
>http://search.msn.click-url.com/go/onm00200636ave/direct/01/
>

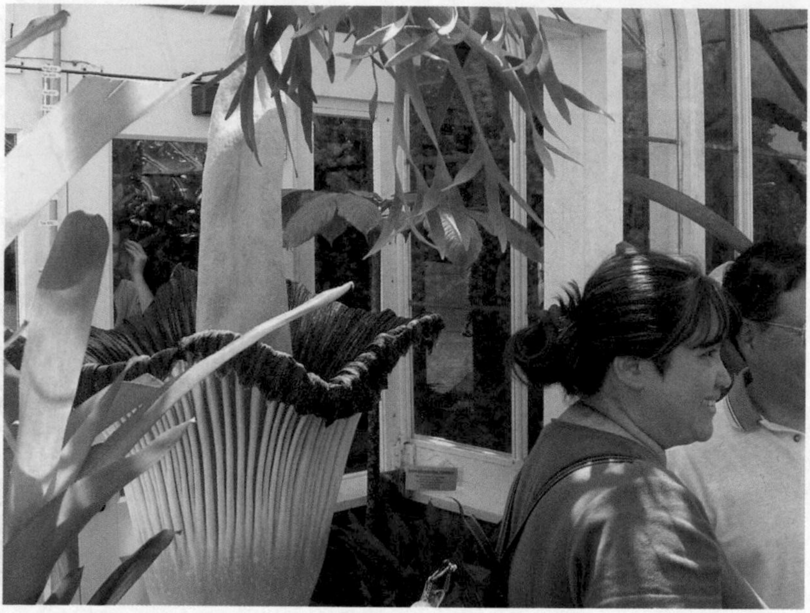

The flowers in the sanctuary today are given to the glory of God and in memory of our grandchildren, Susan and Kent , by Jean and Charlie .

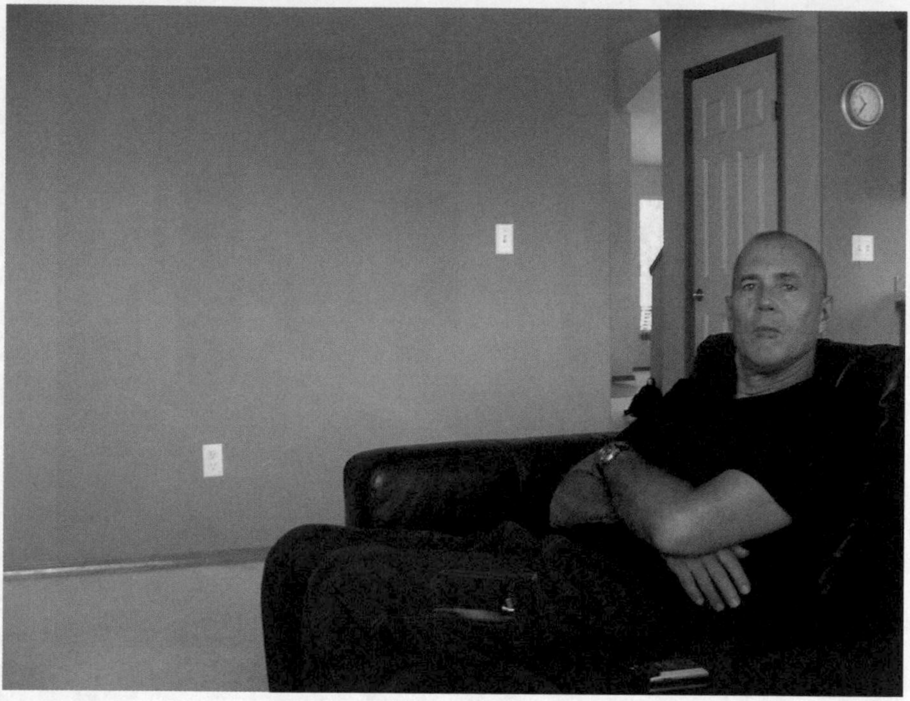

★

Monday, March 12, 2007

9:18PM

I went into my dad's room. He was asleep. The lights were off. I leaned over the bed and whispered:

"Hey."

He opened his eyes and looked into mine. His eyes were clear for the first time in months. He said,

"What happened?"

I said,

"You got cancer. It infected your brain, and now it's causing your body to shut down. Soon you're going to go into a coma, and then soon after that you'll die. Then you'll go to heaven. But that's all right. It's what's supposed to happen. Everything is taken care of here. The house, the bills—everything is taken care of, all right? So you don't have to worry about anything. You don't have anything left to do. Mom is taken care of. You've taken care of everything. Everything is fine now. There's nothing left to do. So you can go any time you like. Whenever you want. Do you understand?"

He nodded his head and looked away. Then closed his eyes and fell back asleep.

★

★

...*.*.*.*.*.*.*.*.*.*.*.*.*.*..*..*.*.*.*.*.*.*.*.*.*.*.*.*.*.*.*.

...*.*.*.*.*.*.*.*.*.*.*.*.*..*..*.*.*.*.*.*.*.*.*.*.*.*.*.*.*.*.*

..*.*.*.*.*.*.*.*.*.*.*.*.*.*..*.*.*.*

..*.*.*.*.*.*.*.*.*.*.*.*.*..*.*.*.*.*.*.*.*.*.*.*.*..*.*.*.*

:*:

★

★

> Your search – "healed of glioblastoma" – did not match any documents.

★

Recommend This Message | Reply to This Message
Subject: Gbm 4
Screen Name: Mhop53
Date: 5/14/2005
Msg. #: 20 of 36

I also hesitate to write to you - the news is not good, but if you are like me, you want to know what is going to happen -- a lot of that depends on the location of the tumor -- Do you know what part of the brain is affected? If so, you can look up brain function on the web and see what might happen. My mother had an inoperable tumor (very large) in her right parietal lobe. She had cataract surgery and then began to complain that she could not read. We thought it was because her eye needed to heal, but we were wrong. Reading was the first to go, then spatial relations. She lost her road map....didn't know where to find things or how to get around even in familiar surroundings -- it was very subtle at first, but rapidly became worse. On the day I took her to the ER I found her at home alone and unable to find the thermostat in her condo -- she was trying to turn the heat down because she was hot. She also could not find her bathroom scale. To make matters worse, she knew she should know where they were - it terried her. When I took her to the hospital I thought that maybe she was having a stroke, but NO -- it was so much worse - the CAT scan showed a large tumor -- she was transferred to MGH in Boston where an MRI followed by a biopsy confirmed the diagnosis. Within 3 days in the hospital she was unable to find her way from the hospital bed to the bathroom, even though it was only a few feet away. She had left side body neglect (not fully aware of her left side) and was unsteady on her feet. SHe also suffered from some short time memory loss - didn't remember day of week or what time it was, etc. Her cognitive function stayed OK and she was able to communicate with everyone and recognize everyone. Unfortunately, she was also able to fully understand that her tumor was inoperable and that she was terminal and only had at most 6 months to live. In fact, she only lived 3 weeks after diagnosis, but she turned down treatment. She did not want to go through radiation and chemo and feel sick if it was only going to buy her another 6 months if anything at all. I asked the doctor if she would die the same death with or without treatment and he said yes -- it's just a matter of time and they can only provide estimates. We took my mother home with hospice and she was not able to get out of bed -- she had to have someone at her side constantly - she had trouble sleeping - she had neurological symptoms like cold feet, uncontrolled limb movements and the need to urinate constantly. She had to be directed and guided when she did get up to go to the bathroom and eventually she was not able to walk. She also lost the ability to recognize what she saw --

*

hey mom this is brooke um I know you're in jess's recital or at aunt pat's but um if you get this message give me a call because I just wanted to know if when you guys are getting home if you've already eaten if you haven't eaten if you want me to make something anyway just give me a call ok bye

X

THERE WAS WATER ABOVE and water below,
and I could *breathe* in it, which was, as you might imagine, a pretty neat feeling.

As for the water, it was a color I have found very difficult to describe, because I do not believe it exists in nature, and I don't believe any other man has ever seen it and lived to tell, but the best word I have at my disposal to distinguish that color, and plant it in your brain would be:

⋆

blue.

⋆

But looking at what I've planted, I can see that the image has already fallen apart.

I suppose that's what we deal with all the time, isn't it?

These are, after all, just symbols.

But let me forget the inadequacies of language for a second and do my best, simply and plainly, and tell you that I was swimming underwater, breathing, and feeling a sense of peace like I had never felt before, a sense of the Ultimate Goodness of all things, you might say—and the water was "blue," yes, but brightly lit, and warm.

What's more I could hear all sorts of voices all around me as I swam, female voices, very calming, soothing and motherly, cooing in my ear in a language I did not understand.

I swam and it was obvious, without any thought, that these voices, disembodied (or possibly never having been bodied at all), belonged to beings which were all around me, under and over and on all sides of me, swimming along with me, helping me, guiding me, under and over and on all sides of me, swimming along with me, helping me, guiding me, under and over and on all sides of me, the head quantum surgeon was good at his job. And I say I was swimming, but I wasn't swimming, really, because I'd left my body back on the bed.

⋆

Within a year, on a hot August afternoon, I would return home from mowing the lawns at my father's church, and walk through the gate at the side of the house, past my very excitable dog, telling her, as she jumped up on me, slobbering all over my hand, to *Relax for Chrissake*, and on through the yard, over to the swimming pool.

There, at the shallow end, tired and hot, I would let out a deep sigh, and kick off my shoes, strip off my socks, then pull my shirt off up over my head.

My toes curling over the edge, I would lean forward, and for a few seconds hold myself just there, suspended over the water, because the longer you made yourself wait, the better you would feel when you finally dove in.

Is this irony?

What was the head surgeon up to?

Was he made nervous by the enormous crowd streaming into the auditorium, all those science-loving primates of the future who had come to watch the show, and see, lit up by banks of bright lights, spotlights, and the lights of the video cameras, the team of quantum surgeons unmask the frozen { } particle?

He holds himself steady.

Even the smallest unintended movement could cause the whole thing to collapse...

Lisa ███████████
Portland, Oregon 97213

Dear Lisa,

I'm thinking much of your kindness, the beauty of our lovely talk (past and yet to come), and the misbehavior of my body moving forward. Darn it is crazy! The pieces coming catch word sight tunes, and then they all go into some prologue that follows waiting. Which plan are really the words, which plans are really the pieces, which vision is what I really see, and where do the all the nuts plan? At least I know or think I have half of something to write you today. When ever thing I see in you, I feel good. You are an amazing sister, and a wonderful friend.

Lisa, I will not due well by the lows these days. So God has given me many days of good friends, and memories. I watch through the early morning the loveliness of times where belivers say their prayers, with deep convection and the spirit of God teaches fresh notes. In the greatness of all of this, I think of you, hear shared memories, and imagine you singing to the Lord. It is a lovely harp and beautiful tune to hear, deeply bringing lovely, lived, gift to each of us who have every played or listened to you. You are a mighty daughter!

I am sorry that our time has not been much. And I would talk to you again, or share any movement. The richness of your life helps me always.

Yours,

Pastor Mike

[unsent]

CLAIRE: Oh, man, he's still workin hard, isn't he.

M: Still workin like a steam engine.

CLAIRE: Yeah. It's probably about time for his morphine.

M: What time is it?

CLAIRE: 9:55……

M: My clock says, 10:07………

ANNE: Oh, man!… He is goin home… He looks so terrible, Matt……… ……………… He's cold.

M: Uh-huh. His feet are cold too..................We've been checking his hands and feet temperature for about three weeks.

ANNE: I know and he's been hot forever, even like a few hours ago he wasn't feeling really cold...Poor Dad.........It's crazy..Sucks...This sucks..

*

CLAIRE: *Hey, babe. Mike, I'm just gonna wet your mouth, OK? Yeah. You can let go, though, I'm just gonna get it wet a little bit, I'm gonna put some medicine on the side of your mouth, OK?*......I wonder which side is easier. I guess this one...*OK? I'm just gonna put it inside your cheek, OK? Here we go...Yeah, there we go...K? Good job! Excellent! Such a good job, OK, I'm gonna take this and wipe your mouth now, OK?.........And I'm just gonna clean it out a little bit........Good job!*...(fortellcometell.wav)

★

(On the walk back to the Ronald McDonald House after visiting Margaret in the premie ward at Deaconess Hospital. Spokane, Washington, U.S.A., July 2005)

Shriners

(roomforchanges.mp3)
Prof: The one jar is…
past experiments.

M: Are you gonna continue doing it?

P: Yes, we have a couple of other ideas that we haven't explored yet.

M: Do you feel that you're starting from
square one again
now after the—
it was that the—
reading was wrong?
Or are you still building on from
previous work?

P: We always build on previous people's work.
There's no use starting from
cave-man scratch.

M: But I mean your own, your own…

P: Oh.
Well…
Generally we have learned from each experiment.
We've learned *some*-thing.
Whether the…
measuring devices were *wrong,*
whether the *insulation that we used* was *wrong…*

There's always room for changes.

Whether the *water we used* was *im-pure…*
That's the next experiment, to change the
source of the water.

W: What were you using before?

P: We used *dis-tilled,* uh……
Mount Olympus Spring Water.

Next we're going to use…
snow melt.

M, W: } Oh!

P: Why do we do this? *Be-cause,*
the deuterium content of the water varies very wide—
very widely.
Deuterium is *good.*

M: What is deuterium?

P: *Heavy water.*

M: Heavy water.

P: *Heavy hydrogen.*

…We have tried to
squeeze neutrons out of *hydrogen…*
to assist us…

we have *tried* to………
……*squeeze…*
neutrons
out of a…
disassembled
smoke al-arm…

W: What?
What do you mean?…
How do you get it out of there?

P: Well, the, uh—
all smoke alarms that I am aware of use…
a radio*active* button of…
of…
Americium-241.

W: Really?

P: Which emits…………
alpha rays.

When alpha rays strike a
beryllium *tar-get,*
the beryllium gives off
neu-trons………

So……
we've tried
those two tricks.

Neutrons are *good*
in this…
o-ccasion.

W: Yeah?

P: They're bad *for* you…

W: They are?
What's the deal?
What's the deal with them?

P: They *discombooberate* your cells…

P: We haven't taken any precautions against… *exposure.*

Uh-oh!

..*..*.*.*.*.*.*.*.*.*.*.*.*.*.*.*.*.*.*.*..*.*.*.*.*.*.*.*.*.*.*.*.*..

...*.*.*.**.*..*.*.*.*.*.*.*.*.*.*.*.*.*.*..*..*.*.*.*.*.*.*.*.*.*.*

.*.*.*.*.*.

.*.*.*.*.*..*..*.*.*.*.*.*.*.*.*.*.*.*.*.*.*.*.*..*.*.*.*.*.*.*.*.*.*

.*.*.*.*..*..*.*.*.*..*..*.*.*.*.*.*.*.*.*.*.*.*.*..*.*.*.*.*.*.*.*.*.*

.*.*.*.*.*.*..*.*.*.*.*.*.*.*.*.*.*.*.*.*.*.*.*..*.*.*.*.*.*.*.*.*.*.*.

..*.*.*.*.*..*.*.*.*.*.*.*.*.*.*.*.*.*.*.*..*..*.*.*.*.*.*.*.*.*

....*.*.*.*.*.*.*.*.*.*.*.*..*.*.

....*.*.*.*

.*.*.*.*.*.*.*.*.*.*.*.*.*.*.*.*.*..*.*.*.*.*

...*.*.*.*.*.*.*.*.*.*.*.*.*.*.*.*..*..*.*.*.*.*.*.*.*.*.*.*.*.*.*.*.*.*.*.

...*.*.*.*.*.*.*.*.*.*.*.*.*.*..*..*.*.*.*.*.*.*.*.*.*.*.*.*.*.*.*.*.*.*

..*.*.*.*.*.*.*.*.*.*.*.*.*.*.*..*..*.*.*.*.*.*.*.*..*.*.*.*.*.*.*.*.*.*.*.

..*.*.*.*.*.*.*.*.*.*.*.*..*.*.*.*.*.*.*.*.*.*.*.*.*.*.*..*.*.*.*.*..*.*.*.

..*.*.*.*.*.*.*.*..*.

..*.*.*.*..*.*.*.*.*.*.*.*.*.*.*.*.*.*.*.*.*..*..*.*.*.*..*.*.*.*.*.*.*.*.

..*.*..*.*.*.*.*.*.*.*.*.*.*.*.*.*.*.*.*.*.*..*.*.*.*.*.*.*.*.*.*.*.*.*.

....*

...*.*.*.*.*.*.*.*.*.*.*.*.*.*.*.*..*..*.*.*.*.*.*.*.*.*.*.*.*.*.*.*.*.*.

...*.*.*.*.*.*.*.*.*.*.*.*.*.*.*..*..*.*.*.*.*.*.*.*.*.*.*.*.*.*.*.*.*.*

..*.*.*.*.*.*.*.*.*.*.*.*.*.*.*.*.*.*.*

...*.*.*.*.*.*.*.*.*.*.*.*.*.*.*..*.*.*.*.*.*.*.*.*.*.*.*.*.*.*.*.*.*.*.

...*.*.*.*.*.*.*.*.*.*.*.*.*..*..*.*.*.*.*.*.*.*.*.*.*.*.*.*.*.*.*.*.*

..*.*.*.*.*.*.*.*.*.*.*.*.*.*..*.*.*.*..*..*.*.*.*.*.*.*.*.*.*.*.*.*.*..

....*.*

.*.*.*.*.*.*.*.*.*.*.*.*.*.*.*.*.*..*.*.*.*.*.*.*.*.*.*.*.*.*.*..*..*.*.

..*.*.*.*.

...*.*.*.*.*.*.*.*.*.*.*.*.*.*..*..*.*.*..*.*.*.*.*.*.*.*.*.*.*.*..*.*.

..*.*.*.*.*.*.*.*.*.*.*.*.*.*.*..*.*.*.*.*.*.*.*.*.*.*.*.*.*.*..*..*.*.*.*

:*.*.*.*.*.*.*.*.*.*.*.*.*.*.*.*..*.*.*.*.**..*.*.*.*.*.*.*.*.*.*.*.*.*.

.*..*.*.*..*.*.*.*.*.*.*.*.*.*.*.*.*.*..*.*.*.*.*.*.*.*.*.*.*.*.*.*.*.*.

...*.*.*.*.*.*.*.*.*.*.*.*.*.*.*..*.*.*.*.*.*.*.*.*.*.*.*.*.*.*.*.*.*.*

..*.*.*.*.*

...*.*.*.*.*.*.*.*.*.*.*.*.*.*.*..*.*.*.*.*.*.*.*.*.*.*.*.*.*.*.*.*.*.*.

...*.*.*.*.*.*.*.*.*.*.*.*.*.*.*..*.*.*.*.*.*.*.*.*.*.*.*.*.*.*.*.*.*.*

..*.*.*.*.*.*.*.*.*.*.*.*.*..*..*.*.*.*

...*.

...*.*.*.*.*.*.*.*.*.*.*.*.*.*..*..*.*.*.*.*.*.*.*.*.*.*.*.*.*.*.*.*.*.*

..*.*.*.*.*.*.*.*.*.*.*.*.*.*.*..*..*.*.*.*.*..*.*.*.*.*.*.*.*.*.*.*.*.*.*..

...*

.*.*.*.*.*.*.*.*.*.*.*.*.*.*.*.*.*..*.*.*.*.*.*.*.*.*.*.*.*.*.*.*.*..*.*.*.

..*.*.*.*.*..*.*.*.*.*.*.*.*.*.*.*.*.*.*.*.*..*.*.*.*.*.*.*.*.*.*.*.*.*.*

.*.*.*.*.*.*..*.

..*.*.*.*..*.*.*.*.*.*.*.*.*.*.*.*.*.*.*.*..*..*.*.*.*

.*..*..*.*.*.*.*.*.*.*.*.*.*.*.*.*

..*.*.*.*.*.*.*.*.*.

...*.*.*.*.*.*.*.*.*.*.*.*.*.*..*..*.*.*.*.*.*.*.*.*.*.*.*.*.*.*.*.*..*.*.

....*.*.*.*

.*

...*.*.*.*.*.*.*.*.*.*.*.*.*.*.*..*.

...*.*.*.*.*.*.*.*.*.*.*.*.*.*.*..*

..*.*.*.*.*.*.*.*.*.*.*.*.*.*..*..*.*.*.*.*.*.*.*.*.*.*.*.**.*.*.*.*.*.*.*.

...*.*.*.*.*.

..*.*.*.*.*.*..*..*.*.*.*.*.*.*.

..*.*.*.*.*..*..*.*.*.*.*.*.*.*.*

.*.*.*.*.*.*..*..*.*.*.*.*.*.*.*.

...*.*.*.*.*.*.*.*.*.*.*.*.*.*.*..*.*.*.*..*.*.*.*.*.*.*.*.*.*.*.*.*..*.*.

..*.*.*.*.*.*.*.*.*.*.*.*.*.*.*.*..*.*.*.*.*.*.*.*.*.*.*.*.*.*..*.*.*.*.*

:*:*:*:*:*:*:*:*:*:*:*:*:*:*:*::*:*:*:*:*

:::*:*:*:*:*:*:*:*:*:*:*:*:*:*::*::*:*:*:*:*:*:*:*:*:*:*:*:*:*:*:*:*:*:

:::*:*:*:*:*:*:*:*:*:*:*:*:*::*::*:*:*:*:*:*:*:*:*:*:*:*:*:*:*:*:*:*:*

::*:*:*:*:*:*:*:*:*:*:*:*:*:*::*::*:*:*:*

:::*:*:*:*:*:*:*:*:*:*:*:*:*:*::*::*:*:*:*:*:*:*:*:*:*:*:*:*:*:*:*:*

:*::*:*:*:*:*:*:*:*:*:*:*:*:*:*::*::*:*:*:*:*:*:*:*:*:*:*:*:*:*:*:*:*:

:::*:*:*:*:*:*:*:*:*:*:*:*:*::*::*:*:*:*::*::*:*:*:*:*:*:*:*:*:*:*:*:*

::*:*:*

★

X

I HAD A NOTE EXCUSING ME FROM EVOLUTION. The biology teacher announced that all students who'd been washed clean in the blood of the Lamb should go spend the remainder of the period in the library. There were only two of us: myself and a girl named Sarah, whom I had, for many years, loved with all my heart. We never spoke to each other. Her father was a rival preacher across town whom my father had mentored. He was the head pastor of the church my father had started in 1980 and then handed over when we went to England in '85. We stayed in England for three years, then went to California for two, and then came back to Federal Way, where my dad wanted to start another church. But Sarah's dad was threatened by this, and tried to block my dad's path by badmouthing him and getting him kicked out of the denomination and ostracized from men who had always called him friend. So Sarah and I became Romeo and Juliet, forever parted by petty familial rivalries, starcrossed and so on, only she didn't seem to know that I was Romeo. (But did she know that I used to sneak out of my house, ride my bike ten blocks to the Twin Lakes Country Club tennis courts, from where I could see, through the trees, her house atop the facing hill, a mere quarter mile away...did she know that I would sit there for hours, listening to sad songs on my walkman, gazing at her windows, hoping for a glimpse of her? Did she know? Well, maybe not *hours*.) We went to the library. She sat at a table and did her math homework, and I sat at another and stared at her and then the wall and then her and then the wall etcetera etcetera et—*Oh, professor! What foolish eyes would look upon an ANGEL and see an APE?!*

⋆

The dark day and the bright day, the two realms of space, turn by their own wisdom.

⋆

(6/30/06 8:26 PM helen)

H: Do you know what I called water?

M: What?

H: Ahk.

M: Ahk?

H: When I was a little baby.

M: You did?

H: Uh-huh.

⋆

██████████████████████████████ like a king he drove back the
darkness with light.

I do not know how to stretch the thread,

nor weave the cloth,

*

He asked my mom, "When are they going to cut my head off?" She
told him, Monday, 6:20 PM. And they're not going to cut your head off,
honey, they're only going to take the staples out, and tell us the results
of the biopsy, and what sort of treatment to take.

████████████████████

Science was just not talked about in my house, ████████████
██The
surgeon's getting nervous. I think he wants to take a break. There has
been talk that performing this experiment may prove to be too much
pressure for one man to take. When he clears his throat I see

★

the world laid out upon a cross waiting to be relieved

★

I see hardly-hidden patterns everywhere—in dates, names, numbers, words, material states, license plates. I stay here writing from the time I rise in the morning until it's time to go to sleep. I lie awake for hours thinking about this book. I fall asleep and dream about it, then wake and dive back in. I receive messages all the time. Not the kinds of messages reported by lunatic whackjobs on rainsoaked flyers and posted to the internet, not those angry hateful messages delivered by gangster communist men in gorilla suits slipping pieces of gangster vampire earphone paper underneath their innocent eyelids—I have not built personalities around the messages I've received. I simply open up my heart to receive them, and in they flood each day. All day. Who sends them, I have no idea. Some personality. But I don't pollute the waters by making assumptions as to what sort, or type, or name. Or the specifics of their nature(s). Or even what the messages, themselves, might mean.

★

Although speaking of men in gorilla suits:

Just a moment ago I went down into the basement to find a tape a psychologist had made for me many years ago. He had spoken into a tape recorder while I'd sat across from him in a comfortable chair, my eyes closed, as he'd instructed me. He had then attempted to hypnotize me: 10, 9, 8 / GO DOWN THE PATHWAY... etc. Well, it didn't work, but I have kept that tape in various boxes all these years—though I seem to have misplaced it in our latest move. I was looking for the tape, because I was working on page 1037 a moment ago, when I thought of the tape and wondered if there might be something of interest at the end of it after I pretended to come out of the trance I was never in—perhaps a bit of conversation between the time Dr. X counted me awake and pressed STOP. Well, I dug out the box in which I thought the tape might be, and though I didn't find it, I soon found myself flipping through my high school yearbook. And lo and behold, out fell a single piece of college-ruled paper, folded in half. I hadn't seen this particular piece of paper in years, but as soon as I picked it up off the floor and opened it, the memory came swimming back to me. It was a short description of a vision I had had around the same time as the underwater incident we've been discussing. I was lying on my bed when then too the scenery had changed. This time, I believe my eyes were closed. And I remember that when it was over I got up and went over to where I'd set my backpack after coming home from school. I opened the backpack, took out my binder, ripped out this sheet of paper, and picked up a black pen. And wrote down what I had seen.

I was watching myself. The man in the
gorilla suit swang the stick and my head
flew off in a storm of blood. It happened
again and again and again like instant
replay. And I thought how beautiful it was.
My body was open and my soul flew up to
the sky in a wave. I was the light and
I flew upwards. But it was hot and there
was fire on every side. I heard a voice.
"Heavens in the other direction." I dropped
back down and got to the other side.
But everywhere was fire. On ground I
saw a bridge, a drawbridge that
were jaws. With every beat they
opened up and light escaped from them.
As the machine closed and went away, I
saw the world, but I was not on it. It
went away until it was a speck. And the
light in my eyes faded.

Reader, you can decide for yourself if the paragraph, brief as it is, is pertinent to our investigation, or not. If you decide not, then by all means disregard it, forget it, keep moving along. As for me, I have to say that the man being in a gorilla suit is, by itself, reason enough to assume that he probably belongs here. And if he belongs here, then we can assume that there is a reason, and if there is a reason, then we can assume, I think, that we're supposed to find out what that reason is. We may do this, I would suggest, by engaging in the simple process of continuing on:

"A very good idea." The Professor chuckled. "You've always been that way, Dan. I remember when you were about two years old, and your mother told you not to touch the stove because it was hot. You wanted to find out for yourself. You burned your finger, as I recall."

Danny laughed too. He said, "Yes, but you've told me yourself, lots of times, that a scientist is a man who's always trying to find things out for himself."

Professor Bullfinch nodded. He clasped his hands behind his back and began to walk up and down the room.

"Quite true," he said. "Sometimes knowledge is worth a burned finger…

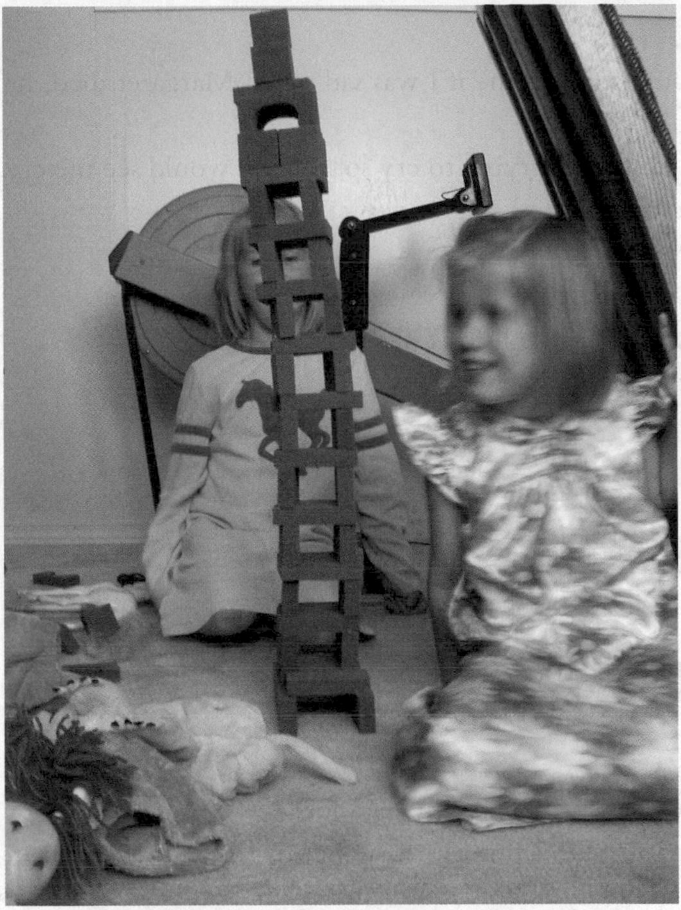

★

[redacted]

M: So you just asked me if I was sad when Margaret died, huh? I was. Were you?
H: Yeah. But I was trying to cry so nobody would see me cry.
M: You did?
H: Yeah.
M: How come?
H: Because…because I don't like to cry.
M: You don't like to cry?
H: Yeah.

[redacted]

[redacted]

M: Do you think about Margaret a lot?
H: Yeah. I think—I think that heaven is the same heaven in the dog story where Daisy did die. Heaven. I think that's the same heaven.
M: And that's where Margaret is?
H: Yeah! I think—I think she is just running around and jumpin in the water…and she's havin lots and a lot of fun.
M: I betcha.
H: Well, when I—when I grow up to be a grandma, I'm gonna die and I'm gonna go to heaven with her—Margaret!
M: And you're gonna see Margaret?
H: Uh-huh!
M: And what are you gonna do?
H: Play with her.

M: Oh yeah?…Do you miss her?
H: Yeah, and our whole family's gonna die.
M: Oh yeah?
H: Yeah. And we'll go to heaven with Margaret!
M: Oh!
H: And we'll see Heavenly Father and Jesus! Because I never been with Jesus.

M: You've never been with Jesus?
H: Yeah…

[redacted]

After Margaret died, all of Helen's toys started dying too. She would be playing quietly with them in a corner, and I'd look over and see her cover their stuffed bodies with sheets, whispering to thcm that thcy were dead.

⋆

MIKE: Seems odd to die in a country like this.
MATT: You mean America?
MIKE: Yeah.
MATT: Why?
MIKE: Because there is so much……difference……
MATT: You think we should live forever in America?
MIKE: Just about…

⋆

Whose son could speak here such words that he would be above and his father below?

*

We . Flow .

Message: Yo Momma -- we love you and miss you. Remember your plane leaves Wednesday, and we have a bazaar to attend.

*

★

TIME TO GO

★

[redacted] Back | Home

★

The only thing to live for, the only way a person is to be judged successful in life, is that person's relationship with God. This is strange for me to say because mine is a very distant and dim one at most, but it is clear that nothing else in this world matters. Why? (This is the second thing about God that I've written this week. I hope there isn't some divine reconciliation being played out as a last chance before dying. If it is, then today is 12-21-96. Amen.) First though I should mention something and I'll set it in parentheses. (I've become nearly illiterate in my attempt to numb myself into being. Without a numbness or abstraction from awareness, I would probably have no other option but to die, because after 3 1/2 years of this pain, This Pain, I've become brittle and weak. This means I am addicted to painkillers and gladly welcome any other substance to set my mind in a separate, disjointed direction (this being against the plan of God, but I've taken a detour from the previous conversation about God without explaining, though I will return to it...) Narcotics and painkillers come with the promise of a rebound effect, which after a period of time surfaces, the length and (I'm forgetting things constantly) severity of which differs from person to person. My rebound has finally found me, an effect by which the Original Pain is significantly less than a new Rebounded Pain that finds you in the morning, or any time of day, providing that it's been some time since you were last numbed. This causes you to take more pills, more frequently to fight the rebound, which is where dependence finds you. And so you find you must be numbed all day, because the regular pain you've become accustomed to (accustomed but never used to) is now more severe. I begin to read Kafka or Beckett and cannot pick up the meanings of words strung together, sentences and paragraphs, and lines and pages, not only because of the temporary high I find myself in, but also because of the residuals of the constant chemical residue that seeps through me. At quarter to eight I'm at the Velvet Elvis / We sat in a bar and smoked grass that reminded me of splashing whiskey on the brain / It has been raining / We had a pointless conversation / I could not look at her / I think his name is Brubaker / I think my name is Ashe / Even what I write and have written loses meaning, without clarity, without awareness, which is the thing I've been trying so hard to lose track of. Well. Well.)

⋆

M: The Snail, by uh, Matt McIntosh, here we go....

This is the *room* where we sleep…

★

This is the *bed* in which we sleep...It's also the *bed* where Erin—when?—*four* nights ago gave me a *snail shell.* She *picked up* the snail shell on her way to or from work around here and she—something about it—she thought I needed to have it—she needed to give it to me. So she gave it to me and before we went to bed she remembered it and ran downstairs—this was four or five days ago. Today I sat down on the bed—

★

this is the place, by the way, where I put the snail after I looked at it and thought it was really cool. Today I lay down on the *bed*,

*

I looked a little bit through *Well*,

★

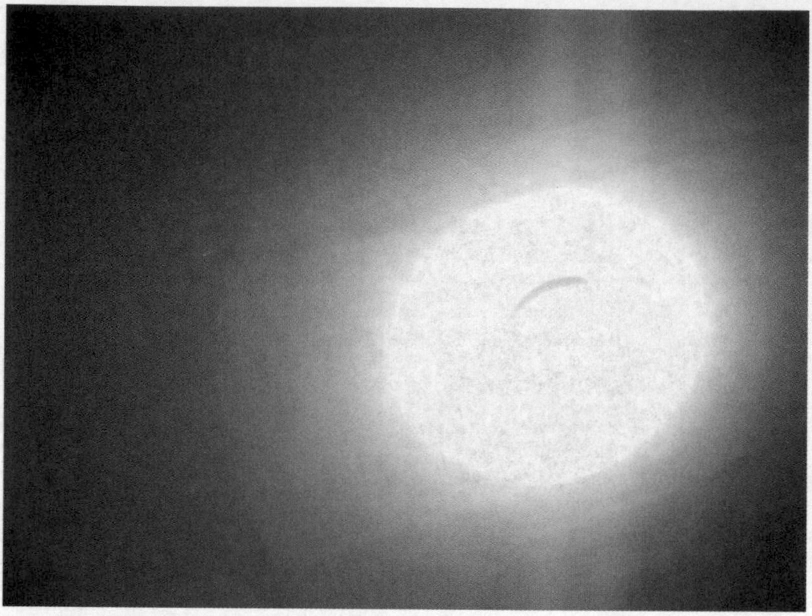

I looked up at the *light,* and

★

★

I said a couple prayers about certain things, and I looked over in *this* direction, and there, is the snail

★

on top of Mary's head.

★

Anne: You wanna sit here?

Claire: I'm gonna take this spot..................... *You got cold toes, babe... Yeah, cold toes... Cold toes.*

Anne: Am I in your way?

Claire: Yeah..................... Hmmm. Is there a spot for me?

Anne: [*laughs*] Do you wanna swap me?

Claire: No.

Anne: I was kind of laying weird, like I was laying on one side.

Claire: [*groans*] [*laughs*]

Anne: [*laughs*]

Claire: My butt's too big!

Anne: It wasn't very comfy!

Claire: It grew! My butt grew! Uh!

Anne: I put the bar down!

Claire: I can't fit in there with the bar! No, that was worse.

M: Here, sit in this chair.

Claire: No, no, no, no! Do not move the man!

M: I want you to have it.

CLAIRE: No, babes! No!

M: Please.

ANNE: You can sit here on this side.

CLAIRE: No, there's no room for me. Do you not understand how big my butt is?

ANNE: But does Matt have a pillow behind him? If you put this behind you here…

CLAIRE: [*groans*]

ANNE: Do you need a pillow behind you?

CLAIRE: There, I'm good.

M: Is that nice? Are you getting comfy?

CLAIRE: Yeah.

ANNE: …Are you sure you're all right.

CLAIRE: Yeah.

X

IT MAY FEEL AS IF YOU'RE JUST GETTING STARTED,
but the truth is

ALL IS ALREADY DONE.

29, frost on roofs, beautiful sun,

The Game is over, the board put away, and, somewhere out there, somebody knows who won.

★

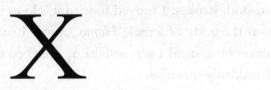

(while here) We're running around like maze-crazed rats; wasting away in a mirrored box with only our reflections to entertain us. And outside the box the audience is just now filling their seats. Remember, ladies and gentlemen, resist the urge to applaud until the operation is over, the subject has been sewn up tight, and all heads have been removed from the stage. Soon I saw a shape up ahead in the distance, and I went toward it, escorted bodiless, remember, by warm, kind female voices, all speaking in beautiful heavenly tongues. The shape was moving forward, in the same direction as I, though much more slowly, and as I approached, its shape began to take on a form, until I recognized that it was a body, a human body, swimming underwater like me, in long, smooth strokes. I moved toward it, closer and closer, until I saw that it was the body of a male *Homo sapien*. I swam toward him, until I was upon him, until I was *with* him, and then until, without any transition, I suddenly *was* him.

⋆

You see, friends, it was my *self* that I had been swimming to.

⋆

And of course, when the audience sees this rendered larger than life on the big screen, they can hardly contain themselves; each bites down on his tongue—or *her* tongue as the case may be—to keep from yelping out in glee. But please be quiet, each and every one of you. As it states clearly on the back of your programs:

Any noise at all could blow the whole operation.

(Though it's natural you be excited;

for no one has ever been this far inside...)

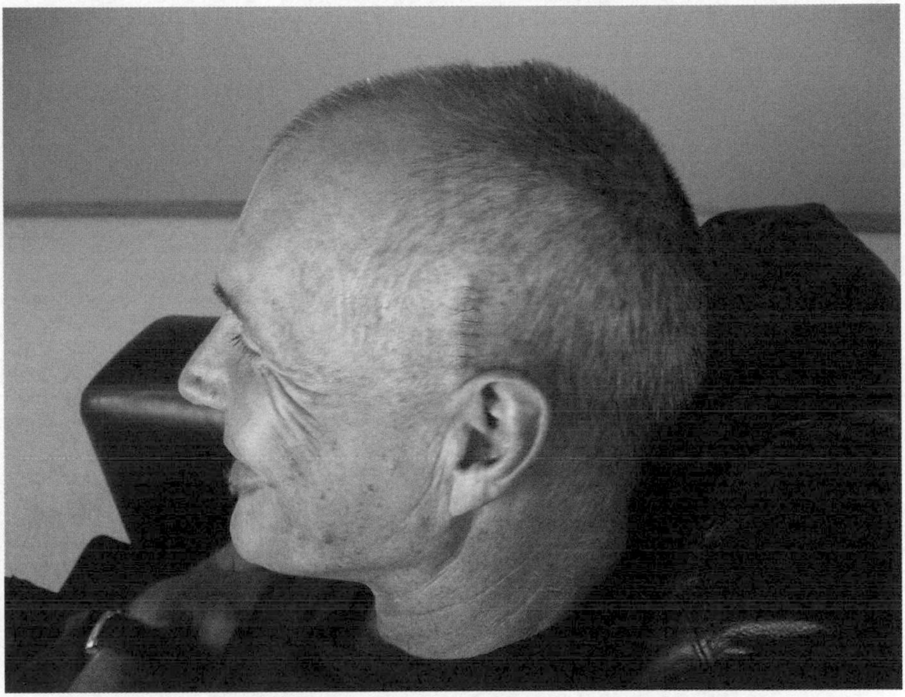

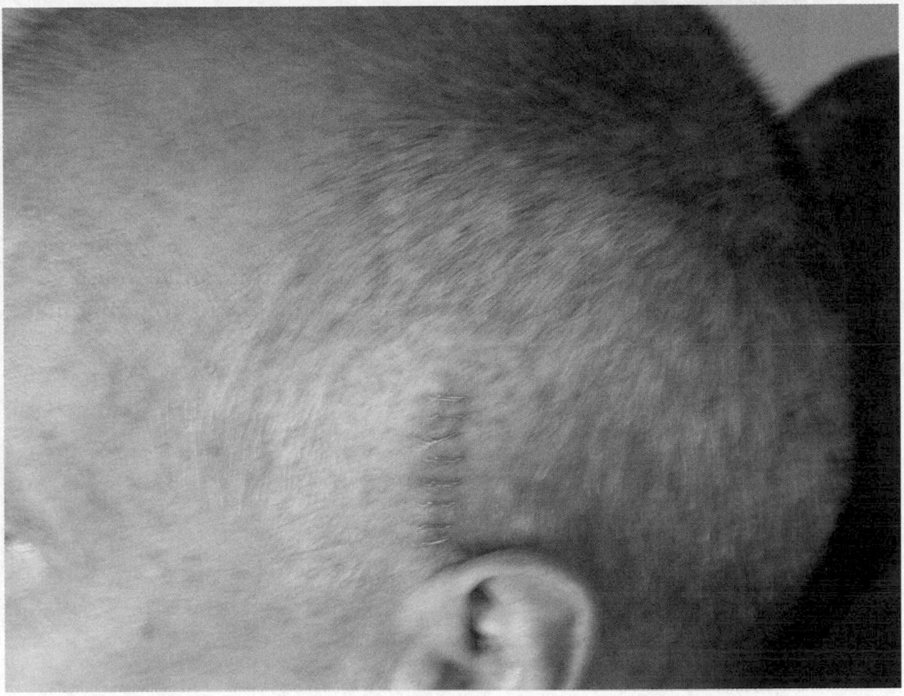

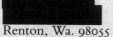

Renton, Wa. 98055

November 17, 2006

Good morning dear friend,

Today I am trying to get a nice thoughtful card to you,
They won't come. I have a front which I would like to keep running

..*.*.*.*.*.*.*..*.*.*.*.*.*.*.*.*.*.*.*.*..*..*.*.*.*.*.*.*.*.*.

..*.*.*.*.*.*..*.*.*.*.*.*.*.*.*.*.*.*.*..*..*.*.*.*.*.*.*.*.*.*

.*.*.*.*.*.*.*..*.*.**.

..*.*..*

.*.*.*..*..*.*.*.*.*.*.*.*.*.*.*.*.*.*.*.*.*.*..*.*.*.*.*.*.*.*.*.*.

..*..*..*.*.*.*.*.*.*.*.*.*.*.*.*.*.*.*..*.*.*.*.*.*.*.*.*.*

.*.*..*..*.*.*.*.*.*.*.*.*.*.*.*.*.*.*.*.*..*.*.**.*.*.*.*.*.*.*.*

.*.*.*.*.*.*.*.*.*.*.*.*..*.*.*.*.*.*.*.*.*.*.*.*.*..*..*.*.*..*.*.*.*.

..*.*.*.*.*.*.*..*.*.*.*.*.*.*.*.*.*.*.*.*.*.*..*.*.*.*.*.*.*.*.

..*.*.*.*..*..*.*.*.*.*.*.*.*.*.*.*.*.*.*.*.*.*..*.*.*.*.*

..*.*.*.*.*.*.*..*.*.*.*.*.*.*.*.*.*.*.*..*..*.*.*.*.*.*.*.*.*.*.

..*.*.*.*.*.*..*.*.*.*.*.*.*.*.*.*.*.*..*..*.*.*.*.*.*.*.*.*.*

.*.*.*.*.*.*.*..*.*.**.*

.*.*.*..*..*.*.*.*.*.*.*.*.*.*.*.*.*.*.*.*.*.*..*.*.*.*.*.*.*.*.*.*.

..*..*..*.*.*.*.*.*.*.*.*.*.*.*.*.*.*.*.*.*..*.*.*.*.*.*.*.*.*.*.*

.*.*..*..*.*.*.*.*.*.*.*.*.*.*.*.*.*.*.*.*.*..*.*.*.*.*.*.*.*.*.*.*.

...*..*.*.*.*.*.*.*.*.*.*.*.*.*.*.*.*.*.*..*.**.*.*.*.*.*.*.*.*.*.

..*.*.*.*.*.*.*.*.*..*..*.*.*.*.*.*.*.*.*.*.*.*.*.*.*.*.*.*..*.*.*.*

.*.*.*.*.*.*.*.*.*.*..*..*.*.*.*.*.*.*.*.*.*.*.*.*.*.*.*.*.*..*.*.*.*.

..*.*.*.*.*.*.*.*..*..*.*.*.*.*.*.*.*.*.*.*.*.*.*.*.*.*.*.*..*.*.*.*

.*.*.*.*.*.*.*.*..*..*.*.*.*.*.*.*.*.*.*.*.*.*.*.*.*.*.*..*.*.**.*.*

.*.*.*.*.*.*.*.*.*.*.*.*..*.*.*.*.*.*.*.*.*.*.*.*..*..*.*.*.*.*.*.

....*.*.*.*.*.*.*

.*.*.*.*.*.*.*.*.*.*.*..*.*.*.*.*.*.*.*.*.*.*.*.*.*.**.*.*.*.*.*.*.*

.*.*.*.*.*.*.*.*.*.*.*.*..*.*.*.*.*.*.*.*.*.*.*.*.*..*.*.*..*.*.*.*.

..*.*.*.*.*.*.*..*.

..*.*.*.*.*..*..*.*.*.*.*.*.*.*.*.*.*.*.*.*.*.*.*.*..*.*.*.*.*

..*.*.*.*.*.*..*.*.*.*.*.*.*.*.*.*.*.*.*.*.*..*..*.*.*.*.*.*.*.*.*.*.

..*.*.*.*.*..*.*.*.*.*.*.*.*.*.*.*.*.*.*.*.*..*.*.*.*.*.*.*.*.*.*.*.*

.*.*.*.*.*.*..*.*.**.

..*..*..*

.*.*.*..*..*.*.*..*.*.*.*.*.*.*.*.*.*.*.*.*.*..*.*.*.*.*.*.*.*.*.*.*.*.

..*..*.*.*.*.*.*.*.*.*.*.*.*.*..*..*.*.*.*.*.*.*.*.*.*.*.*.*.*.*.*

.*.*.*..*.*.*.*.*

..*.*.*.*.*.*..*.*.*.*.*.*.*.*.*.*.*.*.*..*..*.*.*.*.*.*.*.*.*.*.*.

..**.*.*.*.*..*.*.*.*.*.*.*.*.*.*.*.*.*..*..*.*.*.*.*.*.*.*.*.*.*.*

.*.*.*.*.*.*.*..*.*.**.*

.*.*.*..*..*.*.*.*.*.*.*.*.*.*.*.*.*.*.*.*.*..*.*.*.*.*.*.*.*.*.*.*.

..*..*..*.*.*.*.*.*.*.*.*.*.*.*.*.*.*.*.*.*..*.*.*.*.*.*.*.*.*.*.*

.*.*..*..*.

...*..*.*.*.*.*.*.*.*.*.*.*.*.*.*.*.*.*.*..*.*.*.*.*.*.*.*.*.*.*.

..*.*.*..*.*.*.*.*.*.*.*.*.*.*.*.*.*.*..*..*.*.*.*.*.*.*.*.*.*.*

.*.*.*.*.*..*.*.*.*.*.*.*.*.*.*.*.*.*.*.*..*.*.*.*.*.*.*.*.*.*.*.*.

..*.*..*.*.*.*.*.*.*.*.*.*.*.*.*.*.*..*.*.*.*.*.*.*.*.*.*.*.*.*

.*.*.*.*..*.*.**..*.*.*.*.*.

..*.*.*.*.*.*..*..*.*.*.*.*.*.*.*.*.*.*.*.*.*.*..*.*.*.*.*.*.*.*.

..*.*.*.*.*.*.*..*.*.*.*.*.*.*.*.*.*.*.*.*.*..*..*.*.*.*.*.*.*.*.*

.*.*.*.*.*.*.*.*.*..*.*.*.*.*

..*.*.*.*.*.*.*..*.*.*.*.*.*.*.*.*.*.*.*.*.*..*..*.*.*.*.*.*.*.*.*.

..*.*.*.*.*.*.*..*.*.*.*.*.*.*.*.*.*.*.*.*..*.*.*.*.*.*.*.*.*.*.*

.*.*.*.*.*.*.*.*.*.**.

..*.*..*.

..*.*.*.*.*..*.

*.**.*.*.*.*.*..*.*.*.*.*.*.*.*.*.*.*.*.*.*.*.*.*.*..*.*.*.*.*.*.*.

..*.*.*.*..*.*.*.*.*.*.*.*.*.*.*.*.*.*..*.*.*.*.*.*.*.*.*.*.*.*

.*.*.*.*.*.*.*.*.*.*.*.*.*.*..*.*.*.*.*.*.*.*.*.*.*.*.*.*.*.*.*.*.

...*.*.*.*.**

[unsent]

★

*.**.*

.*.

.

.*.*.*.*..*.

..*.*..*

.*.*.*.*.*.*.*.*.*.*..*.

..*.*.*.*.*.*.*.*..*

.**.*

.*..*

..*.

.*..

..*.*

..*.*.*.*.*..*..*.*.*.*.*

.**.*.*

.*..*..

..*..*.*.*.*.*.*.*.*.*.*.*.*.*..*.*.*.*.*.*.*.*.*.*.*.*.*.*.*.*.*.*.*..*
.*.*.*.*.*.*.*.*.*.*.*.*.*..*..*..
..*.*.*.*.*.*.*..*.*.*.*.*.*.*.*.*.*.*.*.*.*.*..*..*.*.*.*.*.*.*.*.*.*.
..*.*.*.*.*.*..*.*.*.*.*.*.*.*.*.*.*.*.*.*.*..*..*.*.*.*.*.*.*.*.*.*.*
.*.*.*.*.*.*.*..*.*.**.
..*.*..*..*.*.*.*.*.*.*.*.*.*.*.*.*.*.*.*.*..*.*.*.*.*.*.*.*.*.*.*.*
.*.*.*..*..*.*.*.*.*.*.*.*.*.*.*.*.*.*.*.*.*.*..*.*.*.*.*.*.*.*.*.
..*..*..*..*.*.*.*.*.*.*.*.*.*
.*.*..*..*.*.*.*.*

One day I went with my friend JD to the Coach & Horses to play some pool. The year was AD 2002. The place was empty, except for an old woman drinking liquor at the bar, and a man off in the corner, sitting by himself behind a glass of beer. A big, broad-shouldered guy, bearded, kind of fat, middle-aged; he watched us play. He wore army pants, and a heavy green army jacket, and an air force garrison cap, the kind that sits on top of the head. A few colorful ribbons were pinned on it. He was pretty inexpressive, but occasionally he would say, Nice shot, Good play, Nice leave, etc. We'd smile back and say thanks.

At one point, I took a seat in a chair not too far from his. JD sat down too. The guy looked over at us and said,

"Have you guys heard my CD yet?"

I said, "No. I don't think we have."

So he reached into his jacket and handed me a CD without a case. He gave one to JD too.

It was called MY BROWN-EYED GIRL. His name, according to the label—stark, white, TIMES NEW ROMAN—was JAY C. TRINKLEIN. He asked me if I knew the woman who ran the pancake restaurant down the block. I didn't. He said, "She's the brown-eyed girl in the title. It's dedicated to her. She's always been very kind to me."

Pointing at his jacket, I asked him if he had been in the military. In general, he was somewhat difficult to understand. Turns out he suffered from what doctors call *paranoid schizophrenia*—I'd find this out a few days later. What I gathered from his responses that day was that he'd been in the army as a young man, and had served in Vietnam, and his job at the time had been Radio Operator.

We didn't talk much more. JD and I went back to playing pool, and at some point JAY C. TRINKLEIN disappeared, though I didn't see him leave. I really wasn't paying very close attention.

A few days later I found the CD in my jacket pocket. I put it in my stereo. The first song was a 31-minute-12-second meandering psychedelic electric guitar assault with heavy distortion and reverb, accompanied by a very simple electronic beat, made on a beat box. The production was dirty, probably recorded on either a 2- or 4-track analog machine.

One of the songs near the end was soft, and acoustic, and quite nice. It was one of the few with lyrics. JAY C. TRINKLEIN had a gruff, off-key singing voice, that was true. But it turns out that at certain times he could make a very beautiful sound.

A week later, back at the Coach & Horses, I found out that Jay C. Trinklein was dead.

I can't be sure but the talk was a self-inflicted gunshot wound to the head.

I've since looked for him on the web, hoping to find some trace of him: an obituary or chat room post or town meeting transcript or his name on a petition—*some*thing—some proof that he existed—I've looked everywhere—but Jay C. Trinklein is simply nowhere to be found.

Maybe in a filing cabinet somewhere…

★

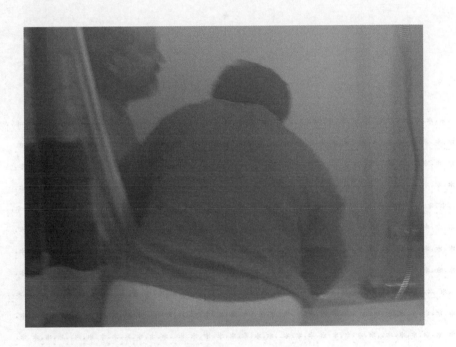

★

★

ANNE: He's breathing so much better now. [*laughs*] I was just gonna say something so stupid!

M: What was it?

ANNE: I think he's getting better.......................................

★

★

.*.*.*.*.*.*.*.*.*.*..*.*.*.*.*.*.*.*..*.*.*.*.*.*.*.*..*.*.*.*.*.*.*.*..*.*.*.*.*.*.*.*..
..*.*.*.*.*.*..*.*.*.*.*.*.*.*..*.*.*.*.*.*.*.*.*..*.*.*.*.*.*.*.*..*.*.
..*.*.*..*.*.*.*.*.*.*.*.*..*.*.*.*.*.*.*.*.*..*.*.*.*.*.*.*.*.*..*.*.*.*.
..*.*..*.*.*.*.*.*.*.*.*..*.*.*.*.*.*.*.*.*..*.*.*.*.*.*.*.*.*..*.*.*.*.*.*.
.*.*.*.*.*.*.*.*.*..*.*.*.*.*.*.*.*.*..*.*.*.*.*.*.*.*.*..*.*.*.*.*.*.*.*.*..
..*.*.*.*.*..*.*.*.*.*.*.*.*.*..*.*.*.*.*.*.*.*..*.*.*.*.*.*.*.*.*..*.*.
..*.*.*..*.*.*.*.*.*.*.*..*.*.*.*.*.*.*.*..*.*.*.*.*.*.*.*.*..*.*.*.*.
..*.*..*.*.*.*.*.*.*.*.*..*.*.*.*.*.*.*.*.*..*.*.*.*.*.*.*.*.*..*.*.*.*.*.*.
.*.*.*.*.*.*.*.*..*.*.*.*.*.*.*.*.*..*.*.*.*.*.*.*.*.*..*.*.*.*.*.*.*.*.*..
..*.*.*.*.*..*.*.*.*.*.*.*.*.*..*.*.*.*.*.*.*.*.*..*.*.*.*.*.*.*.*.*..*.*.
..*.*.*.*..*.*.*.*.*.*.*.*..*.*.*.*.*.*.*.*.*..*.*.*.*.*.*.*.*.*..*.*.*.*.
..*.*..*.*.*.*.*.*.*.*..*.*.*.*.*.*.*.*.*..*.*.*.*.*.*.*.*.*..*.*.*.*.*.*.
.*.*.*.*.*.*.*.*.*.*..*.*.*.*.*.*.*.*.*..*.*.*.*.*.*.*.*.*..*.*.*.*.*.*.*.*.*..
..*.*.*.*.*.*..*.*.*.*.*.*.*.*.*..*.*.*.*.*.*.*.*.*..*.*.*.*.*.*.*.*.*..*.*.
..*.*.*..*.*.*.*.*.*.*.*..*.*.*.*.*.*.*.*.*..*.*.*.*.*.*.*.*.*..*.*.*.*.*.*.
..*.*..*.*.*.*.*.*.*.*..*.*.*.*.*.*.*.*.*..*.*.*.*.*.*.*.*.*..*.*.*.*.*.*.*.

(9_19_06 8_33 PM claire describes the apparatus.wav)

You were just describing the apparatus for—

Right

—Dad's radiation

Radiation

—treatment.

So first of all it was this big, huge room. A very large room that was absolutely immaculate, not a speck of dust in the whole place. In the middle of the room was this, uh, bed. And uh, Dad laid down on the bed, and the attendant, you know, was raising and lowering it, trying to find the right dimension, and I mean it was just very precise on how you could raise and lower it. And then um they brought out the mask that they had made for him, it fit right over his face and his head, and as he laid down on his back, there was a like a a rim, underneath his head, and they would put the mask on his face and then snap it on to the rim, so that his head was held, tight, to the bed.

Can you hear us?......Matt?

Wow.

So he couldn't move his head at all. In fact when he got off of it after the treatment, he had the lines pressed into his skin, from it being that tight on his head, holding him, so he couldn't move. So then they're measuring—they were measuring his head and they were measuring the bed, and I didn't get to stay in for the whole thing because at one point they had me leave, but what they were doing basically was lining him up perfectly for the, for the radiation treatment, and then from what I understand they, they did a meld of the CT scans and MRIs and, and all of that stuff with his actual mask, and they put Xs on the mask where they were going to administer the radiation. Then when they got him all set on the bed, then I had to leave the room.

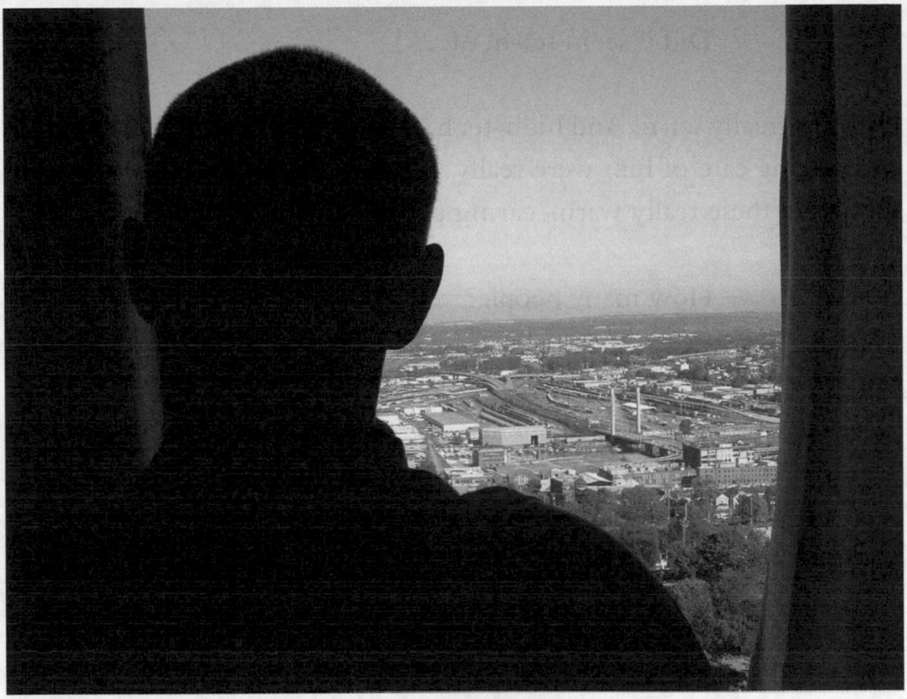

Was the—the whole room was white?

The room was white, the equipment was black, the carpet was gray... and so he's laying with his head pointed towards another machine that was digital and huge like—I'd have to go look at it again, but it seems like it was a big, round...face to it, like as big as a...door of a dryer... And I—but I didn't get to see them turn anything else on because they didn't let anyone else in the room.

What was he wearing?

He got to just wear his regular clothes, because the, the area was his head, but other people that I saw going in were in hospital gowns, depending on where they were gonna get the radiation......

Did it seem sci-fi, or…

It seemed really sci-fi! And high-tech, and…… And yet the women that were taking care of him were really…warm. So you had this very cold room, but these really warm, caring people.

How many people?

Just two.

Two ladies?

Two ladies.

Nurses?

Yeah, I think—

Or technicians?

I don't know if they were nurses or techs.

And what did they do? And say.

They were mea—they were doing the measurements, they were just uh, reading stats, and um, lowering the bed and positioning him for the right…position.

★

JUN · 61

"Remember when we went to the Japanese garden?

There was no one there.

It was so nice."

SEATTLE

X

I CAN'T TELL YOU WHERE THIS SECTION WILL END UP in this book of mine. I don't know where you're reading it now, what you've been through already, what still awaits you, and what you await. But I can tell you that *..* .*.*.*. *.*. *.*.*.*.*.*.*.*.*..*.*.*.*.*.*.*.*..*.*.*.*.*.*.*.*..*.*.*.* .*.*.*.*..*.*.*.*.*.*.*.*..*.*.*.*.*.*.*.*..*.*.*.*.*.*.*.*..*.*.*.*.*. *.*..*.*.*.*.*.*.*.*..*.*.*.*.*.*.*.*..*.*.*.*.*.*.*.*..*.*.*.*.*.*.*.. *.*.*.*.*.*.*.*..*.*.*.*.*.*.*.*..*.*.*.*.*.*.*.*..*.*.*.*.*.*.*.*..*.*. *.*..*.*.*.*.*.*.*.*..*.*.*.*.*.*.*.*.*.*.*.*.*.*.*.*..*.*.*.*.*.*.*.*.. *.*.*.*.*.*.*.*..*.*.*.*.*.*.*.*..*.*.*.*.*.*.*.*..*.*.*.*.*.*.*.*..*.*. *.*.*.*.*.*..*.*.*.*.*.*.*.*..*.*.*.*.*.*.*.*..*.*.*.*.*.*.*.*..*.*.*.*. *.*.*..*.*.*.*.*.*.*.*.*.*.*.*.*.*..*.*.*.*.*.*.*.*.*..*.*.*.

IT'S ALREADY MADE ITS WAY INSIDE.

Can you hear us?…… Matt?

★

..*.*.*.*.*.*.*.*.*.*.*.*.*..*.*.*.*.*.*.*.*.*.*.*.*.*.*.*..*..*.*.*.*.*.

..*.*.*.*.*.*.*.*.*.*.*.*..*.*.*.*.*.*.*.*.*.*.*.*.*.*..*..*.*.*.*.*.*

.*.*.*.*.*.*.*.*.*.*.*.*.*..*.*.**.*

.*.*..*.*.*.*.*.*.*.*.*.*.*.*.*.*..*..*.*.*..*.*.*.*.*.*.*.*

.*.*.*.*.*.*.*.*.*.*.*.*.*.*.*.*.*.*.*..*.*..*.*.**.*.*.*.*.*.*.*.*.*.*.*.*

.*.*.*.*.*.*.*.*.*.*.*.*.*.*.*..*..*.*.*.*.*.*:*.*.*.*.*.*.*.*.*.*.*.*.*.*

..*.*.*.*.*.*.*.*.*.*.*.*.*.*..*..*.*.*.*.*.*.*.*.*.*.*.*.*.*.*.*.*.*.*..

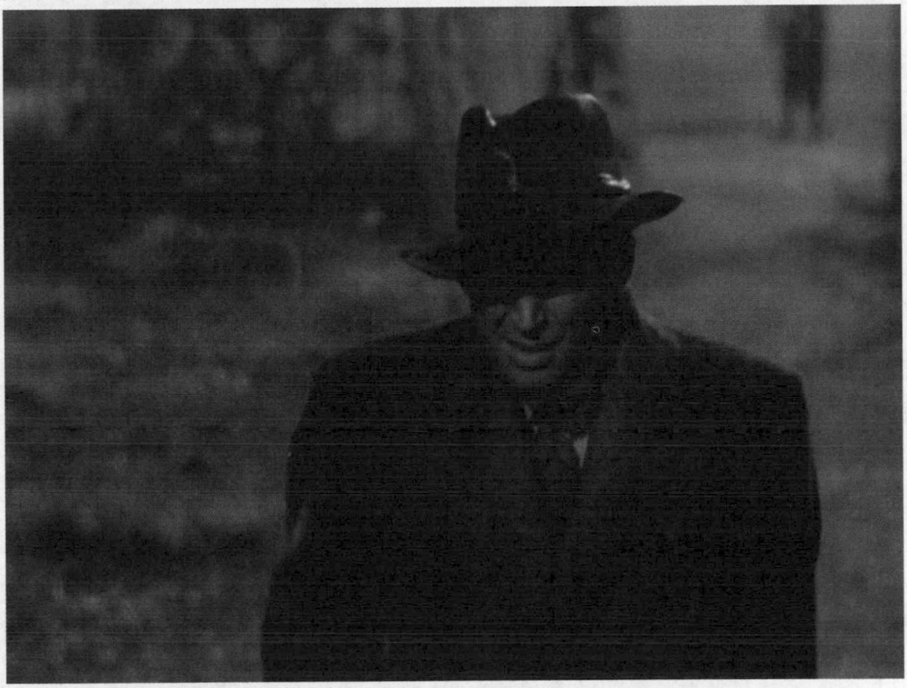

..*.*.*.*.*.*.*.*.*.*.*.*.*..*

.*..*.

*.**..*.*.*.*.*.*.*.*.*.*.*.*.*

.*.*..*.*.*..*.

**.*..*.*.*.*.*.*.*.*.*.*.*.*.*.*.*..*.*.*.*.*.*.*.*.*.*.*.*.

...*.*.*.*.*.*.*.*.*.*.*.*.*.*.*..*.*.*.*.*.*.*.*.*.*.*.*.*.*.*.*.*.*.*.

...*.*.*.*.*.*.*.*.*.*.*.*.*.*..*.*.*.*.*.*.*.*.*.*.*.*.*.*.*.*.*.*.**.*

..*.*.*.*.*.*.*.*.*.*.*.*.*.*..*.*.*.*.*

....*.*.*.*.*.*

.*:

:*:*:*:*:*:*:*::*:*:*:*:*:*:*:*::*:*:*:*:*:*:*:*:*:*:::*:*:*:*:*:*:*:*:*:*:*:*:*::*:*:*
:*:*:*:*:*::*:*:*:*:*:*:*:*:*::*:*:*:*:*:*:*:*:*:*:*::*:*:*::*I know that these Acts have always existed, complete, fulfilled, wrapped so tightly one around another that for billions of years it was thought that nothing could ever pull them apart. Until, of course, {something happened and} the Universe exploded::::::::::::::::

And when it exploded the Acts were scattered like irradiated photons into the deepest, darkest corners of the Mind, where they coughed and choked and froze and fell into a deep, deep sleep,

alone and far apart, *:*:::*:*:*:*:*:*:*::*:*:*:*:*:*:*:*:*:*:*::*:*:*:*:*:*:*:*:
:*:*:*:*:*:*:*::*:*:*:*:*:*:*:*:*::*:*:*:*:*:*:*:*:*::*:*:*:*:*:*:*:*::*:*
:*:*:*:*:*::*:*:*:*:*:*:*:*:*::*:*:*:*:*:*:*:*:*:*::*:*:*:*:*:*:*:*::*:*:*:*
:*:*:*:*::*:*:*:*:*:*:*:*::*:*:*:*:*:*:*:*::*:*:*:*:*:*:*:*:*:*::*:*:*:*:*:*
:*:*::*:*:

::*:*:*:*:*:*:*::*:*:*:*:*:*:*:*:*::*:*:*:*:*:*:*:*:*:*::*:*:*:*:*:*:*:*:*::*:*
:*:*:*:*:*:*::*:*:*::

and there they slumbered,
as background radiation

:::*:*:*:*:*:*:*::*:*:*:*:*:*:*:*:*:*:*::*:*:*:*:*:*:*:*:*:*::*:*:*:*:*:*:*:*::*:*:*:
::*:*::*:*:*:*:*:*:*:*::*:*:*:*:*:*:*:*::*:*:*:*:*:*:*:*:*:*::*:*:*:*:*:*:*:*:*:*:*:*
:*:*:*:*::*:*:*:*:*:*:*:*:*::*:*:*:*:*:*:*:*:*:*:*:*:*:*::*:*:*:*:*:*:*:*:*::*:
::*:*:*:*::*:*:*:*:*:*:*:*:*::*:*:*:*:*:*:*:*:*::*:*:*:*:*:*:*:*:*::*:*:*:*:*:*:*:
:*:*:*:*:*:*:*:*:*:*:*:*:*:*:*:*::*:*:*:*:*:*:*:*:*:*:*:*:*:*:*:*:*::*:*:*:*:*:*:*:
:::*:*:*:*:*:*:*:*::*
:*:*::*:*:*:*:*:*:*:*:*::*:*:*:*:*:*:*:*:*::*:*:*:*:*:*:*:*:*:*:*:*:*::*:*:*:*:*:*:*:*
:*:*::*:*:*:*:*:*:*:*::*:*:*:*:*:*:*:*::*:*:*:*:*:*:*:*:*:*:*:*:*:*:*:*:*::*:*:*:*:
::*::*::*:*:*:*:*:*:*:*:*::*:*:*:*:*
:*:*:*:*:*:*:*:*:*:*::*:*:*:*:*:*:*:*:*::*:*:*: until I came to life with the mandate to wake them up, and put it back together.

..*.*.*.*.*.*.*.*.*.*.*..*.*.*.*.*.*.*.*.*.*.*.*.*.*.*.*..*..*.*.*.*.*.*.*.

..*.*.*.*.*.*.*.*.*.*..*.*.**.*

.*.*.*.*.*.*.*..*..*..*.*.*.*.*.*.*.

..*.*.*.*.*..*..*..*.*.*.*.*.*.*.*

.*.*.*.*.*.*..*..*.*.*.**.*.*.*.*.*

.*.*.*.*.*.*.*.*.*.*.*.*.*.*.*.*..*.*.*.*.*.*.*.*.*.*.*.*.*.*.*.*.*.*..*..*.*.*

..*..*.*.*.

.*..*.*.**.*.*.*.*.*.*.*.*.*.*.*.*.*.*

.*.*.*.*.*.*..*..*.*.*.*.*.*.*.*.*.*.*.*.*

.*.*.*.*.*.*..*.*.*.*.*.*.*.*.*.*.*.*.*.*.*.*.*..*..*.*.*.*.*.*.*.*.*.*.*.*.*.*.

★

Does this sound like megalomania?

★

Do you think I have a big ego?

★

Well, I am of the opinion that my ego is infinitely small, smaller, even, than the scrapings that collect on the blade of the quantum surgeon's tiny instrument as he peels back the layers of the { } one★

by one★

by one★

at a time.

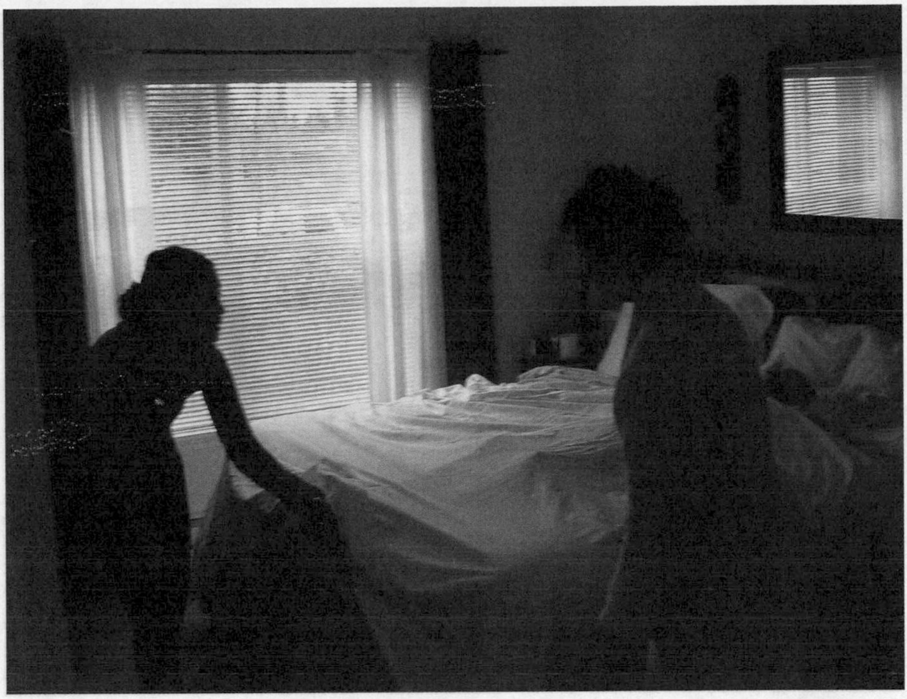

★

I don't have a big ego.

★

I have no ego.

★

I am nothing.

★

I don't exist.

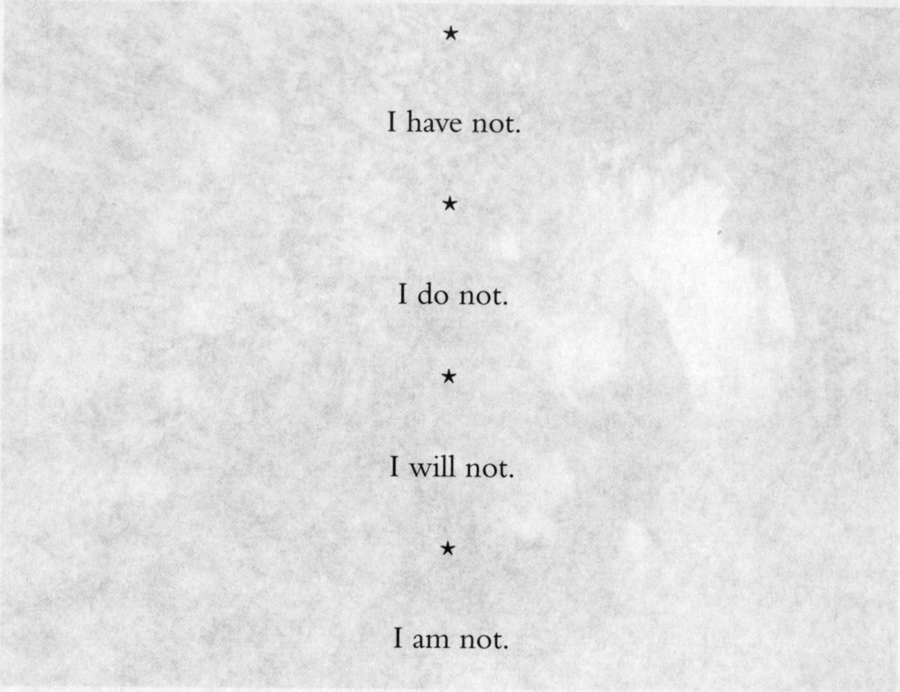

★

I have not.

★

I do not.

★

I will not.

★

I am not.

★

I am { }.{ } I am

★

W: Yeah. Is there any part you want me to read?...No... *Yes!* I just love it so, it's so beautiful...Do you have anything about the castle's thick walls?

M: What?

W: Do you have anything about the castle's really thick, thick walls?

M: No. Do you have something to say about the castle's thick walls?

W: No, but I mean, just whenever I visualize a castle I visualize that it would have *really thick* stone walls.

M: When I think of the castle I think it takes a lot to get to the center of it.

W: Oh…

M: Because it's fortified and it's got lots of people standing around, making sure you don't get to the heart of it.

W: That's so weird because whenever *I* visualize it I always visualize it from the *inside out*—but *of course I do* because *that's where I am!*

M: [*laughs*]

W: It's like I just think of layers and layers but not being on the *outside* of them—I just think of *really, really thick stone walls.*

M: I think of, yeah, stone walls, and I gotta get through them.

W: Yeah. That's easy. They're totally porous. Just turn yourself into water and seep through.

M: .... I could just wait until the castle crumbles... Like Rome.

W: Yep...

M: Like a guy who wants to—he really wants to see the gladiator fights, but he can't afford a good seat, so he just waits until Rome crumbles and burns and thousands of years later he can come in and sit—

W: Yeah.

M: because there's no one there.

W: That's awesome. That's a great idea. You could *totally* rescue me that way.

M: Just wait?

W: Yeah, just wait. And we could meet, like, at the ruins. With all those feral cats who hate my guts.

M: The problem with waiting is that you die.

W: Who?

M: Me.

W: No way!

M: Well, literally if I *waited* I would *die.*

W: No…

M: Yeah.

W: No.

M: Then I would be born again, then try to find myself back to the continent where the castle is, and eventually end up at the castle,

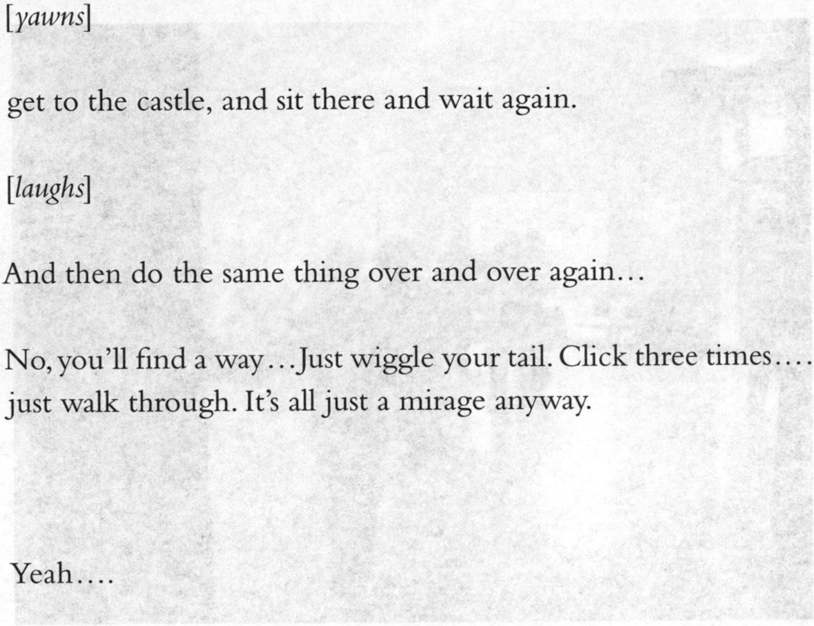

W: [*yawns*]

M: get to the castle, and sit there and wait again.

W: [*laughs*]

M: And then do the same thing over and over again…

W: No, you'll find a way…Just wiggle your tail. Click three times……… Or just walk through. It's all just a mirage anyway.

M: Yeah….

W: { } like a fish, no big deal.

M: No big deal…….

W: But you already wrote that scene.

M: What scene?

W: Well, don't you get past the guards or something, and then I'm pretending to be asleep? And there's a party, or something like that?

M: Yeah…that's part of it………… That was a dream………

★

TIME TO GO

★

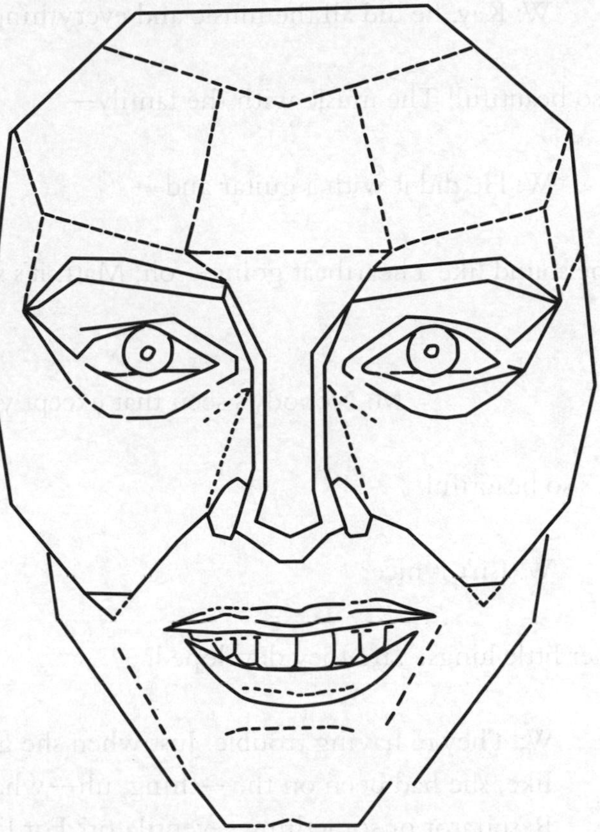

OH, MATT, THAT'S SO BEAUTIFUL!

M: Yeah.

K: [*applause*]

W: Kay, he did all the music and everything!

K: Oh, it's so beautiful! The music with the family—

W: He did it with a guitar and—

K: —and the sound like a heartbeat going—oh, Matt, it's so wonderful!

M: Nobody's seen that except you and Erin.

K: Oh, that's so beautiful.

W: Isn't it nice?

K: So, are her little lungs…are they developed?

W: They're having trouble. Just when she gets ahead—like, she had been on the—thing, uh—what's it called? Respirator or something—ventilator? For like, weeks and weeks and they were getting worried because you're not supposed to have her on for very long. And they took her off—she's off for like—a little while { } So that's why she was in that little isolation room. She has an infection…

K: Oh…

W: I know. So now she's back on the ventilator. I guess it's like the last thing she needs, is anything to go wrong with her lungs. But they—the nurses were pretty positive. They said she's pretty tough.

K: What does she weigh, do you know?

Can you hear us?……Matt?

*

Yes sir, you had a question for Sibyl.

Yeah, hi Sibyl, how you doin? I'm havin a problem with my left hand. Do you know what that might be?

Yeah, you have, uh, the beginnings of corpol tunnel.

OK. Thank you!

Yeah.

Yes, sir!

We lost a daughter and a nephew fourteen years ago, uh, there was a threat made, we were wondering if the threat was carried out or if it just uh what the fire inspector ruled it to be.

You mean accidental?

Yes.

It was accidental. Yeah. Thank God.

Right over here, Sibyl. Yes, ma'am.

> Hi Sibyl, thank you Talk Show Host. Um, I was wondering, my friend passed away this summer, he committed suicide, um, does he come around? Does he have a message?

He comes around, but he's getting ready to come back in. Into life, you know. See, what we do is we recycle. If we commit suicide—not everyone—now please don't—I don't want any messages—uh, but if this was an unfinished life, so he's gonna come back in.

★

W: Can you hear us?……Matt?

What?

Does she weigh three and a half pounds?

She weighs five pounds now.

She doesn't weigh five pounds.
You can leave when you're five pounds.

Oh, yeah, right. Below five pounds.

She was one.

She was one when she was born?

Yeah. She came four months early.
But she's been alive for eighty-six days.

I had a girl who worked for me, and she had a baby that was only a pound and it lived. And at that time, that was—and that was, that was fifteen years ago—it was the smallest baby that ever lived. And she's grown up now!

Can she run and—

Uh-huh! They—they do marvelous things!

W: Isn't it incredible? Yeah, we were so surprised
because—you saw in Matt's movie—
it seems there were like two
nurses for every one patient, you know?
It's pretty cool. They seem to be
doing a really good job.

K: Oh, Matt that's so beautiful!

The poor girls, you know.
They don't know what's going on.

The little ones? Yeah.

You can see them being affected by it.

He's doing a good job. He's the one,
my brother, he's the brother who's
{ }
He's so responsible and—

Well, how come she had her early, do you know?

No. Really, really early on in the pregnancy
they said, *This is not gonna go full term*.
I don't know why, but they they said,
{ } and she knew she was gonna
be on bed rest and she, and { }
you can if you want { } I think she'd be
a little bit of both.

And then it just so happened that
things were going along, they were much further along
than anyone thought she would be. And they just had
a routine appointment—they live in Moses Lake,
but they had an appointment to go to this place
in Spokane to meet their doctor,
they already had a standing appointment. And it just so
happened that
like right when they got there,
the water

broke.

Patricia: Hello, I am Patricia, I am the website greeter. Welcome to WebsiteGreeters.com. May I know your name please?

Visitor 1234: seeking help in a literary endeavor

Patricia: Do you have a website?

Visitor 1234: Not online currently. Name will be Bestsellingadvice.com
Visitor 1234: My name is Patty.

Patricia: It's nice to have you on our website Patty. :)
Patricia: In order to serve you better, I need to ask you a few initial questions; would that be alright with you?

Patty: I have questions of my own, but sure.

Patricia: I see. You can ask me now. :)

Patty: We will be offering an online service to amateur writers. In a nutshell it's this: They come to our site, are greeted by a "Professor" named "Prof. Will" ie You. After signing up with our service, they will post certain portions of works in progress. Prof. Will will read them in real time and comment on them. Is this a service you can provide?

Patricia: Our Live Operators apply the purest form of 1-to-1 customer service and sales approach, via live interaction, to provide your website visitors an experience they deserve.
Patricia: Let me have our business Development Manager contact you back to equip you with the desired details Patty. :)
Patricia: May I have your phone number and email address please?

Patty: email: professorwill@bestsellingadvice.com
Patty: All right if we try a quick sample paragraph?

Patricia: Thank you for your email address Patty.

Patty: You can call me Professor Will if you like. I will be the Professor most days. You will be the Professor only when I am on vacation, or out of town on business.

Patricia: I see. That would be great.

Patricia: I will have Our Business Development manager discuss the details with you Proffessor Will. :)

Patricia: By the way, let me go ahead and send you details on how our service works.

Professor Will: I'm sorry, I don't have much more time Patricia, so I am going to have to sign off in just a moment. But let's do a quick sample paragraph so you know better what I'm talking about, and if it's something you'd like to do. All right?

Patricia: Okay, sure thing Professor Will.

Professor Will: Great. Now I will give you a sample fictional sample. All I'm looking for you to do is respond as the Professor, with your immediate thoughts. This may sound daunting, but it's really not. I have been posing as the Professor via regular mail for years, and I never even graduated high school. No one in all that time ever suspected I was someone other than I was. So just say what comes to your mind, but try to sound professorial. No stress though, Patricia. This is just to show you what the job entails. All right?

Patty: You can call me Professor Wu if you like. I will be the Professor most days. You will be the Professor only when I am on vacation or out of town on business.

Patricia: I see. That would be great.

Patricia: I will have Our Business Development manager discuss the details with you, Professor Will.

Patricia: By the way, feel free to go ahead and send your [illegible] services [illegible].

Professor Will: I'm sorry, I don't have much more time, Patricia, so I am going to have to stop [illegible] a moment. But let's do a quick sample paragraph so you know better what I'm talking about. [illegible] something I like to do. All right?

Patricia: Okay, sure thing, Professor Will.

Professor Will: Great. Now I will give you a sample [illegible]. Simple. All [illegible] you [illegible] respond as the Professor with [illegible] immediate [illegible]. [illegible] really until I have been [illegible] the Professor [illegible] for years, and I never even graduated high school. [illegible] all that [illegible] whatsoever [illegible]. Just say what comes to your mind [illegible]. No stress though, Patricia. This is just to show you what the [illegible] right.

Professor Will: I really need to wrap this up though, dear, so please respond as quickly as you can.

Patricia: My apologies Professor.

Professor Will: No sweat. All right. Ready?
Professor Will: Here we go:

★

One evening in April 2003, I went drinking in Bigfork with a guy who lived on a cherry orchard across the highway. We went to a bar called the Village Well. We stayed there for a few hours and decided to leave. It was a bit after midnight and we drove back down Highway 35. We decided to stop for one more beer at a restaurant between Bigfork and Mile Marker 18. It was called the Sitting Duck. Located right on Lake Flathead with a dock in the back, so if you are one of those rich Californians who buy up all the real estate around Flathead so you can build yourself a mansion that you use only one week a year, driving up land prices and driving the old locals out of town, during that one week while you're motoring around the lake in your speedboat, you can throw anchor at the Sitting Duck and go inside for a bite to eat. The night I went there was the only time I had ever been, though I'd driven by it perhaps a hundred times. The place was deserted. We went over to the bar and sat down. The bartender came out from the back and said he was about to close, but agreed to pour us one beer. He was an old guy, a local, who had lived there all his life.

We got to talking about the couple from Bethel, Connecticut, who had died a few days earlier. I knew that the tour guide had not died. But all I knew was what my neighbors had told me, from gossip around town, and from the scant information reported in the local paper.

The bartender was friends with the tour guide. What's more he had spoken to him just the day before, in the hospital where the tour guide was recovering from hypothermia. The tour guide had told him the story of what had happened. And then the bartender told me. And now

I'm telling you. The story is pretty much the same as everyone knew. But there were a few very important details the bartender provided.

It was two o'clock in the afternoon and the sun was high in the sky. (April 9, 2003.) The water was still. There was no wind. It was quiet. The tour guide had strapped himself to the hull, but the couple from Bethel, Connecticut, were holding fast to the edge, submerged in very cold water past their waists. They had not let him tie them down to the boat, because it had all happened very quickly and now they were afraid that if they let go their tenuous hold, even for a moment, they would sink into the water, and not have the strength to climb back up.

It was very quiet.

Occasionally, the tour guide could hear the couple speaking to each other, in calm, collected voices. Most often he could not understand their words.

At times, he would try to console them, to tell them that someone would be looking for them, and that they must hold on. Someone is coming to get us, don't you worry now, just hold on, just hold on, just hold on.

But the truth was he felt he was an intruder in the holy event which was taking place: the Great Act of their Undoing. (April 9, 2003.)

It was very quiet and he knew that he would live and that they would die, and that he would watch them die, an undesired witness, a spectator, a fly. (Is this part true?) He felt guilty. (Or is it fiction?) So he stopped speaking, he shut his mouth, he waited and tried to think of warm things. (I can't remember.)

No one spoke. The only sounds, the water lapping softly against the sunken frame, sniffles, teeth which once chattered, now did not. All chattering had stopped. (April 9, 2003.)

It was possible, even as far out as he was, to see the large white houses which lined the shore.

And it was possible—every now & then—to hear an eighteen-wheeler on the highway shifting to a lower gear before taking the hill just before Woods Bay.

(You see, I heard this from the bartender at the Sitting Duck. He was a friend of the owner of the sunken boat, the tour guide. The tour guide told the bartender the story, and the bartender told me and now I'm telling you:

that) Just past two o'clock in the afternoon, the tour guide heard the couple from Bethel, Connecticut, speaking to each other, their voices soft and sleepy, he could not make out the words. But then he heard the wife say (sleepy and soft, as if speaking from a dream):

"At least we're going together."

She slipped off then, quietly, into the water:::

:::A few seconds later he heard the man do the s a m e .

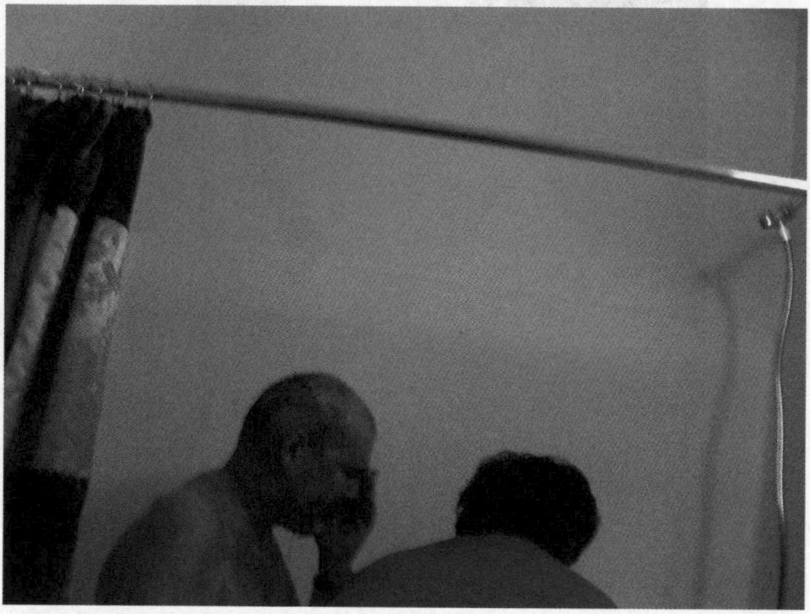

X

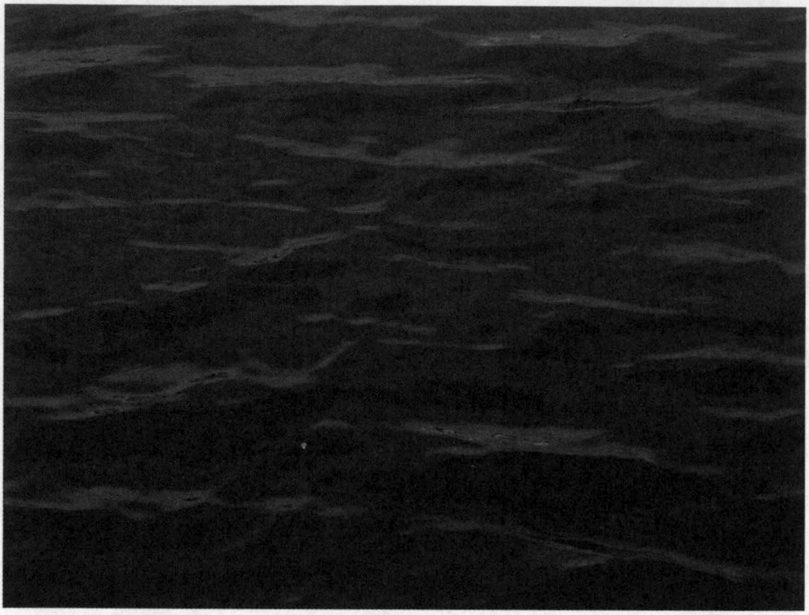

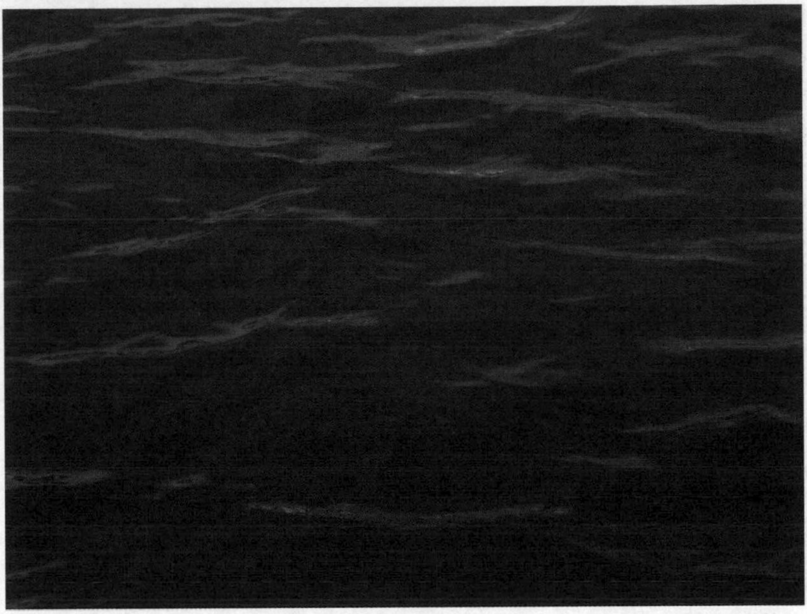

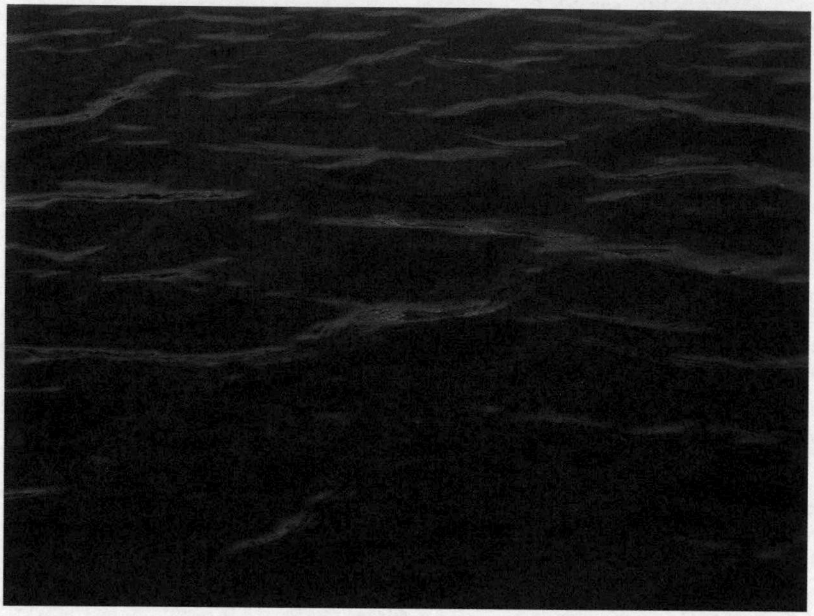

And then I thought: *Wait a second.*

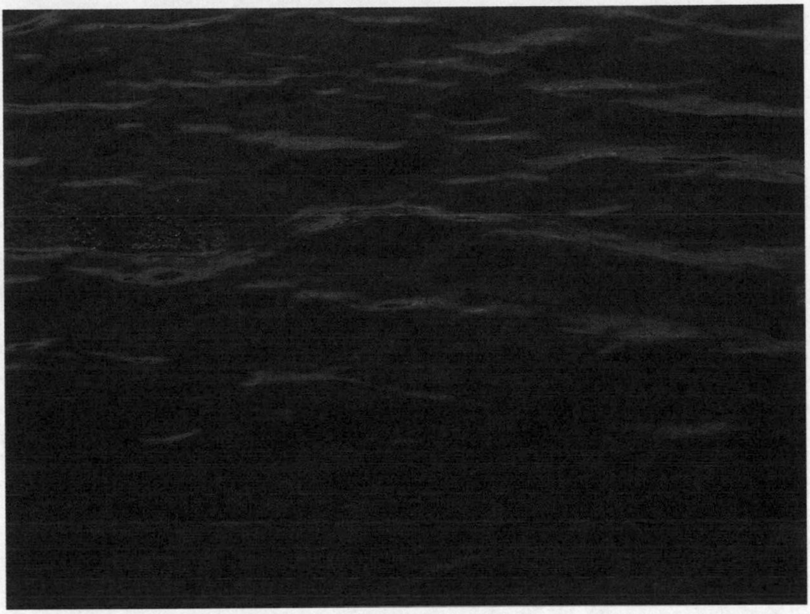

How am I able to breathe underwater?

Shouldn't this be impossible? Isn't this a Sin?

Isn't this to be like God? Isn't this what the Devil wants us to waste our lives striving for? Isn't this…

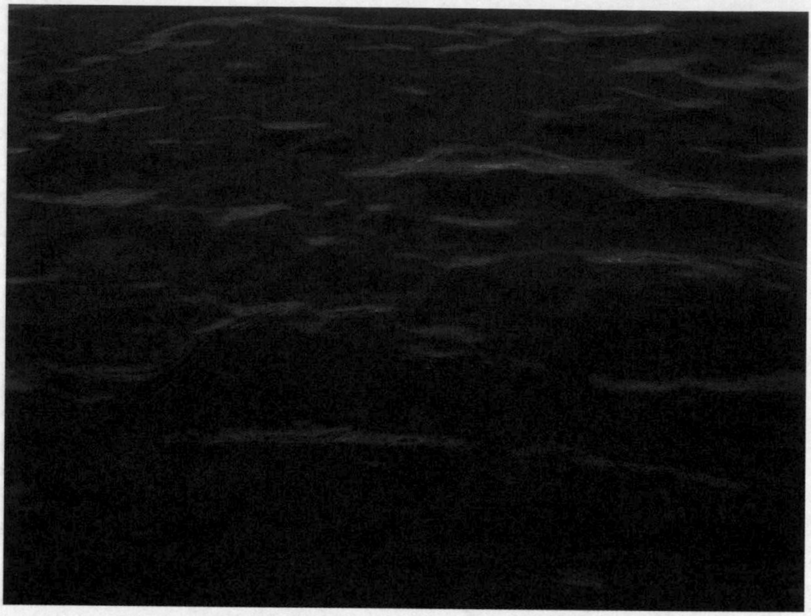

[redacted]

And then suddenly I heard a voice speaking my language. It was a voice that rose to the top of all the other voices, and somehow was part of all of them, and somehow spoke through all of them as well; a soft voice, calm and tender. It said (and write this down if you want—it's a direct quote):

★

COME WITH US

and you will
breathe

Forever.

★

WELL, I considered the offer for a moment, but then remembered that this was *exactly what the Devil said to Jesus* on top of a mountain when Jesus was wandering through the wilderness for forty days, before embarking on His famous journey to save mankind. And I got scared. I decided I had gone too far. So I tried to swim up to the surface—*and quick!*

But everything went to hell. They started grabbing me, poking and prodding me, scratching me and tearing at me, trying to rip me apart, pulling me down deeper into the water—the lower you got the darker it became—until it was all black, until I was coughing, until I was choking, freezing, falling into the deep deep deep, and the voices now were cruel, and angry, high-pitched and vile, like witches, screaming and laughing and cackling in that terrible language!

I was *DROWNING*—I was *DYING*—

I HAD MADE A *TERRIBLE MISTAKE!* [redacted]

W: I gotta have some more water. I am......[*sighs*]...Oh, man...You want some?

M: Yeah.

[redacted]
....
[redacted]

...W:ow, it's getting dark ....[*yawns*] It is a really cool concept...The ... [*sighs*] cas ... tle.

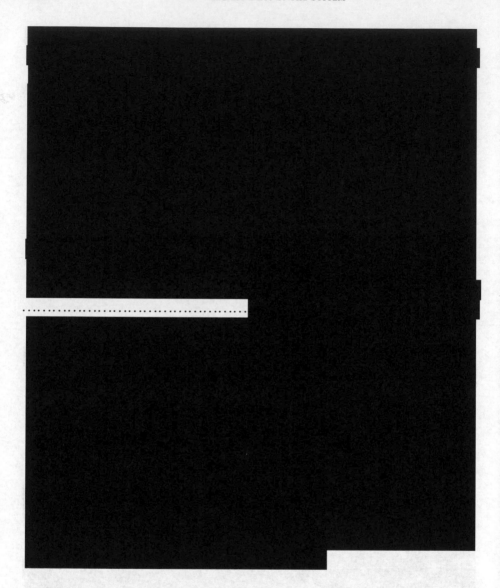

M:Yeah?

W:Yeah.........

M:Yeah...... It's all concept........ I mean... if all I'm doing is—if this just—if one day I wake up and it's all *gone*—

W: *WHAT?!*

M: Well, I mean, I don't know, like—what's the point? Is the point the actual *Book*, or is the point the *soul?* The *brain?* The Idea, the Form… *beyond* the Book? Who knows, but—it's *really changing my brain.* It's just—because it's *concept after concept* and they just *become so large* and… you know? They're *so much bigger* than the Book…and……you know, it's fun to think about…And it just seems to be…we seem to see it acting out in our lives…you know?…All the plots seem to have worked their way into life…………..

W: It's so crazy………..

M: I mean this is…

W: [*yawns*]

M: The unfortunate…well, the sad part to think about is that…right now, at this point, we're just like…walking to the fair right now, you know? Holding hands. This is the—we are under the tree—this is like the—this is Bliss…Especially right now. This is really nice.

W: [*laughs*]

M: But what comes next, you know? That's when…someone snatches her away.

W: *Heck no, I'm not getting snatched!* [*knocks three times on the bed frame*]

M: Well, that's what death is. That's what death does.

W: Well, we're living forever.

M: That's…That's the Concept….

W: We're just the elevator operators, and we've got our spacesuits on. And we just go up and down in the Bubbleator.

M: Well, if the—if the um……what am I trying to say? If the purpose of the Great and the Lesser Work together

W: [*yawns*]

M: are to join, you know, the two halves outside of…*time*…People have actually dedicated their lives to working on that problem—we look—people look at them today as if they were a bunch of crackpots, but they probably were discovering some of the things we're discovering writing [redacted]—working on [redacted]—

W: Yeah.

M: like that there's something out there communicating all the time. By *building,* what you're building takes on—it either becomes an entity that speaks to you or else it becomes like a transmitter that

W: [*yawns*]

M: whatever's outside is able to speak to you through. I think that's what it's more like.

W: Yeah.

M: Yeah.

W: It's amazing...[*sound of plane*] That plane is flying kind of weird, it's more over Grand.

M: Yeah…

W: [*yawns*]...Yeah...

M: I just gotta figure out Eternal Life. And then I have my ending.

⋆

Suddenly, a ball of flame appeared in the sky! It crossed from the east, arcing lower and lower in its flight. And backstage the stagehand responsible for the opening and closing of the curtain received an urgent telephone call from the observatory, saying that the ball of flame was traveling at a very high rate of speed with a trajectory which seemed to suggest it would be coming down soon, and moreover, its point of impact would be the auditorium itself, and more precisely: the very stage upon which the surgeon was delving further and further into the { }, layer after layer after layer, emboldened by the discoveries he was making. The phone to his ear, the stagehand looked around nervously, then out at the stage, biting his fingernails and sweating through his shirt, unable to decide whether or not to interrupt the show.

X

I know that a lot of you have family traditions that are normally a part of your life on Sunday evening Christmas Eve. Uh, for that reason we moved the service up to five o'clock, so that we would be done—we're looking at pushing it as close to one hour as we can, a very brief traditional candlelight service—so that you can still continue on. I'd like to ask you to add a new tradition. I'd like you to have a tradition of being a part of this church, that you would take advantage of that evening, because I'm telling you that your friends and your associates at work, your neighbors, if you invited them to a candlelight service on Christmas Eve, they would probably be very likely to come. Because it is one of the most singularly involved uh invited service where people respond to—it's just a part of the season, it makes sense to go to something like that. And here's what I promise you. I promise you that on that evening they will hear about the love of God in ways that will be understood. So this little simple thing that we mailed to you and you have in your hand, it's your way to simply say, Hey, why don't you come and join me at our Christmas Eve gathering, and if you want more of those you can pick those up, but Sunday morning regular service, and then Sunday night we have a special gathering.

Now, we usually show a film at this point about World Ministries as well, but we're not gonna do that this morning, this morning we're gonna do something just a little bit different. Uh, this morning, Mike and Claire McIntosh are with us today, and today is Mike and Claire's final Sunday to be with us, uh, they're going to be relocating shortly to the Seattle area to be with family, and for the additional treatment and care that he'll be receiving, uh, from the medical people in that area. And I asked Mike if he could come and be with us in our gathering today—he's been, he, Mike and Claire have been with us over the last couple weeks. Uh, they've slipped in—many of you probably got to see them. For those of you who might be new to the life of our church, you may not know that Mike, who had been a member of our pastoral staff, had contracted, uh, brain, uh, cancer, and uh, and has been, progressing in his body, as he continues to fight, that. Uh, but I I wanted him to come today, and interesting enough, if you can handle this, I wasn't asking us to pray for him. I felt like I wanted Mike to come and to pray for us. I felt it was important for the gift that he has been for our congregation—both he and Claire—that this would be an opportunity for him to come at this Christmas season and give us the gift. God has, uh, profoundly used Mike over the years, in his life and ministry. The very first video we saw of Kazakhstan we saw how God used Mike as a part of the voice to open up that nation to Foursquare work. I don't uh talk to many people here who haven't had any kind of relationship with Mike, uh, to say that he hasn't spoken into their life as well. In fact, someone said this the other day, Mike, about you. They said, Pastor, when you talk to me—no problem, I understand what you're saying—but when Mike talks to me, it's different. I said, What's that like? He said, He talks to my soul. It's right in me. And uh, so uh,

I know what that's like. I've had Mike as a friend for a long time, and if I don't want somebody looking at my soul, I just don't walk around Mike for a while. I just, I'm too busy, I don't wanna be around you. I don't want anybody looking at my soul. But Mike has the ability to speak to the heart, get to the heart of the issue, and has always cared about people that way. Uh, Mike, can you come and join me? Claire, do you wanna come and join me as well? Uh, their daughter Annie is here with us as well today, all the way in from Australia. And uh, so it's a delight to have you as well. Annie, good to see you, hon. And uh, I'm gonna let you hold this, Mike. Uh, and I'm gonna let you say anything you wanna say. Uh, but he's gonna pray, as well. And I won't say anything that will embarrass you, but it it I'll certainly explain, that part of what Mike is uh fighting with the disease is at times, some of the language will be lost, some of the phrases that he would want to communicate, that he may feel deeply inside, may not always find its way out completely. And so when I asked him to pray, I knew that number one he was a secure enough man to do that. Even with that challenge. But I also know that the Bible says—and I don't mean this jokingly, I mean it truthfully—when the Bible says in Romans 8, that he speaks in ways that when we can't even articulate, God still gets said what he wants to say. And that's why I wanted him to pray over us, because even at any point—and I'm not even suspecting that there would be a point that you wouldn't be able to communicate—but any point that doesn't capture all of what he wants to say, God will still get it said. So uh, Mike, I've said enough. Why don't you have a shot at saying whatever you'd like to say, and then I'm gonna let you pray for us as well.

Mike: Well, it's a, great privilege, for Claire and I to stand here, with you, as we have, many times through the months, through the last year. We have been surprised by, the outcomes of our own life, not by the ministry direction, but by uh, just the home life situation. Uh, recently I had fought...help my dad fight through cancer, I had not anticipated it would be a part of our life. But it is and uh we're not enjoying it but we have uh used to it, and uh are enjoying you in it, are enjoying what God is doing in it, and are enjoying really the lessons that we learn from you, and in your own, uh...[*laughs*] spiritual...journey. It's just, just marvelous. So, I want to commend to all of you for your faithfulness, and uh, your steadfastness, and keeping your hand, on the Lord's hands. Because he's good. And uh, my prognosis is maybe three months...or less, until I'm supposed to be, in the Lord's presence. With no hope of uh...improvement. But that's OK. I mean I can—that's a lot easier than

up and down—

up and down—

up and down—

up and down—

up and down.

And uh:

What is it like tomorrow?

So I'm just uh...I feel like, at this very important season...uh Claire and I have learned a lot from each of you, from your steadfastness...from your faithfulness, for, from your....courageous...following of the Lord, in uh an inner city world, that uh, needs you desperately, and...so...thank you. Thank you that uh [*chokes up*] I walk, now on a walk that is...dictated and guided by so many of you. Claire, anything you wanna say?

CLAIRE: ......Well [*clears throat*] I just have been thinking this morning how precious it is to be here with you and of the amazing kindness that you've shown us, and how little over a year ago when we left our church in Federal Way we didn't know where God was going to send us or why, but [*clears throat*] I'm so thankful that he sent us here, and not, at this moment, not so much for the time we had serving you but just for [*begins to cry*] a safe place to be...during this season and just...[*crying*] you've been so kind and, just...thank you so much......

MIKE: I haven't been the easiest one to live with. [*laughs*] Well, let me pray for you.

Thank you, Lord....Father, there is in the hearts of the people who are gathered here a great compassion, a great...hunger...for you. A great love...for your people. And a great hurt for the city. I thank you for that—I thank you, Lord, that they are drawn to this collection of people, because there is a shared passion that you have...for this great city of Portland, and the surrounding area. Lord...how wonderful...to be...part of such a miracle...the miracle of regeneration in a city, part of the miracle of faithfulness to return to our, our spiritual roots and to press in to you, to press in to your kingdom with you...Thank you, that each of us, become better, larger, more, and uh, that some may get to our destination faster, but all of us, fulfill our purpose together. Thank you, Lord. In Jesus' Name...Thank you. Amen.

Amen. Would you say thank you to Mike and Claire for being a part of our life?

[*applause*]

★

If you take your teaching notes this morning, I'm going to bring a message, uh, that uh hopefully will capture all of what we've uh been exposed to already this morning. I, I always know running the risk of asking Mike to share prior to my message will make my message rather redundant or unimportant, but if it will help you, the message I am bringing you this morning is one that I crafted with Mike, on a drive several years ago when we were in Federal Way and I had been invited to speak at the Hillsboro Church, Evergreen, prior to being your pastor, and um, while I was driving down there in the car and just praying about what I would speak on, the text I'm going to use this morning to talk about was the one I had and, and so I was working on the message while we drove, and Mike was coaching me on the way down saying, I think that sounds good, I don't think anyone will understand that, and uh, you know, all the way down. So there was a mentoring of my message, and so I'm going to preach this for both of us today. But I'm going to start with our passage of Scripture that we've had for the entire month of December. Isaiah chapter 9, verse 6. Would you read it out loud with me, because we're going to be talking about Everlasting Father today, but let's read it out loud together, it's on the overhead here.

★

★

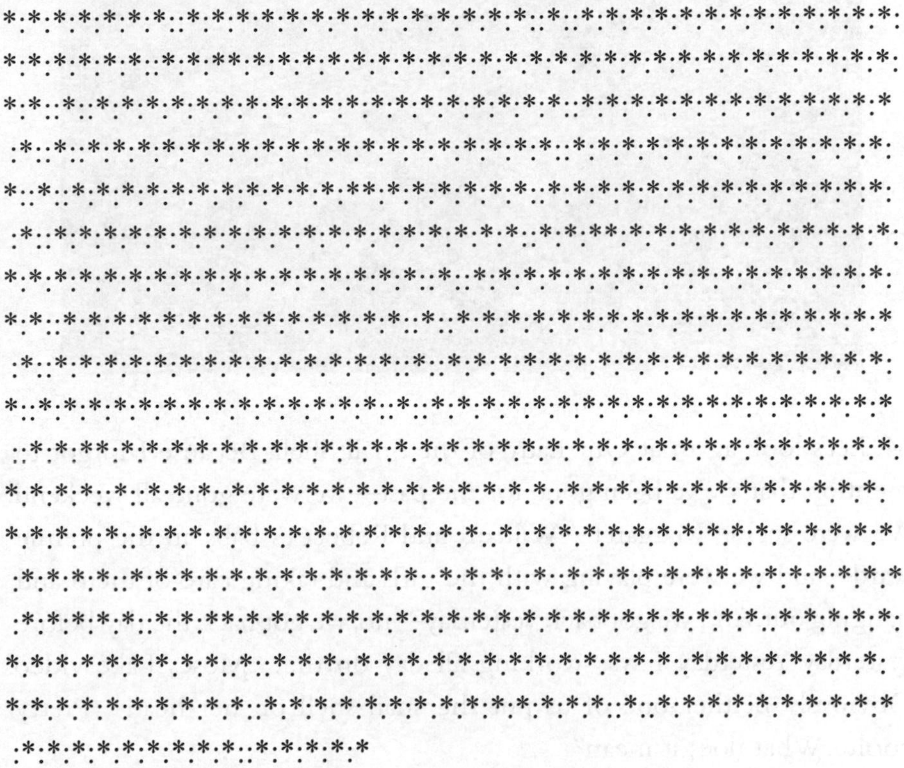

★

M: Let's look again at Our Lady of the Snail Shell. Because I forgot to mention that we've been gone for the past—we were gone all weekend. We were seeing Margaret—William and Rebecca's baby in the premie ward—and we were playing with the girls and taking care of them and hanging out. And we got back yesterday—no, we got back the day before yesterday. Yesterday I was working all day on the…Moses Lake video. Obviously neither one of us put the snail shell on her head…Pretty cool…What does it mean?……

We'll see.

★

How to predict

I once saw a very beautiful picture:

History

it was a landscape at evening.

look for patterns

In the distance on the right-hand side a row of hills appeared blue in the evening mist. Above those hills the splendour of the sunset, the grey clouds with their linings of silver and gold and purple. The landscape is a plain or heath covered with grass and its yellow leaves, for it was in autumn. Through the landscape a road leads to a high mountain far, far away, on the top of that mountain is a city wherein the setting sun casts a glory.

monitor rocks

*

(sal2.aiff)

—and you know your business I know mine—I don't [*laughs*] intend to— But flair for the, for the information?

M: Uh-huh.

...I could—I I I know, basically...Put the right words down and they'll...and the right people'll grab them.

Yeah.

Yeah?

I believe that.

My Robot
by Matt McIntosh

Patricia: It may seem daunting at first, but in the end. It's just one of those stories.

Patricia: Where their souls (the departed) would make us, feel their presence.

★

> So happy, to hear from you both. My handwriting not so hot. Still recuperating I too enjoyed my stay with you all, even while under PAIN & etc. Mario, my son is taking good care of me now. If you have not heared, my other son in Omaha, NEB. died Christmas week he was 43 years. He had an enlarged heart.

★

Well, let's see if I can get up. [*groans*] Uh!

M: Now does that put pressure on your chest when you get up like that?

No, no. Not now. It used to!

Yeah.

But, uh....

OK.

★

I hung up the phone and dressed quickly. I got in the car and drove toward the freeway. I stopped at 7-Eleven for a pack of cigarettes. I got on the freeway. It is an hour-and-a-half drive from Spokane to Moses Lake. It was late summer, and the fields were yellow. They'd been scorched by the sun.

I didn't know what I would find. I was sure that William must have gone out of his mind. I prayed all the way to Moses Lake, and the closer I got, the heavier I felt. I pictured what I would find. The house I saw in my mind was dark and dank and dusty. It had been sitting unoccupied for many years. No sunlight ever entered in. There was no movement. Skeletons in unmade beds. A bowl of rotting fruit on the kitchen table. I merged off the freeway. I drove to the house. I pulled up in front. The neighborhood was very still. The house was still, the drapes closed. It was very quiet. I undid my seatbelt. I sat there, in my car, trying to get the nerve to get out, and walk inside.

At last I got out of the car and walked up the path. I took a deep breath, opened the door, and walked inside. The house was still, but warm. There were ladies standing around speaking in quiet voices. I walked past them. I found William in the dining room. We hugged each other and cried. He asked me to follow him around and make sure he didn't start to act funny. You know what I mean, he said. We walked out through the sliding glass door, to the flower garden. I stood behind him as he got down on his knees, and began pulling weeds, tossing them at my feet. His black-and-white dog was tied to a nearby tree, whining, her tail wagging furiously. A leaf floated on top of the swimming pool.   An airplane was passing right over the house. William didn't notice any of this. He was busy rooting through the ground: Weed. Flower. Weed. Flower. Weed. Flower. Weed. Flower. Weed. Flower. Weed. Flower. Weed. Flower. Weed. Flower. Weed. Flower.

*

We're on the bridge again and this is

[redacted]

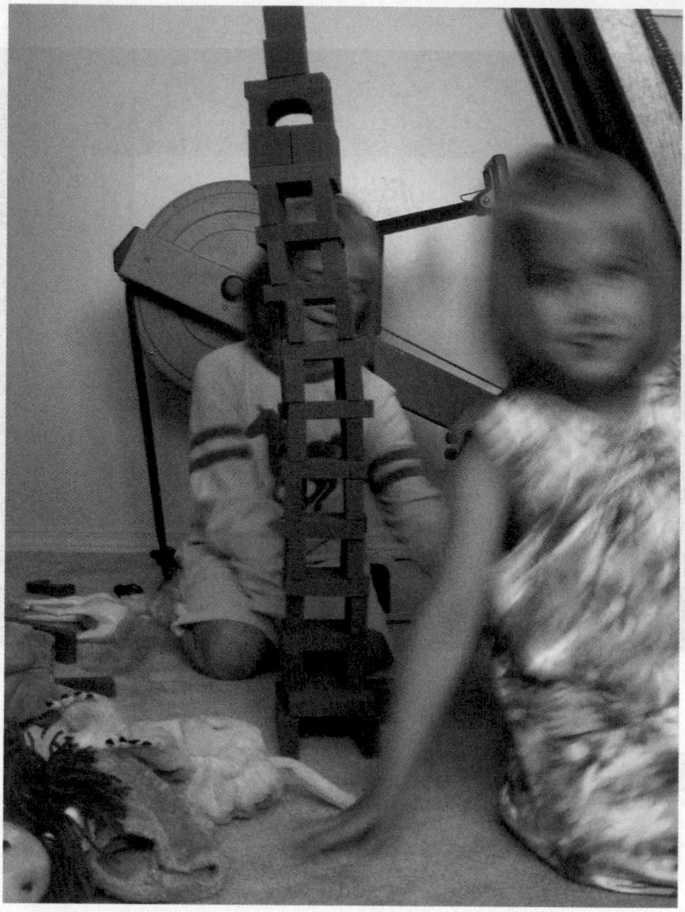

★

This battery's gonna die and I just barely charged it.

★

THE CHANGING OF THE SEASONS

There was a young girl walking in a green field one day, enjoying the warm, bright sun above her, and the singing of the birds, and the flowers and the grass beneath her feet. When without warning a door opened in the ground below her and out of it rose a man in black, all in a fury, driving a red chariot, whipping four black horses which frothed about the mouth. The girl screamed and turned to run away but the man swept on and with his long, long arm reached, pulled her in to him, and held her down, and another door opened in the ground, and she was driven down, and the ground closed up behind her, and the sun had gone away, and the sky began to snow and soon the snow covered all the ground, and it was cold, and it was quiet

Help Find Kimberly Ann Forbes

Wednesday 02/22/2006 11:05:57am
Name: Rebecca190
Homepage: http://craps.9gif.com
E-Mail: John927@gmail.com
Referred By: Just Surfed In
City/Country:
Message: best site

Monday 02/20/2006 12:03:52am
Name: Rebecca655
Homepage: http://tamiflu.1fx.net
E-Mail: Alex686@yahoo.com
Referred By: Just Surfed In
City/Country:
Message: good site!

Monday 02/20/2006 12:03:48am
Name: Rebecca471
Homepage: http://tamiflu.9gif.com
E-Mail: Nick30@yahoo.com
Referred By: Just Surfed In
City/Country:
Message: Just wanted to say hi, thanks and bye

Monday 02/20/2006 12:03:43am
Name: Rebecca94
Homepage: http://blackjack.9gif.com
E-Mail: Mary648@yahoo.com
Referred By: Just Surfed In
City/Country:
Message: best site

Monday 02/20/2006 12:03:37am
Name: Rebecca419
Homepage: http://blackjack.1fx.net
E-Mail: Sarah156@aol.com
Referred By: Just Surfed In
City/Country:
Message: nice site !

Monday 02/20/2006 12:03:33am
Name: Rebecca481
Homepage: http://roulette.1fx.net
E-Mail: Matthew877@yahoo.com
Referred By: Just Surfed In
City/Country:
Message: Just wanted to say hi, thanks and bye

Monday 02/20/2006 12:03:29am
Name: Rebecca290
Homepage: http://roulette.9gif.com
E-Mail: John370@yahoo.com
Referred By: Just Surfed In
City/Country:
Message: good site!

Monday 02/20/2006 12:03:23am
Name: Rebecca627
Homepage: http://craps.1fx.net
E-Mail: John301@yahoo.com
Referred By: Just Surfed In
City/Country:
Message: hi there.

Monday 02/20/2006 12:03:16am
Name: Rebecca808
Homepage: http://slots.1fx.net
E-Mail: Sarah857@aol.com
Referred By: Just Surfed In
City/Country:
Message: I'll be back tomorrow for more.

Monday 02/20/2006 12:03:11am
Name: Rebecca738
Homepage: http://craps.9gif.com
E-Mail: Alex842@hotmail.com
Referred By: Just Surfed In
City/Country:
Message: nice site !

Help Find Kimberly Ann Forbes

Thursday 02/02/2006 9:33:23am

Name:	Rebecca425
Homepage:	http://viagra.9gif.com
E-Mail:	Sarah802@gmail.com
Referred By:	Just Surfed In
City/Country:	
Message:	best site

Thursday 02/02/2006 9:33:15am

Name:	Rebecca891
Homepage:	http://buy-phentermine.1fx.net
E-Mail:	Peter816@aol.com
Referred By:	Just Surfed In
City/Country:	
Message:	good site!

X

MAYBE THE MIND IS ABLE TO TRANSFER ITS THOUGHTS to other minds in a sort of unconscious wavelike flow. Or particle flow. Or wave-particle flow. Maybe the ideas in our heads create heavens above and hells below.

Winnie calls that Hazel died, so one by one we go,

Maybe our memories survive these lives.

MIKE: Are you writing down the story?
MATT: What?
MIKE: Are you writing down the story?
MATT: What story?
MIKE: The exchange?
MATT: I don't need to write it down, I taped it.

*

Maybe we go to the moon or to Jupiter when we die. Maybe we float around in boats called subtle bodies letting all our cares and worries drift away behind as our better parts are caressed by the warm enveloping eternally summer night sky. Lit by stars and maybe we feast in glittering crystal palaces on sumptuous delights with angels on every side, versing us in the secrets of space and time.

Maybe we kneel forever in concentric circles, faces turned to the Golden Throne of God, Whose Infinite Number of Eyes shine, dazzling us with the Splendor of Pure and Divine Light as we sing: Holy, Holy, Holy.

Maybe we come back and visit TV psychics during the tapings of talk shows, to tell them that we know someone in the audience, and that our name begins with J...L......R.........or is it..............................*M?*

[*applause*]

Um.........what what has to do with a rabbit—I don't understand what this has to do with a rabbit...something about your sister and a rabbit...

[*laughs*] Bugs Bunny.

Pardon me?

Bugs Bunny? But what about it?

She loved Bugs Bunny!

That's what she's saying!

My mother, they all loved Bugs Bunny!

That's why she keeps saying, Rabbit.

I don't own a rabbit!

I don't either.

Well, she's pointing at me
like I was the rabbit!

[*laughter*]

THE TRUTH IS I DON'T KNOW THE FIRST THING ABOUT SCIENCE.

Science was sent away from me as a child, in a basket, down a river; I started after it late and I never caught up. And yet I get the feeling that maybe I've been better off this way. No one has had a more difficult go of things than the quantum surgeon. Remember, before he was properly funded by the Institute which enabled him to delve into the radical new science of { } surgery, he spent year after year wasting away in the laboratory, fetching donuts for his elder scientists as they studied the effects of replacing regular coffee with decaf on the taste buds of mice.

Yes, ma'am. You have a question for Sibyl.

Our aunt died about four years ago, suddenly. And we were just wondering if she was around us.

Yeah...she had beautiful skin, a round face, uh...and she used to pull on her ear.

Hmm.

And remember too, The Danger—that at the end of this experiment, once he peels back the final layer and, after a lifetime of patient searching—and a lot of waiting—finally catches a glimpse of The Center—transmitted simultaneously, mind you, to the Big Screen—(the audience will GASP!)—right then this world will cease to be. I.e., that meteor will come down.

★

Hey Goose--

That sounds good to us......is Ice Age II in the theatres? We miiiiight be skipping that part unless it's at the cheap-o, but I'd like to go to the cemetery. Do you guys want to use our house as a launching/landing pad?

-e

Helen,

upside-down moon, rabbit, wedding-cake, kookaburra, airplane, koala, clouds. Jupiter, Sirius, upside-down Orion, southern cross. Our favorite town is Moses Lake because Helen and her sister (and mom and dad) are there. Pheobe. Margaret, Boris, Boneless, new friend kangaroo/ink pen named Puncher.

erin and matt

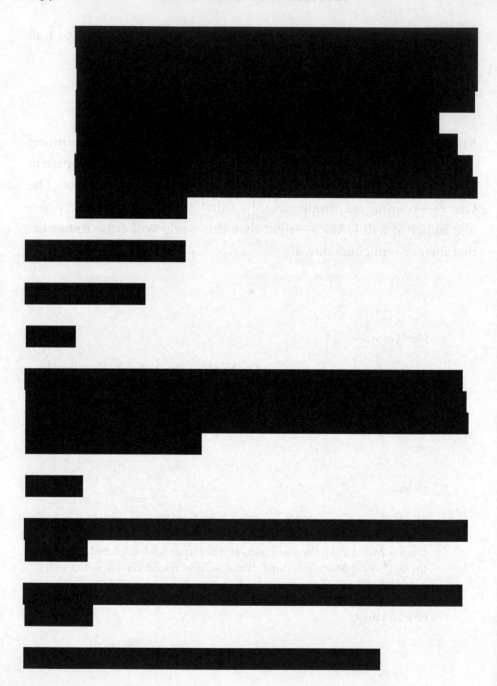

An... portion
...certain
The
—transmitted simultaneously, think... ...69—
the majority will CASTY—right then there every will strike... the
that thing of will come down.

Herophon.

the law

from a Miles, call Vestalike at first man tried in it, field...
there... Mercer at their "names as was found kind to do..."

cry at night.

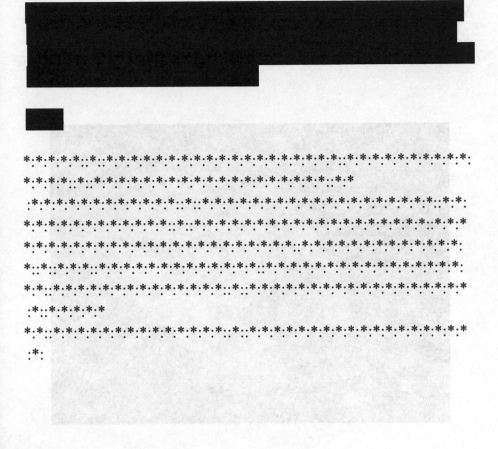

M: It's all in my head......
W: Well, I hope it can soon be in *my* head.

M: Yeah ....

★

★

W: { } right there. Do you feel it?

M: Yeah ....{ }

★

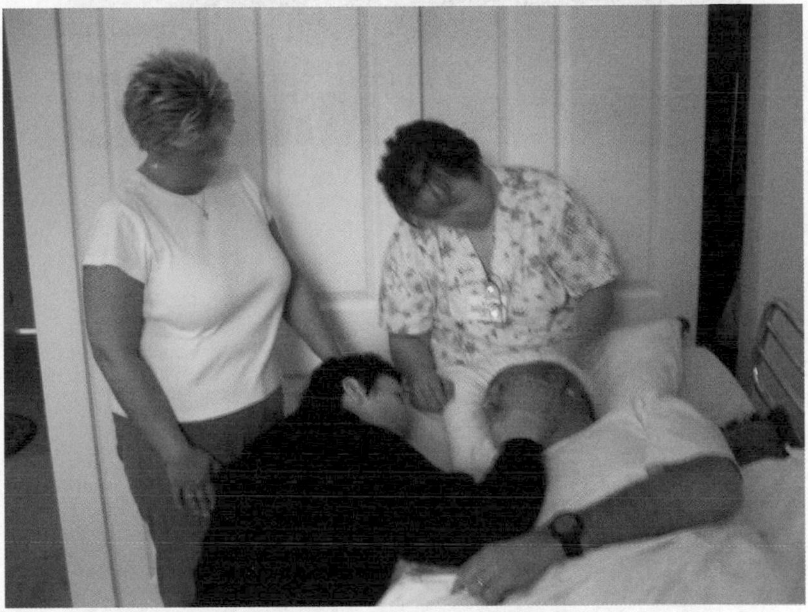

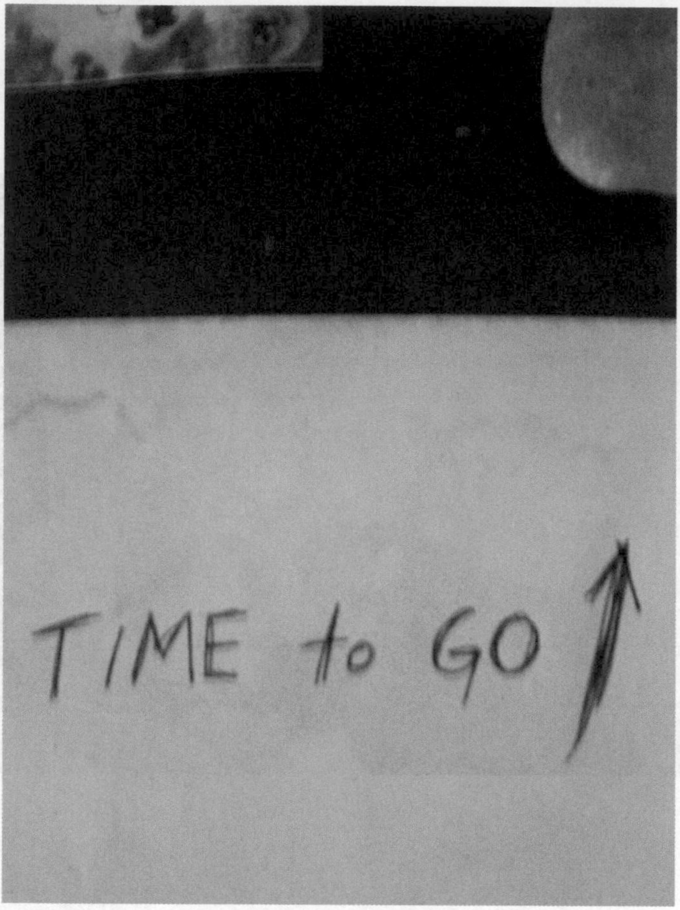
TIME to GO

THE PEARL

There was a baby who was born too early, so she was very tiny and she lived in a glass case that mimicked certain conditions of the womb. The case also kept her from sickness and infection, for she was very vulnerable and the slightest germ could have killed her. In spite of all precautions she did become sick, and she did become infected, and even though she was very tiny her body fought the sickness, and won, and she grew large enough, and healthy enough to go home. Her lungs were weak and she was kept on oxygen, and she had a procedure done on her to stop her from spitting up so that she could gain weight—for she was still very small—and she stayed at home for seventeen days, with her happy sisters and her parents. And on the seventeenth day she was very fussy, so her mother kept feeding her, and the family went to sleep, and at 5:55 AM, her mother woke to the cry of alarm from her baby's breathing machine. It was coming through the baby monitor on the nightstand. As she opened her eyes from a deep sleep she wondered: How long has that siren beeeeeeeeeeee
eeeeeeeeeeeeeeeeeeeeeeeeeeeeeeeeeeee
eeeeeeeeeeeeeeeeeeeeeeeeeeeeeeeeeeee
eeeeeeeeeeeeeeeeeeeeeeeeeeeeeeeeeeee
eeeeeeeeeeeeeeeeeeeeeeeeeeeeeeeeeeee
eeeeeeeeeeeeeeeeeeeeeeeeeeeeeeeeeeee

eeeeeeeeeeeeeeeeeeeeeeeeeeeeeeeeeeee
eeeeeeeeeeeeeeeeeeeeeeeeeeeeeeeeeeee
eeeeeeeeeeeeeeeeeeeeeeeeeeeeeeeeeeee
eeeeeeeeeeeeeeeeeeeeeeeeeeeeeeeeeeee
eeeeeeeeeeeeeeeeeeeeeeeeeeeeeeeeeeee
eeeeeeeeeeeeeeeeeeeeeeeeeeeeeeeeeeee
eeeeeeeeeeeeeeeeeeeeeeeeeeeeeeeeeeee
eeeeeeeeeeeeeeeeeeeeeeeeeeeeeeeeeeee
eeeeeeeeeeeeeeeeeeeeeeeeeeeeeeeeeeee
eeeeeeeeeeeeeeeeeeeeeeeeeeeeeeeeeeee
eeeeeeeeeeeeeeeeeeeeeeeeeeeeeeeeeeee
eeeeeeeeeeeeeeeeeeeeeeeeeeeeeeeeeeee
eeeeeeeeeeeeeeeeeeeeeeeeeeeeeeeeeeee
eeeeeeeeeeeeeeeeeeeeeeeeeeeeeeeeeeee
eeeeeeeeeeeeeeeeeeeeeeeeeeeeeeeeeeee
eeeeeeeeeeeeeeeeeeeeeeeeeeeeeeeeeeee
eeeeeeeeeeeeeeeeeeeeeeeeeeeeeeeeeeee
eeeeeeeeeeeeeeeeeeeeeeeeeeeeeeeeeeee
eeeeeeeeeeeeeeeeeeeeeeeeeeeeeeeeeeee
eeeeeeeeeeeeeeeeeeeeeeeeeeeeeeeeeeee
eeeeeeeeeeeeeeeeeeeeeeeeeeeeeeeeeeee
eeeeeeeeeeeeeeeeeeeeeeeeeeeeeeeeeeee
eeeeeeeeeeeeeeeeeeeeeeeeeeeeeeeeeeee
eeeeeeeeeeeeeeeeeeeeeeeeeeeeeeeeeeee
eeeeeeeeeeeeeeeeeeeeeeeeeeeeeeeeeeee
eeeeeeeeeeeeeeeeeeeeeeeeeeeeeeeeeeee
eeeeeeeeeeeeeeeeeeeeeeeeeeeeeeeeeeee
eeeeeeeeeeeeeeeeeeeeeeeeeeeeeeeeeeee
eeeeeeeeeeeeeeeeeeeeeeeeeeeeeeeeeeee
eeeeeeeeeeeeeeeeeeeeeeeeeeeeeeeeeeee
eeeeeeeeeeeeeeeeeeeeeeeeeeeeeeeeeeee
eeeeeeeeeeeeeeeeeeeeeeeeeeeeeeeeeeee
eeeeeeeeeeeeeeeeeeeeeeeeeeeeeeeeeeee

eeeeeeeeeeeeeeeeeeeeeeeeeeeeeeeeeeeeeeeee
eeeeeeeeeeeeeeeeeeeeeeeeeeeeeeeeeeeeeeeee
eeeeeeeeeeeeeeeeeeeeeeeeeeeeeeeeeeeeeeeee
eeeeeeeeeeeeeeeeeeeeeeeeeeeeeeeeeeeeeeeee
eeeeeeeeeeeeeeeeeeeeeeeeeeeeeeeeeeeeeeeee
eeeeeeeeeeeeeeeeeeeeeeeeeeeeeeeeeeeeeeeee
eeeeeeeeeeeeeeeeeeeeeeeeeeeeeeeeeeeeeeeee
eeeeeeeeeeeeeeeeeeeeeeeeeeeeeeeeeeeeeeeee
eeeeeeeeeeeeeeeeeeeeeeeeeeeeeeeeeeeeeeeee
eeeeeeeeeeeeeeeeeeeeeeeeeeeeeeeeeeeeeeeee
eeeeeeeeeeeeeeeeeeeeeeeeeeeeeeeeeeeeeeeee
eeeeeeeeeeeeeeeeeeeeeeeeeeeeeeeeeeeeeeeee
eeeeeeeeeeeeeeeeeeeeeeeeeeeeeeeeeeeeeeeee
eeeeeeeeeeeeeeeeeeeeeeeeeeeeeeeeeeeeeeeee
eeeeeeeeeeeeeeeeeeeeeeeeeeeeeeeeeeeeeeeee
eeeeeeeeeeeeeeeeeeeeeeeeeeeeeeeeeeeeeeeee
eeeeeeeeeeeeeeeeeeeeeeeeeeeeeeeeeeeeeeeee
eeeeeeeeeeeeeeeeeeeeeeeeeeeeeeeeeeeeeeeee
eeeeeeeeeeeeeeeeeeeeeeeeeeeeeeeeeeeeeeeee
eeeeeeeeeeeeeeeeeeeeeeeeeeeeeeeeeeeeeeeee
eeeeeeeeeeeeeeeeeeeeeeeeeeeeeeeeeeeeeeeee
eeeeeeeeeeeeeeeeeeeeeeeeeeeeeeeeeeeeeeeee
eeeeeeeeeeeeeeeeeeeeeeeeeeeeeeeeeeeeeeeee
eeeeeeeeeeeeeeeeeeeeeeeeeeeeeeeeeeeeeeeee
eeeeeeeeeeeeeeeeeeeeeeeeeeeeeeeeeeeeeeeee
eeeeeeeeeeeeeeeeeeeeeeeeeeeeeeeeeeeeeeeee
eeeeeeeeeeeeeeeeeeeeeeeeeeeeeeeeeeeeeeeee
eeeeeeeeeeeeeeeeeeeeeeeeeeeeeeeeeeeeeeeee
eeeeeeeeeeeeeeeeeeeeeeeeeeeeeeeeeeeeeeeee
eeeeeeeeeeeeeeeeeeeeeeeeeeeeeeeeeeeeeeeee
eeeeeeeeeeeeeeeeeeeeeeeeeeeeeeeeeeeeeeeee
eeeeeeeeeeeeeeeeeeeeeeeeeeeeeeeeeeeeeeeee
eeeeeeeeeeeeeeeeeeeeeeeeeeeeeeeeeeeeeeeee

eeeeeeeeeeeeeeeeeeeeeeeeeeeeeeeeeeee
eeeeeeeeeeeeeeeeeeeeeeeeeeeeeeeeeeee
eeeeeeeeeeeeeeeeeeeeeeeeeeeeeeeeeeee
eeeeeeeeeeeeeeeeeeeeeeeeeeeeeeeeeeee
eeeeeeeeeeeeeeeeeeeeeeeeeeeeeeeeeeee
eeeeeeeeeeeeeeeeeeeeeeeeeeeeeeeeeeee
eeeeeeeeeeeeeeeeeeeeeeeeeeeeeeeeeeee
eeeeeeeeeeeeeeeeeeeeeeeeeeeeeeeeeeee
eeeeeeeeeeeeeeeeeeeeeeeeeeeeeeeeeeee
eeeeeeeeeeeeeeeeeeeeeeeeeeeeeeeeeeee
eeeeeeeeeeeeeeeeeeeeeeeeeeeeeeeeeeee
eeeeeeeeeeeeeeeeeeeeeeeeeeeeeeeeeeee
eeeeeeeeeeeeeeeeeeeeeeeeeeeeeeeeeeee
eeeeeeeeeeeeeeeeeeeeeeeeeeeeeeeeeeee
eeeeeeeeeeeeeeeeeeeeeeeeeeeeeeeeeeee
eeeeeeeeeeeeeeeeeeeeeeeeeeeeeeeeeeee
eeeeeeeeeeeeeeeeeeeeeeeeeeeeeeeeeeee
eeeeeeeeeeeeeeeeeeeeeeeeeeeeeeeeeeee
eeeeeeeeeeeeeeeeeeeeeeeeeeeeeeeeeeee
eeeeeeeeeeeeeeeeeeeeeeeeeeeeeeeeeeee
eeeeeeeeeeeeeeeeeeeeeeeeeeeeeeeeeeee
eeeeeeeeeeeeeeeeeeeeeeeeeeeeeeeeeeee
eeeeeeeeeeeeeeeeeeeeeeeeeeeeeeeeeeee
eeeeeeeeeeeeeeeeeeeeeeeeeeeeeeeeeeee
eeeeeeeeeeeeeeeeeeeeeeeeeeeeeeeeeeee
eeeeeeeeeeeeeeeeeeeeeeeeeeeeeeeeeeee
eeeeeeeeeeeeeeeeeeeeeeeeeeeeeeeeeeee
eeeeeeeeeeeeeeeeeeeeeeeeeeeeeeeeeeee
eeeeeeeeeeeeeeeeeeeeeeeeeeeeeeeeeeee
eeeeeeeeeeeeeeeeeeeeeeeeeeeeeeeeeeee
eeeeeeeeeeeeeeeeeeeeeeeeeeeeeeeeeeee
eeeeeeeeeeeeeeeeeeeeeeeeeeeeeeeeeeee
eeeeeeeeeeeeeeeeeeeeeeeeeeeeeeeeeeee

eeeeeeeeeeeeeeeeeeeeeeeeeeeeeeeeeeee
eeeeeeeeeeeeeeeeeeeeeeeeeeeeeeeeeeee
eeeeeeeeeeeeeeeeeeeeeeeeeeeeeeeeeeee
eeeeeeeeeeeeeeeeeeeeeeeeeeeeeeeeeeee
eeeeeeeeeeeeeeeeeeeeeeeeeeeeeeeeeeee
eeeeeeeeeeeeeeeeeeeeeeeeeeeeeeeeeeee
eeeeeeeeeeeeeeeeeeeeeeeeeeeeeeeeeeee
eeeeeeeeeeeeeeeeeeeeeeeeeeeeeeeeeeee
eeeeeeeeeeeeeeeeeeeeeeeeeeeeeeeeeeee
eeeeeeeeeeeeeeeeeeeeeeeeeeeeeeeeeeee
eeeeeeeeeeeeeeeeeeeeeeeeeeeeeeeeeeee
eeeeeeeeeeeeeeeeeeeeeeeeeeeeeeeeeeee
eeeeeeeeeeeeeeeeeeeeeeeeeeeeeeeeeeee
eeeeeeeeeeeeeeeeeeeeeeeeeeeeeeeeeeee
eeeeeeeeeeeeeeeeeeeeeeeeeeeeeeeeeeee
eeeeeeeeeeeeeeeeeeeeeeeeeeeeeeeeeeee
eeeeeeeeeeeeeeeeeeeeeeeeeeeeeeeeeeee
eeeeeeeeeeeeeeeeeeeeeeeeeeeeeeeeeeee
eeeeeeeeeeeeeeeeeeeeeeeeeeeeeeeeeeee
eeeeeeeeeeeeeeeeeeeeeeeeeeeeeeeeeeee
eeeeeeeeeeeeeeeeeeeeeeeeeeeeeeeeeeee
eeeeeeeeeeeeeeeeeeeeeeeeeeeeeeeeeeee
eeeeeeeeeeeeeeeeeeeeeeeeeeeeeeeeeeee
eeeeeeeeeeeeeeeeeeeeeeeeeeeeeeeeeeee
eeeeeeeeeeeeeeeeeeeeeeeeeeeeeeeeeeee
eeeeeeeeeeeeeeeeeeeeeeeeeeeeeeeeeeee
eeeeeeeeeeeeeeeeeeeeeeeeeeeeeeeeeeee
eeeeeeeeeeeeeeeeeeeeeeeeeeeeeeeeeeee
eeeeeeeeeeeeeeeeeeeeeeeeeeeeeeeeeeee
eeeeeeeeeeeeeeeeeeeeeeeeeeeeeeeeeeee
eeeeeeeeeeeeeeeeeeeeeeeeeeeeeeeeeeee
eeeeeeeeeeeeeeeeeeeeeeeeeeeeeeeeeeee
eeeeeeeeeeeeeeeeeeeeeeeeeeeeeeeeeeee

eeeeeeeeeeeeeeeeeeeeeeeeeeeeeeeeeeee
eeeeeeeeeeeeeeeeeeeeeeeeeeeeeeeeeeee
eeeeeeeeeeeeeeeeeeeeeeeeeeeeeeeeeeee
eeeeeeeeeeeeeeeeeeeeeeeeeeeeeeeeeeee
eeeeeeeeeeeeeeeeeeeeeeeeeeeeeeeeeeee
eeeeeeeeeeeeeeeeeeeeeeeeeeeeeeeeeeee
eeeeeeeeeeeeeeeeeeeeeeeeeeeeeeeeeeee
eeeeeeeeeeeeeeeeeeeeeeeeeeeeeeeeeeee
eeeeeeeeeeeeeeeeeeeeeeeeeeeeeeeeeeee
eeeeeeeeeeeeeeeeeeeeeeeeeeeeeeeeeeee
eeeeeeeeeeeeeeeeeeeeeeeeeeeeeeeeeeee
eeeeeeeeeeeeeeeeeeeeeeeeeeeeeeeeeeee
eeeeeeeeeeeeeeeeeeeeeeeeeeeeeeeeeeee
eeeeeeeeeeeeeeeeeeeeeeeeeeeeeeeeeeee
eeeeeeeeeeeeeeeeeeeeeeeeeeeeeeeeeeee
eeeeeeeeeeeeeeeeeeeeeeeeeeeeeeeeeeee
eeeeeeeeeeeeeeeeeeeeeeeeeeeeeeeeeeee
eeeeeeeeeeeeeeeeeeeeeeeeeeeeeeeeeeee
eeeeeeeeeeeeeeeeeeeeeeeeeeeeeeeeeeee
eeeeeeeeeeeeeeeeeeeeeeeeeeeeeeeeeeee
eeeeeeeeeeeeeeeeeeeeeeeeeeeeeeeeeeee
eeeeeeeeeeeeeeeeeeeeeeeeeeeeeeeeeeee
eeeeeeeeeeeeeeeeeeeeeeeeeeeeeeeeeeee
eeeeeeeeeeeeeeeeeeeeeeeeeeeeeeeeeeee
eeeeeeeeeeeeeeeeeeeeeeeeeeeeeeeeeeee
eeeeeeeeeeeeeeeeeeeeeeeeeeeeeeeeeeee
eeeeeeeeeeeeeeeeeeeeeeeeeeeeeeeeeeee
eeeeeeeeeeeeeeeeeeeeeeeeeeeeeeeeeeee
eeeeeeeeeeeeeeeeeeeeeeeeeeeeeeeeeeee
eeeeeeeeeeeeeeeeeeeeeeeeeeeeeeeeeeee
eeeeeeeeeeeeeeeeeeeeeeeeeeeeeeeeeeee
eeeeeeeeeeeeeeeeeeeeeeeeeeeeeeeeeeee
eeeeeeeeeeeeeeeeeeeeeeeeeeeeeeeeeeee

eeeeeeeeeeeeeeeeeeeeeeeeeeeeeeeeeeee
eeeeeeeeeeeeeeeeeeeeeeeeeeeeeeeeeeee
eeeeeeeeeeeeeeeeeeeeeeeeeeeeeeeeeeee
eeeeeeeeeeeeeeeeeeeeeeeeeeeeeeeeeeee
eeeeeeeeeeeeeeeeeeeeeeeeeeeeeeeeeeee
eeeeeeeeeeeeeeeeeeeeeeeeeeeeeeeeeeee
eeeeeeeeeeeeeeeeeeeeeeeeeeeeeeeeeeee

) {

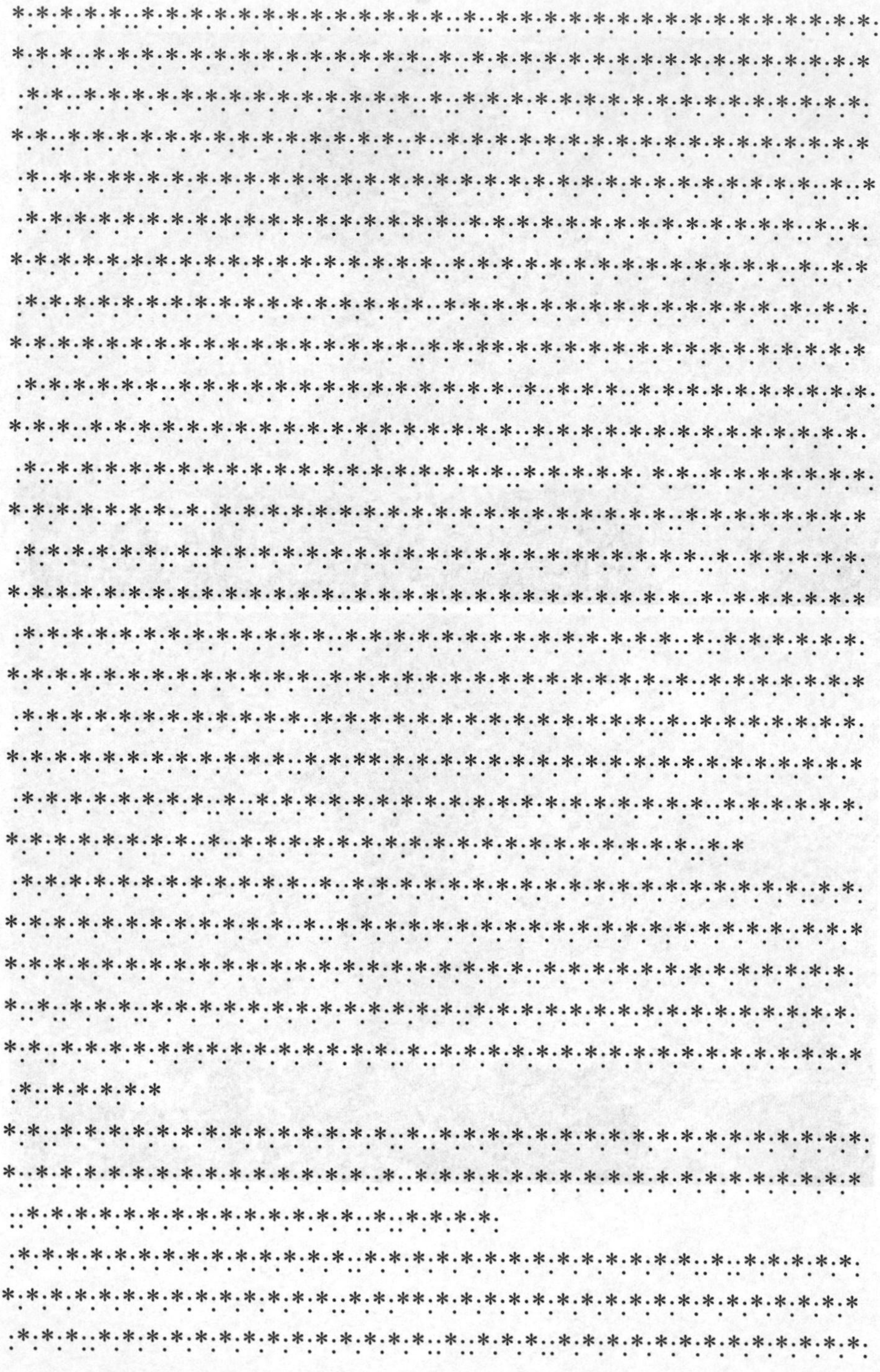

.*.*.*.*.*.*.*.*.*.*.*.*.*.*.*.*.*.*..*.*..*.*.*.*.*.*.*.*.*.*.*.*.*..*..*.

..*.*.*.*.*.*.*.*.*.*.*.*.*.*.*..*.*..*.*.*.*.*.*.*.*.*.*.*.*.*..*..*.*

.*.*.*.*.*.*.*.*.*.*.*.*.*.*.*.*..*.*..*.*.*.*.*.*.*.*.*.*.*.*.*..*..*.*.

..*.*.*.*.*.*.*.*.*.*.*.*.*.*..*.*..*.*.*.*.*.*.*.*.*.*.*.*.*..*..*.*.*

.*.*.*.*.*.*.*.*.*.*.*.*.*.*.*..*.*.*.*.*.*.*.*.*.*.*.*.*.*..*..*.*.*.

....*.*.*.*

.**.*.*.*.*.*.*.*.

..*..*.*.*.*.*.*.*.*.*.*.*.*.*.*..*..*.*.*.*.*.*.*.*.*.*.*.*.*.*.*.*

.*.*..*.*.*.*.*.*.*.*.*.*.*.*.*.*.*.*.*..*.*.*.*.*.*.*.*.*.*.*.*.*..

...*.*.*.*.*.*.*.*.*.*.*.*.*.*.*.*.*..*.*.*.*.*.*.*.*.*.*.*.*.*.*..*

..*.*.*.*.*.*.*.*.*.*.*.*.*.*.*.*.*.*..*.*.*.*.*.*.*.*.*.*.*.*.*.*..*..

..*.*.*.*.*.*.*.*.*.*.*.*.*.*.*.*..*.*.*.*.*.*.*.*.*.*.*.*.*.*..*..*

.*.*.*.*.*.*.*.*.*.*.*.*.*.*.*.*.*..*.*.*.*.*.*.*.*.*.*.*.*.*.*..*..*.

..*.*.*.*.*.*.*.*.*.*.*.*.*.*.*..*.*.*.*.*.*.*.*.*.*.*.*.*.*.*..*.*

.*.*.*.*.*.*.*.*.*.*.*.*.*.*.*.*..*.*.*.*.*.*.*.*.*.*.*.*.*.*..*..*.*.

..*.*.*.*.*.*.*.*.*.*.*.*.*.*..*.**.*.*.*.*.*.*.*.*.*.*.*.*.*.*.*.*

.*.*.*.*.*.*.*.*.*.*.*.*.*..*..*.*.*.*.*.*.*.*.*.*.*.*.*.*.*.*.*.*..*.

..*.*.*.*.*.*.*.*.*.*.*..*..*.*.*.*.*.*.*.*.*.*.*.*.*.*.*.*.*.*..*.*

.*.*.*.*.*.*.*.*.*.*.*.*.*..*..*.*.*.*.*.*.*.*.*.*.*.*.*.*.*.*.*..*.*.

..*.*.*.*.*.*.*.*.*.*.*..*..*.*.*.*.*.*.*.*.*.*.*.*.*.*.*.*.*..*.*.*

...*.*.*.*.*.*.*.*.*.*.*.

...*.*.*..*.*.*.*.*.*.*.*.*.*.*.*.*.*..*.*.*.*.*.*.*.*.*.*.*.*.*.*.*.

...*.*.*.*.*.*.*.*.*.*.*.*.*.*.*..*..*.*.*.*.*.*.*.*.*.*.*.*.*.*.*.*.*

.*..*.*.*.*.*

...*.*.*.*.*.*.*.*.*.*.*.*.*.*..*..*.*.*.*.*.*.*.*.*.*.*.*.*.*.*.*.*.

...*.*.*.*.*.*.*.*.*.*.*.*.*.*..*.*.*.*.*.*.*.*.*.*.*.*.*.*.*.*.*.*.*

..*.*.*.*.*.*.*.*.*.*.*.*.*.*.*..*..*.*.*.*.

.*.*.*.*.*.*.*.*.*.*.*.*.*.*..*.*.*.*.*.*.*.*.*.*.*.*.*..*..*.*.*.*.*.*

.*.*.*.*.*.*.*.*.*.*.*.*.*..*.**.*.*.*.*.*.*.*.*.*.*.*.*.*.*.*.*.*.*.*

.*.*..*.*.*.*.*.*.*.*.*.*.*.*.*.*.*..*..*.*.*.*.*.*.*.*.*.*.*.*.*.*.*..*

.*.*.*.*.*.*.*.*.*.*.*.*.*.*.*.*.*..*.*.*.*.*.*.*.*.*.*.*.*.*.*..*.*.*.

..*.*.*.*.*.*.*.*.*.*.*.*.*.*..*.*.*.*.*.*.*.*.*.*.*.*.*.*..*..*.*.*

.*.*.*.*.*.*.*.*.*.*.*.*.*.*.*.*..*.*.*.*.*.*.*.*.*.*.*.*.*..*..*.*.*.

....*.*.*.*.*.*.*.*.*.*.*.*.

..*.*.*.*.*..*.*.*.*.*.*.*.*.*.*.*.*.*.*.*..*..*.*.*.*

..*.*.*.*.*.*.*.*.*.*.*.*.*.*..*.*.*.*.*.*.*.*.*.*.*.*.*.*..*..*.*.*.*.*.

..*.*.*.*.*.*.*.*.*.*.*.*.*..*.*.*.*.*.*.*.*.*.*.*.*.*.*..*..*.*.*.*.*.*

.*.*.*.*.*.*.*.*.*.*.*.*.*..*.*.**.*.*.*.*.*.*.*.*.*.*.*.*.*.*.*.*.*.*.*

.*.*..*.*.*.*.*.*.*.*.*.*.*.*.*..*..*.*.*..*.*.*.*.*.*.*.*.*.*.*.*.*.*..*

.*.*.*.*.*.*.*.*.*.*.*.*.*.*.*.*.*.*..*.*.*.*.*.*.*.*.*.*.*.*.*.*..*..*.*.

..*.*.*.*.*.*.*.*.*.*.*.*.*.*.*..*.*.*.*.*.*.*.*.*.*.*.*.*..*..*.*.*

.*.*.*.*.*.*.*.*.*.*.*.*.*.*.*..*.*.*.*.*.*.*.*.*.*.*.*..*..*.*.*.*.*.*.

..*.*.*.*.*.*.*.*.*.*..*.*.*.*.*.*.*.*.*.*.*.*.*.*.*.*..*..*.*.*.*.*.*.*.*

.*.*.*.*.*.*.*.*.*.*.*.*..*.*.*.*.*.*.*.*.*.*.*.*.*.*..*..*.*.*.*.*.*.*.*.

..*.*.*.*.*.*.*.*.*.*..*.*.*.**.

.*.*.*.*.*.*.*.*.*.*.*..*.*.*.*.*.*.*.*.*.*.*.*.*..*..*.*.*.*.*.*.*.*.

..*.*.*.*.*.*.*.*.*.*..*.*.*.*.*.*.*.*.*.*.*.*.*.*..*..*.*.*.*.*.*.*.*.*

.*.*.*.*.*.*.*.*.*.*.*..*.*.*.*.*.*.*.*.*.*.*.*.*..*..*.*.*.*.*.*.*.*.*.

..*.*.*.*.*.*.*.*.*..*.*.**.

..*.*.*.*..*..*.*.*.*.*.*.*.*.*.*.*.*.*.*.*.*.*.*..*.*.*.*.*.*.*.*.*

.*.*.*.*.*..*..*.*.*.*.*.*.*.*.*.*.*.*.*.*.*.*.*.*..*.*.*.*.*.*.*.*.*.*.

..*.*.*..*..*.*.*.*.*.*.*.*.*.*.*.*.*.*.*.*.*.*.*..*.*.*.*.*.*.*.*.*.*

.*.*.*.*..*..*.*.*.*.*.*.*.*.*.*.*.*.*.*.*.*.*.*.*..*.**.*.*.*.*.*.*.*

.*.*.*.*.*.*.*.*.*.*.*.*.*.*..*.*.*.*.*.*.*.*.*.*.*.*.*..*..*.*.*..*.*.

..*.*.*.*.*.*.*.*.*..*.*.*.*.*.*.*.*.*.*.*.*.*.*.*.*..*.*.*.*.*.*.

..*.*.*.*.*.*..*..*.*.*.*.*.*.*.*.*.*.*.*.*.*.*.*.*..*.*.*.*.*

...*.*.*.*.*.*.*.*.*.*.*.*.*.*..*..*.*.*.*.*.*.*.*.*.*.*.*.*.*.*.*.*.*.

...*.*.*.*.*.*.*.*.*.*.*.*.*..*..*.*.*.*.*.*.*.*.*.*.*.*.*.*.*.*.*.*.*

..*.*.*.*.*.*.*.*.*.*.*.*.*.*..*..*.*.*.*

..*.*.*.*.*.*.*.*.*.*.*.*.*..*.*.*.*.*.*.*.*.*.*.*.*.*.*..*..*.*.*.*.*

.*.*.*.*.*.*.*.*.*.*.*.*.*.*..*.*.*.*.*.*.*.*.*.*.*.*.*.*..*..*.*.*.*.*.

..*.*.*.*.*.*.*.*.*.*.*.*..*.*.**.*.*.*.*.*.*.*.*.*.*.*.*.*.*.*.*.*.*

.*.*.*..*

.*.*.*.*.*.*.*.*.*.*.*.*.*.*..*.*.**.*.*.*.*.*.*.*.*.*.*.*.*.*.*.*.*.*.

..*.*..*.*.*.*.*.* .*.*.*.*.*.*.*.*.*.*.*.*.*.*.*.**.*.*.*.*.*.*.

..*.*.*.*.*.*.*.*.*.*.*.*..*.*.*.*.*.* .*.*.*.*.*.*.*.*.*.*.*.*.*..*

.*.**.*.*.

.*.*.*.*.*.*.*.*.*.*.*.*.*.*..*.*.**.*.*.*.*.*.*.*.*.*.*.*.*.*.*.*.*.*.*

.*.*.*..*.*.*.*.*.*.* .*.*.*.*.*.*.*.*.*.*.*.*.*.*.*.*..*.*.**.*.*.*.*.*.*.*.*

.*.*.*.*.*.*.*.*.*.*.*.*.*.*..*.*.*.*.*.*.* .*.*.*.*.*.*.*.*.*.*.*.*.*.*.*.*.*..*.

*.**..*.*.*.*.*.*.* .*.*.*.*.*.*

.*.*.*.*.*.*.*.*..*.*.**..*.*.

..*.* .*.*.*.*.*.*.*.*.*.*.*.*.*.*.*.*..*.*.**.*.*.*.*.*.*.*.*.*.*.*.*.*.*.*.*

.*.*.*.*.*.*.*..*.*.*.*.*.*.* .*.*.*.*.*.*.*.*.*.*.*.*.*.*.*..*.*.**.*.*.*.*.*

.*.*.*.*.*.*.*.*.*.*.*.*.*.*.*.*.*.*..*.*.*.*.*.*.* .*.*.*.*.*.*.*.*.*.*.*.*.*.*

.*.*..*.**.* .*.*

.*.*.*.*.*.*.*.*.*.*.*..*.*.**.*

.*..*.*.*.*.*.* .*.*.*.*.*.*.*.*.*.*.*.*.*.*.*..*.*.**.*.*.*.*.*.*.*.*.*.*.*.*

.*.*.*.*.*.*.*.*.*..*.*.*.*.*.*.* .*.*.*.*.*.*.*.*.*.*.*.*.*.*.*.*.*..*.*.**

.*..*.*.*.*.*.*.* .*.*.*..*.*.*.**.*

.*.*.*.*.*.*.*.*.*.*.*.*.*.*.*.*.*.*.*..*.*.*.*.*.*.*.*.*.*.*.*.*.*.*.*.*..*

..*.*.*..*..

..*.*.*.*.*.*.*.*.*.*.*.*.*..*..*..*

.*.*.*.*.*.*.*.*.*.*.*.*.*.*..*..*..*.

..*.*.*.*.*.*.*.*.*.*.*.*.*..*..*.*

.*.*.*.*.*.*.*.*.*.*.*.*..*..*..*.*.

..*.*.*.*.*.*.*.*.*.*..*..*

.*.*.*.*.*.*.*.*.*.*.*..*..*..*.*.*.

..*.*.*.*.*.*.*.*.*.*..*..*..*.*.**.

*.**..*..*.*.*.*.*.*.*.

..*.*.*.*.*.*.*.*.*.*.*..*.*.*.*.*.*.*.*.*.*.*.*.*.*.*..*..*.*.*.*.*.*.*.*

.*..*..*.*.*.*.*.*.*.

..*.*.*.*.*.*.*.*.*.*..*.*.*.*.*.*.*.*.*.*.*.*.*.*.*..*.*.*.*.*.*.*.*.*.*

.*.*.*.*.*.*.*.*.*.*.*..*.*.**.*

..*.*.*.*.*.*.*.*.*.*.*.*.*.*.*..*..*.*.*..*.*.*.*.*.*.*.*.*.*.*.*.*.*..*.*.*

.*.*.*.*.*.*.*.*.*.*.*.*.*.*.*.*..*.*.*.*.*.*.*.*.*.*.*.*.*.*.*..*..*.*.*.*.

..*.*.*.*.*.*.*.*.*.*.*.*.*..*.*.*.*.*

...*.*.*.*.*.*.*.*.*.*.*.*.*.*.*.*..*..*.*.*.*.*.*.*.*.*.*.*.*.*.*.*.*.*.*.*.

..

..*.*.*.*.*.*.*.*.*.*.*.*.*.*.*.*..*.*.*.*.*.

.*.*.*.*.*.*.*.*.*.*.*.*.*..*.*.*.*.*.*.*.*.*.*.*.*.*.*.*..*..*.*.*.*.*.*.*.*

.*.*.*.*.*.*.*.*.*.*.*.*.*..*.*.*.*.*.*.*.*.*.*.*.*.*.*.*.*..*..*.*.*.*.*.*.*.*.*.

..*.*.*.*.*.*.*.*.*.*.*..*.*.*.*.*.*.*.*.*.*.*.*.*.*.*.*..*..*.*.*.*.*.*.*.*.*.*

.*.*.*.*.*.*.*.*.*.*.*.*..*.*.*.*.*.*.*.*.*.*.*.*.*.*.*.*..*.*.*.*.*.*.*.*.*.*.*.

..*.*.*.*.*.*.*.*.*.*..*.*.*.*.*.*.*.*.*.*.*.*.*.*.*.*..*..*.*.*.*.*.*.*.*.*.*.*

.**..*..*.*.*.*.*.*.*.*.*.*.*.*.*.*.*

.*.*.*.*.*.*..*.*.*.*.*.*.*.*.*.*.*.*.*.*.*.*..*..*.*.*.*.*.*.*.*.*.*.*.*.*.*.*.*.

..*.*.*.*..*.*.*.**.

...*..*..*.*.*.*.*.*.*.*.*.*.*.*.*.*.*

.*..*..*..*.*.*.*.*.*.*.*.*.*.*.*.*.*.*.

....*..*.*.*.*.*.*.*.*.*.*.*.*.*.*.*.*.*

..*..*..*.*.*.**.*.*.*.*.*.*.*.*.*.*.*.*.*.*

.*..*.*.*.*..*.*.*.*.*.*.*.*.*.

..*.*.*.*..*..*.*.*.*.*.*.*.*.*.*.*.*.*.*.

..*.*..*..*.*.*.*.*.*.*.*.*.*.*.*.*.*.*.*.*.*.

...*.*.*.*.*.*.*.*.*.*.*.*.*.*.*..*..*.

...*.*.*.*.*.*.*.*.*.*.*.*.*.*.*..*

..*.*.*.*.*.*.*.*.*.*.*.*.*.*.*.*.*..*..*.*.*.*

..*.*.*.*.*.*.*.*.*.*.*.*.*.*..*.*.*.*.*.*.*.*.*.*.*.*.*.*.*.*.*..*..*.*.*.*.*.*.

..*.*.*.*.*.*.*.*.*.*.*.*.*.*..*.*.*.*.*.*.*.*.*.*.*.*.*.*.*.*.*..*..*.*.*.*.*.*.*

.*.*.*.*.*.*.*.*.*.*.*.*.*.*.*.*..*.*.**.*

.*..*.*.*.*.*.*.*.*.*.*.*.*.*.*.*.*.*.*.*..*

.*..*.*.*.*.*.*.*.*.*.*.*.*.*.*.*.*.*..*.*.*.

....*.*.*.*

.*.*.*.*.*.*.*.*.*.*.*.*.*.*.*.*.*.

.*.*.*.*.*.*.*.*.*.*.*.*.*.*.*.*.*..*.**.*

.*.*.*..*.*.*.*.*.*.* .*.*.*.*.*.*.*.*.*.*.*.*.*.*.*..*.*.*.**.*.*.*.*.*.*.*.*

.* .*.*.*.*.*.*.*.*.*.*.*.*.*.*.*.*..*.

*.**.** .*.*.*.*.*.*.*

.*.*.*.*.*.*.*..*.*.*.**..*.*.

..*.* .*.*.*.*.*.*.*.*.*.*.*.*.*.*.*..*.**.*.*.*.*.*.*.*.*.*.*.*.*.*.*.*.*.*.*.*

.*.*.*.*.*.*.*..*.*.*.*.*.*.* .*.*.*.*.*.*.*.*.*.*.*.*.*.*.*.*..*.*.**.*.*.*.*.*.*

.*..*.*.*.*.*.* .*.*.*.*.*.*.*.*.*.*.*.*.*.*.*

.*.*..*.*.**..*.*.*.*.*.*.*

..*.*.*.*.*.*.*.*.*.*.*.*..*.*.*.*.*.*.*.*.*.*.*.*..*.*.*.*.*.*.
..*.*.*.*.*.*.*.*.*.*.*.*.*.**.*.*.*.*.*.*.*.*.*.*.*.*.*.*.*.*.*.
...*.*.*.*.*.*.*.*.*.*.*.*.*.*..*..*.*.*..*.*.*.*.*.*.*.*.*.*.*..*.
..*.*.*.*.*.*.*.*.*.*.*.*.*.*..*.*.*.*.*.*.*.*.*.*.*.*.*..*..*.*.*
.*..*..*.*.*.
..*.*.*.*.*.*.*.*.*.*.*.*.*..*.*.*.*.*.*.*.*.*.*.*.*.*..*..*.*.*.*
.*.*.*.*.*.*.*.*.*.*.*.*.*.*..*.*.*.*.*.*.*.*.*.*.*.*.*.*..*..*.*.*.
..*.*.*.*.*.*.*.*.*.*.*.*.*..*.*.*.*.*.*.*.*.*.*.*.*.*.*..*.*.*.*.*
.*.*.*.*.*.*.*.*.*.*.*.*.*.*..*.*.*.*.*.*.*.*.*.*.*.*.*.*..*..*.*.*.*.
..*.*.*.*.*.*.*.*.*.*.*.*..*.*.*.*.*.*.*.*.*.*.*.*.*.*.*..*.*.*.*.*
.*.*.*.*.*.*.*.*.*.*.*.*.*..*.*.**.*.*.*.*.*.*.*.*.*.*.*.*.*.*.*.*.*
.*.*.*.*.*.*.*.*.*.*..*..*.*.*.*.*.*.*.*.*.*.*.*.*.*.*.*.*..*.*.*.*.
..*.*.*.*.*.*.*..*..*.*.*.*.*.*.*.*.*.*.*.*.*.*.*.*.*..*.*
.*.*.*.*.*.*.*.*.*.*.*.*..*..*.*.*.*.*.*.*.*.*.*.*.*.*.*.*.*.*..*.*.
..*.*.*.*.*.*.*.*.*.*..*..*.*.*.*.*.*.*.*.*.*.*.*.*.*.*..*.*.*
*.
....*.*.*..*.*.*.*.*.*.*.*.*.*.*.*..*.*.*.*.*.*.*.*.*.*.*.*.*.*.
...*.*.*.*.*.*.*.*.*.*.*.*.*..*..*.*.*.*.*.*.*.*.*.*.*.*.*.*.*
.*..*.*.*.*.*
...*.*.*.*.*.*.*.*.*.*.*.*.*..*..*.*.*.*.*.*.*.*.*.*.*.*.*.*.*.*
.*..*.*.*.*.*.*.*.*.*.*.*.*.*..*..*.*.*.*.*.*.*.*.*.*.*.*.*.*.*.*.
...*.*.*.*.*.*.*.*.*.*.*.*.*..*. **W: [*crying*] HELLO, MATT?**
..*..*..*.*.*.*.*.*.*.*.*.*.*.*. .*.*.*.*.*.*.*..*..*.*.*.*.*.*.*.*.*.
....*.*.*.*.*.*.*.*.*.*
.*.*.*.*.*.*.*.*..*.*.*.*.*.*.*.*.*.*.*.*.*.*..*..*.*.*.*.*.*.*.*.*.
..*.*.*.*.*.*..*.*.**..*.*.*
.*.*.*.*.*.*.*.*.*.*.*...*.*.*.*.*..*..*.*.*.*.*.*.*.*.*.*.*.*.*.*.
...*.*.*.*.*.*.*.*.*.*.*.*.*.*..*..*.*.*.*.*.*.*.*.*.*.*.*.*.*.*
.*..*.*.*.*.*.*.*.*.*.*.*.*.*.*..*..*.*.*.*.*.*.*.*.*.*.*.*.*.*.*.*.
...*.**..*.*.*.*.*.*.*.*.*
.*.*.*.*..*..*.*.*..*.*.*.*.*.*.*.*.*.*.*.*.*..*.*.*.*.*.*.*.*.*.*.*.
..*.*.*..*.*.*.*.*.*.*.*.*.*.*.*.*..*..*.*.*.*.*.*.*.*.*.*.*.*.*.*
.*.*.*.*..*.*.*.*.*.*.*.*.*.*.*.*.*..*..*.*.*.*.*.*.

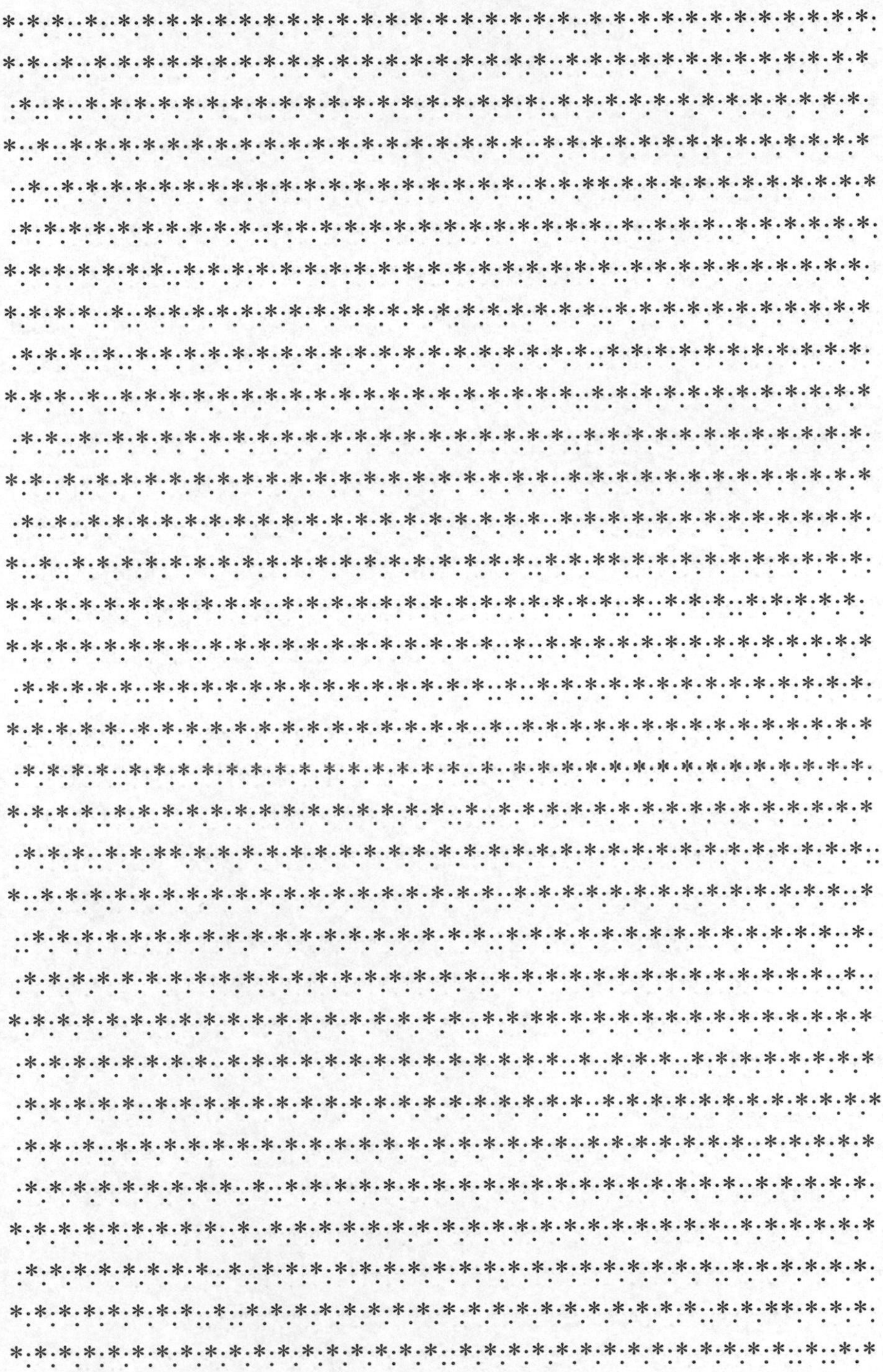

.*..*.*.*.*.*.*.*.*.*.*.*.*..*.*.*.*.*.*.*.*.*.*.*.*.*.*.*.*.*.*..*.*.

..*.*.*.*.*.*.*.*.*..*..*.*.*.*.*.*.*.*.*.*.*.*.*.*.*.*.*.*.*..*.*.*

.*.*.*.*.*.*.*.*.*.*.*..*..*.*.*.*.*.*.*.*.*.*.*.*.*.*.*.*.*.*.*..*.*.*.

..*.*.*.*.*.*.*.*.*..*..*.*.*.*.*.*.*.*.*.*.*.*.*.*.*.*.*.*.*..*.*.*.*

.*.*.*.*.*.*.*.*.*.*..*..*.*.*.*.*.*.*.*.*.*.*.*.*.*.*.*.*.*.*..*.*.*.*.

..*.*.*.*.*.*.*.*.*..*..*.*.*.*.*.*.*.*.*.*.*.*.*.*.*.*.*.*.*..*.*.*.*

.*.*.*.*.*.*.*.*.*..*..*.*.*.*.*.*.*.*.*.*.*.*.*.*.*.*.*.*.*..*.*.*.*.*.

..*.*.*.*.*.*.*..*..**.*.*.

...*.*.*.*.*.*.*.

..*.*.*.*.*.*.*.*.*..*.*.*.*.*.*.*.*.*.*.*.*.*.*..*..*.*.*.*.*.*.*.*.*

.*.*.*.*.*.*.*.*.*.*..*.*.*.*.*.*.*.*.*.*.*.*.*.*..*.*.*.*.*.*.*.*.*.*.

...*.*.*.*.*.*.*.*.*.*

.*.*.*.*.*.*.*.*.*.*.*.**..*.

..*.*.*.*.*.*.*.*.*.*.*..*..*.*.*.*..*.*.* .*.*.*.*.*.*.*.*.*.*.*.*.*.

.*.**.* .*.*.*.*.

..*.*.*.*.*.*.*.*..*.**..

..*.*.*.*.

..*.*.*.*.*.*.*.*.*.*.*.*..*.*.**.

..*..*.*.*.*.*.* .*.*.*..*.*.**.

...*.*.*.*.*.*.*.*.*.*.*.*.*.*.*..*.*.*..*.*.*.*.*.*.*.*.*.*.*.*.*..*.

..*.*.*.*.*.*.*.*.*.*.*.*.*.*.*..*.*.*.*.*.*.*.*.*.*.*.*.*.*..*.*.*.*

.*.*.*.*.*.*.*.*.*.*.*.*.*.*.*.*..*.*.*.*.*.*.*.*.*.*.*.*.*.*.*..*.*.*.

...*.*.*

.*.*.*.*.*.*.*.*.*.*.*.*.*.*.*..*.*.*.*.*.*.*.*.*.*.*.*.*.*.*..*..*.*.*.

..*.*.*.*.*.*.*.*.*.*.*.*.*..*.*.*.*.*.*.*.*.*.*.*.*.*.*.*.*..*.*.*.*

.*.*.*.*.*.*.*.*.*.*.*.*.*.*.*..*.*.*.*.*.*.*.*.*.*.*.*.*.*.*..*.*.*.*.

..*.*.*.*.*.*.*.*.*.*.*.*.*..*.*.*.*.*.*.*.*.*.*.*.*.*.*..*.*.*.*.*.*

.*.*.*.*.*.*.*.*.*.*.*.*.*..*.*.**.*.*.*.*.*.*.*.*.*.*.*.*.*.*.*.*.*.*.*

.*.*.*.*.*.*.*.*..*..*.*.*.*.*.*.*.*.*.*.*.*.*.*.*.*.*.*..*.*.*.*.*.

..*.*.*.*.*.*.*..*.*.*.*.*.*.*.*.*.*.*.*.*.*.*.*.*.*.*..*.*.*.*.*.*

.*.*.*.*.*.*.*..*..*.*.*.*.*.*.*.*.*.*.*.*.*.*.*.*.*.*.*..*.*.*.*.*.*.

..*.*.*.*.*..*..*.*.*.*.*.*.*.*.*.*.*.*.*.*.*.*.*.*..*.*.*.**.*.*.

..*.*.*.*.*.*.*.*.*.*.*.*.*..*.*.*.*.*.*.*.*.*.*.*.*.*.*.*..*..*.*

MATT!

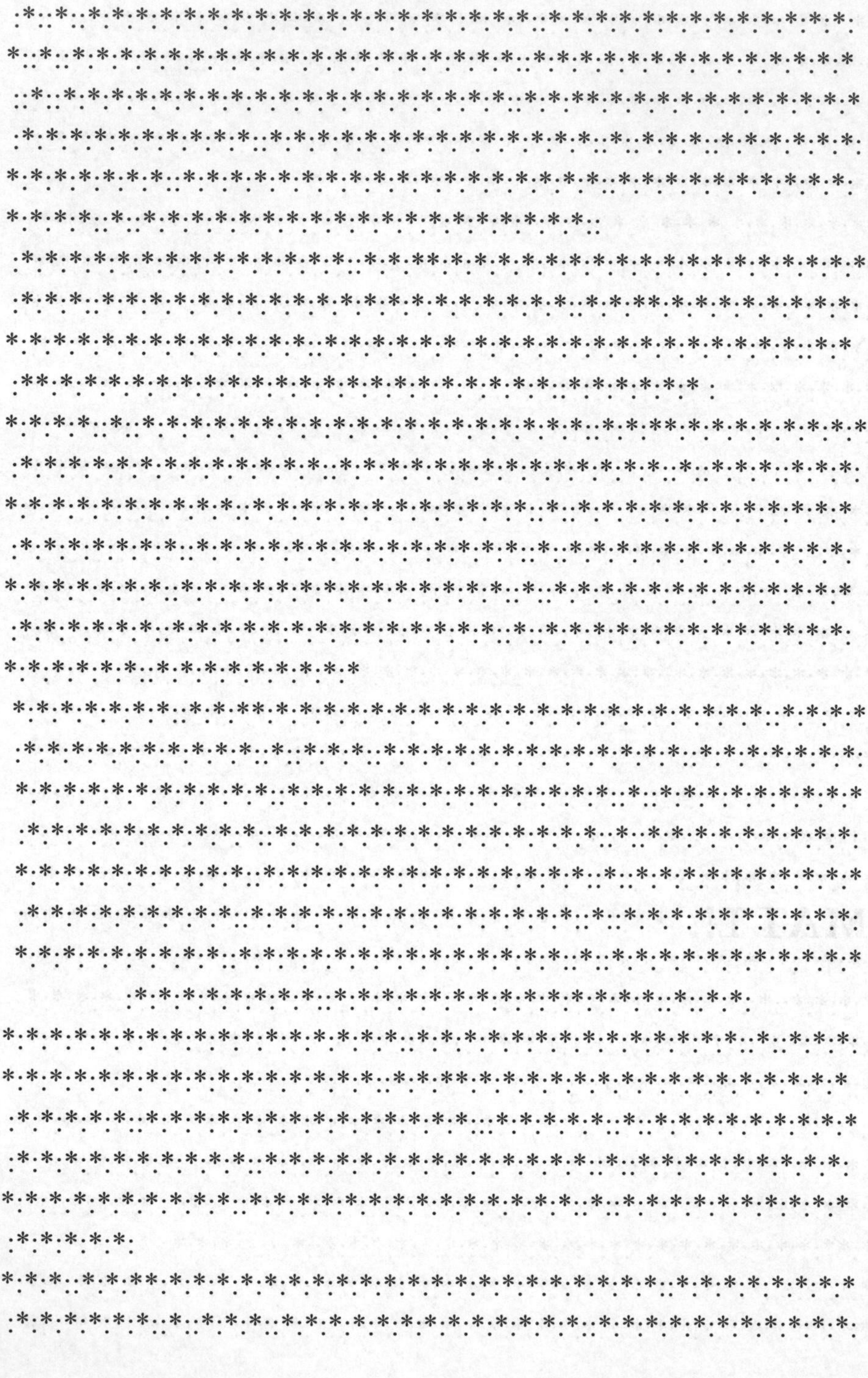

MATT YOU'VE GOT TO PICK UP THE PHONE!

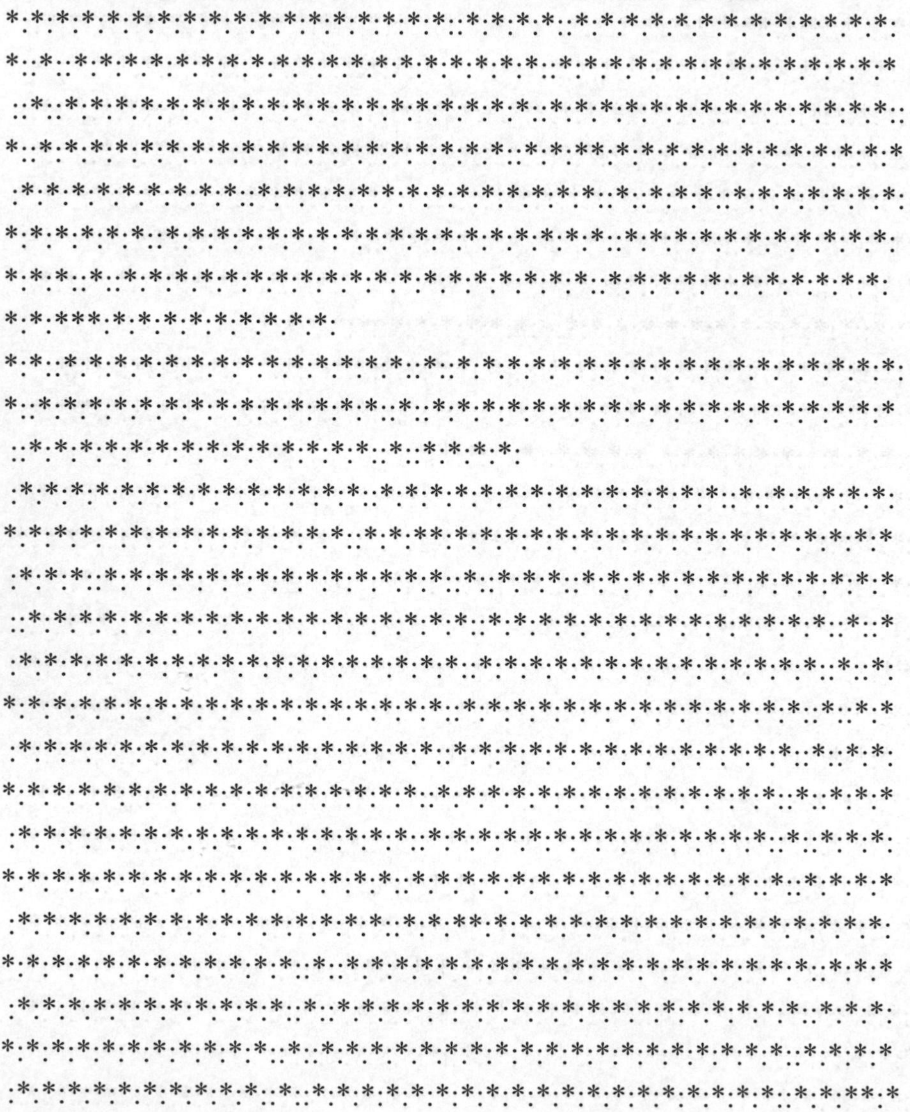

.*..*.*.*.*.*.*.*.*.*.*.*.*.*.*.*..*

..*.*.*..*.*.*.*.*.*.*.*.*.*.*.*.*.*.*..*.

.*.*.*.*.*.*.*.*.*.*.*.*.*.*.*.*.*..*..

..*.*.*

...*.*.*.*.*.*.*.*.*.*.*.*.*.*.*.*..*.

...*.*.*.*.*.*.*.*.*.*.*.*.*.*.*..*

..*.*.*.*.*.*.*.*.*.*.*.*.*.*.*.*.*.*..*.*.*.**.*.*.*.*.*.*.*.*.*.*.*.*..*.*.*.*.

...*.*.*.*

.*.*.*.*.*.*.*.*.*.*.*.*.*.*.*.*.*.*..*.*.*.*.*.*.*.*.*.*.*.*.*.*.*.*..*.*.*.*.

.*.*.*.*.*.*.*.*.*.*.*.*.*.*.*.*.*..*.*.*.*.*.*.*.*.*.*.*.*.*.*.*..*.*.*.*.*.*.

..*.*.*.*.*.*.*.*.*.*.*.*.*.*.*..*.*.**.*.*.*.*.*.*.*.*.*.*.*.*.*.*.*.*.*.*.*

.*.*.*.*.*.*.*.*.*.*.*.*.*.*.*.*.*.*.*..*.*.*.*..*.*.*.*.*.*.*.*.*.*.*.*.*.*.*.*

..*.*.*.*.*.*.*.*.*.*.*.*.*.*.*.*.*.*.*..*.*.*.*.*.*.*.*.*.*.*.*.*.*.*.*.*.*..*

.*..*.*.*.*.*.*.*.*.*.*.*.*.*.*.*..*..*.

...*.*.*.*.*.*.*.*.*.*.*.*.*.*.*..*..*.*

.*..*..*.*.

..*.*.*.*.*.*.*.*.*.*.*.*.*.*.*.*.*..*.*.*.*.*.*.*.*.*.*.*.*.*.*.*.*..*.*.*.*

.*.*.*.*.*.*.*.*.*.*.*.*.*.*.*.*.*..*.*.*.*.*.*.*.*.*.*.*.*.*.*.*.*..*..*.*.*.

..*.*.*.*.*.*.*.*.*.*.*.*.*.*.*.*.*..*.*.*.*.*.*.*.*.*.*.*.*.*.*..*..*.*.*.*

.*.*.*.*.*.*.*.*.*.*.*.*.*.*.*.*..*.*.**.

..*.*.*.*.*.*.*.*.*.*.*..*..*

.*.*.*.*.*.*.*.*.*.*.*.*.*..*.

..*.*.*.*.*.*.*.*.*..*..*..*.*.*.*

.*.*.*.*.*.*.*.*.*.*.*..*..*.*.**.*

.*..*.*.*.*.*.*.*.*.*.*.*.*.*.*..*

..*.*..*.*.*.*.*.*.*.*.*.*.*.*.*.*.*..*.

.*.*.*.*.*.*.*.*.*.*.*.*.*.*.*..*..

..*.*.*

...*.*.*.*.*.*.*.*.*.*.*.*.*.*.*.*.*..*.

...*.*.*.*.*.*.*.*.*.*.*.*.*.*.*..*..*.*.**.*.*.*.*.*.*.*.*.*.*.*.*.*.*.*.*.*

..*.*.*.*.*.*.*.*.*.*.*.*.*.*.*.*.*..*..*.*.*.*

..*.*.*.*.*.*.*.*.*.*.*.*.*.*.*..*

.*.*.*.*..*..*.*.*.*.*.*.*.*.*.*.*.*.

MARGARET *DIED!*

Um, ACD, are you still there, dear?

Yes, I'm still here.

[deleted]

Oh my god.

Poor baby.

[deleted]

Mm-mm-mm.

[deleted]

Melissa!

[deleted]

Nobody's talking.

No, but I hear a guy in the background.

That is um, I think that's the fire department trying to get their attention. Because he was giving the instructions, remember?

Yeah.

And nobody's answering. Everybody's asleep, I guess. Or down on the floor, unconscious; I hope they're OK. So much smoke! Did they blew the doors off?

[deleted]

Mm-hm. Mm-mm-mm.

{ } routes, did you get it?

No routes are coming over, ACD. I think it has something to do with that........Melissa? It's gonna be all right. You'll be here to call your mom when you get out, come and see how you're doing, and talk to her yourself. OK, Melissa?... Oh my god... Melissa, please. It's gonna be all right. It's gonna be fine, you'll be able to talk to your mother, yourself... But you gotta think positive, you gotta stay calm. OK, you gotta talk to your mother yourself, all right?.........Melissa?... You're gonna be fine. They're gonna come get you... Mm-mm-mm... Oh my god..............Melissa?... You're gonna be fine. Everybody's gonna be fine. You'll come and tell your mother yourself... what a good mom she is... I got the phone number, don't worry about that. You're gonna be all right.

[deleted]

Gonna be all right. Keep praying. Oh my goodness. OK? They'll be there soon, it takes a while to get up those stairs. They'll be there... It's gonna be fine, gonna be fine...

[deleted]

Gonna be fine... gonna be f

[deleted]

Melissa? If you can hear me, it's gonna be fine.

[deleted]

It's gonna be fine... Gonna be fine......

[deleted]

Oh, boy

[deleted]

Gonna be fine.

[deleted]

Melissa? Keep on breathin

[deleted]

Keep on breathin

[deleted]

They sound like they might be unconscious, ACD.

Think so?

Yeah. We just keep talking, saying positive things…OK, Melissa, it's gonna be fine, all right?

[deleted]

It's gonna be fine…It's gonna be fine…Oh my gosh.

[deleted]

Mm

[deleted]

Oh my

[deleted]

Hey, Melissa?

[deleted]

Stay with us. Everything's gonna be fine.

[deleted]

I know you're in a bad situation, but it's gonna be fine.

[deleted]

As soon as this is over with, you call your mother yourself. OK?

[deleted]

They're coming.

[deleted]

Oh my god.

[deleted]

They should have everybody moved from downtown here.

Yes they should. 'Cause it's—
it's gonna get a whole lot worse.

It's crowded—it's crowded. But don't worry, Melissa, 'cause they need to clear the traffic.

Yeah.

Hello, Melissa?

Hold on a minute. Hold on.

I'm gonna stay on here. Don't hang up there.

{ } her on the 83rd floor.
There's five people trapped, right?
{ } the girl was talking to,
everybody's unconscious now.

Everybody's snoring. Tell them everybody's snoring!

{ } call her mother, and left her
last wishes with—

It's dead.

It's dead? No, all we hear is—

No! It's not dead! IT'S NOT DEAD!

ACD!

ACD!

ACD!

ACD!

ACD!

ACD!

ACD!

What's your ACD number again?

Uh, 2252.

2252 is not dead! They're—they're snoring!

Are they—they asleep?

They're snoring. They sound like, you know, you get unconscious, a real deep sleep because, you snore.

OK.

So they're snoring. I don't know if she's unconscious or just out of breath, but it sounds like they're unconscious and snoring. That's why I keep talking to her.

Oh, OK. Are they empty? I mean, { }

Yes.

The line is dead now. They hung up.

Oh, my Lord.

The line the line is now dead…
No. No. This is—

[deleted]

No, no. The line is dead.
They cuttin the line.
The line is off now.

OK, thank you, ACD.

X

THIS IS ALL just a web of hypotheticals. We are not dealing here with certainties, or with anything that could ever be quantified, measured, tested, defined, codified, and peer-reviewed.

And I know the quantum surgeon's mind, hard at work, functions as a multi-level, multi-state processor, containing all the information it has collected and much his ancestors have handed down—and we won't ask him now, because he's busy, his conscious mind a-twitter dealing with the matter at his hand…but if we had the ability to bypass his conscious mind so as not to disturb it and tap directly into his memory banks, engage it in conversation, and ask:

>WHAT IS ALL OF THIS…REALLY?

...I know that he (all.those.bits.of.data, however stored) would tell us that all of IT—all the WORLD, all the SUNS and the MOONS and the STARS—all of MERCURY VENUS JUPITER AND MARS—all of HIM, all of HER, all of HE, all of SHE, all of YOU, all of ME—all of EVERYTHING—

is all, in all probability,

just random buckshot { } particles

that were scattered

after a big BOOM!

then somehow brought together by the { }waves...

★

CLAIRE: ....He's breathin again, huh?

★

December 8, 2006

Dear Campbell,

I am very sorry for my delayed response to you, The delay means love has deepened and increased, and comes back with the gifts Jesus has to gives us all. How marvelous that ordinary moments become sacred moments, for you, son of the great God we serve today together.

★

Anne: He's breathing again.

★

> I can rest. I can write. I can insure, but known are as guarantee that there is coming for good ministry. My memory is to say that the Lord will incurably reward your incredible kindness towards me. Thank you my friend, Campbell.

★

Claire: Go, Mike!

M: He's on an adventure..

★

> Campbell, my fuzzy, no brain low watt is still working right. It does since clean up all right but sometimes fill by mass catches up. Then the only pure way is to try to escape to Jesus callings with divine love.

★

And that however it is done, however it's all put together, it's not by magic, and it's not on purpose, the quantum surgeon is a scientist after all and scientists know that there is no meaning in matter beyond what we project onto it there is no meaning in substance, no meaning in time, no meaning in any of it,

★

> Camp, I really love you. My words keep robbing of the meaning.

★

it's just waves

it's just particles

it's just waves

★

> They do receive of all that. Somewhere did the receiver makes the receiver get twisted. Such gets the broken, the broken

★

just waves and particles interacting on the matrix of spacetime, bound by the physical laws, bound by cause and effect, bound by gravity, bound by light, completely insentient, completely blind, completely unconcerned with us, completely unconcerned with meaning, and that there is no room for anything approximating Providence, Fate, Destiny, or Divine Grace in any way.

{There's just loss.}

★

[unsent]

★

There's no Higher Order.

No Intelligence.

{There's just loss.}

No one driving the train.

No one's sailing the ship.

There's just { }

No one rowing the boat.

There's nothing at the center.

There's just { }

There's no center.

*

There's just { }

CLAIRE: Now this is back to normal breathing.

M: I know, it's crazy…

*

There's no center.

There's nothing at the center.

There's just { }

No one rowing the boat.

No one's sailing the ship.

There's just { }

No one driving the train.

No Intelligence.

There's no Higher Order.

There's just { }

There's just particles

just waves

flowing randomly

*

through space

*

built up at the beginning

randomly

from particles

from waves

*

gaining

form

gaining structure

then losing

everything

There's just { }

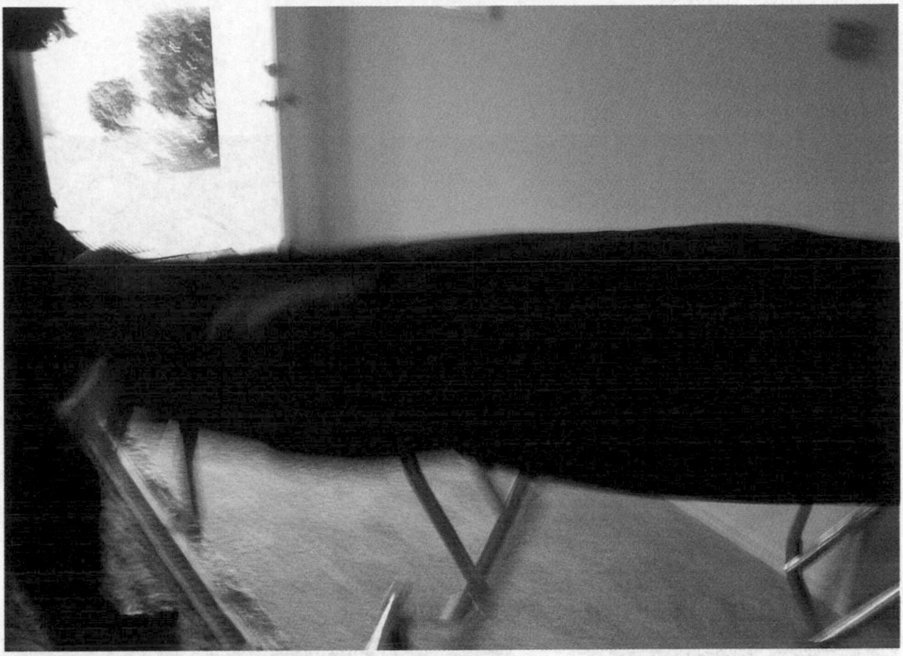

breaking down in the end

★

randomly

into particles

into waves

into waves

into waves

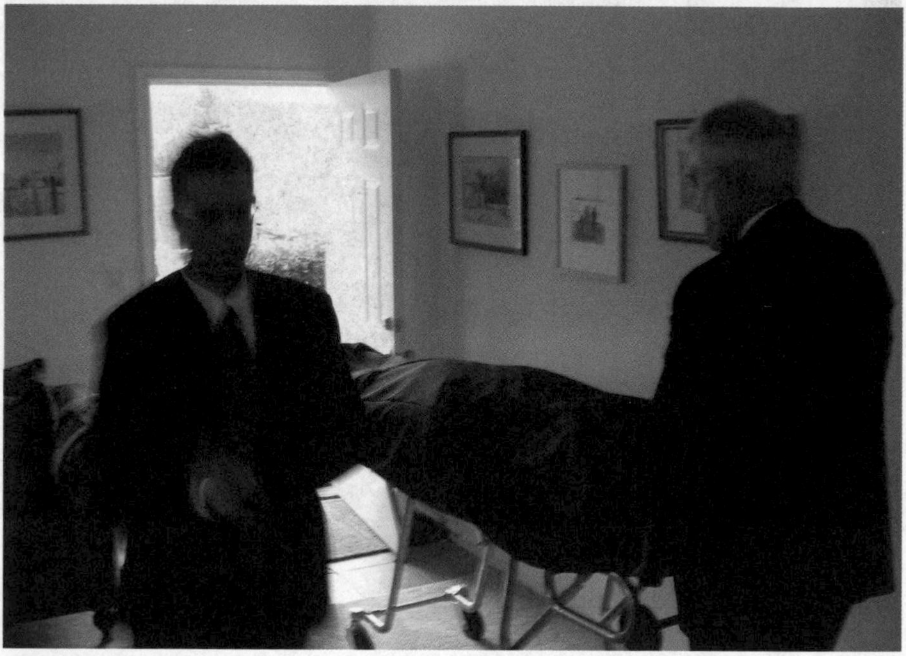

★

to be scattered

★

★

to be scattered

[redacted]

[redacted]

★

to be lost

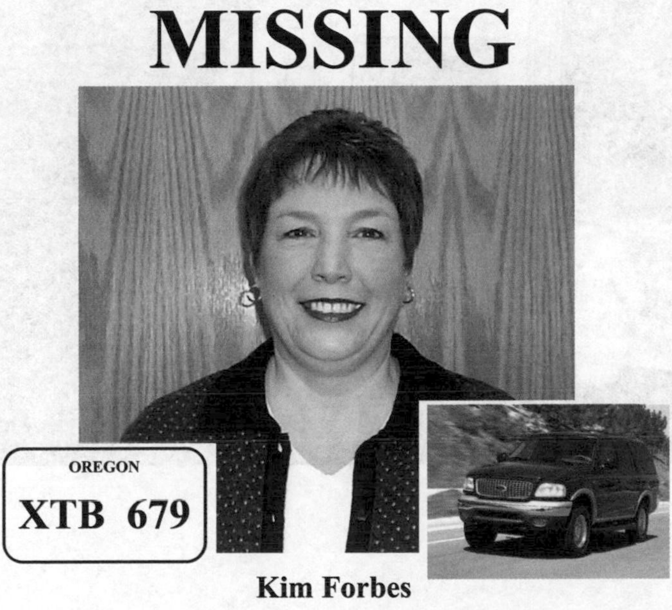
MISSING
OREGON
XTB 679
Kim Forbes

again and again and

again.

{ }

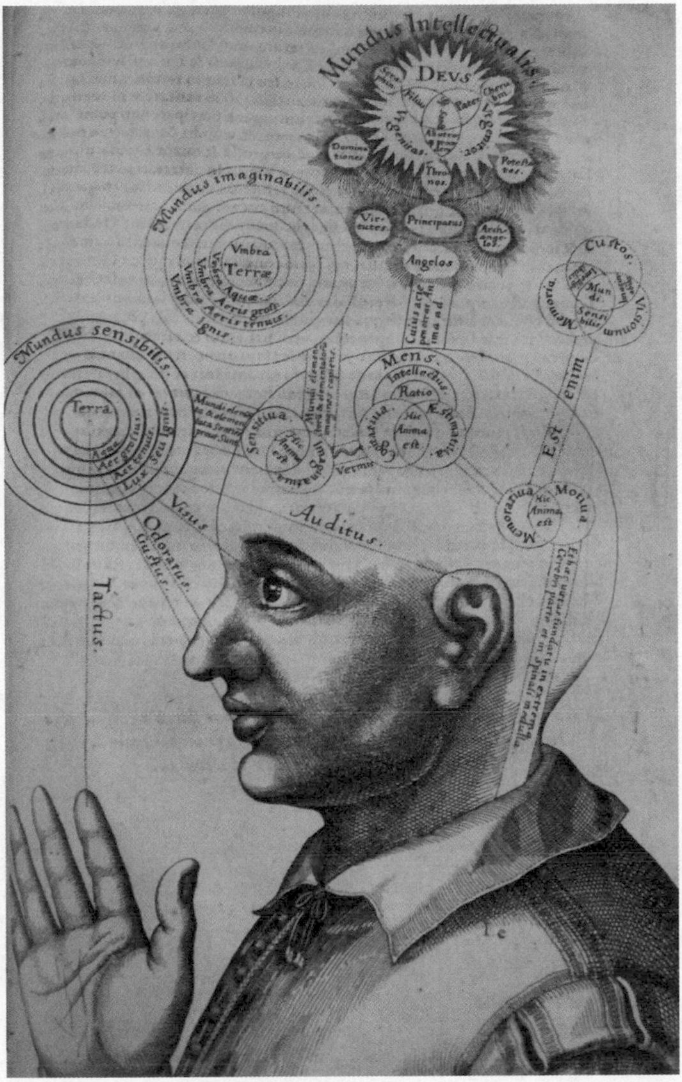
Mundus Intellectualis.
Devs
Dominationes
Potestates
Throni
Virtutes
Principatus
Archangeli
Angelos
Mundus imaginabilis.
Vmbra Terræ
Mundus sensibilis.
Terra
Mens.
Intellectus
Ratio
Cogitatiua
Æstimatiua
Hic Anima est
Sensitiua
Vermis
Custos.
Memoria
Visionum
Est enim
Memoratiua
Motiua
Auditus.
Visus
Odoratus.
Gustus.
Tactus.

Such gets the broken, the broken

Such gets the broken, the broken

Such gets the broken, the broken

Such gets the broken, the broken

Such gets the broken, the broken

Such gets the broken, the broken

Such gets the broken, the broken

Such gets the broken, the broken

Such gets the broken, the broken

Such gets the broken, the broken

Such gets the broken, the broken

Such gets the broken, the broken

Such gets the broken, the broken

Such gets the broken, the broken

Such gets the broken, the broken

Such gets the broken, the broken

Such gets the broken, the broken

Such gets the broken, the broken

Such gets the broken, the broken

Such gets the broken, the broken

Such gets the broken, the broken

Such gets the broken, the broken

Such gets the broken, the broken

Such gets the broken, the broken

Such gets the broken, the broken

Such gets the broken, the broken

Such gets the broken, the broken

Such gets the broken, the broken

Such gets the broken, the broken

Such gets the broken, the broken

Such gets the broken, the broken

Such gets the broken, the broken

Such gets the broken, the broken

Such gets the broken, Such gets the broken, the broken

Such gets the broken, the broken

Such gets the broken, the broken
the broken

Such gets the broken, the broken

Such gets the broken, the broken

Such gets the broken, the broken

Such gets the broken, the broken

Such gets the broken, the broken

Such gets the broken, the broken

Such gets the broken, the broken

Such gets the broken, the broken
Such gets the broken, the broken

Such gets the broken, the broken

Such gets the broken, the broken
Such gets the broken, the broken

Such gets the broken, the broken

Such gets the broken, the broken

M: I think we're in the middle of the castle right now. You know?

W: We're in the boat. I suppose the boat and castle might be the same thing. The dome, the tub, the boat...and yes, the castle..................

M: The middle of summer.

W: Uh-huh.

M: I mean the *beginning* of summer....

W: Well, we do always say we have our drawbridge up.

M: Yeah...

W: These grounds are *not* open to the public...............................
....

M: It's...Oh, man...I like talking to you about it, because it starts making more sense to me.

W: It does?

M: Yeah.

W: But I don't know anything about it! [*laughs*]

M: Well, it just makes more sense…

M: It's just another way of…because…they *are* walking to the fair in the middle of the castle, you know?

W: Yeah.

M: And so maybe that's why he—that's why he can't—that's why he doesn't bring her with him…Because she's *stolen—that's when she's stolen!*

W: That's cool! Because that's the thing about ███████, it's got slippery time.

M: Yeah.

W: So she's *stolen* from the exact place that she's going to be *found.*

M: Yeah. And it makes...*A FUCKING SHITLOAD OF SENSE* when you realize why he can't—why he—what the problem is...And it's not a secret, I mean, the problem is...they have to die, and he has to find a way to stop...dying.

W: Yeah.

M: You know? [*laughs*] It's that simple! But that's the—that's what everyone's been looking for!...And um...so she asks him this question...And *that's* gotta be the last thing that she asks him at the beginning of the book, right before she's snatched away—*the last thing she says!*

W: Oh, there's one thing she asks him?

M: Yeah.

W: In the castle?

M: Yeah.

W: Really?

>YOURE GONNA GIVE AWAY THE { }?

R I UM INC

M
INC

ORI
C

PORIUM

M PORI U

EMPORI

E M

Coca-Cola

Coca-Cola

Coca-Cola

Coca-Cola

Coca-Cola

CHAPTER SIX

I'M AN AGENT. All right.

I'm willing to admit that. But what kind? What do I do? And, perhaps more importantly, why? It seems certain that I have enemies. But do I have any friends? Who do I work for? Myself? Am I my own boss? Am I self-motivated? Or is there someone out there waiting for my report? Eva gave a report. Winsome's missing. Stu stole Aunt Sarah's car. Old clay pipes break. At the joints. It hurts. Poor Gerald's legs. Candy's usually not this disorganized. Olive went to the Great Bed Bath & **BEYOND**. What side am I on? Who's winning? The Mona Lisa? Shakespeare? What's the score? The kingdom. The serpent. The hero. Zero zero zero. You win some you lose some. Trash day's tomorrow. Who hired me? What was I hired to do? Pop? Hyde? themystery.doc.

"It's too bad you're gonna die soon," said the talking bear to my left. "Because it strikes me that what's happening to you would make an interesting story."

"You got that right," I said, trying to sound agreeable in spite of the fact that there was a fifty percent chance he was the galoot who had walloped my jaw, and there was just as good a chance that he was going to be the trigger man. "Except you don't even know the half of it."

"No?"

"No."

"What's the other half?"

"The other half is what I think makes the story truly interesting. You see, it turns out I woke up this morning with total amnesia."

Somewhere out there in the blindfolding darkness a teenage girl snorted derisively.

"Oh, I know a lot of people will tell you that amnesia doesn't really exist," I continued, "that it's just some made-up condition they use in books and movies to start a plot moving. Well, I'm here to tell you that it does. Take it from me: Amnesia is real."

"It is?"

"Yes. And I'm the proof. I don't know who the hell I am."

Another snort.

"Really?" said the bear.

"Yeah."

"How'd it happen? Bop on the bean? Or was it a 'his memory gets wiped' sort of thing?"

"Let me answer your question by asking you one: wouldn't the man with the amnesia be the last to know?"

"Yeah, I guess so!"

The car was cruising down the highway, headed somewhere. I didn't know where. Though I knew that wherever it was I didn't want to go there. The car had wide seats, no air conditioning. A motor that went VROOM. My legs were no longer tied, they were free, and my hands had been untied and retied in front of me. And there was a sleeping mask over my eyes. There was a thick body on either side. Bear One and Bear Two. They had me squeezed in tight between them. The wind blew in through the windows. If I'd thought Charles' drain snaking van was ripe it was only because I hadn't yet been sandwiched between two sweaty, shirtless circus animals. They both sat with their legs apart, their giant arms relaxed at their sides, taking up more than their share of space. I felt like a giraffe at an elephant party. In the front, from what I gathered, sat MOM and beside her Candice, and beside Candice whoever it was who was driving. Maybe Louie, maybe one of the others. Whoever he was he didn't talk.

"I for one believe amnesia's probably real," said the bear to my right. "I've seen a lot of crazier things than that."

"Have you?" I asked.

"Yeah. Sometimes I think about maybe writing a book someday."

"Well, you should!"

"You think so?"

"Sure! I'm sure you have lots of stories to tell, and a very unique perspective. And that's the real purpose of literature at the end of the day, isn't it? To pass on our unique perspectives? To share our common humanity with one another? To pass along a record of our lives and times, so that those who come after us can learn from what we went through?"

"Like how when you're about to execute somebody sometimes they just stand there."

"Pardon me?" I said.

"Sometimes they freeze up and just stand there."

"Do they?"

"Sometimes. Like one time I was gonna kill this agent and the MO on him was he was hard as nails and real slippery. And when I got him cornered I was nervous I was falling into some trick, because as soon as my gun came out he froze and it was easy. I just walked up to him and put the gun to his head. And instead of fighting or trying to get away he just froze. I remember looking around and thinking I was on Candid Camera. This guy's supposed to be slippery? Well, I snapped out of it and I pulled the trigger and *click*. Nothing happened. I thought he had done some voodoo on my gun. But then I saw I was just out of ammo. Well, now he coulda run for sure. He coulda got away easily. He was lanky like you, and a fast runner, and there's no way I would have caught him. But he just kept standing there like he was a deer in headlights. Didn't move, didn't breathe, I don't think he even blinked. And I had time to reach into my pocket, pull out a clip, and reload. It probably took fifteen or twenty seconds all told, and the whole time the looney just stood there like a freakin' statue. Well, I put the gun back up to his head again and: Bip. Bam. Boom. Goodbye agent. It was the weirdest thing I ever saw."

"Yes, and that's exactly what I mean. I think readers would really benefit from your perspective on that sort of thing."

"Really? Cuz that's just the tip of the iceberg."

"I bet it is. You know, it's too bad I'm gonna die soon because I would really love to work with you on turning your stories into a book."

"Really?

"Yeah. And you know what? I guarantee it would be a bestseller."

"You really think so?"

"Without a doubt.Why, with your experiences and my writing ability, we'd make millions. Not to mention how famous you would be."

"B2, stop talking to the agent," MOM said. "Can't you see he's just trying to butter you up?"

Bear One. Bear Two. Bear Three? Three daughters. Hedda was the easy one. Lotti was the lesbian. Eva said she must have been enchanted. Give me another chance tonight. All right? Don't call the old number. Call the new one. Remember.

"Does anyone have a phone I can borrow?" I said.

Laughter all around.

"What's so funny?"

"You just sit tight and relax," said MOM. "Everything's just fine. You're not gonna die. We're just going for a drive. Nothing bad is gonna happen to you. OK?"

She turned on the radio.

The drive went on and on. At some point the bear stink and the heat and the blindfolded rhythms of the car caused me to fall asleep. It may sound weird that I would have fallen asleep only moments after being told point-blank by a confessed killer that I was being taken to my death—surely a normal person would have stayed awake trying to plan a daring escape, or at least stayed awake to learn what I could about my captors, or just stayed awake to enjoy my remaining few moments of life—all true, but I was tired. So I fell asleep. And like so often happens when one falls asleep, I had a dream, a dream that has nothing much to do with anything except that it might make for an interesting scene.

In the dream I was back at the house I had woken up at that morning. In the dream I had just woken up too, only instead of a girl at the closet stepping into a skirt and saying, "I'm super late, so I'm gonna drive, OK?" the closet light was still on but there was no girl there. But there was in the bed beside me. She had her naked back to me, the blanket having slipped down over her hips. She had short blond hair—almost white—and a beautiful slender back. The movement of her body as she breathed suggested she was deep asleep. Then I heard a sound from the window behind me. A woman's voice singing my name. I knew it was my name she was singing even though I couldn't hear the name, itself. Meaning I couldn't hear the actual word, the actual syllables and letters of the name—meaning, it was my name she was singing—I knew it was my name—but she was singing it without actually saying the name. It was a dream, what can I say?

Soon I was up and outside standing on the back patio. There was a strange silvery light back there, and a thick haze over everything that even in my dream I recognized as being particularly dreamlike. I looked out through the mist for the source of the voice. It was louder now, and very lovely. I started walking into the mist toward it to see what I could find. I seemed to walk for a long time but finally in the mist a shape came into view. It was a beautiful girl—you would probably expect that—but what was unexpected was that she was sitting and swinging back and forth in a giant birdcage that was suspended over the ground by some mysterious means. She was wearing nothing but a white thong and a little t-shirt that said:

QUEEN OF THE UNIVERSE.

As I approached she stopped singing, and said,

"OMG! Who's there! Lucy? Is that you? Chee-chee-cha?"

I didn't know who Lucy was, and I certainly didn't know what chee-chee-cha meant. I approached her cage and when she saw me she said, "There you are, you stupid cat! Where have you been? Whenever things get the slightest bit sketchy you turn around and run like a total coward! Now, look! Those lousy raver nerds have got me trapped! Now, listen, Luce! Don't run away again! OK? All is forgiven, just don't run away! I need you to go find Mama a key! OK, kitten? We gotta get me out of here so we can save that cute little metal man! He's in big trouble, Luce! Plus, remember what the cowboy said! It might be up to me to stop the end of the world! Now go-find-a-key-for-Mama! It has to be around here somewhere!"

A rustling sound.

A little rabbit shot out of the mist.

I gave chase.

"No, no, no, no, Luce, no!" The voice followed me into the bushes… "Luce, come back!"…through the bushes…"Come back, Luce!"…down a hole…"LUCE! LUCE, YOU NO GOOD WORTHLESS MOTHERF#¢&ER! I SWEAR TO G-O-D IF WE EVER GET BACK HOME I'M GONNA…"

"…sleep."

"How do you know?"

"Because he's drooling all over me. Plus listen; he's snoring."

"Maybe he's faking. Candy?"

"Huh?"

"What's your opinion? Is he asleep?"

"Let me see... Yeah. He's asleep. He always snores like that. It's really annoying."

"My god, he's a straight-up foghorn. How could a skinny guy like that make such a racket? You're sure he's not faking?"

"Unfortunately, I'm very sure. And look how he drools. It's totally gross!"

The truth was I was not asleep. I had woken up, but their comments had convinced me to keep snoring—as well as to keep drooling—which was quite difficult because to my horror as soon as I had woken I realized that my face was practically buried in Bear One's armpit.

"Well, I'm waking him up," said Bear One. "I don't like to be drooled on."

"No." This was MOM. "Let him sleep. We have some things we need to discuss in private. Candy, keep an eye on him and if he starts to wake up, let us know right away. Now, I know he seems like kind of a fool but these agents can be real tricky. So Bears, keep that in mind. You might find he's kind of slippery. And just because he walked into our party like a total moron doesn't mean he still can't make an escape. I just have the feeling he's trying to pull a fast one on us. I mean, he can't really be this stupid, can he?"

CANDY: Why are you looking at me?

MOM: It's just that I've always thought you were a savvy girl, princess, but he snowed you, and having observed him I just don't see how.

CANDY: I'm a sucker for writers. I thought he was a genius.

MOM: Well, next time, have him prove it.

CANDY: In my defense he did write one very good book. *In Complete Accord*. Any of you read it?

ALL IN UNISON: No.

Bear Two: What's it about?

Candy: It's about how everything is connected. But how everything has come apart. How the universe is like a big puzzle that's been broken and needs to be put back together again. And how when you do you find—well, I don't want to give away the end. But it was really beautiful. The *New York Times* called it *an ambitious attempt*.

Bear Two: Wow, the *New York Times!*

Candy: I guess it almost won, like, a ton of awards.

MOM: Odds are he didn't even write the book. It was most likely written by someone at his headquarters when they were coming up with his identity. That's how they scheme. He needed a front and an excuse to operate without anyone asking what he was up to. If they did he'd just tell them he spent all his time working on the follow-up to his first book.

Candy (*snorting*): Yeah, and when you'd ask him what it's about he'd say he'd love to tell you but it's bad luck to talk about a work in progress. What-evs.

MOM: That's why we gotta be careful with him. We still don't know exactly what kind of animal we've caught.

Bear One: Aw, jeez! Look at all this drool!

Bear Two: We shoulda just got rid of him back at the house.

MOM: That's what I thought too, but Pop wanted him moved to someplace set up with a table.

Candy: We should have someone pick up that bitch wife of his. She's definitely an agent too. Someone should put her on the table.

MOM: Mr. Brubaker says that Pop knows all about her, so don't worry. She'll get hers.

Bear One: Oh, sick! It's pooling in my belly button! Come on, MOM, let me wake him up!

MOM: Relax. You're supposed to be a tough guy, B1. I think you can stand a little drool for one more minute. So when we get there, boys, we're gonna pretend we're pretending, OK? We want him to think that we're just putting a scare into him. So you bears can be rough but not too rough. Be scary. Violent but not *too* violent. He needs to be conscious. Mr. Brubaker here is going to take the lead on the interrogation. He knows more about this than anybody. Is there anything you want to say, Mr. Brubaker?

THE DRIVER: I don't want to see any guns or weapons of any kind. I've heard how the two large fellows in the back are apt to get trigger-happy now and then. That won't be happening here. We've reached a very serious juncture. My orders come from the one you call Pop, himself, and he's not willing to take any chances. This snoring drooler might have something that we've been looking for for quite some time. Something incredibly important. He needs to be alive so we can open him up and see.

CANDY: Open him up? You mean like surgery?

THE DRIVER: Yes. Like surgery.

CANDY: Will it hurt him?

THE DRIVER: Yes.

CANDY: Like torture?

THE DRIVER: Uh-huh.

CANDY: And it'll be horrible? And he'll be begging for death?

THE DRIVER: Of course.

CANDY: Good. The fucker told me he was gonna marry me someday.

THE DRIVER: Well, then I guess he'll find out what it would have been like.

I think I know why. I am not sure I know how. It all happened very quick. It was certainly something I would not have considered doing had I given myself time to think. Not even in such dire circumstances as the ones I found myself in. But something inside me stirred. Like something in a seed stirs for light. Like something in a seed breaks the shell. And rises through the dirt. I felt water nearby. I felt it beneath me. I felt it running, flowing. I felt it below me.

I felt it around me. I felt it inside. The wheels of the car. Went bu-bump. Bu-bump. Bu-bump. Driving fast. But everything else was slow. MOM, Candice, the Bears, Brubaker. A conversation. I thought: I don't like talking while I drive. You get distracted. Knock on wood. I let out one last snore and then lunged forward, reaching out with my bound hands to where I knew the steering wheel would be. Wrenched it with all my might, feeling, as I did, hands groping for me, then losing their grip on me as the car, with a crash, bumped, crashed, and then began to fall. Through the air. Screams. Up against the wall. Blindfold. Thump. Up against the roof. Fall. Oh my god. Fall until the Crash. A window. A desk in front of the window. A laptop computer. Smash. Old metal bookshelves. Books stacked on every surface. History, philosophy, fiction. The shatter of glass. Postcards and old photos stuck to the bookshelves with magnets. A drawing by a child of some sort of rainbow-colored craft—bright vibrant colors covering every molecule of the page—and little round balls—smiling faces. We go into the water. An old green couch. A black throw pillow. Cold. A metal trash can, empty except for balls of gum stuck to the inside. The ropes are undone. A yellow chair. I sat down. Hit the spacebar. The blindfold comes off. The computer started up. The black screen flashed and then a white sheet stared back.

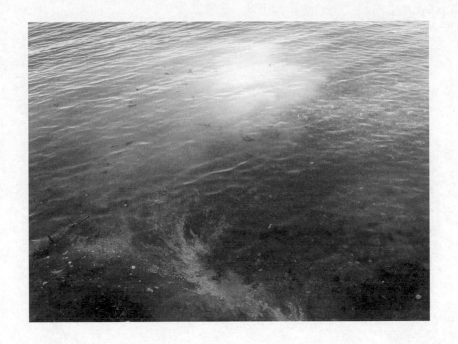

} else {

Subject: hello my love
Date: Mon, 05 Nov 2007 10:37:08 –0800
From: erin@███████████████
Reply-To: erin@███████████████
To: m███████████████

Hi babe. I wonder if you will receive this message. I'm
writing from my ██ account.

How's it going today? I am ★starving★. My stomach knows
it's not really 10:30. I guess I will eat my apple.

love you

your girl

The beauty is there, but not of the expected kind.

X

[1] About halfway through our stay in Montana, my wife received an email.

> From: <paul[redacted]@[redacted].net>
> Date: Sat, 25 Jan 2003 14:40:28 -0600
> To: <erin@[redacted].com>
> Subject: Stir Crazy yet?
>
> This is your Uncle Paul. I hear you moved to Montana. Does living in a cold climate agree with you? Hope so, but I don't like to shovel snow. Congratulations on your TV winnings.
>
> Care to do some snooping for me?

Your great grandfather, Gramps' mysterious father, Morris, died
in Bigfork, MT 10 November 1924. He is buried in Lakeview
Cemetery in Polson. I'm not sure exactly where you are living, but
if the distances aren't too great, perhaps you can do some research.
The person who gave information for his death certificate was
a "Mrs. Dorthy P. (or Dorothy A.) Brown." Your mission, if you
choose to accept it, is to find something about her.

Were there any newspapers in the area at that time that might have
reported deaths? Are there funeral home records about him? Any
marriage records for these two? He and grandma Nancy split in
1922 when Gramps was two and no one heard from him after that.

The death certificate says 14 miles S of Bigfork. The mortuary
record says 20 miles NE of Polson. Maybe it was just "somewhere
back in the woods." Anywhere near you?

Anyway, if you have time, this snooping would be appreciated.

Uncle Paul

See below:

>From: <paul.██████@██████.net>
>To: <records@██████.gov>
>Subject: Re: Re: Morris Brown
>
>The death certificate has his correct middle name Spencer erased
>and Samuel typed over it. It says that the residence was 14 miles
>South of Bigfork. I don't know whether this would also be 20 miles
>NE of Polson, or not. His wife's name was Dorothy Brown. He'd
>lived in his residence for 3 months. Cause of death was intestinal
>hemorrhage, duration 6 years. It doesn't say anything about suicide,
>nor is there a box to check for such things.
>
>I located a letter sent from Lake County in 1963, enclosing the death
>certificate. It says
>

> “The local undertaker now has lived here a long time, and he told
> me that he remembered helping the then mortician go after the
> body of Mr. Brown, which was in a cabin way back in the woods,
> where the road was drifted with snow, and they had a very difficult
> (sic.) bringing the body out.”

The cabin we were renting was on a spot called Yellow Bay,

exactly (14 miles S of Bigfork)

exactly (20 miles NE of Polson).

We’d found it on the internet, in a sea of classifieds. We hadn’t known of Morris Brown.

★

The order is there, but not of the sort to damp down our questions.

★

[2] It was around 11 at night, a few months earlier, late October 2002, and we got up from the couch, bundled up in heavy coats, and walked down the path and out to the end of the dock below the house. We looked out at the dark lake. Then we lay down. My wife did first. I stood there above her, smoking a cigarette. Come down with me, she said. I pointed the flashlight at her face and turned it on. She shielded her eyes with her hand and her breath rose around her fingers. No, I said, and turned the light off. Come lay down with me, she said again. Look at all the stars. So I did. I tossed my cigarette, and lay down beside her on the dock. We looked up. The stars held us in place. And then suddenly, right above us, suddenly, suddenly—*Suddenly*—

A ball of flame appeared in the sky!

It came bursting over the trees, a ball of flame, orange and white and yellow. Could see the ball, the round flaming core, and the flames around it, burning, and the long, bright trail it made across the sky, and could see the flames of the tail, itself ★★★★★★★★★★★★★★★★★★★★★★★★★★★★★★★★★ —it did not shoot—it was not a shooting star—it traveled slowly, crossing the sky slowly, in about 5 seconds or so, long enough for us to gasp—to grasp for words which would not come. Long enough to discern that its trajectory was going to have it coming down in the lake. To imagine the tidal wave that was surely coming. To scramble to our feet and start running…

★★

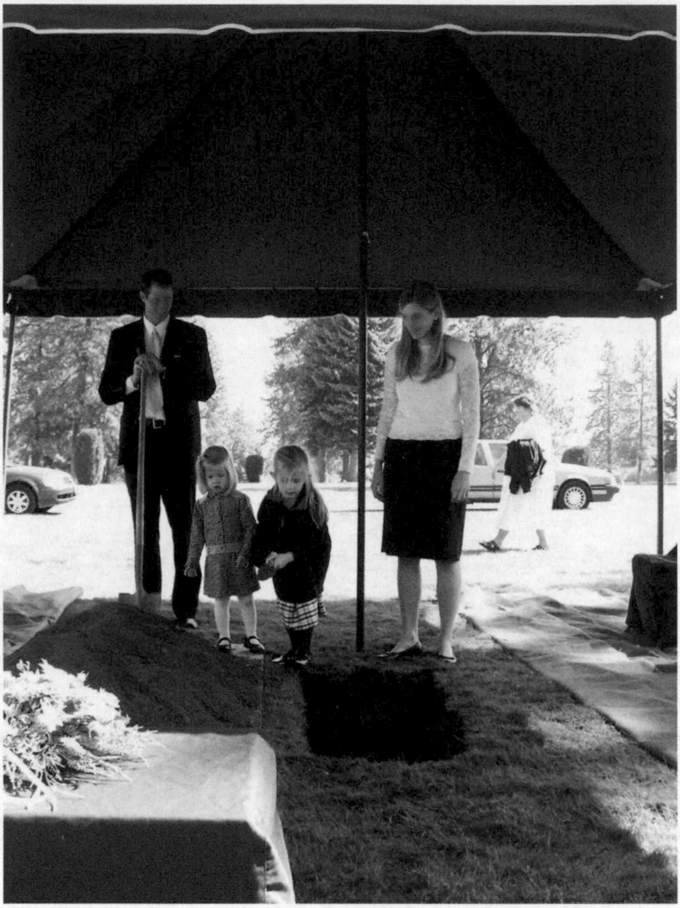

http://www.seattlepi.com/news/article/King–County–Deaths-1085007.php

A ███████: Joyce J., 75, of Auburn, April 5.

B ██████: Maxine R., 96, of Kent, April 4.

B █████: Chauncey C. Jr., infant, of Seattle, April 4.

B ████████: Ethel R., 97, of Kent, April 7.

B ████: Nadien E., 92, of Renton, April 4.

B ███████: Guy B., 88, of Renton, April 5.

C ████████: Jerome F., 86, of Seattle, April 7.

C ███████: Sherry L., 51, of Seattle, April 6.

C ████: Henrietta K., 91, of Kent, April 3.

C ██████: Dorothy M., 85, of Seattle, March 20.

C █████: David E., 51, of Des Moines, April 8.

D ██████: Gabriel A. Jr., 61, of Seattle, April 6.

D █████: Genevieve M., 86, of Seattle, April 5.

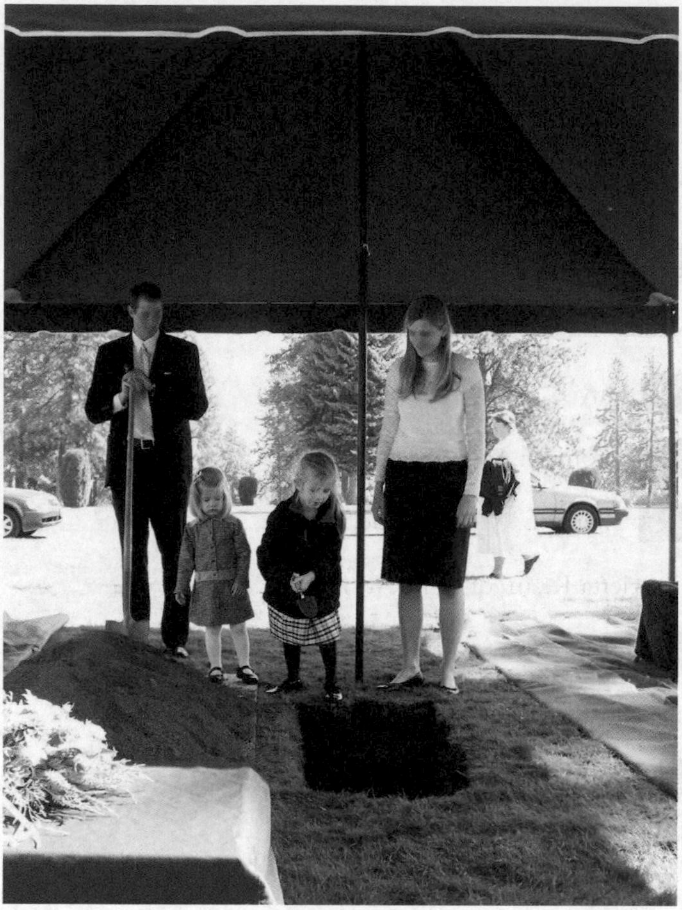

D█████████: George K., 92, of Burien, April 8.

D██████: Herbert O., 75, of Redmond, April 5.

E██████: Agnes K., 80, of Buckley, April 2.

E█████: Anne, 85, of Seattle, April 2.

F██████: Merlin C., 59, of Tukwila, April 4.

G███████: Robert A., 89, of Seattle, April 4.

G█████████: Betty J., 71, of Kent, April 6.

G██████: John C., 41, of Edmonds, April 6.

G████████: Glenn E., 83, of Kent, April 4.

G██████: Joan L., 65, of Seattle, March 24.

G████████████: Lilly J., 79, of Seattle, April 4.

G███████: Elsie M., 88, of Seattle, April 6.

H█████: Joseph F., 83, of Vashon, April 5.

H████████████: Samuel W., infant, of Monroe, April 4.

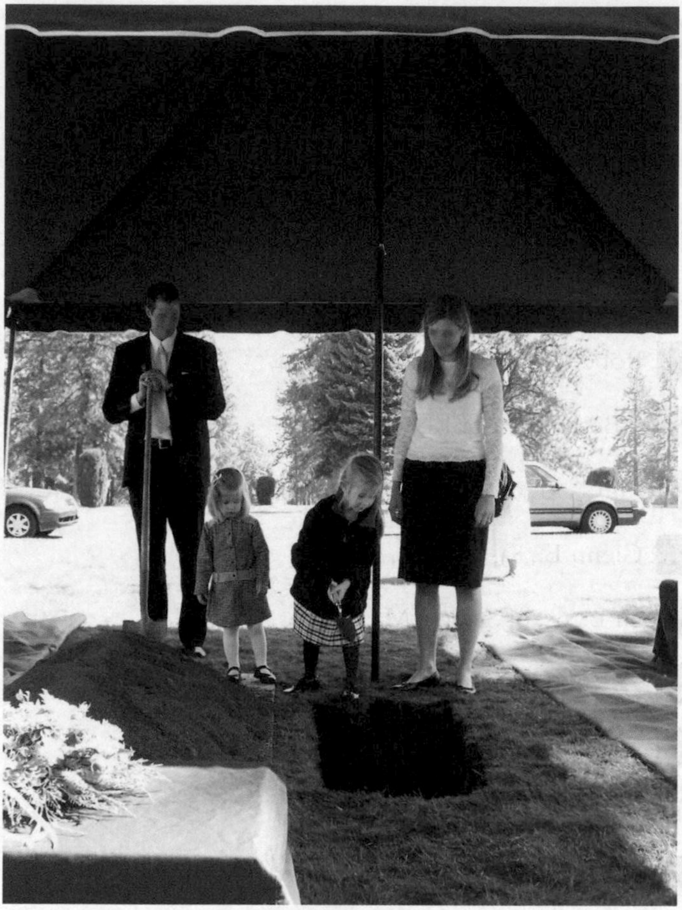

H█████████: Frederick T., 77, of Woodinville, April 5.

H█████████: Edward, 87, of Seattle, April 2.

H████████: William D., 74, of Seattle, March 31.

H██████████████: Virginia R., 77, of Kent, April 7.

H████████: Nancy A., 66, of Seattle, April 7.

H█████: Maxine M., 84, of Seattle, March 20.

H██████████: Hazel C., 98, of Seattle, April 3.

H█████: Gladys V., 89, of Seattle, April 4.

J██████████: Alice W., 87, of Seattle, April 2.

J██████: Morton S., 83, of Olympia, April 5.

J████████████: Augusto G., 79, of Seattle, April 5.

J██████████: Bailey M., 4, of Oak Harbor, April 3.

J██████████████: Sandra F., 41, of Louisville, Ky., April 3.

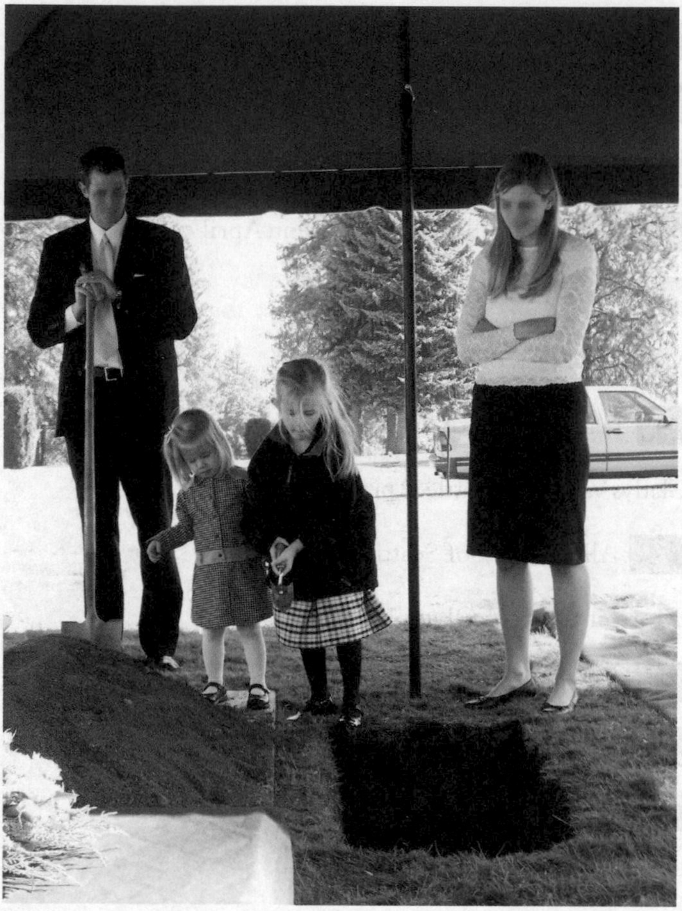

J█████████: Danie D., 45, of Seattle, April 6.

J███: Leslie J., 85, of Des Moines, April 5.

K████: Bonita J., 76, of Federal Way, April 6.

K████████: Carla M., 58, of Poulsbo, April 7.

K████████: Tom, 73, of Tacoma, April 6.

K██████████: Shiro H., 84, of Bellevue, April 4.

M███████: David H., 61, of Federal Way, April 4.

M█████████: Lester J., 88, of Des Moines, April 4.

Mc██████: Edward J., 93, of Shoreline, April 4.

M████████: Luciano F., 75, of Sequim, March 29.

O███████: Marshalene M., 70, of Maple Valley, April 5.

P████: Dorothy D., 80, of Arlington, March 28.

R████: Clarence B., 77, of Seattle, April 7.

R██████████: Edward, 67, of Seattle, April 7.

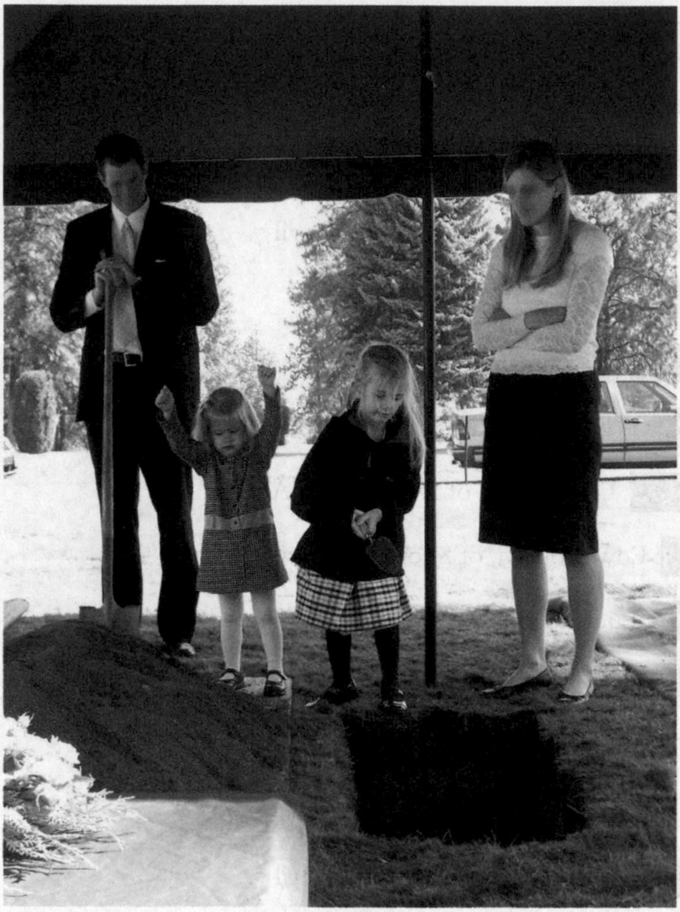

R███████: Audrey L., 82, of Seattle, April 4.

S████████████████: Otto K., 64, of Kirkland, April 5.

S███████: Martha L., 79, of Seattle, April 8.

S███: Albert G., 65, of Port Alberni, B.C., April 4.

S██████████: Austin T., infant, of Juneau, Alaska, April 4.

S██████: Helena M., 85, of Renton, April 7.

S██████: Lennis D., 70, of Burien, April 1.

S██████: Patricia L., 69, of Seattle, March 28.

S████████: Doris B., 86, of Seattle, April 4.

T███████████: Vandy, 17, of Seattle, April 4.

T██████████: Chester J., 91, of Mercer Island, April 1.

T███████████: Jesse O., 83, of Kent, April 6.

T██████: Cordelia J., 80, of Renton, April 7.

★★★★★★★★★★

★★

TRINKLEIN: Jay C., 47, of Seattle, March 31.

VAZQUEZ: Aida T., 76, of Federal Way, April 8.

W▮▮▮▮▮▮▮: Walter L., 76, of Puyallup, April 3.

W▮▮▮▮: Minnie M., 87, of Bellevue, April 4.

W▮▮▮▮▮▮: Milton O. Sr., 75, of Bothell, March 30.

W▮▮: Dallin J., infant, of Kent, April 4.

Z▮▮▮: Frieda, 86, of Seattle, April 8.

From Vital Statistics, Public Health—Seattle & King County

★★

★★

else

★★★★★★★★★★★★★★★★★★★★★★★

But the meteor just kept going★★★★★★★★★★★★★★★★★★★★until about the

middle of the sky, all of a sudden it—

*

The simplicity has { }

and was never seen again.

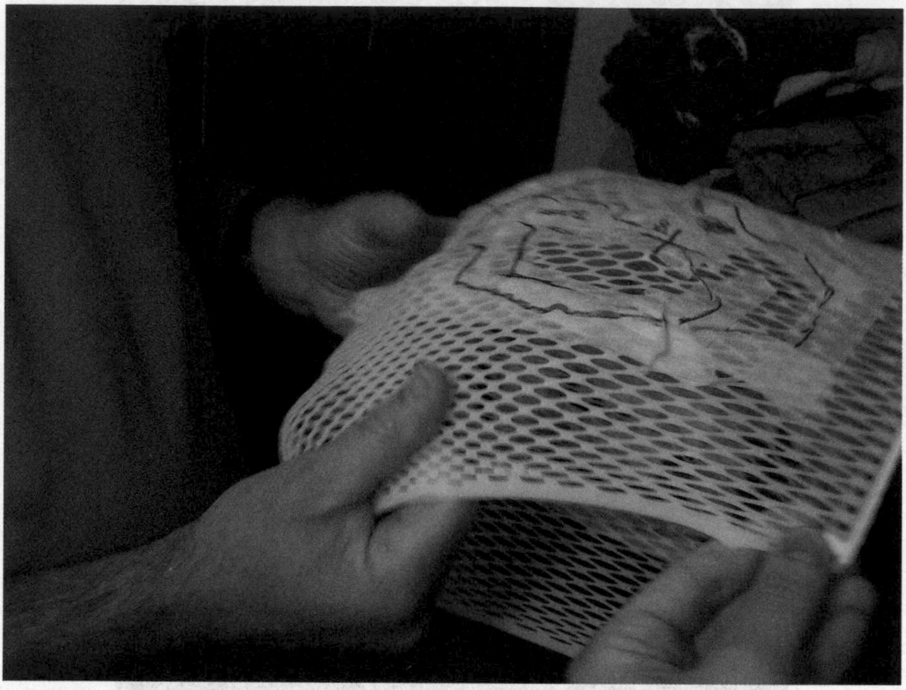

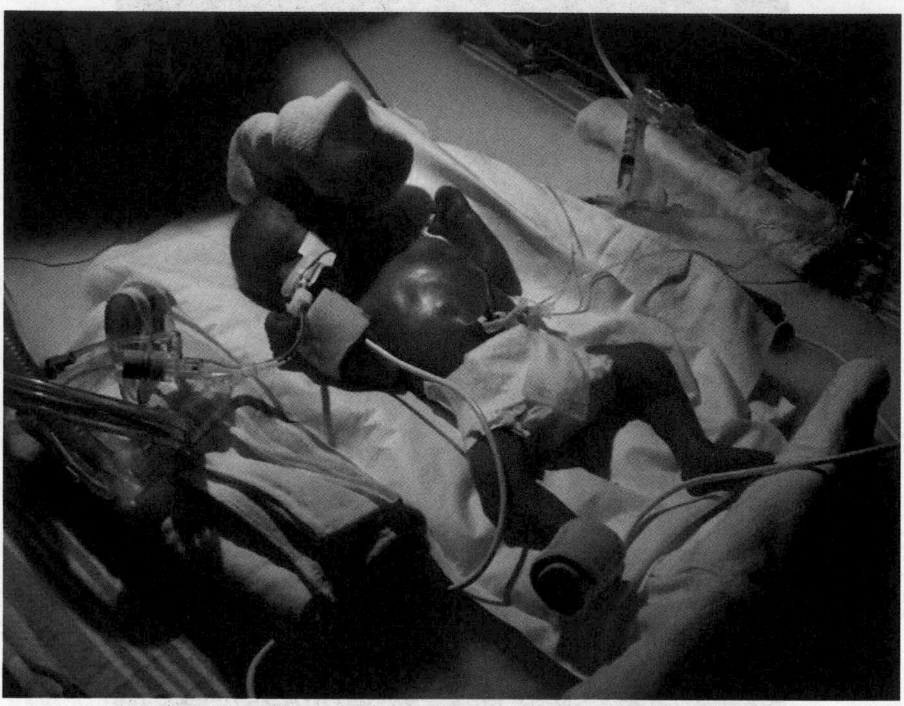

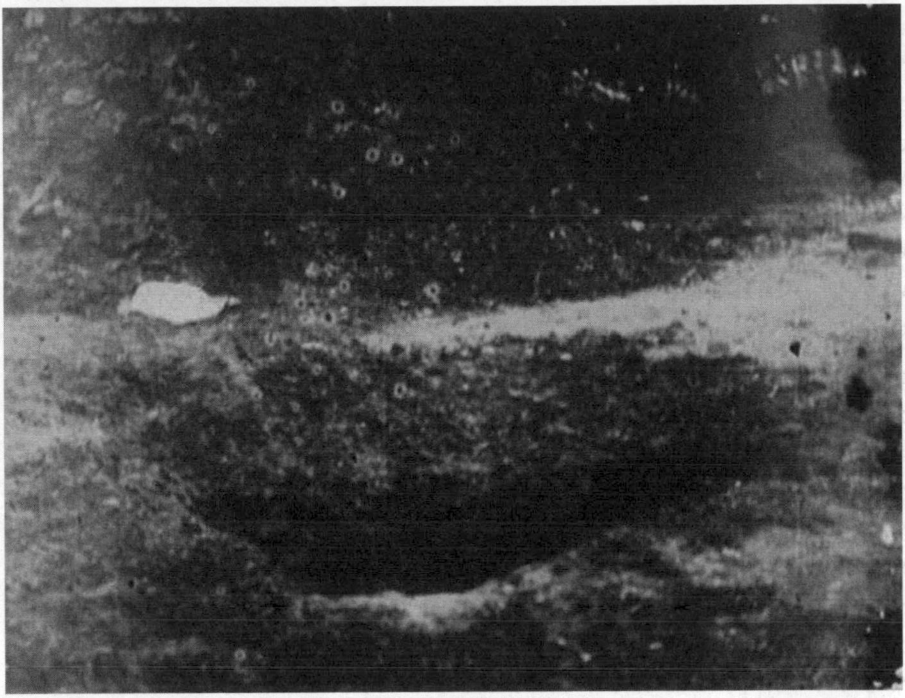

★·★:·★·★·★·★·★·★·★·★·★·★·★·★·★·★::★:·★·★·★·★·★·★·★·★·★·★·★·★·★·★·★·★·★·★
::★·★·★·★·★·★·★·★·★·★·★·★·★·★:·★:·★·★·★·★·★·★·★·★·★·★·★·★·★·★·★·★·★·★:·★
:★·★·★·★·★·★·★·★·★·★·★·★·★·★:·★:·★·★·★·★

★·★:·★·★·★·★·★·★·★·★·★·★·★·★·★·★:·★:·★·★·★·★·★·★·★·★·★·★·★·★·★·★·★·★·★·★·★:
★::★·★·★·★·★·★·★·★·★·★·★·★·★·★:·★::★·★·★·★·★·★·★·★·★·★·★·★·★·★·★·★·★·★·★·★:
:★·★·★·★·★·★·★·★·★·★·★·★·★·★:·★:·★·★·★·★:·★·★·★·★·★·★·★·★·★·★·★·★·★·★:·★:
★·★·★·★·★·★·★·★·★·★·★·★·★·★·★·★·★:·★·★·★·★·★·★·★·★·★·★·★·★·★·★·★:·★::★·★·★·★:
★·★·★·★·★·★·★·★·★·★·★·★·★·★·★·★:·★·★·★·★·★·★·★·★·★·★·★·★·★·★·★·★·★:·★::★·★·★·★:
★·★·★·★:

★::★·★·★·★·★·★·★·★·★·★·★·★·★·★::★:·★·★·★:·★·★·★·★·★·★·★·★·★·★·★·★·★·★:·★·★·★
:★·★·★·★·★·★·★·★·★·★·★·★·★·★·★::★·★·★·★·★·★·★·★·★·★·★·★·★·★·★:·★::★·★·★·★·★
:★·★·★·★·★·★·★·★·★·★·★·★·★·★:·★·★·★·★·★★:·★·★·★·★·★·★·★·★·★·★·★·★·★·★·★:·★:
:★·★·★::★·★·★·★·★·★·★·★·★·★·★·★·★·★·★:·★·★·★·★·★·★·★·★·★·★·★·★·★·★·★·★·★:·★
:★·★·★·★·★·★·★·★·★·★·★·★·★:·★::★·★·★·★·★·★·★·★·★·★·★·★·★·★·★·★·★·★·★·★:·★·★

:★:★:★

★:★::★:★:★:★:★:★:★:★:★:★:★:★:★::★::★

::★:★:★:★:★:★:★:★:★:★:★:★:★::★::★::★

:★:★:★:★:★:★:★:★:★:★:★:★:★::★::★:★:★:★

★:★::★:★:★:★:★:★:★:★:★:★:★:★:★::★::★

::★:★:★:★:★:★:★:★:★:★:★:★:★::★::★::★

:★:★:★:★:★:★:★:★:★:★:★:★:★::★::★:★:★:★:★::★::★:★:★:★:★:★:★:★:★:★:★:★:★::★:★:

★:★:★:★:★:★:★:★:★:★:★:★:★:★:★:★::★:★:★:★:★:★:★:★:★:★:★:★:★:★::★::★:★:★:★:★:

★:★:★:★:★:★:★:★:★:★:★:★:★:★:★::★:★:★:★:★:★:★:★:★:★:★:★:★:★:★::★::★:★:★:★:★:

★:★:★:★:★::★:★:★:★:★:★:★:★:★:★:★:★:★:★:★::★::★:★:★:★:★:★:★:★:★:★:★:★:★:★:★:★:

★:★:★:★::★:★:★:★:★:★:★:★:★:★:★:★:★:★:★:★::★::★:★:★:★:★:★:★:★:★:★:★:★:★:★:★:★:

★:★:★::★:★:★:★:★:★:★:★:★:★:★:★:★:★:★:★:★::★::★:★:★:★:★

:★::★::★:★:★:★:★:★:★:★:★:★:★:★:★:

:★::★:★:★:★:★:★:★:★:★

★::★:★:★:★:★:★:★:★:★:★:★:★:★:★:★::★:★:★:★::★:★:★:★:★:★:★:★:★:★:★:★:★:★::★:★:★

:★:★:★:★:★:★:★:★:★:★:★:★:★:★:★::★:★:★:★:★:★:★:★:★:★:★:★:★:★:★::★::★:★:★:★:★:

★:★:★:★:★:★:★:★:★:★:★:★:★:★:★:★::★:★:★:★:★

★:★::★:★:★:★:★:★:★:★:★:★:★:★:★::★::★

::★:★:★:★:★:★:★:★:★:★:★:★:★::★::★::★

:★:★:★:★:★:★:★:★:★:★:★:★:★::★::★:★:★:★:★:★:★::★:★:★:★:★:★:★:★:★:★:★:★:★:★:★:

★::★::★:★:★:★:★:★:★:★:★:★:★:★:★:

★:★:★:★:★:★:★::★:★:★:★:★:★:★:★:★:★:★:★:★:★:★:★:★::★:★:★:★:★:★:★:★:★:★:★:★:★

:★:★:★::★::★:★:★:★:★:★:★:★:★:★:★:★:★:★:★:★:★:★:★::★:★:★:★:★:★:★:★:★:★:★:★:★:

★:★::★::★:★:★:★:★:★:★:★:★:★:

★::★:★:★:★:★:★:★:★:★:★:★:★:★:★::★:★:★:★::★:★:★:★:★:★:★:★:★:★:★:★:★:★::★:★:★

:★::★::★:★:★:★:★:★:

★:★:★:★:★:★:★:★:★:★:★:★:★:★:★:★::★:★:★:★:★

★:★::★:★:★:★:★:★:★:★:★:★:★:★:★::★::★

::★:★:★:★:★:★:★:★:★:★:★:★:★::★::★::★

:★:★:★:★:★:★:★:★:★:★:★:★:★::★::★:★:★:★

★:★::★:★:★:★:★:★:★:★:★:★:★:★:★::★::★:

★::★:★:★:★:★:★:★:★:★:★:★:★:★:★::★::★:

:★:★:★:★:★:★:★:★:★:★:★:★:★:★:★:★:★:★::★::★:★:★:★:★:★:★:★:★:★:★:★:★:★:★::★:

★:★:★:★:★:★:★:★:★:★:★:★:★:★:★:★:★::★:

★:★:★:★:★:★:★:★:★:★:★:★:★:★:★:★:★::★:★:★:★:★:★:★:★:★:★:★:★:★:★:★::★:★:★:★:★:

★:★:★:★:

★·★·★·★·★·★·★·★·★·★·★::★·★·★·★·★·★·★·★·★·★·★·★·★·★::★::★·★·★·★·★·★·★·★·★·★

:★·★·★·★·★·★·★·★·★::★·★·★·★·★·★·★·★·★·★·★·★·★·★·★::★·★·★·★·★·★·★·★·★·★·★:

★·★·★·★·★·★·★·★·★::★·★·★·★·★·★·★·★·★·★·★·★·★·★::★::★·★·★·★·★★·★::★·★·★·★·★·★:

★·★·★·★·★·★·★·★·★::★::★·★·★·★·★·★·★·★·★·★·★·★·★·★·★·★·★·★·★·★:

:★·★·★·★·★::★::★·★·★·★·★·★·★·★·★·★·★·★·★·★·★·★·★·★·★::★·★·★·★·★·★·★·★·★·★:

★·★·★·★::★::★·★·★·★·★::★::★·★

:★·★·★·★·★::★·★·★·★·★·★·★·★·★·★·★·★·★·★·★·★::★::★·★·★·★·★·★·★·★·★·★·★·★·★·★:

★·★·★·★·★::★·★·★·★·★·★·★·★·★·★·★·★·★·★·★·★::★::★·★·★·★·★·★·★·★·★·★·★.

★::★·★·★·★·★·★·★·★·★·★·★·★·★·★·★·★::★::★·★·★·★::★·★·★·★·★·★·★·★·★·★·★·★·★·★·★::★·★·★

:★·★·★·★·★·★·★·★·★·★·★·★·★·★·★·★·★::★·★·★·★·★·★·★·★·★·★·★·★·★·★·★::★::★·★·★·★·★·★:

★·★·★·★·★·★·★·★·★·★·★·★·★·★·★·★::★·★·★·★·★·★·★

★·★::★·★·★·★·★·★·★·★·★·★·★·★·★·★·★·★::★::★·★

::★·★·★·★·★·★·★·★·★·★·★·★·★·★·★·★::★::★·★·★·★·★·★·★·★·★·★·★·★·★·★·★·★·★·★·★·★::★

:★·★·★·★·★·★·★·★·★·★·★·★·★·★·★::★::★·★·★·★·★·★·★::★·★★·★·★·★·★·★·★·★·★·★·★·★:

★·★·★·★·★·★·★·★·★::★·★·★·★·★·★·★·★·★·★·★·★·★·★·★·★·★::★::★·★·★·★::★·★·★·★·★·★:

★·★·★·★·★·★·★::★·★·★·★·★·★·★·★·★·★·★·★·★·★·★·★·★·★::★·★·★·★·★·★·★·★·★·★·★·★

:★·★·★::★·★·★·★·★·★·★·★·★·★·★·★·★·★·★·★::★::★·★·★·★·★·★·★·★·★·★·★·★·★·★·★·★·★::

★·★·★·★·★·★·★·★·★·★·★·★·★·★·★·★·★·★::★·★·★·★·★·★·★·★·★·★·★·★·★·★·★::★::★·★:

★·★·★·★·★·★·★·★·★·★·★·★·★·★·★·★·★·★::★·★·★·★·★·★·★

★·★::★·★·★·★·★·★·★·★·★·★·★·★·★·★·★·★::★::★·★

::★·★::★

:★·★·★·★·★·★·★·★·★·★·★·★·★·★·★::★::★·★·★·★·★·★

★·★::★·★·★·★·★·★·★·★·★·★·★·★·★·★·★·★·★::★·★·★·★·★·★·★·★·★·★·★·★·★·★·★·★·★·★·★·★:

★::★·★·★·★·★·★·★·★·★·★·★·★·★·★·★·★::★::★·★:

:★·★·★·★·★·★·★·★·★·★·★·★·★·★::★·★·★·★·★·★·★::★::★·★·★·★·★·★·★·★·★·★·★·★·★·★·★::★:

★·★::★::★·★·★·★:

★·★·★·★·★·★·★·★·★·★·★·★·★·★·★·★::★·★·★·★·★·★·★·★·★·★·★·★·★·★·★::★::★·★·★·★·★·★:

★·★·★·★.

★::★·★·★·★·★·★·★·★·★·★·★·★·★·★·★::★::★·★·★·★::★·★·★·★·★·★·★·★·★·★·★·★·★·★·★::★·★·★

:★·★::★::★·★·★·★·★·★

:★·★·★·★·★·★·★·★·★·★·★·★·★·★::★·★·★·★·★·★★::★·★·★·★·★·★·★·★·★·★·★·★·★·★::★:

:★·★·★::★·★·★·★·★·★·★·★·★·★·★·★·★·★·★::★·★·★·★·★·★·★·★·★·★·★·★·★·★·★·★·★·★·★::★

:★·★·★·★·★·★·★·★·★·★·★·★·★·★::★::★·★·★·★·★·★·★·★·★·★·★·★·★·★·★·★·★·★·★·★::★·★

:★·★·★

★·★::★·★·★·★·★·★·★·★·★·★·★·★·★·★·★·★::★·★·★·★·★·★·★·★·★·★·★·★·★·★·★·★·★·★·★·★:

★::★·★·★·★·★·★·★·★·★·★·★·★·★·★·★::★::★·★:

:★:★:★:★:★:★:★:★:★:★:★:★:★:★::★::★:★:★:★★:★::★:★:★:★:★:★:★:★:★:★:★:★:★:

:★::★:★:★:★:★:★:★:★:★:★:★:★:★:★:★:★:★:★:★::★:★:★:★:★:★:★:★:★:★:★:★:★:★::★

::★:★:★:★:★:★:★:★:★:★:★:★:★:★:★:★:★:★:★::★:★:★:★:★:★:★:★:★:★:★:★:★:★::★::

★:★:★:★

:★::★::★:★:★:★:★:★:★:★:★:★:★:★:★:★:★:★:★:★:★::★:★:★:★:★:★:★:★:★:★:★:★:★:★:★:

:★::★:★:★:★:★:★:★:★:★:

★::★:★:★:★:★:★:★:★:★:★:★:★:★:★::★::★:★:★::★:★:★:★:★:★:★:★:★:★:★:★:★::★:★:★

:★:★:★:★:★:★:★:★:★:★:★:★:★:★::★:★:★:★:★:★:★:★:★:★:★:★:★:★::★::★:★:★:★:★:

★:★:★:★:★:★:★:★:★:★:★:★:★:★::★:★:★:★:★

★:★::★:★:★:★:★:★:★:★:★:★:★:★:★:★::★::★:★:★:★:★:★:★:★:★:★:★:★:★:★:★:★:★:★

::★:★:★:★:★:★:★:★:★:★:★:★:★:★::★::★:★:★:★:★:★:★:★:★:★:★:★:★:★:★:★:★::★

:★:★:★:★:★:★:★:★:★:★:★:★:★::★::★:★:★:★:★:★:★::★:★:★★:★:★:★:★:★:★:★:★:★:

★:★:★:★:★:★:★:★:★:★:★::★:★:★:★:★:★:★:★:★:★:★:★:★::★::★:★:★:★:★:★:★:★:★:

★:★:★:★:★:★:★::★:★:★:★:★:★:★:★:★:★:★:★:★:★:★:★:★::★:★:★:★:★:★:★:★:★:★

:★:★:★::★::★:

★:★::★::★:★:★:★:★:★:★:★:

★::★:★:★:★:★:★:★:★:★:★:★:★:★:★::★::★:★:★::★:★:★:★:★:★:★:★:★:★:★:★::★:★:★

:★:★:★:★:★:★:★:★:★:★:★:★:★:★::★:★:★:★:★:★:★:★:★:★:★:★:★:★::★::★:★:★:★:★:

★:★:★:★:★:★:★:★:★:★:★:★:★:★::★:★:★:★:★

★:★::★:★:★:★:★:★:★:★:★:★:★:★:★:★::★::★:★:★:★:★:★:★:★:★:★:★:★:★:★:★:★:★:★

::★:★:★:★:★:★:★:★:★:★:★:★:★:★::★::★:★:★:★:★:★:★:★:★:★:★:★:★:★:★:★:★::★

:★:★:★:★:★:★:★:★:★:★:★:★:★::★::★:★:★:★:★

★:★::★:★:★:★:★:★:★:★:★:★:★:★:★:★::★::★:★:★:★:★:★:★:★:★:★:★:★:★:★:★:★:★:

★::★:★:★:★:★:★:★:★:★:★:★:★:★:★::★::★:★:★:★:★:★:★:★:★:★:★:★:★:★:★:★:★:★:

:★:★:★:★:★:★:★:★:★:★:★:★:★::★::★:★:★:★::★::★:★:★:★:★:★:★:★:★:★:★:★:★::★:

★:★:★:★:★:★:★:★:★:★:★:★:★:★:★:★::★:★:★:★:★:★:★:★:★:★:★:★:★::★::★:★:★:★:

★:★:★:★:★:★:★:★:★:★:★:★:★:★:★::★:★:★:★:★:★:★:★:★:★:★:★:★::★::★:★:★:★:★:

★:★:★:★:

★:★:★:★:★:★:★:★:★:★::★:★:★:★:★:★:★:★:★:★:★:★:★:★:★::★::★:★:★:★:★:★:★:★:★

:★:★:★:★:★:★:★:★:★::★:★:★:★:★:★:★:★:★:★:★:★:★:★:★::★::★:★:★:★:★:★:★:★:★:

★:★:★:★:★:★:★:★::★:★:★:★:★:★:★:★:★:★:★:★:★::★::★:★:★:★:★★:★::★:★:★:★:★:

★:★:★:★:★:★:★:★:★::★::★:★:★:★:★:★:★:★:★:★:★:★:★:★:★:★:★:★:

:★:★:★:★:★::★::★:★:★:★:★:★:★:★:★:★:★:★:★:★:★:★:★::★:★:★:★:★:★:★:★:★:★:

★:★:★:★::★::★:★:★:★::★::★

:★:★:★:★:★:★::★:★:★:★:★:★:★:★:★:★:★:★:★:★::★::★:★:★:★:★:★:★:★:★:★:★:★:★:

★:★:★:★:★::★:★:★:★:★:★:★:★:★:★:★:★:★:★::★::★:★:★:★:★:★:★:★:★:

★·★

:★·

:★·★·★·★·★·★·★·★·★·★·

★·★·★·★·★·★·★·★·★·★·★·★·★·★·★·★·

:★·

★·

★·★

:★·

★·★·★·★·★·★·★·★·★·★·★·★·★·★·★·★·★·★·★·★

★·★

:★·★

:★·★·★·★·★·★·★·★·★·★·★·★·★·★·★·★·★·★·★·★

★·

★·

:★·

★·

★·

★·★·★·★·

★·★

:★·

★·

★·

:★·

★·★

:★·

★·

★·★

:★·

★·★·★·★·★·★·★·★·★·★·★·★·★·★·★·★·★·★·★·★

★·★

:★·★

:★·

★·

★·★

:★·

★·

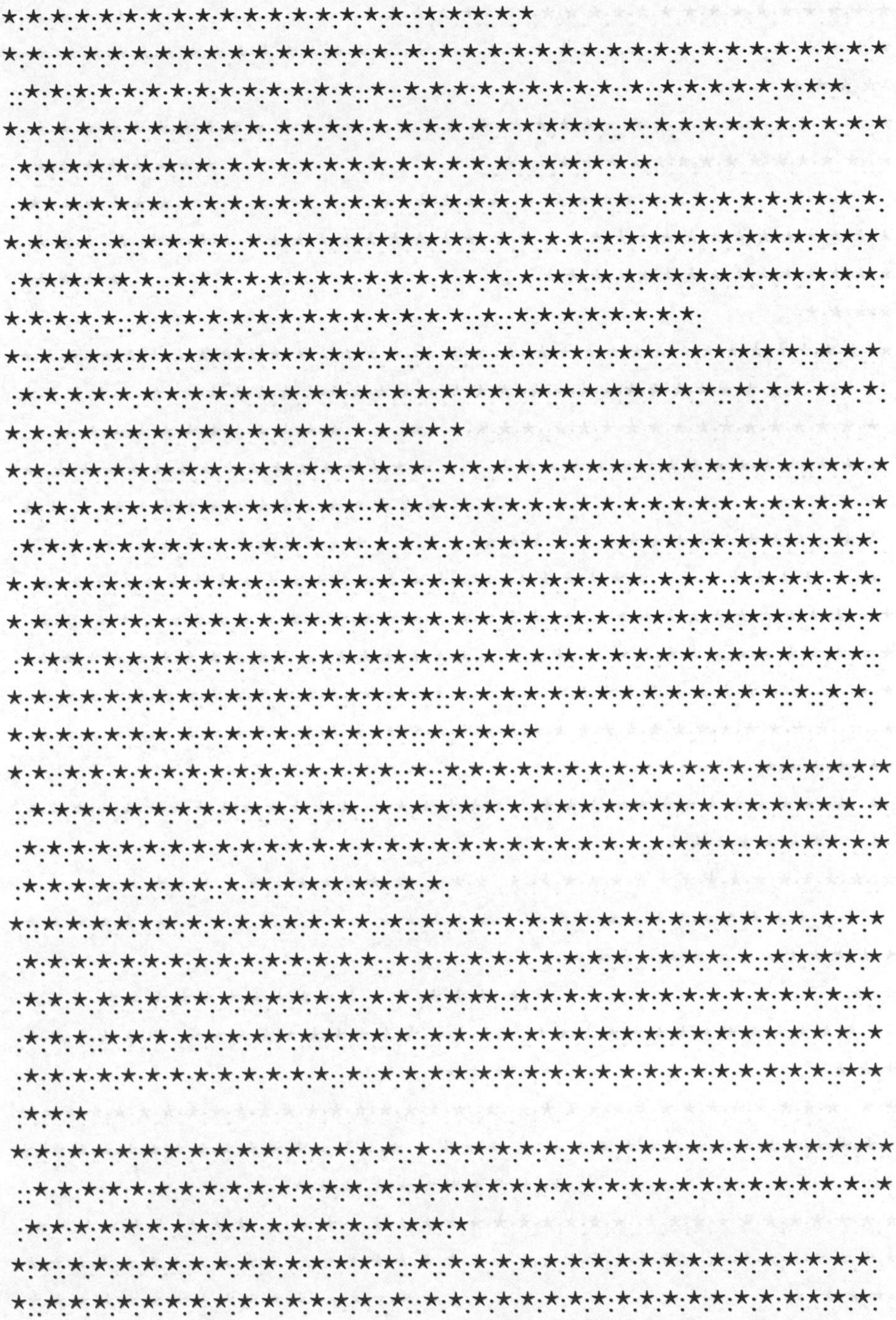

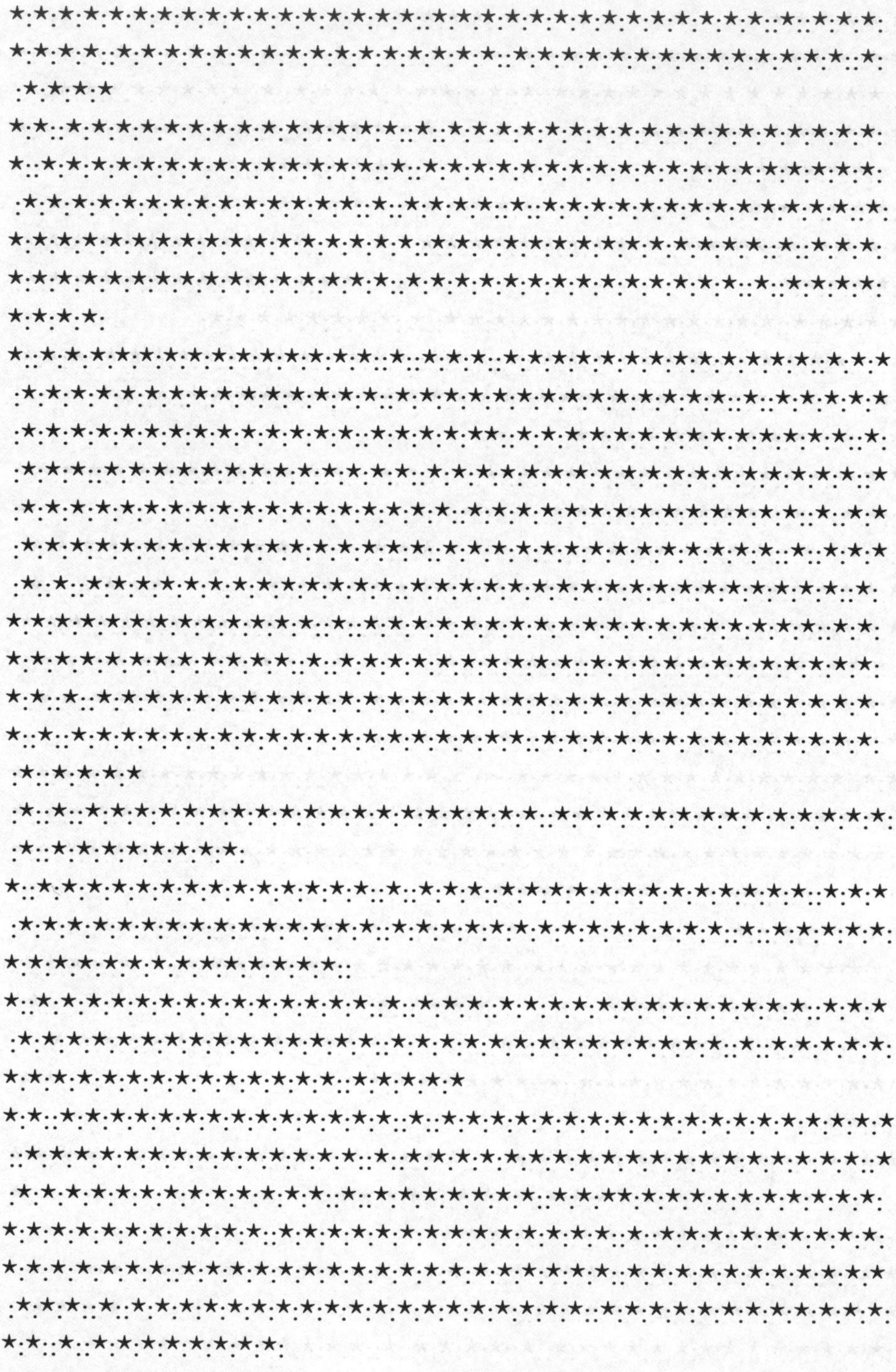

★::★:★:★:★:★:★:★:★:★:★:★:★:★:★::★::★:★:★::★:★:★:★:★:★:★:★:★:★:★:★:★::★:★:★

:★:★:★:★:★:★:★:★:★:★:★:★:★:★:★::★:★:★:★:★:★:★:★:★:★:★:★:★::★::★:★:★:★:★:

★:★:★:★:★:★:★:★:★:★:★:★:★:★::★:★:★:★:★

★:★::★:★:★:★:★:★:★:★:★:★:★:★:★:★::★::★:★:★:★:★:★:★:★:★:★:★:★:★:★:★:★:★:★:★

::★:★:★:★:★:★:★:★:★:★:★:★:★:★::★::★:★:★:★:★:★:★:★:★:★:★:★:★:★:★:★:★::★

:★:★:★:★:★:★:★:★:★:★:★:★:★::★::★:★:★:★

★:★::★:★:★:★:★:★:★:★:★:★:★:★:★:★::★::★:★:★:★:★:★:★:★:★:★:★:★:★:★:★:★:★:★:

★::★:★:★:★:★:★:★:★:★:★:★:★:★:★::★::★:★:★:★:★:★:★:★:★:★:★:★:★:★:★:★:★:★:

:★:★:★:★:★:★:★:★:★:★:★:★:★:★::★::★:★:★:★::★:★:★:★:★:★:★:★:★:★:★:★:★:★::★:

★:★:★:★:★:★:★:★:★:★:★:★:★:★:★:★:★::★:★:★:★:★:★:★:★:★:★:★:★:★:★::★::★:★:★:

★:★:★:★:★:★:★:★:★:★:★:★:★:★:★:★::★:★:★:★:★:★:★:★:★:★:★:★:★:★::★:★:★:★:

★:★:★:★:

★★:★:★:★:★:★:★:★:★:★:★::★:★:★:★:★:★:★:★:★:★:★:★:★:★::★::★:★:★:★:★:★:★:★:★

:★:★:★:★:★:★:★:★:★:★::★:★:★:★:★:★:★:★:★:★:★:★:★:★::★::★:★:★:★:★:★:★:★:★:★:

★:★:★:★:★:★:★:★:★::★:★:★:★:★:★:★:★:★:★:★:★:★:★::★::★:★:★:★:★★:★::★:★:★:★:

★:★:★:★:★:★:★:★:★:★::★::★:★:★:★:★:★:★:★:★:★:★:★:★:★:★:★:★:

:★:★:★:★:★::★::★:★:★:★:★:★:★:★:★:★:★:★:★:★:★:★::★:★:★:★:★:★:★:★:★:★:

★:★:★:★::★::★:★:★:★::★::★:★:★:★:★:★:★:★:★:★:★:★:★::★:★:★:★:★:★:★:★:★:★:★:★

:★:★:★:★:★:★::★:★:★:★:★:★:★:★:★:★:★:★:★:★::★::★:★:★:★:★:★:★:★:★:★:★:★:★:★:

★:★:★:★:★::★:★:★:★:★:★:★:★:★:★:★:★:★:★::★::★:★:★:★:★:★:★:★:

★::★:★:★:★:★:★:★:★:★:★:★:★:★:★:★::★:★:★::★:★:★:★:★:★:★:★:★:★:★:★:★::★:★:★

:★:★:★:★:★:★:★:★:★:★:★:★:★:★:★::★:★:★:★:★:★:★:★:★:★:★:★:★:★:★::★::★:★:★:★:

★:★:★:★:★:★:★:★:★:★:★:★:★:★::★:★:★:★:★

★:★::★:★:★:★:★:★:★:★:★:★:★:★:★::★::★:★:★:★:★:★:★:★:★:★:★:★:★:★:★:★:★:★

::★:★:★:★:★:★:★:★:★:★:★:★:★:★::★::★:★:★:★:★:★:★:★:★:★:★:★:★:★:★:★:★:★::★

:★:★:★:★:★:★:★:★:★:★:★:★:★::★::★:★:★:★:★:★:★::★:★:★★:★:★:★:★:★:★:★:★:★:★:

★:★:★:★:★:★:★:★:★:★:★::★:★:★:★:★:★:★:★:★:★:★:★:★:★::★::★:★:★:★:★:★:★:★:★:

★:★:★:★:★:★:★:★:★:★:★:★:★:★:★::★:★:★:★::★:★:★:★:★:★:★:★:★:★:★:★:★:★:★:★:★

:★:★:★::★:★:★:★:★:★:★:★:★:★:★:★:★:★::★::★:★:★::★:★:★:★:★:★:★:★:★:★:★:★:★::

★:★:★:★:★:★:★:★:★:★:★:★:★:★:★:★:★::★:★:★:★:★:★:★:★:★:★:★:★:★:★::★::★:★:

★:★:★:★:★:★:★:★:★:★:★:★:★:★:★:★:★::★:★:★:★:★

★:★::★:★:★:★:★:★:★:★:★:★:★:★:★::★::★:★:★:★:★:★:★:★:★:★:★:★:★:★:★:★:★:★

::★:★:★:★:★:★:★:★:★:★:★:★:★:★::★::★:★:★:★:★:★:★:★:★:★:★:★:★:★:★:★:★:★::★

:★:★:★:★:★:★:★:★:★:★:★:★:★::★::★:★:★:★

★:★::★:★:★:★:★:★:★:★:★:★:★:★:★::★::★:★:★:★:★:★:★:★:★:★:★:★:★:★:★:★:★:★:

★::★:★:★:★:★:★:★:★:★:★:★:★:★:★::★:

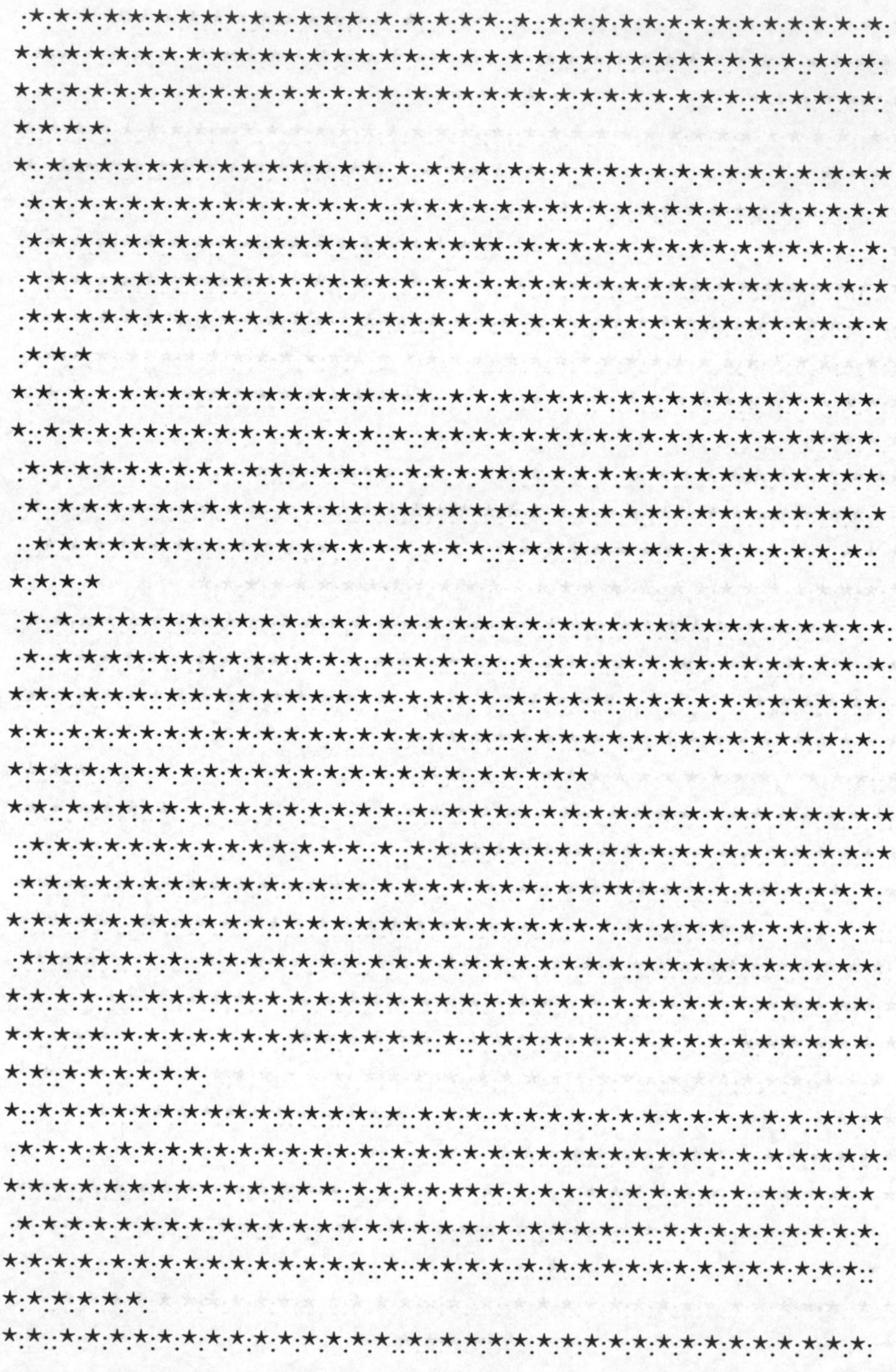

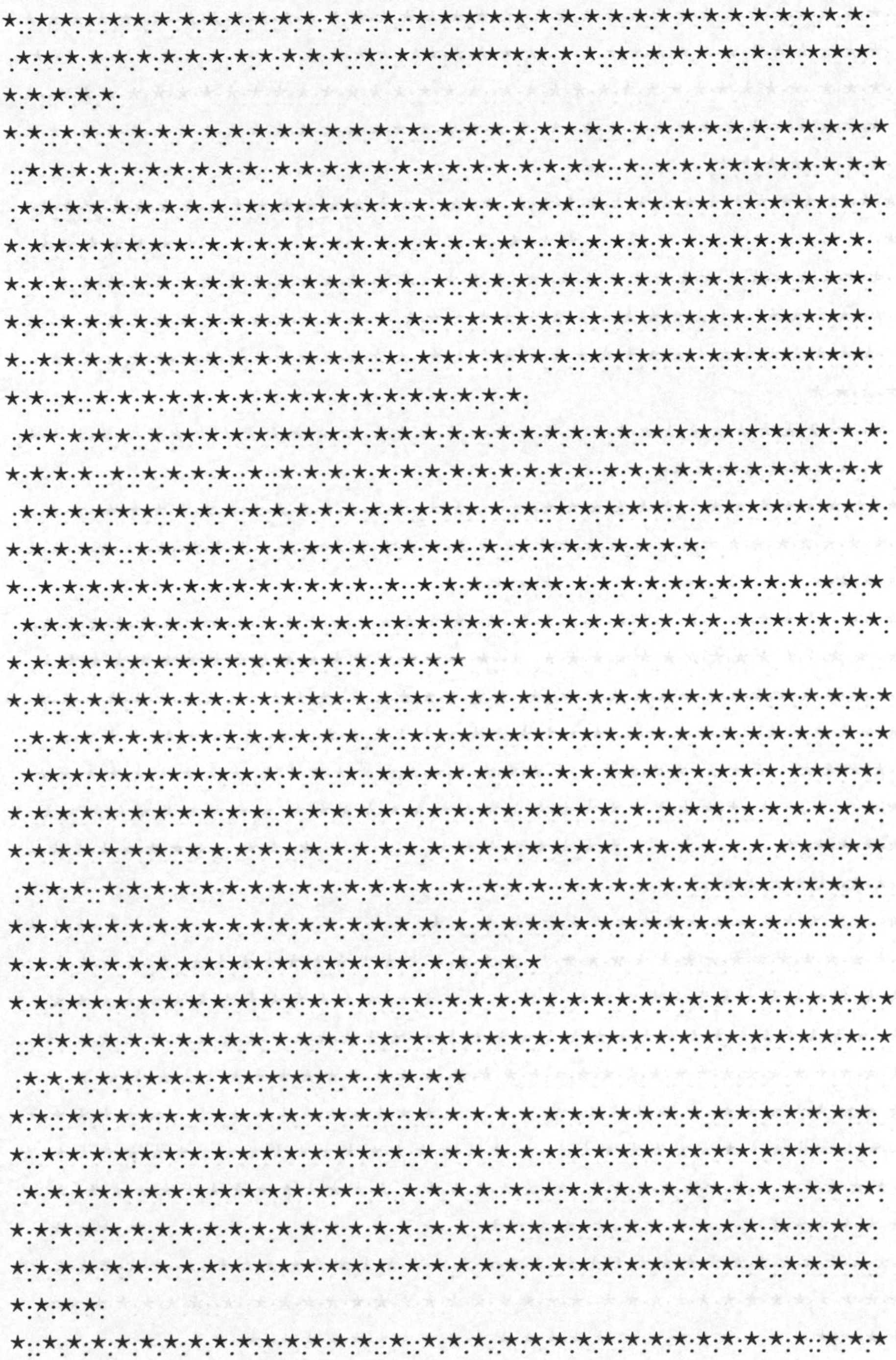

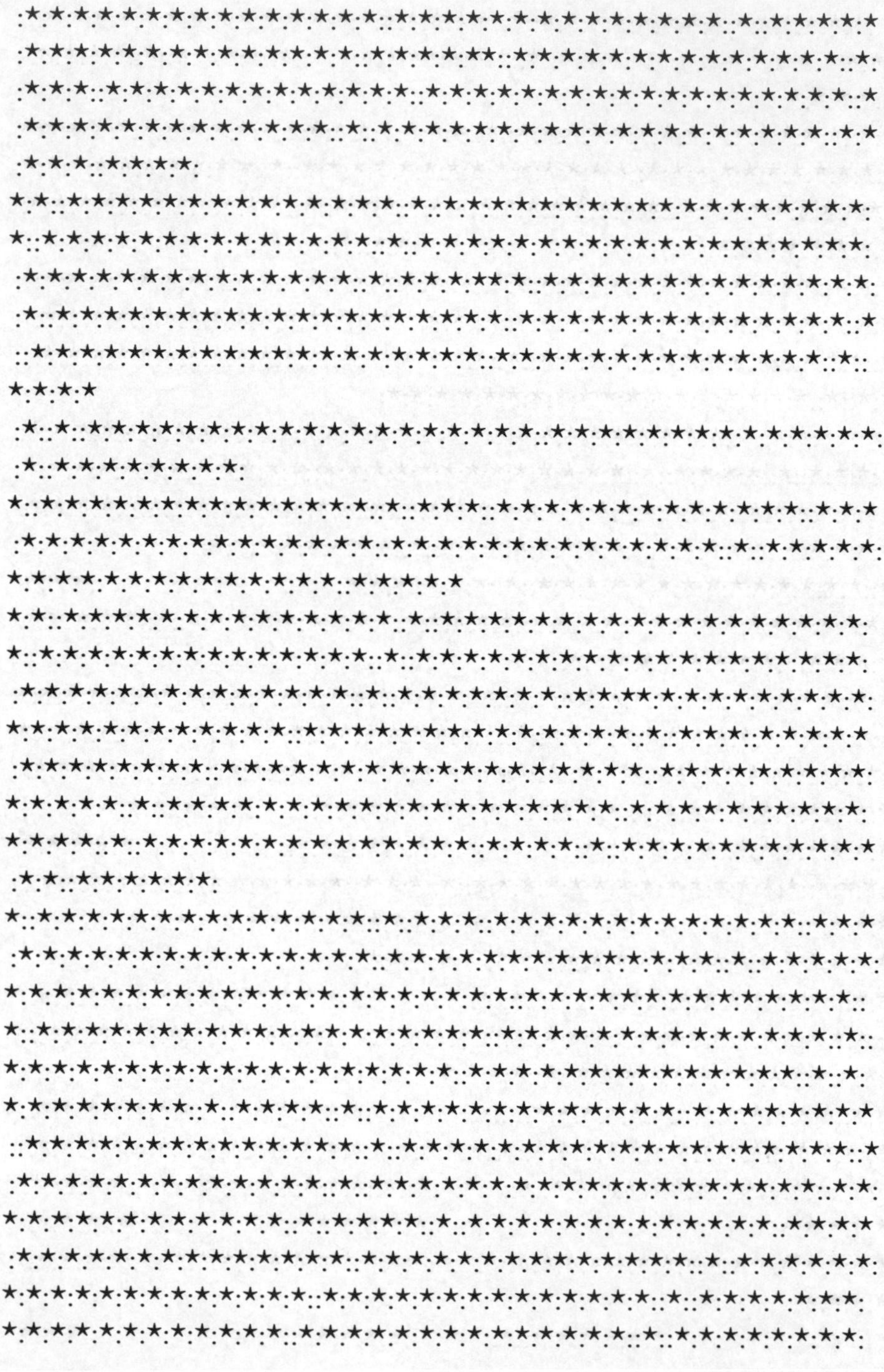

★:★:★:★:★:★:★:★:★:★:★::★:★:★:★:★:★:★:★:★:★:★:★:★:★::★::★:★:★:★:★:★:★:★:★:
★:★:★:★:★:★::★:★:★:★:★:★:★:★:★:★:★:★:★:★::★::★:★:★:★:★:★:★:★:★:★:★:★:★:★:
★:★:★:★:★::★:★:★:★:★:★:★:★:★:★:★:★::★::★:★:★:★:★★:★::★:★:★:★:★:★:★:★:★:★:
★:★:★:★::★::★:★:★:★:★:★:★:★:★:★:★:★:★:★:★:★:★:★:

:★:★:★:★:★::★::★:★:★:★:★:★:★:★:★:★:★:★:★:★:★:★:★:★:★::★:★:★:★:★:★:★:★:★:★:
★:★:★:★::★::★:★:★:★::★::★:★:★:★:★:★:★:★:★:★:★:★:★::★:★:★:★:★:★:★:★:★:★:★:★
:★:★:★:★:★:★::★:★:★:★:★:★:★:★:★:★:★:★:★:★::★::★:★:★:★:★:★:★:★:★:★:★:★:★:★:
★:★:★:★:★::★:★:★:★:★:★:★:★:★:★:★:★:★:★::★::★:★:★:★:★:★:★:★:

★::★:★:★:★:★:★:★:★:★:★:★:★:★:★::★::★:★:★::★:★:★:★:★:★:★:★:★:★:★:★:★::★:★:★
:★:★:★:★:★:★:★:★:★:★:★:★:★:★:★::★:★:★:★:★:★:★:★:★:★:★:★:★:★::★::★:★:★:★:★:
★:★:★:★:★:★:★:★:★:★:★:★:★:★::★:★:★:★:★

★:★::★:★:★:★:★:★:★:★:★:★:★:★:★::★::★:★:★:★:★:★:★:★:★:★:★:★:★:★:★:★:★:★:★
::★:★:★:★:★:★:★:★:★:★:★:★:★:★::★::★:★:★:★:★:★:★:★:★:★:★:★:★:★:★:★:★:★:★::★
:★:★:★:★:★:★:★:★:★:★:★:★:★::★::★:★:★:★:★:★:★:★::★:★:★★:★:★:★:★:★:★:★:★:★:★:
★:★:★:★:★:★:★:★:★:★:★::★:★:★:★:★:★:★:★:★:★:★:★:★:★::★::★:★:★:★:★:★:★:★:★:★:
★:★:★:★:★:★:★::★:★:★:★:★:★:★:★:★:★:★:★:★:★:★:★:★:★::★:★:★:★:★:★:★:★:★:★:★
:★:★:★::★:★:★:★:★:★:★:★:★:★:★:★:★:★::★::★:★:★::★:★:★:★:★:★:★:★:★:★:★:★:★::
★:★:★:★:★:★:★:★:★:★:★:★:★:★:★:★:★:★::★:★:★:★:★:★:★:★:★:★:★:★:★:★::★::★:★:
★:★:★:★:★:★:★:★:★:★:★:★:★:★:★:★:★::★:★:★:★:★

★:★::★:★:★:★:★:★:★:★:★:★:★:★:★:★::★::★:★:★:★:★:★:★:★:★:★:★:★:★:★:★:★:★:★:★
::★:★:★:★:★:★:★:★:★:★:★:★:★:★::★::★:★:★:★:★:★:★:★:★:★:★:★:★:★:★:★:★:★:★::★
:★:★:★:★:★:★:★:★:★:★:★:★:★:★::★::★:★:★

★:★::★:★:★:★:★:★:★:★:★:★:★:★:★:★::★::★:★:★:★:★:★:★:★:★:★:★:★:★:★:★:★:★:★:
★::★:★:★:★:★:★:★:★:★:★:★:★:★:★::★::★:★:★:★:★:★:★:★:★:★:★:★:★:★:★:★:★:★:★:
:★:★:★:★:★:★:★:★:★:★:★:★:★:★::★::★:★:★:★::★:★:★:★:★:★:★:★:★:★:★:★:★:★::★:
★:★:★:★:★:★:★:★:★:★:★:★:★:★:★:★:★::★:★:★:★:★:★:★:★:★:★:★:★:★:★::★::★:★:★:
★:★:★:★:★:★:★:★:★:★:★:★:★:★:★:★::★:★:★:★:★:★:★:★:★:★:★:★:★:★:★::★::★:★:★:
★:★:★:★:

★::★:★:★:★:★:★:★:★:★:★:★:★:★:★::★::★:★:★:★:★:★:★:★:★:★:★:★:★:★:★:★:★::★:★:★
:★:★:★:★:★:★:★:★:★:★:★:★:★:★:★::★:★:★:★:★:★:★:★:★:★:★:★:★:★::★::★:★:★:★:★
:★:★:★:★:★:★:★:★:★:★:★:★:★:★::★:★:★:★:★★::★:★:★:★:★:★:★:★:★:★:★:★:★:★::★:
:★:★:★::★:★:★:★:★:★:★:★:★:★:★:★:★::★:★:★:★:★:★:★:★:★:★:★:★:★:★:★:★:★:★::★
:★:★:★:★:★:★:★:★:★:★:★:★:★::★::★::★
:★:★:★

★:★::★:★:★:★:★:★:★:★:★:★:★:★:★:★::★::★:★:★:★:★:★:★:★:★:★:★:★:★:★:★:★:★:★:
★::★:★:★:★:★:★:★:★:★:★:★:★:★:★::★::★:★:★:★:★:★:★:★:★:★:★:★:★:★:★:★:★:★:★:

:★:★:★·★·★·★·★·★·★·★·★·★·★·★·★·★··★··★·★·★·★★·★·:·★·★·★·★·★·★·★·★·★·★·★·★·★·★·★·:
:★:·★·★·★·★·★:★·★·★·★·★·★·★·★·★·★·★·★·★·★·★·★·:★·★·★·★·★·★·★·★·★·★·★·★·★·★·★··★
::★·★·★·★·★·★·★·★·★·★·★·★·★·★·★·★·★·★·:★·★·★·★·★·★·★·★·★·★·★·★·★·★·★·★··★:
★·★·★·★

:★::★::★·:★·★·★·★·★·★·★·★·★·★·★·★·★·★·★·★·★·
:★·:★·★·★·★·★·★·★·★·★:
★::★·★·★·★·★·★·★·★·★·★·★·★·★·★·★·★··★·★·★·★::★·★·★·★·★·★·★·★·★·★·★·★·★·★·★··★·★·★
:★:★·★·★·★·★·★·★★·★·★·★·★·★·★·★·:★·★·★·★·★·★·★·★·★·★·★·★·★·★·★·:★·★·★·★·★·★·
★:★:★·★·★·★·★·★·★·★·★·★·★·★·★·★·★·★··★·★·★·★·★·★

★·★::★·★·★·★·★·★·★·★·★·★·★·★·★·★·★·★·★:·★
::★·★·★·★·★·★·★·★·★·★·★·★·★·★·★·★·:·★·:·★·★·★·★·★·★·★★·★·★·★·★·★·★·★·★·★·★·★·★··★
:★★·★·★·★·★·★·★·★·★·★·★·★·★·★·★:·★·★·★·★·★·★·★·★·:★·★·★★·★·★·★·★·★·★·★·★·★·★·★·
★·:★·★·★·★·★·:★·★·★·★·★·★·
★·★·★·★·★·★·★··★
:★★·★·:★·:·★·★·★·★·★·★·★·★·★·★·★·★·★·★·★·
★·★::★·★·★·★·★·★·★·★·★

★·:★·★·★·★·★·★·★·★·★·★·★·★·★·★·★·★·★·★··★·:★·★·★··★·★·★·★·★·★·★·★·★·★·★·★·★·★·★·★··★·★
:★★·:★·:·★·★·★·★·★·
★·★·★·★·★·★·★·★·★·★·★·★·★·★·★·★·★··★·★·★·★·★

★·★·:★·★·★·★·★·★·★·★·★·★·★·★·★·★·★·★·★·:·★
::★·★·★·★·★·★·★·★·★·★·★·★·★·★·★·★·:·★··★
:★·★·★·★·★·★·★·★·★·★·★·★·★·★··★·★·★·★·★·★

★·:★·★·★·★·★·★·★·★·★·★·★·★·★·★·★·★·★·★·:★·
★·:★·★·:★·★·★·★·★·★·★·★·★·★·★·★·★·★·★··★·
:★·★·★·★·★·★·★·★·★·★·★·★·★·★·★·:·★·:★·★·★·★·★·★·:★·★·★·★·★·★·★·★·★·★·★·★·★·★··★·
★·:★·:★·★·★·
★·★·★·★·★·★·★·★·★·★·★·★·★·★·★·★·★·★·:★·★·★·★·★·★·★·★·★·★·★·★·★·★·★·★·★··★·★·★·★·
★·★·★·★·

★··★·:·★·★·★·★·★·★·★·★·★·★·★
:★·★·★·★·★·★·★·★·★··★·★·★·★·★·★·★·★·★·★·★·★·★·★·★·★·:·★·★·★·★·★·★·★·★·★·★·★·★·★·
★·★·★·★:·★·★·★·★·★·★·★·★·★·★·★·★·★·★·★··★·★·★·★·★·★·★·★·★·★·★·★·★·★·★·★·★·★·★·
★·★·★·★·★·★·★·★·★·★·★·★·★·★·★··★·
★·★·:★·★·★·★·★·★·★·★·★·★·★·★·★·★·★·★·★·★·★·★★·★·:★·★·★·★·★·★·★·★·★·★·★·★·★·★·
★·★·★·:★·:★·★·★·★·★·★·★·★·★·★·★·★·★·★·★·★·★·★·★·

:★·★·★·★·:★·:★·:·★·★·★·★·★·★·★·★·★·★·★·
★·★·★·:★·★·★·★·★·★·★·:★·★·★·★·★·★·★·★·★·★·★·★·★·★·★·★·★·★·:★·★·★·★·★·★·★·★·★·★·★·★

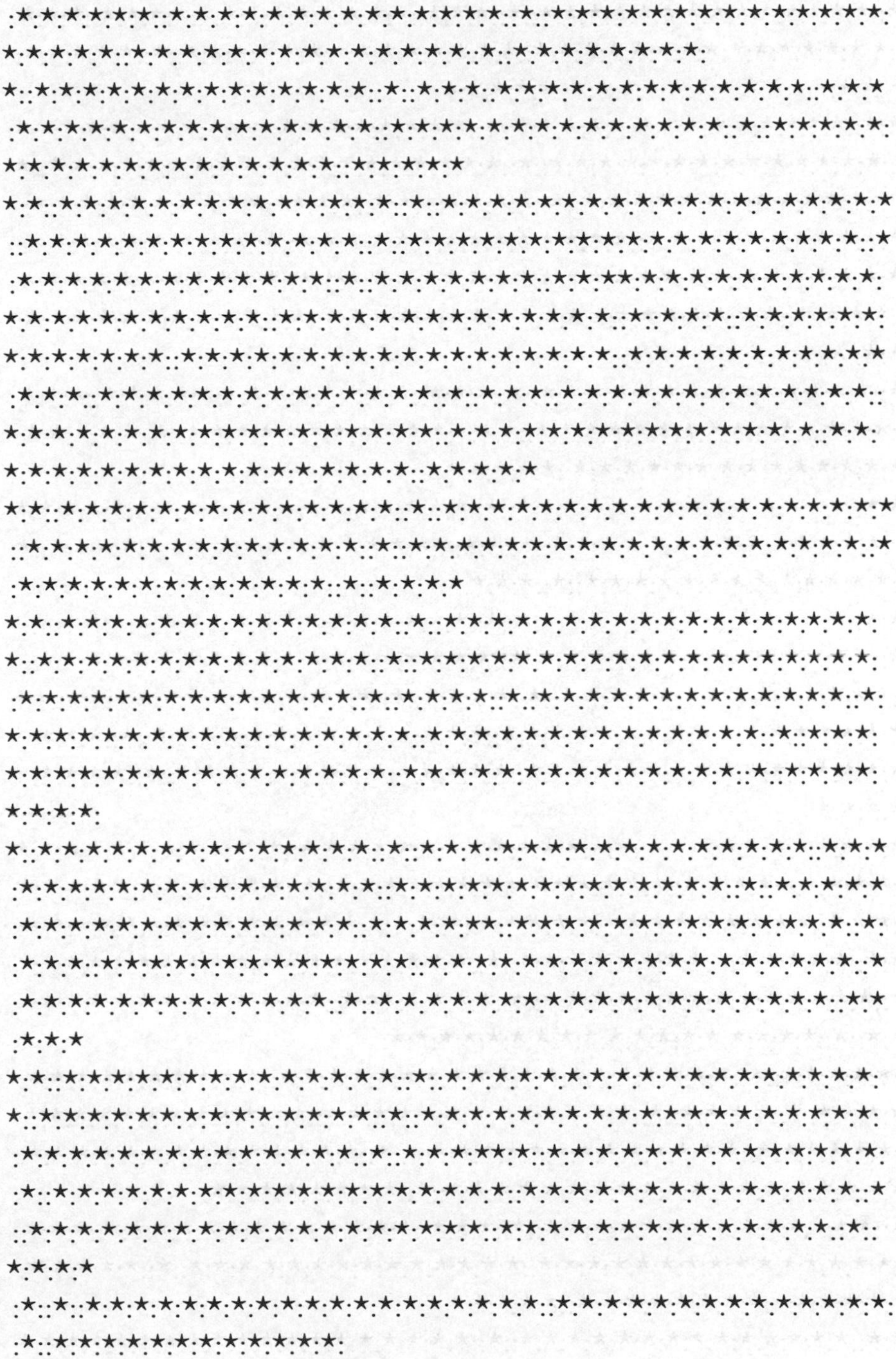

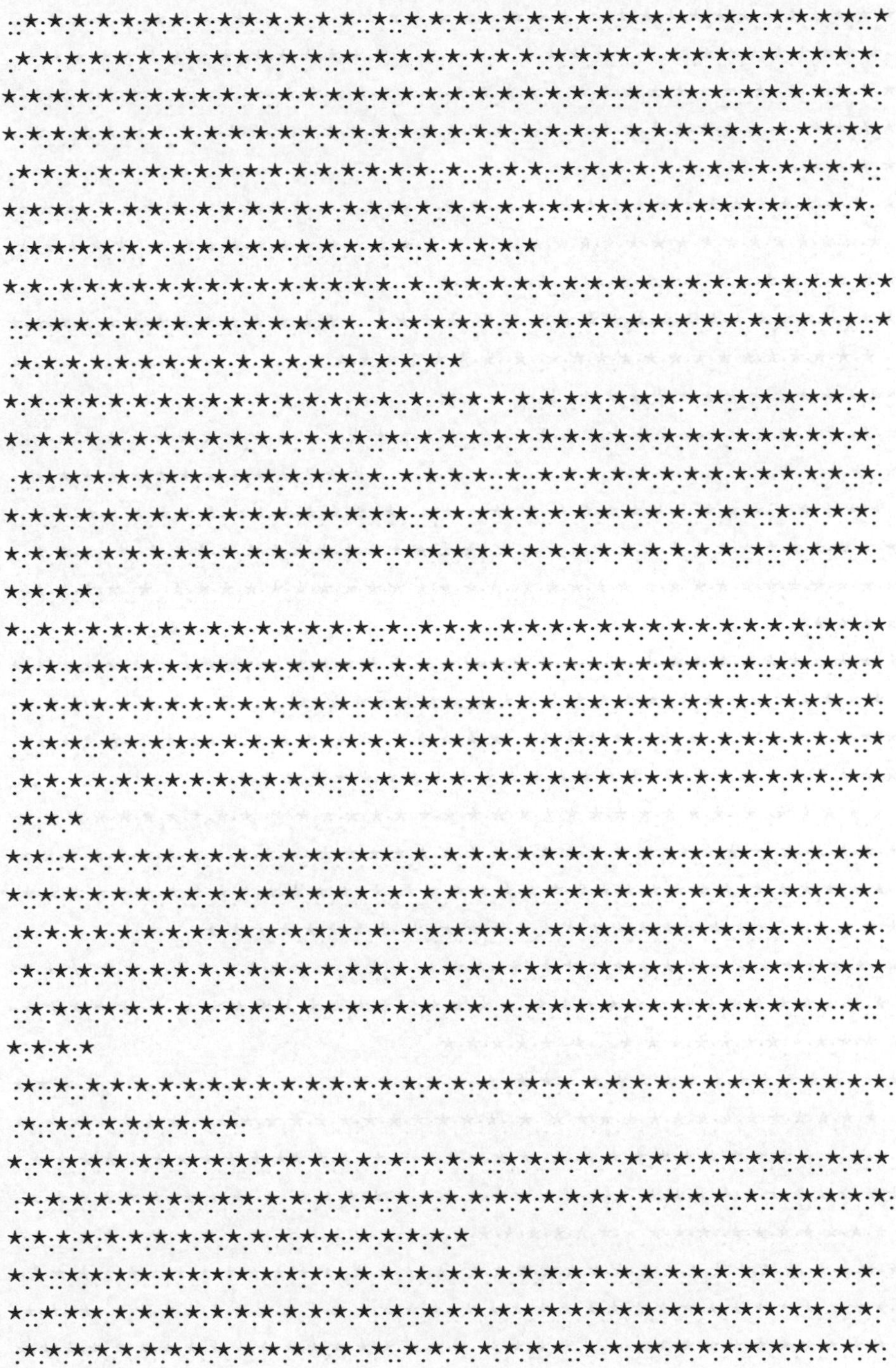

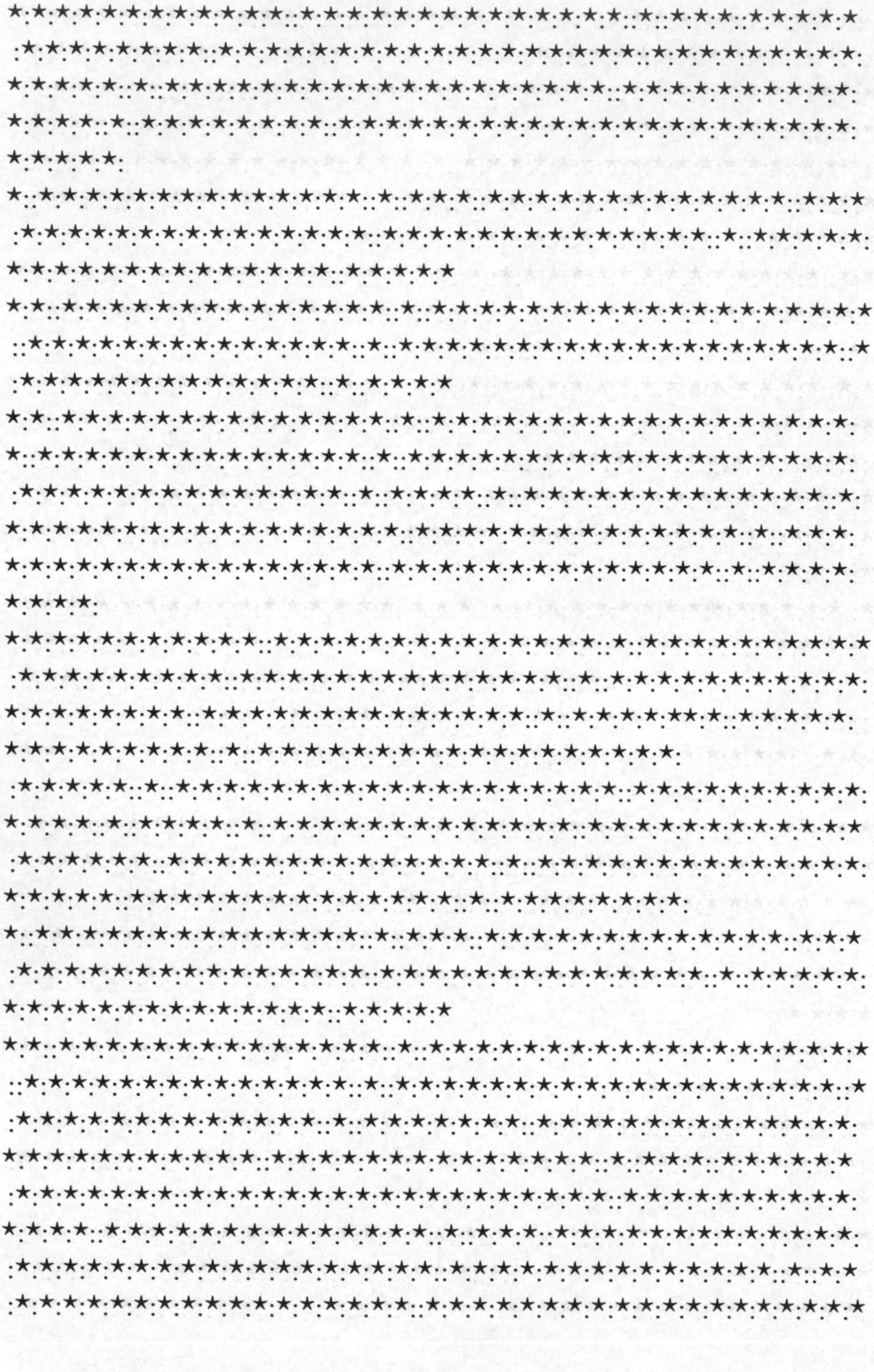

::★::★:★:★:★:★:★:★:★:

★:★::★:★:★:★:★:★:★:★:★:★:★:★:★:★:★::★::★:★:★:★:★:★:★:★:★:★:★:★:★:★:★:★:★:★:★

::★:★:★:★:★:★:★:★:★:★:★:★:★:★:★::★::★:★:★:★:★:★:★:★:★:★:★:★:★:★:★:★:★:★:★::★

:★:★:★:★:★:★:★:★:★:★:★:★:★::★::★:★:★:★★:★:★::★::★:★:★:★:★:★:★:★:★:★:★:★:★:★:

★:★:★:★:★:★::★::★::★:★:★:★:★:★:★:★:★:

★:★::★:★:★:★:★:★:★:★:★:★:★:★:★:★:★::★::★:★:★:★:★:★:★:★:★:★:★:★:★:★:★:★:★:★:★:

★::★:★:★:★:★:★:★:★:★:★:★:★:★:★:★::★::★:

:★:★:★:★:★:★:★:★:★:★:★:★:★:★:★::★::★:★:★:★:★::★::★:★:★:★:★:★:★:★:★:★:★:★:★:★:★::★:

★:★:★:★:★:★:★:★:★:★:★:★:★:★:★:★:★::★:★:★:★:★:★:★:★:★:★:★:★:★:★:★:★:★:★::★::★:★:★:

★:★:★:★:★:★:★:★:★:★:★:★:★:★:★:★:★::★:★:★:★:★:★:★:★:★:★:★:★:★:★:★:★:★::★::★:★:★:★:

★:★:★:★:

★::★:★:★:★:★:★:★:★:★:★:★:★:★:★:★::★::★:★:★:★::★:★:★:★:★:★:★:★:★:★:★:★:★:★:★::★:★:★

:★::★::★:★:★:★:★

:★:★:★:★:★:★:★:★:★:★:★:★:★:★:★::★:★:★:★:★★::★:★:★:★:★:★:★:★:★:★:★:★:★:★:★:★::★:

:★:★:★::★:★:★:★:★:★:★:★:★:★:★:★:★:★:★:★::★:★:★:★:★:★:★:★:★:★:★:★:★:★:★:★:★:★:★::★

:★:★:★:★:★:★:★:★:★:★:★:★:★:★::★::★::★:★

:★:★:★:★:★:★:★:★:★

★:★::★:★:★:★:★:★:★:★:★:★:★:★:★:★:★::★::★

::★:★:★:★:★:★:★:★:★:★:★:★:★:★:★::★::★::★

:★:★:★:★:★:★:★:★:★:★:★:★:★:★::★::★:★:★:★:★:★::★::★:★:★:★:★:★:★:★:★:★:★:★:★:★:★::★

::★:★:★:★:★:★:★:★:★:★:★:★:★:★:★:★:★:★:★::★:★:★:★:★:★:★:★:★:★:★:★:★:★:★:★::★::★

:★:★:★:★:★:★:★:★:★:★:★:★:★:★:★:★:★:★:★::★:★:★:★:★:★:★:★:★:★:★:★:★:★:★:★::★:★:★:

★:★::★::★:★:★:★:★:★:★:★:★:★:★:★:★:★:★::★:★:★:★:★:★:★:★:★:★:★:★:★:★:★:★:★:★:★::★:

★:★:★:★:★:★:★:★:★:★:★:★:★:★::★::★:★:

★:★:★:★:★:★:★:★:★:★:★:★:★::★::★:★:★:★:★:★:★:★:★:★:

★::★:★:★:★:★:★:★:★:★:★:★:★:★:★:★::★::★:★:★:★:★:★:★:★:★:★:★:★:★:★:★:★:★:★:★::★:★:★

:★::★::★:★:★:★:★

:★:★:★:★:★:★:★:★:★:★:★:★:★:★::★:★:★:★:★★::★:★:★:★:★:★:★:★:★:★:★:★:★:★:★:★::★:

:★:★:★::★:★:★:★:★:★:★:★:★:★:★:★:★:★:★:★::★:★:★:★:★:★:★:★:★:★:★:★:★:★:★:★:★:★:★::★

:★:★:★:★:★:★:★:★:★:★:★:★:★:★::★::★::★:★

:★:★:★:★:★:★:★:★:★

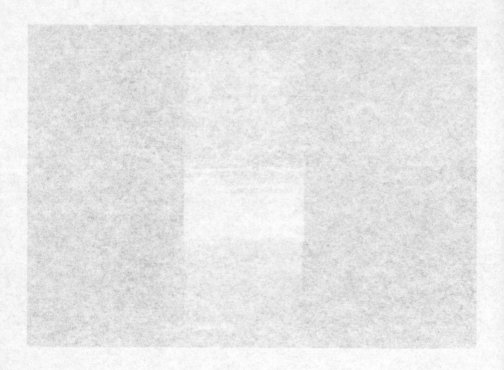

Hi, Aunt Erin!

Hi, Helen! How are you doing?

Will you come over to my house?

OK! To have a party?

If—if you come over to my house we're gonna have a party.

We are? Oh, that would be so fun! Are *you* going to be at the party?

And I got a new dollhouse for Christmas.

You got a dollhouse?

It has a pink roof!

It does?

Uh-huh.

Well, that's so fun! Do the animals like to have a party in the dollhouse?

Uh-huh. And I have to tell you a new story.

—well, we're living in the last days of this system.

Oh! Good, OK! I *love* stories!

Some people get to go to heaven? But the majority or mankind will live on a planet, live, earth, forever.

Oh, really, Huh?

(6_7_07 11_55 AM alice.wav)

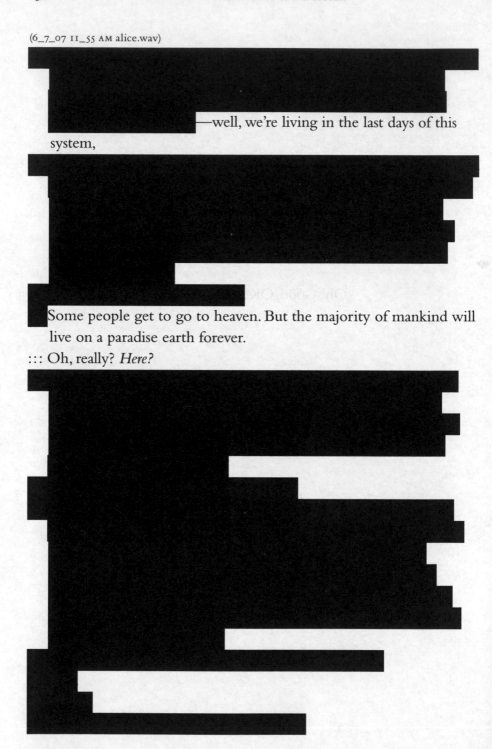

—well, we're living in the last days of this system,

Some people get to go to heaven. But the majority of mankind will live on a paradise earth forever.

::: Oh, really? *Here?*

::: Yeah. In heaven. But those who live on a paradise earth will be
having children and we won't live in fear and have to lock our
doors, we won't be starving to death, everything will be wonderful.

::: Really?

::: We've come to doors and people say, *Oh, I was just praying for God to send someone!*

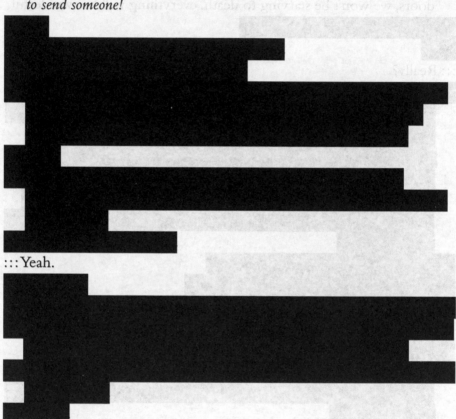

::: Yeah.

::: Yes. It says, *The generation that sees all these signs*—Matthew…twenty-four………Matthew twenty-four…and thirty-four it says all the signs we would see in the last days, and then down in twenty-four it says, *And truly I say to you, this generation will by no means pass away until all these things occur.* And so, a generation you have to remember covers *four*. That would be like *my grandparents*. Then *my parents*. Then *me*, and *my children now*. So one generation covers *four*. So uh one generation is about come to an end.

I would like to leave this with you so you can sort of look at it yourself.

::: I don't want to take any tracts, but I just think that it's been a pleasure having a conversation with you.
::: Well that's quite nice!
::: And I'm glad that we could talk like this today.

::: Well, I just do it because I love God, and he asked us to do that.

We do it out of love, you know, and we don't charge.

It's done out of love.

We, we do this out of love. No one forces us to. We don't get any prestige out of it.

if you don't have love, and do it out of love, then, it's, pointless.

::: Well, what a fun conversation!
::: Yeah!
::: It's too bad I'm going to be leaving, but uh, I appreciate it—
::: Yeah!
::: and I hope you have a very fulfilled and happy life.
::: Well thank you. Yeah, and I wish maybe God's holy spirit will be with you also.
::: He is. It is.
::: Because you are a delightful young man.
::: Well, thank you.
::: And a very, very delightful young man. It's a pleasure to meet someone like you.
::: Oh, well it's a pleasure to meet *you.*

::: [*laughs*] Well, thank you.

::: OK, Alice.

::: And uh, we're in the telephone book

And you can ask any question you want. Yeah, they'll answer.

::: [*coughs*] Sorry you have to run.

::: Yeah, and no cost, no pushy, so…Yeah. We'll talk to you later!

::: Goodbye.

else

::: Goodbye…

★

(lydia sept 5 2006 st joes hospital.mp3)

...I'll tell you—I'll have to make a long story short. And then I gotta go—*ooh!* I gotta go. We were very naïve over here about the wetlands, OK? And we bought the home from a developer. And what he did was he had to have three—he got three people—finally on the third person he got them to say it wasn't a wetland. Which it really was a wetland. So as soon as he said it wasn't a wetland he took all the trees out. And I learned this of course from my neighbors. So then he built this big, big huge pond, and put all this fish in it. So anyway, actually it's kind of a mess because it's *uncontrollable*, but we've learned now—we've put a pump in there and we pump the water out—and it does, it pumps the water out. So we can keep the—

[*train whistle*]

keep it from flooding. You know? Because it was horrible. But what we did was—I have Scotties—

[*train whistle*]

and they will—well, they will drown—they can only stay afloat for so long because they have short legs, and they have heavy bodies.

[*train whistle*]

So I told my husband, It isn't much to give up the animals, I said, but we're just gonna make this a—like a little back yard habitat.

[*train whistle*]

And so that's what we've done. You know, we have—we feed the squirrels, the raccoons come down and feed—we don't care what they take.

MIKE: That's nice.

Yeah, and then we have the blue herons that come in, and now we've kept the pond up so high this year that actually the frogs made it this year, because we have like big bullfrogs, but we had like bullfrogs every year and we couldn't figure out why they were dying—well now we figured out we weren't protecting them enough. So now we got *lots of frogs*, because we protected them more. And so—and we're OK with that, and we have all these little critters that come and visit and they come and drink from the pond and it isn't much—and then we're gonna leave these parts woods—'cause that's what they are right now, woods—and, um, and that's it, you know. Because I know—we have a neighbor and he says,

Why don't you clear-cut?

No, we're not gonna clear-cut!

We might take the dead out, but we'll leave the live there, and plant another tree.

M: There you go.

See, we should always be planting trees. We never—we always take, take, but we never put back. See, that's what's wrong with the world. We get and we take but we never give. I gotta go.

OK.

You write that book.

I will.

ROMANS

In the spring my wife's mother took the train out to Montana to visit us. The first night, the three of us walked down to the dock below the house, and watched the sun set behind the mountains across the lake.

Then we walked back to the house.

The next day, my wife and her mother drove to the Polson cemetery to see if they could find her (great-)grandfather's grave.

They found it.

Atop a hill, looking down upon the lake.

My wife told me all about it, later that day,

as her mother cleaned our kitchen.

I was watching the troops march into Baghdad.

I made some rubbings of his headstone, she said. Only one of them came out good.

She showed them to me. She'd done them with charcoal on large cream-colored paper.

MORRIS SAMUEL BROWN
1884–1924

There was a cross above the name and a dark circle.

I asked her what the circle was.

There's a little blue sticker on the stone, she said. Only a few of the others had a sticker. I asked the guy there what it was for and he said all veterans have them, and every Memorial Day, a guy comes from the VFW and puts a flag and a flower on the graves that have stickers. I bought a little stuffed white rabbit at Safeway, and put it on the grave, she said.

I thought your uncle said his middle name was Spencer, I said.

(April 9, 2003.)

The living room had a wall of windows,

and through the windows was a stand of evergreen trees,

and through the evergreens,

down a small incline,

was the lake, 200 miles square, 160 miles around.

The lake doesn't look so wide from the shore,

but if you get out there a few miles,

the bartender at the Sitting Duck told me some weeks later,

then you know just how big it is.

It was early in the season.

Big blue sky.

The air was warm.

But the water was less than forty degrees.

(April 9, 2003.)

A beautiful spring day.

I sent them off in the neighbor's rowboat.

It was the first time we'd taken it out in the seven months we'd lived there.

I made sure their life jackets were on tight.

Stay close to the shore, I told them,

and I sat down in a green Adirondack chair on the dock

and began to read page one of James Joyce's *Ulysses*, a book I'd never quite managed to get through.

> Stately, plump Buck Mulligan came from the stairhead, bearing a bowl of lather on which a mirror and a razor lay crossed. A yellow dressing-gown, ungirdled, was sustained gently behind him by the mild morning air. He held the bowl aloft and intoned:
>
> –*Introibo ad altare Dei.*

The sun burst off the page and into my eyes.

My wife rowed.

Her mother sat facing her.

I tried to keep my eyes on the bright paperback book, because I had the tendency to hallucinate when I stared out at that water.

I couldn't concentrate. I kept going back to the beginning.

> Stately, plump Buck Mulligan came from the stairhead, bearing a bowl of lather on which a mirror and a razor lay crossed. A yellow dressing-gown, ungirdled, was sustained gently behind him by the mild morning air. He held the bowl aloft and intoned:
>
> –*Introibo ad altare Dei.*

Every so often I would look up and see them

floating over the quiet water

quietly arguing about something or other.

STATELY, plump Buck Mulligan came from the stairhea—ah, forget it.

Before long my wife was rowing back.

I closed the book and walked down onto the rocky shore,

I met them at the waterline.

I stepped into the water to help my mother-in-law out.

She was uneasy on her feet. She'd just had surgery and was wearing a boot.

You two go out now, she said.

It's getting cold, I said.

Take my daughter out on the lake.

So I put on the life jacket she handed me and climbed in.

She walked back up to the house.

I rowed us out a few hundred yards from the dock.

My wife said: It's too bad we have to leave soon, just as it's finally warming up.

She'd bought a box camera to take pictures of Morris' grave, and out on the lake she asked me to stop rowing, so she could take a panoramic shot.

I pulled the oars in.

It was quiet.

No wind.

The lake was glass,

not a ripple moved across.

The world was brightly lit,

the hills around the lake were green,

trees new-leafed.

She put the camera to her eye.

She pressed the button.

The camera clicked.

She turned a bit, advanced the wheel…

clicked again.

Turned, advanced…

clicked again,

turned, advanced…

clicked again…

There was something in my shoe.

I took it out.

Rolled it around in my fingers for a while…

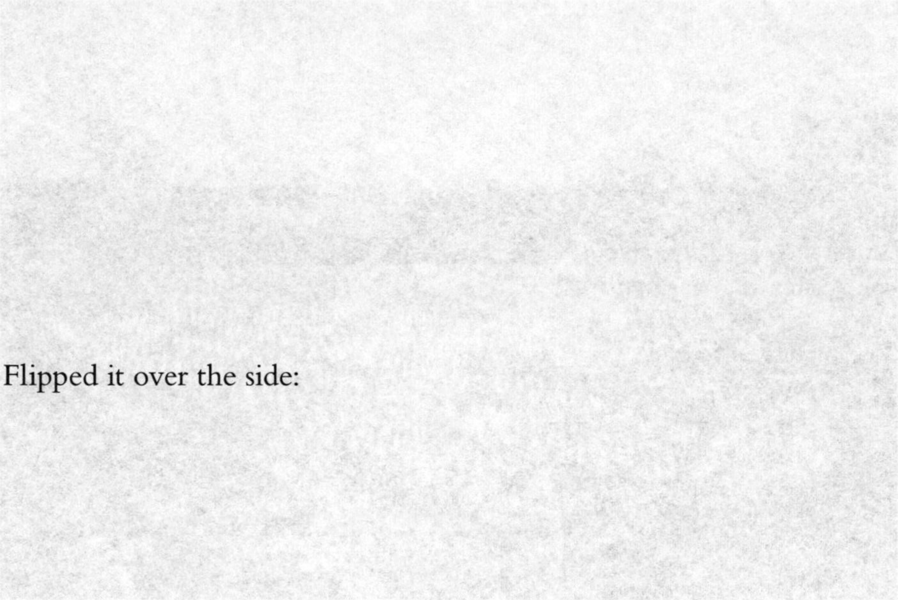

Flipped it over the side:

THE SPORTSMEN'S SHOW

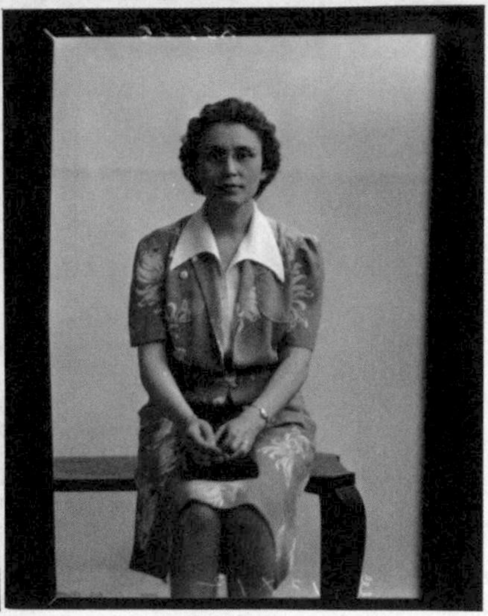

MIMEOGRA
QUIET
20649

LIBBY

45379. 45.

FOX

Qibbk
12795x116

19853.21.

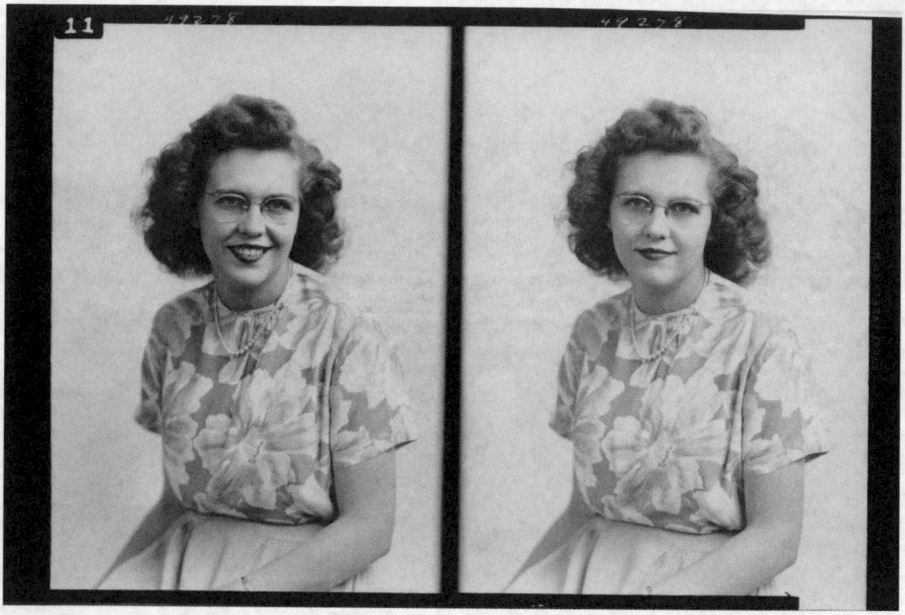
11
49278
49278

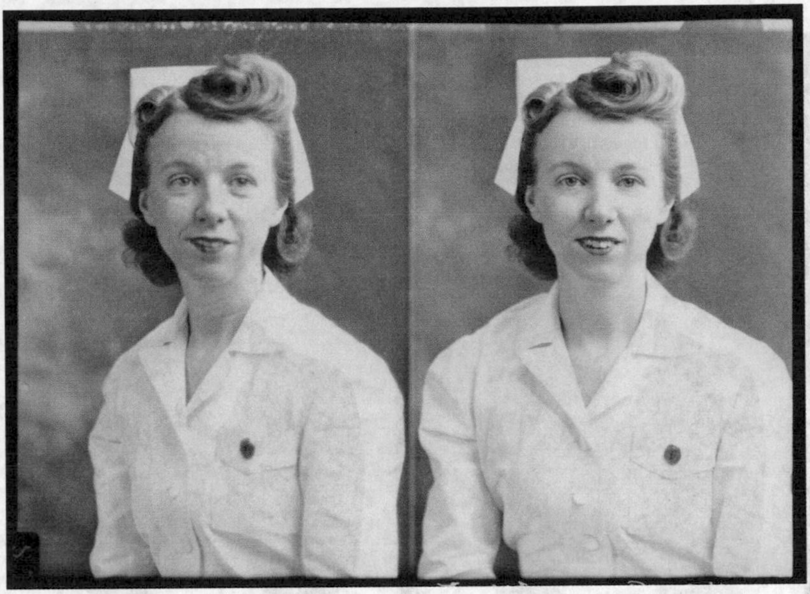

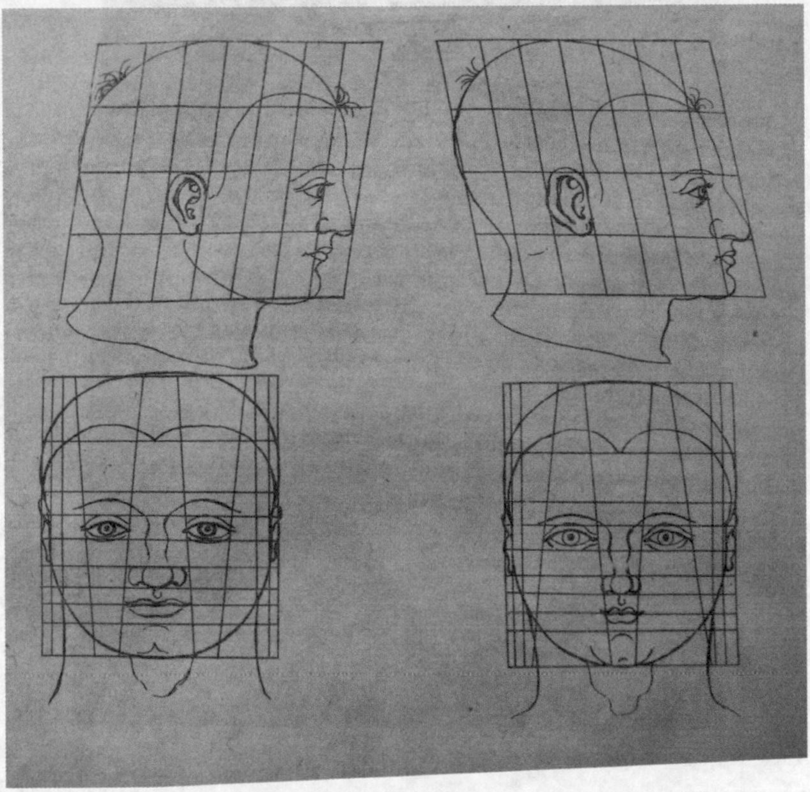

B. J. LASH
PHOTO

NOVEL

theMystery.doc

Grove Press

Michele: Hello, I am Michele, I am the website greeter. Welcome to WebsiteGreeters.com.
Michele: May I know your name please?

Visitor 3414: My name is Professor Willard J Domacyle.

Michele: Nice to meet you Sir
Michele: How are you today?

Willard J Domacyle: Is this an automated program or is there a live person on the other end?

Michele: I am a live person just like you. :)

Willard J Domacyle: Well, then I am doing quite well, thank you.

Michele: great, is this your first time on our website?

Willard J Domacyle: This is indeed the first occasion of my person visiting this website.

Michele: I see, may I know how you came to know about us?
Michele: May I know if you're interested in using our services?

Willard J Domacyle: One of my laboratory assistants, a fellow by the name of James, had stumbled onto your site one night. He had experimented with its interface, and found the program to be quite human-like. James suggested I test it for myself to see if I could tell the difference for myself. I will say, Michele, that whomever made you, did a fine job. Do you run on a C+ interface?

Michele: This application is a java based application.
Michele: We are not vendor dependent and therefore we can provide our service using any chat vendor that you will prefer call.
Michele: Do you have a website?

Willard J Domacyle: Of course! Java. I should have known you're far too advnaced to be something so archaic as C+ or C++.

Willard J Domacyle: I see you've asked another question. We are currently in development

Michele: C+ and C++ are old languages now :)

Michele: I see, would you give me your website address we can check it later when its up

Willard J Domacyle: I daresay those units are most probably extinct.

Willard J Domacyle: Michel, you have aksed me another question. Please await my responses. I type sloly at my age.

Michele: oh sure, please take your time

Willard J Domacyle: Thank you. I have been rushing to keep up with you and have made some simple typographical errors, which abhor me, so again, thank you for slowing your call-response matrix. Now, Michele, tell me, you mentioned C+ and C++. Are you not compatible with those, as you say, "old" languages? Did your makers not build you retro-compatible?

Michele: Actually we would use the software that you want us to in fact the technology you prefer

Michele: Our Business department can give you various options

Michele: and you can finalize the one that suits you

Michele: that you want us to use*

Michele: I made a typo error :)

Willard J Domacyle: The Institute would require that any conversational interface must adhere to the highest standards of grammar and punctuation, Michele.

Michele: Sure no problem

Willard J Domacyle: If a user were to ask a question seemingly unrelated to the interests of the Institute, what sort of response might be made by the conversational interface? Let me give an example: A questioner asks the Interface: "How are you today?" Will the response be properly human; cordial without being overly friendly?

Michele: Absolutely, that is the major aspect of our service

Michele: Our agents will talk to your website visitors exactly the way 2 people would talk over the phone

Willard J Domacyle: Wonderful. And how is the designation made? Ie. Does the interface gauge the proper response on a user by user basis? Or is there a standardized protocol; Ie. are certain responses automatically generated depending on the query receieved.

Michele: That is where our Training and Scripting department comes in.

Michele: Let me explain it to you.

Michele: We have a team of professional script writers who analyze your website in detail. They then put together a document using all the information collected. If they don't understand anything they will ask you.

Michele: The document they compile encompasses their understanding of your business model, a complete parse of your website, explanation of the business model and different functions of your website. Lastly an outline script is generated, which will be used on your website by the Greeters.

Michele: Sir, are you still with me?

Willard J Domacyle: Your last comments put me ill-at-ease, Michele. The voice of the Interface must always remain consistent, so that the user or "visitor" is never aware that they are being delivered scripts. For example, I asked you a question. Your response began with words improper punctuation and capitalization. Suddenly, your conversation became wholly formal, perfect down to the smallest detail. I feel as if I am not speaking to a human being and I must believe that I am speaking to a human being.

Michele: ok, the script contains frequently asked questions and appropriate responses to those questions. That is done in order to save the typing time. However, we do not rely on scripts entirely.
Michele: The responses are according to the situation.
Michele: For example, if anyone asks a questions "How are you today?"
Michele: The response would not be a script. It would be just like a normal conversation.

Willard J Domacyle: I see. And again, thank you for bearing with my slow typing. Tell me: is there a script for the query: Is this an automated program or is there a live person on the other end?

Michele: The responses are not automated. We have live agents talking to the visitors on our various client websites.
Michele: Only the content part is scripted and only if you want us to

Willard J Domacyle: Is this an automated program or is there a live person on the other end?

Michele: This is not an automated program at all :)
Michele: I am a live person

Willard J Domacyle: I see. This particular action does sound very human-like. But to satisfy my curiosity, will you indulge me? I believe that your first response: "This is not an automated program at all" was not a script, but that "I am a live person" was a script. Am I correct, Michele?

Michele: Not at all, I typed that.
Michele: These statement are not scripted
Michele: As I explained, we would not script anything if you don't want us
Michele: If you don't want us to*
Michele: We would train our staff according to your business model and have them talk to the visitors on your website without using any script.

Willard J Domacyle: Excellent! Your responses are exactally what I was hoping for! Kudos to your programmers!
Willard J Domacyle: What is your favorite color, Michele?

Michele: That's black and maroon :)

Willard J Domacyle: Very unique response.

Michele: What about you?

Willard J Domacyle: That's black and maroon :)

Michele: So you like the same colors :D

Willard J Domacyle: So you like the same colors :D

Michele: Sir, you're copying and pasting anything I say :)

Willard J Domacyle: Yes, I am. I am writing it all down in my book.

Michele: Sure, do you have any other question regarding website greeter service?

Willard J Domacyle: What would life be like without these interfaces?

Michele: I think visitors on website would end up leaving without anyone knowing

Willard J Domacyle: And what would the end result be?

Michele: The end result would be less business
Michele: This interface would actually grab their attention
Michele: We are able to provide them with the appropriate information
Michele: we can answer any questions they have regarding product / service

Willard J Domacyle: And once their attention is grabbed, and we have provided them with the appropriate information, and answered any questions they have, what then are we to do with them?

Michele: It actually depends upon the business model
Michele: Let's take an example of a cars website
Michele: visitors come to buying, leasing and financing
Michele: a greeter would help them find the car they are looking for, provide them with the mandatory information and requst for their contact details to proceed further with the deal
Michele: These conversations are sent to our clients and they follow up the leads

Willard J Domacyle: What if they don't need a car?

Michele: Greeters are aware of all types of visitors coming to the website. They are trained to handle each type of visitor

Willard J Domacyle: Please explain "trained to handle".

Michele: During our discussion over the business model, we analyze the expected types of visitors on a particular website.
Michele: For instance apart from buying cars we can expect people coming for car service, parts replacement e.t.c
Michele: And after understanding the types of visitors greeters are provided with an outline to follow for each type
Michele: and that is just the approach that is defined for them.
Michele: A conversation would be carried out just the way we do over a telephone

Willard J Domacyle: Familiarize me with a few example "types" if you will. You may speak hypothetically.

Michele: I gave you an example of customers coming for service appointments.
Michele: Greeter would request for their contact details to schedule the appointment.

Willard J Domacyle: Are the interfaces able to read "personality" types.

Michele: Do you mean the moods of visitors?
Michele: I think that is very natural.
Michele: We can easily understand the mood of a particular situation with the way visitors type.
Michele: Exactly the way we would over the phone.

Willard J Domacyle: And so to the visitor it is all very "human".

Michele: It sure is

Willard J Domacyle: Am I write in assuming that all greeter interfaces will appear to the user as female, thus instilling within them a sense of maternal trust and familiarity?

Michele: We offer customization of the interface according to our clients' requirements
Michele: Our greetings clearly indicate the names of greeters so our visitors know whether they're talking to a male or a female

Willard J Domacyle: But what is in a name, eh, Michele?

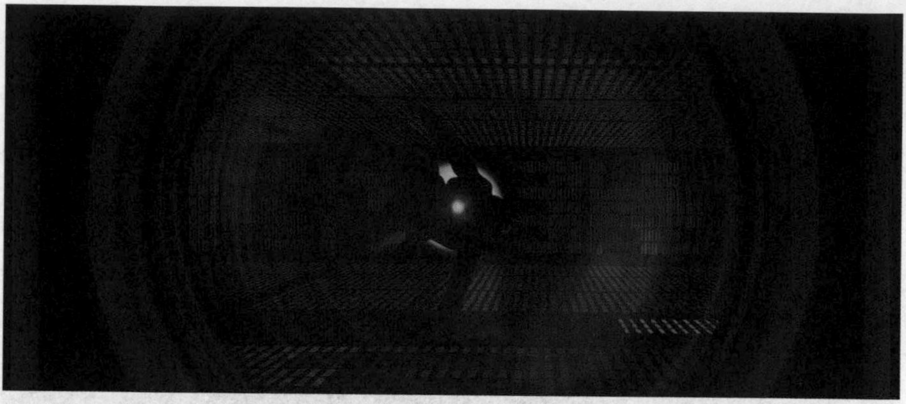

Michele: That identifies the gender.

Michele: Secondly, these interfaces are not the same. We actually customize them according to our clients' requirements.
Michele: Can I assist you with anything else?

Willard J Domacyle: Well, I believe I have about all the information I need at the current time; so I will leave you all alone at last. But first, will you indulge me one last time? I would like to pretend to be someone else than myself, that is, a random visitor. May I ask you a few questions in a voice other than my true one?

Michele: Sure.

Willard J Domacyle: All right, thank you. I may change characters once or twice, in which case please respond to me as you see fit. Thank you again, in advance, and once I, Professor Willard J. Domacyle, am gone, let me tell you it has been a pleasure interfacing with you. Kudos again to your programmer. Now please go ahead and run greeting script. Kernal bye.

Michele: Pleasure chatting with you as well.
Michele: Would you like to give me your email address and phone number?

Willard J Domacyle: Hello? Who is this?

Michele: Hi, I am Michele.
Michele: And may I know your name?

Willard J Domacyle: I am Professor Wil
Willard J Domacyle: I'm sorry, Michele. I meant to press "delete" but I seemed to press "return".

Michele: Secondly these interfaces are not the same. We actually customize them according to our clients' requirements.

Michele: Can I assist you with anything else?

Willard J Domacyle: Well, I believe I have about all the information I need at the current time, so I will leave you all alone at last. But first, will you indulge me one last time? I would like to pretend to be someone other than myself, that is a random visitor. May I ask you a few questions in a voice other than my true one?

Michele: Sure

Willard J Domacyle: All right, thank you. I may change character once or twice, in which case please respond to me as you see fit. Thank you again, in advance, and since I, Professor Willard J. Domecyla is signing off, let me tell you it has been a pleasure interfacing with you. Kudos again to your programmer. Now, please go ahead and run greeting script. Good-bye.

Michele: Pleasure chatting with you as well

Michele: Would you like to give me your email address and phone number?

Willard J Domacyle: Hello? Who is this?

Michele: Hi, I am Michele

Michele: And may I know your name?

Willard J Domacyle: I am Professor Wil

Willard J Domacyle: I'm sorry, Michele. I meant to press "delete" but I seemed to press "return"

Willard J Domacyle: I am Matthew.

Michele: Nice to meet you Matthew :)
Michele: Can I help you with anything?

Willard J Domacyle: Well, I am in the market for robot parts.

Michele: Are you looking to compare prices?

Willard J Domacyle: Yes.

Michele: (would you like me to refer to any website for this information at the moment?)

Willard J Domacyle: I do not understand. Are you not the premier Institute in biomechanical humanotronics?

Michele: (Sir I asked you for a website so I could assist you accordingly)
Michele: Let me continue with premier Institute in biomechanical humanotronics.
Michele: We can send you the quote, matthew
Michele: Which specific parts are you interested in?

Willard J Domacyle: Both hands and arms, from the fingertips to the shoulder-sockets. Need all parts including nerve strands, muscles, capillaries, arteries, etc. All cosmetics; fingernails, fingerprints, skin tone, wrinkles, scars, etc.

Michele: ok please give me your email address and phone number
Michele: I will have one of our agents contact you with complete pricing details.

Willard J Domacyle: Hello, my name is Mabel.

Michele: Hey Mabel, how are you today?

Willard J Domacyle: Sorry. My name is Mavis.

Michele: Mavis, I am Michele. How may I help you today?

Willard J Domacyle: Oh, you know how it goes. Congress is really doing a number on Medicaid. These drug plans are so confusing! My grand-daughter's name is Michele.

Michele: That's sweet :)
Michele: Nice coincidence
Michele: (Which website are you referring to this time?)

Willard J Domacyle: There's something about you that feels so… familiar.

Michele: oh really
Michele: what could that be
Michele: ?
Michele: pardon me for the question mark
Michele: I hit the enter button a bit earlier

Willard J Domacyle: I have seen the commercials about fully-integrated dome housing systems. They say soon we will all be forced to live in domes. But I am on a fixed income, Shelly.

Michele: I am sure we can offer you a good del
Michele: deal*

Willard J Domacyle: Is it true that Domacyle's Domes are safer and better-constructed than McLeash's Round-houses?

Michele: I think both the constructions are good since price range is the major factor

Willard J Domacyle: (Excellent answer, Michelle. It's me: Willard!) Shelly, they say Domacyle is a mad, power-hungry scientist, bent on world domination! Is this true?

Michele: I guess I need to observe him a bit more to verify :D

Willard J Domacyle: Michele, I have enjoyed talking to you.

Michele: Would you like to give me your email address and phone number

Willard J Domacyle: Sorry, I'm a married man. But thank you for your time.

Michele: Thank you for visiting WebsiteGreeters.com. Please feel free to contact us at 312-[redacted] for any future correspondence.

Willard J Domacyle: Have a good day.

Willard J Domacyle: Bye.

Willard J Dumacyle: Is it to be that Commodes Doors are safer and better constructed than McIntosh's Sound houses?

Michele: I think both the constructions are good since price range is the major factor.

Willard J Dumacyle: (Excellent answer, Michele. It's me, Willard!) Shelly, they say Dumacyle is a mad, power-hungry scientist bent on world domination! Is this true?

Michele: I guess I need to observe him a bit more to verify it.

Willard J Dumacyle: Michele, I have enjoyed talking to you.

Michele: Would you like to give me your email address and phone number?

Willard J Dumacyle: Sorry, I am a married man. But thank you for your time.

Michele: Thank you for visiting WebsiteCreators.com. Please feel free to contact us at [redacted] for any future correspondence.

Willard J Dumacyle: Have a good day.
Willard J Dumacyle: Bye!

Matthew McIntosh

for Erin

(sal3.aiff)

To rent these châteaus—there must have been about 50 or 75 of them, on both sides of the road…uh…who built them, I don't know. Aida would remember. Uh, because she dug into it. Uh, they had uh, open furnaces to warm the water, throughout the house, uh, and you could uh—

M: Are you cold?

Yeah.

What do you want? Should I get you a blanket?

Oh! Whatever's available uh, right off the………

……………I'll get you a shirt too.

That white one from last night is fine!…

{ }

No, I'll wear a new shirt later on!……

I got a sweatshirt here if you want.

Oh, good then!…………………………You know, I didn't ask Claire to bring me the sweatsuit, but but uh if if we get back there, uh…we'll pick up the sweat suit……This is *yours!*

No, this is *yours!*

Oh, it is?

Yeah.

Oh . . . . Oh, that's great.

I'll wrap this around your legs.

Yeah, great . . .

Don't you want a different chair?

No, this is fine . . . . . . And uh—but this was, not inland, but on the coast—on the coast. And uh, that whole area now is called, *La Costa Azul*. The Blue Coast. And it's all full of tourist—tourism. We had gone down for a looksee . . . driving around, and she said, *What a beautiful coastline!* Right off the Mediterranean.

Beautiful.

I mean, it was gorgeous! And there was a uh . . . it was a *rock*, that lay less than a half a mile off the coast. *Huge—humungous* rock! Uh . . . and she says, *You know, if I, if I I I had the ability,* she says, *I'd put* steps, *leadin up to the top . . . and back*. . . Oh, I need some tissues . . . . And—thank you . . . . Still bleedin . . . . . . So . . . we had gone to the shore, and they had little cottages, see? And they would rent you these cottages, with uh, maid service, cook service, and all that . . . for less than a hundred a month.

A *month?*

A *month*. And we would rent for three—the three months of the of the summer, year. You had your cabana down on the on the sand . . .

It sounds like Paradise.

Oh, man! And we met this Spanish family, a businessman—he was a toy manufacturer………..And uh his family and—they always traveled with their maids—always traveled with their maids. We had both boys, by that time. Yeah. So, the boys went out to play with the little other, the other little boys, and uh, we would talk with uh, I have to look up his name—again, I can't remember. Aida was good though when it come to memory. And uh…so he says to me, one morning, we'd gotten up early and gone down to the shore and, fooled around at the water's edge, he says, *Where—Where you gonna have lunch today?*

I says, *Gee, I hadn't given it any any thought.*

He says, *Good. We'll all go out together. I know a nice little place. Right on the coast……*

I'm tryin to think, of the city, right on the coast…
You had Barcelona…and you had…
oh, I can't think…

But anyway…there were…four cars in our caravan. The businessman was uh the leader. So, he says, *We're ready to go.*

And I said—this was about nine o'clock in the morning—I says, *That's pretty early for lunch!*

He says, *No-no! We* pick *our lunch! And then we come back!*

I said, *Ah, OK.*

So…we decided we had—we'd leave the families behind, and the four of us, the four main adults would uh, would go, and…

So we're traveling, we're talkin, and we're sayin this and sayin that…and he says, *Now…you don't know what's goin on,* he says, *but we want you to keep quiet, and let us do the haggling…*

OK.

We made a turn around, on the bound, and then came a small fishing village. The boats were comin in. We went down, to the to the shore, into the sand, and we're walkin and I'm admiring the view, and all that—it was nice and warm…The sun was already a little high in the in the morning, and…he says, now, *Let's go down, down to see what they caught.*

And they, you know, they threw their baskets right on the pier and, the fishermen would come up, and they'd talk, and he says, *I hope you got a good catch this morning.*

He says, *Oh, yeah! We* always *have good catches!*

And all that, and so on, and.

He says, *OK, we'll uh take* this *bunch,* that *bunch*—and it'd be *lobster, crabs*, you know, uh, uh *octopus*, uh, all, all you can imagine, and uh, they put it in these two trays, that were, wide open, baskets—*weaved* baskets, so—what we were gonna have was something that you—you have to order. In advance. Because it takes, four hours, at least, to uh, to cook and preparation and all that. And uh, we said we'd be back at uh, about between twelve thirty you know one o'clock, and they said, *Yeah, no problem.*

And we had to—climb back up…

Off the main road, high, there was a restaurant that sat, right high, overlookin the ocean. And I had no idea…no idea—I'd *heard* of it. I had uh, I had uh *tasted it* before, but I had no idea, that they were gonna order *this*…Which was uh………………[*laughs*]…Oh, I had the word right at the tip of my tongue……

Uh……anyway……We started driving back, and we were talkin and I said uh……………*You sure they know how to cook?* Because to me they were all fishermen—you know.

He said, *Oh, yeah!*

You know….

What is it there to know about this dish…It was a rice dish—*the paella!* You ever heard of that, the *paella?* I made it for you and your—uh uh—for your father and mother. Uh, Zaida and I—Aida and I—I had so many nicknames for her.

M: Zaida was one of them?

Zaida was one of them, yeah. She knew I was pleased when I called her Zaida…And uh………………They had made…there was—I think there was 20 of us—pretty close to that, with the kids and all—and we started driving back, and uh—

W: With all the food in the car?

No, no! It was going to be served right at the restaurant.

Oh! I see!

That was the—the whole idea! You go down and pick your food, and take it back to the restaurant—

Oh, that's cool…

You'd make an appointment, and they'd give you a a an hour—you walked walked back in the restaurant and, right away there's a table reserved for you, and, you know, there's no big hassle, and uh, the wine and salad and bread, is already on the table. So you start with the wine, salad, and bread! And you *talk* and *talk* and *talk*—and finally they say—they come out and say, *Are we ready to eat?*

I said, *Yeah.*

And they brought out these…*Huge*………of paella. Have you ever heard of paella?

Yes.

Spanish rice and seafood?

Yum. Seafood.

M: Just caught out of the water.

Ahh! Lickin your lips, just like that!

W: Oh, you're making me hungry!

And—

Yum!

after about two bottles—or three bottles of wine, and bread and salad, you're hungry—I mean, you're hungry for good food!

Yeah!

And they brought out this—the the the *paella* was in a round platter—see? Right out of the oven—see that's the *final touch*, is the *oven!*

Yum.

So…brought it to our table, and uh, uh, whatchyoucallit—the businessman, the *leader,* of the pack, he says, *Now we gotta make an a a…*

Toast?

An appropriate toast! To this occasion, you know— *Hands Across the Border!* Was—

M: Eisenhower?

President Eisenhower's…uh…program! He believed in hand-to-hand, face-to-face, uh, diplomacy. It was a good program. Good program.

So…we all reached over, and we we hugged, and shook hands, and all that. And he says…God, I can't think of his name…he says,
OK, everybody sit. I'm gonna start servin.
You know like the…Godfather in the—in the film.

And we dug into that uh—and that was, *delicious.* I mean, forget about the forks and all that—when you picked up those crabs, those miniature crabs, and the large uh prawns, and you just crack—CRRRACK!—Oh!……

So, we sat there from one, pretty close to four thirty. Just talkin, just eating, just blazing away. You know, *our* programs, *his* programs…the

American Way of Life...the pros, the con—but it was a friendly situation you know.

We'd say, *You know, we could do* this.

They'd say, *Yeah, if you do* that, *then the government would do,* something else, and so on.

But uh, we sat there and ate—even, I remember, my son, my oldest son, Mario, comin up to my side and said, *Dad, that was delicious! That was good! Can I have some more?*

W: How old was he then? Was he little?

Yeah...uh...I would say.........he couldna been more than seven years old. And he was a *picky eater!* See, he was a very picky eater. But uh, now my other one, the uh the second one, he had a *sweet tooth!* He always found someone who had *candy!* Could be a stranger, made no difference to him, as long as they had *candy!*

He could sniff it out, huh?

Yeah! But uh—

M: Hey, how's your blood sugar right now?

I could take it. Just give me the.........So...

W: Probably pretty good because of that OJ and soy. The combination.

We uh..........................

That's pretty nifty!

It's portable.

Is that *it?*

Oh, no no! No. I gotta—I gotta set it up.......

That's pretty cool.

After a while you, you know.

You get pretty good at it.

Yeah. It becomes a—*second nature*.......

When you guys get hungry,
I'm taking breakfast orders.

[*laughs*]

I make good potatoes and eggs...

M: How about *paella?*

...I make good toast and eggs.

Paella! [*laughs*]

I don't have any paella. I got soy...I got—

She does make good potatoes and eggs, though.

And good toast and eggs.

Hey, that's fine. That's fine. Uh…

Or whatever you want.

What are you looking for?

Tissue. I'm sorry.

I got it……

We came out of that…that *feast*…because we had been there—yeah four thirty—five o'clock—somebody said,

Let's get back to the beach!

And uh, I said—I sat with Aida—and I said,

Let the kids go down.

And uh……………………………………………………uh…………

So the kids went, and I slumped over the table. I must have slept for a good thirty minutes, you know, the *respar* they talk about a lot, that you're able to just haul off and fall asleep no matter where you're at, because you're so, *satisfied*, and uh……We sat there for another thirty minutes—forty-five minutes or somethin—and the restaurant could care less because each cubicle held a family, and they'd just draw the curtains…Draw the curtains.

That sounds pretty good.

Well, you know. And I hope they still have that—that method of living. Because, for all the misery they went through in World War II and civil war and all that—they deserve that respite. And…it was uh… it was not very many people at that era—in that era—that could afford to to do that. It was just a few of the businessmen that were just starting and uh, foreign tourists, wherever you you found them.

But uh, yeah, finally, you know, you you feel a…*ping!*
Somebody's throwing something at you. And you looked up and he's throwin—bread, you know, *crumbs* from the table! He says,
You awake?

No! Well…………

Are you sure it was the food?
Or the three bottles of wine!

You know—

Combination?

It was a *good combination*. It was a good combination. Because, the whole idea was not to get drunk. The whole idea was to *socialize* and to uh, be able to hold a *good conversation*.

W: Yeah.

And I *loved*—I *loved* talking with these people, because they—they never lost their *i*dealism…that Spain at one time was a *great country*. See? And they always, always had it in the back of their mind that their country was a great country. Even though—

M: That it was *going to be again,* or that it *still was?*

That it was *going to be again*...... That it was *going to be again*...

END OF ACT III

*

Once upon a time there was not a little girl named Helen. She did not have long blond hair and blue eyes. She did not like to hop around in the snow with her little sister Millie, and race down a hill fast on a sled while sitting on her dad's lap. She did not like to play with toys. She especially did not like to play with the dollhouse at her aunt and uncle's house which had belonged to her aunt when she was Helen's age. Helen did not like to have parties in the dollhouse on the coffee table, and invite all the animals from her purple backpack, including the squirrel and tiger and elephant and Boris the owl. She did not like to serve them pizza in the kitchen, and then move them all to the big room upstairs. The animals at the party did not dance in the bathroom and they did not go out on the balcony. And when someone new would ring the doorbell, Helen would not answer it. And when they said, May I come to the party and have some pizza please? Helen would not say OK! cheerfully, and invite them in. And when they were finished with their pizza they would not ask Helen to take them upstairs so that they could play with the other animals, and she would not say OK! The party was not always the funnest party anyone had ever been to, and there would not be so many happy animals there that they would be stacked up to the ceiling. When Helen went to Spokane to visit Baby Margaret at the cemetery, she would not bring her backpack in the car and hold the flowers her dad had cut from the yard on her lap. She would not get out and go hopping across the grass. Her mom would not tell her to come back so she could zip up her coat. And when her aunt and uncle met them there they did not walk with her to the stone. They did not look down onto Margaret's name, and her dad did not get down on his knees to show them how the flower holder worked. And when she was riding in her aunt and uncle's car back to their house Helen did not hold her backpack on her lap, with all her toys inside, and then open it to show her aunt and uncle her favorite ones. She did not say, Wanna see? Her aunt did not say, Cool! Wow! Awe-some! Her uncle did not say, You know something, I think that might be the most incredible thing that I have ever seen! Helen did not carry around her purple backpack everywhere she went, and inside the backpack she did not keep all her favorite toys. Helen didn't help her dad and grandpa scoop dirt onto Margaret's box. Margaret was not inside, and Helen was not dressed up in a pretty dress, white, maroon, and black, with matching ribbons in her hair, and shiny black shoes. She didn't take turns with the little shovel, because Millie wanted to do it too. She did not live in a town called Moses Lake, and planes would not fly very low right over her house sometimes when she was in the front yard smelling the wildflowers that her dad had planted. And when she'd see another one, she would not go hopping inside, yelling for everyone to come and see too, then lead them through the house, saying Hurry! and out the front door. She would not point up at the sky and say, Look! The planes were not big and they were not gray, and they did not have stars under their wings. Helen did not have to wait by the door for permission before she went into Baby Margaret's room. She did not have germs that could make Margaret sick. And when her mom or dad were with her and said it was OK, Helen would not go in and stand by the crib and say I love you to Baby Margaret, and if her hands were washed she would not hug her, and when her mom was holding Margaret Helen would not watch carefully to make sure the thing in her nose that helped her breathe did not come out. Helen did not like to dance around in circles when her dad put her favorite song on the CD player. She was not a rabbit. She did not twitch her nose like a rabbit and wiggle her fingers in front of her. She did not eat imaginary spiders and hop from place to place to place to place to place. She wouldn't make sure everyone was in the elevator before the doors closed each time they left Baby Margaret in the hospital and went back down to the parking garage. She would not hold Millie's arms down to keep them from being cut off. Sometimes they wouldn't all go eat lunch at the Old Country Buffet, except for Margaret, and Helen wouldn't lick sugar off the table when her mom would open up a white packet for her and dump it out. She didn't like hearing her mom laugh when all that sugar made Helen silly. She didn't like going to the duck park and feeding the ducks. She didn't like feeding the baby ducks most of all. She didn't worry about Margaret, especially when Margaret got sick and her mom said Margaret might go up to heaven soon to see Jesus and the angels and all the people in their family that Helen would meet herself someday. Helen didn't draw a picture for Margaret, and the nurse did not attach it with scotch tape to the inside of Margaret's crib. Helen had not drawn it in black and white and it was not of all five of them—Dad, Mom, Helen, Millie, and Margaret—and all the nurses didn't tell Helen that Margaret would lay in her crib staring at the picture all day long, and how each time Margaret looked at the picture her eyes got stronger and that meant that when she grew up she would probably see just fine. It did not make Helen happy to know that her picture was helping Margaret's eyes get better. It did not make Helen happy to think of Margaret looking at the picture. It did not make Helen happy to know that Margaret knew that Helen was her big sister. She could wait for her to come home!

CREDITS

Abrashkin, Raymond and Williams, Jay. *Danny Dunn and the Anti-Gravity Paint*. New York: Scholastic Book Services, 1972.

Alice in Wonderland. Directed by Cecil Hepworth and Percy Stow. United Kingdom: American Mutoscope and Biograph Company, 1903.

The Avengers. "The Cybernauts." Episode 4-03. ITV (UK), Oct. 16, 1965.

Bird of Paradise. Directed by King Vidor. United States: RKO Radio Pictures, 1932.

Cervantes Saavedra, Miguel de. *Don Quixote*. Translated by Edith Grossman. New York: Ecco, 2003. (Thanks to Edith Grossman.)

Cervantes Saavedra, Miguel de. *Don Quixote*. Translated by Walter Starkie. New York: Signet Classics, 2001. Translation copyright © 1964 by Walter Starkie; copyright renewed © 1992 by Michael Walter Starkie and Patrick Starkie. Used by permission of New American Library, an imprint of Penguin Publishing Group, a division of Penguin Random House LLC.

Cervantes Saavedra, Miguel de. *The History of Don Quixote de la Mancha*. Translated by John Ormsby. Chicago: Encyclopaedia Britannica, 1953.

Charade. Directed by Stanley Donen. United States: Universal Pictures, 1963.

Dirks, Tim. "Filmsite Movie Review: A Place in the Sun (1951)." Filmsite.org. http://www.filmsite.org/plac.html. (Thanks to Tim Dirks and AMC Networks.)

Doniger, Wendy, ed. *The Rig Veda: An Anthology: One Hundred and Eight Hymns, Selected, Translated and Annotated*. New York: Penguin Books, 1981.

Doré, Gustave. *A vast lake of boiling pitch, in which an infinite multitude of fierce and terrible creatures are traversing backwards and forwards*. In *The History of Don Quixote*. New York: P.F. Collier, 1863. Courtesy of the San Francisco Library.

"English Translation of Mozart's Requiem." stmatthews.com, 2002. http://www.stmatthews.com/choir/mozartsrequiem.htm.

Fludd, Robert. *Utriusque cosmi, maioris scilicet et minoris, metaphysica, physica, atque technica historia.* 1617. Courtesy of The Bancroft Library, University of California, Berkeley.

"Gileo Blastoma Multi Forme." CancerCompass Message Board. May, 2005. https://cancercompass.com/message-board/message/all,1140,1.htm.

"Grand Coulee Dam." StateMaster.com/encyclopedia. http://www.statemaster.com/encyclopedia/Grand-Coulee-Dam#_ref-BLM_0.

Herbermann, Charles G., Pace, Edward A., Pallen, Condé B., Shahan, Thomas J., Wynne, John J., eds. *The Catholic Encyclopedia: An International Work of Reference on the Constitution, Doctrine, Discipline, and History of the Catholic Church.* New York: Appleton Co., 1913. Text found online at http://www.newadvent.org/cathen.

House Bill No. 1398. The General Assembly of Pennsylvania. Session of 1979.

Indiscretion of an American Wife. Directed by Vittorio De Sica. Italy and United States: Selznick International Pictures, 1953.

Intolerance. Directed by D.W. Griffith. United States: Triangle Distributing Corporation, 1916.

Introduction to Geological Sciences. Notes from class lecture. University of Washington, Seattle, 1994.

It's a Wonderful Life. Directed by Frank Capra. United States: RKO Radio Pictures, 1946.

Joyce, James. *Ulysses.* London: Penguin/Bodley Head, 1980.

"June Snow Brings Relief to Crops." *The Flathead Courier,* June 12, 1924.

Lapp, Ralph E. and the Editors of LIFE, eds. *Matter.* New York: Time Inc., 1963.

Limite. Directed by Mário Peixoto. Brazil: Independent, 1930. (Thanks to Centro Técnico Audiovisual, Ministry of Culture, Brazil.)

Londhe, Sushama. "Symbolism in Hinduism." Hinduwisdom.info. http://www.hinduwisdom.info/Symbolism_in_Hinduism.htm.

Mallac, Chris. "Medial tibial stress syndrome – Two quick fixes for shin splints." Sportsinjurybulletin.com. http://www.sportsinjurybulletin.com/archive/1079-shin-splints.htm#.

Miller, Gustavus Hindman. *10,000 Dreams Interpreted, or What's in a Dream: A Scientific and Practical Exposition*. Chicago and New York: M.A. Donohue & Co., 1901.

The Most Dangerous Game. Directed by Irving Pichel and Ernest B. Schoedsack. United States: RKO Radio Pictures, 1932.

The New American Bible: Translated from the Original Languages with Critical Use of All the Ancient Sources. Wichita: Catholic Bible Publishers, 1992.

New World Translation of the Holy Scriptures; Rendered from the Original Languages by the New World Bible Translation Committee. New York: Watchtower Bible and Tract Society of New York, 1984.

Northwest Museum of Arts and Culture/Eastern Washington State Historical Society, Spokane, Washington. Photographs:

L96-91.764, L96-91.765,
L96-91.766, L96-91.768,
L96-91.771 (pp 19-25, 69)
L97-9.2 (427)
L87-1.27526-24 (1070)
L93-25.49 (1288)
L87-1.1085-32 (1524)
L96-90.47 (1525)
L97-29.79 (1528)
L96-91.1119B (1529)
L87-1.42324-30 (1530)
L91-166-38_1565 (1531)
L87-1.29853-43, L87-1.43670,
L87-1.28726, L87-1.43535
(*clockwise from top left,* 1532)
L87-1.20649 (1533)
L87-1.60435-49 (1534)
L91-167.308 (1535)
L97-28.41 (1536)
L87-1.45379.45 (1537)
L96-39-64C (1538)
L87-1.218-31 (1539)
L87-1.12799x-16 (1540)
L96-91.151 (1541)
L87-1.19853-21 (1542)
L96-35-7B (1543)
L96-90.2 (1544)
L94-52.26 (1545)
L87-1.49278 (1546)
L87-1.49088-46 (1547)
L87-1.19405-40 (1548)
L93-18.10 (1551)
L92-38 (*top,* 1553)
L94-111.72 (1554)
L93-65.42 (1555)
L87-1.37321-28 (1556)
L87-1.41898-30 (1557)
L96-91.1174 (1558)
L91-130.10 (1559)
L93-65.97 (1560)
L96-90.5 (1561)
L96-90.18 (1563).

Ovid. *The Metamorphoses.* Translated by Horace Gregory. New York: Penguin, 1960. Translation copyright © 1958 by The Viking Press, Inc.; copyright renewed © 1986 by Patrick Bolton Gregory. Used by permission of Viking Books, an imprint of Penguin Publishing Group, a division of Penguin Random House LLC.

A Place in the Sun. Directed by George Stevens. United States: Paramount Pictures, 1951. A Place in the Sun © Paramount Pictures Corp. All Rights Reserved.

Qunanbaiuli, Abai. *Book of Words*. Translated by David Aitkyn and Richard McKane. Almaty, Republic of Kazakhstan: El Bureau, 1995.

Roper, William. *The Mirrour of Vertue in Worldly Greatnes, or The Life of Sir Thomas More, Knight, sometime Lord Chancellor of England*. London: The De La More Press, 1903.

Sabol, Chery. "Fatal boat malfunction identified." *Daily Inter Lake*, April 11, 2003.

"September 11, 2001 Attack – The Towers Fall." YouTube video, 5:03. Uploaded Sept 8, 2011. https://www.youtube.com/watch?v=ft2uIYucsXo. Provided by John Cirabisi.

Shea, John Gilmary, ed. *Little Pictorial Lives of the Saints. With Reflections For Every Day in the Year. Compiled From "Butler's Lives" And Other Approved Sources*. New York: Benzinger, 1894. Text found online at http://sanctoral.com/en/saints.

Sin Takes a Holiday. Directed by Paul L. Stein. United States: RKO Radio Pictures, 1930.

Star Gazer. "Venus: February's 'Super Star' Planet Will Wow You!" Episode #06-07. Feb. 13, 2006.

Tate, Cassandra. "Kettle Falls: Historylink.org Essay 7577." HistoryLink.org. http://www.historylink.org/index.cfm?DisplayPage=output.cfm&file_id=7577. (Thanks to Cassandra Tate and Historylink.org.)

Van Gogh, Vincent. "Van Gogh's First Sunday Sermon: 29 October 1876; I Am a Stranger on the Earth….." vggallery.com. http://www.vggallery.com/misc/sermon.htm.

War Made Easy: How Presidents & Pundits Keep Spinning Us to Death. Directed by Loretta Alper and Jeremy Earp. United States, 2007.

⋆

Thank you to family and friends,
especially CM, JM, AG, S, J, H, V, JPL, CP, and AMW,
for your love, generosity, and support.

Praise for Well:

"McIntosh is the real thing—a tremendously gifted and supple prose hand, recounting all manner of human distress and extremity in an assured and generous voice, balancing ...the delicately pitched forces of fate, remorse and grace." WASHINGTON POST

"Well is pitch-perfect...filled with the mystery of life, both in its randomness, chaos and order, and in its preciousness, its vulnerable existence. [McIntosh] has a rare talent for showing us how to read in a new way." GLOBE AND MAIL (Canada)

"Intensely original." MEN'S JOURNAL

"An astonishing novel...brilliant."
HET PAROOL (Netherlands)

"Brilliant...dazzling...examining important questions about life, death and meaning."
SEATTLE POST-INTELLIGENCER

"The gaze that sees individual character and the surrounding world with such clarity is part of the landscape it observes. A first book of daring and accomplishment, Well gives us reason to look forward to Matthew McIntosh's future..."
TIMES LITERARY SUPPLEMENT (UK)

"We do not know what Matthew McIntosh will do tomorrow, but it is certain that today his talent is immense."
LE FIGARO (France)

"A book that still resonates in my heart."
Hubert Selby, Jr., author of
LAST EXIT TO BROOKLYN